CRIME AND PUNISHMENT

Fyodor Dostoyevsky

Translated and
with an Afterword by
Sidney Monas

Introduction by Leonard J. Stanton
and James D. Hardy, Jr.

A SIGNET CLASSIC

SIGNET CLASSIC
Published by New American Library, a division of
Penguin Putnam Inc., 375 Hudson Street,
New York, New York 10014, U.S.A.
Penguin Books Ltd, 80 Strand,
London WC2R 0RL, England
Penguin Books Australia Ltd, 250 Camberwell Road,
Camberwell, Victoria 3124, Australia
Penguin Books Canada Ltd, 10 Alcorn Avenue,
Toronto, Ontario, Canada M4V 3B2
Penguin Books (N.Z.) Ltd, 182–190 Wairau Road,
Auckland 10, New Zealand

Penguin Books Ltd, Registered Offices:
Harmondsworth, Middlesex, England

Published by Signet Classic, an imprint of New American Library,
a division of Penguin Putnam Inc.

First Signet Classic Printing, February 1968
First Signet Classic Printing (Stanton and Hardy Introduction), February 1999
20 19 18 17 16 15 14 13 12

Cover painting (detail): *The Arrest of a Propagandist* by Ilya Repin. The
Tretyakov Gallery, Moscow. Courtesy of the Elsie Timbey Collection, Society
for Cultural Relations with the USSR.

Library of Congress Catalog Card Number: 98-19279

Printed in the United States of America

TRANSLATOR'S PREFACE

It has become the fashion in translating Russian novels to drop the use of patronymics, nicknames, and diminutives, but I have decided to keep them as much as possible, even though the American or English reader may find them a little odd and awkward. When Raskolnikov is addressed as Rodion Romanovich (or Rodion Romanych) it is, in terms of formality, about halfway between being called Rodion and Mr. Raskolnikov. It seems to me a healthy reminder to the reader that he is, after all, supposed to be in Russia, not America or England; and not too taxing on his memory, really. In some cases, at least, Dostoyevsky probably attached some allegorical shade of meaning to the patronymic, as he obviously did in almost all cases to the family names. Diminutives and nicknames, as terms of intimacy or endearment, convey a special feeling, and, unless they seemed genuinely awkward, I have retained them. Here is a list of the most commonly rung changes on first names:

> Rodion—Rodia—Rodenka
> Dmitry—Mitia—Mitry—Mitka
> Nikolay—Mikolay—Nikolka—Mikolka—
>   Nikolashka—Kolia
> Nastasia—Nastenka—Nastia
> Avdotia—Dunia—Dunechka
> Polia—Polenka—Polechka
> Sofia—Sonia—Sonechka
> Praskovia—Pashenka
> Phillip—Fil'ka
> Lida—Lidochka

Lida, the Marmeladov girl, her father's favorite, turns into Lenia at the end—normally a boy's name, but clearly in this instance still a girl's.

Dostoyevsky wrote in a hurry and for serial publication, and so left some inconsistencies. At the beginning, the police station is on the fourth floor; at the end, on the third. Escap-

ST. PETERSBURG
AT THE TIME OF
CRIME AND PUNISHMENT

Petersburgsky Island

BOLSHOY PROSPECT

Place of Svidrigailov's Suicide

Nevka River

TUCHKOV BRIDGE

The Little Neva

Vasilevsky Island

The River Neva

BOLSHOY PROSPECT

The Winter Palace
and The Hermitage
(Tsar's Palaces)

Falconnet's Statue
to Peter the Great

NEVSKY PROSPECT

KONOGVARDEYSKY BLVD

GORAKTAVYA ST.

The Admiralty Building

The Senate

KAMENY BRIDGE

Raskolnikov's Room
(No. 9, Srednaya Meshchanskaya St.)

VOZNESENSKY PROSPECT

STOLIARNY LANE

Sonya's Room

KOKUSHKIN BRIDGE

The Pawnbroker's Room

Haymarket Square
(Where Raskolnikov Bows
And Kisses The Earth)

EKATERINGOFSKY PROSPECT

KOBUKHOVSKY PROSPECT

Yusupov Gardens

ing after the murder, Raskolnikov goes down three flights
of stairs where clearly two are meant. I have corrected the
latter error, but allowed the former to remain.

Streets and bridges are, for the most part, not named in
the original text, but given merely with their first initial.
Their names are fairly obvious; and after some thought I
concluded that retaining only the initial served no purpose,
while using the name might help the reader who so desired
to plot the novel on a map (see opposite page). The novel
is easy to locate geographically, and Dostoyevsky himself
used to live in a house roughly seven hundred and thirty-
two steps from the house of the old pawnbroker woman.
One discovers, too, that the place of Svidrigailov's suicide is
not far from the bush where Raskolnikov had the dream of
the horse, and *"that very bush"* under which Svidrigailov
first intended to kill himself might well have been *that
very bush*!

Dostoyevsky is an obsessive user of certain words, and it
is a characteristic of his style to repeat key words over and
over again. "Suddenly" is one of the most frequently used
words in *Crime and Punishment.* I have occasionally substi-
tuted "all of a sudden," but not because I think the repetition in itself is an accident or a defect of style. Just as
Dostoyevsky's repeated "perhaps" is a constant calling into
question, his repeated "suddenly" emphasizes the disconti-
nuity, the unexpected and seemingly unreasonable welling
up of the unconscious. "Suddenly" is the adverb of
revelation.

The horse in Raskolnikov's dream, an important image in
the novel, is, in Russian, *kliacha*, a worn-out old mare, a
jade. I have preferred to translate her with the more familiar
American "nag," which I use consistently throughout, or try
to, though there is some problem of unwanted connotation
when Katherine Ivanovna refers to herself as "an old nag."

Each character is in some way or other associated with
words that come up like a leitmotif in opera when he appears. For Sonia the word "together" has great importance.
The translator is often faced with the choice of losing the
effect of repetition or of losing a certain dimension of meaning, a connotation that a single word, or even a single
phrase, cannot convey in English. For instance, I decided to
retain the word "disgust" in connection with Raskolnikov,
though in some places "revulsion" might be more apt. In
connection with Porfiry Petrovich, there is a certain play of

words that have *kon-* ("end," "finish") for a root. Porfiry refers to himself, though he is only thirty-five, as a man who is "used up" (*zakonchenny*) or "finished" (*nakonchenny*)—the echo of the Russian is inevitably lost.

Razumikhin uses quite frequently, and at one point even launches into a little lecture on the meaning of, the Russian word *vran'e* and its verbs. It has the connotation of something not true, yet not really an out-and-out lie (which would be *lozh'*), not really told with the intent to deceive. It means laying it on thick, twisting things a bit, getting carried away, talking nonsense. I have tried to be as repetitive as I could and still convey some sense of what Razumikhin is saying. Again, there is an important play on *prestuplenie* ("crime," as in the title) and *perestupit'*, to transgress, to overstep, to step over, to stride across.

The family names are allegorically significant; I think some of the first names and patronymics are, too. The following list may be of some help to the reader:

Raskolnikov—*raskolnik*=schismatic, sectarian.

Razumikhin—*razum*=good sense, intellect; his first name, Dmitry, is the Russian masculine form of Demeter, and suggests the earth.

Marmeladov—*marmelad*=marmelade, jam. Katherine Ivanovna may suggest the Empress Catherine who copied much from Beccaria in her *Nakaz,* or Instruction, of 1767, which was never really implemented with concrete and effective legislation as may or may not have been intended. The suggestion comes up mainly because Katherine Ivanovna's prevailing passion is for justice, and because she labors under the delusion that somehow this world, while it may not be the theater of happiness, must surely be the theater of justice. Her patronymic is also the same as that claimed by Frau Lippewechsel, her German landlady, whom Marmeladov endows with a different patronymic, however, at the beginning of the book. *Sonia* is a diminutive for Sofia, which means wisdom, and in the Orthodox Church is associated with St. Sophia, or heavenly wisdom, as opposed to the worldly kind.

Luzhin—*luzha*=puddle, pond, pool; or might be derived from *luzhionny,* canned; that is, not fresh.

Lebeziatnikov—*lebezit'*=to fawn on somebody, to cringe; also suggests *lebed',* a swan.

Porfiry Petrovich—he alone among the major characters

has no family name. At one point he is supposed to have kidded Razumikhin and his associates by telling them he was going to join a monastery; but there is in fact something monkish about him. *Porfiry* is the royal purple of Byzantium; whereas his patronymic means "the son of Peter" and may suggest Peter the Great, implying that he is also a civil servant on the Western model, combining traditional Byzantine with Western virtues. Technically, he is a *sudebny sledovatel'*—a "court investigator." This was a position created by the law reforms of 1864 (new at the time Dostoyevsky wrote), and means that he was not a police inspector of the American kind, or a district attorney. He was *supposed* to be impartial—neither on the side of the criminal nor on that of the police. Even for a court investigator, however, Porfiry Petrovich's behavior during his last and genuinely "paternal" visit to Raskolnikov must have been rather extraordinary.

Svidrigailov—if his family name has any symbolic significance I have not been able to discover it. His first name, however—*Arkady*=Arcadian, someone who lives in Arcadia—is another matter.

In transliterating names I have followed, with some slight variation, the system of the Library of Congress.

—SIDNEY MONAS

INTRODUCTION
A Soul's Journey

I. PERSPECTIVES

Crime and Punishment has been read as a psychological thriller, as a case study of the criminal mind, and as a treatise on social problems. It is highly regarded as a work of philosophy, as an allegorical prose poem rich in symbolism, and as a classic tragedy. Readers of the original serialization (1866) found it rich in themes that dominated the periodical press at the time: crime and legal reform, social justice and the status of women, poverty and wealth, education, urban problems, the shape and promise of the future. This is a lot to ask from one book, but it is what readers in Dostoyevsky's Russia expected to find in a novel. Moreover, Dostoyevsky was looked upon in his own time as a kind of seer. Today, more than a century after his death, no aspect of his work remains fresher or more vital than its contemplative vision.

As a heroic type, Rodion Raskolnikov has many cousins. He has the compassion of the Buddha and the anger of Achilles. But Raskolnikov's closest literary ancestors are to be found in the Lives of the Saints. He is the notorious sinner destined to repent and ultimately to achieve great holiness. In his poverty, Raskolnikov resembles a hungry desert ascetic. And in his delirium and madness, there is even something of the "holy fool"—a rude and ragged freak sitting in the dusty heat of a public square—a figure venerated throughout the Christian East as a vessel of spiritual knowledge beyond the ken of science or conventional logic.

In terms of literary form, the novel's closest antecedents are confessional. In the West, Rousseau and Pascal had worked in a related vein. But after Dante (d. 1321), the West's literature of introspection undertook new avenues, exploring psychology and ethics in increasingly narrower ways. The Russian religious mind remained robustly medieval well into the nineteenth century; it perceived the cosmos as a great chain of being in which angels and men, plants and animals, and even the demons in hell are brought together under the loving rule of divine justice. Though Raskolnikov's problem is contemporary—How can I find my way back to God in the modern city?—still, the way he is destined to travel is perennial. None described that way better than St. Augustine in his *Confessions*, and it is to him we will turn for a model of Dostoyevsky's spiritual imagination in *Crime and Punishment*.

Russia's prominence in European affairs grew following Emperor Alexander I's defeat of Napoleon in 1815, and so did the size, acumen, and seriousness of the Russian reading public. Russia possessed a mighty army, but its laws, administration, and economic and political institutions were inefficient and desperately antiquated. Its social and religious structures were lumbering, patriarchal, even cruel. Historians, then poets stepped to the forefront of the debate over the "accursed questions"—Where is Russia going? and What is to be done about Russia?—a land so poor and yet so rich, so promising and yet so abject, so holy and yet so wicked.

Behind this verbal wrangling lay yet another question: Who will speak for Russia? That prerogative had traditionally belonged to the crown, and every Russian ruler up to 1917 spoke in the imperial "We." Challenges to imperial authority were not taken lightly. Dostoyevsky had been condemned to death in 1849 for having given a private reading of a letter by the literary critic Vissarion Belinsky to the novelist Nikolai Gogol. It was a brilliantly acerbic attack on serfdom, on the Orthodox Church's abnegation of responsibility for society, and on the overall malaise affecting Russia from top to bottom. Emperor Nicholas I personally commuted the sentence to four years of hard labor in Siberia and service as a soldier in the ranks, but only after the prisoner had been dressed and shriven for execution and was standing at the scaffold.

With the death of Nicholas in 1855, the iron grip of autocracy was loosed. Censorship was relaxed. By the time of Dostoyevsky's return to St. Petersburg in 1859, novelists and essayists (like the fictional Raskolnikov) led public debate. Emperor Alexander II's Great Reforms of the 1860s brought the power and prestige of the crown to bear in addressing the nation's problems. But the emperor could no longer claim sole right to speak for Russia. From below, in thick monthly journals such as the *Russian Messenger*, where

Crime and Punishment appeared, a babel of competing voices clamored for the nation's ear. Dostoyevsky himself was a Native-Soil Conservative (*Póchvennik*), a moderate sort of Slavophile—one of those groups on the edge of the political map that only a few dreary professors bother to think about today. In this intellectual fray, novelists enjoyed extraordinary prestige. They were looked upon—and looked upon themselves—as social critics, prophets, and visionaries.

The most important of the Great Reforms were the Emancipation of the serfs in 1861 and a comprehensive reform of the judiciary begun in 1864. The liberation of the peasants from the bonds of serfdom shook foundations of Russian society that extended back to the Middle Ages and earlier. The masters were no longer masters, and they now had to establish a new economic relationship with their peasants. Traditionally, all law had been thought to derive from the person of the emperor, God's anointed vicar in affairs of state. Now other sources of law were being proposed, with bases in reason and individual conscience. What was one to think of these changes? If the old ways had indeed come to an end, whose word would have authority now? Was every man suddenly a Napoleon, free to usurp the throne, a law unto himself?

Freedom is a test as well as a gift. Without it a man is but a cog in a machine, an ant in an anthill. Exercised to an extreme, one man's freedom is the instrument of another's enslavement or even death. Reason doesn't mitigate the tragedy of freedom. The hero of Dostoyevsky's *Notes from Underground* decries rationalism's exaltation of that one-twentieth part of man's being as if it were the *summum bonum* of human existence. Equally abhorrent to Dostoyevsky was the notion, seriously floated since the European Enlightenment, that history may soon witness the evolution of a new species of man, mentally, physically, and *morally* improved over his forebears.

If the old ethics were founded on the commandment to love God and one's neighbor, then the new code would center on love-of-self tarted up as "rational self-interest." And what of the injunction "Thou shalt not kill"? Dostoyevsky repeatedly pairs tyrant with victim to dramatize every ramification of the new law; again and again, the novel gives us nightmare images of the violent inheriting the earth, of the merciful obtaining scorn.

The Russian word for crime, *prestuplénie*, means "step-

ping over." Can murder be the means whereby Raskolnikov
will enter the ranks of extraordinary men? By acting the
tyrant, Raskolnikov seems to destroy his compassionate side,
that part which appears to him in a dream as a suffering
horse with meek, beautiful eyes. Having crossed the line,
can Raskolnikov ever return?

The novel's landscape reverberates with these questions.
This almost kinetic stage, as well as incredible propinquities
of kinship, place of residence, and chance meetings endow
Dostoyevsky's Petersburg with an atmosphere that can seem
more mythic and symbolic than realistic. In every door,
every bridge and waterway, every street and dusty square,
and every window staring back toward the eyes of the be-
holder—we feel a struggle of spirit with matter, of faith with
reason, of good with evil.

II. THE UNFOLDING OF RASKOLNIKOV'S SOUL

As the novel unfolds, event by event, interview by interview,
dream by dream, character by character, the personality and
attitudes of Raskolnikov emerge with it. Dostoyevsky does
not establish his personality all at once, and then follow him
as a fixed character through assorted adventures. That is
the technique of a whodunit, and *Crime and Punishment* is
emphatically not a detective story. Dostoyevsky's leisurely
narration of Raskolnikov's encounters—with himself as well
as with his surroundings—is also an equally leisurely explo-
ration of the contents, contradictions, and ambiguities of
Raskolnikov's character. The reader sees Raskolnikov
through events, through time within the novel; and Raskolnikov understands himself the same way. Not until the second Epilogue can the reader understand the ultimate
direction of the novel, and only then does Raskolnikov begin
to fathom the true direction and meaning of life. Only at
the very last does Dostoyevsky reveal the crucial element in
Raskolnikov's soul—hitherto inadequately developed, though
instinctually present, hidden both from the readers and from
Raskolnikov himself. That element is love.

The progressive unfolding of Raskolnikov's character
through illustration, encounter and meditation, as if in the
opening of a rose, holds the key to understanding the essential meaning of the events themselves and of the novel as a
whole. The reader necessarily searches for clues that can
illuminate the meaning of the novel. And there are many

clues. They are not, of course, about the transgression itself;
that has been established in the first pages when a confused
Raskolnikov wonders "Can I do *that*, really?" Along the
trail of clues concerning the novel as a whole, Dostoyevsky
comments on divers topics, ranging from the cultural, such
as the idea of progress or the growing role of foreign attitudes and values in Russia, to the social, including drunkenness, urban class structure, poverty, the role of women and
the geography of St. Petersburg. But these, we maintain, are
fustian. The meaning of the novel as a whole unfolds in the
soul of Raskolnikov.

Dostoyevsky reveals the soul of Raskolnikov in three
ways: through his dreams, emotions and meditations;
through his instinctive revulsion toward Svidrigailov as the
embodiment of evil; and through his encounters with Porfiry
Petrovich and Sonia. Here, and particularly, we suggest, in
the encounters with Porfiry Petrovich and Sonia, are the best
vantage points from which to see the rose unfold.

In part 3, chapter 5, Raskolnikov has his first interview
with Porfiry Petrovich, the court investigator. Much of the
interview is taken up with discussing Raskolnikov's article
"Concerning Crime," written in support of the exceptional
man who would speak the "new word" and bring about the
New Jerusalem. Porfiry asks directly:

"So you still believe in the New Jerusalem?"
"I believe," Raskolnikov answered firmly.

Porfiry Petrovich presses further. Was Raskolnikov himself
an exceptional man, and hadn't it been just such a man
who murdered the pawnbroker? Raskolnikov is invited to a
second "little talk," which produces the court investigator's
confident assertion that the murderer will not flee but will
instead provide his own proof of guilt. A third interview,
at Raskolnikov's lodgings, might have been the climactic
scene in the novel were *Crime and Punishment* a story of
deduction and detection with Porfiry Petrovich the Russian Sherlock Holmes. When Raskolnikov asks who killed
the pawnbroker and her sister, Porfiry Petrovich almost
whispers:

"What do you mean, who killed?" he asked as though
he could not believe his own ears. "Why, Rodion Romanych, *you* killed! You committed the murders, yes."

But the reader knows, as Rodion Romanych does not yet know, that murder is only an incident on a long journey, that the heart of the novel is elsewhere.

The place to look, we suggest, is with Sonia, in particular the scene in part 4, chapter 4, when Raskolnikov comes "straight to the house on the canal embankment where Sonia lived." Surprised to see Raskolnikov, Sonia is as ill at ease as he is, but discomfiture does not stifle her almost "insatiable compassion." Raskolnikov prostrates himself before Sonia, in honor of her suffering, of all suffering, and at his request she reads the story of the raising of Lazarus from the dead (John 11: 1–44). In reply Raskolnikov expresses to Sonia his sense of disbelief, along with a homily from his new word:

> Freedom and power, but the main thing is power! Over all trembling flesh and over the whole ant heap! . . . That's the goal!

But Sonia only replies with terror. And terror is appropriate. Raskolnikov is the one who is dead. Sonia—the embodiment of Hagia Sophia, holy wisdom—will be the instrument of his rebirth.

III. THE AUGUSTINIAN JOURNEY

In the first paragraph of his *Confessions*, Augustine tells the reader what the book means, what students ought to take with them from this autobiography of spiritual journey. Addressing God, Augustine states that "You made us for Yourself" and that "our hearts are restless until they rest in Thee." Such a thing could be known only through personal experience of a journey not completed but nonetheless illuminated. The image of a journey became the standard metaphor within Western Christianity for a person's life. Dante adopted it for the *Commedia* and Milton for *Paradise Lost*, and it received equivocal acceptance by Chaucer. So standard was this metaphor that it acquired purely secular connotations, as in a people's common historical journey toward national identification, or in the nineteenth-century fondness for the *Bildungsroman*, the novel of personal development. By Dostoyevsky's time, journey had become the common metaphor for character development.

As Augustine defined the human journey in *The Confessions*, the secular theme of personal development was not only incidental, it was downright insignificant. The Augustinian journey was a lifetime of spiritual formation. Through God's grace, given out of love, the journey led away from the things of the world to salvation and the heart's "rest in Thee."

The journey consists of three stages. It begins in a condition of *aversio*, a turning away from God and toward things of the world, the flesh, and the devil. In such a state of bewilderment and restlessness—a perfect description for Raskolnikov until the second Epilogue—one loves the lesser things of this world more than the God who created them. Such love is misdirected and disordered, according to Dante, or idolatrous, according to Augustine and Milton, and utterly hollow for Raskolnikov. In a condition of *aversio*, one is given not only to sin but also to misunderstanding the nature of life, to supposing that there could even exist a "new word" or that some extraordinary person could speak it. But *aversio*, Augustine explains, is the common condition of all humanity. For the truly lost, it persists an entire lifetime; for those who obtain grace, it is the first stage on the journey to salvation.

Grace is always seeking the repentant heart, that a person "may turn from his wickedness and live." For those in whom the restlessness becomes intolerable, a *retorqueo*—a movement of turning from the idols of the imaginary "new word" to the love of God—reorients life in the direction of grace and love rightly ordered. This turning came for Augustine as a single tearful and ecstatic moment, the result of reading Paul's letter to the Romans. For Raskolnikov, the explosion of tears and love occurs in the second Epilogue:

> Love resurrected them; the heart of one contained infinite sources of life for the heart of the other.

Raskolnikov has been converted. As was the case with Augustine before him, his past now seems unreal:

> Everything—even his crime, even sentence and exile—seemed to him now, in his first outburst of feeling, strange and superficial, as though it had not actually happened to him.

Like Augustine, Raskolnikov reaches for the New Testament. Life, of course, would remain the same for the exile and prisoner. But he himself was new. And that was appropriate.

Everything had to change now, did it not?

Both Augustine and Dostoyevsky end their accounts of the spiritual journey to renewal in the immediate aftermath of the salvific moment. For Raskolnikov, life after the *conversio*, the conversion to a right understanding of love and God, is described only in generalities, and was to be "the subject of a new tale." Entirely proper—the turning from the idolatry of *aversio* to the love of *conversio* is so overwhelming that all before seems unreal, just as everything afterward seems illuminated by grace.

Conversio can not come without premonitory hints as to the right path. One of the preliminary moments for Raskolnikov came at the Haymarket, in part 6, chapter 8. At Sonia's urging, Raskolnikov had gone there to kiss the earth, to confess his crime, to accept and acknowledge responsibility. He pushed into the square and—disgusted by the jostling drunken crowd—wondered if this was the right thing to do. As he knelt and kissed the ground, "Everything seemed to melt inside him, and tears flowed." True repentance had begun. A confession to the police followed, but it was anticlimactic. Indeed, Porfiry Petrovich—the exemplum of wisdom in the *civitas terrena*, the earthly city—was absent. His work was done. But Sophia was there. And she sensed his conversion in his embrace and the wordless torrent of tears.

> She jumped up and looked at him and shivered. But at the same time, at that very moment, she understood everything. A boundless joy illuminated her eyes. She understood. For her there was no longer any doubt he loved her. He loved her infinitely. At long last the moment had come. . . .

The mark of his conversion is that he has regained the ability to love.

IV. THE "NEW LIFE" AND THE NEW TALE OF *CONVERSIO*

Only at the very end, the last two paragraphs of the second Epilogue, did Dostoyevsky confirm that *Crime and Punishment* expressed an Augustinian journey. Sonia and Raskolnikov were then "at the beginning of their happiness," though

Rodia did not yet know what Sonia so clearly had always known,

> . . . that a new life had not been given him for nothing, that it would have to be bought dearly, that he would have to pay for it with a great deed in the future . . .

The "new life," that is the key—a new life that begins "a new story." That new story would be, clearly and unmistakably,

> . . . the story of a man's gradual renewal and rebirth, of his gradual transition from one world to another. . . .

Dostoyevsky thus ends where Augustine had ended, with the turning to accept the conversion experience. The great Christian novel parallels the great Christian autobiographical spiritual journey. Raskolnikov will come to know,

> . . . a new reality of which he had previously been completely ignorant.

The readers of *Crime and Punishment* know what that reality is. It is the "subject of a new tale," one in which Raskolnikov's heart is at rest, in which he gives over being the theorist of the "new word" and becomes the bearer of the true Word.

—LEONARD J. STANTON
AND JAMES D. HARDY, JR.

PART ONE

1

Early one evening, during an exceptional heat wave in the beginning of July, a young man walked out into the street from the closetlike room he rented on Stoliarny Place. Slowly, as though he could not make up his mind, he began to move in the direction of the Kokushkin Bridge.

He had managed to avoid meeting his landlady on the stairs. He lived practically under the roof of a five-floor house, in what was more a cupboard than a room. In an apartment one flight below lived his landlady, from whom he rented this garret, dinner and service thrown in. Every time he went out he had to pass her kitchen door, which almost always stood open facing the stairs. When he walked past, he felt a nauseous, cowardly sensation; it made him wince, and he was ashamed of it. He was deeply in debt to his landlady, and he feared meeting her.

Not that he was cowardly or abject; quite the contrary. For some time, though, he had been tense and irritable, in a state resembling acute depression. He had plunged so far within himself, into so complete an isolation, that he feared meeting not only his landlady but anyone at all. He had lately ceased even to feel the weight of the poverty that crushed him. He had completely lost interest in his day-to-day affairs, and he had no wish to recover such interest. It was not landladies he feared, no matter what this one happened to be plotting against him.

To find himself stuck on the stairs, though, and forced to listen to the whole range of her nonsense and offensive rubbish for which he had absolutely no concern; forced to listen to her pesterings for payment, her threats, her appeals; and he himself all the while prevaricating, making excuses, lying . . . No. Better somehow to slink down the stairs like a cat and slip away unseen.

As he came out onto the street the terror that had gripped him at the prospect of meeting his landlady struck even him as odd. "Imagine being scared of little things like that, with the job I have in mind!" he thought, smiling strangely.

"Well, now . . . it's all in a man's hands. And if he lets it slip away . . . it's because he's a coward, and that's that . . . yes, an axiom. . . . And what scares people the most? It's a new step, an authentic new word, that's what. . . . Anyway, I jabber too much. That's why I don't do anything. Because I jabber. Or maybe it's the other way around. I jabber because I don't do anything. I really taught myself jabbering this last month, lying in my corner days on end, thinking . . . about King Never. All right, then: why am I going now? Can I do *that,* really? Is *that* serious? No, it's not. So. I'm kidding myself. I'm indulging a daydream. Idle games! Yes, that's just what it is, idle games!"

Outside, the heat had grown ferocious. Closeness, crowds, scaffolding, with lime and brick and dust everywhere, and that special summer stench familiar to every Petersburger who cannot afford a summer cottage: it all jarred instantly and unpleasantly on the young man's nerves, which were tense enough already. The intolerable stench of the saloons, especially numerous in that part of town, and the drunks he came upon continually in spite of the fact it was a working day, contributed to the melancholy and repulsive tone of what confronted him. An expression of the deepest loathing flashed for a moment across his sensitive face. He was, incidentally, a remarkably good-looking young man, above average in height, slender and well built, with beautiful dark eyes and darkish blond hair.

He soon plunged into deep thought, or rather, into a kind of oblivion. He walked on without noticing his environment, without wanting to notice it. Every so often he would mutter something to himself. It was that propensity for monologues he had already acknowledged as a peculiarity of his. At that moment, he knew his thoughts were confused. He knew he was very weak. For the second day now, he had scarcely touched food.

He was badly dressed; so badly, it would have embarrassed a tramp to go out in such rags in the daytime. In that neighborhood, though, nothing could surprise anybody. Close to the Haymarket, thick with whorehouses, it swarmed with a population of tradesmen and jacks-of-all-trades who combined to make those central streets of Petersburg flash with a panorama in which almost nothing or nobody could cause any surprise.

And in spite of his occasional quite youthful fastidiousness, his rags bothered him least of all when he was out in the street—such bitter contempt he felt for the world. Meeting old friends or people he had known was another matter. He did not, in general, like to run into them. Yet just then a drunk rode past him on the street, in an enormous cart drawn by an enormous dray horse; he was being carted off somewhere for some unknown reason; and he suddenly cried out: "Hey, you in the goddamn German hat!" The drunk bellowed and waved at him. And the young man stopped suddenly and grasped convulsively at his hat. It was a tall, round Zimmerman top hat, quite worn out, altogether faded, all holes and stains, brimless, and cocked at a most unseemly angle. Not shame, but an altogether different feeling, more like fear, took hold of him.

"I thought so!" he muttered in confusion. "I thought so! The last straw! A dumb trick like that, the merest little thing like that—it could spoil the whole scheme! Yes. The hat stands out. . . . It's absurd. That's why it stands out. . . . To go with my rags, I need a worker's cap. Obviously. Anything, but not this monstrosity! Nobody wears them. It would be noticed a mile away. It would be remembered. . . . Oh, yes, it would be remembered. It's evidence. You've got to be as inconspicuous as possible. . . . Little things. Little things are what count. Little things like that—why, they could ruin everything, once and for all. . . ."

He did not have far to go. He even knew how many steps it was from the gateway of his house. Seven hundred and thirty steps. Lost in dreams, he had somehow counted them once. He himself had not believed much in his dreams at the time. He had merely allowed their hideous but seductive audacity to play upon him. A month later, he was beginning to look at them differently. To be sure, there were all those undermining monologues dealing with his own impotence and indecision, but in spite of them, somehow, and even against his will, the "hideous" dreams had turned into a project, though he did not yet quite believe in it. Now he was going to *size up* the project. With every step he grew more and more excited.

He approached a huge house, facing a canal on one side, Sadovaia Street on the other. His heart was pounding, his nerves twitching. The house consisted of small apartments, and petty entrepreneurs of all kinds lived in it: tailors, mechanics, cooks, assorted Germans, prostitutes, office workers, and so on. People scurried in and out both entrances and around both courtyards, where three or four janitors were stationed. Quite satisfied that he had encountered none of them, the young man slipped unnoticed through the gateway on the right, and up the stairs.

The stairway was dark and narrow (a back stair), but he had known all that before. He had gone over it carefully; it pleased him. In such darkness even an inquisitive glance did not matter.

"I'm so scared now, I wonder what it would be like if I were doing *that*?" The question occurred to him as he came to the fourth floor. Moving men, carrying furniture out of one of the apartments, blocked his way. A German (a government clerk) and his family, as he knew beforehand, had occupied this apartment. "So, he's moving out now. That means, along the stairs on the fourth floor, the old woman's apartment is the only one that's going to have somebody living in it for some time. Well, now . . . Good . . ."

He went over all this again as he rang the bell to the old woman's apartment. The bell rang feebly, as though it were made of tin and not of brass. In the cramped little apartments of such houses, there are always bells that sound like that. Its tone had slipped his mind. Now this peculiar tone reminded him suddenly of something. His nerves were so overwrought, he flinched.

In a little while, the door was opened a tiny crack. Through the crack the tenant observed her visitor with evident distrust. Only a small pair of eyes could be seen, glittering from out the darkness. Since there were a number of people on the landing she grew bolder, and opened the door all the way. The young man crossed the threshold into a dark anteroom divided by a partition behind which was a tiny kitchen. The old woman stood there silent and looked at him inquiringly. She was a dry crumb of a little old woman, about sixty, with sharp, nasty little eyes and a small, sharp nose. She was bare-headed, her almost colorless hair, turned only slightly gray, thickly plastered with grease. A flannel rag of some sort was tied around her neck, which, long and scrawny, resembled a rooster's claw. In spite of the heat, she wore a threadbare, faded fur jacket flung over her shoulders. She kept coughing and groaning. The young man must have been looking at her with a rather peculiar expression, for distrust flared up again in her eyes.

"I'm Raskolnikov, a student, I came here about a month ago," the young man hastily muttered. He knew he had to be more polite, so he made a half bow.

"Oh, I remember, my good man, I remember quite well that you were here," the old woman said sharply. But she did not take her inquisitive eyes from his face.

"Well, you see, ma'am . . . I'm here on the same business again. . . ." Raskolnikov went on. He was troubled and a bit surprised the old woman should distrust him so.

"But maybe she's always like that, and last time I just didn't notice it," he thought, feeling disturbed.

The old woman was silent, as though mulling it over. Then she stepped aside, motioned her visitor to the door, and said: "Go on in."

The small room into which the young man stepped—yellow wallpaper, windowsill geraniums, chintz curtains—was at that moment vividly illuminated by the setting sun.

"That's how the sun will be shining *then*!" flashed as if by chance through the mind of Raskolnikov. With a swift glance, he took in everything in the room. He was using the opportunity to study and fix in his memory the disposition of things.

Yet there was nothing special in the room. The furniture, all quite old and of yellow wood, consisted of a couch with an enormous curved wooden back, an oval table in front of the couch, a dressing table and mirror between the windows, chairs along the walls, and two or three cheap pictures in yellow frames—German maidens, birds in their hands. That was all the furniture. In a corner, before a small icon, burned an oil lamp. Everything was very clean. Furniture and floor were polished to a gloss. Everything shone.

"Lizaveta's work," the young man thought. Not a grain of dust in the whole apartment. "It's in the rooms of nasty old widows that one finds a shininess like this." Curious, he touched the chintz curtain that hung over the door to the second small room, where the old woman's bed and bureau stood, and into which he had not yet peered. These two rooms made up the whole apartment.

"What is it you want?" the old woman said sternly, entering the room. As before, she stood directly in front of him so she could look straight into his face.

He pulled an old, flat silver watch out of his pocket. "Here, ma'am. I brought something to pawn!" There was a globe engraved on the back. The chain was of steel.

"The time is up on your last pledge. The month was up the day before yesterday."

"Just be *patient*. I promise I'll bring you the interest, all right."

"That's for me to say. I could sell your pledge right now."

"How much for the watch, Aliona Ivanovna?"

"The stuff you bring me is junk. Look here. It's worthless. Last time I gave two good paper rubles for that ring of yours. I could have bought it new for a ruble and a half at a jeweler's."

"Let me have four rubles. I'll redeem it. It's my father's. I'm getting some money soon."

"A ruble and a half, interest in advance, take it or leave it."

The young man cried: "A ruble and a half!"

"Take it or leave it." The old woman handed him back the watch. The young man was so angry he wanted to leave, but he thought better of it at once, remembering there was nowhere else to go. And after all he had come here for another reason as well.

"Give it here," he said rudely.

The old woman reached into a pocket for her keys, then went behind the curtain into the other room. Left alone, the young man listened eagerly and followed her in his mind's eye. He could hear her open the bureau. "Must be the top drawer," he reckoned. "She carries her keys in the right-hand pocket, no doubt. . . . All in one bunch on a steel ring . . . One key three times as big as the others, with a notched tip, obviously not to the bureau . . . Must be another chest, or a strongbox . . . Funny. Strongboxes all have keys like that. . . . What a lousy business . . ."

The old woman came back.

"Here you are. Ten kopecks a month to the ruble, fifteen kopecks deducted from your ruble and a half for a month in advance. And for the two rubles already on account, at the same rate, twenty kopecks. So that comes to thirty-five. That means you get a ruble fifteen kopecks for your watch. Here."

"So you've got me down to a ruble fifteen, have you!"

"That's it. Exactly."

The young man did not argue. He took the money. Looking at the old woman, he seemed to be in no hurry to leave, as though he still had something he wanted to say, but did not quite know himself what it was. . . .

"I might bring you something else in a day or so, Aliona Ivanovna. . . . It's a good . . . silver . . . it's a cigarette case . . . I'm getting it from a friend of mine. . . ." He became confused and fell silent.

"We'll talk about it when the time comes, my good man."

"Good-bye, ma'am. . . . Oh, yes, by the way. Isn't your sister ever around? Are you always at home alone?" As he was walking into the anteroom he tried to ask this as casually as he could.

"What business is that of yours?"

"Nothing special. I was just asking. And here you're already . . . Well, good-bye, Aliona Ivanovna!"

Raskolnikov left in a great ferment. This ferment kept mounting in intensity. On his way down the stairs he paused several times, each time as though something had suddenly struck him. Finally, out on the street, he exclaimed: "My God! How disgusting! Can I, can I . . . Oh, no! Nonsense. Stupid nonsense!" he added decisively. "How could I get an atrocity like that into my head? Into what filth my impulses . . . The first point is that it's filthy, lousy, foul, foul! . . . And for a whole month I . . ."

But neither words nor expletives could express his agitation. Even while he was still on his way to the old woman's, a feeling of endless disgust had pressed on his heart, twisting it out of shape; and now, this disgust made itself felt so palpably he did not know where he could flee to hide from his anguish. He walked like a drunkard along the sidewalk, heedless of passersby, occasionally bumping into them. He was a long block away before he came to his senses.

He looked around. He was standing in front of a saloon that one entered by stairs leading down from street level to a basement. At that moment two drunks were coming out of the doorway. They were leaning on each other, swearing loudly as they picked their way back to the street. Without stopping to think about it, Raskolnikov made his way down.

He had never gone into a saloon before, but his head whirled and a burning thirst oppressed him. He wanted a drink of cold beer, and he attributed his sudden weakness to the fact that he was hungry. In a dark, dirty corner, at a sticky table, he found a seat. He ordered some beer and drank the first glass down greedily. Immediately he felt better, and his thoughts grew clearer.

"The whole thing's absurd," he said hopefully, "no reason to get all worked up! It's only physical. A glass of beer, a cracker, presto, my mind gets a grip on itself, I can think clearly and my intentions grow firm! God, what appalling pettiness!" And he spat.

In spite of the scorn he had just expressed, he seemed happy now, as though he had suddenly freed himself of a terrible burden. His eyes embraced the denizens of that cellar in a friendly spirit. But even then he had a vague foreboding that this whole shift to the better was pathological too.

Not many people were in the saloon at that time. The two drunks had been followed up the stairs by a group of five men and a girl carrying an accordion. After they left, it seemed quiet and empty. There was a man planted behind his beer, and he looked lower middle-class, drunk, but only slightly. He had a companion: a stout, enormous man in a Siberian jacket, with a gray beard, who was very far gone indeed. He had dozed off on a bench, but every once in a while, in a kind of half sleep, he would jerk his arms upward and apart, and snap his fingers. Without rising from the bench, he would sway the upper part of his body and sing some trashy song, straining to remember such verses as:

> "He cuddled his wife all of a year.
> He cuddled his wife all of a year."

Or, once he had jogged himself awake again:

> "Walking out on Clergy Lane,
> He came upon his former flame. . . ."

But no one shared his fun. Through all these outbursts his silent companion looked at him with hostility and distrust.

There was another man present, who looked like a retired government clerk. He sat apart, a pitcher of vodka before him. Sometimes he took a drink, or, at long intervals, he looked around him. He, too, seemed a bit agitated.

2

Raskolnikov was not used to crowds and had been avoiding company, especially recently. Yet something now suddenly began to draw him to people. Something new was taking place within him, and with this went a kind of craving for people. After a whole month of concentrated melancholy and gloomy excitement, he was so weary he wanted to take breath in some other world, no matter what kind, and even if only for a moment. In spite of all the dirt around him, it was actually with pleasure he lingered in the saloon.

The owner was in another room, but every now and then he descended by some steps into the main room. First a pair of quite fancy boots with large red overflaps would appear; then a long vest, no tie, a very dirty black satin jacket; and the face, which seemed smeared in grease, as though it were an iron padlock. Behind the counter stood a boy of about fourteen; a younger boy waited on customers. Here and there were sliced pickles, black crusts, and fish cut up in chunks. It all had a bad smell. Unbearably stale, the atmosphere was so thoroughly soaked with alcohol, it seemed you could get drunk in five minutes here, from the air alone.

There are some people who interest us immediately, at first glance, before a word is exchanged. The customer sitting by himself who looked like a retired government clerk had this effect on Raskolnikov. Later, Raskolnikov would recall that first impression and think of it as an omen. He kept staring at the clerk just because the latter also was gazing uninterruptedly at him. The clerk apparently very much wanted to strike up a conversation. He looked at everyone else in the saloon, including the owner, with a bored stare that assumed the familiarity of all it met, not without a trace of arrogance, as though he were looking at people socially and intellectually beneath him, with whom he could find little to talk about.

He was a man in his early fifties, of average height and solid build. He had a graying fringe of hair and a large bald spot. His face, puffed out from steady drinking, had taken on a yellow, even a greenish tinge, and he had swollen eyelids from under which flashed slits of tiny but animated reddish eyes. Yet there was something very strange about him. When he looked at you there was the flash of a kind of exaltation and perhaps even intelligence, too, and sense; but also the glitter of a kind of madness. He was dressed in an old black, quite ragged frock coat, and its buttons were missing. He sat with the one button that still hung by a thread buttoned up, as though he were clinging to this last shred of respectability. A shirttail stuck out from under his nankeen jacket, and it was crumpled, soaked, and soiled. As a government clerk, once upon a time, he had kept clean-shaven, but now his face displayed a thick bluish-gray bristle. There really was something solidly official about his manner. Yet he was in distress. He kept running a hand through his hair, or sometimes he propped exposed elbows on the wet, sticky table, gloomily supporting his head with both hands. Finally he looked straight at Raskolnikov and said loudly and firmly: "May I be so bold, my dear sir, as to engage you in polite conversation? Although you are not well dressed, my experience discerns in you an educated man and one unaccustomed to strong drink. I myself have always respected learning when it is combined with sincere feelings. Moreover, I am a titular councillor. Marmeladov is my name: Titular Councillor Marmeladov. May I be so bold as to inquire—are you in the government service?"

"No, I'm studying. . . ." the young man answered. Marmeladov's peculiarly florid turn of speech surprised him. Raskolnikov did not like the way the conversation immediately focused upon himself. Although he had been longing but a moment ago for almost any kind of human community, the first word actually addressed to him induced a feeling of disgust. Such talk, from a stranger, or even a mere allusion to himself as a subject, always made him feel that way.

"A student or former student!" the government clerk shouted. "I thought so! Experience tells, my dear sir, long experience!" He tapped his finger to his forehead in a sign of self-esteem. "I knew immediately that you were from somewhere in the world of learning! But permit . . ." He rose, staggered, seized his glass and pitcher, and sat down closer to the young man, almost diagonally across from him. Though drunk, he spoke sonorously and fluently, only occasionally stumbling here and there and dragging out his speech. As though he too had spoken to no one for a whole month, he fastened on Raskolnikov with a certain desperation.

"My dear sir," he began almost solemnly, "poverty's no vice, and that's the truth. Drunkenness, however, is no virtue; and that's the truth, too, only more so. But destitution, my dear sir, destitution is most certainly a vice. You may be poor, yet still retain a certain inborn nobility of feeling. When you are destitute, there is nothing, there is nobody. When you are destitute, they don't use a stick to chase you away. When you are destitute, they sweep you clear of human companionship; and just to make it more insulting they use a broom. And rightly so. When I am destitute no one is quicker to humiliate me than I myself. And the next

step is the bottle! It was a month ago, my dear sir, that Mr.
Lebeziatnikov beat my wife. Do you know what that means?
Mind you, my wife is not what I am! Allow me to ask you
another question, just out of curiosity. Have you ever spent
a night on the Neva, on the hay barges?"

"No," said Raskolnikov. "What are you driving at?"

"Well, now, I just came from there . . . fifth night
now. . . ."

Filling his glass, he drank it down and paused reflectively.
There were bits of hay clinging to his clothes and in his hair.
He had probably not undressed or washed for five days.
His hands were especially dirty, greasy, red from exposure,
fingernails black.

His talk seemed to elicit general if idle interest. The boys
behind the counter began to snigger. Even the host seemed
to wander down from the room above on purpose to listen
to "the clown." He sat down lazily at a distance and yawned
pompously. Evidently, Marmeladov was well known here
and had acquired that rhetorical flair of his in many such
talks in many such saloons. There are heavy drinkers who
become compulsive talkers, especially those who are hen-
pecked at home, and they are always trying to persuade
their drinking companions to show them some justice and
maybe even, if possible, some respect.

"Clown!" the host resonantly proclaimed. "Why aren't
you working? If you're a civil servant, why don't you serve?"

"The reason I do not serve, my dear sir," rejoined Marmeladov, but addressing himself exclusively to Raskolnikov,
as if he had asked the question, "ah, yes, the reason I do
not serve? Rest assured, sir, that because I grovel in the
dust as I do, my heart aches, and I know, I know it is to no
avail. And when, a month ago, Mr. Lebeziatnikov beat my
wife with his own hands while I was lying there drunk—did
I not suffer? Permit me, young man, has it ever happened to
you . . . hmm . . . well, to ask for a loan, without a chance?"

"It has . . . but what do you mean 'without a chance'?"

"I mean without the ghost of a chance of getting it, when
you know, you know beforehand that you won't get anywhere. When you know beforehand and you know it well
that such and such respectable, most worthy, and most supremely important sir would not even dream of giving you
any money. And why should he, I ask you? After all, he
knows I *won't* give it back. Out of compassion? But Mr.
Lebeziatnikov, that follower of modern ideas, took pains to

explain the other day that in our time compassion is actually forbidden us by science, and that where political economy is practiced, compassion is already abolished by law. *Why,* I ask, should he give? Well, so you know ahead of time he won't give, but you go anyway. You go anyway, and—"

"And why do you go?" Raskolnikov joined in.

"Yet if you do not go to him, you have nowhere else to go! And everyone needs a somewhere, a place he can go. There comes a time, you see, inevitably there comes a time you have to have a somewhere you can go! When my only daughter took to the streets for the first time, I had to go, too. . . . For my daughter lives by the yellow ticket. . . ." he added parenthetically, and he looked at the young man with a certain distress. "It's nothing, my dear sir, nothing!" he immediately hastened to declare, apparently calmly, when both boys behind the counter snorted and the host himself smiled. "Nothing, sir! This shaking of the heads does not disturb me in the least, for the cat is altogether out of the bag, and I regard this not with scorn but with humility. So be it! So be it! 'Behold the man!' Permit me, young man, perhaps you might . . . Ah, no, permit me to put it more bluntly and more vividly. Not, 'perhaps you might,' oh, no, but *do you dare*—you, who gaze on me as I am now—do you dare state definitely that I am not a pig?"

The young man said not a word in reply.

The orator waited for the laughter in the room to subside and continued. "Well, then," he said solemnly, with an access of dignity, "well, then, so be it. I am a swine. But *she* is a lady! I am the shape of a beast, but Katherine Ivanovna, my wife—she is an educated person, she was born the daughter of a staff officer. So be it, so be it. I am a scoundrel, while she is lofty in spirit, and her feelings have been ennobled by education. Ah, still . . . if she only pitied me! My dear sir, why, my dear sir, everyone needs a small such somewhere, where he knows he will be pitied! Katherine Ivanovna—she's magnanimous, mind you. But she's unjust. . . . I know, of course, I know myself that when she pulls my hair, she pulls my hair out of pity. For I repeat without shame, young man, she does pull my hair." He confirmed this with special dignity, after hearing the sniggering once again. "But, oh, God, if she would only once . . . Ah, no, no! What am I talking about, what am I talking about! It's happened more than once, what I wished for, and I was pitied after all . . . but that's the way I am. I'm a beast by nature!"

"You said it!" the host remarked with a yawn.

"Oh, that's the way"—Marmeladov pounded his fist on the table—"that's the way I am! Do you know that I even drank up her stockings? Not her shoes, mind you, for that might still fall within the natural order of things, not her shoes, my dear sir, but her stockings. I drank up her stockings! Her mohair shawl—yes, I drank that up, too. The one she used to own. It was a present, her own property, not mine at all. It's chilly where we live. This past winter she caught cold and started to cough. Now she's coughing blood. We have three small children, and Katherine Ivanovna works at them morning to night. She combs and washes and scrubs those kids. You see, she's used to being clean, used to it from childhood. But she has a weak chest and a tendency to consumption, and, you know, I feel this. Oh, don't I feel it, though? And the more I drink the more I feel it. That's why I drink. Because when I drink, I look for compassion, I look for feeling . . . I drink because I want to suffer!" And as if in desperation, he leaned his head upon the table.

"Young man"—he raised his head again and continued—"I read a certain sorrow in your face. As soon as you came in, I noticed it, and that is why I turned to you. The reason I tell you the story of my life is not because I desire to make a spectacle of myself before these idlers. They know it all anyway. I am looking for a sensitive and educated man. You should know that my wife received her education in an exclusive gentry institute in the provinces. At commencement she danced the shawl dance in the presence of the governor and other dignitaries, and she won a gold medal and a citation for it. The medal . . . well, the medal, yes . . . it was sold . . . some time ago . . . hmm . . . the citation lies in the bottom of her trunk to this day. She was showing it to our landlady not long ago. She fights with the landlady all the time, mind you. Still, she wanted to show off a bit and talk to someone about happy days past. And I don't condemn it, I don't condemn it. This is all she can scrape from the last of her memories, everything else is gone to dust! Yes, yes: a willful, proud, and passionate lady . . . Washes her own floors and eats black bread, but she'll allow no disrespect. She would not suffer Mr. Lebeziatnikov's rudeness, and that's why; and when Mr. Lebeziatnikov beat her for it, she took to her bed. Not so much from the blows as from her feelings. When I married her she was already a widow with three children, each one smaller than the next. Her first husband was an infantry officer, and she married him out of love. They eloped. She loved this first husband very much, but he took to cards, wound up in court, and then he died. Toward the end he used to beat her. And while she didn't just let him get away with it (I know this very well, my dear sir, there is documentary proof), still, to this day she remembers him with tears in her eyes, and she throws him up to me. And I am glad. I am glad she sees herself, even though it's in her fancy, as happy once upon a time. . . . When he died she was left with three small children in a remote and barbarous province, where I also happened to be at the time. She was left in such hopeless destitution that I, though I've seen quite a bit of the world, could not even begin to describe it. Her relatives wouldn't have anything to do with her. She was proud, you see, thoroughly proud. . . . And at that time I was a widower, too, my dear sir, at that time. I had a fourteen-year-old daughter by my first wife. I offered her my hand. I could not bear to look on such suffering. You may judge for yourself, sir, how hard up she was. She agreed to marry me! The well-bred, well-educated daughter of a distinguished family! But she did! Yes, weeping and wailing and wringing her hands, she did! Because there was nowhere to go. Do you understand now, my dear sir, what it means having nowhere to go? No! You wouldn't understand that yet. . . . For a whole year I did my duty honorably and in good faith. I did not touch the stuff"—he tapped his finger on the pitcher—"for I want you to know that I'm a man of feeling. Even so, I had no power to please. And then I lost my job. It wasn't even my own fault that time; the staff was being reorganized. Then I started hitting the bottle really. . . .

"A year and a half ago it was, we found ourselves at last, after many wanderings and numerous calamities, in this metropolis so superbly ornamented by innumerable monuments. And I found a job here, too . . . I found a job, and I lost it again. See? This time it was my own fault. The way I really am, it finally caught up with me. . . . Next thing you know we were living in that corner we rent at our landlady's. Amalia Fiodorovna Lippewechsel. How we live, what we pay her with, I cannot tell you. We are not the only ones who live there, needless to say. . . . A most disorderly Sodom . . . hmm . . . yes . . . My daughter—the daughter of my first marriage—grew up meanwhile. What she suffered in her growing up from her stepmother—about that I will not speak. Katherine Ivanovna overflows with magnanimity, mind you, but she is a lady of temperament, she has her nerves, and she will break out. . . . Yes, well, no point in lingering on it! As for my poor Sonia's upbringing, as you may well imagine, she received none. Four years ago I tried to teach her a little geography, with some world history thrown in. But I was not very strong in these subjects myself, and we had no appropriate texts, because whatever books we had had . . . hmm . . . well, we did not have them anymore. Well, that put an end to her instruction. We stopped at Cyrus the Persian. Later, when she was grown up, she read a few books of a romantic nature, and not long ago, through Mr. Lebeziatnikov, she read Lewes' *Physiology*. Do you by any chance know it? She read it with great interest and even read some passages aloud to us. And that's the whole of her education. Now, my dear sir, I would like to turn to you on my own account with a personal question. Do you think a poor but honorable girl can earn much by honest labor? If she is honorable and has no special talents, she will not, sir, earn fifteen kopecks a day, and I mean working without a stop! Then there is State Councillor Ivan Ivanovich Klopstock. Do you know him? To this day he has not paid her for the half-dozen holland shirts she sewed. Not only that, he drove her off with an insult, stamped his feet and shouted obscenities at her, claiming a collar was askew, not sewn according to specifications. And so the little ones go hungry. . . . And so Katherine Ivanovna paces the room, wringing her hands, and red stains come out on her cheeks the way they do when you have that disease. 'Just look at you, you parasite, sponging off us! You eat, you drink, you keep warm. . . .' *What* she's eating and drinking, God knows. Even the kids hadn't seen a crust of bread for three days! I was down on the floor then . . . well, I won't deny it, I was down on the floor drunk and I hear Sonia talking . . . she is meek, her voice is so mild . . . blonde little creature, face always kind of pale, skinny . . . she says, 'Katherine Ivanovna, you don't really want me to do a thing like that, do you?' There was a wicked woman named Daria Frantsovna, well known to the police, who had tried a couple of times to get in touch with her through the landlady. 'And why not?' answers Katherine Ivanovna in mockery, 'what are you saving it for? Some treasure!' But you mustn't blame her, you mustn't blame her, my dear sir, you mustn't blame her! She was not in her right mind. She was consumed by a wasting disease, her feelings were all upset, she heard the weeping of her hungry children. And it was said more to wound than in the precise sense. . . . Because that is Katherine Ivanovna's nature, and if the children should burst out weeping, even though they do it because they are hungry, right away she starts to beat them. I think it was close to six o'clock. I look and see my Sonia get up. She puts on her cape and kerchief and she leaves the apartment. It was around nine when she returned. She returned, walked straight up to Katherine Ivanovna, and quietly put thirty rubles on the table in front of her. She did not utter a word, she did not even look. She took our large green light wool shawl (we have a light wool shawl that we all use), and she hid her head and face in it and lay down on the bed with her face to the wall. Her body and shoulders kept trembling. . . . And I lay there, just as I was. . . . Then after that, young man, I saw Katherine Ivanovna go to my Sonia's bed. She spent the whole evening on her knees at Sonia's feet; she kissed her feet and did not want to rise. And then they fell asleep in one another's arms . . . both . . . both . . . yes, sir . . . but I . . . I, sir, was lying there drunk."

Marmeladov fell silent, as though his voice had dried up. Suddenly he poured himself a drink, hastily drank it down, and grunted. After a certain silence he continued.

"From that time, sir, from that time, because of one unfortunate occurrence and because malicious people reported her—and it was Daria Frantsovna who urged all that along; it seems she felt she had not been shown sufficient respect—from that time, my daughter, Sofia Semionovna, had to register as a prostitute and carry the yellow ticket, and for that reason she could no longer live with us. Our landlady, Amalia Fiodorovna, would not allow it (she was in league with Daria Frantsovna herself at first, mind you), and Mr. Lebeziatnikov . . . hmm . . . That incident between him and Katherine Ivanovna was on Sonia's account. First he tried to get at Sonia himself, then suddenly he stood back on his dignity: 'How can a man as enlightened as myself live in the same rooms with the likes of that?' But Katherine Ivanovna would not have it; she went up to him, and, well, it happened. . . . Now it's mostly after dark my Sonia comes to us. She helps Katherine Ivanovna and provides what she can. . . . She lives in an apartment at the tailor Kapernaumov's place. She rents an apartment there. Kapernaumov is lame, and he stutters, and everyone in his whole large family stutters. And his wife stutters, too. . . . They live in one room, and Sonia has her own room, with a partition. . . . Hmm, yes . . . The poorest kind of people, and they all stutter . . . yes . . . And then when I rose in the morning I put on my rags and patches, I raised my hands to heaven, and I went to see His Excellency, Ivan Afanasievich. Do you happen to know His Excellency, Ivan Afanasievich? No? Well, it is a man of God that you do not know. This man is wax . . . wax before the Lord's face; even as wax melteth! . . . And when he heard my story he wept. 'Well, Marmeladov,' he says, 'I've been disappointed in you once. . . . I'll take you again, on my own responsibility,' that is the way it was put. 'Remember!' he said, and 'You may go now.' I kissed the dust at his feet—metaphorically, of course, for he would never actually have permitted it; he is a state dignitary and a man of modern education and statesmanlike ideas. I returned home, and when I declared I had a job again and would receive a salary, Lord, what went on. . . ."

Marmeladov paused again, very much aroused. At that moment, a party came in from the street. They were all drunk. The sound of a hired barrel organ came from the entrance, and the cracked childish voice of a seven-year-old singing "The Farm." It grew noisy. The host and staff occupied themselves with the newcomers, to whom Marmeladov, however, paid no attention. He resumed his story. Apparently he had weakened considerably, yet the more drunk, the more fluent he became. Remembering his recent success in the service seemed to enliven him and to imbue his face with a kind of radiance. Raskolnikov listened attentively.

"All that happened five weeks ago, my dear sir. Yes. . . . No sooner had they heard about it, Katherine Ivanovna and my Sonia, when, Lord, it became exactly as though I'd been transported into the Kingdom of Heaven. The way it used to be, I'd be lying there, and they'd treat me as though I were cattle, nothing but abuse! And now they're suddenly walking around on tiptoe, hushing the children: 'Semion Zakharych has been working hard, he needs to rest, ssssh!' Before I went off to work they made coffee for me, and boiled cream for it. Real cream they started to feed me, mind you! And how they scraped up eleven rubles fifty kopecks so I could have a decent uniform I do not understand.

Boots, linen shirt-fronts—the best kind—and my everyday
uniform. They scraped it all together in the most remarkable
way, all for eleven and a half. My first day home from work
for lunch, I took a look: there was soup and corned beef
with horseradish, two whole courses Katherine Ivanovna had
prepared. That would have been unheard of before. She has
no clothes, mind you, really none at all . . . and here I see
she's dressed up as though she were going to a party. She
didn't have a thing, but somehow these women can make
everything out of nothing: a little fixing up of the hair, a
neat, clean little collar of some kind, some cuffs, and lo and
behold she looks like an altogether different kind of person,
younger and prettier. My Sonia, my dove, helped only with
money. 'It's too early,' she says, 'I can't come personally. If
I come to see you too often, it's awkward, unless I come
after dark when no one will see me.' Do you hear that? Do
you hear? After dinner I lay down for a nap, and what do
you think, Katherine Ivanovna could scarcely hold back any
longer. Not more than a week ago, she and the landlady,
Amalia Fiodorovna, had blown up at each other. Now Katherine Ivanovna suddenly calls her in for a cup of coffee.
They sat together for two hours and hashed it all over in
whispers. 'You see, Semion Zakharych is back in the service
now and receiving a salary. He appeared before His Excellency, and His Excellency came out in person. His Excellency ordered everybody else to wait, but Semion Zakharych
he led by the hand, past them all, right into his office.' Do
you hear that? Do you hear? ' "Of course, I remember your
past services, Semion Zakharych," he says, "and I know you
used to have this little weakness, but things have gone badly
here without you, and since you've promised—" ' Do you
hear that? Do you hear? ' "I depend on you," he says, "and
on your word of honor!" ' Everything I'm telling you, all of
it, she made it up herself, but you mustn't think she was
just foolishly bragging! Oh, no, she believed every bit of it
herself, she was comforting herself with her fantasies! And,
by God, I don't blame her! No, I do not blame her for it!
Six days ago I brought her my first full pay, twenty-three
rubles forty kopecks. And she called me her little minnow.
'Little minnow,' she says, 'you are my little minnow!' We
were alone by ourselves, mind you. I'm no beauty, and what
kind of a husband am I, after all? And yet she pinched my
cheek. 'You are my little minnow!' she says."

Marmeladov paused. He wanted to smile, but his chin

suddenly began to quiver. Yet he restrained himself. The saloon, the man's dissipated appearance, his five nights on the hay barge, and with all this his morbid love for wife and family, bewildered Raskolnikov, who was listening intently but with a morbid sensation. He regretted having come here.

Marmeladov recovered himself. "My dear sir, my dear sir!" he exclaimed. "Oh, my dear sir, perhaps it all seems a laughing matter to you as it does to others, and I merely annoy you with the stupid, miserable details of my domestic life. But to me it is not a laughing matter! For I can feel it all. . . . All that heavenly day of my life and that whole evening I allowed myself to be carried away by fleeting dreams. I would fix everything, buy clothes for the little ones, comfort my wife, rescue my only daughter from dishonor and bring her back into the bosom of the family. . . . And so on, and so on. . . . It's understandable, sir. Well, then, my dear sir"—Marmeladov suddenly winced, raised his head, and gazed steadily at his listener—"well, then, after all those dreams, on the very next day, five days ago exactly, as evening came on, like a thief in the night I used a sly trick, I pried loose the key to Katherine Ivanovna's strongbox, and I took out what was left of the pay I brought home. How much it was I don't remember. And—mind you, look at me—that—look at me now—that was all! It is my fifth day away from home. They are looking for me there. And my job is done with. And my uniform lies in a saloon near the Egyptian Bridge. I picked up this outfit instead . . . and everything is finished!"

Marmeladov pounded himself on the forehead with his fist, ground his teeth, closed his eyes, and leaned his elbow heavily on the table. Yet after a moment his face changed suddenly. It was with a certain self-indulgent slyness and affected bravado that he threw Raskolnikov a quick glance, laughed, and said: "I was at Sonia's today. I went and I asked her for cash to buy me a snifter! He-he-he!"

From among the crowd that had just come in, someone shouted and laughed out loud: "Don't tell me she gave it to you?"

"You see this half pitcher here; I bought it with her money," said Marmeladov, addressing himself exclusively to Raskolnikov. "She gave me thirty kopecks with her own hands, the last she had, everything, I could see that myself. . . . She said nothing. She only looked at me in silence. . . . Not as it is done here on earth, but *there* . . .

where they sorrow over people, where they weep, and where
they do not reproach, no, they do not reproach! Yet it hurts
worse, it hurts much worse, when they do not reproach. . . .
Thirty kopecks, yes, sir. And suppose she needed them?
Suppose she needed them right now? Ah? What do you
think, my dear sir? She has to keep up a neat, clean style
now, her polish. That neat, clean style costs money, you
understand, that something extra. . . . You understand, don't
you? Well, she has to buy makeup, too, can't do without it.
Starched petticoats, and a little slipper to display her foot
more enchantingly as she steps over a puddle . . . You understand, don't you, sir, what this kind of polish means? Well,
then, here I am, her own blood father, and I took her thirty
kopecks to go and get myself drunk! And I dri-i-ink! And
it's all gone! . . . Well, who is going to be sorry for the likes
of me? Ah? Are you sorry for me, sir, are you sorry for me
now or not? Go on and say it, sir. Are you sorry or are you
not? He-he-he-he!"

He wanted to pour himself another drink, but none was
left by now. The half-bottle was empty.

"Why should anybody be sorry for you?" shouted the
owner, who was near them.

There was an outburst of laughter and swearing. Those
who had been listening laughed and swore; and so did those
who had not been listening, but merely caught a glimpse of
the singular figure of the former clerk.

"Feel sorry! Why should anyone feel sorry for me!" Marmeladov suddenly sang out. He rose, hand stretched forward, positively inspired, as though all along he had been
merely waiting for these very words. "Why feel sorry, you
say? Oh, yes, there is no reason to feel sorry for me! I
need to be crucified, not pitied! Crucified! Crucify, O Judge,
crucify, and when you have crucified, then take pity! If you
do that, I will come and ask for crucifixion, for it is not
merriment I crave, but tears and sorrow! Think you, publi-
can, your bottle has been a sweetness unto me? It has been
a sorrow. I have sought sorrow in its dregs, sorrow and tears,
and I found and savored them. He will feel sorry for us who
has felt sorry for all and understood each and everyone: He
alone is Judge. On the day of His coming He will ask:
'Where is the daughter who sold herself for the sake of a
bad-tempered and consumptive stepmother, for the sake of
someone else's little children? Where is the daughter that
felt sorry for her earthly father, an obscene drunkard, fear-

ing not his beastliness?' And He will say: 'Come! I have already forgiven thee once. . . . Once already I forgave thee . . . Thy sins which are many are forgiven thee for thou hast loved much. . . .' And He forgives my Sonia; forgives, why, I *know* that He forgives. . . . When I was with her not long ago, I felt this in my heart! And He will judge and forgive all, the good and the evil, the wise and the humble. . . . And when He has finished judging all, He will summon us, too: 'You, too, come forth,' He will say, 'Come forth, you drunkards; come forth, you weaklings; come forth, you shameless ones!' And we will all come forth unashamed. And we will stand before Him, and He will say: 'You are swine, made in the image of the Beast, with his seal upon you: but you, too, come unto me!' And the wise and the clever will cry out: 'Lord! why dost thou receive these men?' And He will say: 'I receive them, O wise and clever ones, because not one among them considered himself worthy of this. . . .' And He will stretch out His hands unto us, and we will fall down before Him and weep . . . and we will understand everything . . . and Katherine Ivanovna . . . she will understand, too. . . . O Lord! Thy kingdom come!''

He dropped to the bench, weak and exhausted, and he looked at no one, as though oblivious to his surroundings and deep in thought. His words had produced a certain impression. For a moment silence reigned. Then the laughter and swearing broke out again.

"He has it all figured out!"

"Talking through his hat!"

"A fine civil servant!"

And so on, and so on.

"Let us go, sir," Marmeladov said suddenly, lifting his head and addressing Raskolnikov. "Take me home . . . Kozel's house, in the yard. It's time . . . to get back to Katherine Ivanovna. . . ."

Raskolnikov had long since wanted to leave, and it had occurred to him to help Marmeladov, who seemed much weaker on his feet than in his speech. He leaned heavily on the young man. They had perhaps two or three hundred paces to go. As they approached the house, fear and confusion possessed the drunkard more and more.

"I am not afraid of Katherine Ivanovna now," he muttered in agitation, "and it's not because she starts pulling my hair that I'm afraid. What do I care about hair! Hair doesn't mean a thing! If she starts pulling, it is even better.

That is not what I am afraid of. . . . I am . . . afraid of her eyes . . . yes . . . her eyes. . . . I am also afraid of those red stains on her cheeks. . . . And I am afraid of the way she breathes. . . . You know how they breathe when they have this disease . . . when their feelings are all tense and excited? I am also afraid of the children's weeping. . . . Because if Sonia did not bring them food . . . Well, I don't know, I just don't know! But I am not afraid of blows. . . . You must realize, sir, that such blows not only fail to inflict pain, they are actually a pleasure. . . . I could not get along without them. It is better. Let her beat me; it distracts her. . . . It is better. . . . Ah, there's the house. Kozel's house. He's a mechanic, a German, rich. . . . Lead on!"

They entered from the yard and climbed up to the fourth floor. The further they mounted the darker the stairs became. It was almost eleven by then. There was no real night in Petersburg at this time of year, but at the top of the stairs it was quite dark.

At the very top of the stairs a small, grimy door stood open. A candle butt illuminated a squalid room about ten paces long. Everything in it was visible from the landing. The room was in terrible disorder, with all kinds of rags scattered about, especially children's old clothes. A tattered bed sheet stretched across the far corner, probably with a bed behind it. There were only two chairs, and an extremely battered couch with some kind of water-repellent covering. In front of this stood an old pine kitchen table, unpainted and uncovered. At one edge stood a burned-down tallow candle butt in an iron holder. The Marmeladovs, it seemed, lived in a room of their own, not in a corner of someone else's room, but their room served as a passageway. The door that led to the other rooms or cubicles into which Amalia Lippewechsel's apartment was divided stood ajar. It was loud and noisy there. Someone laughed. They were playing cards and drinking tea. Every now and then the most unceremonious words came flying out.

Raskolnikov immediately recognized Katherine Ivanovna. A delicately built woman, fairly tall and well proportioned, with still attractive dark brown hair, she had grown terribly thin, and her cheeks had turned red as though with stain. She paced that small room, hands folded across her chest, lips parched, her breath coming in broken and irregular gasps. Her eyes flashed as though with fever, yet her gaze was sharp and steady. In the last flickering of the burned-down candle butt, this consumptive and agitated face produced a painful impression. To Raskolnikov she seemed about thirty; she was obviously much younger than Marmeladov. She seemed immersed in a kind of oblivion and did not notice them as they came in. She did not see and she did not listen. Though the room was stifling, she did not open the window. A stench wafted up the stairs, but the door onto the landing was not closed. Through the partly open door from the inner quarters waves of tobacco smoke drifted. She coughed, but did not shut the door. The youngest child, a girl of about six, sat on the floor asleep, her head buried in the couch. A boy, a year or so older, stood in a corner, quivering and weeping. He must have been beaten not long ago. The elder daughter, about nine, stood in the corner by the side of her small brother. She was rather tall, and spindly as a matchstick, and had on a threadbare, tattered chemise under a shabby light wool cape that was flung over her naked shoulders. The cape had probably been made for her some years back, since it did not now reach anywhere near her knees. Her long, wizened, matchsticklike arm was draped about her brother's neck, and she seemed to be soothing him, whispering to him, restraining him somehow so he no longer whimpered. At the same time she was following her mother with her huge, dark, terror-stricken eyes, which tended to seem even larger in that meager and frightened little face.

Marmeladov did not enter the room, remaining on his knees in the doorway, but he pushed Raskolnikov on ahead. Seeing a stranger, the woman paused distractedly in front of him and came to herself for a moment, as though she were groping to imagine what in the world he had come for. An explanation seemed to come quickly to mind, perhaps to the effect that he must be on his way to one of the other rooms, since hers was a passageway. She then paid no further attention to him, but walked toward the door to shut it. Seeing her husband on his knees at the threshold, she cried out.

"Aaaah!" she screamed in a frenzy, "he's come back! The monster! The hoodlum! Where's the money? What's in your pocket? Show me! Those aren't your clothes! Where are your clothes? Where's the money? Speak up! . . . ."

She fell to searching him. Marmeladov immediately stretched his hands to both sides, humbly and obediently, in order to make her search of his pockets easier. There was not a kopeck.

"Where's the money?" she yelled. "O Lord, he's drunk it all up! But there were twelve rubles left in the box!" Suddenly she seized him in a frenzy by the hair and dragged him into the room. Marmeladov made it easier for her by meekly sliding after her on his knees.

"And I tell you I enjoy it! I tell you I feel no pain, but I actually enjoy it, my dear sir!" This he shouted out as he was being shaken by the hair, and once his forehead even struck the floor. The youngest child, asleep on the floor, woke and wept. The boy in the corner lost control, trembled violently, screamed, and flung himself upon his sister, terror-stricken, almost in a fit. Half awake, the older girl shook like a leaf.

"He drank it up! He drank it all up! Everything!" the poor woman shouted out in her desperation, "and his clothes are not the same! They're hungry! Hungry!" Wringing her hands, she pointed to the children. "Oh, damn this life! And you, there!" Suddenly she hurled herself on Raskolnikov. "Aren't you ashamed? So you were drinking with him at the saloon, were you? You were drinking with him, too? Get out!"

Without saying a word, the young man hastened to depart. By now, the inner door was wide open and from the threshold peered several curious onlookers. Brazen, laughing faces pushed their way in, cigarettes or pipes dangling from their mouths, skull caps on their heads. Some were in their bathrobes, some quite unbuttoned, scantily and immodestly dressed and in disarray; some still held playing cards in their hands. They laughed with particular amusement when Marmeladov, pulled by the hair, shouted out that he enjoyed it. Some of them even came into the room. At last an ominous shriek was heard, and that was Amalia Lippewechsel, who now pushed her way forward. She was going to settle things in her own way. For the hundredth time she was going to threaten the poor woman to force her to move out by to-morrow. As he was leaving Raskolnikov managed to thrust his hand into his pocket and pull out whatever coins he had left in change from his ruble. He put them unnoticed on the windowsill. Later, on the stairs, he had second thoughts and wanted to turn back.

"What the hell am I doing," he thought. "I need that money myself, and they have their Sonia, after all." But he decided it was impossible to take the money back. Even if it hadn't been impossible, he would not in any case have taken it back. He waved his hand and set out for his own apartment. "Sonia needs makeup, after all," he continued as he strode along the street. He smiled caustically. "That kind of polish costs money. . . . Hmm! And maybe our Sonia herself will go broke today, because, after all, there *is* a risk involved, hunting big game . . . or prospecting for gold. . . . Without my money they might not have a thing tomorrow. . . . Ah, Sonia, Sonia! That's quite a gold mine they've got, and they know how to dig! They do know how to dig, though! And they've gotten used to it. They wept, and then they got used to it. That scoundrel, man—he gets used to anything!

"Well, and what if I'm wrong," he suddenly exclaimed involuntarily. "What if man really isn't a *scoundrel*, man in general, that is, the race, I mean the whole human race? Then the rest is—prejudice? Empty fear? And there are no barriers, and everything is as it should be!"

3

The next morning, after a troubled sleep, a sleep that had not refreshed him, he woke up late. He woke up tense, bilious, and irritable, and looked with hatred at his tiny room. It was a minute cubicle, six steps long. Peeling off the wall in strips, the dusty yellow wallpaper gave the room a most sorry appearance. The ceiling was so low that a man of any height could not stand there without the sense that he was about to bump his head. The furniture matched the room. There were three old chairs. In the corner was a painted table, not quite level, and on it lay several books and notebooks which, covered with dust, apparently had not been touched for quite some time. Finally, a large, clumsy couch occupied almost the entire wall and half the width of the whole room. Once upholstered in chintz, it was now badly tattered. This couch served Raskolnikov as a bed. Often he dropped off to sleep on it as he was, without undressing, without a sheet, covering himself with his dilapidated old student's overcoat. He rested his head on a small pillow under which he stuffed all the linen he had, clean or dirty, to prop it up a little higher. In front of the couch stood a small table.

To let himself go more than he had, to sink lower, would have been difficult. Yet Raskolnikov, in the mood he was in, actually found this state of things agreeable. He had withdrawn from everything, like a turtle into his shell. Even the face of the maid whose job it was to look after him, and who occasionally threw a glance into the room, roused his bile and filled him with disgust. With certain monomaniacs who have been concentrating on something for too long, that is the way it goes. Since two weeks ago his landlady had stopped sending him up food. But he went without his dinner and never thought of having the issue out with her. Nastasia, the landlady's cook and only servant, seemed willing enough to humor this inclination of his. She had entirely abandoned sweeping and tidying up his room. It was only once a week that she would mosey in behind a broom, accidentally as it were. She woke him up now.

"Get up, now's no time to sleep!" she shouted, bending over him. "It's ten o'clock. I brought you some tea. Want some tea? Wouldn't surprise me if you was near starved."

He opened his eyes, shuddered, and recognized Nastasia.

"The landlady send this tea up, or what?" he asked. He propped himself up on the couch slowly and with a pained look.

"What do you mean, the landlady!"

She put her own cracked kettle down in front of him, poured out some weak tea, and deposited two yellowish lumps of sugar.

"Here, take this please, Nastasia," he said, rummaging about in his pockets (he had fallen asleep fully dressed) and fishing out a few mixed copper coins. "Go buy me a roll. And maybe a little sausage. The cheapest kind."

"I'll go get you a roll this minute, but instead of the sausage, wouldn't you rather have some cabbage soup? It's good. It's yesterday's. I saved some for you yesterday, but you didn't get in till late. It's good cabbage soup."

When the cabbage soup came and he began on it, Nastasia sat down beside him on the couch and began to chat. She was one of those country women who love to jabber away.

"Praskovia Pavlovna wants to complain to the police about you," she said.

He frowned. "To the police? Why?"

"You won't pay up and you won't move out. What she wants is clear."

"Eh, to hell with her," he muttered, grinding his teeth. "That's all I needed. . . . No . . . I can't have that right now. . . . She's a fool," he added loudly, "I'll go talk to her today."

"She's a fool, I'm a fool, and what are you? You're smart all right, lying around like a lump, no good to anybody. Before, you used to go out and teach kids, you said, but why don't you do a damn thing now?"

"I do. . . ." Raskolnikov said sternly and reluctantly.

"What do you do?"

"Work. . . ."

"What kind of work?"

"I think," he answered seriously, after a short silence.

Nastasia rocked with laughter. She was prone to laughter, and when it seized her she laughed inaudibly, heaving and shaking with her whole body until she felt positively ill.

"Do you make a lot of money thinking?" she finally managed to ask.

"I can't go out to teach if I don't have a decent pair of shoes. And I'm fed up; I spit on them all."

"Don't spit in your own well."

"You don't make anything teaching kids. What can you do with small change?" he went on distastefully, as though he were answering his own thoughts.

"You want to make a fortune all at once?"

He looked at her strangely. "Yes," he answered firmly after a pause, "a fortune all at once."

"Well, for goodness' sake, take it easy. You scare me. . . . Shall I go get the roll or not?"

"As you like."

"Oh, I forgot! There was a letter for you yesterday while you were out."

"A letter! For me! From whom?"

"I don't know from whom. I paid the mailman three kopecks, my own money. You going to pay me back?"

"Bring it here, for God's sake, bring it here!" Raskolnikov, quite beside himself, cried out. "Oh, Lord!"

The letter appeared, and it was from his mother, from Riazan Province. He turned pale as he picked it up. He had received no letters for a long time. But now it was not that, it was something quite different that gave his heart a twinge.

"Go, Nastasia, for God's sake. Here are your three kopecks, but for God's sake, go. Quickly!"

The letter trembled in his hands. He did not want to open
it in her presence. He wanted, with this letter, to be *alone*.
When Nastasia left, he quickly lifted it to his lips and kissed
it. For a long time he stared at the address on the envelope,
at his mother's dear, familiar, delicate, slanted handwriting.
She had taught him how to read and write, once upon a
time. He delayed. He seemed to be afraid of something.
Finally he opened it. The letter was a long one: the small,
delicate handwriting densely covered two large pages of
stationery.

My dear Rodia, it is a little over two months now since
I've chatted with you by mail, and this has caused me
some distress and I've even lain awake nights thinking
about it. But you won't blame me for my involuntary
silence. You know how much I love you. You are all
we have left, Dunia and I, you are our everything, all
our wishes and all our hope. How it stunned me when
I learned you left the university some months back
because you had no means to support yourself, that
the lessons you were giving and the other things you
were doing had ceased! With only my hundred-
twenty-rubles-a-year pension, how could I help you?
The fifteen rubles I sent you four months ago I borrowed, as you know yourself, on the credit of this
pension from our local merchant, Afanasy Ivanovich
Vakhrushin. He is a good man and was a friend of
your father's. Having turned over to him the right to
receive my pension until the debt was paid, I had to
wait. It has only just been paid, and in all this time
there was nothing I could send you. Thank God, I
now seem to be able to send you something. As a
matter of fact, it seems we can thank our lucky stars
all the way around, and I now hasten to tell you all
about it. First of all, I wonder if you know, Rodia
dear, that your sister has been living with me this past
month and a half, and in the future we will no longer
be separated from each other. Thank the Lord, her
sufferings are over, but I will tell you everything in
order, everything we have kept from you, and how it
all was. About two months ago, when you wrote me
you had heard from someone that Dunia had a good

deal to put up with in the Svidrigailov household, and you asked me for a precise explanation—what could I then write you in reply? If I had written you the whole truth, you would certainly have abandoned everything and come to us, on foot if need be, for I know your character and feelings, and you would not let your sister be insulted. I was desperate myself, but what could I do? At that time even I did not know the whole truth. The main trouble was that when Dunia went to work as governess in their house a year ago, they paid her a hundred rubles in advance on her salary, a certain amount to be taken out every month. It was impossible for her to quit her job before she had paid back her debt. In taking this money, her main motive (now I can tell you all about it, Rodia, my precious) was to send you sixty rubles—of which you were in such need, and which you received from us this past year. At that time we deceived you. We wrote you that it came out of money Dunia had saved up from before. But that was not true. Now I will tell you the whole truth, because everything has suddenly changed, by God's will, for the better; and now you may know how great is Dunia's love for you, and how precious. Actually, Mr. Svidrigailov treated her extremely rudely from the beginning, and at table perpetrated a number of jokes and discourtesies at her expense. . . . But I do not want to go into all these unfortunate details; I do not wish to disturb you in vain, especially since it is all over now. In short, in spite of the fine and decent way that Martha Petrovna (Mrs. Svidrigailov) and all the domestics treated her, it was very difficult for our Dunia, especially when Mr. Svidrigailov, relapsing into his old regimental habit, found himself under the influence of Bacchus. The motive for his deplorable behavior was made clear only later. Can you imagine, this madman, some time ago, actually conceived a passion for Dunia, but he concealed it and pretended to be rude to her and to hold her in contempt. Perhaps when he had a look at himself—well on in years and the father of a family—he felt ashamed of himself, and horrified to be caught up in such foolish desires. Perhaps that is why he had it in for Dunia, in spite of himself. Or it may be that by his rudeness and his jokes he hoped to hide the truth from others. In the end, he no longer restrained himself, and went so far as to proposition Dunia directly, openly, shamelessly, promising her all sorts of things, offering moreover to give everything up and run away with her to another village, or even, if you please, abroad. You can imagine yourself what she suffered! She could not, at the time, leave her job; not only because of the money she owed, but also to spare Martha Petrovna, whose suspicions would suddenly have been aroused, to prevent discord within the family. It would also have made a great scandal for our Dunia, inevitably so. For a number of different reasons, Dunia could not count on escaping from that terrible household in less than six weeks. Of course, you know Dunia. You know how clever she is, what a strong-minded character she has. Our Dunia can bear a lot. Even in the most extreme circumstances she has reserves of magnanimity, she is strong-minded. About all this, she did not even write me—in order not to upset me—and, mind you, we corresponded frequently. The resolution came as a surprise. Martha Petrovna accidentally overheard her husband while he was imploring Dunia in the garden. Misinterpreting, she blamed Dunia for everything, thinking somehow that Dunia was responsible. A terrible scene in the garden followed. Martha Petrovna even struck Dunia. She would listen to nothing, shouted steadily for a whole hour, and at last gave orders that Dunia be driven off to my place in town, immediately, in a peasant cart, into which all her things were thrown—linen, dresses, everything as it came, unpacked and helter-skelter. Then it began to rain hard, and Dunia, insulted and humiliated, had to ride with a peasant, twelve miles in an open cart. Think, then, how could I have answered that letter of yours I received two months ago? What could I have written? I myself was desperate. I did not dare to write you the truth. You would have been extremely unhappy; you would have been outraged and angry. And what, after all, could you have done? You could only have ruined yourself. Dunia forbade it. Simply to fill a letter with little things of one kind or another when inside I felt so badly—I was not up to it. For a whole month nasty rumors about this episode circulated in the town, and

things went so far that Dunia and I could no longer
go to church, because of the suspicious glances and
the whispering; and there were even conversations
aloud in our presence. Our acquaintances began to
avoid us, no one even said hello to us, and I learned
that some store clerks and officeboys were preparing
to insult us in a low way, to smear the gates of our
house with tar. And our landlord began asking us to
move out of our apartment. Martha Petrovna was the
reason behind it all. She had accused and blackened
Dunia in all homes. She knew everyone we knew.
That month she drove into town frequently, and since
she was a bit of a gossip and enjoyed telling her family
affairs, and especially loved complaining about her
husband to each and all, she managed in a short time
to spread the whole story, and not only in the town
but throughout the whole district. I took sick. Dunia
proved stronger-minded than I. If you had only seen
how she survived it all, and comforted me and gave
me courage! She is an angel! By God's mercy, however, our torments came to an end. Mr. Svidrigailov
took hold of himself and repented. Probably he pitied
Dunia, and he presented Martha Petrovna with full
and obvious proof of our Dunia's innocence; specifi-
cally, a letter Dunia had written and handed to him
sometime before that incident in the garden. The letter requested an end to the secret meetings and personal explanations on which he had been insisting. Mr.
Svidrigailov kept it after Dunia left. She reproached
him in this letter most vigorously, thoroughly indignant at his treatment of Martha Petrovna, reminding
him that he was a father and a family man and, finally,
how vile it was on his part to torment and make miserable a defenseless girl who had already suffered misfortune enough. In short, Rodia my dear, this letter
was written in such a touching and noble manner that
I wept when I read it, and I have not been able to
read it without weeping since. I should add that the
servants came to Dunia's defense as witnesses. As always happens in such cases, they had seen and they
knew much more than Mr. Svidrigailov imagined.
Martha Petrovna was quite taken aback, and as she
told us herself, "struck dead anew." She was in any
case fully convinced of our Dunia's innocence, and on

the very next day, Sunday, went straight to church, prayed on her knees, with tears in her eyes, to our Sovereign Mistress to give her the strength to bear this new trial and to do her duty. Straight from the cathedral she came to us. She told us everything, wept bitterly, and fully repentant, embraced Dunia and implored her to forgive her. That very morning, without any delay, she went straight from our place to every home in town. Everywhere, in phrases that were most flattering to Dunia, tears flowing all the while, she vindicated Dunia's innocence and the propriety of Dunia's feelings and behavior. What is more, she showed everybody Dunia's original letter to Mr. Svidrigailov and read it aloud and even (as she had me previously) let them copy it (which would seem to me to be going a bit too far). She spent several days in this way, trying to reach everyone in town, for some people had been offended that others had been shown preference. Thus, a kind of pecking order was established, and each household knew ahead of time that on such a day Martha Petrovna would be in such and such a place to read the letter. And at every reading many people gathered who had already heard the letter several times in their own homes and in their friends' as well. In my opinion, a good deal of this, quite a good deal, was unnecessary. But that is Martha Petrovna's character. At least she vindicated Dunia's honor completely. The whole infamy and shame of the affair lay indelibly upon her husband, and I even began to feel sorry for him. That was being altogether too stern with such a madman. Dunia was requested to give lessons in several homes, but she refused. In general, everyone started to treat her with special deference. And all this helped bring about an unexpected event, through which one might say our entire lot has been altered. You must know, Rodia my dear, that Dunia has been offered a proposal of marriage and she has already deigned to consent, and I hasten to inform you of this as quickly as possible. Although it was done without your advice, I trust you will not hold that against either your sister or myself. You will see for yourself that putting things off until you replied was impossible. And you would not have been able to judge properly without being here yourself. This is the

way it came about. He is already a court councillor,
this Peter Petrovich Luzhin, and he is a distant relative
of Martha Petrovna's. Indeed, she helped a good deal
in arranging everything. He began by conveying to her
a desire to make our acquaintance. He was properly
invited, we had coffee, and on the very next day he
sent a letter in which he quite courteously explained
his proposal and requested a quick and definite answer. He is a man of affairs, and busy. At present he
is off to St. Petersburg, and he values every moment.
Of course, we were a bit taken aback at first, because
it all happened so quickly and unexpectedly. That
whole day we thought the thing over together. He is
a promising and prosperous man, has two official jobs,
and already has money of his own. True, he is forty-
five, but rather good-looking and still attractive to
women. He is in general quite a solid and reliable
man. A bit morose, perhaps, and haughty. But this
may be merely a first impression. And let me warn
you, Rodia dear, when you see him in Petersburg,
which you will very soon now, don't judge him too
quickly or impulsively in that way you have, if your
first impression of him strikes you as not quite right.
I say this just in case, though actually I am convinced
he will impress you pleasantly. And anyway, in order
really to get to know any man, one must do it gradually and cautiously, so as not to fall into prejudice or
to make a mistake which would be rather difficult to
correct or smooth over later. Peter Petrovich, according to many indications, at least, is an extremely
worthy man. At the time of his very first visit, he
declared to us that he was a practical man, but that he
shared in many things "the convictions of our younger
generation," as he put it, and that he was against all
forms of prejudice. He said a good deal beside, for he
is just a little bit vain and enjoys having people listen
to him; but this is a small vice. Of course, I did not
understand much of it, but Dunia made it clear to
me that, though he is a man of little education, he is
nevertheless intelligent; and, it would seem, kind. You
know your sister's character, Rodia. She is a strong-
minded girl, clever, patient, and magnanimous, though
she has a fervent heart, a trait I have come to know
well in her. Of course, love is not especially involved,

either on her side or on his; but Dunia is, in addition to being a clever girl, a noble creature, like an angel, and would make her husband's happiness her duty. I am sure he would concern himself for his part over her happiness, too. At least, we have no good reason to doubt that he would, though it must be admitted that arrangements were made rather quickly. Moreover, he is a very shrewd man, and he will naturally see for himself that his own marital happiness will be the greater the happier Dunia is with him. And if there is a certain unevenness to his character, if there are certain odd habits, and some disagreement as to ideas (impossible to avoid even in the happiest of marriages)—Dunia has told me that she counts on herself in these matters, that there is little cause for anxiety, and that she could bear a great deal as long as their basic relationship remained honest and true. At first he seemed to me a bit abrupt, but this may actually be due to the fact that he is a straightforward kind of person, and just can't help it. During his second visit, for example, after he had received our consent, he said in the course of our conversation that even before he had met Dunia he had intended marrying an honorable girl who had no dowry and who knew what it was like to be poor; for, as he explained, a husband should not be obliged to his wife for anything, since it is much better the other way around, if the wife considers the husband her benefactor. I must in all fairness add that he put it somewhat more softly and delicately than I have, since I have forgotten what he actually said and remember only the idea. Moreover, all this was said without aforethought, but obviously spontaneously in the heat of conversation, and later he even tried to qualify and soften it a bit. Nevertheless, I thought it was a little abrupt, and I told Dunia as much. But she replied indignantly that "word and deed are two different things," and that is of course true. Before she arrived at her decision, Dunia spent a sleepless night. Assuming that I was already asleep, she got up from her bed and paced up and down her room all night long. Finally she went down on her knees before the icon and prayed long and fervently, and in the morning she let me know that she had decided.

I have already mentioned that Peter Petrovich is on his way to Petersburg. He has important business there and wants to open a lawyer's office in Petersburg. He has been practicing law for some time, and only the other day he won a very important case. He has to be in Petersburg because he has an extremely important case coming up before the Senate. He may, incidentally, be quite useful to you in this way, Rodia my dear; in fact, in all kinds of ways. Dunia and I have supposed that you might definitely begin on your future career from this very day and regard your lot as clearly settled. Oh, if this could only be! It would be such a benefit as would have to be considered a blessing on us straight from the Almighty. Dunia dreams only of this. We have already ventured to say a few words to Peter Petrovich on this subject. He replied cautiously to the effect that since he could not get along without a secretary, naturally it was better to pay a salary to a relative than to a stranger, provided he showed an aptitude for the job (as though there were any doubt you would show an aptitude for it!), yet he expressed some doubt as to whether your university studies would leave you time for work in his office. We ended on that for the time being, but Dunia has since thought of nothing else. For the last few days she has been in a kind of fever and has composed an entire project pointing out how you could become Peter Petrovich's assistant and eventually perhaps even his partner, especially since you are studying law yourself. I agree with her completely, Rodia, and I share all her plans and hopes, and I think they are quite realistic. Dunia is firmly convinced, in spite of Peter Petrovich's present quite understandable evasiveness (after all, he does not know you yet), that she will be able to arrange everything through her good influence on her future husband, and she is convinced of it. Of course, we have been careful about mentioning our more remote plans to Peter Petrovich, especially your becoming his partner. He is a practical man and might take this rather coldly, since all this might seem to him mere dreaming. Nor have Dunia and I mentioned our strong hope that he will help us pay for your university education. We did not mention it, first of all, because later on it will no doubt come of itself. Peter Petrovich will do it on his own, without any waste of words—as though he could refuse our Dunia this—particularly since you might become his right hand in the office, and so you'd be receiving this assistance not as charity, but as a salary earned. That is the way Dunia would like to manage it, and I agree with her completely. Secondly, we did not mention it because I particularly wanted you to feel on an equal footing when you met him, as you will shortly. When Dunia proudly told him about you, he replied that one had to observe a man for oneself, as closely as possible, before one could judge him, and that he proposes to get to know you and form his own opinion about you. Do you know, my priceless Rodia, I have been thinking about it, and it seems to me (it has nothing to do with Peter Petrovich, it is just one of my own personal old ladyish whims) perhaps it would be better if, after their marriage, I lived alone as I live now, and not with them. I am quite convinced that he will be well bred and tactful enough to ask me himself to live with them, so that I should not be separated from my daughter any longer, and that if he has not yet mentioned it, of course, that is because it is self-understood. Nevertheless, I will refuse. I have more than once noticed in the course of my life that mothers-in-law do not much endear themselves to husbands, and not only do I not want to be the least burden to anyone, but I wish to be fully free myself as long as I have a crust to eat and children such as you and Dunia. If possible, I will settle down near both of you; and, Rodia, I have saved the most pleasant news of all for the end of my letter. My dear, you should know that we shall be together again very soon now, and the three of us can embrace after a separation of almost three years! It has been settled *for certain* that Dunia and I are setting out for St. Petersburg; I do not know exactly when, but in any case very very soon, perhaps within a week. It all depends what arrangements Peter Petrovich makes. As soon as he has had a chance to look around in Petersburg, he is going to let us know immediately. He would like for some reason to speed up the ceremonial as much as he can, and even, if possible, have the wedding before Shrovetide; but if not (there isn't much time, after all) then immediately after Assumption. Oh, how good it will be to put my arms around you! Dunia is overjoyed at the prospect of seeing you again, and she has even told me, as a joke, of course, that she would marry Peter Petrovich for this alone. She is an angel! She is not going to write you anything now, but she asks me to tell you that she has so much to say to you, so much, that she does not dare pick up her pen, for in a few lines one can say nothing and one only gets oneself all worked up. She asks me to send you her love and innumerable kisses. Although we will be seeing you very soon in person, I am going to send you some money in a day or so anyway, as much as I can. Since everybody has learned that Dunia is about to marry Peter Petrovich my credit has suddenly zoomed, and I am sure that Afanasy Ivanovich will trust me on the pledge of my pension for as much as seventy-five rubles, if need be, so I will send you perhaps twenty-five or even thirty rubles. I would send more if I were not worried about our expenses for the journey. Although Peter Petrovich has been kind enough to assume part of our expenses—he has undertaken to have our luggage and large trunk conveyed at his expense (he is going to arrange this through people he knows)—we still have to reckon on our arrival in Petersburg, where we cannot do without money, at least not for the first few days. Dunia and I have figured it all out together in detail, and as we figured it, our expenses for the road should not be much. It is about sixty miles from where we are to the railroad, and we have already made a bargain with a peasant cabdriver we know. Dunia and I can travel quite comfortably third-class. So I think I will be able to send you thirty, not just twenty-five rubles. But enough. I have filled two large pages on both sides, and there is no more room to squeeze anything in. It is our whole story. My, how one thing has piled on top of another! For now, Rodia my precious, I embrace you until we meet soon, and I send you a mother's blessing. Love your sister Dunia, Rodia. Love her as she loves you; and know that she loves you infinitely more than she loves herself. She is an angel; but you, Rodia, you are all we have—all our desire and all our hope. If only you are happy, we will be happy. Do you say your prayers, Rodia, as you used to do? and do you believe in the goodness of our Creator and Redeemer? I fear in my heart that you may have been visited by the latest fashionable unbelief. If so, I pray for you. Remember, my dear, how when you were still a child, when your father was still alive, you used to babble your prayers on my knee and how happy we all were then! Good-bye. Or, better, till soon! I embrace you tightly, tightly, and I kiss you, kisses without number.

Yours till the grave,
Pulcheria Raskolnikov

From the beginning and for most of the time that he was reading the letter, Raskolnikov's face was damp with tears. But when he finished it was pale, distorted by a twitch. A heavy, bilious, angry smile played around his lips. He lay back his head on his meager and bedraggled pillow, and he thought. He thought for a long time. His heart beat powerfully, and powerfully his thoughts tumbled upon each other. At last he felt it grow close and stuffy in that little yellow room so much like a chest or a cupboard. Both his gaze and his thought craved space. He grabbed his hat and left. This time he did not even worry about meeting anyone on the stairs; he had forgotten about it. He started out in the direction of Vasilievsky Island by way of Voznesensky Prospect as though he were in a hurry and had some purpose in mind. But he walked as he usually did, without looking where he was going, whispering to himself and even addressing himself aloud occasionally, which very much surprised the passersby, many of whom took him for drunk.

4

His mother's letter made him suffer. About the most important point, however, the fundamental issue, he had no doubt at all, not for a moment, not even while he was reading the letter. On the essential point, his mind was made up, once and for all. "As long as I'm alive this marriage will not take place; Mr. Luzhin can go to hell!

"Because the whole thing is clear as day," he muttered to himself, grinning and gloating in advance over the success of his decision. "No, Mother dear; no, Dunia; you don't fool me! . . . So they even apologize about not asking my advice and settling this thing without me! I'll say! They think it can't be broken off now, but we'll see whether it can or not! What a marvelous excuse: 'Well, you see, he's a busy, practical man, Peter Petrovich, such a busy, practical man he has to get married on the hop, practically right on the train.' No, my Dunia, I see through it, and I know what you want to talk to me about *so much.* And I know what you were thinking about as you paced up and down your room that night, and what you were praying about to the Holy Mother of Kazan in Mother's bedroom. It's a hard climb to Golgotha. Hmm . . . So it's all definitely settled, is it? You've decided to marry a rational, practical businessman, Avdotia Romanovna, one who has money of his own (already has money of his own—ah, that sounds more solid, more inspiring)—one who holds down two official jobs, who shares the convictions of our *younger* generation (as our dear mother writes), and who '*seems* kind,' according to Dunia herself. That *seems* is the most marvelous of all! So our Dunia is about to get married for the sake of that *seems!* . . . Marvelous! Just marvelous!

"Curious: why did Mother write me about our 'younger generation'? Was she trying to tell me what he was like, or did she have something else in mind—maybe to get me to look at Mr. Luzhin with more favorable eyes? Oh, they are sly! I'd like to know one more little detail. How frank were they with one another that day and that night and all the time since? I wonder if they spoke to each other directly *in words,* or if they understood without saying anything that their feelings and thoughts were the same, and so it was better not to say anything aloud, and there was nothing to talk about. Probably that's more or less the way it was. The letter makes it clear. To Mother he seemed abrupt—*a little*— and Mother even implied as much to Dunia. And she, of course, lost her temper and 'replied indignantly.' I'll say! Who wouldn't get mad when the case was clear without any naïve questions, and it was understood that it was useless to talk about it. And to me she writes: 'Love Dunia, Rodia, for she loves you more than she loves herself.' Why, it's remorse, secretly making her suffer, for she has consented to sacrifice a daughter for a son. 'You are our hope, you are our all!' Ah, Mother dear . . ."

Anger flared up in him more and more strongly, and if at

that moment he had met with Mr. Luzhin he probably would have killed him.

"Hmm, it's true," he continued, pursuing the storm of thoughts that tossed about in his brain, "it's true that 'in order really to get to know any man, one must do it gradually and cautiously.' But Mr. Luzhin is clear. The main point is, 'he's a practical businessman and *seems* kind.' After all, he's having the trunk carted up at his own expense, and the luggage, too! That's not unkind, is it? And those two, both of them, the *bride* and her mother, are hiring a peasant and his cart, and the cart's covered with matting (I know what it's like, I've traveled that way myself!)—but that's nothing! Why, it's only sixty miles, and then 'we will travel third-class quite comfortably' for another seven hundred miles. It's reasonable: you cut clothes to the shape of your cloth. But what about you, Mr. Luzhin? After all, she's your bride. . . . And you couldn't help but know, could you, that her mother is borrowing money on her pension for the trip? Of course, it's all one of your general commercial transactions, a mutually profitable enterprise, equal shares, half and half on expenses; food on the house but pay for your own tobacco. Well, at this point their practical businessman seems to have come out slightly ahead. The luggage doesn't cost as much as their trip, and I rather suspect he'll get it carted free. Don't they see all this, or don't they want to see it? And they are content! Satisfied! Pleased! Remember, these are only the blossoms; the fruits are yet to come! What's important is not the miserliness, the mean scrimping, it's the *tone* of the whole thing. That's going to be his tone after they get married: a prophecy. . . . Yes, and what about Mother? Why is she throwing her money around like that? How much will she have left when she shows up in Petersburg? Three silver rubles or two 'paper'?—as that one . . . the old woman says . . . hmm! What does she think she is going to live on in Petersburg? Somehow she has grasped that she will not be *able* to live with Dunia after the marriage, even at first. The dear man probably just *let it slip out,* though Mother would throw up her hands at the suggestion: 'I shall refuse on my own account.' What does she have to live on but a hundred and twenty rubles' pension, not counting the debt to Afanasy Ivanovich. She'll knit shawls and embroider cuffs, and she'll ruin her eyes. And the shawls will bring in another twenty rubles a year to add to the hundred and twenty, I know it well. So they must be depending on Mr.

Luzhin's noble feelings: 'He will suggest it himself, he will insist. . . .' Fat chance! And that's the way it always is with these Schilleresque 'beautiful souls.' They dress a man up in peacock feathers and insist on looking at him that way. Up to the very last moment they hope for the best. They have a kind of foreboding as to what's on the other side of the coin, all right, but they wouldn't breathe a word of it, perish the thought! They keep pushing the truth away with both hands. Until such time as the peacock man steps out of his feathers and personally crowns them fools . . . I wonder if Mr. Luzhin has been decorated. I bet there's a St. Anne's ribbon in his buttonhole and he wears it when he goes out to dinner with contractors and merchants. I bet he'll wear it at his wedding! Oh, to hell with him, Goddamn him!

"Well, never mind Mother. She is what she is. But what about Dunia? Ah, Dunia, my dear, how well I know you! Last time I saw you, you were nineteen; but your character—I understood it even then. As Mother has written: 'Our Dunia can bear a lot.' That I knew. I knew it two and a half years ago, and I've been thinking about it for two and a half years, about just that point, that 'our Dunia can bear a lot.' If she could bear Mr. Svidrigailov and all the consequences, I guess that means she really can bear a lot. Now, though, she and Mother have gone and imagined she can bear Mr. Luzhin, too, who expounds the theory of the superiority of wives rescued from a life of poverty by their husbands, who expounds this theory, indeed, practically at their first meeting. Well, let's suppose he 'let it slip out,' though he's a rational man (so maybe it did not 'slip out,' but he deliberately and as quickly as possible made clear what was what)—Dunia, what about Dunia? She must see through this man—but then, to go and live with him . . . She would live on a diet of black bread and water, yet she would not sell her soul, nor would she give up her moral freedom for a life of comfort. She would not give it up for all Schleswig-Holstein, let alone a creature like Mr. Luzhin. No, the Dunia I used to know was not like that . . . and I don't expect she's changed a bit! There's no denying, the Svidrigailovs are hard to take. It's hard to take wandering about the provinces all your life as a governess at two hundred rubles a year. Nevertheless, I know that my sister would sooner work like a Negro slave on a plantation or like a Lett peasant for a Baltic German landowner than debase her soul and her moral sense by marrying a man she does not respect and with whom she has nothing in common, and for life, just for her personal gain! And even if Mr. Luzhin were all of purest gold or solid diamond, even then she would not agree to become the legal concubine of Mr. Luzhin! So why, then, has she agreed? What's going on here? What's the answer to the riddle? The case is clear. For herself, for her own comfort, she would not do it; she would not sell herself even to escape death. For someone else, though—yes, she would; she'd sell herself! She'd sell herself for a man who is dear to her, for a man she worships! That's what is going on here: for her brother, for her mother—she'd sell herself! She'd sell everything! Oh, in a case like that we strangle our moral sense. Freedom, peace of mind, conscience even—everything, we take it all to the flea market. Let life go hang, as long as these loved ones of ours are happy! We invent our own casuistry, what's more, we take lessons from the Jesuits, and in time we even manage to calm ourselves down, and we persuade ourselves that it was necessary, really necessary, and for a good cause. That's the kind of people we are, and it's all clear as day. It is clear that the number one attraction on the stage here is none other than Rodion Romanovich Raskolnikov. Well, why not. She can make him happy, support him at the university, make him a partner in the law firm, provide him with security for the rest of his life. Later on, he may even get to be a rich man, respected, distinguished, and maybe by the time he dies he'll even be famous! And his mother? Well, never mind. Have a look at Rodia, though—precious Rodia, the firstborn! For a firstborn son like that how could you not sacrifice even such a daughter! O loving and overpartial hearts! And what! We would even go the same way as Sonia! Dear little Sonia, Sonia Marmeladov, eternal Sonia as long as the world endures! Has either of you plumbed your sacrifice to the depths? You have? Are you up to it? Will it do any good? Does it make sense? Do you realize, Dunia dear, that little Sonia's lot is not in any way more squalid than life with Mr. Luzhin? 'Love is not involved,' Mother writes. And if there cannot only not be love, but no respect, either? What if, on the contrary, there is already disgust, contempt, loathing—what then? Then it will turn out you have to '*keep up your polish.*' Not so? Do you understand, do you understand, do you, do you understand what that polish means? Do you understand that Mrs. Luzhin's polish is quite the same as little Sonia's, maybe even worse, nastier, fouler; because you, dear Dunia, will still have some scrap ends of comfort, while there, it's a case of death from hunger! 'It costs, it costs a lot, Dunia dear, to keep up that polish of yours!' Well, and what if you're not up to it after all, will you repent? Think of the humiliations, the sorrows, the curses, the tears, kept secret, of course; for after all, you are not Martha Petrovna, are you? And what will become of your mother then? Why, even now she's ill at ease, she makes herself suffer; what will happen when she sees everything clearly? And me? What in the world did you take me for? I don't want your sacrifice, Dunia; I don't want it, Mother dear! As long as I live it shall not come to that! It shall not, shall not come to that! I refuse to accept it!"

Suddenly he recollected himself, and paused.

"Shall not? What can you do to prevent it? Forbid it? By what right? What can you promise in return to claim such a right? Dedicate your life, your future to them—*after you get your degree and find a job?* We've heard all that; just dandy; but what about now? Because something has to be done *now,* understand? And what *are* you doing now? You are robbing them, that is what you are doing. They get that money from the pension, and by borrowing from the Svidrigailovs! O future millionaire Zeus, you with their fate in your hands! how do you propose to save them from the Svidrigailovs and from Afanasy Ivanovich Vakhrushin? Are you going to save them ten years from now? In ten years your mother will have gone blind knitting those damn shawls and weeping, and she'll be wasted away from lack of food. And your sister? Can you imagine what your sister will be like ten years from now or during those ten years? Can you guess?"

So he tormented himself, fretting at himself with these questions, and he even took a certain pleasure in it. None of these questions was new; he had suffered them all, since long ago. Since long ago they had been rending him, and they had rent his heart asunder. Long, long ago his present anguish had taken shape within him, had grown and developed, and had recently ripened and become dense, assuming the form of a terrible, wild, fantastic question, exhausting him, mind and heart, implacably demanding resolution. Now his mother's letter struck him like a thunderbolt. It was clear that he should no longer be moping, suffering passively, brooding over the problem's being insoluble; he ought to be doing something right away, immediately, as soon as possible. He had to come to a decision at all costs, or else . . .

"Or else renounce life altogether!" he cried out in a frenzy, "humbly accept my fate as it is, once and for all, strangle everything I have within me, and give up every right I have to act, to live, and to love!"

"Do you understand, my dear sir, do you understand what it means when you have nowhere to go?" Suddenly he remembered Marmeladov's question of yesterday. "For every man needs to have at least a somewhere he can go . . ."

And he shuddered. A certain thought, also yesterday's, once again flashed through his mind. But he did not shudder at the flash of the thought. For he had known, he had *felt* that inevitably it would "flash," and he had been waiting for it. Yet this thought was not altogether yesterday's. The difference was that a month ago, and even yesterday, it had been a mere dream; and now, suddenly, it manifested itself not as a dream, but in a new and terrifying form that he had not known before. And suddenly he became aware of this. . . . The blood rushed to his head and his sight dimmed.

He looked around quickly, searching for something. He wanted to sit down and looked for a bench. At the moment, he was walking along Konnogvardeisky Boulevard. About a hundred steps ahead was a bench. He walked as quickly as he could, but on the way he became absorbed in a little incident which for a few minutes took all his attention.

Looking for the bench, he had noticed a woman who was also walking along the street, about twenty steps ahead of him. At first he had paid no more attention to her than to any of the objects that flickered before his gaze. He often walked home without at all remembering the way he had come, and he had gotten used to walking like that. Yet there was something rather strange about the woman walking ahead of him, apparent from the first glance, so that little by little his attention fastened on her, at first involuntarily and even against his will, then more and more irresistibly. He felt a sudden desire to know what was actually so strange about her. First of all, she seemed quite young, and she was walking in the hot sun without a hat or parasol or gloves, waving her arms about in a rather foolish way. She wore a dress of light silky material, but it was oddly put on, scarcely fastened, and torn open in back at the top of the skirt near the waist. A whole shred of material was torn off and hung loose. About her bare neck a small kerchief was tied, but crookedly and askew. Moreover, she was unsteady on her feet, stumbling and even staggering from side to side. At last this encounter aroused all of Raskolnikov's attention. He overtook the girl at the bench. As soon as she reached it, however, she collapsed on it, in the corner. She threw her head against the back rest and closed her eyes, apparently from sheer exhaustion. Once Raskolnikov had a good look at her, he immediately realized that she was quite drunk. It was a strange and savage sight. He even wondered if he could have been mistaken. He saw before him a very young face—about sixteen, perhaps only fifteen—small, fair, and attractive, but all flushed and apparently slightly swollen. The girl seemed to be in a coma. As she crossed one leg over the other she exposed much more of it than was proper. She seemed to be but dimly aware that she was out in the street.

Raskolnikov did not sit down, but he did not want to leave. He stood there indecisively in front of her. This boulevard was usually empty; and on such a hot day, past one o'clock, there was almost no one about. And yet, off to one side, on the edge of the street fifteen steps or so away, a gentleman was lingering, who evidently also wanted very much to approach the girl, with intentions of his own. He, too, had probably noticed her at a distance and overtaken her, but now Raskolnikov prevented him from following through. He threw angry glances at the young man, but covertly, impatiently awaiting his opportunity when this annoying tramp would be gone. It was clear. The gentleman was a thickset, stout, quite fashionably dressed man of about thirty, with a strawberry and cream complexion, rosy lips, and a small moustache. Raskolnikov lost his temper. Suddenly he wanted to insult this fat dandy in some way. He left the girl for a moment and went up to the gentleman.

"Hey, you! Svidrigailov! What are you up to here?" he shouted, clenching his fists and laughing, his mouth foaming with rage.

"And what is the meaning of this?" the gentleman asked sternly, frowning, with a look of haughty astonishment.

"Get out of here, that's what!"

"How dare you, you scum!"

He brandished his cane. Raskolnikov rushed at him with his fists, without even considering that the thickset gentleman was more than a match for two like him. But at that moment someone seized him powerfully from behind. Between them stood a policeman.

"That's enough, gentlemen. No fighting in public places." He turned sternly to Raskolnikov, having noted his rags. "What are you up to? Who are you?"

Raskolnikov looked at him intently. He had a frank soldier's face, with a gray moustache and whiskers, and a sensible look about him.

"You're just the man I want," he exclaimed, seizing the policeman by the hand. "I'm a former student. My name's Raskolnikov. . . ." He turned to the thickset gentleman. "You might as well know that, too. But officer, come here. I'll show you something. . . ."

Having taken the policeman by the hand, he dragged him to the bench.

"Here, look. She's drunk. She's been walking along the boulevard. God knows who she is or where she's from, but she doesn't look like she's in the trade. Most likely somebody got her drunk somewhere and seduced her . . . for the first time . . . understand? And then he just dumped her out on the street. Look at how her dress is torn, look at how it was put on. She was dressed, you see, she didn't dress herself, and the hands that dressed her were pretty clumsy at the job, man's hands. That's clear. Now look over there. This dandy I was about to tangle with, I don't know him, I see him for the first time. But he noticed her on the street just now too, drunk as she was, lost in a daze, and he wanted very much to come up and grab her in the state she's in and take her off somewhere. . . . It's true. I assure you I am not mistaken. I saw him myself, watching and following her, only I got in his way and he was waiting for me to leave. So he went off to the side a bit and pretended to roll a cigarette. . . . What do you say we don't let him have her? Let's think how we can get her home!"

The policeman understood the situation immediately. The thickset gentleman was easy to understand; there remained the girl. He bent over to examine her more closely, and a look of sincere compassion came into his face.

"Ah, what a pity!" he said, shaking his head. "Why, she's only a kid. She's been seduced, that's clear. Listen, miss," he began calling to her, "where do you live?" The girl opened her tired, bleary eyes, looked dully at her questioners, and waved them away.

"Listen," said Raskolnikov. "Here." He fumbled in his

pocket and dug out twenty kopecks he found there. "Take it. Call a cab and ask him to drive her home. But we've got to know the address!"

"Miss, ah, miss?" the policeman began again, having taken the money. "I'm going to call a cab now and I'm going to take you home myself. Where to? Ah? Where do you live?"

"G'way! . . . p'st'r'ng me!" the girl muttered, and again she waved them away.

"Oh, it's bad, bad! You ought to be ashamed of yourself, miss; oh, what a shame!" Again he shook his head, shocked, sympathetic, and indignant. "There's a job, though!" Turning to Raskolnikov, he gave him a quick sharp look from head to foot. He, too, seemed a strange figure, dressed in such rags and handing out money!

"Where did you find them? Was it far from here?" he asked the young man.

"I tell you she was walking in front of me, staggering down the boulevard. As soon as she got to the bench she collapsed."

"Oh, the shame that's done in the world now, Lord! A little kid like that, and look at her, drunk! Seduced, that's how it was! And you can see the dress is torn. . . . The lewdness nowadays! She looks like she's from a good family, too, maybe poor. . . . Nowadays there are many like that. She looks delicate, too, like she was a lady." And once again he bent over her.

Perhaps he, too, had daughters who "looked delicate" like ladies, with genteel manners and pretensions to fashion. . . .

"The main thing," pleaded Raskolnikov, "is not to let her fall into the hands of this scoundrel! Why should he too outrage her! What he wants is clear. Look at the scoundrel, he's not going away!"

Raskolnikov spoke loudly and pointed straight at the man, who listened and seemed to want to make a show of anger again, but thought better of it, limiting himself to a single contemptuous glance. He walked away another ten steps and once more paused.

"No, we won't let her fall into his hands," the policeman replied, thinking aloud. "If only she'd say where to take her . . . Miss, ah, miss!" And he bent over her again.

She suddenly opened her eyes wide, looked about intently as though something had just sunk in, rose from the bench, and crossed over to the side of the street from which she had come.

"Fff! Brazen! Pestering!" she said, waving them off once more. She walked quickly, but as before, staggering a lot. The dandy followed her, if not immediately, without letting her out of his sight.

"Don't worry," the policeman said decisively, "I won't let him." And he followed.

"Eh, the lewdness nowadays!" he said again, with a sigh.

At that moment something seemed to sting Raskolnikov. It seemed in a flash to turn him inside out.

"Hey! Listen!" he shouted to the policeman, who turned around.

"Stop! Why bother? Let it go! Let him have his fun." He pointed to the dandy. "What's it to you?"

The policeman stared at him without understanding. Raskolnikov laughed.

"A-a-ach!" muttered the policeman, with a gesture. Then he followed after the dandy and the girl, probably taking Raskolnikov for cracked or for something worse.

"There he goes with my twenty kopecks," Raskolnikov, left alone, muttered angrily. "Well, let him take something from the other guy, too, then let the girl go off with him, and that's that. . . . Why the hell did I have to butt in! Is it my business to help? Do I have a right to help? Suppose they swallow each other alive, what's it to me? How dare I give those twenty kopecks away, as though they really belonged to me?"

In spite of these strange words, he felt quite depressed. He sat down on the deserted bench. His thoughts were scattered. . . . To think about anything at all at that moment made him feel depressed. He would have liked to forget everything, forget completely, and wake up and begin anew. . . .

"Poor girl!" he said, looking at the empty corner of the bench. "She'll come to, she'll cry. . . . Then her mother will find out. First she'll give her a smack. Then she'll beat her till she aches with shame. Then she'll chase her out. . . . If she doesn't chase her out, some Daria Frantsovna will get wind of her all the same, and she'll start going out on calls here and there, my girl will. . . . Then right away the hospital (that's the way it goes with girls like that living respectably with their mothers and skipping out on the sly), well, and then . . . then the hospital again . . . drink . . . saloons . . .

and again the hospital . . . two, three years and she's a human wreck, and that's her life only eighteen or nineteen years from the time she was born. . . . Haven't I seen these things? And how do they happen? Fff! Just like that, that's all. So there you are! That's the way it goes, they say. They say a certain percentage are bound to go to the devil every year. Bound to, so the rest can stay fresh and healthy. A certain percentage! That's marvelous, isn't it, so comforting, so scientific! As soon as you say 'a certain percentage' you can see right away there's practically nothing to worry about. If you used another phrase, maybe it would be more disturbing. . . . And what if my Dunia falls into a certain percentage! If not this one, some other?. . .

"Where am I going?" he thought suddenly. "Strange! I had some reason, though. I started out as soon as I read the letter. . . . To Vasilievsky Island, to Razumikhin, now I remember, that's where I was going. But for what? Why did the idea of going to see Razumikhin pop into my head now of all times? That's remarkable."

He surprised himself. Razumikhin had been a fellow student of his at the university. It was a curious fact that Raskolnikov had had almost no friends at the university, had felt estranged from all, went to see no one, and had been reluctant to invite anyone to come see him. Everyone soon began to avoid him, too. He took no part in the student get-togethers, conversations, amusements, or in anything. He worked hard, without sparing himself, and for this he was respected; but no one liked him. He was poor, and somehow stiff, proud, and uncommunicative, as though he were keeping something to himself. Some of his fellow students felt that he looked down on them, and on everyone, as though they were children, as though he were ahead of them not only in development and knowledge but in the quality of his convictions, and that he regarded their convictions and interests as inferior.

With Razumikhin, though, he had for some reason become friends. Not that they really became friends, that is, but Raskolnikov was more communicative with him, more open. It was impossible to be any other way with Razumikhin. He was an extraordinarily gay and communicative fellow, good-natured to the point of simplicity. Beneath this simplicity, however, there were a hidden depth and a dignity. His best friends understood this, and everybody liked him. He was far from stupid, though he really was a bit simple sometimes. Tall, thin, black-haired, and always badly shaved, his appearance was quite striking. He brawled sometimes and was supposed to be pretty strong. One night, out with a party, he had knocked a huge policeman flat with one blow. His capacity for drink was limitless, but he could as well go without drinking. Sometimes he played practical jokes and even went too far; but he could just as easily not play any practical jokes. Razumikhin was also remarkable for the fact that no failure daunted him, and unfavorable circumstances seemed unable to keep him down. He could make himself at home even on a rooftop, he could stand terrible hunger and extreme cold. Though he was very poor, he made his own way entirely, earning money at various odd jobs. He knew a fantastic number of ways of making money. Once he went a whole winter without heating his room, insisting it was pleasanter that way, and one slept better in the cold. At present, he, too, had been obliged to leave the university, but not for long, and he was doing his best to make it possible to continue with his education. It was four months now since Raskolnikov had seen him, and Razumikhin did not even know where Raskolnikov lived. Once, about two months ago, they had passed by chance on the street, but Raskolnikov had turned around and even crossed over to the other side of the street so the other would not notice him. Razumikhin had noticed him nevertheless. But he had passed on by, not wishing to disturb a *friend*.

5

"As a matter of fact, I did want to go ask Razumikhin for some work, see if he could get me some lessons or something. . . ." Raskolnikov was thinking. "But how can he help me now? Supposing he gets me some lessons, supposing he shares his last kopeck with me (if he has a kopeck) so I can buy myself a pair of shoes and fix up my clothes and get in shape to go give lessons . . . hmm. . . . Well, what then? I'll earn a few grubby coins, and then what? What do I care, now? Going to Razumikhin's was a foolish idea, really . . ."

The question of why he was now going to see Razumikhin disturbed him more than he himself realized. Uneasily, he kept trying to find some ominous implication in this apparently quite ordinary act.

"Did I really think I could settle the whole business and find a way out just by going to see Razumikhin?" he asked himself with astonishment.

He rubbed his forehead and went on thinking. A strange business: suddenly, after long reflection, almost spontaneously and as if by chance, the strangest notion came into his head.

"Hmm . . . to Razumikhin's," he said suddenly, quite calmly, as though a conclusive decision had been reached. "I'll certainly go see Razumikhin. . . . But not now. . . . I'll go . . . the day after *that;* I'll go when *that* will be over and done with, when everything will begin anew. . . ."

Suddenly he realized what had been going on inside him.

"After *that!*" he exclaimed, tearing himself from the bench, "but will *that* come to pass? Will it really happen?"

He left the bench and walked away, almost ran. He wanted to go back home, but suddenly the idea of returning home appalled him terribly. There, in his corner, in that terrible cupboard, for more than a month now, all *this* had been ripening. He walked where his eyes led him.

His nervous tremor passed into a kind of feverish shivering. He felt a chill. Even in the intense heat he remained cold. With some effort, almost unconsciously, by a kind of inner necessity, he began to stare at everything he passed, as though looking desperately for something to distract his attention; but he succeeded badly at this, and in a moment fell to brooding. When he raised his head again with a start, he immediately forgot what he had been thinking about and where he had gone. In this manner he passed across all of Vasilievsky Island, came out at the Little Neva, crossed the bridge, and turned in the direction of the islands.

At first the greenery and the freshness pleased his weary eyes, accustomed as they were to the city dust, to the lime, and to the huge houses that hemmed him in and seemed to weigh upon him. Here there was not that closeness, nor the bad smell, nor the saloons. Soon, however, even these new, pleasant sensations turned painful and irritating. Sometimes he would pause before some brightly painted summer cottage among the trees. He would look over a fence and peer into the distance at balconies and terraces, at the well-dressed women and the children running about in the garden. He paid special attention to the flowers. At them he looked longest of all. He came across luxurious carriages and men and women on horseback. He followed them with curious eyes and forgot about them even before they disappeared from sight.

Once he stopped and counted up his money. He had about thirty kopecks left. "Twenty to the policeman, three to Nastasia for the letter . . . That means I gave around forty-seven, fifty kopecks to the Marmeladovs yesterday," he thought, for some reason reckoning it all up, but soon forgetting why he had taken his money out. He remembered while passing a restaurant, a tavern of sorts, and feeling hungry. He went in, drank a glass of vodka, and ate some kind of meat pie, which he took out with him to finish on the road. Although he had drunk only a very small glass, it was a long time since he had had any vodka, and it went to his head immediately. His feet grew suddenly heavy, and he became very drowsy. Returning home, he got as far as Petrovsky Island and stopped, unable to go on. He left the road, made his way into the bushes, dropped onto the grass, and fell instantly sound asleep.

In pathological states dreams are often distinguished by an uncommon vividness and sharpness of focus and by an extraordinary conjunction with reality. The scene unfolded may be a monstrous one, and yet the setting and the means of presentation not only probable, but subtly detailed, full of surprises, and at the same time artistically in key with the scene as a whole, so that the dreamer himself, though he were an artist of the caliber of Pushkin or Turgenev, could never have invented them awake. Such dreams, pathological dreams, make a powerful impression on man's disordered, already aroused organism, and are always remembered for a long time.

Raskolnikov dreamed a terrible dream. He dreamed of his childhood, and the small town where his family had lived. He was seven, it was a holiday, and he was out for a walk with his father just outside the town. It was getting on toward evening after a dull and sultry day. The neighborhood was very much as he remembered it, though he did not remember it as clearly as he saw it in his dream. The town lay spread before them, exposed, without even a willow around. At a point very far away, a small wood darkened the rim of the sky. A few steps from the town's last kitchen garden stood a tavern, a big one, one which, whenever he strolled past it on walks with his father, made the most unpleasant impression on him and even made him feel

afraid. It was always so crowded, the people made so much
noise, they laughed, they cursed, they sang hoarsely and
tunelessly, and so often they brawled. And around the tavern such sotted and frightening figures were always
slouching. . . . He would pull himself closer to his father and
tremble. A road led past the tavern, always dusty, the dust
always black, winding on into the distance. About three hundred steps beyond, it took a bend to the right, skirting the
town cemetery. In the middle of the cemetery was a stone
church with a green cupola, where he used to go to morning
mass twice a year with his father and mother, when a service
was held in memory of his grandmother, who had long been
dead and whom he had never seen. They always took a
special funeral cake with them on a white plate wrapped in
a napkin, a sugar and rice cake, with raisins pressed into the
rice in the shape of a cross. He loved that church and the
old icons in it, icons for the most part without settings, and
the old priest whose head quivered. Beside his grandmother's grave, which was marked by a stone, was the small grave
of his younger brother, who had died at the age of six
months and whom he also had never known and could not
remember. But he had been told that he had a little brother,
and every time he visited the cemetery, respectfully and reli-
giously, he crossed himself over the grave, bowed down and
kissed it. Now he dreamed that he and his father were walking along the road to the cemetery and they were passing
the tavern. He was holding his father's hand and looking
fearfully at the tavern.

A particular circumstance attracts his attention. Something special seems to be going on, a celebration. There is
a crowd of townspeople all dressed up, peasant women, their
husbands, all kinds of riffraff. They are all drunk, all singing
songs. Near the front steps of the tavern stands a wagon, a
strange wagon, though. It is one of those big wagons used
to carry boxes or wine barrels, usually drawn by huge dray
horses. He always liked watching those huge horses, with
their long manes and thick legs, plodding calmly and deliberately on, drawing practically a whole mountain of goods, yet
scarcely straining, almost as though it were easier going *with*
a load than without one. Now, though—strangely enough—
a small, skinny sorrel mare was hitched to one of those big
wagons. This peasants' nag was the kind that (and he had
seen it often) finds pulling even an ordinary cart difficult if
it is piled high with wood or hay, and especially if it gets

stuck in the mud or in a rut. Every time this happens peasants beat her painfully, so painfully, with whips, right along
the muzzle and around the eyes, and he always grieved so,
grieved so to be watching this, that he almost wept, and it
always ended with his mother leading him away from the
window. Suddenly a noisy din goes up: hulks of peasants
come pouring out of the tavern, shouting, singing, balalaikas
strumming, drunk, blind drunk, in red and blue shirts, coats
flung over their shoulders. "All aboard, everybody get in!"
one yells. He is still young. He has a thick neck and a beefy
red face. "All aboard, I'll take everybody!" Laughter and
exclamations ring out. "Look at that nag! He says he's going
to take everybody!"

"What's wrong with you, Mikolka, you nuts or something,
hitching that little mare up to the big wagon!"

"Listen, you guys, I bet that sorrel's twenty if she's a day!"

"All aboard, I'll take you all," Mikolka shouts again. He
leaps first onto the wagon, takes the reins up front, and
stands at full height. "Matvey took the bay," he shouts from
the wagon, "but this little mare, I tell you, you guys, she
breaks my heart. She don't earn her keep, so if I kill her,
so what! All aboard, I say! I'll make her gallop! She'll gallop, all right!" He takes the whip in his hands and gets ready
gleefully to flog the sorrel.

"Well, come on, let's get aboard!" the crowd laughs. "Did
you hear that, she's gonna gallop!"

"She ain't galloped for ten years!"

"She'll skip!"

"Don't worry, you guys, take your whips. Come on, let's
go!"

"Okay, let her have it!"

They pile into Mikolka's wagon, laughing and joking. Six
men climb aboard, and there is room for more. They take
a fat, red-faced peasant woman along with them. She wears
a red calico dress; she is plumed and beaded, with high-top
shoes on her feet; she is cracking nuts and laughing. In the
crowd all around they're laughing too, and to tell the truth,
it's hard not to laugh: such a miserable runt of a mare trying
to gallop with a load like that! Two fellows in the wagon
start using their whips, helping Mikolka. They all shout
"Gee-up!" and the mare strains with all her might, but not
only does she not gallop, it is all she can do to move forward
at all. Her legs make pathetic little pawing motions; she
groans and cowers as the blows of three whips drop on her

like hailstones. The laughter in the crowd and in the wagon doubles, but Mikolka is beginning to lose his temper, and he flogs the little mare furiously, with quickened blows, exactly as though he really believed she could gallop.

"Let me get on, too, you guys," shouts a young fellow from the crowd who had worked up a taste for the occasion.

"All aboard! All aboard, everybody!" Mikolka yells. "She'll pull everybody! I'll whup 'er!" And he lashes and lashes, no longer knowing why, hitting out in a frenzy.

"Daddy, Daddy," he shouts to his father, "Daddy, what are they doing! Daddy, they're beating the poor horsie!"

"Let's go, let's go," his father says. "They're drunk, they're fooling around, they're idiots. You mustn't look, let's go!" His father tries to lead him away, but he tears himself loose from his father's hands and, beside himself, runs toward the horse. For the poor horse, things are in a bad way. She is breathing hard, stopping, straining again, almost falling.

"Whup 'er to death!" Mikolka yells. "I don't mind. I'll whup 'er myself!"

An old man shouts indignantly from the crowd: "How come there's a cross on you? You're no Christian, you're a devil!"

Another adds: "You can see the horse can't pull a load like that!"

A third shouts: "You're doing her in!"

"Mind your own business! I'll do what I please. All aboard, everybody! Everybody aboard! I want her to gallop, and she'll gallop!"

Suddenly a volley of laughter erupts that drowns out everything else. Unable to stand the intensified beating, the little mare in her impotence had begun to kick. Even the old man, unable to restrain himself, breaks out laughing: "Imagine, a bag of bones like that, and yet she kicks!"

Two young fellows from the crowd arm themselves with whips, intending to flog her, one from each side.

"On the muzzle! Hit her around the eyes! Right around the eyes!" Mikolka shouts.

"Hey, you guys," somebody shouts from the wagon, "let's have a song!" And everybody in the wagon joins in. There is a rowdy song, the clash of tambourines, shrill whistling during the refrains. The peasant woman goes on cracking nuts and laughing.

He runs up to the mare, he runs out in front of her a little, he sees how she's being whipped around the eyes, right around the eyes! He weeps. His heart heaves; his tears flow. A blow glances across his face, but he does not feel it. He wrings his hands, he shouts, he pushes his way toward the old graybeard shaking his head, disapproving of all this. A woman takes him by the hand and tries to lead him off, but he tears himself away and runs back to the horse. She is on her last legs, but once again starts to kick.

"You damn bloody devil!" Mikolka screams out in a fury. He throws away his whip, bends down, and fishes a long, thick shaft out from the bottom of the wagon. Taking hold of it by one end with both hands, with an effort he swings it over the sorrel.

The shout goes up: "He's going to let her have it! He'll kill her!"

"It's my business!" Mikolka yells, and he brings the shaft down with all his might. There is the sound of a heavy blow.

Voices shout from the crowd: "Whup 'er! Whup 'er! Why stop!"

Mikolka swings again, and another blow comes down hard on the back of the unfortunate mare. She sinks back on her haunches, only to leap up again. She strains and strains with all the strength she has left, trying first in one direction and then in another to move the wagon. Whichever side she tries, however, she is met by six whips, and the shaft rises again and falls a third, and then a fourth time, slowly and with great force. Mikolka is furious at not being able to kill her with one blow.

"She's got a lot of spunk!" they shout.

One of the sports shouts from the crowd: "She's had it now, you guys! This is the end of her."

And someone else shouts: "Go get an ax! Finish her off quick!"

"Eh, eat bugs, you crapper!" Mikolka yells furiously at the mare. "Let me through!" He throws down the shaft, bends down into the wagon again, and comes up with a crowbar. "Watch it!" he shouts, and with all his might he deals the poor horse a shattering blow. The mare staggers, sits back, is about to try pulling again, but the bar comes down full force on her back. She falls to the ground as though all four legs had been knocked out from under her at once.

Beside himself, Mikolka, leaping from the wagon, yells: "Let her have it!" A few drunk, red-faced young fellows grab what comes their way—whips, canes, a shaft—and run up to the dying mare. Mikolka stands to one side and starts beating her across the back at random with the crowbar. The mare stretches out her muzzle, draws a heavy breath, and dies.

"You butchered her!" they shout in the crowd.

"Why wouldn't she gallop?"

"It's my business!" Mikolka shouts, the crowbar in his hands, his eyes all bloodshot. He stands there as though he were sorry there is nothing more to whip.

"Well, anybody can see you don't wear no Christian cross!" comes from a hubbub of voices in the crowd.

But by now the poor boy is beside himself. With a shout he plunges through the crowd to the sorrel, embraces her dead, bloodstained muzzle, and he kisses her, kisses her on the eyes, on the mouth. . . . Suddenly he leaps up and flings himself on Mikolka, striking out in a frenzy with his fists. At that moment his father, who has been pursuing him for some time, catches hold of him at last and carries him out of the crowd.

"Let's go, let's go!" his father says to him. "Let's go home!"

"Daddy, why . . . why did they . . . the poor horse . . . they killed her!" he sobs, but his breath catches and the words come as cries from his heaving breast.

"They're drunk, they're fooling around, it's not our business, let's go!" his father says. He throws his arms around his father, but his chest feels very tight. He wants to draw breath, to cry out. And he wakes up.

He woke up drenched in sweat. His hair was damp with sweat, he was panting, and he rose in terror.

"Thank God, this is only a dream!" he said, sitting down at the foot of a tree and inhaling deeply. "What's it all about, though? Am I coming down with a fever, or what? Such a hideous dream!"

His whole body felt as though it had been shattered. In spirit he felt troubled and dark. Propping his elbows on his knees, he supported his head with both hands.

"God!" he exclaimed. "Will I really? . . . Will I really take the ax, will I really hit her on the head, split open her skull . . . will I really slip in the sticky warm blood, break open the lock, steal, and shiver . . . and hide, all bloody . . . with the ax. . . . Good Lord, will I really?"

As he said it he shook like a leaf.

"What's the matter with me, though!" he continued, sitting up again, deeply astonished. "Didn't I know I could never go through with it? So why have I been making myself suffer? Even yesterday, why, even yesterday when I went to size up that . . . *project*, even yesterday I understood that I'd never make it. . . . So why am I stewing now? Why have I been in doubt up to this very moment? When I was going down the stairs yesterday, why, I said myself it was filthy, lousy, foul, foul. . . . *Awake*, the very idea turned my stomach and filled me with horror. . . .

"No, I won't make it, I won't make it! Although, although in all that reckoning there is no doubt, although every conclusion I came to this last month is clear as day and true as arithmetic. God! All the same, I can't bring myself . . . I won't make it, I won't make it! Why, up to . . . up to this very moment . . ."

He got up and looked around him in surprise, as though wondering why he had come here, and he walked to the Tuchkov Bridge. He was pale; his eyes were burning, he felt weary in every limb, yet suddenly he seemed to be able to breathe more freely. He felt that he had flung off the fearful burden that had for so long weighed upon him, and he felt suddenly at ease and calm within himself. "O God!" he prayed, "show me the way . . . I renounce that damned . . . dream of mine!"

As he crossed the bridge, he gazed calmly and quietly at the Neva, at the bright glow of the bright red sunset. In spite of his feebleness, he did not feel especially tired. It was as though the abscess in his heart, gathering all that month, had suddenly burst. Freedom, freedom! He was free now from that witchcraft, that devilment, that spell, that obsession!

Subsequently, when he recalled everything that happened to him in those days, moment by moment, point by point, bit by bit, he was always struck, almost superstitiously, by that one circumstance, not in itself unusual, but which afterward constantly seemed to him a kind of predestined turning point of his fate. Actually, he could not at all understand or explain to himself why, weary and exhausted as he was, instead of going home by the shortest and most direct route, he went via the Haymarket, which was out of his way. The detour was not a long one, but obviously a detour and unnecessary. Dozens of times, of course, he walked home without remembering the streets along which he had come. Yet why, he always asked, why did such an important meeting, for him so decisive and yet so extraordinarily accidental, take place in the Haymarket (where he had no reason to be going) just then at just that hour at just that moment of his life when he happened to be in just the mood and under just those circumstances when that meeting alone could have exerted the most decisive and the most conclusive influence on his entire destiny? It was as though it had purposely been lying in wait for him!

It was almost nine when he came walking along Haymarket Square. All the tradespeople at the tables, at the trays, in the stores and in the stalls, were closing their establishments or clearing off and packing up their goods and, like their customers, about to go home. At the entrances of eating houses, on the lower floors, in the dirty, fetid yards of the houses of Haymarket Square, and most of all in and around the saloons, a large and varied crowd of peddlers and ragpickers gathered. In his aimless street wandering, Raskolnikov liked these places and the neighboring alleys above all. Here his rags attracted no one's arrogant attention, and he could go dressed as he pleased without scandalizing anybody. At the corner of Konny Place a street peddler and his wife had been displaying their goods on two tables: thread, lace, chintz cloth, and so forth. They had been preparing to go home, but lingered on to talk to a woman they knew who had come by. This was Lizaveta Ivanovna, or simply Lizaveta, as everyone called her, the younger sister of Aliona Ivanovna, the old pawnbroker woman whom Raskolnikov had been to see yesterday, to pawn his watch and size up his *project*. . . . He had known all about this Lizaveta for a long time, and she even knew him slightly. She was a tall, awkward, shy, meek woman, a bit feeble-minded, thirty-five years old, completely in thrall to her sister, working for her day and night, trembling before her, and suffering even her blows. She stood hesitantly holding a bundle, in front of the peddler and his wife, and she was listening to them attentively. They seemed to be explaining something to her especially heatedly. When Raskolnikov suddenly caught sight of her a strange feeling, something like the most profound astonishment, possessed him, although there was nothing astonishing in this meeting.

"You better make up your mind yourself, Lizaveta Ivanovna," the peddler was saying loudly. "Come tomorrow, around seven. They'll be here then."

"Tomorrow?" Lizaveta drawled thoughtfully, as though she could not make up her mind.

"Eh, what a panic Aliona Ivanovna's got you in!" gabbled

the peddler's wife, a sharp little woman. "Look at you, you're just like a little kid. She's not even your sister, just a stepsister, but, boy, has she got you under her thumb!"

"I'd advise you this time not to say anything to Aliona Ivanovna," her husband interrupted. "Just come without asking her. It will be worth your while. Your sister won't mind later."

"Mmm, come?"

"Seven o'clock tomorrow. They'll send somebody, too, and you can make up your own mind."

"And we'll have some tea," added the wife.

"All right, I'll come," Lizaveta said, still hesitant, however, and she began slowly walking away.

Raskolnikov had already passed by and heard no more. He had walked by quietly, unnoticed, intent not to miss a single word. His initial astonishment gave way to horror, as though a chill had crawled down his back. He had learned, he had learned suddenly, all at once, and altogether unexpectedly that tomorrow at seven in the evening, Lizaveta, the old woman's sister and the only person who lived with her, would not be home, and therefore the old woman at exactly seven o'clock in the evening *would be home alone.*

He was only a few steps from his house. He entered his room like a man condemned to death. He had not chosen and was not capable of choosing. Yet suddenly with all his being he felt that he no longer had any freedom of choice—that he had no alternative and that suddenly everything had been conclusively decided.

And even if he waited for years on end, with his plan always in mind, for a similar opportunity, he could not have found any more obvious for carrying out his intention successfully than the one which suddenly presented itself. In any case, he would have found it difficult indeed to discover on the very eve, and for certain, with greater accuracy or less risk, without dangerous inquiries and investigations, that the next day at such and such an hour, such and such an old woman against whose life an attempt was being prepared would be at home, and absolutely alone.

6

Afterward Raskolnikov happened to find out why the peddler and his wife had actually invited Lizaveta to come see them. It was the most ordinary business matter, and there was nothing special about it. A family newly arrived in St. Petersburg, and impoverished, was selling off its women's clothes. Since they would get little for them on the market, they were looking for a middleman, and Lizaveta was engaged in this kind of work. She dealt in second-hand clothes on commission and she had a large clientele, since she was quite honest and always set the best price; and whatever price she set, she stuck to it. As a rule she did not talk much, and was, as already mentioned, quite meek and timid. . . .

Recently, however, Raskolnikov had grown superstitious. Traces of superstition remained in him for a long time afterward, too. And he was always inclined to see a certain strangeness, a mystery, in the whole affair; he assumed the working of special influences and coincidences. The previous winter, a student he knew named Pokorev, about to leave for Kharkov, had somehow in the course of a conversation given him Aliona Ivanovna's address, just in case he might have to pawn something. For a long time he did not go see her. He was working at giving lessons, and somehow he managed. Six weeks ago he had remembered the address. He had two things that were suitable for pawning: his father's old silver watch and a gold ring with three small red stones, given him as a keepsake when he said good-bye to his sister. He decided to pawn the ring. When he saw the old woman for the very first time, before he knew anything special about her, he conceived for her an insurmountable disgust. She gave him two "paper" rubles. On the way home he dropped in at a nasty little restaurant, ordered tea, sat down, and fell to brooding. As a chick scratches its way out of the egg, a strange thought was scratching its way into his conscious mind. It fascinated him.

Almost next to him, at another table, sat a student he did not know at all and a young officer. They had been playing billiards and had stopped for some tea. Suddenly he heard the student telling the officer about the pawnbroker woman, Aliona Ivanovna, and giving him her address. This already seemed a bit strange to Raskolnikov; he had just come from there, and here they were talking about her. It was, of course, a coincidence, but he could not free himself somehow from a decidedly peculiar impression as though someone were catering to his inmost wish. Then the student began to communicate various details about this Aliona Ivanovna to his companion.

"She's quite a girl," he said. "Rich as a Jew, she's always got money around. . . . She could lend out five thousand just like that, yet she wouldn't turn down a pawn worth a ruble. A lot of our guys have been to her. Only she's a terrible skin-flint. . . ."

He began telling how capricious and bad-tempered she was, how one only had to be a day late in redeeming a pawn and the thing was gone. And she would only give a quarter of what anything was worth, charging interest of 5 to 7 percent a month, and so forth. The student chattered away. He mentioned that the old woman had a sister, Lizaveta, and though the old woman was only a shrunken little hag, she beat her sister, holding her virtually in thrall, as though she were a small child, whereas this Lizaveta was actually at least six feet tall. . . .

"There's another phenomenon for you!" the student exclaimed, and laughed.

They started talking about Lizaveta. The student talked about her with a certain special pleasure, laughing frequently, and the officer listened with great interest and asked the student to send this Lizaveta to him to mend his linen. Raskolnikov, who did not miss a single word, learned everything at one stroke: Lizaveta was the old woman's younger stepsister (they had different mothers), and she was thirty-five years old. She worked for her sister day and night, and served at home in place of a cook and laundress; in addition, she mended, and hired herself out to wash floors. Everything she earned she gave to her sister. She did not dare accept an order or any kind of work without her sister's permission. The old woman had already made out her will, the contents of which were well known to Lizaveta, who received nothing from it except a few chairs and things like that. The money was all going to a particular monastery in Novgorod Province for eternal remembrance of the old woman's soul. Lizaveta was of lower sociàl status than her sister, who had married into the civil-service class. She was unmarried, terribly uncouth, remarkably tall, with big splay feet always in battered goatskin shoes, and she kept herself very clean. What really surprised the student and made him laugh was that Lizaveta was always pregnant.

"But you say she's a freak?" the officer remarked.

"Well, she's a bit dark, and she looks like a soldier in disguise. But, you know, she isn't really a freak. Her face and eyes are rather kind. Yes, very much so. Proof is, there are lots who like her. She is very quiet, very meek, very timid, and agreeable, agreeable to everything. And she has a very sweet smile."

"You like her too, do you?" The officer laughed.

"For her strangeness. I tell you what, though," the student added heatedly, "I could rob and murder that damned old woman and I assure you I wouldn't have a twinge of conscience."

The officer laughed again, but Raskolnikov shuddered. How strange it was!

"If you don't mind, I'd like to ask you a serious question," the student continued warmly. "Of course, I was kidding. But look. On the one hand we have a stupid, senseless, insignificant, bad-tempered, sick old hag, needed by no one and harmful to all. She herself does not know what she is living for, and she might just as easily die tomorrow of natural causes. Do you see what I mean?"

"I see what you mean," replied the officer, watching his excited companion attentively.

"Well, listen. On the other hand, we have fresh young elements going under with no help—by the thousands, everywhere! This old woman's money, which is going to be sequestered in a monastery, could beget a hundred, a thousand good deeds and fresh starts! Hundreds, perhaps thousands of lives could be put on the right path, dozens of families rescued from poverty, from ruin, from collapse, from decay, from the venereal wards of the hospitals—all this with her money! Kill her, take her money, dedicate it to serving mankind, to the general welfare. Well—what do you think—isn't this petty little crime effaced by thousands of good deeds? For one life, thousands of lives saved from ruin and collapse. One death and a hundred lives—there's arithmetic for you! What does the life of this sickly, stupid, bad-tempered old woman mean anyway in the balance of existence? No more than the life of a louse or a cockroach. Not that much—because the old woman actually does harm. She eats up other people's lives. The other day she bit Lizaveta's finger in a fit of temper, and it almost had to be amputated!"

"Of course she doesn't deserve to live," observed the officer. "But—that's nature."

"Ah, my friend, nature has to be shaped and directed, or we'd all drown in prejudice. Or there would not be a single great man. People say: 'Duty. Conscience.' I won't say anything against duty or conscience, but how do we interpret them? Wait, I'd like to ask you another question. Listen!"

"No, you wait. I'd like to ask you a question. Listen!"

"Well!"

"Here you go on talking, making speeches all over the place. But tell me. Would *you* murder the old woman, or wouldn't you?"

"Of course not! I am for justice. . . . But it's none of my business. . . ."

"Well, if you want to know what I think, I think if you won't do it yourself there's no justice in it! Let's get back to the game!"

Raskolnikov was greatly agitated. Of course, this was all the most usual kind of intellectual discussion among young people, and he had heard it all before, if on somewhat different themes. But why had it come to pass that he overheard just this conversation and just these ideas at a time when *the same ideas exactly* were stirring in his own mind? And why now, with the germ of his idea fresh from the old woman's place, had he stumbled straightaway onto a conversation about the same old woman? This coincidence would always seem strange to him. This trivial conversation overheard in a shabby restaurant had a very great influence on him as the affair developed further, as though it actually had been a kind of prefiguration, a sign. . . .

On returning from the Haymarket, he flung himself on his couch and sat there a whole hour without moving. Meanwhile it grew dark. He had no candles, and to light one would never have occurred to him anyway. Was he thinking anything, then? He would never be able to remember. At last he felt feverish again, shivered, and became pleasantly aware that he could stretch out on the couch if he wanted to. Soon a strong, leaden sleep seemed to press down upon him.

He slept unusually long, without dreaming. Nastasia, who came into his room at ten o'clock the next morning, had trouble waking him. She brought him tea and bread. The tea was again twice-boiled, and again she brought it in her own kettle.

"My, how he sleeps!" she cried indignantly, "he sleeps and sleeps and sleeps!"

He raised himself with an effort. His head ached. He rose to his feet, took a turn in his garret, and collapsed again on the couch.

"Going back to sleep!" Nastasia exclaimed. "You sick, or what?"

He did not answer.

"Tea?"

"Later," he pronounced with an effort, closing his eyes again and turning to the wall. Nastasia stood over him.

"He must really be sick," she said, turned, and went out.

She came back at two with some soup. He lay as before, and the tea was untouched. Nastasia felt hurt and began to shake him angrily.

"Why don't you get up!" she cried, looking at him with disgust. He raised himself to a sitting position, but said nothing to her and stared at the floor.

"Are you sick or not?" Nastasia asked, but received no answer.

"You ought to go out," she said, calming down, "and get a breath of fresh air. You gonna eat something?"

"Later," he said weakly. "You can go." He dismissed her with a wave of his hand.

She remained a little longer, looked at him with compassion, and went out.

A few minutes later, he raised his eyes and looked for a long time at the tea and at the soup. He took the bread, picked up a spoon, and started to eat.

He ate little, without appetite, three or four spoonfuls, almost mechanically. His head ached less. Having eaten, he again stretched out on the couch. This time he could not sleep, and he lay there motionless, prone, face buried in his pillow. He kept daydreaming, and his daydreams were very strange. He fancied he was somewhere in Africa, in Egypt, somewhere on an oasis. A caravan was resting; the camels lay quietly. Palm trees grew about in a circle. Everyone was eating dinner. He was drinking water, though, straight from a flowing, murmuring spring. And it was so cool, and such marvelous blue water, marvelously cold, pouring over colored stones and along such clean, gold-flashing sand. Suddenly he distinctly heard a clock strike. He gave a start, came to, raised his head, and glanced at the window, estimating the time. Suddenly he leaped up as though someone had torn him from the couch. He went to the door on tiptoe, opened it quietly, and stood listening for sounds from below on the stairs. His heart pounded fearfully. But on the stairs all was quiet. Everyone was asleep. . . . It seemed wild and strange to him that he could sleep so oblivious for so long; that he had done nothing yet, and had prepared nothing. For all he knew, the clock might have struck six. . . . And sleep and torpor gave way to an unusual, feverish, and somewhat distraught activeness. Not much needed to be prepared, however. He strained his attention to think of everything and forget nothing. His heart was pounding so heavily that it became difficult for him to breathe. First, a sling had to be made, and sewn into his overcoat; that would only take a minute. He dug into the laundry crammed under his pillow and searched out one of his tattered old unwashed shirts. He tore off a strip a couple of inches wide and a little over a foot long. He folded this strip in two, took off his broad sturdy summer overcoat, made of some kind of thick cloth (the only real overcoat he owned), and began to sew both ends of the strip to the inside just below the left armhole. His hands trembled as he sewed, but he managed. Nothing was visible from the outside when he put the coat on again. The needle and thread he had prepared a long time ago, and they had remained on the table wrapped in a sheet of paper. As for the sling, it was his own quite clever invention. The sling was designed for the ax. He could not possibly carry an ax in his hands through the streets. If it were hidden under the coat, a hand would still be needed to hold it there; and that might be noticed. Now all he had to do was insert the ax blade in the sling, and it would hang inside the coat under his arm safely all the way. From the left pocket of his coat he could hang on to the ax handle so it wouldn't swing. Since the coat was very broad, a regular sack, no one would notice him supporting something with his hand through the pocket. The sling was also something he had thought of two weeks ago.

That done, he thrust his fingers into a small slit between his "Turkish" couch and the floor, fumbled about near the left corner, and withdrew the "pledge" he had prepared a long time ago and concealed there. This was not really a pledge at all, but just a smoothly planed piece of wood the size and thickness of a silver cigarette case. He had found

it accidentally in a workshop in the wing of a certain courtyard on one of his walks. To it he attached a thin, smooth
iron strip, some sort of fragment he had also found in the
street at about the same time. The iron was a little smaller
than the wood. He bound them firmly together by tying
them criss-cross with thread. Then he wrapped them carefully and neatly in clean white paper and tied it so it would
not be easy to unwrap. When the time came, the old woman's attention would be distracted; she would be fiddling
with the knot; and so, he would have a spare minute. The
purpose of the iron strip was weight, so the old woman
wouldn't guess immediately the thing was wood. He had
saved all this under his couch until the time came. As he
picked up the pledge he suddenly heard a shout from somewhere in the courtyard.

"It struck six long ago!"

"Long ago! My God!"

He rushed to the door, listened, seized his hat, and cautiously began climbing down his thirteen steps, inaudibly,
like a cat. The most important thing was stealing the ax
from the kitchen. He had decided long ago that it had to
be done with an ax. He had a pocket knife, too, but he
could not rely on the knife, and especially not on his own
strength, so he decided conclusively on the ax. We may note
one peculiarity in passing with regard to all the resolute
decisions he had already made in this matter: the more resolutely they were made, the more grotesque and the more
absurd they instantly became in his eyes. In spite of all his
agonizing inner struggle, he could not in all this time believe
for one moment in the carrying out of his plans.

If he had actually managed at some point to examine
everything and decide every last little detail conclusively, if
doubt no longer remained—at just this point apparently he
would have rejected it as absurd, monstrous, impossible, and
refused to go through with it. There remained, however, a
whole abyss of doubts and unresolved details. As to where
he would get an ax he was not much troubled. Nothing could
be easier. As a matter of fact, Nastasia frequently was out,
especially in the evenings. She ran over to the neighbors',
or down to the store, and she always left the door wide
open. The landlady was always yelling at her for this. All
one had to do was enter the kitchen quietly at the right time
and take the ax; and then an hour later (when everything
was done) enter and put it back. Still, there were doubts:

suppose he entered an hour later to put back the ax, but
Nastasia had by chance returned. Then he would have to
walk on past and wait till she went out again. But suppose
she missed the ax in the meantime, started looking for it,
and raised an outcry: that would mean suspicion, or at least
the chance of suspicion.

But these were all little things about which he had not
started thinking, and indeed he had no time to think about
them. He thought about the main thing and put off the
little things until he *could believe in it all*. But that seemed
completely unattainable. So it seemed to him, at any rate.
He could not imagine, for instance, that the time would
come when he would stop thinking, get up, and—just go
there. . . . Even sizing up that *project* of his (his visit of not
long ago, with the intention of looking the place over) had
been, after all, only sizing up a project, had not been "for
real," but only more or less as follows: "Suppose I have a
look? Why just go on dreaming about it?" And he had not
been able to stick it out. He had run away, and he had been
furious with himself. And yet it would seem that the whole
analysis he had made, his attempt to find a moral solution
to the problem, was complete. His casuistry had been honed
to a razor's edge, and he could no longer think of any objections. Yet all told he simply had no faith in himself, and he
was looking everywhere, like a slave, for valid objections,
groping his way, as though someone were forcing and pushing him. This last day, however, which had so unexpectedly
decided everything at once, had caught him up almost automatically, as if by the hand, and pulled him along with unnatural power, blindly, irresistibly, and with no objections
on his part; and he was caught, as if by the hem of his coat
in the cog of a wheel, and being drawn in.

At first (and it was a long time ago) one question had
concerned him: why almost all crimes were so easily de-
tected and solved and why almost all criminals left such
transparent clues behind. Little by little, he came to curious
and complex conclusions. He believed that the most important reason had not so much to do with the practical impossibility of concealing a crime as with the criminal himself.
While committing his crime, almost every criminal seemed
subject to a failure of judgment and of the will, which gave
way to a phenomenal, childish recklessness at the very moment when he needed caution and judgment the most. He
became convinced that this failure of judgment and collapse

of will take hold of a man like a disease, develop gradually, and mount in the intensity of their possession until just before the crime is committed. At the moment of the crime, and for some time thereafter, the process continues, depending on the individual. Then, like any disease, it passes. Whether the disease produced the crime, or whether crime by its own innate peculiarities was always accompanied by something like disease, he did not as yet feel he was able to answer.

Having reached such conclusions, he decided that he personally was immune; while he carried out his plan, his judgment and will would remain sound, for the simple reason that what he planned to do was "not a crime."

We omit the process by means of which he arrived at this last conclusion; as it is, we are a bit ahead of ourselves. We add merely that the practical, purely material difficulties involved played an altogether secondary role in his mind. "One only needs to bring to bear all one's will and all one's judgment, and all difficulties can in due time be overcome, as one grows familiar with all the details of the matter, down to the least little item. . . ." But the matter had not yet begun. He particularly ceased to believe in his own most resolute decisions. And when the hour struck, everything turned out rather differently, somehow inadvertently, and even unexpectedly.

One trivial circumstance had him baffled even before he had descended the stairs. Reaching the landlady's kitchen— wide open as usual—he gave it a cautious glance to make sure in advance the landlady was not there while Nastasia was out; and, if she was not, to make sure the door to her room was well shut and she would not be likely to stick her head out from there as he entered for the ax. To his astonishment, however, he suddenly saw that Nastasia was not only at home this time, in the kitchen where she belonged, but that she was still busily at her job. She was taking laundry out of a basket and hanging it on the line! Seeing him, she stopped hanging clothes, turned toward him, and watched him all the time he was walking past. He dropped his eyes and hurried by as though he noticed nothing. But the matter was at an end. There was no ax! He was dumbfounded.

"What made me assume," he thought as he went out by the gate, "what made me assume that at this moment inevitably she would not be at home? Why, why, why was I so certain of that?" He was crushed, somehow even humiliated. He wanted to laugh at himself with rage. . . . A blind and brutal rage boiled up inside him.

He stopped below the gates and thought things over. Going out for a stroll like this, just to keep up appearances, went against his grain; returning to his room, even more so. "What a chance I muffed for good!" he muttered, standing there aimlessly below the gates, right across from the janitor's dark little room, which was open. In the janitor's little room, not more than two steps away, under a bench on the right, something that flashed caught his eye. . . . He looked about; there was no one. He entered on tiptoe, went down two steps, and called the janitor in a weak voice. "So. He's not home. He's not far off, though, must be in the yard, because his door is wide open." He went straight for the ax (it was an ax), and removed it from under the bench where it had been lying between two logs. On the spot, he attached it to the sling, thrust both hands into his pockets, and walked out of the janitor's room. No one saw him. He thought, "If judgment fails, the devil takes a hand!" and laughed strangely. This incident encouraged him amazingly.

He walked calmly along, *taking his time,* not hurrying, in order to avoid suspicion. He hardly looked at passersby and tried not to glance at their faces at all, so he himself would remain unnoticed. Then he remembered his hat. "My God! The day before yesterday I had the money, and I didn't get myself a cap!" He swore.

Out of the corner of his eye he glanced accidentally into a store window, noticing by the wall clock that it was already ten minutes past seven. He had to hurry. He would have to make a detour, approaching the house by its entrance on the far side.

When he had imagined all this before, he had thought sometimes that he would be very much afraid. He was not much afraid now. He was not afraid at all. At the moment his thoughts were incidental and fleeting. Passing Iusupov Park, he thought of the advantages of high fountains, and how much fresher they would make the public squares. Gradually he came to the conclusion that if the Summer Park could be extended to include all of the Mars Field and even united with the Mikhailovsky Palace Gardens, the result would be, practically and esthetically, a great improvement for the city. Then he wondered why it was that in all the great cities, and not merely or exclusively because of necessity, but rather because of some special inclination, people settled and lived in those parts of the city where there were neither parks nor fountains, but dirt and stench and slime of all kinds. Then he remembered his own walks across the Haymarket, and for a moment he seemed to come to. "Ridiculous," he thought. "It's better not to think at all!

"Those who are led off to execution—no doubt their thoughts fasten on anything, just like mine." It flashed into his head, but merely flashed, like lightning. He stifled this thought as quickly as he could. . . . But now he was already near. There was the house. There were the gates. Somewhere a clock struck once. "Not half past already? Can't be! Probably fast . . ."

At the gates, luck was still with him. Not only that, but just then, as though on purpose, a huge load of hay was passing through the gates, hiding him completely, and as soon as the wagon emerged from the gateway into the yard, he slipped away to the right. As he walked beside the wagon he heard several voices shouting and quarreling, but no one noticed him and nobody passed him coming the other way. Many windows looking out on this huge, square yard stood open at the moment, but he did not lift his head, for he had no strength. The stairs that led to the old woman's were close at hand; from the gates, to the right. . . . He was already on the stairs.

Catching his breath, clutching at his pounding heart, groping for the ax and setting it straight, he began cautiously, quietly, to climb the stairs, pausing every now and then to listen. But the stairs were empty. All the doors were closed. He encountered no one. On the second floor, it is true, in one wide open vacant apartment, painters were working; but they did not look up. He paused, reflected, and went on. "It would be better, of course, if they weren't there . . . but there are two more floors over them."

There was the fourth floor. There was the door. There was the apartment opposite. It was empty. The apartment directly below on the third floor was, by all signs, empty too. The name card tacked to the door had been removed. . . . He was out of breath. The thought flashed into his mind: "Should I leave?" He provided himself with no answer, however, and began to listen at the old woman's apartment: dead silence. Then he listened again at the stairs, for a long time, intently. . . . Then he looked about for the last time, once again set straight and tested the ax in the sling. "Maybe I'm . . . too pale," he thought, "maybe I look too nervous. . . . She's very suspicious. . . . Maybe I should wait awhile . . . till my heart stops pounding. . . ."

But his heart would not stop pounding. As though on purpose, it started pounding harder and harder and harder. . . . He couldn't stand it. Slowly he reached his hand to the bell and rang. In half a minute he rang again, louder.

No answer. No point just ringing. In fact, it was not a good idea. The old woman was home, all right, but she was alone, and suspicious. He knew some of her habits. He put his ear up against the door again. Either his senses had grown especially keen (and that was unlikely), or it could be heard quite distinctly. There was the cautious rustle of a hand at the doorknob, and something like the swish of a dress right near the door. Someone was standing silently at the threshold, and exactly as he was doing on the outside, was lurking and listening within; also, it would seem, with an ear to the door. . . .

He stirred and shuffled on purpose, muttering aloud, so as not to give the impression that he was lying in wait. He rang a third time; calmly, with authority, without any bustle of impatience. In later recollections, this moment was engraved sharply and clearly and forever. He could not understand from what source he had drawn so much cunning, especially since his mind went blank for moments at a time, and he had almost no sense of his body. . . . A moment later he could hear the latch being removed.

7

As before, the door opened a tiny crack, and as before, two sharp and distrustful eyes stared at him from the darkness. Then Raskolnikov lost his head and almost made a big mistake.

Assuming that the old woman would be afraid of their being alone, and without much confidence that his appearance would reassure her, he grabbed the door and pulled it toward him to prevent her from closing it again. Seeing this, she did not pull the door back toward her, but she did not let go of the knob, either, and he almost dragged her out onto the stairs clinging to the door. When he realized, however, that she was blocking the entrance and would not let him in, he went right up to her. She hopped back in panic, tried to say something, but seemed unable to. She looked at him with eyes wide open.

"Hello, Aliona Ivanovna," he began as casually as he could, but his voice would not obey him, broke off and trembled. "I've . . . brought you . . . something. . . . Come . . . maybe we better . . . go over here . . . to the light. . . ." He brushed straight by her and walked uninvited into the room. The old woman rushed in after him. Her tongue loosened up now.

"Good God, what are you up to! Who are you, anyway? What do you want?"

"Please, Aliona Ivanovna . . . You know me . . . I'm Raskolnikov. . . . Here. I brought the pledge I said I would the other day. . . ." And he held out the pledge to her.

The old woman threw a quick glance at the pledge, then immediately fixed her eyes straight on the eyes of her uninvited visitor. She stared intensely, angrily, and suspiciously. A minute passed. He thought he saw something like mockery in her eyes, as though she already knew everything. He felt himself losing his grip, and he felt scared, so scared that if she went on staring at him like that, if she went another half minute without saying a word, he would have run away.

"Why are you staring at me as though you didn't know who I was?" he said suddenly, even with a note of anger. "If you want it, take it. If you don't, I'll go somewhere else. I don't have much time."

He had not even thought about saying this. Somehow it was said of itself, just like that.

The old woman remembered. Her visitor's firm tone seemed to encourage her.

"But why so all of a sudden, my good man. . . . What is it, anyway?" she said, glancing at the pledge.

"It's a silver cigarette case. I told you before."

She held out her hand.

"But why are you so pale? Look at your hands shake! Have you been at the baths, or what?"

"Fever," he answered abruptly. "You can't help looking pale . . . if you don't get enough to eat," he added, scarcely enunciating the words. His strength was failing him again. Yet his answer seemed reasonable. The old woman took the package.

She looked at Raskolnikov intently and weighed the pledge in her hand. "What is it?" she asked.

"The thing . . . it's a cigarette case . . . silver . . . take a look."

"Doesn't seem like silver, somehow. . . . You certainly wrapped it up."

Trying to untie the knot, she turned to the light that came from the window. In spite of the closeness, the windows were all shut. For a few seconds she had her back turned toward him. He unbuttoned his overcoat and freed the ax from the sling. He still did not draw it out all the way. He merely held it under the coat with his right hand. His hands were terribly weak. He could feel them becoming stiffer and he numbered every moment. He was afraid he would drop the ax . . . and suddenly his head seemed to whirl.

"He certainly did a job of wrapping it up!" the old woman exclaimed indignantly, and made a movement as though she were about to turn to him.

There was not a moment to lose. He drew the ax out all the way, raised it back with both hands, hardly aware of what he was doing; and almost without effort, almost automatically, he brought the blunt side down on her head. He seemed to have no strength. Yet the moment he started bringing the ax down, strength sprang up in him.

The old woman was bareheaded as usual. Her thin, light, gray-streaked hair, as usual greasy and streaked with oil, was in a rat's-tail plait, fastened under what was left of a broken horn comb that stuck out at the nape of her neck. She was small, and the blow had struck her on the very crown of her head. She had cried out, but quite feebly. Then she suddenly sank in a heap to the floor, though first she managed to raise both hands to her head. In one hand she still held the pledge. He struck once more, then again, full strength, with the blunt side of the ax, and on the top of her head. The blood gushed as from an overturned glass, and the body fell backward. He stepped back to let her fall, and immediately bent over her face. She was dead. Her eyes were staring as if they wanted to leap out. Her forehead and her whole face were terribly contorted and drawn by a convulsion.

He laid the ax beside the dead woman on the floor. At once he felt in her pocket, taking care to avoid the flowing blood; that same right pocket from which he had seen her take the keys last time. The dark spots and the spinning of his head no longer troubled him. He was in full possession of his mind. Yet his hands trembled. He remembered later that he was particularly cautious and alert, and tried not to get himself smeared.

Then he took out the keys. As they had been before, they were all on one chain, on one steel ring. He ran immediately into the bedroom with them. It was a very small room with a huge icon case. By the far wall stood a large clean bed with a silk patchwork quilt. Against the third wall was a bureau. Strange: as soon as he tried fitting the keys to the bureau drawers, as soon as he heard the jingling of the keys, something like a spasm passed over him. Suddenly he wanted to abandon everything and leave. This was only for a moment. It was too late to leave. He was even beginning to laugh at himself when another alarming thought suddenly struck him. He suddenly began to imagine that the old woman was still alive and might actually come to. Abandoning keys and bureau, he ran back to the body, seized the ax and lifted it once more over the old woman. But he did not let it fall. There could be no doubt she was dead. He bent down and examined her more closely. He saw clearly that the skull was fractured, and even slightly battered in on one side. He wanted to feel it with his finger, but then withdrew his hand quickly. It was clear enough as it was. Meanwhile, a whole pool of blood had formed on the floor. He suddenly noticed a string on the old woman's neck and pulled at it, but the string was sturdy and did not break. And it was wet with blood. He tried pulling what was attached to it out from the bosom of her dress, but something got in the way, and it stuck. In his impatience, he lifted the ax again, to break the string on the body then and there, from above. But he did not dare. With difficulty, getting his hands and ax all blood-smeared, he cut the string after two minutes' harried effort and removed it, without touching the ax to the body. He had not been wrong. There was a purse. On the string were two crosses, one of Cyprus wood and one of brass, and there was an enameled icon in addition. Along with these hung a small, greasy suede purse with a steel rim and ring. The purse was crammed full. Without looking at it, Raskolnikov stuffed it in his pocket, dropped the crosses on the old woman's chest, and taking the ax with him this time, rushed back to the bedroom.

He was in a terrible hurry, snatched at the keys, and again began trying them. Somehow, none of them worked. They would not fit the locks. Not only were his hands shaking, he kept making mistakes. For example, he would see that a key was not the right one, that it would not fit, yet he insisted on trying it. Suddenly he remembered that the big key with the deep notch, dangling there along with the small ones, could not possibly belong to the bureau (this had even occurred to him before) but must belong to a strongbox of some sort, and perhaps in that very strongbox everything lay hidden. Knowing that old women usually keep strongboxes under their beds, he abandoned the bureau and began to feel under the bed. So it was: there was a good-sized chest, about a yard long, with a curved top, surfaced in red leather, studded with steel nails. The notched key fitted at once, and the chest opened. On top, under a white sheet, lay a hareskin coat, trimmed with red brocade. Under it was a silk dress, and then a shawl, and then below that, it seemed, there were only odds and ends of clothes. First, he tried to wipe his bloodstained hands on the red brocade. "It's red," he reckoned. "Blood will be less noticeable on red." And suddenly he remembered himself and thought in a panic: "Good Lord! Am I going out of my mind, or what?"

But as he was shuffling through the odds and ends, a gold watch slipped out from under the fur coat. He started going through everything. Sure enough, some gold objects were scattered among the clothes—all pledges, probably, redeemed and unredeemed—bracelets, chains, earrings, brooches, and similar items. Some were in cases, others simply wrapped in newspaper, but neatly and carefully folded, in double sheets, and tied around with tape. He began to cram them hurriedly into the pockets of his trousers and coat without examining or opening the packets or cases. But he did not manage to take many. . . .

Suddenly he heard someone walking in the room where the old woman was. He froze, and remained still as death. Everything was quiet. He must have imagined it. Suddenly he distinctly heard a soft cry, as though someone softly and abruptly moaned and then fell silent. And then for a minute or two there was deathly silence once more. He crouched by the strongbox, waiting, scarcely breathing. Then he leaped up suddenly, seized the ax, and ran out of the bedroom.

Lizaveta was standing in the middle of the room with a large bundle in her arms, staring stupefied at her murdered sister, white as a sheet and unable to cry out. She saw him as he ran out, and trembled like a leaf, small, shuddering twitches crisscrossing her whole face. She raised an arm and opened her mouth, but did not cry out. Slowly she started backing away from him into a corner, staring at him steadily and persistently, but not screaming, as though she had no breath left with which to cry out. He rushed at her with the ax. Her mouth was twisted pathetically out of shape, in the manner of very small children who are getting ready to be afraid of something, who keep staring steadily at the object of their fear as they are about to cry out. And this unfortunate Lizaveta was so simple and squashed and absolutely afraid, she did not even raise her arms to protect her face, although at the moment that would have been the most natural and inevitable gesture, since the ax was raised directly over her face. All she did was lift her free left hand a little at a distance from her face, slowly stretching it out toward him, as though to keep him off. The sharp end of the ax struck her directly on the skull, splitting instantly the whole upper part of her forehead almost as far as the crown. She collapsed. Raskolnikov nearly lost control of himself. He seized her bundle, threw it down again, and ran into the anteroom.

Panic was taking hold of him more and more, especially after this, the second and quite unexpected murder. He wanted to run away from there as quickly as possible. If at that moment he had been in condition to choose rationally or to see more clearly, if he could even have imagined all the difficulties of his situation, how altogether desperate, hideous, and absurd it was, and if at the same time he could have grasped how many difficulties he would still have to overcome, how many villainies he might perhaps still have to commit, in order to get out of there, in order to get himself as far as home—quite likely he would have abandoned everything and gone immediately to give himself up, and not because he was afraid for himself, but entirely from horror and disgust for what he had done. Disgust especially surged up within him and grew stronger every minute. For nothing in the world would he now have gone back to the strongbox or even into those rooms.

Little by little a kind of absentmindedness, even a kind of reverie, began to take hold of him. He forgot himself for minutes on end, or rather, he forgot what was important and fastened on little things. Looking into the kitchen, he saw half a bucket of water on the bench, and decided to wash his hands and the ax. His hands were sticky with blood. He immersed the ax blade in the water, grabbed a piece of soap that was lying on the windowsill on a broken dish, and started washing his hands right in the bucket. When he had washed them, he took out the ax and washed the blade. It took him a long time, about three minutes, to wash off the wood where it was bloodstained. Then he wiped it with a piece of laundry drying on the clothesline that stretched through the kitchen. Then he took the ax to the window and examined it carefully. There were no traces left, though the wood was still wet. He carefully inserted the ax into the sling under his coat. As much as light permitted in that dim kitchen, he then examined coat, trousers, shoes. From outside and at first glance there seemed to be nothing; only on the shoes was there a stain. He moistened the rag and washed off the shoes. He had a feeling, though, that his examination had not been thorough, and there might be something he had not noticed that actually flaunted itself to the eye. He paused in the middle of the room, absorbed in his thoughts. A dark, tormented thought swelled up within him: the thought that he was going out of his mind and that at the moment he lacked the capacity to make a rational choice or to protect himself, and that perhaps something quite different needed to be done from what he was actually doing. . . . "Good God! I've got to run, run!" he muttered, and hurried into the anteroom. But in the anteroom a horror awaited him the like of which he had never experienced before.

He stood there, looked, and could not believe his eyes. The door, the outside door from the anteroom to the stairs, the very door where he had stood ringing the bell not long ago, the door through which he had entered, stood unfastened and a hand's length open. All that time it had been neither locked nor fastened! The whole time! The old woman, perhaps out of caution, had not fastened it behind him. But, good God! He had seen Lizaveta after that! And how had it not occurred to him that she must have come in from somewhere! Certainly not through the wall!

He dashed to the door and fastened the latch.

"But no. Again that's not it! I've got to get out of here, to get out . . ."

He removed the latch, opened the door a little, and listened at the stairs.

He listened a long time. Somewhere far below, probably at the gateway, two voices were shouting something loudly and shrilly, arguing and quarreling. "What is that?" He waited patiently. Things quieted down all at once, as though cut short. They had gone. He was about to leave now, but suddenly a door was flung noisily open on the floor below, and somebody went down the stairs humming a tune. "Why do they all have to make so much noise!" flashed into his head. He closed the door again and waited. At last everything fell silent; there was not a breath. He had already taken a step onto the stairs when suddenly he heard a new set of footsteps.

Far, far off he heard these footsteps, at the very bottom of the stairs, but later he clearly remembered that from the first sound he heard he began for some reason to suspect that these footsteps moved inevitably *there,* to the fourth floor, to the old woman's. Why? What was so special about them? The footsteps were heavy, steady, unhurried. *He* now passed the first floor, still climbing; more and more distinctly audible. He could hear the heavy breath of the man who approached. On his way to the third floor now . . . *This* way! Raskolnikov suddenly felt turned to stone, as in a dream when you dream you are being pursued; they are getting close; they intend to kill; and you stand rooted to the spot, unable to move your arms.

At last, when the visitor was beginning to mount to the fourth floor, he gave a violent start, and somehow managed swiftly and skillfully to slither back from the landing into the apartment and close the door behind him. Then quietly, inaudibly, he grasped the latch and slipped it into place. His instinct helped him. He crouched breathlessly right by the door. The uninvited visitor was also at the door by then. They stood now one opposite the other, as he and the old woman had recently been standing, when the door alone separated them, but now he was doing the intent listening.

The visitor panted heavily several times. "He must be a big, stout man," Raskolnikov thought, clenching the ax. It all seemed as though he were dreaming it. The visitor seized the bell and rang hard.

As soon as the bell rang and he heard the tinny sound, Raskolnikov suddenly had the feeling that something in the room was moving around. For a few seconds he even listened quite seriously. The stranger rang again, went on waiting, but then suddenly, in his impatience, began to shake the doorknob with all his strength. Raskolnikov looked in horror at the hook of the latch hopping about in its place and waited in blank panic for the moment that the latch would leap out. The door was being so powerfully shaken, it really seemed possible. He thought of holding the latch with his hand, but then *he* might guess. Once again his head started to spin. "I'm going to faint!"

he thought in a flash, but the stranger started speaking and he immediately recovered himself. "What the he-e-ell's going on here! They snoring away, or somebody strangle them?" he roared in a booming voice. "Hey, Aliona Ivanovna, you old witch! Lizaveta, you fabulous beauty! Open up! Oof, hell! They asleep, or what?"

And again, enraged, he pulled at the bell with all his might about a dozen times. He certainly seemed to be a man of authority and at home in this house.

At that very moment, though Raskolnikov did not hear them at first, there were light, hurried footsteps on the stairs. Someone else was approaching.

"Nobody home?" the newcomer shouted gaily and resonantly, going straight up to the first visitor, who was still pulling on the bell. "Hello, Koch!"

"He must be quite young, judging by his voice," Raskolnikov thought.

"Who knows. I damn near broke the lock," Koch answered. "How come you know my name?"

"Aha! Why, the day before yesterday at Gambrinus' I beat you at billiards three times in a row."

"O-o-o-oh."

"So they're not in? Strange. Dumb, what's more. Terrible. Nuisance. Where would the old woman go? I've got business."

"Well, I've got business, too, my good man."

"Well, what's to be done? Means, back. E-e-ekh! But I thought I'd get some money!" the young man cried out.

"Sure, that means I have to come back. But why did she make the appointment? She made my appointment herself, the witch. It's out of my way. And how she manages to go gallivanting off to some bloody devil I'm sure I don't know. All year long she sits home, the witch; she mopes, her feet hurt. . . . Now all of a sudden she goes out on a stroll!"

"Maybe we should ask the janitor?"

"What?"

"Where she went and when she's coming back?"

"Hmm . . . ask . . . hell . . . She doesn't *go* anywhere, though. . . ." Once again he pulled at the knob. "What the hell can we do? Let's be on our way."

"Wait a minute," the young man suddenly exclaimed. "Look. See what the door does when you pull on it?"

"So?"

"That means it's not locked. It's on the latch. On the hook, that is! Do you hear how the latch rattles?"

"So?"

"Don't you get it? That means somebody's home. If nobody was home, they'd lock the door from outside with a key, not on the latch from inside. Hear how the latch rattles? To lock the door on the latch from inside, somebody's got to be home. Understand? It means they're sitting at home and not opening up!"

"Goddamn if you're not right!" the astonished Koch cried out. "What the hell are they up to!" He began furiously shaking the door.

"Wait!" the young man called out again. "Wait a minute! Something's wrong here . . . you rang and you beat at the door. They don't open. That means either they both passed out, or . . ."

"What?"

"I tell you what. Let's go get the janitor. Let him wake them up."

"Right!" They started making their way down.

"Wait a minute! You better stay here. I'll run down and get the janitor."

"Why should I stay?"

"Better had . . ."

"If you say so . . ."

"You see, I'm going to be a public investigator! And it's obvious, it's o-o-obvious that something is wrong here!" the young man exclaimed heatedly, and rushed hastily down the stairs.

Koch remained. He pulled the bell again, softly this time. It gave a single ring. Then quietly, as though he were inspecting it and thinking deep thoughts, he started turning the doorknob, twisting it and letting it go as though to convince himself all over again that the door was only on the latch. Then, panting, he bent down and started looking through the keyhole. But the key was in it on the inside, and he could see nothing.

Raskolnikov stood there, clenching his ax. He was in a kind of delirium. He was even ready to tangle with them the moment they stepped in. While they were knocking at the door and talking together, he even thought several times of putting an end to it all, of yelling out all at once from behind the door. At times he wanted to start swearing at them, taunting them, until they opened it. "Get it over with!" flashed through his mind.

"What's the devil doing in there. . . ."

Time passed. A minute, another. No one came. Koch started shuffling about.

Suddenly he cried out impatiently: "He is a devil, though!" Abandoning his post, he, too, made his way downstairs, hurrying along, clopping on the stairs with his shoes. His footsteps passed on into silence.

"Lord, what is to be done?"

Raskolnikov removed the latch and opened the door. He could hear nothing. Suddenly, without thinking about it, he left. As securely as possible, he closed the door behind him, and plunged down the stairs.

When he had already gone down two flights of stairs, he suddenly heard a great commotion below. Where could he hide! There was no place to conceal himself. He was about to run back up to the apartment.

"Hey, you bastard, you goblin, you devil! Hold up there!"

With a yell someone burst out of one of the apartments below, and not only ran but practically fell downstairs, shouting loudly: "Mitka! Mitka! Mitka! Mitka! Mitka! You fool, blast you!"

The shout ended in a yelp. The last sounds already came from the yard. Everything quieted down. At that very moment, however, several men, speaking to each other loudly and at frequent intervals, started climbing the stairs noisily. There were three or four. He could distinguish the resonant voice of the young man. "It's them!"

In sheer despair, he walked straight toward them. If they stopped him, all was lost. If they let him by, all was still lost—they would remember him. They were approaching each other. There was only one flight of stairs between them. And suddenly—rescue! A few steps away, on the right, empty and wide open, was the apartment; that very same apartment on the second floor that the workmen had been painting, and which they had now left, as though on purpose. It must have been they who had just run out with all that shouting. The floor was freshly painted. In the middle of one room stood a small tub and a crock with paint and a brush. He darted through the open door in a flash and hid himself against the wall. And just in time. They were already on that very landing. Then they walked on up and past, to the fourth floor, talking loudly. He waited, went out on tiptoe, and ran down.

There was no one on the stairs! . . . or at the gateway.

Swiftly he passed through the gates and turned to the left along the street.

He knew very well, he knew most excellently well, that at this moment they were already in the apartment, that they were astonished to find it open since it had been closed but a little while before, that they were already looking at the bodies, and that not more than a minute would pass before they fully grasped that the murderer had just been there, and had managed to conceal himself somewhere, slither past them, and escape. They would also grasp that he had actually been trapped in the vacant apartment as they were ascending the stairs. Meanwhile, he dared not quicken his pace in any way, though he still had about a hundred steps before the first turning. "Shouldn't I slip in some gate and wait on the stairs somewhere till it all dies down? No, that's bad. Shouldn't I throw the ax away somewhere? Shouldn't I take a cab? No, that's bad! bad!"

At last he reached Stoliarny Place. Half dead, he turned into it. Here he was almost safe, and he knew it. There would be fewer suspicious about his presence here. The crowd was thick, and he lost himself in it like a grain of sand. All his torments had weakened him so much, however, that he could scarcely move. The sweat rolled off him in drops, and his neck was soaked. As he came out onto the bank of the canal, someone shouted at him: "You've sure had it, brother!"

He hardly knew what he was doing himself now, and the further he went the worse it got. He did remember, though, suddenly coming out onto the canal bank, feeling scared because there were so few people here and he might therefore be more conspicuous, and wanting to turn back to Stoliarny Place. In spite of the fact that he almost collapsed, he made a detour and arrived home from a different direction.

Nor was he in full command of himself as he went through the gate of the house; at any rate, he was already as far as the stairs before he remembered the ax. And yet he was confronted with a very important problem; how to put it back while attracting the least possible attention? He was no longer capable, of course, of appreciating that it might be much better for him not to put the ax back in its former place at all, but to dump it down somewhere quietly in somebody else's backyard, later if necessary.

Everything turned out well, though. The door to the janitor's room was closed but not locked, which would make it seem likely the janitor was in. Yet he had so far lost his capacity to take such things into account that he walked straight up to the janitor's door and flung it open. If the janitor had asked, "What do you want?" he would have been quite capable of simply handing him the ax. Once again, however, the janitor was not in, and he managed to put the ax back where it had been before under the bench. He even hid it with a log, as it had been partly hidden before. From that time until he reached his own room he met no one, not a solitary soul. The landlady's door was closed. He went into his room and threw himself down on the couch, just as he was. He did not sleep, but lay there in a state of oblivion. Had anyone entered his room, he would have leaped up immediately and cried out. Fragments and shreds of thoughts swarmed in his head; but he could not get hold of a single one, he could not linger over a single one, in spite of all his trying. . . .

PART TWO

1

He lay like that for a very long time. From time to time he seemed to wake up, and then he noticed that it was long since night, but it never occurred to him to rise. At last he noticed that it was daylight. He was lying stretched out on the couch, still numb from his recent oblivion. The terrible, desperate shouts that he heard every night under his window after two o'clock came to him now sharp as a knife from the street. That was what wakened him. "Ah! the drunks are coming out of the saloons," he thought. "It's after two. . . ." Suddenly he leaped up, as though he had been ripped from the couch. "What! After two!" He sat down again on the couch. And then he remembered everything. In a single flash he suddenly remembered everything.

At the first moment he thought he would go mad. A terrible chill seized him; but the chill was from a fever that had begun some time ago in his sleep. Now, though, such a fit of shivering suddenly struck him that he all but felt his teeth jarred loose, and he trembled and shook all over. He opened the door and listened. Everyone in the house was sound asleep. He looked at himself, he looked at everything in the room around him, and he was amazed. How could he have come in like that yesterday without putting the door on the hook, flinging himself down on the couch, not only not undressing, but with his hat on. It had fallen off, and lay on the floor near his pillow. "If anyone had come in, what would he have thought? That I was drunk, but . . ." He hurried to the window. The light was sufficient, and he examined himself hastily from head to foot, all his clothes. Were there any traces? That was no way to go about it, though. Shaking and shivering, he took off all his clothes and examined them all over once more. He turned everything inside out, scrutinized every thread and patch, and since he did not trust himself, repeated the process about three times. But there seemed to be nothing, no traces. Only in one place, where his trousers had been badly frayed, some thick traces of dried blood clung to the frayed edge. He seized his large clasp knife and cut off the frayed edge. That seemed to be all there was. Suddenly he remembered that the purse and all the things he had taken out of the old woman's chest had been in his pockets all along! He had not even thought of removing and concealing them before this! He had not even thought of it while examining his clothes! What was the matter with him? In a flash he hastened to take them out and spread them on the table. He spread them all out, and even turned his pockets inside out to make sure nothing was left. Then he collected everything in a heap and carried it into a corner. There, in that very corner, down toward the floor, the wallpaper had come unstuck from the wall and was torn in one place. He immediately began to stuff everything into this hole behind the paper. "Made it! Everything's out of sight. The purse, too!" he thought joyfully, and he stood there staring blankly into the corner at the hole, which bulged out more now. Suddenly he started with horror. "My God," he whispered desperately, "what's the matter with me? Do I call that *hidden*? Is that a way to hide things?"

True, he had thought there would be only money and had not counted on the things; and so he had not prepared a place ahead of time. "But now, what was there for me to be so pleased about just now?" he thought. "Is that a way to go about hiding things? My intelligence has really left me!" He sat down helplessly on the couch, and an unbearable fit of shivering shook him again immediately. With a mechanical gesture he reached for what had once been a student's great-coat, lying on a chair nearby. It was still warm, but almost in shreds. He covered himself with it, and instantly sleep and fever together possessed him again. He sank into oblivion.

Not more than about five minutes had passed, however, when he leaped up and began rushing in a frenzy to his clothes again. "How could I go back to sleep when nothing has been done! That's it, that's it! The sling under the armhole—I haven't removed it yet! I forgot. I forgot! It's evidence!" He ripped the sling off and tore it into little pieces as quickly as he could, stuffing them into the laundry under his pillow. "Pieces of torn linen are not suspicious, anyway. Yes, apparently. Apparently not," he repeated. Standing in the middle of the room, with a tension that amounted to pain, he began to look around him again, at the floor, everywhere. Was there something he might still have forgotten?

The conviction that everything, even his memory, even common sense, was departing, began to torment him unbearably. "What, is it beginning already, is it my penalty approaching? Aha, that's the way it is!" Indeed, what caught his eye first were the frayed pieces he had cut from his trousers and strewn over the floor in the middle of the room! "What is the *matter* with me!" he cried again, like one lost.

Then a strange thought occurred to him. Maybe all his clothes were bloody, maybe there were stains all over, and he could not see them, did not notice them, because his mental powers were failing, splitting up, his mind clouding. . . . Suddenly he recalled that there had been blood on the purse, too. "Damn! There must be blood inside my pocket, then. I stuffed the purse into my pocket while it was still wet!" Instantly he turned the pocket inside out, and so it was. There were bloodstains on the lining. "So my intellect hasn't altogether left me, so I still have a mind and a memory! After all," he thought with pride, "I figured it out for myself!" He inhaled deeply and joyfully. "I was just weak with fever, momentarily delirious!" He ripped out the whole lining of his left trouser pocket. At that moment, a shaft of sunlight fell on his left shoe. There seemed to be some traces on the bit of the sock that peeped out from his shoe. He flung off the shoes. "Traces indeed! The whole edge of the sock is coated with blood." He must have been careless enough to step in the puddle. . . . "But what can I do with it now? Where can I hide the sock, this frayed part off my pants, this pocket?" He gathered it all in his hand and stood in the middle of the room. "In the stove? That's the first place they'd look. Burn them. But with what? I don't have any matches. No, I better go out somewhere and get rid of it. Yes! Better get rid of it!" he repeated, sitting down on the couch again, "and right now, this minute, no delay!" Instead, however, he lay his head down on the pillow again. An unbearable shivering shot through him like ice. Again he pulled the coat over him. For a long time, for several hours, he was dimly aware of sudden outbursts through his sleep: "Got to go right now, right away, get rid of it all, out of sight, soon as possible, soon as possible!" He wanted to get up from the couch several times, but could not. At last it was a loud knock on the door that wakened him.

"Open up! You dead or alive? Snoring away as always!" Nastasia shouted, beating her fist against the door. "Snoring away for days and days! In broad daylight, like a dog! Just like a dog! Open up, huh? It's past ten."

"Maybe he ain't home," a man's voice said.

"Damn! That's the janitor's voice . . . what does he want?"

He sat bolt upright on the couch. His heart was pounding so it hurt.

"Then who put the door on the latch?" Nastasia said. "All we need now is for him to start locking himself in! Does he think somebody's going to rob him, or what? Open up, my brainy one! Wake up!"

"What do they want? Why the janitor? It's all up. Should I resist or should I open? Come what may . . ."

He stood up, bent forward, and took off the hook. The room was so small that he could take the door off the hook without leaving his bed. Nastasia and the janitor were standing there.

Nastasia looked at him a bit strangely. He glanced at the janitor with a defiant and desperate air. Silently the latter handed him a gray sheet of paper folded in two, sealed with bottle wax.

"Summons from the station," he announced, handing over the paper.

"What station?"

"Police. Means they want you to show up at the station. What station is clear."

"Police! Why?"

"How should I know? They ask, so you go." The janitor looked at him carefully, looked all around, and turned to go.

"But he's really sick," Nastasia remarked, "isn't he?" She did not take her eyes off him. The janitor turned his head for a moment. "Been in a fever since yesterday," she added.

He did not reply. He held the paper in his hands without breaking the seal.

"Don't bother getting up," Nastasia said. Seeing him about to lift his feet from the couch, she suddenly felt sorry for him. "Don't go. You're sick. It won't burn down. What's that you've got there?"

He looked. In his right hand he was holding the cut bits of frayed trouser, the sock, and the scraps of the ripped-out pocket. He had slept holding them like that. Afterward he recalled that even when he had half wakened during the bout of his fever, he had clasped the rags more tightly in his hand and fallen asleep like that again.

"Oh, my, such rags he collects, and he sleeps with them like with a treasure. . . ." Nastasia went off into her hysterical laughter. Instantly he stuffed everything under his coat, fixing her steadily with his eyes. Though there was little he could fully and rationally comprehend at the moment, nevertheless he sensed that a man about to be taken off would not be handled this way. "But . . . the police?"

"Would you drink some tea? I'll bring some, eh? There's some left. . . ."

"No . . . I'll go. I'll go right now," he muttered, rising to his feet.

"But you couldn't get down the stairs, could you?"

"I'll go. . . ."

"As you like."

She followed the janitor out. Immediately he dashed to the light to examine the sock and the piece of frayed trouser. "There's a stain, but not really noticeable. Everything's all dirty, torn, and faded. If you didn't know you wouldn't notice. From a distance Nastasia couldn't have seen a thing. Thank God!" He unsealed the summons with a tremor and began to read. He kept reading for quite a while, until at last it sank in. It was an ordinary summons from the district police station, asking him to appear that day at half past nine in the office of the district superintendent.

"What's going on here, though? I've never had anything to do with the police! Why all of a sudden today?" he thought in agonized bewilderment. "Lord, let it be over as quick as possible!" About to drop to his knees in prayer, he burst out laughing—not at the prayer, but at himself. He began to dress himself hastily. "If I'm through, I'm through. It doesn't matter!" Suddenly he thought: "I'll put on the sock! It will get dustier, and the traces will disappear." As soon as he put it on, however, he tore it off again with disgust and horror. He tore it off, but realizing that he had no other, he picked it up and put it on again, and again he burst out laughing. "It all depends, it's all relative, just a matter of form," he thought in a flash, but only in one corner of his mind, as his body trembled all over. "Well, didn't I put it on! I did, and that's that!" But his laughter gave way immediately to despair. "No, I won't make it," he thought. His legs were trembling. "From fear," he accused himself. His head whirled and ached from fever. "It's a trick! They want to get me down there and all of a sudden pull a fast one," he went on murmuring to himself as he walked out to the stairs. "It's bad luck I'm almost delirious . . . I might let something stupid slip out."

On the stairs he recalled leaving all the things in the hole behind the wallpaper. "They probably want to search while I'm out," he reminded himself, and paused. Suddenly such despair possessed him, and such indifference to his own ruin, that he merely waved his hand and moved on.

"If they'd only just get it over with!"

In the street it was unbearably hot again. Scarcely a drop of rain had fallen all these days. Again, dust, brick, and lime; again, that stench from the stalls and the saloons; again, the numerous drunks, the Finnish peddlers, the half broken-down horse-cabs. The sun flashed in his eyes; it hurt him to look, and his head whirled—the usual state of a man in high fever who suddenly goes out into the street on a bright, sunny day.

As he came to the corner that turned off into *yesterday's* street, he looked down it at *that* house . . . and immediately he turned his eyes away.

"If they ask, maybe I'll tell them," he thought as he approached the station.

The station was a few blocks away, having just been moved into a new building, to the fourth floor. He had once been to the old quarters on some trifling errand, but that had been a long time ago. As he entered the gate he saw stairs on the right, and a peasant with a small book in his hands coming down them. "Must be a janitor. The station must be up here." It was a guess, but he started to go up. He did not want to ask anybody about anything.

As he came to the fourth floor he thought: "I'll go in, I'll fall on my knees and I'll tell all. . . ."

The stairs were narrow, steep, and wet with slops. All the kitchens of all the apartments on all four floors opened out on the stairs and stayed open almost all day. There was a terrible closeness. Up and down the stairs went janitors with house registers under their arms, policemen, and men and women—visitors. The station door was also wide open. He went in and paused in the anteroom. Some peasants were standing about waiting. Here, too, it was extremely close; there was, in addition, the nauseating smell of paint still raw over stale oil in the newly painted rooms. He decided to move on into the next room. The rooms were very small and low. Terrible impatience egged him on and on. No one noticed him. In the second room, some clerks sat writing.

They were dressed not much better than himself, and they seemed a queer lot. He turned to one.

"What is it?"

He showed the summons.

The clerk asked: "Are you a student?" He had glanced at the summons.

"I used to be a student."

The clerk looked at him, but without any curiosity. Unkempt in appearance, there seemed to be something rigid in his glance.

"Won't learn anything from him," Raskolnikov thought. "To him everything is the same."

"Go in there, to the chief clerk," he said, motioning him forward, pointing with his finger to the very last room.

The room was the fourth in a row; as he entered, it was stifling and crowded, but by people somewhat better dressed than in the other rooms. Among those waiting were two ladies. One was in mourning, poorly dressed, sitting behind a desk opposite the chief clerk, writing down something he dictated to her. The other, a woman of full figure and a purplish blotched complexion, rather luxuriously dressed and wearing a brooch on her bosom the size of a saucer, stood to one side and was waiting for something. Raskolnikov handed the chief clerk the summons. He gave it a quick look, said, "Wait," and continued to occupy himself with the lady in mourning.

Raskolnikov relaxed a little. "It can't be that!" Gradually he regained his confidence, and began to concentrate on keeping himself in hand.

"If I'm stupid, if I'm not careful even about petty details, I could let it all slip out! Hmm . . . pity there's no air in here," he added. "Stifling . . . Head's going around more and more . . . brain, too . . ."

He was aware of a terrible disorder within himself. He was afraid he could not keep himself under control. He tried to concentrate on something, to think of something altogether incidental, anything at all. He did not succeed. And the chief clerk interested him. He wanted to figure him out, to learn something about him from his face. A young man of about twenty-two, with a dark, mobile face that made him seem older than his years, he was fashionably, foppishly dressed, his hair parted in the middle, all combed and pomaded, and a number of rings on his scrubbed white fingers, and a gold chain on his vest. He even addressed a few words in French to a foreigner who happened to be there, and fairly correctly, too.

"Luisa Ivanovna, would you please sit down," he said to the overdressed purple-faced lady. She had been standing all along as though she would not presume to sit down on her own, although a chair was right beside her.

"Ich danke," she said, and quietly, with a rustle of silk, she dropped into the chair. Her light blue dress trimmed with white lace billowed out around her like a balloon and occupied almost half the room. It was scented. Filling half the room and being so strongly scented evidently embarrassed her; and although she smiled impudently and cringingly at the same time, it was with obvious uneasiness.

At last the lady in mourning finished and began to get up. Suddenly a young police officer entered the room rather noisily, swinging his shoulders oddly at each step. He flung his cockaded cap on the table, and sat down in an armchair. As soon as she saw him the luxurious lady practically leaped from her seat, and with a special kind of rapture fell to dropping curtsies at him. The officer paid not the slightest attention to her, while she on the other hand hardly dared sit down again in his presence. He was the assistant district superintendent, and he had brownish moustaches sticking out horizontally from each side of his face. His face had remarkably delicate features, which expressed nothing special, however, except perhaps a certain arrogance. Every now and then he looked askance and with indignation at Raskolnikov, whose bearing had too little in common with his shabby dress. Raskolnikov was looking at him too directly and too long, and he felt offended.

"And what do *you* want?" he shouted, apparently astonished that such a tramp did not cringe before the lightning-like majesty of his gaze.

"I received . . . a summons. . . ." Raskolnikov somehow replied.

"It's about recovering money from . . . from the *student,*" the chief clerk, tearing himself away from his paper work, put in hastily. "Here you are!" He tossed Raskolnikov a document, and pointed out the place. "Read this!"

"Money? What money?" thought Raskolnikov, "but that must mean it isn't *that!*" And he quivered with joy. He suddenly felt terribly, inexpressibly relieved. It all dropped from his shoulders.

"And at what time, m' dear sir, were you instructed to

appear?" the officer shouted, for some obscure reason more and more offended. "It says nine o'clock, and it's past eleven now!"

"I just received it fifteen minutes ago," Raskolnikov replied loudly, over his shoulder. To his surprise, he, too, grew angry. He even took pleasure in it. "You'd think it was enough I came here as I am, sick with fever!"

"Don't shout!"

"Who's shouting! I'm speaking quite softly, and it's you who are shouting at me. I'll have you know that I'm a student, and don't permit myself to be shouted at."

The assistant superintendent was so furious he could not for the first minute say anything, but only spluttered inarticulately. He jumped to his feet.

"Be si-i-ilent! You are in a government office. Don't you da-a-are be rude, sir."

"You are in a government office, too," cried Raskolnikov, "and not only are you shouting, you are showing disrespect to all of us by smoking a cigarette." Having said this, Raskolnikov felt an ineffable pleasure. The chief clerk looked at them with a smile. The bad-tempered officer had obviously been disconcerted.

"That's no business of yours!" he cried finally, with a kind of unnatural loudness. "Be so good as to make the declaration that's demanded of you. Show him, Alexander Grigorevich. There are complaints against you! You don't pay your bills! That's the fine bird you are!"

But Raskolnikov was no longer listening. Eagerly he grabbed the paper, looking for the quickest possible solution to the riddle. He read it once. He read it again. He did not understand.

"What does it mean?" he asked the chief clerk.

"You are being asked for money according to an I.O.U. of yours. This is a writ. You must either pay it—including all costs, expenses, et cetera—or submit a written declaration stating when you will be able to pay, and at the same time an undertaking not to leave the capital before you pay and not to sell or conceal your property. The creditor is free to dispose of your property and deal with you according to the law."

"But I'm . . . not in debt to anybody!"

"That's not really our business. A duly and legally attested I.O.U. for a hundred and fifteen rubles has been turned over to us for recovery. It was issued by you to the widow of

Collegiate Assessor Zarnitsyn, nine months ago. From the widow Zarnitsyn it was passed on as tender to Court Councillor Chebarov. We summon you therefore to said declaration."

"But she's my landlady. . . ."

"What concern is it of ours that she's your landlady?"

The chief clerk looked at him with an indulgent, sympathetic smile, yet with a certain triumph, as though on a novice under fire for the first time—a sort of "Well, what's it feel like now?" expression. But what did he care. What in the world did he care about an I.O.U., a writ! Was it worth worrying about, was it even worth any consideration! He stood there; he read, he listened, he answered; he even asked an occasional question himself; but all this was done mechanically. A feeling of triumphant security, of rescue from imminent danger, filled his entire being at this moment. He did not look ahead, he did not analyze, he had no suppositions or surmises concerning the future, no doubts and no questions. It was a moment of complete, unadulterated, purely animal joy. At that very moment in the station, though, thunder and lightning struck. Still quite shaken by the disrespect shown him, furious and obviously attempting to repair his wounded vanity, the officer hurled himself with all his thunderbolts on the unfortunate "luxurious lady," who had been looking at him, from the moment he arrived, with the most stupid smile.

"And a fine one you are!" he shouted suddenly at the top of his voice. The lady in mourning had already left. "What was going on at your place last night? Ah? Scandal! Scandal for the whole street. More brawling and drunkenness. Do you want to go to jail, or what? I've warned you ten times that eleven won't do! Now you're at it again. You're a fine one, all right!"

The paper dropped from Raskolnikov's hands. He looked wildly at the luxurious lady, who had been dealt with so unceremoniously. But he soon realized what had happened, and as soon as he did, the whole episode began to amuse him. He listened with pleasure. He wanted to laugh and laugh and laugh. . . . His nerves were that much on edge.

"Ilia Petrovich," the chief clerk began anxiously, but stopped to bide his time. As he knew from his own experience, it was not possible to deal with the enraged officer just then except by force.

As for the luxurious lady, she trembled at first before the

thunder and lightning. Yet, strangely, the more the abuse mounted, the more amiable she became, the more charming the smile she addressed to the dread officer. She shifted restlessly from foot to foot and curtsied incessantly, waiting anxiously that she might at last be permitted to put in her word, too. The opportunity came.

"Dere vas no commotion und no prawling py my blace, Mr. Captain," she began as though scattering peas, in confident if highly Germanized Russian, "und no scandal, no scandal at all. So it vas drunk zey come, und so already about it I have all told, but it vas not mein fault. . . . Mein house iss a respectable house, Mr. Captain, und it iss run respectable, und I alvays don't vant no kind of scandal. But zey vas come all drunk, und zen again for zree pottles zey ask, und zen vun his feet raised und to blay ze biano mit his foot started, und zat iss not good in a respectable house, und the biano he has ganz gebroke, und zere iss no manners here at all, no manners at all, und I have said ziss. Und ziss pottle he took, und everybody he started to hit mit ziss pottle from behind. Und so the janitor I called, und Karl iss come, und he iss Karl taken und in the eye hit him, und Henriette also in the eye he hit, und me five times in ze face. Und ziss iss so pad manners in ein respectable house, Mr. Captain, und I so am yelling. Und ze vindow he opens to ze canal, und like a pig he squeals. Und ziss iss a shame. Und how it iss possible through ze vindow to ze streets to squeal like a pig? Like ziss: Pff-u-u-ui-pfui-pfui! Und Karl from ze vindow py ze coat has pulled him back—ziss iss true, Mr. Captain—und sein Rock has torn. Und zen he has yelled man musz him fine payen fifteen rubles. Und myself I paid him, Mr. Captain, five rubles for sein Rock. Und ziss iss not a respectable guest, Mr. Captain, und has all kind of scandal made! Und I, he says, vill have a great satire on you gedrueckt, because I can write about you in all the newspapers."

"That means he's a writer?"

"Yes, Mr. Captain, und such a not respectable guest, Mr. Captain, und ven he iss in a respectable house—"

"Well, well, well! Enough! I have warned you, though, I have warned you, I have warned you—"

"Ilia Petrovich!" the chief clerk proclaimed weightily again. The officer threw him a swift glance, and the chief clerk tilted his head slightly.

"This much I will tell you, most worthy Luisa Ivanovna, and it is my last word," the officer went on. "If a scandal takes place in your respectable house just once more, then I will personally, as they say in high society, toss you in the clink. Do you hear me? So: a writer, a litterateur no less, took five rubles for getting his coattail torn in a respectable house? That's what they're like—these writers!" And he hurled a contemptuous glance at Raskolnikov. "In that tavern, day before yesterday, there was another story like that. This writer ate his dinner, all right, and then he doesn't want to pay. 'I'll write you up in a satire,' he says, and all that stuff. Last week on the ferry there was another one. He was insulting a respectable family, using the foulest language. To a state councillor and his wife and daughter, mind you. And one was kicked out of a candy shop the other day. That's what they're like, these writers, litterateurs, students, town criers—tffoo! You better go! But I'm going to look in at your place myself sometime . . . then watch out! Do you hear me?"

Luisa Ivanovna began to curtsy in all directions with intensified gratitude. She curtsied herself right up to the doorway. In the doorway, however, she collided with an important-looking officer. He had a fresh, open face and most impressively thick blond sideburns. This was Nikodim Fomich himself, the district superintendent. Luisa Ivanovna made haste to curtsy practically down to the floor, and hopping along with small, rapid steps, flew out of the office.

"Fuss and rattle again, thunder and lightning, hurricanes and waterspouts!" Nikodim Fomich said to Ilia Petrovich in a kind, friendly way. "You are boiling over again! I heard you all the way down the stairs."

"Well, then!" said Ilia Petrovich with refined nonchalance. Swinging his shoulders in a picturesque manner at each step, he went over to a desk that had some papers on it. "Look at this. Here's a writer, or a student, a former student, anyway. He doesn't pay his bills, has handed out I.O.U.'s, won't clear out of his apartment. Complaints coming in about him all the time. And then he has the nerve to complain that I smoke a cigarette in His Majesty's presence! They're bad actors, all of them. Just look at him. Pretty, isn't he?"

"Poverty's no vice, old fellow, and that's about the size of it! You're famous for this; go up like powder, can't stand an insult." Nikodim Fomich turned politely to Raskolnikov. "No doubt something he said offended you and you couldn't restrain yourself," he continued. "But that's a mistake. Why, he's one of the fi-i-inest! I tell you, one of the finest fellows—but powder, sheer powder! Why, he used to lose his temper all the time, boil over, get mad, and then—nothing! It would all roll off! And what was left, sir, was a heart of gold! In the regiment they used to call him Lieutenant Powder. . . ."

"And what a regiment it was!" Ilia Petrovich exclaimed, pleased at the flattery, but still sulking a bit. Raskolnikov suddenly wanted to say something pleasant to them.

He turned suddenly to Nikodim Fomich. "Be so kind, Captain," he began quite familiarly, "put yourself in my position. If I've done anything wrong on my part, I'm ready to beg anyone's pardon. I'm a poor, sick student. Crushed"—he actually used the word "crushed"—"by poverty. A *former* student, because at the moment I cannot support myself. But there's some money coming my way. I have a mother and a sister in Riazan Province. They're going to send me some, and I will . . . pay. My landlady is a kindly woman. She's been angry, though, because I lost the job I had giving lessons. It's over three months I haven't paid her. She doesn't even send up my dinner anymore. I really don't understand what all this is about! She wants cash for my I.O.U.—but how can I pay her, I ask you!"

"That's really not our business," said the chief clerk.

"Please, please, I agree with you completely, but please let me explain," Raskolnikov went on, addressing himself not to the chief clerk, but entirely to Nikodim Fomich. Yet he tried as hard as he could to include Ilia Petrovich, too, even though the latter was doing his best to look occupied with various papers and contemptuously paid no attention to him. "Please let me explain my side of it. Close to three years now I've been living at her house. Since I first arrived from the provinces. And at first . . . at first . . . well, I might as well admit it. From the very first I promised I'd marry her daughter. Nothing in writing, you understand, kind of a gentleman's agreement. This girl . . . anyway, I liked her . . . though I certainly wasn't in love . . . youth, and all that. I mean, what I want to say is, my landlady gave me a lot of credit then, and I would live it up a bit . . . I was a bit wild—"

"No one, my dear sir, is asking you for such intimacies, and we have no time to listen to them," broke in Ilia Petrovich coarsely and triumphantly. With some passion Raskolnikov continued, though speaking had suddenly become extremely difficult for him.

"Please, please . . . Let me tell you everything. How it happened and what I . . . I agree with you, it's all beside the point. . . . But a year ago this girl died of typhus. I stayed on as a tenant, just like before. When she was moving to her present apartment, the landlady said to me, and she said it in a friendly way . . . she had complete faith in me and all that . . . but wouldn't I give her an I.O.U. for a hundred and fifteen rubles, which was what she figured I owed her. Allow me, sir. She actually said all I had to do was make out this paper and she'd be glad to give me as much credit as I wanted and she would never, never—those were her very words, mind you—she would never make use of this paper until such time as I myself could pay. Now, just when I've lost my job and don't have enough to eat— now she goes and takes legal action. . . . What can I say?"

"These sentimental details, m' dear sir," Ilia Petrovich cut in flatly, "do not concern us. You have to make a statement and sign an undertaking. As for your being in love, and all these tragic touches—that is absolutely not our business."

"Come, now . . . you're being a little rough," murmured Nikodim Fomich. He had seated himself at a desk, and he, too, was busy signing documents. Somehow, he felt ashamed.

"Write, please," the chief clerk said to Raskolnikov.

"Write what?" he asked rather rudely.

"I will dictate to you."

It seemed to Raskolnikov that after his confession, the chief clerk's manner toward him had become more casual and more contemptuous. Yet strangely enough he suddenly felt himself completely indifferent as to who thought what about him; and this change occurred in a moment, in a single flash. If he had felt any impulse to reflect a little, it certainly would have astonished him that he had been talking the way he had a minute before, even trying to force his feelings on them. And where had these feelings come from? Now, if the room had suddenly turned out to be full, not of policemen, but of his closest friends, he would not have been able to address a single human word to them, so abruptly had his feelings been drained. He suddenly felt within himself a gloomy sensation of tormented, infinite solitude and estrangement. It was not the humiliation of having poured his soul out before Ilia Petrovich or the humiliation of the officer's triumph over him that caused this sudden change of feeling. What did he care now about his own baseness, all those vanities, those officers, German ladies, legal writs, offices, et cetera, et cetera! If at that moment he had been condemned to burn at the stake, he would not have blinked an eye. He would scarcely have paid any attention to the sentence. Something happened inside him he had never known before, something entirely new, sudden, and unprecedented. Not that he understood it. Yet with every fiber of his being he clearly sensed not only that he would not be able to turn again as he had a little while ago, with a kind of sentimental expansiveness, to the people in the police station, but that he would never again be able to communicate with them about anything—not even if, instead of police officials, they turned out to be his blood brothers and sisters. Until that moment he had never before experienced such a strange and terrible sensation. Most painful of all, it was more a sensation than it was understanding or conscious awareness; an immediate sensation, the most painful of all the sensations he had experienced in his lifetime.

The chief clerk began dictating to him the usual statement in such cases—a statement to the effect that he was unable to pay, promised to do so at such and such a time, would not leave the city or sell his property or give it away, and so forth.

"You can hardly write," the chief clerk noted curiously. "The pen's falling out of your hands. Are you sick?"

"Yes . . . head's going around . . . Read on!"

"That's all. Just sign."

The chief clerk took away the document and began to busy himself with others.

Raskolnikov returned the pen. Instead of getting up and leaving, however, he put both his elbows on the desk and clasped his head in both hands. He felt as though a nail were being driven into his skull. A strange thought suddenly occurred to him: he would get up now, he would walk over to Nikodim Fomich and tell him everything that had happened yesterday, down to the last detail; then he would take him back to the apartment and show him what he had hidden in the hole in the corner. The impulse was so strong he had already risen from his seat to carry it out. "Shouldn't I think it over a little?" dragged across his mind. "No, better not think about it. Better just get it off my chest!" Suddenly he stopped as though petrified. Nikodim Fomich was saying something heatedly to Ilia Petrovich, and he caught the words.

"Impossible. They'll both go free. In the first place, it all contradicts itself. Just think. Why would they call the janitor if they had really done it? Why should they give themselves away? Just to be cunning? No. That would have been *too* cunning! Finally, the janitor and this peddler woman both saw the student Pestriakov right at the gateway the very moment he came in. He was with three friends, and they parted company at the gateway, and he was asking the janitors about the address while his friends were still around. Would he be asking about the address if that was what he had in mind? As for Koch, he spent half an hour with the silversmith down below before he went up to see the old woman. It was exactly a quarter to eight when he went up. Now, just think—"

"But, excuse me, how do you account for this contradiction: they say themselves they knocked and the door was fastened; yet three minutes later, when they came back with the janitor, it turns out the door was open?"

"That's just the point. Undoubtedly the murderer was there and had the door on the latch. Undoubtedly they would have found him there if Koch hadn't been dumb enough to go look for the janitor himself. That was when *he* actually managed to get down the stairs and slip past them. Koch thanks his lucky stars. He says, 'If I'd stayed there, he would have jumped out and murdered me with his ax.' Now he wants to offer up a special service in church, he-he! . . ."

"But nobody saw the murderer?"

"How could anybody see him?" asked the chief clerk, who had been listening in. "The house is a veritable Noah's ark."

"The case is clear," Nikodim Fomich said heatedly, "the case is clear!"

"No," Ilia Petrovich countered, "the case is anything but clear."

Raskolnikov picked up his hat and walked toward the doorway. But he did not get as far as the doorway.

When he came to, he noted that he was sitting in a chair, a young man on his right was holding him up, another man on his left was holding a yellow glass filled with yellowish water, and Nikodim Fomich was standing in front of him gazing at him steadily. He got up from the chair.

"What's the matter?" Nikodim Fomich asked rather sharply. "You ill?"

"He could hardly hold the pen while he signed his name,"

the chief clerk noted. He had taken his place again and was occupying himself with official papers.

"Have you been sick a long time?" Ilia Petrovich called out. He, too, resumed going through the papers. Of course, he, too, had been staring at the sick man as long as the latter was in a faint. As soon as Raskolnikov had come to, he had turned away.

"Since yesterday," Raskolnikov answered.

"Did you go out yesterday?"

"Yes, I went out."

"Even though you were sick?"

"Even though I was sick."

"What time?"

"Eight P.M."

"And where, may I ask?"

"Along the street."

"Brief and to the point."

White as a sheet, Raskolnikov answered in brittle fragments, without dropping his dark, dilated eyes before the gaze of Ilia Petrovich.

"Look," said Nikodim Fomich, "he can hardly stand on his feet, while you—".

"Ne-ver mind!" said Ilia Petrovich in a rather peculiar way. Nikodim Fomich wanted to add something, but he glanced at the chief clerk, who had been looking at him quite steadily, and he remained silent. Suddenly everyone fell silent. It was strange.

"Very well, then," Ilia Petrovich concluded, "we are not keeping you."

Raskolnikov went out. He could still catch the sounds of an animated conversation that sprang up as soon as he left. Most clearly he heard the questioning voice of Nikodim Fomich. . . . In the street he recovered himself completely.

"A search! a search! Now there will be a search!" he kept repeating to himself as he hurried home. "The bastards! They suspect!" His former terror seized hold of him again and shook him from head to foot.

2

"What if there's been a search already? What if they're there now waiting for me?"

There was his room, though. Nothing. No one. Nobody had been looking around. Not even Nastasia had touched anything. But, good God! How *could* he have left the things in that hole?

He rushed to the corner, put his hand under the wallpaper, and began to pull out the things, loading his pockets with them. There were eight items. Two small boxes with earrings or something like that in them; he did not examine them very carefully. Four small morocco-leather cases. One chain wrapped only in newspaper. And something else wrapped in newspaper, a medal or some such thing . . .

To make them as inconspicuous as possible, he thrust the things into different pockets in his coat and in the remaining right-hand pocket of his trousers. He took the purse along, too. Then he went out of the room, leaving the door wide open this time.

He knew what he was doing, and although he felt quite shattered, walked with a quick, firm step. He was afraid of being followed; he was afraid that within half an hour, perhaps a quarter of an hour, there would be an order out to keep track of him. So he had to cover all traces before that time. While he still had some strength and some judgment left, he had to get rid of these things. But where?

Some time ago he had made up his mind: "Throw it all in the canal, all traces into the water, and the business is done." He had made up his mind about this last night, in his delirium, in those moments when, as he recalled, he had felt the repeated impulse to rise and go, "quick, as quick as I can, get rid of it all." Yet getting rid of it all seemed quite a difficult matter.

For half an hour, perhaps longer, he walked along the bank of the Katherine Canal. Several times, as he walked past them, he examined the steps that led down to the canal. It was out of the question, though. Either there were floats at the foot of the steps and women were doing their laundry there, or boats were moored there and people swarmed all over them, as indeed they swarmed everywhere on the banks, on both sides. They could see. They would notice. A man deliberately walking up, stopping, throwing something in the water: that is suspicious. And what about the jewelry boxes—would they sink or float? Certainly float. Everyone would see. As it was, they all stared at him as he walked by. They looked him up and down as though they had nothing to do but look at him. "Why should they? Maybe that's just the way I see it."

Finally he thought somewhere along the Neva might be better. There were fewer people there, he would escape notice more easily, it would be more suitable in every way, and, anyhow, it was further off. And he was suddenly amazed that he could have spent so much time wandering about, alarmed and anxious, in such dangerous places—without having thought of this sooner! And he had killed so much time to no purpose—all because he had made up his mind while he was dreaming and delirious! He was becoming too distraught and forgetful, and he knew it. He would certainly have to get going!

He walked along Voznesensky Prospect in the direction of the Neva, but along the way another thought struck him. "Why in the Neva? Why in the water? Wouldn't it be better to go somewhere far away, maybe to one of the islands again, and somewhere in a lonely place there—in some woods, or under a bush—hide everything, and mark the spot?" Although he felt he was in no shape at that moment to think it through, the idea nevertheless seemed sound to him.

He never got to the islands, though. Something else happened instead. As he left Voznesensky Prospect and came out onto a square, he suddenly noticed an entrance to a yard on his left, enclosed on two sides by blank walls. On the right, directly by the entryway, the blank unwhitewashed wall of a neighboring four-story house jutted into the yard. On the left, parallel to the blank wall, beginning also directly by the entryway, ran a wooden fence—about twenty paces into the yard, with a sharp turn then to the left. It was a vacant, secluded spot, where various odds and ends were lying about. Further on, he could see from behind the fence the corner of a low, sunken stone shed. It had obviously once been part of some kind of workshop. There had apparently been some kind of shop here, a carriage-maker's, or a mechanic's, or something of that sort. A black layer of coal dust covered everything right up to the entryway. "Here's a place I can hide the things, and get away," he thought suddenly. Not seeing anyone in the yard, he walked in, and at once saw, near the entryway, a trough fitted up against the fence (a frequent convenience in such houses, where there are many workers around, cabdrivers and so forth), and over the trough on the fence there was an inscription in chalk, the kind of witticism one usually finds in such places: "Don't just stand here. Do sumting." That meant there would be nothing suspicious about his walking in and standing around, and that was good. "Dump it all here and clear out!"

Having looked around again, his hand already in his pocket, he suddenly noticed between the entryway and the trough, where there was not more than a square yard of space, a large rough stone about fifty pounds in weight against the stone wall that faced the street. Behind that wall was the sidewalk, and one could hear the passersby, and there were always more than a few in the neighborhood. Behind the entryway, though, no one could see him unless somebody walked in from the street. Since this was not at all unlikely, he had to hurry.

He bent down over the stone, grasped the top with both hands, and using all his strength turned it over. Under the stone there was a small cavity. He started shoving everything he took out of his pockets into it. The purse went on top; and there was still some room. Then he grasped the stone again and turned it back over so it dropped exactly where it had been before. Perhaps it seemed just a tiny bit higher; but he heaped up some dirt and tamped down the edges with his foot. Nothing was noticeable.

He left and walked toward the square. Just as it had a little while ago in the station, a powerful, almost unbearable joy possessed him again for a moment. "The traces are buried! And who—who in the world—would think of looking under that stone? Probably been lying there since the house was built. Probably go on lying there for at least as long. Even if they found it—who would think of me? It's all over! Not a clue!"—and he laughed. Yes, later he remembered that he had laughed a slight, nervous, inaudible, prolonged laugh. He had laughed all the while he had been walking across the square. His laughter suddenly ceased when he came to Konogvardeisky Boulevard where, the day before yesterday, he had met that girl. Other thoughts came into his head. The thought of walking by the bench on which he had sat pondering after the girl's departure now seemed to him horribly disgusting, nor did he relish meeting the moustachioed policeman again, the one he had given twenty kopecks. "Damn him!"

Looking distractedly and angrily about him, he walked on. His thoughts circled around something he really knew was the main point, and at that very moment he knew he was confronting the main point, and he was confronting the main point for the first time in two months.

"Damn it all!" he thought suddenly in a fit of boundless rage. "If it has begun, then it has begun! To hell with it! To hell with the new life! God, how stupid it is! How I lied today, how I humiliated myself! How nastily I fawned and played up to that bastard Ilia Petrovich awhile ago! That's dumb, too! To hell with them all, I don't care. I don't care if I played up to them! That's not the point. That just isn't the point. . . ."

Suddenly he stopped. A new, quite unexpected, and extremely simple question perplexed and bewildered him. "If you did this business conscientiously, not like a fool, but if you really had a firm and definite purpose, why is it you haven't looked into the purse, why is it you don't even know what you've got, you don't know why you put yourself to all these torments, don't know why you consciously started out on such a vile, base, low business? A little while ago you were about to throw the purse into the water, along with all the things you haven't even had a good look at yet. Why?"

Yes, that's the way it was, the way it was exactly. He had even known it before, and it was by no means a new question. When his mind had been made up during the night to toss everything into the water, it had been made up without hesitation or doubt, as though that was the way it had to be, as though it could not be otherwise. . . . Yes, he knew all this, he remembered it all; nor had he made up his mind yesterday. He had made up his mind while he squatted over the chest fishing the jewel cases out of it. . . . That's how it was!

"Because I'm so sick," he concluded morosely at last, "I've worried and tortured myself, and I myself don't know what I'm doing. . . . And yesterday and the day before yesterday and all this time I've been tormenting myself. . . . I'll get better. Then I won't torment myself. . . . What if I never get better, though? God, I hate all this!" He kept on walking and did not stop. He yearned terribly for some

diversion, yet he did not know what. With every moment a
new and irresistible sensation held increasing sway over him:
it was a kind of boundless, almost physical disgust for everyone he met and everything around him, obstinate, angry,
and virulent. The people he met seemed loathsome; their
faces were loathsome, their walk, their movements. If anyone had addressed him, he would have been quite capable
of simply spitting on him or biting him.

When he came to the bank of the Little Neva, on Vasilievsky Island near the bridge, he stopped suddenly. "This is
where he lives, in this house," he thought. "I seem to have
come to Razumikhin's somehow on my own! Same story
over again . . . That's really curious, though. Did I come
here because I wanted to, or by chance? And how did I get
here? But it doesn't matter. The day before yesterday I said
I'd go see him the day after *that*. Well, here I am! As though
I couldn't drop in on him even now!"

He climbed up to the fifth floor, to Razumikhin's.

The latter was at home, in his little room. At the moment
he was busy writing something. He opened the door himself.
They had not seen each other for about four months. Razumikhin was lounging around in a dressing gown that had
been worn to shreds, slippers on his bare feet, disheveled,
unshaved, and unwashed. He looked surprised.

"What do you know!" he exclaimed, examining his friend
from head to foot as he came in. Then he fell silent and
gave a whistle.

"Pretty hard up, eh? You seem to've done me one better,
old pal," he added, looking at Raskolnikov's rags. "Sit
down, though, you must be tired!" When Raskolnikov
slumped down on the oilskin-covered Turkish couch (in
worse shape even than his own), Razumikhin suddenly became aware of the fact that his guest was ill.

"You're seriously ill, though, do you know that?" He put
a finger to his pulse. Raskolnikov tore his hand away.

"Never mind," he said. "I came . . . Here's why. I don't
have any lessons . . . I wanted . . . I don't need any lessons, though. . . ."

"You know what? You're raving!" Razumikhin, who had
been observing him steadily, remarked.

"No, I'm not raving. . . ." Raskolnikov got up from the
couch. On the way up to Razumikhin's, he had not really
confronted the notion that he would have to meet the latter
face to face. He realized now, and his experience confirmed

it, that there was no one in the whole wide world he could effectively meet at this moment face to face. His bile rose within him. A self-directed rage had virtually intoxicated him the moment he crossed Razumikhin's threshold.

"Good-bye!" he suddenly declared, and went to the door.

"Where are you going? Wait, wait a minute, you idiot!"

"I don't need any!" Raskolnikov repeated, once more tearing his hand away.

"Why the hell did you come here, then! You gone off your rocker, or what? Why, it's . . . damn near insulting. I'm not going to let you go like that."

"Look. I came here because you're the only one I know who could help . . . to start with . . . because you're kinder than everybody else; I mean cleverer . . . and you have some sense. . . . But now it's clear to me, I don't need anything. Nothing at all, do you hear? No services. No help . . . I myself . . . I am alone. . . . Very well, then! Let me be!"

"Now, wait a minute, you bum! You're absolutely nuts! Do as you like, I don't care. I don't have any lessons myself now, you see. Well, to hell with it. Down at the flea market there's this bookseller Kheruvimov, though, and he's kind of a lesson in himself. I wouldn't trade him for five lessons teaching merchants' kids. He does a little publishing—natural science, stuff like that. And, boy, does his stuff sell! All you really need is the title! Remember, you always used to say I was dumb, old pal. Well, my God, you'd be surprised how many people there are in the world dumber than I am! Now he's taken up the progressive movement, too. He doesn't know beans about it himself, but I egg him on, of course. Here you have a little over thirty-two pages of German text. In my opinion, it's the most blatant fake. Is woman a human being or not a human being? That sort of thing. Well, naturally, you prove triumphantly that she's a human being. Kheruvimov's getting it ready for his feminist section. I'm translating. He'll expand those thirty pages to a hundred. We'll compose the most passionate title, half a page long, and we'll put the thing out for half a ruble. Will it sell! I get about fifteen rubles for the job. I took six in advance. When we finish that, we'll start translating a book about whales, then I've got some of the duller scandals from the second part of the *Confessions* marked out, and we'll translate those. Somebody told Kheruvimov that Rousseau was a Radishchev of sorts. Naturally, I did not contradict. To hell with him! How about it, would you like to translate part two of *Is Woman Human?* If so, you can take the text right now. Take pen and paper. It's all on account. And take three rubles. Because I received an advance for the whole translation, for the first part as well as the second. So three rubles goes straight to you—your share. When you're done you'll get another three. Please don't think I'm doing you a favor in any way. On the contrary. I realized you'd be useful to me the minute you walked in. First of all, my spelling's bad; secondly, my German's a bit *schwach* sometimes, so I mostly just make it up myself, comforting myself with the thought that it's better than the original. Who knows, though, maybe it isn't better after all. Maybe it's worse. Will you take it, or not?"

Silently Raskolnikov picked up the German text, took the three rubles, and left without saying a word. Razumikhin watched him go with astonishment. When he had gone down to the first floor, however, Raskolnikov suddenly did an about-face, mounted the stairs again to Razumikhin's, deposited both the German text and the three rubles on the table from which he had taken them, and left without saying a word.

"You got the D.T.'s, or what!" Razumikhin roared. He had become quite angry at last. "Why are you staging this comedy! You've got me all riled up! Even me . . . What the hell did you come for?"

"I don't need . . . translations. . . ." muttered Raskolnikov, who was already descending the stairs.

"What the hell do you need, then?" Razumikhin shouted from above. Raskolnikov continued silently to descend.

"Hey! What's your address?"

There was no answer.

"Well, then, to he-e-ell with you!"

Raskolnikov was already out in the street. On the Nikolaevsky Bridge something very unpleasant happened to him, which brought him back to himself with a start. A carriage driver hit him squarely across his back with a whip. In spite of the fact that the driver had yelled at him three or four times, he had almost been run over by the horses. The blow of the whip stung, and he hopped over to the parapet. He did not know why he had been walking straight down the middle, where there were vehicles and no pedestrians. He clenched and ground his teeth furiously. People around him were laughing.

"That'll teach him!"

"Sly bastard."

"Sure. Pretends to be drunk, throws himself under the wheels on purpose, then you have to answer for him."

"They earn a living that way, pal, they earn a living that way. . . ."

As he stood at the parapet, still furiously and senselessly staring after the vanishing carriage and rubbing his back, he suddenly felt somebody thrust some money into his hands. He looked. It was a stout merchant woman in a bonnet and goatskin shoes. With her was a girl wearing a hat and carrying a green parasol, probably her daughter. "Take it, my dear man, for Christ's joy." He took it, and they walked past. It was a twenty-kopeck piece. By dress and appearance he might have been mistaken for a professional beggar collecting alms in the street; but for the amount of twenty kopecks he was probably obliged to the blow of the whip, which had aroused their pity.

He clutched the coin in his hand, took about ten steps, and turned to the Neva, facing in the direction of the palace. There was not a cloud in the sky, and the water was almost blue, a rarity for the Neva. The dome of the cathedral, which cannot be seen to better advantage than from this bridge twenty paces from the chapel, glittered marvelously; and through the clear air its every ornament could be seen in vivid detail. The pain from the whip's blow eased off, and Raskolnikov forgot about it. A single restless yet not altogether clear thought possessed him now exclusively. He stood there and stared off into space for a long time, and steadily. The place was very familiar. Often, when he had been attending the university, most frequently on his way home, he would stop at this very place (he must have done it a hundred times) to have a good look at the truly marvelous view. Every time that single unclear and unresolved impression of his would take him almost by surprise. The marvelous view always left him with an unexplained chill; the extravagant panorama seemed to have a soul that was deaf and dumb. . . . This gloomy, puzzling impression took him by surprise every time. He did not trust himself, and had postponed trying to figure it out until some future date. Now, suddenly, he recalled sharply these former doubts and perplexities of his, and it seemed to him not by chance that he remembered them now. Even the fact that he stopped at the accustomed place seemed to him wild and fantastic, as though he somehow imagined it was still possible to think about what he had thought about before, or to interest himself in the same subjects and sights as before, not so very long ago. It struck him as almost funny. At the same time, it weighed on his chest till it hurt. In some depth below, somewhere far beneath his feet and barely discernible, stirred all the life he had lived, the thoughts he had thought, the business that had kept him busy, the subjects that had concerned him, the sights that had impressed themselves on him, and the superb view and he himself and everything, everything. . . . He seemed to be flying away somewhere, higher and higher, and everything was disappearing before his eyes. His arm made an involuntary gesture, and suddenly he became aware of the twenty-kopeck piece he had been clutching in his fist. Unclasping his hand, he gazed steadily at the coin. Then, with a sudden movement, he flung it into the water. Then he turned around and went home. He felt as though he had cut himself off at that moment, with a scissors as it were, from everything and everyone.

He must have been out walking for about six hours, since it was almost evening when he arrived home. How and by what route he had returned he did not recall. After undressing, he lay down on his couch, trembling all over like an overdriven horse. He pulled the greatcoat up over him and slipped immediately into oblivion.

In the dead of night he was wakened by a terrible shriek. God, what a shriek that was! He had never in his life heard such weird sounds—howls, wails, grinding of teeth, weeping, blows, and curses. He could not imagine such brutality, such frenzy. He lifted himself up in terror and sat there on his bed, agonizing through each moment. The blows, the wails, the swearing, grew more intensive. To his great amazement, he could suddenly make out his landlady's voice. She was wailing, screaming, grieving; her words came pouring out so hastily nothing could be made of them, begging for something. Naturally, begging somebody to stop beating her, because somebody on the stairs was beating her mercilessly. The voice of the man who was beating her had already, from rage and fury, turned into a horrible croaking; yet, spluttering and in garbled haste, he, too, was saying something. Raskolnikov began to shake like a leaf. He recognized that voice. It was the voice of Ilia Petrovich. Ilia Petrovich was here. He was beating the landlady! He was kicking her, beating her head against the steps—clearly, you could tell from the sounds, from the wailing, from the blows! What was going on? The world turning over, or what? You could hear it now on all the floors; a crowd was gathering along the stairs, you could hear voices, exclamations, people walking about, knocking, banging doors, running back and forth. "But for what, for what . . . and how come!" he repeated, thinking seriously that he had gone altogether mad. But no. He heard all too clearly! If it were so, that must mean they'd be coming to see him, too, now, "because . . . probably, this is all due to . . . that business yesterday. . . . Good God!" He wanted to put his door on the latch, but he could not move his arm . . . and what good would it do! Terror encased him as with a layer of ice, tormented him and left him numb.

The hullabaloo, which had been going on for about ten minutes, finally began to simmer down. The landlady was moaning and groaning. Ilia Petrovich still threatened and cursed. . . . At last, however, he, too, seemed to quiet down. Then you could not hear him any longer, either. "He's gone! Good God!" Yes, and the landlady was leaving, too, still moaning and weeping . . . her door slammed. . . . The crowd on the stairs was breaking up and returning to the various apartments—exclaiming, quarreling, gossiping—and the sound rose at times to a shout, at times simmered down to a whisper. It must have been a big crowd. Almost everyone in the house had come running, apparently. "But, God, how come! And why, why did he call here!"

Powerlessly Raskolnikov sank back on the couch, but he could no longer close his eyes. For about half an hour he lay there in such torment, with such a sensation of unbearable and boundless horror, as he had never experienced before. A bright light suddenly illuminated his room. Nastasia entered with a candle and a plate of soup. Scrutinizing him carefully and seeing he was not asleep, she put the candle on the table and started uncovering what she had brought: bread, salt, a plate, a spoon.

"I don't suppose you've eaten since yesterday. You've got such a fever, and yet you go running around town all day long."

"Nastasia . . . why were they beating the landlady?"

She looked at him intently.

"Who was beating her?"

"Just now . . . half an hour ago, Ilia Petrovich, the assistant superintendent, on the stairs . . . What was he doing beating her like that? And . . . why did he call?"

Nastasia looked him up and down. She was silent, and

she frowned. She stared at him like that for a long time. It gave him an unpleasant feeling, even frightened him.

"Nastasia, why don't you say something?" he timidly ventured at last in a weak voice.

"It's the blood," she said at last, quietly, as though talking to herself.

"Blood! What blood?" he murmured, and turned pale, moving back toward the wall. Nastasia continued looking at him in silence.

She said in a stern and decisive voice: "Nobody was beating the landlady." Scarcely breathing, he looked up at her.

Even more timidly he said: "I heard it myself . . . I wasn't asleep . . . I was sitting up . . . I was listening a long time. . . . The assistant superintendent called. . . . From all the apartments, everybody ran out on the stairs. . . ."

"Nobody was here. That's the blood clamoring in you. That's what happens when it doesn't have a way out and starts clogging up the livers, then you start seeing things. . . . Would you like to eat something, or what?"

He did not answer. Standing over him, Nastasia kept looking at him intently, and did not leave.

"Let me have something to drink, Nastasia dear."

She went downstairs and returned in a few minutes with some water in a white clay pitcher. He did not remember what happened after that. He only remembered drinking one swallow of cold water and spilling some from the pitcher onto his chest. Then he lost consciousness.

3

He was not completely unconscious all the time he was sick, but rather delirious, in a feverish state of half consciousness. He could recall a good deal later. Once his room seemed full of people, and they wanted to carry him off somewhere, and they fussed and argued a lot about him. Another time he found himself suddenly alone in the room. They had all gone out. They were afraid of him. . . . Yet every so often they would open the door a little to take a look at him. They would threaten him, and talk something over among themselves. They laughed and made fun of him. He remembered Nastasia frequently beside him, and he could make out another man who seemed extremely familiar, but he could not guess who it was, and this bothered him and even made him cry. Still another time he felt as though he had been lying there for a month; and another time as though it were only a day that had passed. About *that,* however— about *that,* he had completely forgotten. Yet he kept having the feeling that he had forgotten something, something he could not afford to forget. He suffered pangs and torments as it nagged at him. He moaned, flew into a rage, or into a terrifying, insufferable panic-fear. Then he would tear himself away and want to run, but somebody always stopped him by force, and he would drop again into impotence and unconsciousness. At long last he recovered.

It happened at ten o'clock in the morning. At this morning hour on bright days a bright sun stripe always passed along the right wall of his room and lit up the corner near the doorway. Nastasia was standing at his bedside with a man he didn't know at all, who was looking at him with a great deal of curiosity. He was a young fellow in a caftan; he wore a goatee and looked like some kind of tradesman. The landlady was peeping through the half-open door. Raskolnikov lifted himself up.

He pointed at the fellow. "Who's that, Nastasia?" he asked.

"Well, it looks like he's come to," she said.

"He's come to," the tradesman echoed. Realizing that he had come to, the landlady, who had been peeping in, closed the door and withdrew. She had always been shy, and managed to endure explanations and conversations with difficulty at best. She was about forty, heavyset, a little on the fat side, dark-eyed, dark-browed, and good-natured, with a kind of lazy fatness. She was actually rather attractive. She had no reason to be so shy.

"Who . . . are you?" Raskolnikov asked, addressing the tradesman. At that moment, however, the door was flung wide open and Razumikhin came in, stooping a little because he was so tall.

"It's called an apartment," he cried out as he came in, "but it's a ship's cabin! Oop, my head! So you've come to, old pal? Pashenka just told me."

"He just came to," Nastasia said.

"He just came to," echoed the tradesman, smiling.

"And who, if you don't mind, may you be?" Razumikhin asked, addressing him. "Vrazumikhin at your service. Not, as they keep calling me, Razumikhin, but—Vrazumikhin, student, son of a gentleman. And this is my friend. Well. And who are you?"

"I work in the office at the merchant Shelopaev's. I'm here on business."

"Sit down in this chair, if you will." Razumikhin sat down himself on the other, on the opposite side of the small table. "Well, old pal, you did a good job, coming to," he went on, addressing Raskolnikov. "You've scarcely had a bite or a drink for four days. They gave you some tea with a spoon, it's true. I brought Zosimov here twice to have a look at you. Remember Zosimov? He looked you over carefully and he said right away nothing was wrong—all in the head; something somehow just struck you—nervous nonsense of some kind or other. Doesn't get enough to eat, he says, doesn't get enough beer and horseradish, so he's sick. But it's nothing. It'll ease off and go away. Quite a guy, Zosimov! A damn good doctor! Well," he addressed the tradesman again, "I don't want to keep you. Why don't you tell us your business? Mind you, Rodia, this is the second time that office sent somebody. He isn't the one who came last time. It was somebody else. We had a talk. Who was the guy who came here before you?"

"The day before yesterday? Must have been Alexei Semionovich. He works in our office, too."

"He's a little brighter than you are, though, wouldn't you say?"

"Ye-e-es. You might say so. He has more weight."

"Nicely put. Well, go on."

"Well, at your mother's request, you see," he began, addressing Raskolnikov directly, "Afanasy Ivanovich Vakhrushin, whom I think you know, sent you a remittance through our office, which we're supposed to hand over to you, provided you're in your right mind. Thirty-five rubles. Semion Semionovich received authorization for said amount from Afanasy Ivanovich at your mother's request in the same way as before. You know about it, don't you?"

"Yes . . . I remember . . . Vakhrushin," said Raskolnikov pensively.

"You hear! He does know the merchant Vakhrushin!" Razumikhin shouted. "How can you say he's not in his right mind? Anyway, it's now clear that you're a bright fellow, too. Well, well! It's always fun listening to clever speeches."

"Oh, yes, it is Mr. Vakhrushin, Afanasy Ivanovich, and at your mother's request, who once had money sent to you the same way before. Nor has she been refused this time. The other day Semion Semionovich deigned to let it be known that thirty-five rubles were to be turned over to you in the hope of better things to come."

"That's good. 'In the hope of better things to come!' That's very good. There's a phrase for you. 'Your mother's request'—that isn't bad, either. Well, what do you say? Is he in his right mind or isn't he, ah?"

"It is perfectly all right as far as I am concerned, sir. I merely stand in need of his signature."

"He'll scribble it for you! You got a book for him to sign or what?"

"Here is the book, sir. Yes, sir."

"Let's have it. Well, Rodia, up a little. Let me give you a hand. Come on, now. Take the pen and sign—Ras-kol-ni-kov—because, old pal, money's the best medicine we've got right now."

Raskolnikov pushed away the pen. "Don't need . . ."

"What do you mean, *don't need?*"

"I won't sign."

"For God's sake! How can we get the money if you don't sign?"

"I don't need . . . the money. . . ."

"So money isn't needed, ah? Well, old pal, you're lying. I can testify to that! Please don't be alarmed. It's just that he's . . . wandering again. He does that sometimes even when he's awake. . . . You are a man of sense, and we will just have to help him along, to put it simply. We'll take him by the hand and he'll sign. Come on, now . . ."

"If you wish I can come back some other time, sir."

"No, no, why go out of your way. You are a man of sense. . . . Come on, now, Rodia, let's not detain your visitor . . . look, he's waiting. . . ." And in all seriousness he was about to guide Raskolnikov's hand.

"Wait. I'll do it myself. . . ." the latter said, took the pen, and signed the book. The visitor counted out the money and departed.

"Bravo! And now, my friend, how about eating something?"

"Yes," answered Raskolnikov.

"Do you have any soup?"

"Yesterday's," Nastasia answered. She had been standing there all this time.

"With potato and rice in it?"

"With potato and rice."

"I know it by heart. Bring the soup. And let's have some tea."

"I'll bring it."

Raskolnikov looked at everything with profound amazement and a vacant, mindless panic. He decided to wait quietly and see what happened next. "Apparently I'm not delirious," he thought, "apparently this is really going on. . . ."

In a couple of minutes Nastasia came back with the soup and said there would soon be some tea, too. With the soup appeared two spoons, two plates, and a whole setting: salt, pepper, mustard for the beef. This had not happened for quite a long time. And the tablecloth was clean.

"It might not be a bad idea, Nastasia dear, if Praskovia Pavlovna could send us up a couple of bottles of beer. I don't think we'd have any trouble putting them away."

"Well, I've sure got to hand it to you!" Nastasia muttered, and left to carry out the order.

Raskolnikov went on looking about him wildly yet with strained attention. Meanwhile Razumikhin sat down on the couch beside him and, clumsy as a bear, put his left arm around Raskolnikov's head, although the latter was quite able to sit up by himself; with his right hand he lifted a spoonful of soup to Raskolnikov's mouth. He did this several times, blowing on the soup first so Raskolnikov would not burn himself, although the soup was barely warm. Raskolnikov greedily swallowed one spoonful, then another, then a third. After several spoonfuls, however, Razumikhin suddenly stopped and said there would have to be a consultation with Zosimov before he could have more.

Nastasia entered carrying two bottles of beer.

"Want some tea?"

"Yes."

"Hop to it and bring some tea, Nastasia. I think we can have some tea without consulting the medical school. But here's some beer!" He sat down again in his chair, pulled the soup over, and fell to as though he hadn't eaten in three days.

"Rodia, old pal, I've been eating like this every day at your place," he muttered as best he could through a mouth full of boiled beef, "and it's your dear landlady Pashenka who's responsible. She does me proud, I must say. I don't insist, of course, but I don't say no, either. Well, here's Nastasia with the tea. Nimble, isn't she! How about some beer, Nastenka?"

"Go on with you!"

"A little tea, then?"

"A little tea, if you like."

"Pour. No, wait a minute. I will pour for you myself. You sit down at the table."

He prepared everything with dispatch, poured one cup, then another, left his lunch and sat down on the couch again. As before, he put his left arm around the sick man's head, braced him, and started feeding him tea with a spoon, blowing incessantly and with a special zeal, as though the patient's recovery depended on this very process. Raskolnikov was silent. He offered no resistance, although he now felt quite strong enough to sit up by himself on the couch without help, and not only could he control himself sufficiently to handle a spoon or cup, but he thought he could even get up and walk. Because of some strange, almost animal cunning, however, he chose to conceal his strength for the time being, lie low, and pretend he still did not quite know what was going on. Meanwhile, he would listen, and try to figure out what was going on. Yet he could not fully control his feeling of disgust. When he had sipped about ten spoonfuls of tea, he suddenly freed his head, pushed away the spoon capriciously, and dropped down on his pillow again. And there were real pillows under his head now, with clean pillowcases, and stuffed with down. He made note of that, too, and took it into account.

"Pashenka's got to send up some raspberry jam, and he can have it in his tea," Razumikhin said. He went back to his seat and took up his soup and beer again.

"Where's she going to get raspberries?" Nastasia asked, balancing her saucer on outspread fingers and sipping tea in the Russian manner, through a lump of sugar she held in her teeth.

"She can get them in the store, old pal. You see, Rodia, there was a lot going on around here while you were conked out. When you left my place in that uncivilized way without giving me your address, I was so damn mad I thought I'd hunt you up and fix you up but good. So that very day I started. Well, I walked around and walked around, asked here, asked there. I'd forgotten about this apartment of yours. Though I don't really see how I could possibly have remembered, because I never knew it. Well, this place you had before, I remembered where it was, at Five Corners, Kharlamov's house. Well, I looked and I looked for this Kharlamov's house, and it turned out not to be Kharlamov's house at all, but Buch's—like sometimes you get the sounds mixed up! Well, then I got mad. I got mad and I thought to hell with it and I went to the address bureau at the police station, and just think—they found you for me in two minutes. They've got you listed."

"Listed!"

"Right. And yet they were looking for some General Kobelev, and all the time I was there they couldn't locate him. But to make a long story short. I got to know all about your affairs almost as soon as I dropped in there. Everything, old pal, everything. I know all about it. If you don't believe me, ask Nastasia. I got to know Nikodim Fomich, and I was introduced to Ilia Petrovich and the janitor and Mr. Zamiotov who's chief clerk in the office there. And finally, Pashenka, too—that was to top it all off. Nastasia knows about it. . . ."

"The way he made up to her, sugar wouldn't melt in his mouth," Nastasia murmured, smiling roguishly.

"Why don't *you* put the sugar *in* your tea, Nastasia Nikiforovna."

"You sure are some dog!" Nastasia burst out laughing. "My patronymic's Petrovna, though, not Nikiforovna," she added suddenly, after she stopped laughing.

"We will make a note of it, *madame*. Well, I'll tell you, old pal, to make a long story short, I wanted to distribute a few lightning bolts around here at first, to get rid of everybody's prejudices right away. But Pashenka won out. Old pal, I didn't expect she'd be so . . . so, well . . . so sort of *avenante* . . . ah? What do you say?"

Raskolnikov remained silent but did not for a moment drop his alarmed gaze, and went on staring at him intently.

"And very much so," continued Razumikhin, unembarrassed by his friend's silence, and as though confirming an answer he had received, "very nice, really, in all her details."

"What a creature!" Nastasia burst out again. This conversation seemed to provide her with some inexplicable joy.

"It's too bad, old pal, that you didn't catch on earlier in the game. You should have handled her differently. Because she's quite a character, really! Well, about her character we'll talk later. . . . How can you explain the fact that she wouldn't send up your dinner, for example? Or, for example,

that I.O.U.? I must say, you really were off your rocker
when you signed that I.O.U.! Or, for example, that marriage
you proposed when her daughter, Natalia Egorovna, was
still alive . . . I know all about it! What's more, I can see
it's a delicate string, and I'm a jackass. You must excuse
me. While we're on the subject of stupidity, though—you
know, Praskovia Pavlovna isn't at all as dumb as you might
at first think, ah?"

"Yes," mumbled Raskolnikov, looking away, but feeling
it was better to keep up the conversation.

"That's the truth, though, isn't it?" Razumikhin cried, apparently delighted he had received an answer. "On the other
hand, she's not bright, either, ah? Quite an unusual character, really! Sometimes I can't figure her out, old pal, I assure
you. . . . She's forty at least. She says thirty-six, and I guess
she has her rights. I assure you I judge her more in an
intellectual sense, according to a certain metaphysic, you
might say. You see, old pal, there's a kind of symbolic relation between us, like algebra! I don't understand any of it!
Well, this is all nonsense, of course. She saw you weren't a
student anymore, you weren't giving any lessons, and you
had no clothes. When the girl died, there wasn't much reason to treat you as an in-law anymore, and suddenly she
panicked. As for you, you just went into your corner and
didn't even try to keep up your former relations. Well, so
she started thinking about getting you out of that apartment.
She'd been brooding about that a long time, but it seemed
too bad to let all the money you owed her go. What's more,
you told her yourself your mother would pay—"

"In my baseness I told her that. . . . My mother is practically forced to beg alms. . . . And I lied so I could keep my
room and get fed," Raskolnikov proclaimed loudly and
distinctly.

"Well, that made sense. But here's the point. This is
where Mr. Chebarov comes in—court councillor and businessman. Without him, Pashenka could never have thought
of it. She'd have been embarrassed. Well, a businessman
doesn't embarrass easily, and right off he naturally poses the
question. Is there any chance of collecting on the I.O.U.?
Answer: Yes, there is. Because he's got the kind of mama
would come to her boy's rescue with her hundred-twenty-
five-ruble pension, though she went hungry herself. He's got
the kind of sister would sell herself into slavery for her
brother. So he made up his mind—Why do you jump like

that? I got to know all your little ins and outs, old pal. It's not for nothing you unburdened yourself to Pashenka when you were still on a family basis with her. Mind you, what I say now I say out of love. . . . That's the way it goes, you know. A sensitive, honest man unburdens himself, but a smart businessman listens and goes on eating. And then he eats you up. So she turns over this I.O.U. as a kind of payment to this Chebarov, and he calls it in officially without feeling any embarrassment at all. When I heard about it, I wanted at first to expose him to a bit of the old lightning treatment, just to clear up everybody's conscience, but then Pashenka and I got to understand each other, and I told her to stop the whole thing at its source, and I gave her my word you'd pay. I vouched for you, old pal, you hear? We called Chebarov, stuffed ten rubles in his teeth, and got back the document. Which I now have the honor of presenting you. They'll take your word for it now. Here, take it. I've torn it in half like you're supposed to."

Razumikhin put the note on the table. Raskolnikov looked at it, but without saying a word, he turned to the wall. This response jarred even on Razumikhin.

"I see, old pal," he said a moment later, "that I've made a fool of myself again. I thought I'd cheer you up and entertain you with my chattering, and all I've done is stir your bile."

After a moment's silence, Raskolnikov asked without turning his head: "Was it you I didn't recognize when I was delirious?"

"It was me, all right. You worked yourself into quite a tizzy over it. Especially when I brought Zamiotov along once."

"Zamiotov? The chief clerk? Why?" Raskolnikov turned swiftly and fixed his eyes on Razumikhin.

"What's wrong? What are you getting so excited about? He wanted to make your acquaintance. Because I'd been telling him so much about you. And he told me a few things—how else could I have found out what I did about you? He's quite a fellow, old pal, really most remarkable . . . in his own way, of course. We're friends now, and see each other almost every day. I moved over to this part of town. Did you know that? Moved a little while ago. We've been to Luisa's together a couple of times. Do you remember that Luisa, Luisa Ivanovna?"

"Did I say something when I was delirious?"

"Did you ever! You certainly were not yourself."

"What did I say when I was delirious?"

"Good Lord, what did he say when he was delirious? It's well known what people say when . . . Well, old pal, mustn't lose any more time. Back to work."

He rose from the chair and reached for his cap.

"What did I say when I was delirious?"

"My, my, how he carries on! Afraid you let some secret out or what? Don't worry. You didn't say a word about the countess. Something about a bulldog of some kind, and about earrings, and some sort of chains, and about Krestovsky Island and some janitor or other, and you said a lot about Nikodim Fomich and Ilia Petrovich, the assistant superintendent. You also seemed to be terribly interested in your own sock, just terribly! You kept begging for it. Give it to me, please. Just like that. Over and over. Zamiotov himself looked for your socks in all the corners and handed you that garbage with his own scented and bejeweled hands. That's what it took to calm you down, and you kept clutching this garbage to you for hours on end. It was impossible to tear it away. Must be somewhere under your blanket even now. Then you kept asking for some frayed ends of trousers, oh, so pitifully! We tried to figure out what kind of frayed ends you might have had in mind, but we couldn't. . . . Well, now, to work! Here are thirty-five rubles. I'm going to take ten of them; and in an hour or so I'll give you an account of what I did with them. I'm going to get ahold of Zosimov, too. He should have been here long ago, anyway. It's past eleven. And you, Nastasia dear, while I'm not here, do see to it that you drop in as often as you can. In case he wants something to drink, or anything like that . . . As for Pashenka, I'll go down myself right now and tell her what's needed. So long!"

"Pashenka, he calls her! My, is he an operator!" Nastasia called after him. Then she opened the door and tried to eavesdrop from there, but lost patience and ran downstairs herself. She seemed terribly interested in finding out exactly what he was saying to the landlady down there. It seemed clear that she was altogether charmed with Razumikhin.

The door had scarcely closed behind her when the sick man threw off his blanket and leaped out of bed as though he were insane. He had been waiting for them to leave, with a burning, convulsive impatience, so that he might get to work as soon as they were gone. Get to work doing what?

As though deliberately, he seemed to have forgotten. "Good God, tell me one thing only! Do they know everything, or do they still not know? And what if they do know and are only pretending, mocking, sounding me out—and then all of a sudden they'll come in and say they knew it all long ago and they were only . . . What was I going to do now? I've forgotten, as though deliberately. Forgotten suddenly what I just remembered!"

He stood in the middle of the room and looked about him in anguished perplexity. He went up to the door, opened it, and listened. That wasn't it, though. Suddenly he rushed as though he remembered to the corner where the hole in the wallpaper was. He put his hand in the hole, rummaged about, started examining everything. But that wasn't it, either. He walked over to the stove, opened it, and started poking about in the ashes. The bits of frayed edges of his trousers and the shreds of his torn pocket were still lying where he had thrown them—which meant that nobody had seen them! Then he remembered the sock that Razumikhin had just been talking about. Sure enough, there it was, under the blanket on the couch; but it was so crumpled and dirty that Zamiotov had certainly not been able to notice anything.

"Zamiotov, damn! . . . The station! . . . Why are they summoning me to the station, though? Where's the summons? Bah! . . . I got mixed up. The other time was when they sent for me! I was examining my sock then, too. Now, though . . . I've been sick. But why did Zamiotov come? Why did Razumikhin bring him here?" he was muttering weakly, and sat down again on the couch. "What's wrong? Am I still delirious, or is it real? Seems to be real. Ah, now I remember! Got to run! Got to run away quick. Got to run away quick! Yes . . . but where? And where are my clothes? No shoes. They took them away! They've hidden them! I understand! There's my coat, though—they overlooked it! And there's the money on the table, thank God! And there's the I.O.U. I'll take the money and go, I'll rent another apartment, I won't be found! But what about the address bureau? They'd find me, all right. Razumikhin would find me. Best of all run . . . *far* away . . . to America—and to hell with them! Take the I.O.U., too . . . might come in handy there. What else should I take? They think I'm sick! They don't know I can walk, ha-ha-ha! . . . I could tell by their eyes that they know it all! If only I could get down the stairs!

What if they've got a police guard there? What's this? Tea? And there's some beer left. Half a bottle. Cold, too!"

He grabbed the bottle, which still contained a whole glass of beer, and drank it pleasurably in one gulp, as though he were putting out a fire inside him. Scarcely a minute passed before the beer started going to his head, and a slight, even rather pleasant shudder ran along his back. He lay down and pulled the blanket over him. His thoughts, sick and disconnected enough before, became increasingly confused, and soon a light and pleasant drowsiness overcame him. Pleasurably he burrowed his head into the pillow, wrapped more securely about him the soft cotton blanket that had replaced his ragged greatcoat, breathed peacefully, and fell into a deep, sound, powerful sleep.

He woke up when he heard someone come into his room. He saw Razumikhin, who had opened the door wide and was standing on the threshold, hesitating as to whether to go in or not. Quickly Raskolnikov raised himself up on the couch and looked at him, as though he were trying to remember something.

"So you're not asleep. . . . Well, here I am! Nastasia, bring that bundle up!" Razumikhin shouted. "Now you'll have an accounting—"

"What time is it?" Raskolnikov asked, looking around in alarm.

"You slept like a soldier, old pal. It's evening. Soon be six. You slept six hours, and a little over."

"Good God! I did that!"

"And why not? It's good for you! Where is there to hurry off to? A tryst, or what? We have all the time in the world. I've been waiting for you three hours now. I came in a couple of times, but you were asleep. Twice I went down to Zosimov's. He's not home, and that's all there is to it! Well, it doesn't matter, he'll come! . . . I've also been off on my own little matters. I moved today, you know. Moved over lock, stock, and barrel to my uncle's. I have an uncle now, you know. . . . Well, to hell with all that, down to brass tacks! . . . Hand that bundle over, Nastenka. That's the girl. . . . And how are you feeling, old pal?"

"I'm all right. I'm not sick. . . . Razumikhin, have you been here long?"

"I told you. I've been waiting three hours."

"No, but before?"

"What do you mean, before?"

"How long is it you've been coming here?"

"But I told you all about it not long ago. Don't you remember?"

Raskolnikov pondered. Something from not long ago flashed in his mind as in a dream. He could not fasten on any one thing, though, and he looked inquiringly at Razumikhin.

"Hmm!" said the latter, "forgotten! I thought some time ago you were not quite yourself. . . . That sleep seems to have done you some good, though. . . . It's true. You look a hell of a lot better. That's the boy! Well, then, to brass tacks! It'll all come back to you any minute now. Just look over here, my dear fellow."

He began to unbundle the package, which apparently interested him very much.

"Believe it or not, old pal, I had a soft spot in my heart for this job. Because we've got to make a man out of you. So, here we go. We start at the top. Do you see this li'l ole hat?" he began, taking out of the bundle a fairly nice-looking yet quite ordinary cheap cap. "Mind trying it on?"

"Later. In a while," Raskolnikov said, querulously waving him away.

"Oh, come on, Rodia old pal, don't say no. Later it'll be late. And I won't get any sleep, because I took a flyer buying it. I didn't know your size. Ah! Right on the button!" he exclaimed triumphantly, trying it for size. "Fits like a glove! The warbonnet, old pal, that's the most important item in your attire. It's a ticket in itself. There's a friend of mine, now—Tolstiakov, maybe you know him—he feels obliged to take his lid off whenever he's anyplace where everybody's standing around in hats and caps. And it's not servility, mind you. He does it because that bird's nest of his embarrasses him. That's how bashful he is. What do you say, Nastenka. Now just compare these two lids, would you. This Palmerston"—he picked up Raskolnikov's battered top hat from the corner; for some unknown reason he called it a Palmerston—"or this jewel of a hat? How much do you think I paid for it, Rodia? Guess. Nastasia dear?" Since Raskolnikov remained silent, he turned to her.

"I bet he gave twenty kopecks for it," Nastasia said.

"Twenty kopecks, now you're being silly," he said, taking offense. "One can't even buy the likes of you for twenty kopecks nowadays. It was eighty kopecks. And only because it was secondhand. True, it's got a guarantee. If you wear it out in a year they'll give you another one free. How about that! Well, now, let's move on to the United States of America, as we used to call them in school. I warn you beforehand, I'm proud of these pants!" And he displayed before Raskolnikov a pair of gray trousers made of a light summer woolen material. "No holes, no stains. Just as good as new. Even though they're not. And there's a jacket to match. The same color, just as fashion requires. As for being secondhand—speaking frankly, that makes it better; softer, more delicate. You see, Rodia, it's my considered opinion that all you have to do to make your way in the world is the right thing at the right time. If you can do without asparagus in January, that puts rubles in your purse. And the same principle applies to this little item. It's summer now, so I bought a summer item; because toward autumn you need warmer material anyhow. You'd have to throw these away whether you wanted to or not . . . especially since they'd probably have disintegrated by then anyhow. From inner inadequacies if not from your increased standard of luxury. Take a good look. Guess how much? Two rubles twenty-five kopecks! With the same guarantee. Wear these out, they'll give you another pair next year, free! That's the way they do business at Fediaev's. Once you pay for anything it's got to last you a lifetime, otherwise you won't go back there again. Well, then, let's be getting on to the boots. How do you like them? Of course, you can see they're secondhand, but they'll do for a month or two. Imported labor and imported material, mind you. A secretary from the English embassy sold them on the flea market last week. He'd only worn them six days. He needed the money badly. Price: one ruble fifty kopecks. Bargain?"

"Maybe they won't fit," said Nastasia.

"Not fit! What do you mean, not fit!" He pulled Raskolnikov's old shoe out of his pocket—full of holes, cracked, caked with dried mud. "I took the old veteran along, and we managed to reconstruct the regular size from this old dinosaur. I might add that the whole transaction was conducted in the proper spirit. As for the linen situation, that was discussed with your landlady. To begin with, here are three shirts. The cloth's a bit coarse, but they've got fashionable fronts. . . . Well, sir, there it is. Eighty kopecks the cap; two rubles twenty-five the rest of the haberdashery, and that makes three rubles five kopecks; a ruble fifty the shoes— they're very good, after all—and that makes four rubles fifty-five kopecks; then, five rubles for underwear—got that wholesale—makes exactly nine rubles fifty-five kopecks. Forty-five kopecks' change in copper coins—here you are, sir, please take them—and in this way, Rodia, as far as clothes are concerned, you are back in full bloom. Because in my opinion your coat is not only good yet, it even has a certain special look of gentility about it—that's what it means to buy your clothes at Charmeur's! As for socks and things like that—I leave it to you. You have twenty-five rubles left. As for Pashenka, paying the rent, and all that— don't worry about it. I spoke to her. Your credit is most unlimited. Now, old pal, let's change your linen, because if you ask me your illness resides in that shirt, and in that shirt alone—"

"Let me alone! I don't want to!" Raskolnikov waved him away. He had listened with disgust to Razumikhin's tensely playful account of his purchases.

"That won't do, old pal," Razumikhin insisted. "What do you think I've been wearing my shoes out for! Nastasia dear, don't be bashful, give us a hand, that's the girl." Raskolnikov's linen was changed in spite of his resistance. He threw himself back on his pillow and for a couple of minutes said not a word.

"It'll be a long time before I get rid of them," he thought. "What money did you buy all this with?" he asked finally, staring at the wall.

"Money? Say, what *about* that! Your own, of course. Not long ago there was a messenger here from Vakhrushin, your mother had him sent. Or have you forgotten?"

"Now I remember. . . ." Raskolnikov said after long and gloomy reflection. Razumikhin frowned, looking at him with some alarm.

The door opened and a tall, solid-looking man came in, who also looked somewhat familiar to Raskolnikov.

"Zosimov! At long last!" Razumikhin cried out, cheering up.

4

Zosimov was a tall, well-fed man, with a puffy, sallow, clean-shaven face and blond straight hair. He wore glasses, and on his fingers, a large gold ring that made the fat bulge out. He was about twenty-seven, dressed in a loose, fashionable light coat and bright summer trousers. In general, everything he wore fitted loosely and was fashionable and brand-new; his linen irreproachable and his watch chain massive. His manner was slow and, as it were, sluggish; yet at the same time of a studied casualness. Though he took pains to conceal it, his self-esteem was always peeping out. Everyone who knew him found him ponderous, but said he knew his business.

"Twice I've been to see you, old pal. . . . Look, he's come to!" said Razumikhin.

"I see, I see. Well, how are we feeling now, ah?" Zosimov addressed Raskolnikov, looking at him intently and sitting down beside him on the couch, at his feet, where he at once made himself as comfortable as possible.

"Still feels blue," Razumikhin went on. "We changed his linen and he almost wept."

"That's understandable. His linen could have been changed later if he didn't want to. . . . Pulse, excellent. And your head, does it still hurt a little, ah?"

"I'm all right. I'm quite all right!" Raskolnikov said emphatically and irritably. He raised himself up on the couch and his eyes flashed, but he sank down on his pillow again immediately and turned to the wall. Zosimov observed him carefully.

"Very good . . . all as it should be," he said languidly. "Did he eat anything?"

They told him, and asked what the sick man could be fed.

"Why, anything. Soup, tea . . . Of course, you don't want to feed him mushrooms or cucumbers just yet, or boiled beef, either, and . . . but I don't have to tell you!" He swapped glances with Razumikhin. "No more prescription, no more anything. I'll look in tomorrow. Maybe I should have looked in today . . . but, well . . ."

"Tomorrow evening I'll take him for a walk," said Razumikhin. "We'll go to Iusupov Park, and then to the Palais de Crystal."

"I don't think I'd move him around much tomorrow. Maybe a little . . . well, we'll see then."

"Ah, pity. I'm having a housewarming today, just a couple steps away. Nice if he could have come. Even if he just stretched out on the couch there! And what about you—will you be there?" Razumikhin suddenly turned to Zosimov. "Don't forget, now. You promised."

"If you like. But a little on the late side. What's the program?"

"Nothing special. Tea, vodka, herring. We'll have some pastry. A few friends."

"Who?"

"Well, they're all from around here, and come to think of it, they're almost all new, except maybe my old uncle, but actually he's new, too. He's here on some kind of business and only arrived in Petersburg yesterday. We see each other about once every five years."

"Who is he?"

"Oh, he's a district postmaster, been vegetating all his life. He's sixty-five and he gets a pension. Hardly worth talking about. Still, I'm very fond of him. Porfiry Petrovich will be there; he's a lawyer . . . our local court investigator. But then, you know him. . . ."

"He's a relative of yours too, isn't he?"

"Oh, very distant, I think. Why the frown? Just because you and he had a little to-do once, does that mean you shouldn't come?"

"To hell with him. . . ."

"That's better. Well. There will be students, a teacher, one official, one musician, an army officer, Zamiotov—"

"Tell me, please, what can there be in common between you, or him there"—Zosimov nodded at Raskolnikov—"and the likes of that . . . that what's-his-name, Zamiotov?"

"Oh, these touchy people! Principles! You're always standing on your principles as if they were stilts. You won't move on your own feet. If you ask me, if a man's all right—there's a principle for you. I don't need to know another thing. Zamiotov's a marvelous man."

"And he takes bribes."

"All right, so he takes bribes, so what do I care if he takes bribes!" Razumikhin was shouting in exasperation. "Do you think I praise him because he takes bribes! I just said that in his own way he was all right. If you insist on looking at everybody that way, how many good people will you find? Why, what do you think I'd be worth, guts and all?—one baked onion, approximately! And the scale wouldn't move much if you were thrown into the bargain, what's more!"

"Come on, now. That's not enough. I'd give two just for you—"

"And I'd only give one for you! Some wit! Why, Zamiotov's still a kid. Maybe I'll even take him across my knees one of these days. You've got to be nice to him, not simply reject him. You can't reform a man by rejecting him, and all the more so with a kid. With a kid you've got to be twice as careful. You squarehead progressives don't understand a thing!

> Do a man dirt;
> Yourself you hurt. . . .

If you really want to know, there's a certain job we've got a common interest in."

"Do tell."

"Well, it's got to do with that case of the painter—the house painter, that is . . . We're trying to get him off. Shouldn't be much trouble now, anyway. The case is altogether and completely obvious now! All we have to do is work up a little more steam."

"What house painter are you talking about?"

"You mean I haven't told you? Really? That's right, I guess I just told you the beginning . . . you know, about that murder. The old pawnbroker woman. Well, now this house painter's gone and gotten himself mixed up in it—"

"Why, I heard about that murder case even before you told me. I'm interested in it in a way . . . for a certain reason. . . . I've been following it in the papers, so—"

"Lizaveta! She was killed too!" Nastasia suddenly blurted out, turning to Raskolnikov. All this time she had remained in the room, leaning back against the door and listening.

"Lizaveta?" Raskolnikov murmured in a scarcely audible voice.

"You know. Lizaveta. She used to sell things. Once in a while she used to come here. Even mended a shirt for you once."

Raskolnikov turned to the wall. He turned to the dirty yellow strips of wallpaper decorated with white flowers, and he chose one clumsy white flower with brownish veins and started examining it: how many leaves it had, and the cut of the scalloped edges of the leaves, and how many veins in each leaf. He felt his arms and legs go numb, as if they had been removed. He did not even try to move, but stared obstinately at the flower.

"Well, what about the house painter?" Zosimov inter-

rupted Nastasia's chatter with marked impatience. She
sighed and fell silent.

"He's been classified as a murderer, too!" Razumikhin
went on heatedly.

"Evidence of some sort, or what?"

"Like hell there's evidence! Well, maybe there is some.
This evidence isn't really evidence, though—that's what we've
got to prove! It's exactly like when they first locked up those
whatchemacallems and kept them under suspicion . . . Koch and
Pestriakov. Oh, hell! It sure is dumb, the way they go about
it, even an outsider can see that. Just sickening. This fellow
Pestriakov—you know, he might be over at my place
tonight. . . . By the way, Rodia, you know this bit, don't
you? Happened before you got sick, the day before that
time you fainted at the police station while they were talking
about it."

Zosimov looked curiously at Raskolnikov, who did not
stir.

"I don't mind telling you, Razumikhin, you really are
quite a busybody," Zosimov remarked.

"Be that as it may, we're going to get him off!" Razumikhin shouted, pounding his fist on the table. "You know
what's most irritating about this whole business? It isn't that
they talk nonsense. You can always forgive somebody talking nonsense. We all have a soft spot in our hearts for somebody who talks nonsense, and there's a kind of nonsense
that leads to sense. No, what's shameful is this. They talk
nonsense and worship their own nonsense. Mind you, I respect Porfiry, but— Do you know, for example, what first
threw them off the scent? The door had been locked. Yet
when they came back with the janitor, it stood open. And
that meant that Koch and Pestriakov committed the murder!
That's the kind of logic they use."

"Don't get so excited. They were just kept in custody.
After all, you can't— What's more, I met this Koch fellow.
Didn't he used to buy unredeemed articles from the old
woman? Ah?"

"Oh, yes, he's a swindler, all right! He buys up I.O.U.'s, too.
Regular entrepreneur. To hell with him. But don't you
understand what makes me mad? It's that lousy, decrepit,
case-hardened routine of theirs makes me mad. Right here,
in this very case, it may be possible to pioneer a new technique. You could show them the right track just by pointing
out the psychological facts alone. 'Oh,' they say, 'we've got

the facts, though!' Yes, but the facts aren't everything. At least half the case is in knowing what to do with the facts."

"And you know what to do with the facts?"

"When you feel it in your bones that you might be some help in the case, you can't just shut up about it. . . . Eh! Do you really know this case in detail?"

"Well, I'm waiting to find out about the house painter."

"Oh, yes! Well, here's the story. Early the third day after the murder, while they were still fussing around about Koch and Pestriakov—mind you, those two had accounted for every step they'd taken, and the obviousness of the whole thing cries to high heaven—suddenly the most unexpected fact came to light. A certain peasant named Dushkin, who keeps a saloon facing that very building, appears at the station and hands over a jewel case with gold earrings and tells a whole story. 'The day before yesterday,' he says, 'around eight o'clock in the evening, this house painter comes running to me . . .' It's the very day and hour of the murder—understand? '. . . and this Mikolay used to come to my place for a drink now and then, and this time he brought me this here little box with gold earrings and stuff, and he asks me to let him have two rubles on them. So I ask him where did he get them, and he says he picked them up off the street. So I let it go at that. . . .' This is Dushkin speaking, mind you. 'So I makes him out a ticket—for a ruble, that is—because I look at it this way: if I don't take it, somebody else will; it's all the same, go down in drink any way you look at it, might as well keep the stuff here with me. Further you hide it, closer you find it, as the saying goes. If I hear any rumors about the stuff I'll turn it in.' Well, he was talking hogwash, of course. I know this Dushkin. He lies like a trooper. He's a fence and a pawnbroker. He didn't pinch a thirty-ruble item from Mikolay just to 'turn it in.' He got cold feet, that's all. But it doesn't matter. So, listen. 'I know this peasant Mikolay Dementiev since he was a kid,' Dushkin goes on. 'We come from the same province, same district. We're both from the Zaraisky District in Riazan. And this Mikolay, well, he's no drunk exactly, but he likes to hit the bottle quite a bit, and I know he's working in that very house. He was painting along with Mitry, and this Mitry, he's from the same place, too. Soon as I give him his ticket he gets it changed and he drinks down two glasses just like that, picks up his change and leaves. Only I didn't see Mitry with him. Next day I hear the news. Aliona Ivanovna and her sister Lizaveta Ivanovna murdered with an ax. I knew them, naturally, so I starts wondering about them earrings. Because I knew the deceased used to lend money on such items. I go to the house where they work, and I start finding out for myself. Carefully. On tiptoe, so to speak. First of all I ask, Mikolay around? And Mitry says Mikolay's been goofing off, came home drunk at daybreak, stayed home about ten minutes, and went out again. Mitry ain't seen him since and is finishing up the job by himself. This job of theirs is along the same stairs as the murdered women, only on the second floor. When I hears all this, I says nothing to nobody'—Dushkin speaking, mind you—'I just try to find out much as I can about the murder, and I go back home and keep wondering. This morning at eight o'clock, though'—that's on the third day, understand—'I see Mikolay coming into my place. He's not exactly sober, but not very drunk either. He can follow what's being said. He sits down on a bench and he shuts up like a clam. There's only one guy besides him in my saloon, a stranger. And another guy, somebody I knew, asleep on a bench. And two of my boys. "Seen Mitry?" I ask. "Nope," he says, "haven't seen him." "You haven't been around!" "Haven't been around," he says, "not since the day before yesterday." "Where did you spend the night?" "Out by the Sands," he says, "at the Kolomna place." "And where did you," I say, "get those earrings from that time?" "Found them on the street," he says, and he says it as though I wasn't going to believe him, without looking me straight in the eye. "Have you heard," I say, "what happened that evening at that time on those very stairs?" "No," he says, "I ain't heard." He's listening, all right, though. His eyes are popping and his face is white as chalk. I'm watching him all the time I'm talking. He starts to reach for his hat. Around this point, naturally, I want to hang on to him. "Wait, Mikolay," I say, "how about another drink?" I give the sign to one of my kids to keep the door shut and I come out from behind the counter. But he gives me the slip and he's out in the street at a run and around the corner. That's the last I saw him. I didn't have much doubt anymore. The sin is on him. That's how it is. . . .' "

"Just so!" said Zosimov.

"Wait! Listen to the ending! Naturally, everybody went out looking for Mikolay. Dushkin, they detained and cross-examined him. Mitry, too. They also gave the Kolomna people a going-over. Then all of a sudden, the day before yesterday, they find Mikolay in person. Near one of the city gates, in a tavern. He was detained. He'd gone there, taken the silver cross off his neck, and asked for a drink in return. They gave it to him. A few minutes later a woman was on her way to the cow shed, and she happened to notice through a crack how he had tied his belt to a beam in the adjoining shed, how he'd made a noose and was standing on a block of wood trying to get the noose around his neck. The woman yelled at the top of her lungs, and people came running. 'What the hell are you up to!' 'Arrest me,' he says, 'I'll confess everything.' So they escort him to the station in proper style. Here, that is. Well, there are questions, et cetera. 'How old are you?' 'Twenty-two.' And so on, and so on. Question: 'When you and Mitry were working, didn't you at such and such or such and such a time notice anybody on the stairs?' Answer: 'Maybe people were walking up and down the stairs—of course—but we didn't notice.' 'Didn't you hear any kind of a noise?' 'We didn't hear anything special.' 'Mikolay, did you or didn't you know that a certain widow woman and her sister were murdered and robbed that very day and hour near those very stairs?' 'I didn't know anything, I didn't hear anything. First I heard about it was from Afanasy Pavlych in the saloon day before yesterday.' 'And where did you get those earrings?' 'I found them in the street.' 'Why didn't you show up for work with Mitry the next day?' 'I was goofing off.' 'Where were you goofing off?' 'Such and such and such and such.' 'Why did you run away from Dushkin?' 'Because I was scared.' 'What were you scared of?' 'That I'd be accused.' 'Why were you scared if you felt you were innocent?' Believe it or not, Zosimov, that question was actually asked, literally in those terms, I know it for a fact! Can you imagine? Can you *imagine?*"

"There is a certain amount of evidence, though."

"Well, it's not evidence I mean. I'm talking about how they do their job! Hell, they pressed him and pressed him, they squeezed and they bullied, and—well, he confessed. 'I didn't find it in the street,' he says, 'I found it in the place where Mitry and me were painting.' 'How?' 'Like this. Mitry and me were painting all day long, you see, till eight o'clock. We were getting ready to go home, but Mitry, he picks up a brush and he gives me a flip of paint across the puss, and then he takes off with me after him. So I'm running after him and yelling at the top of my voice. Where the stairs come out at the gates I bump right into the janitor and some other gentlemen, and how many other gentlemen there were with him I don't remember. The janitor, he was swearing at me because of this, and the other janitor was swearing too, and the janitor's wife, she comes out and she swears at us too, and some gentleman, he comes into the gateway with some lady and he swears at us too. On account of Mitka and me are lying sprawled across the way. So I grabbed Mitka by the hair and I knocked him down and I was giving it to him, when Mitka, he came out from under me and grabbed my hair and started giving it to me. We weren't really mad, though. It was all in fun. Then Mitka, he shakes loose and starts running down the street, me after him. Only I couldn't catch him and there was some cleaning up to do, so I go back to the apartment alone. I start cleaning up and I'm waiting for Mitry in case he comes. Well, right near the doorway, by the corner wall, I step on this here little box. I look. It's lying there wrapped in paper. I take off the paper and I see these teensy little hooks. I unfasten these little hooks . . . and in this here little box are the earrings. . . .' "

"Near the doorway? Lying near the doorway? Near the doorway?" cried Raskolnikov suddenly, casting a troubled, frightened glance at Razumikhin. Leaning on his arm, he slowly raised himself up on the couch.

"Yes. And so? What's the matter with you? Why are you so upset?" Razumikhin, too, rose from his seat.

"It's nothing," Raskolnikov replied, scarcely aloud, dropping to his pillow again, and again shifting over to face the wall. They all relapsed into silence for a while.

"Dozed off—he must have been half asleep," Razumikhin said at last, looking questioningly at Zosimov, who shook his head slightly, in the negative.

"Well, go on," said Zosimov. "What next?"

"What next? Well, no sooner did he see the earrings than he forgot about the apartment and Mitka. He grabbed his hat and ran to Dushkin and, as is known, received a ruble from him and told him that lie about finding the box in the street and started drinking right off. Still, as far as the murder is concerned, he keeps insisting as he did before: 'I don't know anything, I didn't hear anything till the day before yesterday.' 'And why didn't you show up before now?' 'I was scared stiff.' 'And why did you want to hang yourself?' 'I'd been thinking.' 'Thinking about what?' 'About how I'd be judged.' Well, there's the whole story for you. Now, what do you think they've deduced from all that?"

"What do you expect me to think? There's a clue, such as it is. A fact. You wouldn't suggest letting that painter of yours go?"

"Why, they've gone straight off and accused him of murder, though! They don't even have any doubts. . . ."

"Come on, now. You're piling it on a bit thick, aren't you? You're all excited. Well, what about the earrings? You will have to admit that if those earrings managed to find their way from the old woman's strongbox into Nikolay's hands, and on that very day and hour, they must have gotten there *somehow?* In a case like this, even that signifies something."

"So you want to know how he got hold of them!" Razumikhin cried out. "And how can you, a doctor, whose duty it is to study man, you who have more opportunity than anyone else to study human nature, how can *you* fail to see that for Nikolay all this is perfectly in character? How can you fail to see at first glance that everything to which he testified during the examination really is the most sacred truth, so help him God? The earrings got into his hands exactly the way he said they did. He stepped on the box, then picked it up!"

"The most sacred truth! But you have to admit yourself, he lied the first time."

"Listen to me. Listen carefully. The janitor and Koch and Pestriakov and the other janitor and the first janitor's wife and a woman who happened to be sitting in the janitor's cubicle at the time and Court Councillor Kriukov who had just gotten out of a cab and was coming through the gateway with a lady on his arm . . . all these—eight to ten witnesses, mind you—testify unanimously that Nikolay had Dmitry down on the ground and was pummeling him and Dmitry was pulling Nikolay's hair and pummeling him back. They were stretched across the road, blocking the entry. People were swearing at them on all sides, but they, 'like little children'—the literal expression of the witnesses—were pummeling each other, screeching and laughing, egging each other on with laughter, making ridiculous faces at each other. Then they get up and one chases after the other and, like children, they run out into the street. Have you noted all this? Now, note carefully. At this time the bodies upstairs are still warm. Still warm, you hear. That's the way they were found! If the two had killed them, or just Nikolay alone had done it, and gone through the strongbox, or even if he'd just taken part in the robbery, then allow me to put before you just one simple question. How does that childish little brawl at the gate—the squeals, the laughter—really jibe with axes, with blood, with malevolent cunning and planned robbery? Having committed a murder five or ten minutes ago, they go running out like that. The bodies are still warm, and they leave them with the door wide open, knowing that people will be coming along right away, they throw away their loot and go scampering down the road laughing, like little children, drawing all kinds of public attention to themselves—and, mind you, to this we have ten unanimous witnesses!"

"It certainly *does* seem strange. Of course, it's impossible, but—"

"No, my friend, but me no buts. The earrings Nikolay got hold of that very day and hour may be an important piece of circumstantial evidence against him, but they are directly accounted for by his testimony, and therefore they are *dubious* evidence, and one must take into account facts that point to his innocence, too, all the more since these facts are *undeniable*. Yet can you seriously imagine, given the nature of our jurisprudence, that a fact can or will be accepted that rests on a conception of sheer psychological impossibility, that considers a state of mind to be an undeniable fact, and one which sends tumbling all other material and accusatory facts, whatever they might be? No, they will not accept it, for no reason will they accept it, because they found this little box, and the man wanted to do himself in, 'and wouldn't have, if he hadn't felt himself to be guilty!' That's the main problem, that's why I get hot under the collar, see!"

"Well, I can certainly see that you're hot under the collar. Wait a minute. I forgot to ask you if it was demonstrated that the box with earrings really came from the old woman's chest?"

"That's been demonstrated," Razumikhin replied, unwillingly it seemed, frowning. "Koch recognized the item and indicated the man who pawned it, and he in turn testified the thing really was his."

"That's bad. One more thing. Did anybody see Nikolay at the time Koch and Pestriakov were going upstairs the first time, any evidence about that?"

"It's true nobody saw them," Razumikhin indignantly replied, "and that's bad. Koch and Pestriakov didn't notice them as they were going upstairs, though I don't suppose their testimony would actually be worth much now. They say they saw the apartment open and guessed somebody must be working there, but they paid no attention and don't really remember whether the workers were there at that moment or not."

"Hmm. So it turns out their only alibi is that they were pummeling each other and laughing. Let's admit that's powerful evidence, still . . . Allow me. How do you yourself account for this datum entirely? How do you account for his finding the earrings if he really found them the way he says he did?"

"How do I account for it? Why, what is there to account for? It's clear! At least the direction along which to proceed is clearly indicated, and actually it's the little box that indicated it. The real murderer dropped those earrings. He was upstairs while Koch and Pestriakov were knocking. He was locked in. Koch was an ass and went downstairs. This is when the murderer scurried out, and he ran down the stairs too, because there was no other way for him to get out. He managed to hide himself in the empty apartment as Koch, Pestriakov, and the janitor went by. That was just at the time that Dmitry and Nikolay had run out of it, and he stood there behind the door while the janitor and the others walked by and passed on upstairs. He waited until their footsteps died down, and then very quietly he went downstairs. That was just the moment when Dmitry and Nikolay were running out into the street. Everybody had left. There was nobody by the gateway. Maybe he was even seen, but he was not noticed. Quite a few people go in and out. That little box he dropped out of his pocket while he was standing behind the door. He did not notice he had dropped it because that's not what he was thinking about. The box shows clearly that he was actually standing there. That's all there is to it!"

"Ingenious! No, my friend, it certainly is ingenious. It's a bit too ingenious."

"Why, what do you mean? What do you mean?"

"Everything fits together just a little too well. It's too pat. It's exactly as though it were on the stage."

"Oh, come o-o-on!" cried Razumikhin, but at that moment the door opened and a new person came in, a man none of them had ever seen before.

5

It was a gentleman no longer young; stiff, portly, with a wary, querulous face. He began by pausing in the doorway and taking the room in with an unconcealed expression of offended astonishment, as if asking: "What kind of a place *is* this, anyway?" Affecting an air of pained surprise, almost even of injury, he scanned Raskolnikov's low, narrow "ship's cabin." Maintaining the same pose of astonishment, he fixed his gaze on Raskolnikov himself, lying on his dirty miserable couch, undressed, disheveled, unwashed, and staring back fixedly at him. Then, with the same deliberateness, he began scrutinizing the ragged, unshaved, unkempt figure of Razumikhin, who for his part looked him straight in the eyes, boldly and inquiringly, without stirring from the spot. This tense and silent scene lasted a minute or so. Finally, a slight shifting about of props took place, as might have been expected. By this time it must have been abundantly clear to the gentleman who had come in that in this "ship's cabin" his exaggeratedly stern bearing would get him nowhere, and he softened a little, and politely, if not without some severity, addressed Zosimov, emphasizing every syllable: "Mr. Rodion Romanych Raskolnikov, student or former student?"

Zosimov stirred slowly and might have answered, but Razumikhin, who had not been spoken to at all, anticipated him: "That's him lying on the couch. What do you want?"

That familiar "What do you want?" seemed to deflate the stiff gentleman. He was even about to turn to Razumikhin but managed to restrain himself in time, and all the more quickly turned to Zosimov again.

"That's Raskolnikov," Zosimov murmured, nodding at the sick man. He yawned, and as he yawned he opened his mouth unusually wide and kept it that way an unusually long time. Then he reached slowly into his jacket pocket and pulled out an enormous, bulging, muted gold watch. He opened it, looked at it, and slowly and lazily put it back in his pocket again.

All this while, Raskolnikov himself was lying on his back, gazing steadily, though with no sign that he was thinking anything, at the man who had come in. His face, which he had only just turned away from the fascinating flower on the wallpaper, was extremely pale and expressed unusual suffering, as though he had undergone a terrible operation or had just been released from the rack. Little by little, however, the gentleman who had come in began more and more to arouse his interest, then perplexity, then distrust, then, apparently, fear. When Zosimov had pointed him out, saying "That's Raskolnikov," he had quickly lifted himself up, almost jumping. He sat up on his bed, and in an almost defiant, but weak and unsteady voice he said: "Yes. I'm Raskolnikov. What do you want?"

The visitor looked at him carefully and said in a manner meant to impose: "Peter Petrovich Luzhin. I have every reason to hope that my name is not altogether unknown to you."

But Raskolnikov had been expecting something quite different, and looked at him stupidly and wonderingly and did not answer, as though he really were hearing Peter Petrovich's name for the first time.

"What? Is it possible that you have as yet received no news?" Peter Petrovich asked, a bit ruffled.

Raskolnikov in reply dropped slowly back on his pillow, put his hands behind his head, and began to stare at the ceiling. A look of dismay came into Luzhin's face. Zosimov and Razumikhin kept looking at him with great curiosity. At last he became visibly embarrassed.

"I calculated and assumed," he murmured, "that a letter sent more than ten days ago, perhaps even two weeks ago—"

"Listen," Razumikhin suddenly broke in, "there's no point standing in the doorway. If you've got something to explain, sit down. You and Nastasia standing there together make a tight squeeze. Step aside, Nastasia dear, and let him by. Come on in. Here's a chair. Have a seat. Squeeze on in!"

He moved his own chair back from the table, made a little space between the table and his knees, and in that awkward position waited a bit until the visitor could "squeeze on in." The moment was so chosen that the visitor could not refuse, and stumbling awkwardly, he squeezed through the narrow space. When he reached the chair he sat down, casting a nervous glance at Razumikhin.

"No need to be embarrassed," Razumikhin said. "This is the fifth day Rodia's been sick. He was delirious for three days. Now he's himself again. He even ate. With appetite. Sitting there is his doctor, who's just had a look at him. And I'm a friend of Rodia's, a former student too, and right now I'm nursing him along. So don't mind us. Don't let us inhibit you. Go ahead with whatever you've got."

"I thank you. But wouldn't I disturb the patient with my presence and my conversation?" Peter Petrovich addressed Zosimov.

"No-o-o," Zosimov murmured, "might even divert him." And again he yawned.

"Oh, he's been himself for quite a while now. Since morning!" Razumikhin went on. His familiarity had the ring of such genuine good nature that Peter Petrovich thought better of it and began to feel encouraged; perhaps in part because this impudent tramp had had sense enough to introduce himself as a former student.

"Your mother—" Luzhin began.

"Hmmm!" Razumikhin exclaimed loudly. Luzhin looked at him inquiringly.

"Nothing. I was just— Go on. . . ."

Luzhin shrugged.

"Your mother began a letter to you while I was still in her presence. When I arrived here I deliberately let several days pass without coming to see you so that I could be certain you would be informed about everything. But now, to my surprise—"

"I know, I know!" Raskolnikov said suddenly with an expression of most impatient annoyance. "So that's who you are? The bridegroom? Well, I know . . . and plenty!"

Peter Petrovich took offense, but remained silent. He made a hasty effort to figure out what it all meant. The silence went on for a minute or so.

Meanwhile Raskolnikov, who had turned a little in his direction in answering, began to scrutinize him intently, as though he had not had time to scrutinize him fully before, or as if something new about the man had just struck him. He even raised himself from his pillow on purpose to do so. There was, actually, something striking about Luzhin's appearance, which seemed to justify the title of "bridegroom" so unceremoniously bestowed on him. First, it was apparent and even all too obvious that Peter Petrovich had been in a fret to use his few days in the metropolis to get himself outfitted and adorned in anticipation of his bride. This, of course, was perfectly innocent and proper. Perhaps even his oversmug awareness of the pleasant improvement in his appearance could be forgiven in view of the occasion, for Peter Petrovich was on the verge of becoming a bridegroom. All his clothes were fresh from the tailor's and of good quality, though too new, perhaps, and making too apparent their intended purpose. The stylish new top hat also testified to this purpose. Peter Petrovich handled it too gingerly, somehow, and held it too cautiously in his hands. A charming pair of lilac-colored gloves, real Jouvenet, if only because they were not worn but merely carried in the hand for display, testified to the same thing. Light and youthful colors predominated. He wore a fine light tan summer jacket, light summer trousers and a vest to match, a light linen shirt that was brand-new, the lightest possible cambric necktie with pink stripes—and actually it all looked very becoming on him. There was a freshness to his rather handsome face, and even apart from that he seemed younger than his forty-five years. Dark mutton-chop whiskers framed the face pleasantly on both sides, thickening attractively near his gleaming, smooth-shaven chin. Even his hair, slightly streaked with gray, combed and curled at the barber's, did not seem absurd or wrong, as is almost always the case with curled hair, for it inevitably makes a man look like a German getting married. If there was anything actually unpleasant or repulsive about this rather handsome and solid-seeming figure, it came from other causes. Having unceremoniously scrutinized Mr. Luzhin, Raskolnikov smiled venomously, sank back on his pillow, and began staring at the ceiling as before.

Mr. Luzhin took a firm grip on himself, though, and seemed to decide to take no notice of all these oddities for the time being.

"I am very, very sorry to find you in such a condition," he began again, breaking the silence with an effort. "If I had known of your bad health I would have come sooner. Business troubles, though, you know . . . What's more, I have rather an important case coming up in the Senate, part of my law firm's affairs. Many little errands, you can imagine, I won't even mention them. From hour to hour I expect your family. Your mother and sister, that is . . ."

Raskolnikov stirred, and he wanted to say something. His expression seemed a little agitated. Peter Petrovich paused, waited, but since nothing followed, he went on.

"From hour to hour. I've found them an apartment for the first part of their stay—"

"Where?" asked Raskolnikov weakly.

"Not very far from here. Bakaleev's house—"

"That's on Voznesensky," Razumikhin broke in. "They rent out two floors there as furnished rooms. Merchant Iushin owns it. I've been there."

"Yes, furnished rooms—"

"It's a terrible joint. Filth, stench, suspicious activities, too. Been quite some deals pulled off there. Devil knows who lives there! The time I was there, it had to do with some scandal. It's cheap, though."

"Naturally, I was in no position to gather such information, since I am a newcomer here myself," said Peter Petrovich. "Nevertheless, they are two very, very clean little rooms, and since it's to be for such a short time . . . And I've already found our regular, that is, our future apartment." He addressed Raskolnikov. "It is being done over now. Meanwhile, I myself am living in crowded furnished rooms, a few steps from here, at Mrs. Lippewechsel's, in the apartment of a certain young friend of mine, Andrey Semionych Lebeziatnikov. He was the one who told me about Bakaleev's house."

"Lebeziatnikov?" Raskolnikov said slowly, as though he were trying to remember something.

"Yes. Andrey Semionych Lebeziatnikov. Who serves in the ministry. Do you know him?"

"Yes . . . No . . ." answered Raskolnikov.

"Excuse me. From the way in which you asked I thought you did. I was his guardian at one time . . . a very nice young man . . . keeps up with things . . . For my part, I am delighted to meet young people. You learn what is new in the world that way." Peter Petrovich glanced hopefully at all those present.

"In what sense?" asked Razumikhin.

"In the most serious sense, that is to say quintessentially," Peter Petrovich responded quickly, as though delighted at being asked. "You see, it is ten years since I last visited Petersburg. All these new trends in our country, these reforms, these new ideas—I do not mean to say that they have not reached us in the provinces, but in order to see life clearly and see it whole, so to speak, you have to be in Petersburg. Well, sir, what I really mean to say is this, you will observe the more and learn the most by keeping a close eye on our young people. And when I looked around I must admit I was pleased."

"With what, exactly?"

"That is a big question. It seems to me—of course, I could be mistaken—that I find a steadier gaze, a more critical attitude, so to speak, more practicality. . . ."

"That's true," murmured Zosimov.

"You're laying it on thick," Razumikhin joined in. "There's no practicality. That's a tough business, practicality, and it doesn't drop from the skies for free. We've been off it almost two hundred years now. . . . Ideas, if you like—lots of those around"—he turned to Peter Petrovich—"and the wish to do good, yes—though it's a bit childish. And there's even a certain amount of honesty, though, God knows, an awful lot of crooks have wormed their way in one way or another. But there's no practicality in any sense! Practicality needs a pair of shoes."

"I don't agree with you," replied Peter Petrovich with apparent relish. "Of course, there are enthusiasms, and some irregularities, but you have to be indulgent. Youthful enthusiasms testify to a passion for the business at hand and to the irregular environment in which the business at hand is to be found. If little has actually been done—well, there has not been much time. About the means I do not speak. I take the personal view, if you please, that although little has been done, new and useful ideas have been disseminated. Yes, new and useful works have been disseminated, taking the place of those old-fashioned, dreamy, and romantic notions. Our literature acquires a more mature tone. Many harmful prejudices have been eradicated. . . . In a word, we have cut ourselves off irrevocably from the past, and I think that is something in itself. . . ."

"He's learned it by heart! He's weasling his way in," said Raskolnikov suddenly.

"What?" asked Peter Petrovich, who could not believe his ears. He received no answer.

"All this is quite true," Zosimov hastened to put in.

"It is true, isn't it?" Peter Petrovich went on, glancing appreciatively at Zosimov. "You yourself will agree," he continued, addressing Razumikhin, but already with a certain shade of triumph and contempt, and he was tempted to add *young man,* "that there has been an improvement, or, as they say nowadays, progress, in the name of science and economic justice. . . ."

"A platitude!"

"No, sir, not a platitude! In the past I was told, for example, 'Love thy neighbor,' and I used to love him, and what came of it?" Peter Petrovich went on with perhaps unseemly haste. "What came of it was that I tore my coat in half and shared it with my neighbor. And we both remained half naked. As the Russian proverb says: Go after lots of rabbits at once, you won't catch one. Now science says: Love yourself above all, for everything in the world is based on self-interest. If you love yourself above all, you will manage your business properly, and your coat will remain whole. Economic science adds that the more successfully private business is run in society and the more (so to speak) whole coats there are, the firmer are its foundations and the more the commonweal flourishes. Thus, while busy acquiring only and exclusively for myself, I actually, at the same time as it were, acquire for all and help bring about a condition in which my neighbor receives something more than a torn coat. And he receives it not from the private charity of a few but as a result of overall improvement. The idea is a simple one. Unfortunately, it has been too long in reaching us. Its development was hindered by exaltation and day-dreaming. It would seem, now, that little wit is needed to perceive—"

"Sorry, I don't have much wit, either," Razumikhin broke in sharply, "so you better stop. When I started I had something in mind. But all this chattering self-deception, these incessant, uninterrupted platitudes—and all the same, all the same—have made me good and sick these past three years, and by God I blush even when it's *other* people that talk like that in my presence. Of course, you'd like to make yourself look good in our eyes, and I don't blame you for that, I don't presume to judge. I just wanted to find out what kind of a man you were. There are lots of different kinds of operators who've been attaching themselves to the common cause lately. They've twisted everything they've touched to their own interest. So much so, they've decidedly fouled up the whole business. Well, sir, why don't we let it go at that!"

"My dear sir," Mr. Luzhin began with extreme dignity, taking offense, "what you want to say in this unceremonious manner is (isn't it?) that I, too—"

"Oh, forgive me, forgive me. . . . How could I! Well, sir, why don't we let it go at that!" Razumikhin turned abruptly to Zosimov to continue their former conversation.

Apparently Peter Petrovich had enough sense to accept this explanation immediately. He had made up his mind that he would leave in a few minutes in any case.

"I hope," he said to Raskolnikov, "that our acquaintance, which has just begun, will, in view of the circumstances that are known to you, become still closer when you recover. . . . I specially wish your health. . . ."

Raskolnikov did not even turn his head. Peter Petrovich started getting up from his chair.

"One of her customers killed her, no doubt about it!" said Zosimov.

"One of her customers, all right!" confirmed Razumikhin. "Porfiry's not letting anything out, but I know he's questioning her customers. . . ."

"He's questioning her customers?" Raskolnikov asked loudly.

"Yes, what about it?"

"Nothing."

"How is he getting them together?" asked Zosimov.

"Koch knew some. The names of others were written on those tags the things had on them. Others came on their own when they heard. . . ."

"Well, he must have been a clever, experienced bastard! What nerve! What presence of mind!"

"That's exactly what he didn't have!" Razumikhin interrupted. "That's what's throwing you all off the track. I tell you he's clumsy and inexperienced and this was probably his first job! If you picture a plan and some clever bastard, the whole thing seems unlikely. If you picture somebody inexperienced, it turns out mere chance alone got him out of trouble. And chance can do anything, can't it? Excuse me, but he probably didn't even anticipate the obstacles! How does he go about it? He takes ten- and twenty-ruble things and stuffs them in his pocket. He mucks around in the old woman's chest, in her old clothes, and all the time there's this box in the upper drawer of her bureau they found fifteen hundred cash in, not counting the notes. No, he wasn't much good at robbing. All he could do was kill! His first job, I tell you, his first job! He lost his head. And it wasn't by plan he got away but by chance."

"You seem to be speaking of the recent murder of the old widow woman," Peter Petrovich put in, addressing Zosimov. He had his hat and gloves in his hands, but he wanted to say something clever before he left. He was anxious to make a good impression, and his vanity overcame his prudence.

"Yes. You've heard about it?"

"Of course. It happened in the neighborhood."

"You know the details?"

"That I cannot say. Another aspect of the case interests me, though—the problem as a whole, so to speak. I am not referring to the fact that among the lower classes the crime rate has been on the increase these last five years. I do not refer to the cases of burglary and arson that take place everywhere and all the time. What strikes me as most strange is that the crime rate has been increasing in the upper classes, too, in exactly the same way, in a parallel manner, so to speak. In one place a former student is reported to have robbed the mail on the highway; in another, highly placed society people have been making counterfeit money. In one place, in Moscow, they caught a whole gang forging state lottery tickets, and among the main culprits there was a university lecturer in world history. In another place, abroad, a legation secretary of ours was killed for some mysterious reason having to do with money. . . . And now we have this old pawnbroker woman who has been killed by someone from the upper ranks of society—for, you know, peasants do not pawn gold objects—how is one to explain this deterioration of moral standards in the civilized part of our society?"

"There have been many economic changes," said Zosimov.

"How is one to explain it?" Razumikhin latched on. "Why, it might really be explained by our inveterate impracticality."

"And what do you mean by that, sir?"

"Well, what did that Moscow University lecturer of yours answer when he was asked why he forged lottery tickets? 'Everybody's getting rich one way or another; so I wanted to get rich quick too.' I don't remember the exact words, but the idea was that he wanted something for nothing, and quick, without work! We're used to living without having to work for it, holding on to somebody else's leading strings, having our food premasticated for us. Well, the great hour struck. Serf emancipation. Then everybody showed himself in his true colors. . . ."

"Morality, though? And the regulations, so to speak—"

"What are you worried about?" Raskolnikov unexpectedly broke in. "All this fits in with your theory!"

"What do you mean it fits in with my theory?"

"If you took what you were preaching a little while ago to its logical conclusion, it would turn out people can be done away with. . . ."

"I beg your pardon!" exclaimed Luzhin.

"No, that surely is not so," Zosimov chimed in.

Raskolnikov lay there, face pale, breathing hard, upper lip quivering.

"There's a limit to everything," Luzhin went on haughtily. "An economic idea is not quite an invitation to murder, and if one merely imagines—"

"And is it true," Raskolnikov suddenly interrupted him again, his voice quivering with rage and a certain delight in insulting him, "is it true that you told your bride . . . at the very time you received her consent, how glad you were that she was a beggar . . . because it's more profitable saving a wife from beggary—you can lord it over her and remind her she's in your debt?"

"My dear sir!" Luzhin cried out angrily and irritably, all flushed and confused, "my dear sir . . . distorting an idea like that! Excuse me, but I am obliged to inform you that the rumors that have reached you, or rather, it would be better to say, the rumors that have been carried to you, have not even the shadow of a solid foundation, and I . . . I suspect who . . . in a word . . . this shaft . . . in a word, your mother . . . She seemed to me . . . I mean, for all her admirable qualities, I thought I noticed a hint of something overenthusiastic, something romantic, you might say, in her thinking. . . . But I was a long way from imagining that she was capable of conceiving or presenting the matter in such a fantastically distorted way. . . . And finally . . . finally—"

"Do you know what?" said Raskolnikov, lifting himself on his pillow and looking at him steadily with a piercing, glittering look. "Do you know what?"

"What, sir?" Luzhin paused, and with an offended and provocative air he waited. For several seconds there was a silence.

"This. If you are so bold as to mention just one word about my mother again. I'll kick you headfirst down the stairs!"

"What's wrong with you!" cried Razumikhin.

"Well! So that's how it is!" Luzhin turned pale and bit his lip. "Listen to me, sir," he began deliberately, restraining himself with all his might, but breathing hard nevertheless. "I guessed your hostility from the very first, but I remained here on purpose in order to find out more. I could forgive a man a good deal who might be a relative and who was sick, but now, sir, you will never—"

"I am not sick!" Raskolnikov cried out.

"So much the worse."

"Go to hell!"

Without even finishing his speech, Luzhin was about to leave of his own accord, sliding through once again between the table and the chair. This time Razumikhin got up to let him by. Glancing at no one, without even so much as a nod to Zosimov, who had some time ago signaled him to leave the sick man in peace, Luzhin left. As he bent over to pass through the doorway, he cautiously lifted his hat to the level of his shoulders. Even the curve of his back seemed to express the notion that he was bearing away with him the burden of a terrible insult.

"How could you, how could you behave like that?" said the perplexed Razumikhin, shaking his head.

"Leave me alone, leave me alone, all of you!" Raskolnikov cried out, beside himself. "Why don't you leave me alone once and for all, you bloody tormentors! I'm not afraid of you! I'm not afraid of anybody now—not anybody! Get away from me! I want to be alone, alone, alone!"

Zosimov nodded to Razumikhin and said: "Let's go."

"But we can't just leave him like that, can we?"

"Let's go!" Zosimov repeated insistently, and went out. Razumikhin pondered, and ran to overtake him.

"If we don't do as he says, it could be worse," Zosimov said. He was already on the stairs. "He mustn't be irritated."

"What's *wrong* with him?"

"If only we could give him a shock of the right kind, that would do it! At first he was feeling all right. . . . You know, he's got something on his mind! Some fixed idea, some obsession weighing on him . . . Yes, I'm afraid so. Certainly!"

"And this Peter Petrovich gentleman! From what they said, seems clear he's about to marry Rodia's sister, and Rodia got some letter about this just before he took sick."

"Yes. Devil knows why he had to show up when he did. May have spoiled the whole business. He's indifferent to everything—didn't you notice?—he responds to nothing. Except one thing. And this one thing puts him beside himself. And that's the murder."

"Yes, yes!" Razumikhin agreed, "I was struck by that. He's interested, frightened. That day he took sick in the police station, they frightened him. He fainted."

"You tell me more about it tonight, and then I'll tell you something. He interests me very much! In half an hour I'll come back and have a look at him. . . . There's no danger of pneumonia, though."

"I'm grateful to you! I'll be at Pashenka's, meanwhile, and I'll keep a watch on him through Nastasia."

Left alone, Raskolnikov looked at Nastasia with impatience and anguish, but she put off leaving.

"Would you drink some tea now?" she asked.

"Later! I want to sleep! Leave me. . . ."

He turned convulsively to the wall. Nastasia left.

6

As soon as she left, however, he rose, put the door on the latch, undid the bundle of clothes Razumikhin had shown him earlier and tied up again, and began to dress. Strange business: suddenly he seemed quite calm. He was neither in the half-conscious delirium that had possessed him at first nor in the panic terror that came later. It was the first moment of some strange, sudden calm. He moved with a clear-cut precision and evidently with a firm purpose. "This very day," he muttered to himself, "this very day!" He realized he was still weak, but his most powerful inward effort had brought him to a point of calm, the point of a fixed idea, and given him strength and self-confidence. He hoped he would not collapse in the street. Dressed entirely in his new clothes, he looked at the money lying on the table, pondered for a moment, then put it in his pocket. Twenty-five rubles. He took the copper coins too, change from the ten rubles Razumikhin had spent on his clothes. Then he quietly unlatched the door, left the room, and went down the stairs. He looked at the wide-open kitchen. Nastasia was standing with her back toward him, bent over the landlady's samovar, blowing on the coals. She heard nothing. Who would suspect that he'd be going out, after all? A minute later he was in the street.

It was eight o'clock. The sun was setting. The former closeness remained. Yet he breathed in eagerly this reeking, dusty, corrupt city air. His head started spinning a little. A kind of wild energy suddenly flashed out from his inflamed eyes and flickered in his wasted yellowish-white face. He did not know where he was going and did not think about it. This much he knew: he had to put an end to all *that,* today, right away, once and for all, otherwise he could not return home, because *he did not want to live like that.* Put an end

to it—but how? By what means put an end to it? About
this he had no conception. He did not even want to think
of it. He drove away thought. Painfully, thought tracked
him down. He only felt, he only knew, one way or another,
everything had to be changed. "Come what may," he repeated, with a desperate fixed self-confidence and determination.

Following the usual direction of the walks he took, he
came by old habit to the Haymarket. On the sidewalk in
front of a small shop just before the Haymarket stood a
young, dark-haired organ-grinder, grinding away at a very
sentimental love song. He accompanied a girl of about fifteen, who stood a little ahead of him on the sidewalk. She
was dressed like a young lady in a crinoline, cloak, gloves,
and a straw hat with a bright red feather, but all very old
and shabby. She sang in a jingling street voice which was
nevertheless pleasant and quite strong, evidently expecting
some coins from the store. Raskolnikov stood beside two or
three of her audience, listened, took out a five-kopeck piece,
and put it in the girl's hand. She suddenly broke off her
song on a sentimental high note, as though she had cut it
off with a knife, called out sharply to the organ-grinder,
"Stop!" and both of them pushed on to the next store.

"Do you like street singing?" Raskolnikov suddenly asked
one of the passersby, a man no longer young, who had been
standing beside him listening to the organ-grinder and who
looked like a *flâneur*. The latter looked at him a bit weirdly
and with some astonishment. "*I* do," Raskolnikov went on,
but didn't at all look as though he were talking about street
singing. "I like it when they sing beside the street organ on
a cold dark damp autumn evening. Yes, it has to be a damp
evening. When all the passersby have pale green sickly faces;
or, still better, when wet snow is falling, straight down, no
wind—you know?—and the gas lamps shining through
it . . ."

"I don't know, sir. Excuse me," the gentleman muttered,
frightened by Raskolnikov's strange appearance as well as
by the question. He crossed over to the other side of the
street.

Raskolnikov walked straight ahead and came to the corner of the Haymarket where the vendor and his wife had
traded—the ones who had once been engaged in conversation with Lizaveta. But they were not there now. He recognized the place, stopped, looked around, and turned to a

young fellow in a red shirt who was lounging around at the entrance to a flour merchant's shop.

"Isn't there a guy keeps a stall here on the corner, with his old woman, ah?"

"We got all kinds here," the fellow answered, looking Raskolnikov condescendingly up and down.

"What's his name?"

"Whatever they baptized him, that's his name."

"Aren't you a Zaraisky man? What province?"

"It's not a province, Your Excellency, it's a district, and it isn't me who left, but my brother. I stayed home. So I wouldn't know. . . . So I hope you'll forgive me, Your Excellency."

"Is that an eating place upstairs?"

"It's a tavern. They've got a pool table. You could find a princess or two. . . . It's quite a joint!"

Raskolnikov walked across the square. There on the corner stood a dense crowd of people. They were peasants. He pushed his way in, glancing at the faces. He was drawn somehow to engage them all in conversation. The peasants, however, paid no attention to him. They were making a hubbub about something among themselves, gathering in small groups. He stood there, pondered, then walked to the right on the sidewalk, going toward Voznesensky Prospect. Crossing the square, he found himself on a side street.

He had often passed through that narrow side street before. Making a sharp bend it led from the square to the Sadovaia. Recently, when he'd begun to feel nauseous, he had felt drawn to lounging around these places, "so he could feel even more nauseous." Now he walked down the street with nothing on his mind. A huge building loomed there. It consisted of saloons and other eating and drinking establishments. From these, women were continually emerging, dressed as though "just visiting a neighbor," bareheaded and coatless. In two or three places they gathered in groups on the sidewalk, mostly near the approaches to the basement, where, down two steps, you could enter some quite festive establishments. At that moment a din and hubbub arose from one of these, and the whole street heard it; a guitar strummed, songs rang out, and it was very gay. A large group of women gathered at the entrance. Others sat on the steps, still others on the sidewalk. Others still stood around and talked. A drunken soldier, cigarette dangling from his mouth, lounged in the road nearby and swore loudly. He seemed to want to go in somewhere but couldn't remember where. A tramp was swearing at another tramp, and somebody was sprawled dead-drunk across the sidewalk. Raskolnikov paused near a large group of women talking in husky voices. They were all bareheaded, and wore cotton dresses and goatskin shoes. Some were around forty, but there were also some around seventeen. To be beaten with fists was part of their trade; almost everyone had a black eye.

For some reason the singing and the din and hubbub downstairs fascinated him. He could hear somebody frantically dancing down there, beating time with his heels to shrieks and laughter and the thin falsetto of a gay song and a guitar. Intent, pensive, gloomy, he listened, stooping at the entrance and peering curiously from the sidewalk into the hall.

> "Soldier sweet of mine,
>   Don't you beat me for nothing!"

pulsed the singer's thin voice. Raskolnikov strained to puzzle out the words, as if everything depended on it.

"Why not go in?" he thought. "They're laughing! It's from drink. But why not get drunk?"

"Why not go in, dear gentleman?" one of the women asked in a quite resonant and not yet coarsened voice. Alone of the whole group she was both young and not bad-looking.

"Why, she's pretty!" he replied, straightening up and looking at her.

She smiled. The compliment pleased her very much.

"You're not bad-looking yourself," she said.

"Bit skinny, though," another broke in, in a bass voice. "Just out of the hospital, or what?"

"Seems they're generals' daughters, but they all got snub noses," a tipsy peasant who had just joined the group suddenly interjected. He wore a peasant's cloth coat, all unbuttoned, and there was a sly smirk on his coarse face. "Well, it's damn good fun!"

"Go on in, since you're here!"

"I'm going, sweet stuff!" And headlong down he went. Raskolnikov walked on.

"Listen, dear gentleman!" the girl called out behind him.

"What?"

She was embarrassed.

"Dear gentleman, I'd always be glad to spend some hours

with you, but just now, somehow, you make me feel shy. Wouldn't you give me six kopecks, my handsome cavalier, for a little drink?"

Raskolnikov gave her whatever he could fish out of his pocket. Three five-kopeck coins.

"Ah, what a kind, good gentleman!"

"What's your name?"

"Just ask for Duclida."

"Well, how do you like that!" one of the group suddenly remarked, shaking her head at Duclida. "I don't know what it takes to beg like that! Why, I'd drop through the sidewalk for shame. . . ."

Raskolnikov gazed curiously at the speaker. She was pock-marked, about thirty, with black and blue marks on her face and a swollen upper lip. She was quiet and earnest as she spoke.

"Where is it," thought Raskolnikov as he walked on, "where is it I was reading somebody condemned to death said or thought an hour before his death that if he had to live somewhere on a crag, on a cliff, on a narrow ledge where his two feet could hardly stand, and all around him there'd be the abyss, the ocean, everlasting darkness, everlasting solitude, and an everlasting storm, and he had to remain like that—standing on a square yard of space—all his life, a thousand years, an eternity, it would still be better to live like that than die at the moment. To live and to live and to live and to live! No matter how you live, if only to live! How true that is! God, how true! What a scoundrel man is! And he's a scoundrel who calls him a scoundrel for that," he added a minute later.

He came out on another street. "Bah! The Crystal Palace! Razumikhin was talking about the Crystal Palace. What the hell was I after, though? Oh, yes—to read up! Zosimov said he read it in the papers. . . ."

He entered a roomy and even rather neat-looking tavern, which seemed fairly empty. "Any newspapers?" he asked. Two or three customers were drinking tea, and a group of about four sat in one of the far rooms sipping champagne. Raskolnikov thought he saw Zamiotov among them, but from a distance it was impossible to make him out clearly.

"And what of it!" he thought.

"Would you like some vodka, sir?" the waiter asked.

"Let me have some tea. And bring me the papers. The old ones, too—for five days back. I'll leave you a tip."

"Yes, sir. Here are today's, sir. And would you like to order some vodka, sir?"

The old newspapers and the tea appeared. Raskolnikov settled down in his chair and began to search: "Izler Mineral Waters . . . Izler . . . Aztecs . . . Aztecs . . . Izler . . . Bartolo . . . Massimo . . . Aztecs . . . Izler . . . oh, damn! Ah, here are the local items. Woman falls down stairs, spontaneous combustion of a drunken shopkeeper, fire at the Sands, fire in Peterburg suburb, another fire in Peterburg suburb, another fire in Peterburg suburb, Izler Mineral Waters, Izler, Izler, Izler, Izler, Massimo . . . Ah, here it is . . ."

At last he found what he was looking for and started reading. The lines leaped at his eyes, but he read the whole story and began eagerly to search the following numbers for the latest additions. As he turned the pages, his hands trembled with a convulsive impatience. Somebody suddenly sat down beside him at his table. He looked, and it was Zamiotov—the very same Zamiotov, looking the same as he had in the police station, with his rings, his watch chain, his black curly pomaded hair parted down the middle, his fancy vest, his somewhat threadbare coat and his not quite clean shirt. He was in a good mood; at least he smiled quite gaily and good-naturedly. His dark face was a little flushed from the champagne he had been drinking.

"Well! You here?" he began, puzzled, yet in a tone that implied they had known each other through all eternity. "And it was only yesterday Razumikhin was telling me you weren't conscious yet. Strange! I was even at your place. . . ."

Raskolnikov had known he would approach him. He put the newspapers away and turned to Zamiotov with a mocking smile. In that smile, a certain new and irritable impatience could be seen.

"I know you were," he replied. "I heard about it. You were looking for my sock. . . . Do you know, Razumikhin's really very fond of you? He says you and he went to Luisa Ivanovna's together. That's the lady you were trying to help that day—remember? You kept winking at Lieutenant Gunpowder, but he didn't get it at all. It was a clear case, though, and he must have been pretty dense, ah?"

"He's a rough man!"

"Gunpowder?"

"No. Your friend Razumikhin."

"You really lead a nice life, Mr. Zamiotov. You get in

free to the most entertaining places! Who's been funneling champagne into you?"

"Why, we were just . . . having a drink . . . What do you mean, *funneling*?"

"An honorarium! You make good use of it!" Raskolnikov laughed. "It's nothing, old boy, nothing!" He clapped Zamiotov on the shoulder. "I'm not really mad at you, you know, 'It's all in fun,' as that house painter of yours was saying about his belting Dmitry—you know, in that case of the old woman."

"How do you know that?"

"Maybe I know more about it than you people do."

"You certainly are a queer duck. . . . I think you're still sick. You shouldn't go out. , . . ."

"I seem queer to you, do I?"

"Yes. What's all this? Are you reading the papers?"

"I'm reading the papers."

"There's a lot about the fires."

"I wasn't reading about the fires." Once again a mocking smile twisted his mouth. "No, I wasn't reading about the fires." He winked at Zamiotov. "Come on, now, old boy, you really would like to know an awful lot what I *was* reading about, wouldn't you?"

"Not at all. I just asked. Can't I ask? Why are you so—"

"Listen, you're an educated man, aren't you? Literary, ah?"

"I did finish high school," said Zamiotov with a certain dignity.

"So you finished high school! Ah, what a fine cock robin! Rings on your finger, fancy part in your hair—why, you're a millionaire! What a nice guy you are!" And Raskolnikov, right in Zamiotov's face, broke into nervous laughter. The latter drew back. He was more astonished than offended.

"You certainly·are a queer duck!" Zamiotov repeated quite earnestly. "I can't help thinking you're still delirious."

"I? Delirious? Nonsense, cock robin! You think I'm a queer duck? I strike you as strange, ah? Strange?"

"Strange."

"You'd like to know what I was reading, wouldn't you? What was I looking for? Look, see how many papers I was going through. Suspicious, ah?"

"Well? Tell me."

"You prick up your ears?"

"What do you mean, I prick up my ears?"

"I'll tell you later. Now, my dear fellow, I declare to you—No, better, 'I acknowledge.' No, that's not quite right, either. 'I hereby make this statement and you take it down'—that's it! I hereby make this statement that I was reading, I was interested in, I was searching out, I was looking for—" He squinted his eyes and paused. "I was looking for—and that is why I came here—news about the murder of the old pawnbroker woman," he uttered at last, almost in a whisper, bringing his face very close to Zamiotov's face. Zamiotov looked at him steadily without flinching and without turning his face away. What afterward struck Zamiotov as the strangest part was that their silence lasted for a whole minute and for a whole minute they were staring at each other like that.

"Well, so what if you were reading about it?" he cried out suddenly in perplexity and impatience. "What do I care! So what?"

"It's the same old woman," Raskolnikov said in the same whisper, without flinching at Zamiotov's exclamation, "the same one, remember. You were starting to talk about her in the police station the time I fainted. Do you understand now?"

Zamiotov was almost in a panic. "What are you talking about? What do you mean, 'Do you understand?' "

Instantly Raskolnikov's blank and solemn expression changed, and he suddenly broke out in that nervous laugh of his, as though he could not restrain himself. And in a single flash he remembered, with an extraordinary vividness of sensation, that moment not so long ago when he was standing behind the door with the ax, the latch jumping about, and on the other side of the door they were swearing and pounding, and suddenly he had wanted to shout at them, stick out his tongue, taunt, mock, and laugh and laugh and laugh!

"Either you're mad, or . . ." said Zamiotov, and he paused, as though suddenly struck by a thought that flashed into his mind.

"Or? Or what? Well? Go on. Say it!"

"Nothing!" Zamiotov replied angrily. "It's all nonsense!"

Both fell silent. After his laughing fit, Raskolnikov suddenly became pensive and sad. Putting his elbows on the table, he propped his head on his hand. It seemed as though he had forgotten about Zamiotov completely. The silence continued a fairly long time.

"Why don't you drink your tea?" Zamiotov said. "It's getting cold."

"Ah? What? Tea? All right . . ." Raskolnikov took a gulp from his glass, stuffed a piece of bread into his mouth, and seemed, as he was looking at Zamiotov, suddenly to come to his senses and pull himself together. His face assumed its former mocking expression. He went on drinking his tea.

"Been a slew of swindles lately," Zamiotov said. "I was reading in the *Moscow News* not long ago that they caught a whole gang of counterfeiters in Moscow. Whole organization. They were forging big bills."

"That was quite awhile ago. Must have been a month ago I read about that," Raskolnikov calmly replied. "So you think they were swindlers, do you?" he added, smiling.

"Do you think they weren't swindlers?"

"Them? Why, they were children. Simple *blancs-becs*. How could you call them swindlers! There were fifty of them! Is that possible? You'd think even three would be too many unless each could trust the other two more than himself! If one talks when he's drunk, the whole business collapses. *Blancs-becs,* I tell you! They took on untrustworthy people and sent them to the bank to change the bills, as though it were the kind of job you trust to the first man who comes along. But suppose it worked—even with *blancs-becs*—and each one made a million. Then what? What about the rest of their lives? They have to depend on each other the rest of their lives! They'd be better off dead! They didn't even know how to change the bills, though. One of them goes into a bank to change the bill. They give him five thousand and his hands are shaking. He counts four, but he takes the fifth without counting. On trust. So he could shove it in his pocket and get out as quick as possible. Well, that was suspicious. And the whole thing went bust because of one fool! It seems incredible."

"That his hands were shaking?" Zamiotov asked. "No. I think it's credible. I'm quite convinced that it's credible. There are times you just can't stand it."

"Something like that?"

"You think you could stand it? I am sure I could not! A terrible risk like that just for a few hundred rubles! Taking a false bill—and where?—to a bank, where they're professionals at spotting things like that! I'd have gotten confused. Wouldn't you?"

Again Raskolnikov felt a terrible impulse to stick out his tongue. Shivers kept running up his back.

"I wouldn't have done it that way," he began from a great distance. "Here's how I'd get the bill changed. I'd count the first thousand four times, backwards and forwards. I'd look at each bill separately. Then I'd take another thousand. I'd start counting it, and count to about the middle. Then I'd pull out some fifty-ruble note and hold it up to the light. Then I'd turn it over and hold it up to the light again. Maybe it's counterfeit? 'I'm afraid,' I'd say. 'One of my relatives lost twenty-five rubles the other day just because she wasn't careful.' And then I'd tell the whole story. As I was starting to count the third thousand I'd say, 'Excuse me, but I think I miscounted,' and I'd put down the third and start counting the second thousand all over again. And so on for all five. And when I was done, I'd take a bill from the fifth and one from the second, and I'd hold them up to the light and I'd express some doubt again. 'Change them, please.' And by the time I was through the clerk would be ready to do just about anything to get rid of me! And when I was finished at last, I'd go and open the door—but no, excuse me, back I'd go again and I'd ask him something, how to get somewhere, or something like that. That's how I'd do it!"

"You certainly talk terrible things!" Zamiotov said, laughing. "It's all just talk, though. If it came to doing, you'd probably slip. When it comes to crime, I think not only you and I, but even a hardened and desperate man, can't always vouch for himself. Why go far afield? Here's an example. In our district an old woman was killed. Some desperado, it would seem. He took all his risks in broad daylight and was saved only by a miracle. Yet his hands were shaking. He didn't manage to steal. He couldn't go through with it. It's clear from the case."

Raskolnikov looked offended.

"Clear! Why don't you catch him, then? Go on, now, why don't you!" he cried out, maliciously provoking Zamiotov.

"Don't worry. He'll be caught."

"Who's going to catch him? You? You think you'll catch him? Why, you're barking up all the wrong trees! The main thing you seem to be on the lookout for is somebody spending money. Somebody who didn't have any money, and who started spending all of a sudden. That must be the man, eh? Why, even a kid could figure that out if he wanted to!"

"Still, that's what they all do," Zamiotov said. "A man

commits a clever murder at the risk of his life. Then he goes straight to a saloon and gives himself away. Starts spending and gets caught. They're not all as clever as you are. You wouldn't go to a saloon, would you?"

Raskolnikov frowned, and looked intently at Zamiotov.

"Seems you've worked up an appetite for the subject, and you'd like to know how I'd have gone about it?" he asked with displeasure.

"I'd like to," the other answered firmly and seriously. He was beginning to speak and to watch a little too seriously.

"Very much?"

"Very much."

"All right," Raskolnikov began, "this is what I would have done." Again he brought his face close to Zamiotov's face; again he looked at him steadily; and again he spoke in a whisper. This time Zamiotov actually shuddered. "This is the way I would have gone about it. I would have taken the money and the things and I would have gone straight off without any detours to some deserted place where there are only fences and practically no one around—a back lot or some such place. I'd have looked the place over beforehand and found a stone somewhere around fifty or seventy-five pounds, in a corner somewhere, near a fence, left over from building a house. I'd lift the stone. Must be a hole under it. I'd put the money and the things in the hole, and put the stone back on top. I'd put the stone back and dig around it a little so it would look just as it did before. I'd tamp it around with my foot, and then I'd leave. For a year, two, maybe even three years, I wouldn't go near the place. And after that, try and find me! I'd be gone."

"You are mad," Zamiotov managed somehow to say, almost in a whisper. For some reason he moved suddenly away from Raskolnikov. The latter's eyes flashed. He turned terribly pale. His upper lip quivered and twitched. He leaned forward as closely to Zamiotov as possible and his lips started to move, but not a word came out. This went on for half a minute. He knew what he was doing, yet he could not restrain himself. The terrible sentence quivered on his lips as the latch had once quivered in its hook. In another moment, it would out. In another moment, he would simply let go. In another moment, he would speak!

"And what if it was I who murdered the old woman and Lizaveta?" he said suddenly. Then he came to his senses.

Zamiotov looked at him wildly and turned as white as the tablecloth. His expression contorted itself into a smile.

"Is it possible, though?" he said, scarcely aloud.

Raskolnikov threw a malevolent look at him.

"You believed me, didn't you? Yes? Surely, yes?"

"Don't be silly! And I believe it now less than ever!" said Zamiotov hastily.

"So now I've got you! Cock robin is caught. If you believe it now less than ever, you must have believed it before."

"Why, don't be silly!" Zamiotov exclaimed, evidently disconcerted. "Is that why you've been scaring me—to lead up to that?"

"So you don't believe it? And what were you talking about behind my back when I left the police station that time? Why did Lieutenant Powder cross-examine me after I fainted? Hey, there!" he called to the waiter, rose, and picked up his cap. "How much do I owe?"

"Thirty kopecks in all, sir," the waiter answered as he came up at a run.

"Here's another twenty kopecks. Buy yourself a vodka on me. . . . Quite a bit of money, eh?" He waved the bills in his trembling hand at Zamiotov. "Red ones, blue ones, twenty-five rubles. Where does it come from? And where does the new suit come from? You remember very well I didn't have a kopeck! And you must have cross-examined my landlady by now. . . . Well enough! *Assez causé.* So long. . . . Best of luck!"

He left, quivering all over with a kind of wild hysteria in which there was also an element of unbearable delight. Yet he was gloomy and terribly tired. His face was contorted, as though after a seizure of some sort. He felt increasingly exhausted. The slightest shock, the least irritation or stimulus, aroused and revived his energies but they subsided as soon as the stimulus was gone.

Left alone, Zamiotov sat for a long time in the same place, deep in thought. Raskolnikov had unwittingly upset all his ideas on a certain point, and had definitely helped him make up his mind.

"Ilia Petrovich is a fool," he declared resolutely.

Raskolnikov opened the door to the street. As he did so, right in the entryway he bumped into Razumikhin, who was on his way in. They did not see each other until they practically knocked heads together. For a little while they examined each other. Razumikhin was astounded. Then anger—real anger—flashed threateningly from his eyes.

"So there you are!" he shouted full throat. "Ran away from your bed! And me looking for you everywhere, even under the couch! We went up to the attic! We damn near gave Nastasia a beating on your account. . . . And here you've been, all along! Rodia! What's the meaning of this? Tell me the whole truth! Out with it! You hear?"

"The meaning is that you all bore me to tears, and I'd like to be left alone," Raskolnikov answered calmly.

"Alone? When you can't even walk yet, and your mug is white as a sheet, and you're gasping for breath! You fool! What were you doing in the Crystal Palace? Out with it! Right away."

"Leave me alone!" said Raskolnikov, and tried to walk past. This put Razumikhin in a fury. He seized Raskolnikov powerfully by the shoulder.

"Leave you alone? How dare you say 'Leave me alone'? Do you know what I'm going to do with you now? I'm going to pick you up, tie you in a knot, take you home under my arm, and put you under lock and key!"

"Razumikhin," Raskolnikov began, quietly and apparently quite calmly. "Listen. Can't you see I don't want your favors? What kind of a game is it, doing favors to people who despise them? To people who loathe favors, I mean? Why did you look me up when I first took sick? How did you know I wouldn't have been delighted to die? Haven't I made it clear enough to you today that you're torturing me, that you make me sick! You seem to get a kick out of torturing people! I assure you that all this prevents me from recovering. Seriously. Because it keeps irritating me. Zosimov, just a little while ago—he went away so as not to irritate me. You leave me alone too, for God's sake! What right do you have, anyway, keeping me by force? Can't you see I'm talking to you in full possession of my faculties? How, how can I persuade you not to pursue me with your favors? I don't care if you think I'm ungrateful, I don't care if you think I'm low, as long as you all just leave me alone—for God's sake, just leave me alone! You hear? Leave me alone!"

He had begun calmly, gloating beforehand over the venom he was going to pour forth, but he was in a rage by the time he finished, gasping for breath, as with Luzhin earlier.

Razumikhin stood there, thought it over, and then let his hand drop.

"You can go to hell!" he said quietly, almost pensively. As Raskolnikov was about to move off he roared: "Wait a minute! Listen. I tell you, you're all, every one of you, a bunch of big talkers and swaggerers! The minute something goes a little bit wrong, you start brooding on it like a mother hen! And you're plagiarists at that. There's nothing original or independent in you! You're made of spermaceti ointment with skimmed milk in your veins for blood! I wouldn't trust any of you! The first thing you always concentrate on is how to avoid resembling a human being! Wa-a-ait a minute!" He saw Raskolnikov was trying again to get away, and he shouted with redoubled fury. "Listen to the end! I'm having a house-warming this evening, you know. They may even be there already. My uncle's receiving the guests—I just left him there. If you weren't a fool, a common garden-variety all-around fool—if you were an authentic original instead of some translation from a foreign language . . . Well, you see, Rodia, I admit you're a clever guy, all right, but still you're a fool! And if you weren't a fool, you'd be better off coming to my place this evening and sitting in on my little party instead of just pounding the pavement for no reason. Since you've already gone out, there's no help for it! I could drag out a nice comfortable armchair for you; my landlords have one. . . . A little tea, some company . . . Or, if you don't want to, I could fix the couch up for you . . . Anyway, you'd be with us. . . . Zosimov will be there, too. You'll come, won't you?"

"No."

"R-r-ridiculous!" Razumikhin impatiently cried out. "How do you know? You can't even speak for yourself! You don't even understand a thing about it! I've had it out with people myself and broken off with them—a thousand times, I tell you—yet I always went back. You start feeling ashamed of yourself, so you go back! Just remember, Pochinkov's house, third floor . . ."

"Why, Mr. Razumikhin, I think you'd actually let somebody beat you up in return for the sheer pleasure of being allowed to do him a favor."

"Who? Me? Come on, now, I'll punch you in the nose! Pochinkov's house, number forty-seven, the clerk Babushkin's apartment—"

"I won't come, Razumikhin!" Raskolnikov turned and walked away.

"I bet you'll come," Razumikhin cried out after him. "Or else you . . . or else I don't want to know you! Hey, wait! Is Zamiotov in there?"

"He's in there."

"You saw him?"

"I saw him."

"You talked to him?"

"I talked to him."

"What about? Oh, to hell with you! Don't tell me if you don't want to. Pochinkov's. Forty-seven. Babushkin's. Don't forget!"

Raskolnikov walked as far as the Sadovaia and turned the corner. Razumikhin watched him thoughtfully. At last he shrugged and went into the building. Halfway up the stairs, however, he paused.

"Damn it," he muttered, "I thought he was talking sense . . . but I'm a fool! Don't madmen talk sense? Apparently that's just what Zosimov was afraid of!" He tapped his finger on his forehead. "Well, what if— How could I let him go like that? He might go drown himself. . . . Oh, that was a boner I pulled. Can't be done!" He ran back in pursuit of Raskolnikov, but had already lost track of him. He spat, and returned swiftly to the Crystal Palace to find out what he could from Zamiotov.

Raskolnikov went straight to the Voznesensky Bridge, stopped halfway across, put both his elbows on the railing, and stared into the distance. Parting with Razumikhin had drained him, and he had barely managed to drag himself this far. He felt like sitting or lying down somewhere on the street. He leaned out over the water and stared mechanically at the last pink reflection of the sunset, the row of buildings that grew darker as the dusk thickened, a small attic window in the distance on the left bank, which, for a moment, a last ray of the setting sun touched as though with flame. He stared at the darkening water of the canal. He seemed to be scrutinizing this water. At last red circles danced before his eyes, the buildings swayed, the passersby, the embankments, the carriages—everything around him began to swirl and dance. All of a sudden he shuddered. A wild and grotesque scene saved him, perhaps, from another fainting spell. Feeling that someone was standing nearby on his right, he looked up and noticed a tall woman with a shawl on her head and a long, yellow, wasted face and bloodshot sunken eyes. She looked right at him, but obviously she saw nothing and could make no one out. All of a sudden she gripped the parapet with her right hand, lifted herself over the railing, and flung herself into the canal. The dirty water parted, took the victim in for a moment, but in a moment the drowning woman bobbed up again and was carried gently downstream by the current, her head and feet in the water, her back up, her skirt gathered up and puffed out over the water like a pillow.

"She's drowning! She's drowning!" dozens of voices shouted. People came running. Both embankments swarmed with on-lookers. People thronged onto the bridge and around Raskolnikov, shoving him and pushing him back.

"Father, save us, it's our Afrosinia!" a woman's tearful outcry could be heard not far away. "Save us, Father! Dear people, pull her out!"

"A boat! A boat!" cried voices in the crowd.

Boats were no longer needed. A policeman ran down to the canal, tore off his coat and boots, and leaped into the water. It didn't take much work. The water carried the drowning woman not more than two yards from the steps. With his right hand he grabbed her clothes; with his left he managed to hang on to a pole that a fellow policeman held out to him; and the almost-drowned woman was promptly hauled out. They stretched her out on the granite flagstones of the embankment. Soon she recovered consciousness, raised herself, sat up, started sniffing and sneezing and senselessly rubbing at her wet dress with her hands. She said nothing.

"She's drunk herself sick, kind people, she's drunk herself sick." It was the same woman's voice, now beside Afrosinia. "She tried to hang herself, and we cut her down. I just went to the store awhile ago and I left my little girl to keep an eye on her and then it happened! She's a friend of ours, sir, yes, just a friend, and she lives near us, second house from the end, right there. . . ."

People began to disperse. The policemen still occupied themselves with the woman, and someone shouted something about the police station. . . . Raskolnikov watched it all with a strange sensation of apathy and indifference. To him it was disgusting. "No, it's foul . . . the water . . . not worth it," he muttered to himself. "I couldn't," he added. "No use waiting. The police station, then . . . But why isn't

Zamiotov at the police station? I know it's open. . . ." He turned his back to the parapet and looked around him.

"Well, that's it, then! And why not!" he said decisively as he left the bridge in the direction of the police station. He felt empty and remote. He did not want to think. Even his anguish had passed. There was no trace of that energy with which he had left home "to put an end to it all." Utter apathy had taken its place.

"Well, it's a way out!" he thought as he walked listlessly along the embankment. "Anyway, I'm putting an end to it because I want to. . . . But is it really a way out? What's the difference! I'll always have my square yard of space—hah! What an ending, though! Can it be the end? Will I tell them or won't I tell them? Oh . . . hell! I'm tired, though. Got to sit down, lie down somewhere! What makes me feel ashamed is the stupidity. Well, to hell with that, too. God, what dumb things I think about . . ."

To get to the police station he had to walk straight ahead and then turn left at the second crossing. From there it was only a few steps. When he reached the first crossing, however, he paused, pondered, turned into a side street, and took a long detour through two streets, maybe for no reason at all, or maybe to gain some time or stretch it out. He walked along, staring at the sidewalk. Suddenly it was as though somebody whispered something into his ear. Raising his head, he saw he was standing near *that* house, at the very gates. Since *that* evening he had not been here; he had not walked past.

An overwhelming and mysterious urge drew him on. He entered the house, passing through the gateway and into the first entrance on the right. He started climbing the familiar stairs to the fourth floor. It was very dark on the steep and narrow stairs. On each landing he paused and looked about with curiosity. On the first landing he noticed that the window frame had been completely removed. "That's not the way it was then," he thought. Here was the apartment where Nikolashka and Mitka had been working. "Closed. And the door's newly painted. That means it's for rent." Here was the third floor . . . and the fourth. . . . "Here!" He felt bewildered. The door was wide open. People in there. Voices audible. Somehow this was not what he had expected. He hesitated, but mounted the last steps and went into the apartment.

This apartment was also being redone. There were workmen inside. This seemed to take him aback. He had imagined he would find it exactly as he had left it. The corpses might even be in the same places on the floor. But the walls were bare now, and there was no furniture. Strange! He walked over to the window and sat down on the sill.

There were two workmen, both young, but one much younger than the other. They were papering the walls with new wallpaper, white with lilac flowers, replacing the dirty, faded old one. Somehow this displeased Raskolnikov terribly. He regarded the new wallpaper with hostility, as though he resented the change.

The workmen had obviously been loitering and were now rolling up the paper in a hurry and getting ready to go home. They hardly noticed Raskolnikov. They were chatting away about something. Raskolnikov folded his arms and listened.

"So she comes to me in the morning," the older one was saying to the younger. "It's damn early and she's dressed fit to kill. So I says to her, what are you orangeading and lemonading in front of me like that for? So she says, Tit Vasilevich, I'd like to be at your mercy completely from now on, if you don't mind, she says. So that's what's up! That's why she's all dressed up like a damn magazine!"

"What's that mean, though, unc, what's a magazine?" the youngster asked. He was obviously used to having his "uncle" instruct him.

"A magazine, old pal, has got colored pictures in it, and every Saturday the tailors get them by mail from abroad. A magazine has got all that stuff in it about who gets dressed up in what, the men just as much as the women. It's quite a picture. The men all wrapped up in furs, and as for the female section, old pal, they got such souffling prompters on, whatever you paid for them it wouldn't be enough."

"What don't they have in Peter!" the youngster exclaimed with enthusiasm. "Except for ma and pa they've got everything!"

"Except for that, old pal, everything's right here handy," the "uncle" sententiously declared.

Raskolnikov got up and went into the other room, where the chest, the bed, and the bureau had stood before. Without furniture, the room seemed terribly small to him. The wallpaper was the same. In the corner the mark showed clearly where the icon case had been. He looked at it, then returned to his window. The older workman kept looking at him askance.

Turning to him suddenly, he asked: "What is it you want here, sir?"

Instead of answering, Raskolnikov rose. He went out into the hall, seized the bell, and pulled. It was the same bell. It made the same tinny sound. He pulled again, and again. He listened. It came back to him. That previous horrible, agonizing hideous sensation came back to him more clearly and vividly. At every ring, he shuddered. And he found it pleasanter and pleasanter.

"What do you want, anyway?" the workman came out and yelled at him. "Who are you?" Raskolnikov went in again.

"I want to rent the apartment," he said. "I'm looking."

"Nobody goes around renting apartments at night. And, anyway, you should've come up with the janitor."

"The floor's been washed. Are they going to paint it?" asked Raskolnikov. "Blood gone?"

"What blood?"

"It's where that old woman and her sister were murdered. There was a whole pool of blood here."

"What kind of a man are you, anyway?" the workman cried out uneasily.

"Me?"

"Yes."

"Would you like to find out? Let's go to the police station. I'll tell there."

The workman looked at him, bewildered.

"It's time for us to go home now, sir. We were dillydallying. Come on, Alioshka. Got to close up," the older workman said.

"Well, let's go," Raskolnikov replied unconcernedly. He left ahead of them, slowly descending the stairs. As he came out by the gate he cried: "Hey, janitor!"

Several people were standing right in the entryway, eyeing the passersby: both janitors, a woman, a vendor in a long coat, and someone else. Raskolnikov went straight up to them.

"What do you want?" one of the janitors asked.

"Have you been to the police station?"

"I just been there. What do you want?"

"Is it open?"

"It's open."

"The assistant super there?"

"He was, awhile back. What do you want?"

Raskolnikov did not reply. He stood there lost in thought.

The older workman came up and said: "This guy came to have a look at the place."

"What place?"

"Where we're working. He asks if they washed off the blood. He says there was a murder, and here I am, says he, I want to rent this place. Then he starts ringing the bell. He pulls it right off, almost. Then he says, let's go. Let's go, says he, let's go to the police station. I'll talk there. I'll tell everything. Couldn't get rid of him."

The janitor frowned and looked at Raskolnikov, bewildered.

"Who are you, anyway?" he said more threateningly.

"I am Rodion Romanych Raskolnikov, a former student. I live in Shil's house, on a side street not far from here, apartment number fourteen. Ask the janitor, he knows me." Raskolnikov said all this languidly, without even turning around. He stared intently at the darkening street.

"Why did you go up there?"

"To look."

"What's there to look at?"

Suddenly the vendor broke in: "Why don't you take him to the police station?" Then he fell silent.

Over his shoulder, Raskolnikov looked at him attentively, and said in the same quiet and lazy voice: "Let's go."

"You better take him," the vendor said, encouraged. "What was he snooping around for about *that?* What was on his mind? Eh?"

"Maybe he's drunk. Maybe not. God knows what they're up to," the workman said.

"What do you want?" the janitor yelled again. He was really beginning to get angry. "What were you hanging around for, anyhow?"

Raskolnikov sneered. "Are you afraid to go to the police station?"

"Afraid of what? Tell me what you were hanging around for."

"He's a fox!" said the woman.

"What we arguing for?" the other janitor said. He was a huge peasant in a short coat, unbuttoned, a bunch of keys at his belt. "You beat it! He's foxy, all right: You just beat it!"

Seizing Raskolnikov by the shoulder, he threw him into the street. Raskolnikov staggered, but did not fall. He recovered his balance, gazed silently at all who were watching him, and walked on.

"That's a queer duck," said the workman.

"They're all queer nowadays," the woman said.

"I still think you should've taken him to the police station," the vendor added.

"Better not to butt in," the huge janitor said. "He was foxy, all right! It's clear he wanted us to drag him there. Once you get mixed up in something like that, there's no getting out of it. . . . We know about that!"

"Go or not go?" thought Raskolnikov. At the crossroads he paused in the middle of the road and looked as though he expected to hear the last word from somebody outside himself. But he heard nothing. Not from anywhere. Everything seemed remote and dead, like the stones along which he made his way; dead for him, for him alone. Suddenly he saw a crowd. It was about two hundred paces away, at the end of the street in the darkness that had come in thick. He heard a hubbub and shouts. In the middle of the crowd a carriage had stopped. A light flared up in the middle of the street. Raskolnikov turned right and walked to the crowd. "What's up?" He seemed to be clutching at anything. As this occurred to him he smiled coldly, for he had definitely made up his mind to go to the police station. He knew for certain everything was over now.

7

A stylish, elegant carriage drawn by a pair of spirited gray horses stood in the middle of the road. There were no passengers. The driver had slid down from his box and was standing by. The horses were being held by the bridle. A crowd swarmed around the carriage, the police in front of everyone. A policeman was holding a lighted lantern. Bending down, he turned it on something that was lying in the road close to the wheels. They were all talking, shouting, exclaiming. The driver seemed bewildered, and every once in a while he would say over and over again: "What rotten luck! God, what rotten luck!"

Raskolnikov got as close as he could, pushing his way through the crowd, and finally saw the object of all this hubbub and curiosity. On the ground lay a man who had been trampled by the horses. He seemed to be unconscious. He was badly dressed and all covered with blood, yet he seemed like a "gentleman." Blood was flowing from his face and head. His face was battered, crushed, and mangled. It was clear that he had really been hit hard.

"Kind peoplé!" the driver wailed. "How could I see him there! Wasn't as if I was going fast, wasn't as if I didn't yell out at him. I was going at a steady, slow clip. You could see I was just clipping along the same as everybody else. We all know a drunk don't walk a straight line. . . . I see him, he's crossing the street, he staggers and just about falls. I yelled out. Once, twice, three times, and I held the horses in, too, but he goes and falls straight under their feet! Maybe he done it on purpose. Maybe he done it because he was that far gone. . . . These horses is young. They scare easy. They pulled. He hollered. They pulled harder. . . . That's how come the rotten luck."

"It happened just like he says!" confirmed someone in the crowd.

"Yell out—yes, he yelled out. That's the truth. He yelled three times," said someone else.

"Three times exactly. Everybody heard it!" said a third.

Actually, the driver was not very frightened or upset. The carriage evidently belonged to a wealthy and distinguished owner who was waiting for it somewhere. Naturally, the policemen were anxious that he not be kept waiting too long. The crushed man had to be taken to the police station and to the hospital. No one knew his name.

Meanwhile, Raskolnikov pushed his way through and bent more closely over the crushed man. The lantern suddenly lit up the unfortunate face, and Raskolnikov recognized him.

"I know him," he shouted, "I know him!" and he pushed all the way forward. "It's the clerk, the retired titular councillor, Marmeladov! He lives near here, in Kozel's house. . . . Somebody get a doctor! I'll pay. Here!" He fished money out of his pocket and showed it to the policeman. He was remarkably excited.

The police were glad to find out who the injured man was. Raskolnikov gave them his own name and address, too, and with all his powers, as though the matter concerned his own father, he persuaded them to carry the unconscious Marmeladov home as quickly as possible.

"This way," he insisted, "three houses down. Kozel's house, the German, rich . . . Making his way home, no doubt, and he was drunk. I know him. . . . He's a drunkard. . . . He's got family at home—wife, children. There's a daughter. Getting him to the hospital would take awhile, and there must be a doctor somewhere right in the building! I'll pay, I'll pay! His family will take care of him here, but if you send him to the hospital he'll die on the way. . . ."

He even managed to slip something quietly into the policeman's hand. Of course it was a clear case, and legal, and help was more easily available here, as he said. They lifted the injured man and carried him with the help of some people in the crowd. Kozel's house was about thirty steps away. Raskolnikov walked behind. He carefully supported Marmeladov's head and told them the way.

"Turn here, this way! Head first up the stairs, so turn around . . . that's the way! I'll pay. I'll be generous," he murmured.

Katherine Ivanovna was pacing up and down her little room as she always did when she had a moment to herself, from the window to the stove and back, arms folded across her chest, talking to herself and coughing. Recently she had begun to talk more frequently and at greater length with her elder daughter, the ten-year-old Polia. A good deal of this talk Polia did not understand, yet she understood very well that her mother needed her, and so she always followed her with her big, clever eyes, and did her best to pretend that she understood everything. This time Polia was undressing her little brother, who had not been well all day, and putting him to bed. The little boy sat quietly on his chair, straight and still, with a serious expression on his face, his feet firmly together and stretched out in front of him, heels toward his sister and toes apart. While waiting for his shirt (the only one he owned, so it could only be laundered at night), he listened to what his mother was telling his sister and sat perfectly still with his eyes wide open and his lips in a pout, as he had been told all clever little boys must sit when they are being undressed to go to bed. The girl, who was even smaller, and was dressed completely in rags, stood near the screen waiting her turn. The outside door was open, for whatever relief it afforded from the waves of tobacco smoke that floated in from the other rooms and provoked the poor consumptive into long and agonized coughing fits. This past week Katherine Ivanovna seemed to have grown even thinner, and the red stains on her cheeks burned even more brightly than before.

"You wouldn't believe it, Polenka, you can't even imagine it," she was saying as she paced the room, "how good we had it, how happily we lived in my papa's house and how this drunkard has ruined me and will ruin you all! My papa had a colonel's rank in the civil service. Almost a governor. He was only one step away from the governorship, so people would come to see him, and they would say: 'Ivan Mikhailych, we consider you as practically our governor.' When I . . . when I . . ." She paused, racked by coughing. "Oh, this damned life!" she burst out. She spat and clutched at her chest. "When I . . . ah, when I was at my last ball . . . at the marshal's . . . Princess Bezzemelny saw me. She was the one who gave me her blessing later on when I married your father, Polia. Right off she asked me: 'Isn't that the sweet girl who danced the shawl dance at graduation?' You must sew up that rip. Take the needle right now and mend it the way I showed you, or else tomorrow"—she coughed—"tomorrow"—the coughing seized her again—"he'll tear it wider!" Trying to get the words out, she almost shouted. "Prince Shchegolskoy, a page of the chamber, had just come from Petersburg then . . . and he danced the mazurka with me, and the very next day he wanted to make me an offer. I thanked him in flattering terms, but I told him that my heart had been for a very long time in the keeping of another. That other was your father, Polia. My papa was terribly angry. . . . Is the water ready? Well, let's have the shirt. And the socks? Lida"—she turned to the little girl—"you best sleep without a shirt tonight, somehow. . . . Lay your stockings out beside it . . . so they can be washed together. . . . What is that rag-picker up to anyway, the drunkard! The boy's shirt's like a dishrag, all worn out. . . . If I could only do them all at once and not have to go through it all two nights running! God!" Again a coughing fit. "Again! What's this?" she cried out. She stared at a crowd on the landing and people who were huddling some kind of burden into her room. "What's this? What are they carrying? God!"

"Where shall we put him?" the policeman asked, glancing around after the blood-streaked and unconscious Marmeladov had already been brought in.

"On the couch! Put him right on the couch, with his head this way," Raskolnikov directed.

"He was run over in the street! Drunk!" somebody out in the hall shouted.

Terribly pale, Katherine Ivanovna stood there breathing with difficulty. The children were terrified. Little Lidochka cried out, flung herself on Polia, clutched at her and trembled all over.

As soon as they put Marmeladov down, Raskolnikov hurried to Katherine Ivanovna.

"Calm yourself, for God's sake, don't be frightened!" he said, speaking very rapidly. "He was crossing the street and a carriage hit him. Don't be alarmed. He'll come to. I had him brought here. . . . I was here once before, remember? He'll come to. I'll pay!"

"He's got his!" Katherine Ivanovna cried out desperately, and rushed to her husband.

Raskolnikov noted quickly that she was not one of those women who go straight into a swoon. A pillow went under the unfortunate man's head in a flash, something no one had thought of before. Katherine Ivanovna began to undress him. Forgetting all about herself, she examined and fussed over him and did not lose her grip, clamping shut her trembling lips and repressing the cries that were ready to burst from her breast. Raskolnikov meanwhile asked somebody to run for a doctor, who, as it turned out, lived one house down.

"I sent for the doctor," he told Katherine Ivanovna. "Don't worry, I'll pay. Isn't there any water? Let me have a napkin, a towel, something, quick. We still don't know where he's hurt. He's hurt, not killed. You can be sure of that. We'll see what the doctor says."

Katherine Ivanovna rushed to the window. There in a corner on a broken chair was a large clay basin with water in it for the night's laundry. Katherine Ivanovna did this herself, with her own hands, at least twice a week, sometimes more often. There was almost no linen to change into, only one set for each member of the family, and Katherine Ivanovna could not bear uncleanliness. She preferred to drive herself at night beyond her strength, when everybody else was asleep, so she could manage to have the wet wash dried on the line by morning and have it clean, rather than see dirt in her home. She picked up the basin to bring it over as Raskolnikov had asked, but she almost fell. Raskolnikov, however, had already managed to find a towel, wet it, and had begun to wipe the blood off Marmeladov's face. Breath-

ing painfully and hugging her arms to her chest, Katherine
Ivanovna stood there too. She needed help herself. Raskolnikov reckoned he had perhaps done badly to have the injured man brought here. The policeman also seemed
perplexed.

"Polia!" Katherine Ivanovna cried. "Run to Sonia. Right
away. If she's not in, say her father's been run over by horses
and she should come here as soon as she gets back. Quick,
Polia! Here. Put on this shawl!"

The little boy on the chair suddenly cried out: "Run fast!"
Then he resumed his motionless straight posture on the
chair, eyes staring, heels forward, toes apart.

The room, meanwhile, filled to capacity and beyond. All
but one of the policemen left. One stayed for a while and
tried to get the crowd that had swarmed up the stairs back
down the stairs again. From the inner rooms, moreover, almost all Mrs. Lippewechsel's tenants had drifted in. At first
they only gathered in the doorway, but soon they plunged
in a mass into the room itself. Katherine Ivanovna was beside herself.

"Can't you even let him die in peace?" she shouted at
the crowd. "What do you think this is, a play! Smoking
cigarettes!" She coughed. "Why don't you put your hats on
while you're at it! . . . And there *is* one with his hat on. . . .
Look at him! Can't you show a little respect for the dead!"

She choked on her cough, but her scolding had done its
work. Evidently Katherine Ivanovna still inspired a certain
awe. One by one the tenants crowded back to the doorway,
with that strange inner feeling of satisfaction that may always be observed in the course of a sudden accident, even
in those who are closest to the victim, and from which no
loving man is exempt, however sincere his sympathy and
compassion.

But behind the door voices could be heard mentioning
the hospital, asserting there was no reason to be disturbing
people unnecessarily.

"No reason to be dying, is there!" cried Katherine Ivanovna. She was about to rush over, open the door, and un-
leash a full-size thunderbolt on them, when she bumped into
Mrs. Lippewechsel herself in the doorway. The latter had
only just got wind of the accident. She was running over to
set everything straight. Mrs. Lippewechsel was a particularly
quarrelsome, confused German woman.

"Ach, my God!" She clasped her hands together. "Your

drunk husband the horse iss run over. To ze hospisstal mit him! I am landlady!"

"Amalia Ludwigovna! I beg you to consider what you say," Katherine Ivanovna began haughtily. To her landlady she always spoke in a haughty tone, so the latter would "remember her place." Even now she could not refuse herself this pleasure. "Amalia Ludwigovna. . . ."

"I am tellinck you vunce for before zat you should never me dare to call Amalia Ludwigovna. I am Amalia Ivan!"

"You are not Amalia Ivan. You are Amalia Ludwigovna. Since I am not one of your base flatterers as Mr. Lebeziatnikov is, who at this very moment is laughing behind the door"—(there really was an outburst of laughter behind the door, and a shout: "They've locked horns!")—"I will always call you Amalia Ludwigovna, though I really fail to understand why this name does not please you. You see yourself what has happened to Semion Zakharovich. He is dying. I beg you to close this door now and not let anyone in here. Let him at least have a little peace to die! Otherwise, I assure you, your act will be known tomorrow to the governor-general himself. The prince knew me when I was still a girl, and he remembers Semion Zakharovich quite well. He has been kind to him many times. Everyone knows that Semion Zakharovich had many friends and patrons whom he forsook out of honorable pride since he suffered from his unfortunate weakness. But now"—she pointed to Raskolnikov—"a magnanimous young man is helping us, who has means and connections, and whom Semion Zakharovich has known since childhood, and you may be certain, Amalia Ludwigovna . . ."

All this was said rapid-fire, faster and faster, but coughing suddenly interrupted Katherine Ivanovna's eloquence. At this moment the dying man came to, and groaned, and she ran to him. The injured man opened his eyes, and still not recognizing anyone or understanding anything, began to stare at Raskolnikov, who stood over him. He breathed slowly, deeply, and painfully. Blood oozed from the corners of his mouth. The sweat stood out on his forehead. Not recognizing Raskolnikov, he began fitfully casting his eyes about. Katherine Ivanovna looked at him sadly but sternly. Tears flowed from her eyes.

"My God! His whole chest is crushed! And blood, look at the blood!" she said in desperation. "We've got to get his shirt off! Turn a little, if you can, Semion Zakharovich," she cried out to him.

Marmeladov recognized her.

"A priest!" he exclaimed in a hoarse voice.

Katherine Ivanovna went over to the window, leaned her forehead against the windowpane, and said in desperation: "Oh, this damned life!"

"A priest!" the dying man said again, after a moment of silence.

"They've go-o-one!" Katherine Ivanovna cried out to him. He heard her and fell silent. His eyes sought her out with a timid and wistful gaze. She turned to him again and stood at the head of the couch. He calmed down a little, but not for long. Soon his eyes lingered on Lidochka (his favorite), who was trembling in the corner as though in a fit, staring at him with her astonished, childishly intent eyes.

"A-a-ah." He motioned to her restlessly, wanting to say something.

"What now?" cried Katherine Ivanovna.

"Barefoot! Barefoot!" he muttered, indicating with a frenzied look the girl's bare feet.

"Shush!" Katherine Ivanovna cried irascibly. "You know why she's barefoot!"

"Thank God, the doctor!" Raskolnikov cried, greatly relieved.

The doctor came in, a precise little old man, a German, looking about him with a distrustful expression. He went up to the injured man, took his pulse, carefully felt his head, and with Katherine Ivanovna's help undid the bloody shirt-front, uncovering the injured man's chest. It was battered, crushed, and torn. Several ribs on the right side were broken. On the left side, just over the heart, was a large, sinister yellowish-black bruise, the cruel blow of a hoof. The doctor frowned. A policeman told him the injured man had been caught in the wheel and dragged along the road for about thirty yards, turning around and around.

"Astonishing he even regained consciousness," the doctor whispered softly to Raskolnikov.

"What do you think?" the latter asked.

"He's dying now."

"No hope, then?"

"None at all! He's at the last gasp. Head's badly injured, too . . . Hmm. If you like I can have him bled, but it wouldn't do any good. In five or ten minutes he'll die anyway."

"Better bleed him."

"As you like. But I warn you, it won't do any good at all."

Just then more footsteps were heard. The crowd on the landing parted and the priest appeared in the doorway with the Sacrament. He was a gray little old man. One of the policemen had gone to fetch him while they were still outside. The doctor immediately made way and exchanged a significant look with him. Raskolnikov begged the doctor to stay, if only for a little while. The latter shrugged his shoulders and remained.

They all stepped back. Confession did not last long. The dying man scarcely understood anything well. He could only utter fragmented, unclear sounds. Katherine Ivanovna took Lida, lifted the boy from his chair, and going off into the corner toward the stove, knelt down and made the children kneel in front of her. The girl merely trembled. On his bare knees, the boy kept lifting his hand with a slow, measured gesture, crossing himself precisely and bowing to the ground, striking his forehead, all of which apparently gave him special pleasure. Katherine Ivanovna gnawed her lips and held back her tears. She, too, prayed, straightening the boy's shirt occasionally, or managing to throw a shawl she got from the bureau around the girl's overly exposed shoulders without rising from her knees or ceasing to pray. Meanwhile, the door from the inner rooms was opened again by the curious. On the landing the onlookers gathered more and more thickly—tenants from all the apartments along the stairs. Yet they did not cross the threshold. A single candle end alone illuminated the entire scene.

Then Polia squeezed in quickly through the crowd on the landing. She had run out to fetch her sister. She came in breathless from her fast run, took off the shawl and searched out her mother with her eyes. "She's coming," she said. "I met her on the street!" Her mother made her kneel beside her. Then timidly and inaudibly a girl squeezed through the crowd. Strange indeed was her sudden appearance in that room, in the middle of beggary, rags, death, and desperation. She, too, was in rags. She was cheaply dressed, but tricked out gutter-fashion, according to the rules and taste of that special world whose shameful purpose was all too apparent. Sonia paused on the landing, right on the threshold. She did not cross the threshold, though, and looked like some lost soul, oblivious of everything, it seemed, unconscious of her fourth-hand gaudy silk dress with its long absurd train and the immense crinoline that filled the entire doorway, so inappropriate here, and her bright-colored shoes, and the parasol she scarcely needed at night, but which she took with her, and her foolish round straw hat with the bright red feather on top. From under this hat, which was cocked at a rakish angle, gazed a thin, pale, frightened little face, with parted lips and eyes immobile in terror. Sonia was a small, thin girl of about eighteen, fairly pretty, blonde, with remarkable blue eyes. She gazed intently at the bed, at the priest. She, too, was out of breath from running. At last the whispering in the crowd probably reached her. She lowered her eyes, took a step over the threshold, and stood in the room, still practically in the doorway.

Confession was over. So was Extreme Unction. Katherine Ivanovna went up to her husband's bed again. The priest stepped back. He turned to say a few words of solace and comfort to Katherine Ivanovna before he left.

She pointed to the little ones. "What am I supposed to do with these?" she said sharply and irritably.

"God is merciful. Look to the Almighty for help," the priest began.

"E-e-eh! Merciful, yes. But not to us!"

"That's a sin, a sin, *madame,*" the priest said, shaking his head.

Katherine Ivanovna pointed to the dying man. "I suppose that's not a sin," she cried.

"Perhaps those who caused the accident without meaning to will agree to compensate you, at least for the loss of his earnings—"

"You don't understand!" Katherine Ivanovna cried irritably, waving her hand. "Why should they compensate me? He was drunk, wasn't he? Wasn't it his own fault he got trampled! And *what* earnings? He didn't bring home any earnings. Just misery. He was a drunkard. He drank everything up. He stole from us, and he took it to the tavern! Thank God he's dying! It's one less mouth to feed!"

"In the hour of death you must forgive. That's a sin, *madame.* Such feelings are a great sin!"

Katherine Ivanovna busied herself about the injured man. She gave him a drink and wiped the sweat and blood from his head. She straightened the pillows. While talking to the priest she went on with her task, and only managed to face him now and then. Suddenly she flung herself on him, almost in a frenzy.

"Eh, Father! Those are words, just words! Forgive! If he hadn't been run over, he would have come home drunk tonight, his only shirt dirty and in shreds, and he would have snored himself to sleep, and I'd be at it till daybreak, washing his clothes and the kids' clothes, and I'd be drying them by the window. When it was dawn I'd be sitting there mending them. That's the way I spend my nights! So what's this talk about forgiveness! As it is, I have forgiven!"

A deep and terrible coughing fit interrupted her words. She coughed up into her handkerchief and thrust it at the priest to show him, painfully clutching at her chest with the other hand. The handkerchief was covered with blood.

The priest bowed his head and said nothing.

Marmeladov was in his last agony. His wife had bent over him again, and he did not take his eyes from her face. He wanted very much to tell her something. He even started to say something, moving his tongue with effort and shaping the words, but Katherine Ivanovna, grasping that he wanted to ask her forgiveness, at once and peremptorily cried out to him: "Qui-i-i-et! You don't have to! I know what you want to say!" The injured man fell silent. At that very moment, however, his wandering gaze fell on the doorway, and he saw Sonia. He had not noticed her until then. She was standing in the corner and in the shadows.

"Who's that? Who's that?" he asked suddenly in a hoarse, gasping voice, greatly agitated, and in horror he motioned with his eyes to the doorway, where his daughter stood, and he tried hard to lift himself up.

"Lie down! Lie do-o-own!" cried Katherine Ivanovna.

With an enormous effort he managed to raise himself on one arm. He stared fixedly and savagely at his daughter for a while, as though he couldn't recognize her. He had never actually seen her dressed like that before. Suddenly he recognized her: dressed up in cheap finery, humiliated, crushed and ashamed, meekly waiting her turn to take leave of her dying father. His face expressed infinite suffering.

"Sonia! My daughter! Forgive me!" he cried, wanting to stretch a hand out to her, but he lost his balance and fell in a heap off the couch with his face straight down. They rushed to pick him up and put him back on the couch, but he was going fast. Sonia cried out weakly, ran up, embraced him, froze in that embrace. He died in her arms.

"He's got his!" Katherine Ivanovna cried, looking at her husband's corpse. "Well, what can I do now! What am I going to bury him with? And *them?* What am I going to feed them with tomorrcw?"

Raskolnikov went up to Katherine Ivanovna.

"Katherine Ivanovna," he began, "this last week your late husband told me the story of his life and all its circumstances. . . . Rest assured that he spoke of you with proud respect. When I learned how devoted he was to you all, and how much, Katherine Ivanovna, in spite of his unfortunate weakness, he loved and respected you, from that evening on we became friends. Let me help . . . now . . . so I can repay my debt to my late friend. Here you are . . . twenty rubles. If that helps, then I . . . in a word, I'll be back. . . . I'll certainly be back. . . . Maybe I'll even be back tomorrow. . . . Good-bye!"

He left the room quickly, pushing his way through the crowd on the stairs as rapidly as he could. In the crowd he suddenly bumped into Nikodim Fomich, who had heard about the accident and who wanted to come down and take charge of the police arrangements personally. They had not seen each other since their encounter in the police station, but Nikodim Fomich recognized him instantly.

"So it's you?" he asked.

"He died," Raskolnikov answered. "There was a doctor, priest, everything in order. Don't disturb the poor woman. She's most unfortunate. On top of everything, she's got T.B. Cheer her up if you can . . . I know you're kind," he added with a smile, looking him straight in the eyes.

"You seem to be soaked in blood," Nikodim Fomich remarked, noticing by the light of his lantern several fresh stains on Raskolnikov's jacket.

"Yes, soaked . . . I'm all bloody!" Raskolnikov said in a kind of special way, and then he smiled, nodding his head, and descended the stairs.

He descended calmly, without haste; feverish, but unaware of it; full of a single immense new sensation of abundant, powerful life surging up in him. This sensation could be compared to the sensation of a man condemned to death who is suddenly and unexpectedly pardoned. Halfway down the stairs the priest, who was on his way home, overtook him. Raskolnikov let him go by in silence, merely exchanging a silent bow. As he descended the last steps, though, he suddenly heard quick footsteps behind him. Somebody was running after him. It was Polia. She ran up behind him and called out: "Wait! Listen!"

He turned to face her. She ran down the last stairs and paused right in front of him, on the step above. A wan light came from the yard. Raskolnikov studied the thin, sweet face of the little girl. She smiled and looked up at him in a gay, childish way. She had come on an errand that she apparently very much enjoyed.

"Listen. What's your name? . . . And also, where do you live?" she asked hastily, in a halting little voice.

He put both hands on her shoulders, and with a kind of joy he looked at her. He felt so good, looking at her. He himself did not know why.

"Who sent you?"

"My sister Sonia sent me," the little girl answered, and smiled even more gaily.

"You know, I knew it was your sister Sonia, somehow."

"My mother sent me, too. When my sister Sonia started sending me, my mother also came up and said, 'Run quick, Polenka!'"

"Do you love your sister Sonia?"

"I love her more than anybody!" Polenka said with special firmness. Her smile suddenly became more serious.

"Will you love me?"

Instead of answering, the girl brought her little face closer to his. Her puckered lips naïvely reached up to kiss him. Suddenly her arms, thin as matchsticks, embraced him powerfully. She leaned her head on his shoulder and wept steadily, pressing her face more and more closely to him.

"It's awful about Papa!" she said. She lifted her stained face and wiped away the tears with her hands. "We've had such bad luck lately," she added unexpectedly, with the special gravity children deliberately assume when they wish to talk like grown-ups.

"Did your papa love you?"

"He loved Lidochka most of all," she went on seriously, without smiling, quite in the manner of grown-ups. "Because she was little, and also because she was sick. He always brought her presents. And he taught us to read, and me grammar and Scriptures and," she added with dignity, "Mama didn't say anything, only we knew she loved it, and Papa knew, and Mama wants me to learn French because it's high time for me to get an education."

"Do you know how to pray?"

"Oh, of course we know how! We learned that a long time ago. I'm so grown up now I pray all by myself, but Kolia and Lidochka pray aloud together with Mama. First they say the 'Hail Mary.' Then another prayer, 'Lord, forgive and bless our sister Sonia.' Then another, 'Lord, forgive and bless our second papa.' Because our first papa was dead already and this is our second one. But we pray for the first one, too."

"My name is Rodion, Polechka. Pray for me sometimes, too—'and Thy servant Rodion.' That's all."

"I'll pray for you the whole rest of my life," the girl promised, and suddenly she smiled again, threw her arms around him, and again hugged him close.

Raskolnikov gave her his name and address and promised to come back the next day without fail. She went away completely enraptured with him. It was eleven o'clock when he came out on the street. Five minutes later he was standing on the bridge at exactly the same place where the woman had jumped not long before.

"Enough!" he said solemnly and resolutely. "No more mirages, no more creeping horrors, no more phantoms! . . . Life is! Wasn't I alive just now? My life didn't go out with the old woman's! Off to heaven with her—that's enough, old girl, high time you were at peace! Now for the kingdom of light and reason and . . . and freedom, and power . . . and now we shall see! Now we shall match wits!" he added arrogantly as though he were addressing some dark force and issuing it a challenge. "And I was already consenting to live on a square yard of space!

"I'm very weak now, but it does look as though my illness is over. And I knew it would pass when I went out not long ago. What's more, Pochinkov's house is only a few steps from here. To Razumikhin's, without fail! I'd go even if he didn't live just a few steps away . . . let him win his bet! Let him, too, be comforted. It's nothing. Let him. Strength. I need strength. Without strength you get nothing. But strength must be won by strength. That's just what they don't know," he added proudly and self-confidently, and he left the bridge, scarcely lifting his feet. His pride and self-confidence grew in him at every moment. He was not the same man he had been a moment before. Yet what had happened that had so remade him? He did not know himself. Suddenly it seemed to him, as to one who grasps at a straw, that he, too, could live, that life *was,* and that his life had not gone out with the old woman's. Maybe he came to this conclusion too hastily. He did not think about that.

"You did ask her to mention 'Thy servant Rodion,' though," he thought suddenly. "Well, yes, that . . . just in case!" he added, and at once he felt an urge to laugh at this schoolboy trick of his. He was in excellent spirits.

Razumikhin was not hard to find. The new tenant was already well known in Pochinkov's house, and the janitor immediately showed him the way. He could hear the noise and animated talk of a big party halfway up the stairs. The door was wide open. Arguments could be heard, exclamations. Razumikhin's room was fairly large. There were about fifteen people at his party. Raskolnikov paused in the anteroom. Here, behind a screen, two of the landlady's maids busied themselves beside two large samovars, near some bottles, plates, pastry dishes, and hors d'oeuvres brought up from the landlady's kitchen. Raskolnikov asked for Razumikhin. He came running, delighted. It was immediately apparent that he had been drinking quite a bit more than usual. Although Razumikhin had a bottomless capacity and never got really drunk, still, you could see the effects this time.

"Listen," Raskolnikov hastened to say, "I just came to tell you. You win the bet. It's true. A man never knows what can happen to him. I can't come in. I'm so weak I'm about to collapse. So, good luck. And good-bye. Come see me tomorrow, though. . . ."

"You know what? I'll see you home. You're weak, as you say, and—"

"And your guests? Who's that curly-haired fellow just looked in?"

"Him? Who the hell knows! Must be some friend of my uncle's, or maybe he dropped in on his own. . . . My uncle can take care of them. He is a most excellent man. Pity you can't get acquainted right now. But what the hell. To hell with all of them! They don't need me now, and actually I could use a little fresh air. So, my friend, you came in the nick of time. Another couple minutes, and by God I'd have been at their throats! They're throwing such bull. . . . You can't imagine how high they can pile it! What am I saying? Of course you can imagine. We do it ourselves. Let them get it out of their system. Then they won't go piling it up later. . . . Sit down a minute. I'll get Zosimov."

Zosimov approached Raskolnikov with a certain eagerness. You could see he had a certain special curiosity. His face soon brightened.

He examined the patient as best he could. "Get some sleep now," he said. "You ought to take something for the night. Will you? I made it up awhile ago . . . it's one powder."

"Two, if you like," said Raskolnikov.

He took the powder then and there.

"Good you'll be taking him home yourself," Zosimov noted to Razumikhin. "We'll see what tomorrow brings. For today, he's really not in bad shape. Quite a change. Well, you live and learn."

"You know what Zosimov whispered to me as we were leaving?" Razumikhin said as soon as they were out in the street. "I'll tell you straight from the shoulder, old pal, because they're fools. Zosimov told me to chat with you along the way, get you to talk, then tell him. Because he has the idea you're . . . mad, or close to it. Imagine that! First of all, you're three times as smart as he is. Second, since you're not off the hinge, you might as well just laugh at the wild bull he thinks up. Third, that hunk of beef—he's a surgeon by profession, and now he's started monkeying around with mental illnesses—what convinced him decisively about you was the talk you had today with Zamiotov."

"Zamiotov told you all about it?"

"All. Good thing, too. Now I understand all the ins and outs, and so does Zamiotov. . . . You see, Rodia, the point is actually . . . I've had a drop too much. . . . That's nothing, though. . . . The point is this idea . . . you understand? They really had it for a while . . . you understand? That is, not one of them dared say it out loud, because it's the silliest wild bull, and especially since they've arrested that painter, it was all cut short and snuffed forever. Why are they such fools, though? I beat Zamiotov up a little. That's between us, old pal. Don't tell anybody you know; I've noticed he's touchy. It was at Luisa's. But today, today everything came clear. That Ilia Petrovich—mostly his fault. He took advantage of your fainting fit at the police station. Later he was ashamed of himself. Don't I know it, though . . ."

Raskolnikov listened eagerly as Razumikhin chattered away in his cups.

"I fainted because it was stifling and there was such a strong smell of linseed oil," Raskolnikov said.

"Still explaining! It sure wasn't the paint alone. For a

whole month your fever has been coming on. Zosimov will swear to that! But you can't imagine how cut down the kid is now! 'I'm not worth that man's little finger,' he says. Yours, that is. Sometimes, old pal, he's not such a bad guy. But the lesson, the lesson you taught him today in the Crystal Palace—that was perfect! You had him scared at first. He almost had a fit. You just about convinced him all over again of all that ghastly nonsense. Then suddenly you stuck your tongue out at him: 'There. Got what you wanted, didn't you!' Perfect! Now he's crushed, annihilated! By God, you're a master. That's the way to handle them, all right. Eh, wish to hell I'd been there! He was awfully anxious to see you just now. Porfiry would like to meet you, too. . . ."

"Ah. Him too. But why did they think I was mad?"

"Well, not mad, exactly. Looks like I'm talking too much, old pal. . . . Some time ago, you see, it struck him you were only interested in this one point. Now it's clear why. Once you know all the circumstances . . . how it rubbed against you then and got all mixed up with your illness . . . I'm a little drunk, old pal. Damn-all knows what idea he's on to. . . . I told you, he's monkeying around with mental illnesses. But you just spit. . . ."

For half a minute both fell silent.

"Listen, Razumikhin," said Raskolnikov. "I want to tell you frankly. I've been at a dead man's just now. A certain clerk just died. . . . I gave away all my money there . . . and what's more, a creature kissed me a little while ago, and if I'd killed anyone, she might still . . . well, I saw another creature there . . . with a red feather . . . but anyhow, I'm talking through my hat. I'm very weak. Give me a hand . . . here's the stairs now. . . ."

"What's wrong with you?" Razumikhin asked, alarmed. "What's wrong?"

"My head's going around a bit, but that isn't the point. The point is I feel so sad, so sad! Like a woman . . . really! Look. What's that? Look! Look!"

"What do you mean?"

"Don't you see? Don't you see? The light on in my room? Through the crack . . ."

They were standing beside the landlady's door facing the last flight of stairs. One really could see a light coming from Raskolnikov's little room.

"Strange! Maybe it's Nastasia," Razumikhin remarked.

"She never comes up at this hour. She's been asleep for a long time. But . . . it's all the same to me! Good-bye!"

"What are you saying! I'll go up with you. We'll go on up together!"

"I know we're going on up together, but I'd like to shake your hand here, and say good-bye to you here. Well, give me your hand. Good-bye!"

"What's wrong with you, Rodia?"

"Nothing. Let's go. You'll be a witness. . . ."

They began climbing the stairs, and the thought flashed through Razumikhin's mind that Zosimov might well have been right. "Eh! I've upset him with my jabbering!" he muttered to himself. Suddenly, as they approached the door, they heard voices in the room.

"What's going on?" shouted Razumikhin.

Raskolnikov reached the door first and flung it wide open. He flung it open and stood on the threshold as though transfixed.

His mother and sister were sitting on the couch. They had been waiting for an hour and a half. He did not know why they had been the last people in the world he had expected, why he had never thought of them, although twice that day he had received news that they were on their way and would be there at any moment. For the hour and a half they had been there, they had cross-examined Nastasia. She had already managed to fill them in, and was still standing there. When they heard he had "run off today," sick, and (as it seemed from the story) practically delirious, they were beside themselves with fear. "Lord, what's wrong with him!" Both had been weeping. Both, during that hour and a half of waiting, had been through agonies of suspense.

A joyful, triumphant outcry greeted Raskolnikov's appearance. Both flung themselves into his arms. Yet he stood there as one dead. A sudden intolerable awareness struck him like a thunderbolt. And he could not even lift his arms to embrace them. His mother and sister enveloped him in embraces, kissed him, laughed, wept. . . . He moved a step, swayed, and collapsed on the floor in a faint.

Commotion, cries of alarm, moans . . . Razumikhin, who had been standing on the threshold, flew into the room, picked up the sick man in his competent arms, and in a flash had him on the couch.

"It's nothing, nothing!" he exclaimed to the mother and sister. "It's a fainting spell, it's rubbish! Why, the doctor was just saying he's much better, he's quite healthy! Water! Well, you see. He's coming to. He's all right!''

He seized Dunia by the hand so fiercely that he almost dislocated her arm, making her bend down to see that he had "already come to." Both mother and sister regarded Razumikhin as providential and looked at him with gratitude and feeling. They had already heard from Nastasia what he had done for their Rodia during the time of his illness—"this efficient young man," as Pulcheria Alexandrovna Raskolnikov herself called him that very evening in an intimate conversation with Dunia.

PART THREE

I

Raskolnikov raised himself a little and sat up on the couch.

Weakly, he signaled Razumikhin to cut short the flow of disconnected and impassioned consolations the latter had been addressing to mother and sister. He took each by the hand and gazed silently for a minute or two, first at one, then at the other. His look frightened his mother. She saw strong feeling, close to torment, flare up in it, yet it had a fixed quality, too, and perhaps even a touch of insanity. Pulcheria Alexandrovna wept.

Avdotia Romanovna was pale. Her hand trembled in her brother's hand.

"Go home . . . with him," he said in a broken voice, pointing to Razumikhin. "Till tomorrow. Tomorrow, we'll— Have you been here long?"

"Since this evening, Rodia," Pulcheria Alexandrovna replied. "The train was terribly late. I wouldn't leave you now for anything, though, Rodia! I'll spend the night here. . . ."

"Don't torment me!" he said with an exasperated wave of the hand.

"*I'll* stay here with him!" Razumikhin cried. "I won't leave him for a moment. To hell with my guests! They can go climb up the walls! Anyway, my uncle's there."

"How can I ever thank you enough!" Pulcheria Alexandrovna began, pressing Razumikhin's hands again, but Raskolnikov interrupted her again.

"I can't stand it, I can't stand it," he repeated irritably. "Don't torment me! Enough. Go away. I can't stand it!"

"Come, Mother, let's go, for a minute, anyway," the frightened Dunia whispered. "It's clear we're driving him to distraction."

"After three years won't I even get a chance to look at him?" Pulcheria Alexandrovna wept.

"Wait!" He stopped them again. "You're always interrupting me and I get my thoughts mixed up. . . . Have you seen Luzhin?"

"No, Rodia, but he does know we are here. Rodia, we

heard that Peter Petrovich was kind enough to drop in on you today," Pulcheria Alexandrovna added with a certain timidity.

"Yes, he was kind enough. . . . Dunia, not long ago I told this Luzhin I'd throw him down the stairs. I chased him off to hell and gone."

"Rodia, what are you saying! Surely, you . . . you don't mean to say . . ." Pulcheria Alexandrovna began in dismay. Looking at Dunia, however, she paused.

Avdotia Romanovna was gazing intently at her brother, waiting for him to go on. Nastasia had told them about the quarrel as best she could, and they were both extremely perplexed and worried about it.

"Dunia," Raskolnikov forced himself to continue, "I don't want you to marry this man. When you see him tomorrow, you tell him where to go, so we don't have to smell his presence around here again."

"Dear God!" Pulcheria Alexandrovna exclaimed.

"Think what you are saying, Brother dear!" Dunia began angrily, but immediately brought herself under control. "You're in no state . . . you're tired. . . ." she said softly.

"Raving? Oh, no. You're marrying Luzhin for my sake. I don't want your sacrifice. Sometime before tomorrow you'd best write a letter, with your refusal. . . . Let me read it in the morning. That's all!"

"I cannot do that!" the offended girl cried out. "By what right—"

"Dunia, darling, you're angry, too. Stop. Tomorrow, don't you see . . ." His mother hurried over to Dunia in alarm. "We better go now."

"He's raving!" Razumikhin yelled tipsily, "or he wouldn't dare! Tomorrow he'll have this foolishness out of his system. . . . Today, though, he really did give the guy the bounce. Oh, he did it, all right. Well, now, the other fellow got mad, mind you . . . He was making speeches at us, showing off his learning. He left with his tail drooping, though."

"It's true, then?" Pulcheria Alexandrovna exclaimed.

"We'll see you tomorrow, Brother dear," Dunia said with compassion. "Mother, let's go. Good-bye, Rodia."

"Sister dear, you listen to me." Gathering his last strength, he echoed her. "I'm not raving. This marriage stinks to high heaven. Maybe I'm vile. But you mustn't be. One's enough.

Even if I'm vile I wouldn't call a sister like that a sister of mine. So it's me or Luzhin! Now, go. . . ."

"Despot! You've gone out of your mind!" Razumikhin roared, but Raskolnikov did not reply. Perhaps he no longer had the strength to reply. He lay down on the couch, completely exhausted, and turned to the wall. Dunia looked curiously at Razumikhin and her dark eyes flashed, and Razumikhin flinched under her gaze. Pulcheria Alexandrovna stood there nonplused.

"I can't possibly leave. I'll stay here somewhere," she whispered to Razumikhin almost in despair. "You see Dunia home."

"You'll ruin the whole thing!" Razumikhin, beside himself, whispered in return. "Anyway, let's go out on the stairs. Nastasia, a light! I assure you," he went on in a half whisper as they came out on the stairs, "he almost attacked the doctor and me this afternoon! Understand? Even the doctor! He went away so as not to irritate the patient, and I stayed downstairs to keep an eye on him. He got himself dressed and slipped by me, though. If you annoy him, he'll slip away, now, too—and at night—and he'll do something to himself."

"What are you saying?"

"What's more, Avdotia Romanovna cannot be left in those rooms you've got by herself! Just think where you're staying! As though that scoundrel Luzhin couldn't have gotten you better rooms . . . Excuse me, you know, I'm a little drunk and that's why my language got a little . . . don't pay any—"

"I could approach the landlady," Pulcheria Alexandrovna insisted. "I'll beg her to let Dunia and me sleep in some corner here tonight. I can't leave him like that, I cannot!"

They said this standing on the stairs right in front of the landlady's door. Nastasia was on the bottom step holding the light. Razumikhin was extremely excited. Half an hour earlier, seeing Raskolnikov home, in spite of the tremendous quantity of liquor he had drunk that evening, he had been perfectly alert and almost clearheaded, though he talked too much, as he himself acknowledged. Now he was on the edge of bliss. At the same time, all the liquor he had drunk seemed to rush at once and double strength to his head. He stood there holding both ladies by the hand, doing his best to persuade them, giving them his reasons with stunning frankness. No doubt to make himself more convincing, with almost every word he spoke he squeezed their hands until they hurt, and without feeling in the least inhibited, he seemed to be devouring Dunia with his eyes. From time to time they withdrew their hands in pain from his immense and bony paw. He not only failed to notice that anything was wrong but drew them to himself again the more strongly. If they had told him to jump down the stairs headfirst for their sake, he would immediately have done so, without thinking and without hesitating. Pulcheria Alexandrovna was worried about her son. This young man was no doubt a little eccentric and he was squeezing her hand a bit painfully; nevertheless, he had been providential for her, and so she had no wish to notice these eccentric little details. Although she shared her mother's anxiety and was not herself of a timid nature, Dunia was astonished and almost even afraid as her eyes met the wild, flashing, fiery glances of her brother's friend, and only the great trust inspired in her by Nastasia's stories about him prevented her from running away from this strange man and dragging her mother after her. She knew, too, that in a way it wasn't possible to run away from him anymore. After ten minutes or so she calmed down considerably. Razumikhin had the gift of being able to express his character instantly and entirely, no matter what mood he happened to be in, and people quickly knew with whom they were dealing.

"You can't go to the landlady, that's preposterous!" he yelled. "Maybe you are his mother, but you'll drive him out of his mind if you stay, and God knows what will happen then! Look. Here's what I'll do. Nastasia will stay with him for now. I'll take you both back to your place. You can't go out in the streets alone. Because in Petersburg we've got . . . well, never mind! . . . Then I'll run right back. I'll let you know how he is in a quarter of an hour, word of honor, whether he's asleep or not and so on. Then, look. Then, in a flash from your place to mine. Guests there. All drunk. I'll fetch Zosimov. He's the doctor who's been looking after him. He's waiting at my place right now. He's not drunk. That one's not drunk. That one is never drunk! I'll take him over to Rodia, then I'll come to your place immediately. That means within the hour you'll have two bulletins on him. And one from the doctor, mind you, from the doctor himself. That's not the same as getting one from me! If anything is wrong, I swear I'll bring you back here myself. If everything is all right, though, you can go to sleep. And I'll spend the night here, in the hall. He'll never know. I'll get Zosimov to spend the night at the landlady's, so he can be on hand. Well, right now, who does he need more, you or the doctor? You have to admit the doctor's more useful. Well, so you better go home! You can't go to the landlady. I can, but you can't. She won't let you, because . . . because she's a fool. She'd be jealous of Avdotia Romanovna, if you want to know, and of you too. Avdotia Romanovna without a doubt. She's quite a character. Quite a character! I'm a fool too, though! . . . Hell with it. Come on, now. Don't you believe me? Well, do you believe me or don't you?"

"Come along, Mother," Dunia said. "I'm sure he'll do as he says. He's brought my brother back to life already, and if the doctor will agree to spend the night here, what could be better?"

"You . . . you understand me—because you're an angel!" Razumikhin exclaimed ecstatically. "Let's go! Nastasia! You go right on up and sit outside with a light. I'll be back in fifteen minutes. . . ."

Although she no longer resisted, Pulcheria Alexandrovna was not fully convinced. Razumikhin took them both by the arm and practically dragged them down the stairs. He worried her. "He's a nice young man and efficient, but is he in any shape to do as he says? The condition he's in—"

"Ah, I understand. The shape I'm in, you think!" Razumikhin guessed her thoughts and interrupted them. He took giant strides along the pavement, and both the ladies had trouble keeping up with him, though he did not notice. "Hogwash! I'm drunk as a mooncalf, that is, but it isn't the point. Not liquor I'm drunk from. It's just that something hit me on the head soon as I saw you. . . . Well, damn me! Pay no attention. I'm laying it on. I'm unworthy of you. Absolutely unworthy! After I take you home I'll come down here to the canal and I'll pour a couple buckets' water on my head and then I'll be all set. . . . If you only knew how much I love you both! . . . Don't laugh. Don't get mad! You can get mad at everything, only don't get mad at me! I'm his friend. That means I'm your friend, too. That's the way I want it. . . . I had a premonition. . . . Last year, I had this feeling once. . . . It wasn't a premonition, really, though, because you just dropped from the blue. You know, I won't be able to sleep all night. . . . A little while ago Zosimov was worried he might go out of his mind. That's why he mustn't be annoyed."

"What do you mean!" exclaimed Raskolnikov's mother.

"Did the doctor himself really say that?" Dunia asked, alarmed.

"He did, but he's wrong, he's quite wrong. He gave him some medicine, powder, I saw it. Then you came. Ah! If you had come tomorrow it would have been better! Good thing we left. Zosimov will report to you in person about everything in an hour. . . . That guy is not drunk, you know! And I won't be drunk, either. . . . And why did I get so plastered? Because they got me into an argument, damn them! I swore I wouldn't argue! It's all bunk! I almost got in a fight! I left my uncle in charge there. . . . They want complete objectivity, that's what they're after. Anything to avoid being themselves! That's what they consider the acme of progress. Oh, if only they talked nonsense in their own original way, but as it is—"

"Listen," Pulcheria Alexandrovna timidly interrupted, but this merely provided fuel.

"Do you think," Razumikhin cried out, raising his voice still higher, "do you think I care if they talk nonsense? Hogwash! I love nonsense! Talking nonsense is man's only privilege that distinguishes him from all other organisms. If you keep talking big nonsense, you will get to sense! I am a man, therefore I talk nonsense. Nobody ever got to a single truth without talking nonsense fourteen times first. Maybe even a hundred and fourteen. That's all right in its own way. We don't even know how to talk nonsense intelligently, though! If you're going to give me big nonsense, better make it your own big nonsense, and I'll kiss you for it. Talk nonsense in your own way. That's almost better than talking sense in somebody else's. In the first case you're a man; in the second just a parrot! Sense will always be there, but life can be fenced in. There have been some sad cases. Well, what about us now? We are all—without exception, I tell you, in science, thought, culture, engineering, ideals, aspirations, in our liberalism, reason, experience, everything, everything, everything, everything, everything—we still sit in the freshman class in high school! We would rather live off other people's ideas—that's what we're used to! Not so? Isn't what I'm saying really so? Isn't it so?" Razumikhin shouted, shaking and squeezing both the ladies' hands. "Isn't it so?"

"Gracious, I don't know," said poor Pulcheria Alexandrovna.

"It's so, it's so . . . but I don't agree with you in every detail," Dunia added gravely, crying out at this point because he squeezed her hand so hard.

"It's so? You agree it's so? Well, after that, you . . . you . . ." he cried out blissfully, "you are the source of goodness, purity, wit, and . . . perfection! Give me your hand! Give it to me. . . . You give me yours, too. I want to kiss your hands. Here and now. On my knees!" He went down on his knees in the middle of the sidewalk, which was at the moment, fortunately, deserted.

"Stop, I beg you! What are you doing?" Pulcheria Alexandrovna cried out, alarmed in the extreme.

"Get up, get up!" Dunia laughed, though she, too, was alarmed.

"No, I won't. Not before you give me your hands! That's right. Okay, enough. Now I'll get up, and on we go! I'm a miserable mooncalf, I'm unworthy of you, and I'm drunk and ashamed of myself besides! I'm unworthy of loving you. But bowing down to you—that's a duty for everybody who isn't an out-and-out swine! And so I bowed down. . . . Here are your rooms. And Peter Petrovich—when Rodia kicked him out awhile ago he got what was coming to him! How dared he put you up in rooms like these! It's a scandal! You know what kind of people come here! After all, you're his bride-to-be, aren't you? Well, let me tell you, if he could do a thing like that, your bridegroom's a bastard!"

"Mr. Razumikhin, I do believe you have forgotten—" Pulcheria Alexandrovna began.

"Yes, yes, you are right! I forgot myself. I'm ashamed!" Razumikhin tried to make amends. "But . . . but . . . you mustn't be mad at me just because I talk like that! Because I really mean it, and not because . . . hmm! that would be vile. In short, it's not because I . . . toward you . . . hmm! Let it pass; I won't, I won't say why, I don't dare! . . . When he came to see us today, though, we all understood this man was not our kind. Not because of the fresh-from-the-barbershop smell he carried in with him, not because he was in such a hurry to show off his brains, but because it's clear that he's a creep and a charlatan, a clown and a Jew. You think he's clever? No, he's a fool. A fool! Well, is he a mate for you? Oh, my God! You see, ladies"—they had already mounted the stairs to their rooms, and he suddenly paused— "the guys over at my place are all drunk, but they're all honest, and though we all talk nonsense—for I must tell you, I talk nonsense too—still, in the long run, we will go on talking nonsense until we climb to something. Maybe to the truth, because we're on the right road, but Peter

Petrovich . . . he's not on the right road. Though I was cursing them out awhile ago—still, I respect them all. Even Zamiotov. If I don't respect him, I like him because he's such a young pup! Even that mule Zosimov—because he's honest and knows his business. . . . Enough, though. All told and forgiven. Forgiven? You do forgive me, don't you? Come on. I know this corridor. I've been here. There was some scandal there, in number three. . . . What's your room number, then? Eight? Well, just so you lock up at night. Don't let anybody in. I'll be back in fifteen minutes with news, half hour later again with Zosimov—you'll see! Good-bye for now, I'm on my way!"

"Good God, Dunia dear, what is going to happen?" Pulcheria Alexandrovna, nervous and afraid, said to her daughter.

"Calm yourself, Mother," Dunia replied, taking off her hat and veil. "Even though he seems to have come straight from a drinking bout, it was God himself sent this gentleman to us. We can depend on him, I assure you. Remember everything he's already done for Rodia—"

"Oh, Dunia, darling, Lord knows whether he'll come or not! How could I have consented to leave Rodia alone! That wasn't at all, not at all, the way I imagined I'd find him! How hard he was, as if he were not even glad to see us. . . ."

There were tears in her eyes.

"No, that's not true, Mother. You didn't really look. You were too busy crying. He's terribly upset because of a serious illness, and that's all."

"Oh, that illness! Something is going to happen, something is going to happen! And the way he spoke to you, Dunia!" her mother said, casting a quick look into her daughter's eyes to see what she was thinking, but already half comforted because Dunia was actually defending Rodia and so must have forgiven him. "I'm sure he'll think better of it tomorrow," she added.

"I'm sure he'll say exactly the same thing tomorrow—I mean, on this subject," Avdotia Romanovna cut in. There was no getting past that. It was precisely the point Pulcheria Alexandrovna was now too frightened to discuss. Dunia went up to her mother and kissed her. Quietly and closely, her mother embraced her. Then she sat down and nervously began waiting for Razumikhin's return. She timidly followed the movements of her daughter, who, also waiting, had folded her arms and started pacing back and forth across the room, lost in thought. This was an old habit of Dunia's, and when she resorted to it her mother somehow always feared breaking in on her meditation.

Razumikhin was funny, of course, the way he had suddenly been smitten with a drunken infatuation for Dunia. If one looked at her now, though, pacing the room with arms folded, and that pensive, melancholy look upon her, one could understand him easily enough, even without taking his condition into account. She really looked quite striking—tall, wonderfully well built, strong, and self-confident in a way that expressed itself in her every gesture yet did not deprive her movements of their own characteristic softness and grace. Her face looked like her brother's, but it was beautiful. Her hair was brown, a little lighter than her brother's. Her eyes were almost black, and they flashed with pride, and yet at times they seemed exceptionally kind. She was pale, but not sickly pale. Her face shone with freshness and health. Her mouth was a little small, her lower lip, which had something vivid and youthful about it, jutted out a little, and so did her chin. The only flaw to her handsome face, this nevertheless endowed it with a particular character, a certain pride. Her facial expression tended to be serious and pensive rather than gay, yet how attractive a smile appeared on that face. The way she laughed—gay, exuberant, wholehearted—also became her. And so Razumikhin, who was impulsive, spontaneously frank, rather simple, honest, strong as an ancient hero, quite drunk, and had never seen anything quite like her, lost his head at first glance. He had seen Dunia for the first time, what is more, at a moment when love and the anticipated joy of meeting her brother made her specially attractive. Then he had seen how her lower lip trembled indignantly in response to her brother's crude accusations. He could not resist.

When he had said drunkenly on the stairs awhile back that Raskolnikov's eccentric landlady, Praskovia Pavlovna, would be jealous, not only on Dunia's account but on Pulcheria Alexandrovna's too, for that matter, he had been telling the truth. Although Pulcheria Alexandrovna was forty-three, she still showed traces of her former beauty and seemed much younger than her years. This is generally true of women who remain serene in spirit, fresh in their impressions, and spontaneously warmhearted right to the edge of old age. One might add that in this way, and only in this way, they retain their beauty in old age too. Her hair was beginning to thin out and turn gray; around her eyes little crow's-feet had appeared some time ago; and her cheeks were hollow and wrinkled with grief and worry. And yet her face was beautiful. It was the image of Dunia's face twenty years later, except, of course, for the expression of the lower lip, which did not in her case jut forward as Dunia's did. She was sentimental, but not cloyingly so; shy and yielding, but only up to a certain point. There was a good deal to which she would defer, a good deal she would agree to, even though it went against the grain of her convictions. Yet there was always a certain borderline of honesty, principle, deep-seated conviction, no circumstances could persuade her to overstep.

Exactly twenty minutes after Razumikhin had left they heard two muffled, hasty knocks on the door. He was back.

"I won't come in, there's no time!" he said quickly when the door was opened. "He's sound asleep, out cold, quiet as can be, and I hope to God he goes on sleeping like that for ten hours. Nastasia's with him. I told her not to leave till I got back. Now I'm going to get Zosimov. He'll report to you. Then you better hit the sack yourselves. I can see you're exhausted."

And off he went, down the corridor.

"What an efficient and . . . devoted young man!" Pulcheria Alexandrovna exclaimed, quite overjoyed.

"He seems like a wonderful person!" Dunia said with a certain warmth, starting once more to pace up and down the room.

About an hour later they heard steps in the corridor and another knock on the door. The women had both been waiting. They had confidence in Razumikhin's promise this time, and as things turned out he actually did manage to get Zosimov. The latter had agreed at once to leave the party and go have a look at Raskolnikov, but it was with considerable reluctance and mistrust that he went to the ladies, not altogether trusting Razumikhin's intoxicated account of them. His vanity, however, was immediately soothed and flattered. He grasped the fact that they had been waiting for him as for an oracle. He stayed ten minutes exactly, and managed to convince Pulcheria Alexandrovna completely, and to calm her down. He spoke very sympathetically, yet with all the dignity and seriousness of a twenty-seven-year-old doctor at an important consultation. He did not digress from the subject or show any inclination to go into more personal or private matters with the two ladies. As soon as he came in he noticed how very good-looking Dunia was. From that moment and for the rest of his stay, he tried hard not to notice her at all and spoke only to Pulcheria Alexandrovna. All this afforded him tremendous inward satisfaction. As far as the patient was concerned, he said, he was in quite good shape at the moment. His observations led him to believe that illness was due not only to the harsh material conditions in which the patient lived, but also to certain emotional problems. "It is the product of a number of complex moral and material influences, so to speak; fears, anxieties, worries, certain ideas . . . and so on." Having noticed out of the corner of his eye that Dunia started listening most attentively, Zosimov expanded a little on this theme. In response to Pulcheria Alexandrovna's hesitant, frightened question as to whether there might be any "suspicion of insanity," he replied calmly with an open smile that this was a great exaggeration. To be sure, he noticed the patient had a certain fixed idea, a kind of monomania. That was because he, Zosimov, was now doing some special research in this extremely interesting branch of medicine. They must bear in mind, though, that right up to that very day the patient had been delirious, and . . . and, of course, the arrival of his family would lend him strength and speed up his recovery. "Provided he manages to avoid any further unusual shocks," he added significantly. Then he got up and sedately and cordially took his leave, as they expressed their blessings, warm gratitude, and entreaties. Dunia even offered him her hand without his having sought it, and he left extremely satisfied with his visit and still more with himself.

"We'll talk about it tomorrow. You've got to get some sleep now!" Razumikhin said as he went out with Zosimov. "I'll be back tomorrow as early as I can with a report."

As soon as they were out in the street, "What a ravishing girl!" Zosimov said, practically smacking his lips.

"Ravishing? Did you say ravishing?!" Razumikhin roared, flinging himself suddenly on Zosimov and seizing him by the throat. "If you ever dare . . . Understand? Eh?" He shook him by the collar, pressed him against the wall, and shouted at him. "Did you get me?"

"Let go of me, you sot!" Zosimov freed himself. When his friend released him, Zosimov looked at him closely and suddenly burst out laughing. Empty-handed, Razumikhin stood facing him, in gloomy and serious thought.

"Of course, I'm an ass," he said, sullen as a storm cloud, "but so are you."

"Oh, no, old pal, not at all. I don't even dream of such foolishness."

They walked in silence. Only as they approached Raskolnikov's place did Razumikhin, who was quite worried, break it.

"Look," he said to Zosimov, "I know you're a nice enough guy. On top of all your bad qualities, though, you're a skirt-chaser, and I know it, one of the worst. You are weak, nervous, self-indulgent trash. You're unreliable. You've grown fat. You can't refuse yourself anything. Now I call that dirty because it leads straight into the dirt. You've been so self-indulgent, I must say I really don't understand how you can go on being a good doctor, and a self-sacrificing one at that. He sleeps on a feather bed (a doctor, mind you!), yet he gets up nights for a patient! Another three years, you won't be getting up for your patient any more. . . . Well, goddamn it, that's not the point. The point is you're going to spend the night in the landlady's apartment (it's all right with her, but don't think it didn't take some persuading!), and I'll be in the kitchen. That'll give you a chance to get to know her a little better. Not what you're thinking! There isn't even a suspicion of that—"

"I'm not thinking at all."

"Here, old pal, you have diffidence, reserve, modesty, fierce chastity, and yet—just take a breath and she melts, she melts like wax! For God's sake, save me from her! She's so goddamned *avenante*! I'll pay you back, I'll give you anything you want!"

Zosimov laughed even more openly than before.

"You've really worked yourself up into a tizzy! What good is she to me, though?"

"She's not much trouble, I assure you. Just gabble away as you like, so long as you sit down beside her and talk. What's more, you're a doctor, aren't you? Start curing her of something. I swear you won't regret it. She's got a piano. I play a little, you know. I've got a song there, a real Russian song, it goes, 'The tears I shed are burning hot . . .' She's got a taste for the real thing. Well, it all started with that little song. You, though, you're a regular virtuoso on the piano, a maestro, a Rubinstein. . . . I assure you you won't regret it!"

"What's up, did you promise her something, or what? Sign anything? Did you maybe promise to marry her?"

"Not at all! Absolutely not! She's not that type. Chebarov was after her, but—"

"Well, drop her, then!"

"You can't just drop her!"

"Why not?"

"Well, just because you can't, that's all! You see, old pal, you kind of get drawn in."

"Why did you lead her on, then?"

"I didn't lead her on at all. I may even have been the one that was led on, because I was so dumb. As far as she was concerned, though, it really wouldn't make any difference if it were you or me sitting beside her and sighing, as long as it was somebody. You see, old pal . . . I'm not sure I can put it into words, you see. . . . Look, now. You're pretty well up on your math, aren't you. . . . Well, why not start explaining the integral calculus to her? I'm not joking, I swear to God. Seriously. I mean it. She really wouldn't care. She'd look at you and she'd sigh. For a whole year on end. I went on telling her about the Prussian Upper House for two days running—because what's there to talk about with her?—and she just simmered and sighed! Don't go saying anything about love, though! She's so shy she goes into paroxysms. Just make it look as if you can't bear leaving her. Well; that's all you need. It's a terribly comfortable place, absolutely like home. You can read, write, lounge around, lie down. . . . If you're careful, you can even kiss her. . . ."

"What's in it for me, though?"

"Ach, I can't seem to get it through to you! Can't you see that you're absolutely made for each other! I thought of you even before. . . . That's the way you're going to end up anyway! Sooner or later, what difference does it make? Look here, old pal, this is the authentic feather-bed principle—oh, and it's not just the feather-bed principle, either! It'll draw you in. It's the world's final resting place, a cosmic anchor, quiet haven, earth's navel, it's the three fishes on which the world rests, quintessence of pancakes and juicy meat pies, the evening samovar, soft sighs, fur-lined coats, and warm, cozy stoves for sleeping! Why, it's practically as good as being dead, only you're alive, and you can enjoy the advantages of both at the same time! Oh, well, old pal, I've been talking nonsense! Time for bed. Look here. I wake up sometimes. Well, I'll go have a look at him. There's nothing to worry about, everything's fine. You might have a look at him once, too—just *pro forma,* you know. If there's anything wrong—delirium or high fever, for example, anything like that—wake me up right away. There couldn't be, though."

2

When Razumikhin woke the next morning between seven and eight he was preoccupied and serious. He had to face many new and unforeseen difficulties. He had never even imagined he would ever wake up this way. Everything that happened yesterday, down to the minutest detail, came back to him. He grasped that something extraordinary had been going on, that he had experienced something he never experienced before. At the same time he clearly understood that the fantasy flaring up within him was quite unrealizable—so much so, that he was ashamed of dreaming it. As quick as he could he transferred his attention to other, more immediate problems and perplexities, the legacy of that "triple-damned yesterday."

His worst memory was of having been so "low-down lousy" yesterday, not just because he'd been drunk but because he had taken advantage of a girl's position, abusing her bridegroom-to-be to her face in the stupidest kind of quick jealousy, without his even having known anything about how things were between them, or for that matter, anything much about the man himself. What right did he have so quickly and so rashly to judge the man? And who had asked him to sit in the judge's chair, anyway? Was it possible that a creature like Avdotia Romanovna would give herself in marriage to an unworthy man just for his money? So he, too, must have some good qualities. And the rooms? Well, when you came down to it, how was he supposed to know the rooms were like that? After all, he was getting an apartment ready. . . . Damn, how low-down it all was! And what kind of an excuse was being drunk? Pretty stupid alibi, made him seem even more low-down, actually. "*In vino veritas,* so I went and blurted out the truth, I mean all the muck of my crude and jealous feelings!" And was it allowed for him, Razumikhin, to entertain a fantasy like that, even an

eensy bit? Compared to a girl like that, who was he? Razumikhin, the drunken brute and rowdy braggart of yesterday?
Could he even make such a cynical, absurd comparison?
Razumikhin blushed in despair, and suddenly, as though on
purpose, he clearly recalled the way he had spoken to them
yesterday as they had all been standing on the stairs, the
way he had told them the landlady would be jealous on
Dunia's account. . . . It was unbearable. He hit the kitchen
stove so hard with his fist he dislodged a brick and hurt
his hand.

"Of course," he muttered to himself a minute later, with
a feeling of self-abasement, "of course I'll never be able to
straighten out those indecencies, ever . . . so I guess there's
not much point thinking about it. So I guess I better just
shut up about it and . . . just do what I've got to do . . .
and shut up about that, too. Not beg anybody's pardon. Not
say anything, and . . . and . . . Of course, it's all over and
done with!"

Nevertheless, he paid more attention to his clothes than
usual as he dressed. He had only one suit. Even if he had
another, he might not have worn it. "I just wouldn't. On
purpose." But he couldn't just be a cynic and a dirty slob.
He had no right hurting other people's feelings, especially
since they needed him and had themselves asked him to
come. He brushed his suit carefully. As for his linen, it was
tolerably clean, since he had always been rather fussy
about it.

He washed thoroughly that morning. Nastasia had some
soap. He washed his hair and his neck and especially his
hands. Then he faced the problem of whether or not he
should shave. (Praskovia Pavlovna had some excellent razors
that she had kept from the days of her deceased husband,
Mr. Zarnitsyn.) He decided rather angrily in the negative.
"Let it stay as it is! What if they thought I shaved to— Of
course, that's certainly what they would think! Damned if I
will! And . . . and the point is I'm crude and dirty, and I've
got saloon manners. And . . . and let's say I know, let's say
I'm, well, at least to some extent, well, a decent kind of
man . . . well, what's there to be so damn proud about, being
a decent man? Everybody ought to be decent. Cleaner, too,
and . . . and anyway (can't help remembering) some things
I've been guilty of . . . not that they were dishonest, but
still! . . . And my thoughts! Hmm. And I want to stack that
up beside a girl like Avdotia Romanovna! Well, to hell with

it! What do I care! I'll be dirty on purpose, and obscene, and I'll keep my saloon manners, and to hell with it! I'll even put it on thick!"

Zosimov, who had spent the night in Praskovia Pavlovna's parlor, found him talking to himself in this way. He was about to go home and was going to look in on the patient before he went. Razumikhin told him Raskolnikov was sleeping like a log. Zosimov left orders not to wake him. He would be back at eleven, he promised.

"And I hope he's still home," he added. "Damned if I know how to cure a patient who won't do as you say! Do you know if he's going to go see them, or whether *they're* coming over here?"

"They're coming here, I expect," Razumikhin answered, having grasped the implied point, "and no doubt they'll be talking about their family affairs. I'll leave. As their doctor, of course, you have more rights than me."

"I'm not their father confessor either. I'll look in, then leave. I've got enough to do at that."

"One thing bothers me," Razumikhin said, frowning. "I came out with some dumb things yesterday when I was drunk . . . I said some dumb things to him . . . well, for example, that you were scared he might be . . . inclined to insanity. . . ."

"You told the ladies that yesterday, too."

"I know it was dumb! I mean, really dumb! Tell me the truth, though. Did you really and truly believe it?"

"It's nonsense, I tell you! I don't believe it at all. When you took me to him you told me yourself he was a monomaniac. . . . Well, we piled on the fuel yesterday, or at least you did, with those stories about the house painter. A great little old subject for conversation, when he could have gone out of his mind! If I'd really known what went on at the police station, those bastards there suspecting him and insulting him and all that—I never would have permitted such a conversation! Monomaniacs are always making mountains out of molehills, though, and always mistaking the ridiculous for the real thing. . . . Far as I remember, Zamiotov's story about half clarified the business. Well, now! I know a case, a forty-year-old depressive who murdered an eight-year-old boy! Couldn't stand being laughed at, at table every day! Now, here's this poor guy all in rags, illness incipient, and along comes a smart-aleck policeman with a suspicion like that! Against a raving depressive! A man of extraordinary, mad vanity! That must be how the whole illness started! Well, now, what the hell! And this Zamiotov isn't such a bad guy, you know, but . . . hmm . . . you know, I don't think he should have been telling all about it yesterday. He's a terrible gossip!"

"Whom did he tell? Me? You?"

"Porfiry, too."

"So what if he told Porfiry?"

"Anyway, look here. Have you got any influence on the mother and sister? They could be a little more careful with him today. . . ."

"They'll manage," Razumikhin replied reluctantly.

"And what's he got against this Luzhin? He's a man with money. She doesn't seem to find him repulsive. . . . And they don't have a kopeck, do they?"

"What business is it of yours?" Razumikhin exclaimed. "How should I know if they've got a miserable kopeck or not? Ask them yourself, if you want to know. . . ."

"My God, you're dumb sometimes! Still drunk, I guess . . . Well, so long. Thank Praskovia Pavlovna for me for letting me spend the night. She locked herself in. I *bon-joured* her through the door, but she didn't answer. She was up at seven, though. She had the samovar brought into her room from the kitchen across the hall. . . . I didn't even manage to catch a glimpse of her. . . ."

At nine sharp, Razumikhin showed up at the rooms in Bakaleev's house. The ladies had long been expecting him with hysterical impatience. They had gotten up about seven or even earlier. He came in looking bleak as night and he greeted them awkwardly, for which he was immediately angry—at himself, of course. He had not reckoned on a reception like that. Pulcheria Alexandrovna rushed at him immediately, seized him by both hands, and all but kissed them. He glanced shyly at Dunia, but even on that proud face there was at that moment an expression of such gratitude and friendliness and, surprisingly to him, such complete respect (instead of the sarcastic looks and involuntary, poorly concealed contempt he expected) that actually he would have found it easier if they had met him with abuse, for this kind of thing was really too embarrassing. Luckily, there was at hand a ready-made theme for conversation, and he latched onto it as quickly as he could.

When she heard Raskolnikov "hadn't woken up yet," but that "everything was fine," Pulcheria Alexandrovna said,

"So much the better!" She needed very, very much to discuss something with him. They ordered tea and asked him to have some with them; expecting Razumikhin, they had not yet had any themselves. Dunia rang. A man in a torn coat appeared in response to the ring. He looked dirty. Tea was ordered and, finally, served, but everything was so dirty and all done in such an unpleasant way the ladies were ashamed. Just as Razumikhin was about to express himself vehemently on the quality of the rooms, he remembered about Luzhin, fell silent, and grew embarrassed. When, finally, Pulcheria Alexandrovna turned to him with an uninterrupted flow of questions, he was absolutely delighted.

He answered them, talking for three-quarters of an hour, constantly interrupted and cross-examined. He managed to convey to them all the most important and essential facts of the last year in the life of Rodion Romanovich as far as he knew them, finishing up with a circumstantial account of his illness. But he left a lot out that was best left out, the scene in the police station among other things, and all its consequences. They listened avidly to his story. Just at the point he thought he had finished, however, and his listeners were satisfied, they seemed to think he had scarcely even begun.

"Tell me what you think about— Oh, excuse me, but I still don't know your name?" Pulcheria Alexandrovna said hurriedly.

"Dmitry Prokofich."

"Well, you see, Dmitry Prokofich, I'd like very, very much to know . . . generally . . . how . . . what . . . what point of view he has now. . . . How shall I say . . . I mean, what's the best way to put it . . . I mean, what he likes and doesn't like? Is he always so irritable? What is it he wants, and what does he dream about, if you know what I mean? Is there anything specially that influences him now? In short, I'd like—"

"Mother, how can anyone answer all that at once!" Dunia said.

"Dear God, I never expected to find him that way, Dmitry Prokofich!"

"Of course, that's natural enough," he replied. "I have no mother, but, well, every year my uncle comes here to see me, and he fails to recognize me almost every time. Not even my appearance, I mean, and mind you, he's a clever man. You've been separated three years, and there's been a lot of water under the bridge. Well, what can I tell you?

I've known Rodion a year and a half. He's morose, gloomy, haughty, and proud. Lately he's been feeling touchy and depressed. Maybe he has been feeling that way a long time. He's magnanimous and kind. He doesn't like expressing his feelings and would rather perpetrate some cruelty than express in words what's in his heart. There are times when he doesn't seem to be suffering from depression at all, and he's just cold and unfeeling to the point of inhumanity, as though he had two contradictory characters that keep changing places. Sometimes he's terribly uncommunicative! No time for anybody, everything's in his way, while actually he's just lying around, not doing a thing. No jokes, and that's not because he lacks wit, but as though he had no time for such trifles. He doesn't listen to what people say. He's never interested in what everybody happens to be interested in at any given moment. He's got an awfully high opinion of himself. And it would seem he's got some right to it. What else can I say? I think your arrival will have an excellent influence on him."

"Would to God it did!" Pulcheria Alexandrovna cried out, greatly disturbed by Razumikhin's account of her Rodia.

At last Razumikhin looked at Dunia more boldly. He had kept glancing at her during the conversation, but furtively, for an instant at a time only, withdrawing his eyes again immediately. Dunia either sat close to the table and listened attentively to what he had to say, or she got up and started pacing the room from corner to corner again in her usual way, arms folded and lips pressed tight, asking a question occasionally without ceasing to pace up and down, lost in thought. She, too, had a habit of not listening to what was said. She was wearing a dark dress of flimsy material, and about her neck was a white transparent scarf. Razumikhin could tell right away that the two women were extremely poor. If Dunia had been dressed like a queen, he would not have been afraid of her at all. Now that he noticed how poorly dressed she was and how hard up they both looked, perhaps for that very reason, fear gripped his heart, and every word he spoke, every gesture he made, frightened him. For a man who even under normal conditions had no great confidence in himself, that was very inhibiting, needless to say.

"You've told us a lot of strange things about my brother's character, and you told it . . . you were very fair. That's good. Before, I couldn't help thinking you were a bit in awe of him," Dunia observed, smiling. "I'd guess it's also true he needs a woman around," she added, lost in thought.

"I didn't say that. Maybe you're right, though. Only—"

"What?"

"He doesn't love anybody. Maybe he never will," Razumikhin said abruptly.

"You mean he's not capable of love?"

"You're an awful lot like your brother, you know, Avdotia Romanovna. I mean in everything!" he blurted out suddenly, much to his own surprise. At the same time he realized what he had just been saying about her brother, and turned red as a lobster. Dunia couldn't help laughing when she looked at him.

"You may both be mistaken as far as Rodia is concerned," Pulcheria Alexandrovna said, a bit piqued. "I'm not talking, Dunia dear, about the way he is now. What Peter Petrovich writes in his letter, and even what you and I presumed, may be mistaken. You simply cannot imagine, though, Dmitry Prokofich, how moody and—how should I put it—how capricious he has always been. I could never trust his character, even when he was only fifteen. I'm convinced he might do something now nobody would think of doing. . . . Why, take something that happened not so long ago. You remember a year and a half ago how he was almost the death of me, what an awful shock he gave me and how he almost drove me out of my mind when he got it into his head to marry that . . . the daughter of that Zarnitsyn, his landlady?"

"Do you know the details of that story?" Dunia asked.

"Do you think," Pulcheria Alexandrovna went on heatedly, "my tears, my appeals, my illness, even the possibility of my dying of grief, could have stopped him? Or our poverty? He would have stepped over all obstacles, perfectly calm. But he loves us, doesn't he? Doesn't he?"

"He never told me anything about that story himself," Razumikhin replied cautiously, "but I did hear something about it from Mrs. Zarnitsyn. She's not much of a storyteller either, and what I heard, well, you see, it's a bit strange."

"What did you hear?" both ladies asked at the same time.

"Actually, it wasn't anything so very special. I learned this marriage—which was all set and didn't come off only because of the bride's death—wasn't to Mrs. Zarnitsyn's liking at all. . . . I also heard the bride wasn't much to look at, rather homely, as a matter of fact . . . and an invalid, and . . .

and a bit strange, and yet she had some real qualities, it would seem. She certainly must have had some real qualities, or the whole thing would be impossible to understand. . . . She didn't have a dowry, either, and he would not have reckoned on a dowry. . . . In general, it's hard to judge a case like that."

"I'm sure she was a nice girl," Dunia said tersely.

"God forgive me, when she died I couldn't help feeling better, though I'm not at all sure which of them would have ruined which—he her or she him," Pulcheria Alexandrovna concluded. Then she began to question him again cautiously about what had taken place the day before between Rodia and Luzhin. She would pause, and was constantly throwing quick looks at Dunia, which apparently Dunia did not like at all. This event seemed to disturb her more than anything else, to the point of real fear. Razumikhin went over the story again. This time, however, he added his own conclusion. He accused Raskolnikov directly of deliberately insulting Peter Petrovich. This time he found very little excuse for him in his illness.

"He made up his mind about it even before he got sick," he said.

"I think so too," Pulcheria Alexandrovna said, looking crestfallen. Nevertheless, it struck her that Razumikhin was cautious talking about Peter Petrovich this time, and even seemed to show him some respect. It struck Dunia, too.

"That's what you think of Peter Petrovich, then?" Pulcheria Alexandrovna could not help asking.

"I could hardly have another opinion about your daughter's future husband," Razumikhin replied firmly and with warmth. "And I'm not saying this out of mere convenient politeness, but because . . . because . . . well, because Avdotia Romanovna herself, of her own free will, has chosen this man as her husband. If I carried on about him yesterday, that was because yesterday I was disgracefully drunk and still . . . beside myself. Yes, I was beside myself, out of my mind, off my rocker. No doubt about it. And today I'm embarrassed!" He blushed and fell silent. Dunia blushed too, but did not break her silence. From the moment they started talking about Luzhin she did not utter a single word. Without her support, Pulcheria Alexandrovna seemed to hesitate. Continually looking at her daughter and faltering, she said finally that there was one thing that bothered her a lot.

"You see, Dmitry Prokofich . . ." she began. "Dunia, dear, is it all right for me to be quite frank with Dmitry Prokofich?"

"Of course," she said seriously.

"Here it is, then," she began hastily, as though relieved by this dispensation to tell of her trouble. "We received a note from Peter Petrovich quite early this morning. This was an answer to the announcement of our arrival. He was supposed to meet us at the station yesterday, you see. He promised he would. He sent some lackey to the station to meet us instead, who was supposed to show us to these rooms, to this address. Peter Petrovich had told him to tell us that he would come see us this morning in person. Instead we got a note from him this morning. . . . You better read it for yourself. There's one point that disturbs me very much. . . . You'll see the point I'm referring to for yourself, and . . . tell me your frank opinion, Dmitry Prokofich! You know better than anyone what Rodia is like, and you're in a better position than anyone to give us advice. I must warn you, Dunia has made up her mind already. She had it made up from the very beginning. But I, I still don't know what to do, and . . . and I was just waiting for you."

Razumikhin unfolded the note, dated the day before, and read:

Dear Madame, Pulcheria Alexandrovna, I have the honor to inform you that, due to unforeseen obstacles, I was unable to meet you at the station platform as planned, but sent instead a very efficient man with that purpose in mind. Because of Senate affairs that brook no delay, I am likewise forced to deprive myself of the honor of meeting you tomorrow morning, and also because I do not wish to stand in the way of your interview with your son, Avdotia Romanovna's with her brother. I hope, however, to have the honor of visiting you and paying my respects to you in your apartment tomorrow evening at eight o'clock precisely. I herewith make so bold as earnestly and sincerely to request in addition to this, however, that Rodion Romanovich not be present in the course of our interview, inasmuch as when I visited him in his illness yesterday he insulted me in an unprecedentedly discourteous manner, and inasmuch also as I would wish to hear from you personally a necessary and circumstantial explanation of a certain point, concerning which I would like to know your personal interpretation. In anticipation, I have the honor to inform you that if, in spite of my request, I meet the aforementioned Rodion Romanovich, I should feel compelled to withdraw myself immediately, and in such an instance you would have only yourselves to blame. I write on the assumption that Rodion Romanovich, who seemed so ill at the time of my visit, suddenly recovered two hours later, and therefore, being in condition to leave his house, may also pay you a visit. Of the aforementioned I was convinced yesterday by my own eyes when I saw him give away, in the apartment of a certain drunkard who had been trampled by horses and killed as a result, to said drunkard's daughter, a young lady of notorious conduct, as much as twenty-five rubles, under the pretext of funeral expenses—a fact which surprised me exceedingly, knowing as I did the trouble you had collecting this sum. Assuring you withal of my pronounced esteem for your honored daughter, I beg you to accept the devotion of, Your humble servant, P. Luzhin.

"What should I do now, Dmitry Prokofich?" said Pulcheria Alexandrovna, almost in tears. "How can I ask Rodia not to come? Yesterday it was he who demanded so insistently that we refuse Peter Petrovich; now we are ordered not to receive him! He'll come on purpose, though, as soon as he finds out. Then what?"

"Do as Avdotia Romanovna has decided," Razumikhin replied calmly and at once.

"Oh, good Lord! She says . . . God knows what she says. She doesn't bother explaining what she means by it to me! She says it would be better, I mean, not just that it would be better, but that it is for some reason absolutely necessary Rodia should be here at eight this evening, and they should meet without fail. . . . I didn't even want to show him the letter, mind you; by hook or by crook I wanted to keep him away, with your help . . . because he's so . . . irritable. . . . And I don't understand any of this business about the drunkard who died, and this daughter of his, or how he could give away all the money he had left . . . money which—"

"Which was so hard to come by, Mother," Avdotia Romanovna added.

"Yesterday he was not himself," Razumikhin said thoughtfully. "If you knew what he did yesterday in a tavern, clever as it was . . . hmm! About the dead man and about the young woman, he actually did tell me something about it last night as we were on our way home, but I didn't understand a word of it. . . . Last night I was myself a bit—"

"I think, Mother dear, we had best go to him ourselves. Once we're there, I'm sure we'll see at once what is called for. And it's high time, too—good Lord, it's past ten o'clock!" she exclaimed, after she glanced at a splendid gold-enameled watch hanging from her neck on a delicate Venetian chain. It clashed badly with the rest of her outfit. "A present from the bridegroom," Razumikhin reflected.

"Oh, it's high time! It's time, Dunia dear, yes, it's time!" Pulcheria Alexandrovna flurried about in alarm. "If we take so long getting there, he might assume we're angry because of yesterday. Oh, good Lord."

She hurriedly put on her hat and veil as she said this. Dunia put on her things, too. Razumikhin could not help noticing that her gloves were not merely shabby, but actually had holes. Yet the obvious poverty of their dress gave both ladies a special aura of dignity. Razumikhin looked at Dunia with awe, and was proud to escort her. "The queen," he thought to himself, "mending her stockings in prison must have looked every inch the queen as she mended, far more than on the most elaborate ceremonial occasions."

"Good Lord!" Pulcheria Alexandrovna exclaimed, "who could have thought I'd be afraid of meeting my own son— my dear, dear, dear Rodia—as I'm afraid of meeting him now. I am afraid, Dmitry Prokofich!" she repeated, looking at him timidly.

"Don't be afraid, Mother," Dunia said, kissing her. "You had best believe in him. I do."

"Oh, good Lord!" the poor woman exclaimed, "of course I believe in him. But I haven't slept all night long!"

They went out into the street.

"You know, Dunia, as soon as I dozed off this morning I started dreaming of poor dead Martha Petrovna. She was all in white. She came up to me. She took me by the hand, shook her head at me, and looked at me so sternly, as though she were blaming me. . . . That's not a good omen, is it? Oh, good Lord, Dmitry Prokofich, I didn't tell you, Martha Petrovna died?"

"No, you didn't. Who is Martha Petrovna?"

"She died suddenly, and can you imagine—"

"Later, Mother," Dunia interrupted. "He still doesn't know who Martha Petrovna is."

"Ah, you don't know? And here I thought you knew all about it. I hope you'll forgive me, Dmitry Prokofich, my mind doesn't seem to be functioning properly these days. True, I tend to think of you as heaven-sent for us, so I was sure you knew all about it. I think of you as one of the family. . . . Don't be angry with me for talking like this. Good Lord, what happened to your right hand! Did you hurt it?"

"Yes, I hurt it," murmured Razumikhin, overjoyed.

"Sometimes I speak out with too much feeling. Dunia scolds me for it. . . . But, good Lord! What a box he's living in! I wonder if he's up yet? And that landlady of his calls *that* a room? Look, you say he doesn't like emotional scenes, so maybe he'd be annoyed with my . . . weaknesses? Won't you tell me what to do, Dmitry Prokofich? How should I behave? You know, I feel as though I were wandering around like a lost soul."

"If you see him frowning, don't question him too closely about anything. Don't ask him too much about his health, especially. He doesn't like it."

"How hard it is to be a mother, Dmitry Prokofich! Well, here are the stairs. What a terrible stairway!"

"Mother, you look so pale, dear, take yourself in hand," Dunia said to her affectionately. "I'm sure, anyway, he'll be happy to see you, and here you are tormenting yourself so," she said. Her eyes were flashing.

"Wait. I'll go look and see if he's awake."

Slowly the ladies followed Razumikhin up the stairs. When they reached the landlady's apartment on the fourth floor, they noticed her door was open a tiny crack, and a pair of swift dark eyes examined them from out the darkness. When their eyes met, the door was suddenly slammed shut. It slammed shut with such a bang that Pulcheria Alexandrovna almost cried out in fright.

"He's well! He's all well!" Zosimov shouted at them as they came in. Having arrived ten minutes earlier, he was sitting on the same corner of the couch as yesterday. Raskolnikov sat in the opposite corner, dressed, washed, and combed, a rather unusual condition for him recently. The room filled up at once, yet somehow Nastasia managed to make her way in behind the visitors and stood there listening.

Raskolnikov actually did seem almost well, especially compared with the way he had looked the night before. Yet he was morose, distraught, and quite pale. He looked wounded, like someone who had sustained great physical injury. His brows were drawn together, his lips compressed, his gaze feverish. He said little, and reluctantly, as though it went against the grain, or as though he were fulfilling some duty. A certain restlessness occasionally expressed itself in his movements.

All he lacked was a sling on his arm or a bandage on his finger to complete his resemblance to a man who has somehow hurt his finger painfully or sprained his arm. When his mother and sister came in, however, even that pale and gloomy face flickered for a moment, as though with light. Yet this merely seemed to replace his former look of melancholy distraction with one of more intense anguish. The light soon darkened, but the anguish remained. Zosimov, observing and studying his patient with all the fresh zeal of a novice, noted with surprise as his mother and sister arrived that he responded to them not with joy but with a certain secret determination to endure another hour or two on the rack, since there was no way out. He noted how almost every word of the conversation that followed seemed to touch some wound of his patient's, irritating it. Yet at the same time he was amazed how yesterday's monomaniac, raging over the least little word, now seemed able to control himself and hide his feelings.

"Yes, I can see it myself, I'm almost well," Raskolnikov said, and politely kissed his mother and sister. Pulcheria Alexandrovna practically beamed. "And I don't say that the way I did *yesterday*," he added. He turned to Razumikhin and gave his hand a friendly squeeze.

"I must say I was actually surprised to find him in such good shape today," Zosimov began. He was grateful to them. He had been quite unable to keep the conversation going for the ten minutes he had been with the patient. "If this keeps up for another three-four days, he'll be back just about where he was a month or two ago, or maybe it was three. . . . This whole business must have been fermenting for quite a while, no? You'll admit now, won't you, that you were at fault?" He smiled cautiously, as though he were still afraid something might irritate the patient.

"It could very well be," Raskolnikov answered coldly.

"I'd go so far as to say," Zosimov continued, having worked up steam, "that your complete recovery depends mostly on you and you alone. Now that I can discuss it with you, I'd like to suggest that you have to root out the original, the radical causes, so to speak, that shaped your illness. You'll really recover only then. You may even get worse if that isn't done. I have no way of knowing what these original causes might be. You surely must know them, though. You're a clever man. No doubt you've been keeping tabs on yourself. It would seem to me that the beginning of your illness coincided with your leaving the university. You can't just go on without doing anything. It would seem to me that work and some definite aim in life might help you a great deal."

"Yes, yes, you're absolutely right. . . . I'll go back to the university as soon as I can. Then everything will really slide, just slick as grease."

Zosimov had started counseling partly to make an impression on the ladies, and he was certainly taken a bit aback when he finished his speech and glanced at his listener, noticing on his face an unmistakably sardonic expression. This lasted only a moment, though. Pulcheria Alexandrovna was very soon thanking Zosimov, especially for his visit to their lodgings the night before.

"You mean you saw him last night?" Raskolnikov asked, seemingly alarmed. "That means even after your trip you didn't get any sleep?"

"That was earlier than two o'clock, Rodia dear. At home, Dunia and I never go to bed before two o'clock anyway."

Raskolnikov added: "I don't know how to thank him either," and he frowned suddenly and looked down. "Leaving the question of money aside"—he turned to Zosimov—"I hope you'll forgive my referring to it, but I just don't know what I've done to deserve all the special attention you've been lavishing on me. I just don't understand . . . and . . . and . . . because I just don't understand, it's hard for me. I tell you this frankly."

"Don't be upset." Zosimov forced himself to laugh. "Put it this way. You're one of my first patients. We doctors, when we start practicing, we love our patients as if they were our children. Why, some doctors practically fall in love with them. And, mind you, I'm not exactly swarming with patients."

"I didn't even mention him," Raskolnikov added, pointing to Razumikhin. "I've given him nothing but trouble and insults."

"My, he's laying it on thick! What's the matter with you, you feeling sentimental today, or what?" Razumikhin roared.

If he had been a shrewder observer he might have noticed that sentimentality hardly entered into it. On the contrary. Avdotia Romanovna noticed, however. She observed her brother steadily and apprehensively.

"As for you, Mother dear, I dare scarcely even say," he went on, as though reciting a lesson learned that morning. "It was only today I could begin to imagine what you must have gone through yesterday while you were waiting for me to return." After he said this he smiled. He held out his hand to his sister silently. This time there was a flash of genuine feeling in his smile. Pleased and grateful, Dunia immediately seized and warmly pressed the hand held out to her. It was the first time he had turned to her since their falling-out of the day before. At sight of this wordless yet decisive reconciliation between brother and sister their mother's face lit up with pride and joy.

"That's what I like about him!" Razumikhin whispered, prone, as usual, to exaggerations, and turning energetically on his chair. "He has these—gestures!"

"And how well he brings it all off," his mother thought to herself. "What noble impulses he has. How simply and delicately he ended that whole misunderstanding of yesterday's with his sister—just stretching out his hand at the right moment and giving her the right look. . . . What beautiful eyes he has, and how beautiful his whole face is! He's even better looking than Dunia. . . . But, my God, what clothes! How horribly he's dressed! Afanasy Ivanovich's errand boy Vasia is better dressed than he is! And I'd like to . . . I'd like to throw my arms around him and hug him . . . and cry a bit. . . . But I'm afraid to. I'm afraid. Somehow, he's . . . oh, God . . . He's talking affectionately now, but I'm afraid! But what am I afraid of?"

"Ah, Rodia," she said suddenly, hastening to reply to his remark, "you won't believe how . . . unhappy . . . Dunia and I were yesterday! Now that it's all over and done with and we're all happy I can tell you. Just think, we come rushing to greet you straight from the train, and this woman—oh, there she is; hello, Nastasia!—well, all of a sudden she tells us that you've been having fever fits and that you've just slipped away from the doctor, delirious, out into the street, and they've just gone off to find you. You can't believe how we felt! Immediately I thought of Lieutenant Potanchikov and how he came to a tragic end. He was an acquaintance of ours, a friend of your father's. You wouldn't remember him, Rodia. He came down with fever fits too. And he ran straight out into the yard and fell into the well, and it was the next day before they could get him out. And of course we thought of even worse things. We wanted to rush out and look for Peter Petrovich, as though he could help us . . . because we were alone, you see, completely alone. . . ." Her voice stretched out on a plaintive note, and suddenly she fell silent altogether. She remembered that in spite of the fact that everyone was "quite happy again," it was still fairly dangerous to mention Peter Petrovich.

"Yes, yes . . . all that. Of course. It's shameful," murmured Raskolnikov in reply, but with such an abstract expression, as though he were not really paying any attention, that Dunia looked at him in surprise.

"Now what was I about to say?" He tried hard to remember. "Oh, yes. Please, Mother dear, and you too, Dunia, you mustn't think I didn't really want to go over to your place today and was just waiting for you to come here first."

"What *are* you talking about, Rodia!" cried Pulcheria Alexandrovna, surprised in turn.

"Is he answering merely because he feels obliged to, or what is it he's doing?" Dunia thought. "He's begging our pardon and making amends as though he were reciting his catechism or some lesson he'd memorized."

"As soon as I woke up I wanted to go, but I couldn't, on account of my clothes. I forgot to tell her yesterday . . . to tell Nastasia . . . to wash out the blood. . . . I've only just gotten dressed."

"Blood! What blood?" cried Pulcheria Alexandrovna in alarm.

"It's . . . please don't fret. The blood is only because yesterday, while I was wandering around in a daze, I came across a man who'd been crushed . . . a certain clerk—"

"In a daze? But you remember it all," Razumikhin interrupted.

"That's right," Raskolnikov replied with a certain special care. "I remember it all. Down to the smallest detail. But if you were to ask why I did it, why I went there, why I said what I did, I couldn't explain very well."

"That's a very well-known phenomenon," Zosimov interjected. "Sometimes you have an action that's performed with superb skill, most subtly, and yet without control, the movements all originating in morbid stimuli. As in a dream."

"I suppose it's a good thing he takes me practically for mad," Raskolnikov reflected.

"I suppose people do things like that even when they're healthy," Dunia said, throwing a disturbed glance at Zosimov.

"That's a fairly accurate observation," the latter replied. "In a way there's only a fine shade of difference between the healthy and the deranged. Maybe those we call 'sick' are a bit more deranged than we are—after all, we need to draw a line somewhere. But there's practically no such thing as a normal man. In ten thousand, it might even take several hundred thousand, you might find one. Even then he'd probably turn out to be a poor example."

They all frowned when Zosimov incautiously blurted out the word "deranged" as he was chattering away. Raskolnikov sat as though indifferent, deep in thought, with a strange smile on his pale lips. He continued to brood.

"I interrupted you," Razumikhin said quickly. "Who was this guy who got trampled, anyway?"

"What?" Raskolnikov seemed to come awake. "Oh, yes. . . . Well. I got blood on me as I was helping carry him to his apartment. . . . You know, Mother dear, one thing I did yesterday was unforgivable. I really wasn't in my right mind. I gave away all the money you sent me . . . to his wife . . . for the funeral. She's a widow now, consumptive, a pathetic woman . . . three small orphans . . . hungry . . . the cupboard's bare . . . and there's one more daughter. . . . If you had seen, you might have given it away yourselves. . . . But I didn't have any right to. I admit it. Especially since I knew how you came by that money. To help others out, you have to have the right. Or else, *Crevez, chiens, si vous n'êtes pas contents!*" He laughed. "Isn't that right, Dunia?"

"No, it's not right," Dunia firmly replied.

"Hah! you and your . . . intentions!" he murmured, sneering, and looking at her almost with hatred. "I should have known. . . . Well, it's a good thing. For you, all the better. But you'll reach a certain point, and if you can't go beyond it, you'll be unhappy. If you go beyond it, though, you might even be more unhappy. . . . But that's all nonsense!" he added irritably, vexed that what he had been saying had involuntarily carried him away. "I only wanted to beg your pardon, Mother," he sharply and abruptly concluded.

"Enough, Rodia. I'm convinced that everything—everything you do—is excellent!" his mother said, overjoyed.

"Don't be too sure," he answered, twisting his mouth into a smile. A silence followed. A certain tension had run through the whole conversation, the silence, the reconciliation, the forgiveness. Everyone had felt it.

"As if they were afraid of me," Raskolnikov thought, glancing at his mother and sister from beneath lowered brows. The longer she remained silent, the more timid Pulcheria Alexandrovna really did become.

"And yet when they weren't around I loved them," flashed into his head.

"You know, Rodia, Martha Petrovna died!" Pulcheria Alexandrovna suddenly burst out.

"Who's Martha Petrovna?"

"Oh, my goodness, Martha Petrovna Svidrigailov, of course! I wrote you about her many times."

"A-a-ah, yes, I remember. So she died? So she really died?" Suddenly he shook himself, as though he were shaking off sleep. "So she died, did she? What of?"

"Just think, it was so sudden!" Pulcheria Alexandrovna hastened to add, encouraged by his curiosity. "At exactly the same time I sent that letter off to you. That very same day! It would seem that horrible man was the cause of her death, too. They say he gave her a terrible beating."

He asked his sister: "Did they really live like that?"

"No. Quite the contrary. He was always very patient with her. Polite, even. I would say he was often a bit too indulgent to her whims, actually. For seven whole years. Then suddenly for some reason he lost patience."

"If he held out for seven years, he couldn't be all that

horrible! You aren't sticking up for him, are you, Dunia dear?"

"No, no, he was a horrible man! I can't imagine anyone more horrible," Dunia, almost with a shudder, responded. She frowned and grew thoughtful.

"It happened in the morning at their place," Pulcheria Alexandrovna hastened to continue. "After he beat her she ordered the horses to be harnessed so she could drive to town after dinner. She always drove to town then. They say she had a good appetite at dinner—"

"Beating and all?"

"Well, you see, it was her . . . habit. As soon as she ate she went straight to the bathhouse so she wouldn't be late for the drive. . . . She was taking some kind of bath cure. There's a kind of cold spring there, and every day she used to bathe in it regularly. Only this time she had a stroke as soon as she entered the water!"

"No wonder!" said Zosimov.

"Did he beat her badly?"

"What difference does it make?" Dunia said.

"Hmm! Yet all this nonsense seems to amuse you," Raskolnikov said irritably and (it almost seemed) desperately.

"What am I supposed to talk about then, darling!" Pulcheria Alexandrovna burst out.

"What's the matter with you, are you afraid of me, or what?" he said with a twisted smile.

"That's actually true," Dunia said, looking directly and sternly at her brother. "She was crossing herself in fear as she came up the stairs."

His face was twisted as though by a spasm.

"Dunia, what are you saying! Please don't be angry, Rodia. . . . Dunia, why do you go on like that!" Pulcheria Alexandrovna said, confused. "This much is true. All the way here in the train I dreamed how we'd be seeing each other, how we'd tell each other all there was to tell. . . . I was so happy, I didn't see the road! But what am I saying! I'm happy now, too. . . . Dunia, you shouldn't talk like that! I'm happy, Rodia, just to be seeing you—"

"It's all right, Mother," he mumbled in confusion, squeezing her hand but not looking at her. "We'll manage to have a talk!"

This was what he said, but suddenly he turned pale. The horrible sensation of a while ago passed through him again with a deathly cold. Suddenly, and with a dazzling clarity, he understood that he had just uttered a terrible lie, that not only would he never be able to manage to have a talk, but that there was no longer anyone to talk to or anything to *say*. The impact of this agonizing thought was so strong, for a moment he almost forgot himself entirely; he rose from his seat, and without glancing at anyone, started walking out of the room.

"What now?" Razumikhin shouted, seizing him by the arm.

He sat down again and began to look around him in silence. They all stared at him, bewildered.

"Well, why are you all being so dull!" he suddenly cried out, quite unexpectedly. "Say something! What's the point of just sitting there! Somebody say something. . . . Here we are, all together, and everybody's quiet. . . . Say anything!"

"Thank God! For a moment I thought what happened to him yesterday was about to start all over again," Pulcheria Alexandrovna said, crossing herself.

"Why did you do that, Rodia?" Dunia asked mistrustfully.

"It's nothing. I just remembered something," he replied. Suddenly he laughed.

"Well, as long as there was something, I guess it's all right. I myself was beginning to think . . ." Zosimov muttered, rising from the couch. "But I've got to go now. Perhaps . . . if you're in . . . I'll call again. . . ."

He took leave of them and went out.

"What a fine man!" said Pulcheria Alexandrovna.

"Oh, yes, a fine man. Excellent. Well educated, clever," Raskolnikov said suddenly, speaking with surprising rapidity and with a certain unusual animation. "I don't remember anymore where it was I met·him before I took sick. . . . Seems I met him somewhere. . . . Well, now, here's a good man, too!" He nodded at Razumikhin. "Do you like him, Dunia?" he asked her, and for some unknown reason he laughed.

"Very much," Dunia replied.

"Ooh, you hog, you!" Razumikhin got up from his chair, terribly embarrassed and blushing. Pulcheria Alexandrovna smiled softly, but Raskolnikov laughed thunderously.

"And where might you be going?"

"I also . . . I need—"

"Stay where you are; you don't need a thing! Just because Zosimov left, you think you've got to. Don't go. . . . But what time is it? Is it twelve? What a nice watch you have,

Dunia! Well, why are you all silent again? Seems I'm the only one around here who talks!"

"It was a present from Martha Petrovna," Dunia replied.

"And a very expensive one," added Pulcheria Alexandrovna.

"And so big! Almost not like a woman's."

"I like it like that," said Dunia.

"So it's not a gift from the bridegroom," Razumikhin thought. For some reason this cheered him.

Raskolnikov said: "And I thought it was a present from Luzhin."

"No. He hasn't given Dunia anything yet."

"Ah!" Then, looking at his mother, he said suddenly, "Do you remember how I was in love and wanted to get married?" She was struck by the unexpected twist and by the tone in which he said this.

"Of course, my dear, certainly!" Pulcheria Alexandrovna exchanged glances with Dunia and Razumikhin.

"Hmm! Yes, but what can I tell you? I don't even remember much. She was quite sick"—he lowered his eyes—"ailing all the time. She used to love giving to beggars, and she was always dreaming about a nunnery. Once when she started to tell me about it, she wept. Yes, I remember . . . I remember that very well. Sort of a . . . homely-looking thing. I don't know why I felt so attached to her, to tell you the truth, maybe because she was always sick. . . . If she had been lame or hunchbacked I might have loved her even more." He smiled thoughtfully. "Yes . . . it was a kind of spring madness. . . ."

"No," Dunia said with animation, "it wasn't just spring madness."

He looked hard and intently at his sister, but either he did not hear what she said or he did not understand her words. Deep in thought, he rose, went up to his mother, kissed her, returned to his place, and sat down.

"Why," said Pulcheria Alexandrovna, touched, "you're in love with her even now!"

"With her? Now? Oh, yes . . . you mean her! No. That's as if it were in another world . . . and so long ago. But then, everything that's going on around me seems as though it weren't going on here. . . ."

He looked at them attentively.

"You, too . . . it's as though I were looking at you from a thousand miles away. . . . Devil only knows why we're talking about it! Why do you ask?" He fell silent, vexed, chewing on his nails and lapsing once more into thought.

"What a miserable apartment, Rodia. It's like a coffin," Pulcheria Alexandrovna, breaking the oppressive silence, said suddenly. "I'm sure your apartment is half the reason you became such a melancholic."

"Apartment?" he vaguely replied. "Yes, the apartment had a lot to do with it. . . . I thought of that too. . . . But if you only knew, Mother dear, what a queer thought you expressed just now," he added suddenly, with a strange smile.

A little more of this company, of these relatives from whom he had been separated for three years, and of the intimate tone of the conversation (while it was quite impossible to talk about anything at all) would certainly have proved unbearable. There was a business matter, however, which could not be put off, which, one way or another, had to be resolved that very day. He had made up his mind about this when he had first wakened. Now he rejoiced in this *business matter* as a way out.

"Listen, Dunia," he began seriously and dryly. "For what happened yesterday, I'm sorry, of course. I do believe it's my duty, though, to remind you that I do not retract my main point. It's either me or Luzhin. Let me be vile. You must not. One's enough. You marry Luzhin, and I no longer consider you my sister."

"Rodia, Rodia! There you go again, the same as yesterday," Pulcheria Alexandrovna cried out in grief. "And why are you always calling yourself vile? I cannot bear it! It's exactly the same as yesterday—"

"Brother dear," Dunia replied firmly, and also dryly, "you are making one little mistake. I spent the night thinking about it, and I found out what it was. It seems to be this. You somehow imagine that I am preparing myself as a sacrifice to someone and for someone. That's not the way it is at all. I'm getting married for my own sake, because I find things hard. Of course, if I could be of some use to my kin, that would please me, but it's not the main reason."

"She's lying!" he thought to himself, chewing angrily at his nails. "She's a proud one! Refuses to admit she wants to play the benefactress! Oh, what low characters! They even love as though they were hating. . . . Oh, how I . . . hate them all!"

"I am, in short, marrying Peter Petrovich because I choose

the lesser of two evils. I intend to go through with everything honestly, everything he expects of me. So I won't be deceiving him. . . . Why did you just smile like that?"

She too flared up, and anger flashed in her eyes.

"So," he asked, smiling poisonously, "you'll go through with everything?"

"Up to a certain point. Both the manner and form of Peter Petrovich's courtship showed me right away what he was after. It may well be, of course, that he values himself too highly, but I hope he values me, too. What are you laughing at?"

"And why are you blushing? You're lying, Sister dear, you're lying on purpose, out of sheer feminine stubbornness, just to get your own way and spite me. . . . You cannot respect Luzhin. I've seen him. I talked to him. You imply that you're selling yourself for money, so you'd be doing something pretty low in any case, and I'm glad that you can at least blush for it!"

"That's not true, I'm not lying!" Dunia cried, losing all her self-possession. "If I were not convinced he values me and has a high opinion of me I would not marry him. I would not marry him if I were not, for my part, convinced I could respect him. Luckily I can get at the truth of the matter, and today at that. Such a marriage isn't vile, as you say it is! But even if you were right, even if I had made up my mind to do something vile, aren't you cruel to talk to me like that? What right have you to demand heroism from me when you may very well not be a hero yourself? That's despotism, that's coercion! If there's anyone I'm about to ruin, it's myself and nobody else . . . I haven't yet killed anybody! Why do you look at me like that? Rodia, why are you so pale? What's wrong? Rodia, darling!"

"Good Lord!" Pulcheria Alexandrovna cried out, "she made him faint!"

"No, no . . . nonsense . . . it's nothing! My head was whirling a bit. I didn't faint at all. . . . You're always worried about me fainting! What was I going to say? Oh, yes. How do you plan to get at the truth of the matter today, to convince yourself you can respect him, that he would . . . value . . . what was it, what did you say? I thought you said you'd— Or didn't I hear correctly?"

"Show him Peter Petrovich's letter, Mother," Dunia said.

Her hands trembling, Pulcheria Alexandrovna handed over the letter. He took it with great curiosity. Yet suddenly, before unfolding it, he looked at Dunia with a certain surprise.

"Strange," he said slowly, as though suddenly struck by a new thought. "Why am I making such a fuss? What is all the hollering about? Marry whom you like!"

He spoke as though to himself, and yet aloud. For some time he looked at his sister as though taken aback. Finally he unfolded the letter, but with that strange expression of astonishment still on his face. Slowly and attentively he began to read. He read it through twice. Pulcheria Alexandrovna was especially uneasy. They all expected something out of the ordinary.

After thinking it over a bit, he began. "I'm astonished," he said, handing the letter back to his mother, but not addressing anyone in particular. "Here he is, attending to matters of business—he's a lawyer, isn't he? And his talk even has a kind of . . . flourish to it . . . yet look how illiterate his writing is."

Everyone fidgeted. This was not what they had expected.

"They all write that way, though," Ruzumikhin noted.

"You've read it, then?"

"Yes."

"We showed him, Rodia, we were . . . putting our heads together, a little while ago," Pulcheria Alexandrovna said, embarrassed.

"It's the legal style, actually," said Razumikhin, "they still write legal papers that way."

"Legal? Yes, that's right, legal, businesslike . . . Not terribly illiterate, really, but not very literate, either. Businesslike!"

"Peter Petrovich does not conceal the fact that he had a poor education. He's proud of having made his own way," Dunia said, a little offended by the new tone her brother had taken.

"Oh, yes, and if he's proud, he's got something to be proud of, I don't deny that. I think you took offense, Dunia, because given that whole letter I chose to make such a frivolous remark. You're thinking I talked about such trifles on purpose, to take my spite out on you. There was something came into my head about his style, though, and it isn't entirely irrelevant. There's an expression he uses: 'You will have only yourself to blame.' It's clear and quite significant. And then he threatens to leave immediately if I show up. That would actually amount to abandoning you both if you're disobedient, and abandoning you after he himself asked you to come to Petersburg. Well, now, tell me, do you think it's all right to feel offended if that's the way Luzhin puts things? Suppose"—he pointed to Razumikhin—"he had written it. Or Zosimov. Or any of us."

"N-no," said Dunia. "I knew, of course, that he put it too crudely and that perhaps he didn't write properly. . . . You have a point there, Rodia. And I didn't expect—"

"It's expressed in legal language, and if you use legal language you can't write any other way. Maybe it came out coarser than he intended. But I'm afraid I have to disillusion you a bit. There's another expression in that letter. It's a slander on me, and it's vile enough. I gave that money yesterday to a crushed widow who has T.B. Not 'under pretext of the funeral,' but actually for the funeral, plain and simple. Not to the daughter—a girl, as he puts it, 'of notorious conduct' (and whom I saw yesterday for the first time in my life)—but directly to the widow. I think he's entirely too eager to smear me and stir up trouble between us. Again, it's expressed legalistically. I mean the intention is all too clear, and it's revealed in too much of a hurry. He's a clever man. To act cleverly, though, cleverness alone isn't enough. All this shows you the man he is. . . . I don't think he has valued you much. I tell you this only for your own benefit. Because I sincerely wish you well . . ."

Dunia did not answer. She had made up her mind some time back. She was only waiting for the evening.

"What have you decided, Rodia?" Pulcheria Alexandrovna asked, disturbed even more than before by his new, *businesslike* tone.

"What do you mean, 'decided'?"

"Well, you see, Peter Petrovich writes that you shouldn't be with us this evening, that he'll go away if you're there. So, will you . . . be there?"

"That isn't up to me to decide, of course. That's up to you two. If you aren't offended by Peter Petrovich making a demand like that, that is. Secondly, it's up to Dunia. I mean, if she's not offended either. For my part," he added curtly, "I'll do what seems best to you."

"Dunia has already decided," Pulcheria Alexandrovna was quick to say, "and I agree with her entirely."

"I've decided, Rodia," Dunia said, "to ask you to be present at this meeting. Earnestly I ask you to be present. Will you come?"

"I'll come."

"I would like to ask you to be with us, too, at eight o'clock," she said, turning to Razumikhin. "Mother, I'm inviting him, too."

"Excellent, Dunia," said Pulcheria Alexandrovna. "Just as you've decided, so let it be. I must say I feel better. I don't like pretending and lying. Better to tell the whole truth . . . Let Peter Petrovich be angry or not, as he chooses!"

4

At that moment the door opened quietly and a girl entered the room. She looked around timidly. Surprised and curious, they all looked at her. It was Sofia Semionovna Marmeladov. At first glance Raskolnikov did not recognize her. The day before he had seen her for the first time, under such circumstances and dressed in such clothes that he seemed to remember an altogether different person. Now he saw a modestly, rather shabbily dressed girl, quite young, still childlike, modest and attractive in manner, with a bright but somewhat cowed face. She was wearing a simple housedress and an old hat, long out of fashion. In her hands, however, she held yesterday's parasol. When she found the room unexpectedly full of people she became not merely embarrassed, she lost her head completely, panicked like a small child, and even made a move to withdraw.

"Ah, it's you?" Raskolnikov said, astonished. Suddenly he became embarrassed himself.

Immediately it occurred to him that his mother and sister knew about a certain girl "of notorious conduct" from Luzhin's letter. He had just protested against Luzhin's slander and had just mentioned having seen this girl for the first time, and suddenly there she was. He remembered that he had not protested the expression "of notorious conduct." This all flashed unclearly through his mind in an instant. When he took a better look, however, he suddenly realized that this downtrodden creature was downtrodden to such a degree that he felt sorry for her. She made a frightened move to run away, and something inside him seemed to heave.

"I wasn't expecting you," he said quickly, stopping her

with his look. "Please sit down. You come from Katherine Ivanovna, no doubt. Not there, please. Over here . . ."

Razumikhin, sitting near the door in one of Raskolnikov's three chairs, had risen as Sonia entered, to give her room. Raskolnikov was about to indicate the edge of the couch where Zosimov had been sitting, but he reflected that since this couch served him as a bed it was too intimate a place, and he hastened to show her to Razumikhin's chair.

"And you," he said to Razumikhin, "sit here," and he indicated the corner where Zosimov had been sitting.

Sonia sat down. She practically trembled from fright, and glanced timidly at both ladies. She obviously did not herself understand how it came about that she was allowed to sit beside them. As she thought about it she became so appalled she suddenly stood up again and, completely embarrassed, turned to Raskolnikov.

"I . . . I . . . just came for a moment, excuse me for bothering you," she said hesitantly. "I come from Katherine Ivanovna. She had nobody to send. She told me to beg you to be at the funeral service in the morning . . . for Mass . . . at the Mitrofaniev Cemetery, then to our place . . . I mean her place . . . for a bite to eat. . . . Do her the honor. . . . She told me to beg you."

Sonia hesitated and fell silent.

"I will certainly try . . . certainly," Raskolnikov replied. He stood up too, and he too faltered and did not finish what he had to say. "Please," he said suddenly, "do sit down. I must talk with you. You may be in a hurry, but please let me have a couple of minutes. . . . Please."

He moved the chair out for her. Sonia sat down again. In a timid and distraught way she glanced again as rapidly as she could at both the ladies, and again, suddenly, she lowered her eyes.

Raskolnikov's pale face took flame. A shudder passed through him. His eyes lit up.

"Mother," he said firmly and steadily, "this is Sofia Semionovna Marmeladov, the daughter of that most unfortunate Mr. Marmeladov who, before my eyes yesterday, was run over by horses, and about whom I've already spoken to you."

Pulcheria Alexandrovna glanced at Sonia and wrinkled her nose a bit. In spite of the embarrassment of Rodia's steady and evocative gaze, she somehow could not deny herself this satisfaction. Dunia confronted the young girl seriously. and intently, staring at her with amazement. On being introduced, Sonia would have raised her eyes again, but she became even more embarrassed than she had been before.

"I'd been meaning to ask you," Raskolnikov addressed her as quickly as possible, "how everything went yesterday. Anybody bother you? The police, for example?"

"No, everything went all right. . . . What he died of was all too obvious. They didn't bother us. But the tenants are angry."

"What are they angry about?"

"The body being there so long . . . you see, it's hot now, the air. . . . So it'll be taken to the cemetery today, before vespers. It will stay in the chapel till tomorrow. At first Katherine Ivanovna didn't want to, but now she sees for herself that you can't—"

"Today, then?"

"She begs you to do us the honor of being at the church service tomorrow, then coming to her place for the funeral feast."

"She's going to put on a funeral feast?"

"Yes, she's going to have snacks. She told me to thank you very much for helping us yesterday . . . without you there'd be nothing to have a funeral with." Suddenly her mouth and chin began to twitch, but she recovered her grip and restrained herself. Again she quickly lowered her gaze.

Raskolnikov had been looking her intently up and down. Kind of thin, pale little face. Very thin. Fairly irregular and kind of sharp, with a small, sharp nose and chin. Not pretty. Yet her blue eyes were so clear, and when they were animated her expression became so kind and good-hearted, you could not help being attracted to her. Face and figure had one outstanding characteristic. Although she was eighteen, she still seemed like a little girl much younger than her years, almost a child. This could be seen in some of her gestures, which seemed almost funny.

"How could Katherine Ivanovna manage even having snacks, though, when she had so little to work with?" Raskolnikov asked, insistently continuing the conversation.

"The coffin will be simple. . . . Everything will be simple . . . so it won't cost much. . . . Katherine Ivanovna and I figured it all out a little while ago, so we'd be sure to have something left for the feast. Katherine Ivanovna wants very much to have one. You can't say no, you see . . . it comforts her . . . it's the way she is. But you know that."

"I understand. Of course I understand. . . . Why are you staring at my room like that? Well, my mother says it's like a coffin, too."

"Yesterday you gave us everything you had!" Sonia replied suddenly in a strong, swift whisper. Suddenly she dropped her eyes again. Her mouth and chin were quivering. She had been struck for some time by Raskolnikov's impoverished circumstances, and her words seemed all of a sudden to fly out as though of their own will. A silence followed. Dunia's eyes glistened. Pulcheria Alexandrovna seemed actually to be gazing benignly at Sonia.

"Of course we'll dine together, Rodia," she said, rising. "Let us go, Dunia. . . . It might do you some good, Rodia, to go out for a little walk. Then you can lie down and rest for a while. Then come to our place nice and early. I'm afraid we've tired you out for now. . . ."

Rising and bustling about, "Yes, yes, I'll be there," he replied. "But I have some business to attend to."

Razumikhin looked at Raskolnikov with astonishment. "You don't mean to tell me you're planning to have dinner somewhere else?"

"Yes, yes, I'll be there, of course, of course. . . . You stay a moment, though. Mother, you don't need him right now, do you? I'm not depriving you of him, am I?"

"Oh, no, no! You will be so kind as to come to dinner, though, won't you, Dmitry Prokofich?"

"Please, do come," said Dunia.

Positively beaming, Razumikhin bowed. For a moment everyone seemed suddenly and strangely embarrassed.

"Good-bye, Rodia. I mean, until soon. I don't like saying good-bye. Good-bye, Nastasia. Ah, there I go again!" Pulcheria Alexandrovna wanted to take her leave of Sonia, too, yet somehow she could not quite bring herself to that. Bustling about, she left the room.

Dunia followed her mother past Sonia as though she had been waiting her turn. But she made a point of saying good-bye to her, with a full and courteous bow, which Sonia, disturbed, returned timidly and hastily, while a pained expression passed across her face, as if Dunia's courtesy and attention were difficult and painful for her to accept.

"Dunia, good-bye!" Raskolnikov shouted. By now he was out in the hall. "Give me your hand!"

"I gave it to you already. Have you forgotten?" Dunia said, awkwardly and affectionately turning to look at him.

"What of it! Give it to me again!"

He squeezed her fingers strongly. Dunia smiled at him, blushed, quickly pulled her hand away, and followed her mother out. For some reason, she, too, was very happy.

"That's wonderful!" he said to Sonia when he came back into the room. He was looking at her brightly. "God's mercy on the dead, and may the living go on living! That's the way it is, isn't it? Well, isn't it?"

Sonia observed the sudden illumination of his face with something close to amazement. Silently and intently for several moments, he stared at her. Her dead father's whole account of her flashed suddenly through his mind.

"Good Lord, Dunia!" Pulcheria Alexandrovna said as soon as they were out in the street. "It almost feels good to be out of there. Easier, somehow. Well, who could have thought that yesterday on the train?"

"I tell you he's still quite sick, Mother. Couldn't you see that? Maybe he got sick worrying about us. You have to make allowances. Then you can forgive a lot. Yes, a lot."

"But *you* didn't make any allowances!" Pulcheria Alexandrovna broke in hotly and jealously. "You know, Dunia, I was looking at the two of you. You're absolutely the image of him. Not so much in looks as in spirit. Both melancholics, both sulky and quick-tempered, both arrogant and both magnanimous . . . You don't think he's an egotist, do you, Dunia? Ah? But when I think of what's going to happen at our place this evening, my heart just shrivels!"

"Don't worry, Mother. Whatever happens will happen as it must."

"But think of the position we're in, Dunia! And," poor Pulcheria Alexandrovna suddenly let slip, "what if Peter Petrovich breaks it off?"

"What would he be worth if he does!" Dunia sharply and haughtily replied.

Pulcheria Alexandrovna was quick to change the subject. "We picked a good time to leave. He was off on some kind of business. Just as well. He'll get some air . . . horribly stuffy in that place. . . . Where can you get any air around here, though? Even outside it's like a room without windows. Good Lord, what a city! Watch, look out! They'll knock you down! They're carrying something. That was a piano they were carrying, wasn't it? My, how they push you around. . . . That girl frightens me, too—"

"What girl, Mother?"

"Why, that Sofia Semionovna who was there just now . . ."

"What do you mean?"

"I have a premonition, Dunia. Believe it or not, as soon as she came in I thought—here we have what's behind it all. . . ."

"There's nothing at all behind it!" said Dunia indignantly. "You and your premonitions, Mother! Really. He only met her the other day. When she came in the room he didn't even know who she was."

"Well, you wait and see! . . . She worries me. You'll see. You will. How frightened I was. She looked at me with such eyes, I could hardly sit still. Do you remember? And he started to introduce her. It seemed strange to me. Peter Petrovich writes about her the way he does, and here Rodia is introducing her to us. To you, even! So she must mean something to him!"

"The things people write! We were talked about, and written about, too. Have you forgotten? I for one am convinced that she's an excellent person and all this is nonsense!"

"I wish to God, for her sake, that were true!"

"And Peter Petrovich is a cheap gossip!" Dunia suddenly burst out.

Pulcheria Alexandrovna fell silent. The conversation lapsed.

"Listen," Raskolnikov said, "here's what I'd like you to do for me," and he led Razumikhin to the window.

"I'll tell Katherine Ivanovna you'll be there," Sonia said hastily, as though about to leave.

"In a moment, Sofia Semionovna. We have no secrets, you're not in the way. . . . I still want to talk to you a bit. . . . Listen"—he turned abruptly to Razumikhin—"you know that what's-his-name, don't you? That Porfiry Petrovich?"

"I should say so! He's a relative. What's this all about, anyhow?" he added, with a burst of curiosity.

"But he's in charge of that case, isn't he? You know what I mean . . . the murder you were talking about the other day. . . ."

"Yes. . . . And so?" Razumikhin's eyes were bulging.

"He's been interrogating the old woman's clients. I left some things there to be pawned myself. Nothing that amounts to much. But my sister's ring . . . She gave it to me as a memento when I went away. And my father's silver watch. Not worth more than five, six rubles in all, but as mementoes they mean something to me. What am I supposed to do, then? I don't want to lose these items, especially the watch. I was afraid a little while ago my mother might ask to have a look at it . . . you know, when she was talking about Dunia's watch. It's all we have left of my father's things. She'd worry herself sick if it got lost! You know how women are! I need your advice. I know you're supposed to report at the police station, but wouldn't it be better to go straight to Porfiry? Ah? What do you think? The business would be over and done with faster that way. By dinnertime my mother will ask for it, wait and see!"

"Not to the station, of course—straight to Porfiry!" Razumikhin shouted. He was more than usually excited. "Well, I certainly am glad! What are we waiting for? It's only a couple of steps. He's sure to be there!"

"All right. . . . Let's go."

"I know he's going to be very very very very glad to meet you! One time or another, I've told him a lot about you. . . . Just yesterday I mentioned you. Let's go. So you knew the old woman? Well, well! It's all turned out splen-diferously! . . . Oh, yes. Sofia Ivanovna—"

"Sofia Semionovna," Raskolnikov corrected. "Sofia Semionovna, this is my friend Razumikhin. He's a fine man. . . ."

"If you've got to go now . . ." Sonia started saying. She did not look at Razumikhin at all, and as a result became even more embarrassed.

"Let's go, then!" Raskolnikov decided. "I'll call on you later today, Sofia Semionovna. Just tell me where you live."

It was not so much that he was confused as that he seemed to be in a hurry and tried to avoid her gaze. Blushing, Sonia gave him her address. They left together.

"Don't you lock up?" Razumikhin asked, as he followed them downstairs.

"Never. But I've been meaning to buy a lock for two years now," he added carelessly. He turned, laughing, to Sonia. "People who don't need a lock are lucky, aren't they?" Once in the street, they stopped by the gate.

"You turn right here, Sofia Semionovna, don't you? Incidentally, how did you manage to find me?" he asked. He seemed really to want to ask her something quite different. He kept wanting to look at her calm, clear eyes. Somehow he could not.

"Why, you gave Polechka your address yesterday."

"Polia? Ah, yes . . . Polechka! That's . . . the little one . . . your sister? And I gave her my address?"

"Surely you didn't forget that, did you?"

"No . . . I remember. . . ."

"My father told me about you, though. . . . Only I didn't know your name yet, and I guess he didn't know it either. . . . This time I came . . . and since I learned your name yesterday, all I had to do was ask, 'Where does Mr. Raskolnikov live around here?' I didn't know you were subletting a place too. . . . Good-bye . . . I'll tell Katherine Ivanovna. . . ."

She was terribly glad to be leaving at last. She hurried away, head lowered, to get out of their sight as quickly as possible any way she could, to make those twenty steps to the corner where she took the turn to the right, so she could be alone at last, hurrying along, looking at no one, noticing nothing, thinking, remembering, reflecting on every word that had been spoken, on every circumstance. Never, never had she experienced anything like it. Dimly and mysteriously a new universe had taken possession of her soul. Suddenly she remembered that Raskolnikov himself intended to call on her that day, that very morning, perhaps, perhaps immediately!

"But let it not be today, please, not today!" she murmured with a sinking heart, as though she were pleading with someone, like a frightened child. "Oh, God! To me . . . to this room . . . he'll see . . . oh, God, God!"

And she could not of course have noticed at that moment a certain gentleman she did not know, watching her closely and following on her heels. He had been following her ever since she went out the gate. When she, Raskolnikov, and Razumikhin had paused for a few words on the sidewalk, the stranger, as he passed them by, heard Sonia say, "And I asked, where does Mr. Raskolnikov live?" and he seemed all of a sudden to give a start. Quickly yet attentively he glanced at all three, but especially at Raskolnikov, to whom Sonia was speaking. Then he looked at the house, taking mental note of it. The stranger, who tried not to show his interest, took it all in instantly as he walked by. Then he slowed down, as though waiting. He was waiting for Sonia. He could see they were saying good-bye and Sonia would now be off for home.

"Where is her home? I've seen that face somewhere," he thought, recalling Sonia's face. "Got to find out."

When he reached the corner, he crossed to the other side

of the street. Turning, he saw Sonia walking behind him in the same direction. She had noticed nothing. When she reached the corner she turned into the same street. He watched her cross, without taking his eyes off her. When she had gone fifty yards or so he crossed over to the same side, caught up with her, and followed along at a distance of five paces.

He was a man of about fifty, taller than average, portly, with broad, sloping shoulders that made him look as though he stooped a little. He was elegantly and comfortably dressed, in the manner of a dignified country gentleman. He held a handsome cane, which he tapped on the sidewalk at every step, and he wore a pair of brand-new gloves. His broad, high-boned face was quite pleasant, with a freshness of color not native to Petersburg. His hair, still quite thick, was very light and lightly streaked with gray, and his wide, thick, spadelike beard was even lighter than the hair on his head. His eyes were deep blue and had a cold, steady, thoughtful look. His lips were perhaps too red. All in all he seemed like an extremely well-preserved man, much younger than his years.

When Sonia emerged on the canal embankment, the two of them were alone on the street. He noticed how lost in thought she was, and how absentminded. She turned in at the gate when she arrived at her house. Following her, he seemed a bit surprised. In the yard she took a turn to the right, to the corner where a stairway led to her apartment. "Aha!" the stranger muttered, and began to make his way up the stairs after her. It was only then that Sonia noticed him. She went up to the third floor, turned down the corridor, and rang at number 9, on the door of which was written in chalk: KAPERNAUMOV, TAILOR. "Aha!" the stranger again exclaimed, surprised at the strange coincidence, and rang next door at number 8. The doors were about six paces apart.

"So you live at Kapernaumov's!" he said, looking at Sonia and laughing. "He fixed my vest for me yesterday. I live right next door here at Madame Gertrude Karlovna Resslich's. Isn't that something!"

Sonia looked at him attentively.

"Neighbors!" he went on, with a kind of special gaiety. "And this is only my third day in town. Well, for the time being—good-bye."

Sonia did not reply. The door was opened, and she went

in quickly. She felt ashamed for some reason, and for some reason even more timid. . . .

Razumikhin, on the way to Porfiry's, seemed especially excited.

"That's great, old pal," he kept repeating, "and I'm glad! I am glad!"

"And what have you got to be so glad about?" Raskolnikov thought.

"I didn't know you had been pawning things at the old woman's too. . . . Was it . . . a long time ago? I mean, when you were at her place?"

"But how naïve can you get!" Raskolnikov thought to himself. He halted, trying to remember. "When? I think I was there a couple days before her death. By the way, I'm not going there now to redeem the things," he said, with a certain special hasty emphasis on "the things." "I've only got about a ruble in silver left . . . thanks to that damned delirium of mine yesterday!" He mentioned the delirium with special emphasis.

"Well . . . yes, yes, yes," for some reason Razumikhin hastily agreed. "So that's why you were a bit . . . shook up then. . . . You know, don't you, that you kept recalling some rings and chains and stuff when you were delirious! Well, yes. . . . Yes, it's clear. It's all clear now."

"Well, that idea certainly has taken hold among them, hasn't it! This fellow here would go to the cross for me, and now he's very glad he can *see* why I kept talking about those rings when I was delirious! But it certainly seems to have taken hold of all of them!" Aloud, he asked: "Will he be home?"

"He's home, he's home," said Razumikhin hastily. "He's really quite a guy, you'll soon see! A bit clumsy. I mean, he's a man of the world, all right; yet in another sense he's clumsy. He's a smart fellow, very smart, not dumb at all, but he has a kind of special way of looking at things. . . . He doesn't trust anybody. He's a skeptic. A cynic . . . likes to fool people. I mean, not fool them exactly, but kid them along. . . . And he goes in for the old circumstantial method. . . . He really knows his business, though. He knows it. Last year he solved a murder case in which nearly all the clues had been lost! He'd like very very very much to get to know you."

"Why so very?"

"That's not what I mean . . . well, you see, lately, seeing as how you've been sick, I mentioned you quite a bit and quite often. . . . Well, he listened, and when he learned you were a law student and too hard up to finish your studies, he said, 'What a pity!' Well, so I came to the conclusion . . . well, I mean, taking it all together, not only that, but yesterday, Zamiotov— You see, Rodia, yesterday when I was drunk I was laying it on a bit thick to you, when we were on our way home. . . . And so, old pal, I'm afraid, I'm worried you might have made too much of what I said, you see. . . ."

"What do you mean? They think I'm crazy? Well, they may be right at that."

He smiled tensely.

"Yes, yes . . . I mean, hell, no! . . . Everything I said, though—I mean about the other things, too—it was all just nonsense, because I was drunk."

"Well, what the hell are you making excuses for, then! How sick I am of the whole thing!" Raskolnikov shouted with hyper-irritability. Yet he was at least in part pretending.

"I know, I know, I understand. Please believe, I understand. I'm ashamed even to talk about it. . . ."

"So if you're ashamed don't talk about it!"

They fell silent. Raskolnikov sensed with disgust that Razumikhin was in seventh heaven. In addition, what Razumikhin had just said about Porfiry alarmed him.

"I'll have to play the part of Lazarus for him too," he thought, turning pale, heart pounding, "and make it sound more natural, too. Most natural would be not to play any part at all. Deliberately not to play a part! No, not *deliberately.* Unnatural again. . . . Well, we'll see how it turns out . . . good or no good. . . . I'm going there now. . . . Candle draws the moth . . . moth can't help it. Heart's pounding, that won't do!"

"In this gray house," Razumikhin said.

"What's most important is whether Porfiry knows or not I was at that witch's place yesterday . . . and asked about the blood. That's what I'll have to find out right away, soon as I'm in, by the expression on his face. Or else . . . Even if I go under, I've got to find out!"

"You know what?" All of a sudden he addressed Razumikhin with a teasing smile. "I noticed you've been unusually excited today, old pal, ever since morning, for some reason. True?"

"What do you mean, excited? I'm not excited at all."
Razumikhin winced.

"No, it's all too noticeable, old pal. You were sitting on
your chair in a way you never sit, right on the edge, and
you kept squirming. And you'd be jumping up for no particular reason. One minute you'd be angry, the next you'd turn
sweet as sugar candy. You even blushed. Yes, when they invited
you to dinner, you blushed. You blushed terribly."

"I didn't really. You're laying it on thick! What's all this
for, anyhow?"

"That's why you're fussing around like a schoolboy!
Damned if he isn't blushing again!"

"What a pig you are, though!"

"Well, what have you got to be so embarrassed about,
Romeo? Wait, I'll tell them the good news! Will that make
my mother laugh! Someone else, too—"

"Listen, listen, listen, this is serious, though, but this is . . .
What could I do then, damn it!" Razumikhin finally lost all
self-possession, turning cold with terror. "What would you
tell them? Old pal, I . . . Phoo, what a pig you are!"

"Why, he's like a spring rose! You've no idea how good
you look. Romeo—six and a half feet tall! My, you've
scrubbed yourself up today. Even cleaned your fingernails,
ah? When did that happen last? Damned if you didn't even
slick down your hair with oil! Bend down!"

"Pig!"

Raskolnikov was laughing so hard, it seemed he could not
hold himself back. He was laughing like that as they entered
Porfiry Petrovich's apartment. Raskolnikov had reckoned it
would need to be like that. From inside you could hear them
both laughing as they came in. You could hear them still
chuckling in the hallway.

"Not a word here, or I'll . . . brain you!" Razumikhin
whispered furiously, grabbing Raskolnikov by the shoulder.

5

He was already on his way into the apartment. He entered
looking as though it were all he could do somehow to prevent himself from bursting into laughter. Behind him came
the shamefaced Razumikhin, gangly and awkward, face red
as a peony, with a completely frustrated and ferocious ex-

pression. At that moment his face and figure were truly comical and justified Raskolnikov's laughter. Raskolnikov, who had not yet been introduced, bowed to their host, who was standing in the middle of the room, looking at them inquiringly; Raskolnikov shook hands with him while still under the apparently extreme effort of suppressing his mirth and at least saying a few words to introduce himself. Scarcely had he managed to assume a serious expression and say something, however, when suddenly, it seemed involuntarily, he glanced at Razumikhin again and could restrain himself no longer. His laughter broke through all the more irresistibly for having so long been held back. The extreme ferocity with which Razumikhin responded to this "hearty" laughter gave the whole episode a tone of the most spontaneous gaiety, and (the main thing) of naturalness. Razumikhin, as though on purpose, helped out even more.

"Damn it!" he roared with a wave of his hand, which glanced at once against a small round table on which stood an empty glass. It flew off and went crashing.

"Gentlemen, why break up the furniture? Remember, it's government property!" Porfiry Petrovich said cheerfully.

The scene arranged itself as follows. Raskolnikov went on laughing, but his hand remained in his host's hand. Aware that he had to go easy, he waited for the most opportune and natural moment to break it off. Razumikhin, embarrassed by the table he'd upset and the broken glass, threw a gloomy look at the fragments, spat, and turned sharply to the window. He stood there with his back to the audience, scowling terribly, staring through the window, and seeing nothing. Porfiry Petrovich laughed quite sincerely. Yet it was obvious he required an explanation. Zamiotov had been sitting on a chair in the corner. When the guests had come in he had risen and stood there expectantly, mouth moving to form a smile. Yet he looked on the scene that followed with bewilderment, almost with disbelief, and at Raskolnikov even with a certain embarrassment. Zamiotov's unexpected presence had an unpleasant impact on Raskolnikov. "I've got to keep that in mind, too!" he thought.

"Excuse me, please," he began, displaying deliberately his embarrassment. "I am Raskolnikov."

"Not at all, it's a pleasure, I'm sure, and that was very nice, the way you came in. . . . What's the matter with him, doesn't he even want to say hello?" Porfiry Petrovich nodded at Razumikhin.

"He's mad at me for some reason, damned if I know why. I just happened to tell him on the way that he reminded me of Romeo, and . . . and I pointed out why. . . . I don't think there was any more to it than that."

"Pig!" Razumikhin exclaimed without turning round.

"He must have had very serious reasons to become so angry on account of one little word." Porfiry laughed.

"Why, you—you investigator! Well, to hell with all of you!" Razumikhin snapped, and suddenly, laughing out loud himself as though nothing had happened, he went up to Porfiry Petrovich.

"Knock off! We're all fools! Down to brass tacks. Here's my friend, Rodion Romanych Raskolnikov. First, you've heard of him and said you wanted to meet him. Second, he's got a little business matter he wants to take up with you. Well, if it isn't Zamiotov! What are you doing here? Didn't know you two knew each other. Been here long?"

"What does that mean?" Raskolnikov thought in alarm. Zamiotov seemed a little embarrassed, but not much. "We met yesterday at your place," he said casually.

"I've been spared the trouble, then. Last week he was nagging me to introduce him to you, Porfiry, but it seems you've managed to sniff each other out without me. Where do you keep the tobacco?"

Porfiry Petrovich was informally dressed. He wore a very clean shirt under his dressing gown, and worn-out slippers. He was a man of about thirty-five, a little below average in height, stout, a bit paunchy even, smooth-shaven, without moustache or sideburns, the hair on his large round head closely cropped. His head had a peculiar outward bulge in back. His puffy, round, slightly snub-nosed face was of a sickly, sallow hue, but quite alert and even ironical. If the expression of his eyes hadn't gotten in the way, he might even have looked benevolent. His eyes had a watery gleam, fringed by almost white, half-closed eyelids that made him look as though he were winking at somebody. The gaze of those eyes seemed strangely out of harmony with the figure as a whole, which seemed to have something almost maternal about it, and endowed him with a much more serious air than might at first glance have been suspected.

As soon as he heard that his guest had a "little business matter" to settle with him, Porfiry Petrovich asked him to sit down on the couch and sat down himself at the opposite end, fixing his attention on his guest as though he expected the nature of his business to be explained immediately. He looked at him with that concentrated, overserious, and embarrassing attention that tends to make one ill at ease from the first, especially when one isn't well acquainted with the other person, and if what one has to say does not seem commensurate in importance with the attention accorded it. Briefly and coherently, however, clearly and precisely, Raskolnikov explained his business. He was even in sufficient control of himself to manage a fairly good look at Porfiry. For his part, Porfiry Petrovich did not take his eyes off him the whole time. Sitting at the same table across from them, Razumikhin followed the explanation with enthusiasm and impatience, constantly casting his eyes from one to the other and back again. That was really a bit thick. Raskolnikov cursed to himself: "The fool!"

"You should make a formal statement to the police," Porfiry, with the most businesslike air, told him. "To this effect. That having heard of such and such event, to wit, this murder, you would like for your part to inform the investigator in charge of the case that such and such things belong to you and that you would like to redeem them . . . or else . . . but in any case they'll write it down for you."

"That's just the point, right now I'm—" Raskolnikov did his best to appear as embarrassed as possible, "right now I'm not exactly in funds . . . and even a trifle like that, I can't . . . you see, I just sort of wanted to make a statement now that these things are mine, and when I get the money—"

"It really makes no difference," Porfiry Petrovich replied, taking the discussion of finances coldly. "If you want, though, you may write directly to me, along the same line, that having learned about such and such, and declaring such and such my things, I request—"

"On ordinary paper?" Raskolnikov broke in, interesting himself once again in the financial aspect of the case.

"Oh, on the most ordinary, if you like!" All of a sudden Porfiry Petrovich looked at him with a kind of unconcealed irony, screwing up his eyes as though he were winking at him. It may, however, only have seemed so to Raskolnikov, for it lasted only a moment. There had at least been something of the sort. Raskolnikov could have sworn he had winked at him, the devil knew for what.

"He knows!" flashed inside him like lightning.

"Excuse me for disturbing you with such trifles," he went on, somewhat disconcerted. "My things are worth about five rubles in all, but they are specially dear to me as mementoes of the people who gave them to me, and I must admit I was quite worried when I learned—"

"So that's why you hit the ceiling yesterday when I told Zosimov that Porfiry was questioning the clients!" Razumikhin put in, obviously on purpose.

That was really intolerable. Raskolnikov could not restrain himself and looked at him furiously, his dark eyes blazing with anger. He recovered himself immediately, however.

"Are you laughing at me, old pal?" he said with skillfully contrived irritation. "Maybe I worry too much about these things, which seem rubbish to you. I agree. That's no reason you should think I'm selfish or greedy, though. These two trivial items might not seem like rubbish to me at all. As I just told you, that silver watch, which, it's true, isn't worth much, was all my father left behind. Laugh at me if you like, but my mother has come to see me"—he turned suddenly to Porfiry—"and if she found out"—he turned abruptly back to Razumikhin, making a special effort to get a tremor into his voice—"this watch was lost . . . I swear she'd be driven to despair! Women!"

"I didn't mean that at all! That's not what I meant! I meant the complete opposite!" said Razumikhin in distress.

"Did it come off?" Raskolnikov wondered anxiously. "Was it natural? Did I exaggerate? Why did I say 'women'?"

"So your mother's come to see you, has she?" Porfiry asked.

"Yes."

"When was this?"

"Yesterday evening."

Porfiry fell silent, as though in thought.

"Your things couldn't have gotten lost in any case," he went on calmly and coldly. "But I've been waiting for you here a long time now."

As though nothing had happened, he thoughtfully started pushing an ashtray over to Razumikhin, who was dropping cigarette ashes uncouthly on the rug. Raskolnikov shuddered, but Porfiry, as though he were still preoccupied with Razumikhin's cigarette, did not seem to notice.

"What's this?" Razumikhin shouted. "You've been waiting! You mean to tell me you knew he'd been pawning things *there*?"

Porfiry turned directly to Raskolnikov. "Both items, the

ring and the watch, were *at her place,* wrapped up in the same sheet of paper on which your name was clearly written in pencil. So was the day and month she got them from you. . . ."

Raskolnikov smiled awkwardly, trying hard to look him straight in the eyes. "How is it you're so observant?" He could not keep it up, though, and suddenly he added: "I said that because there must have been lots of customers . . . so you'd have a hard time remembering them all. . . . It seems, on the contrary, you remember them all clearly, and . . . and . . ."

"That was dumb! Weak! Why did I add that!"

"But we know almost all her customers by now," Porfiry replied with a barely noticeable trace of irony. "You're the only one who hasn't reported."

"I wasn't entirely well."

"I heard about that, too. I even heard you were quite upset about something. You're a bit pale even now, though, aren't you?"

"Not pale at all . . . on the contrary, I'm quite well!" Raskolnikov snapped out harshly and angrily, suddenly changing his tone. Anger welled up within him, and he could not keep it down. "And in anger I shall give myself away!" flashed in his mind. "Why do they torment me?"

"Not *entirely* well!" Razumikhin broke in. "Listen to him, will you, shooting his mouth off! Till yesterday he was delirious, practically stark raving. . . . Well, would you believe it, Porfiry, he could hardly stand on his feet, but as soon as we turned our backs—Zosimov and me, that is—he got dressed and sneaked out and was fooling around somewhere till almost midnight. And all this, I tell you, while he was utterly delirious! A most remarkable case!"

"*Utterly delirious?* You don't say!" Porfiry gave a kind of old womanish shake of the head.

"Rubbish! Don't believe it!" burst out Raskolnikov, too angry to care. "Of course, you don't really believe it anyway!" But Porfiry did not seem to notice these strange words.

"Would you have gone out if you hadn't been delirious?" Razumikhin suddenly flared up. "Why did you go out? For what? And why so sneaky-like? Could you have been in your right mind? Now the danger's past I can talk to you frankly!"

All of a sudden Raskolnikov addressed Porfiry with an

insolently provocative grin: "I got good and fed up with them yesterday, so I ran off to rent an apartment where they couldn't find me, and I took a heap of money with me. Mr. Zamiotov there, he saw the money. Was I in my right mind yesterday, Mr. Zamiotov, or was I delirious? You settle the argument for us." At that moment he could have strangled Zamiotov, he disliked so immensely his look and his silence.

"In my opinion," Zamiotov declared dryly, "you spoke sensibly enough, even cleverly, but you were too irritable."

Porfiry interrupted: "Nikodim Fomich was telling me today he ran into you quite late yesterday in the quarters of a certain clerk who'd been run down by horses—"

"And what about that clerk!" Razumikhin joined in. "Didn't he act like a madman at the clerk's? He gave the widow all the money he had left, for the funeral! Well, he wanted to help, okay, he could have given her fifteen, he could have given twenty, he might have kept just three for himself—but he went and gave away all twenty-five!"

"Maybe I found a treasure somewhere and you don't know anything about it? And that's why I was throwing money away yesterday. . . . Mr. Zamiotov there, he knows I found a treasure! . . . Excuse me"—he turned with trembling lips to Porfiry—"we've been interrupting you with this stupidity for the past half hour. Aren't you fed up with it?"

"Why, bless you, sir, quite the contrary, *quite* the contrary! If you only knew how much you interest me! I'm curious to look and listen . . . and I must admit I'm very glad you finally decided to report. . . ."

"Come on, now, some tea! My throat's bone-dry!" Razumikhin exclaimed.

"An excellent idea! Perhaps you'd all stay. But wouldn't you like something . . . a little stronger, before tea?"

"Come on, now!"

Porfiry Petrovich went out to order tea. In Raskolnikov's head, thoughts whirled like a cyclone. He was terribly irritated.

"The point is they don't even hide it, they don't even want to pretend! Since you don't know me at all, what occasion did you have to talk about me with Nikodim Fomich? It follows that they don't even want to hide the fact they're keeping track of me like a pack of hounds! They spit in my face openly!" He was trembling with rage. "Strike out if you must, but straight. Don't play cat and mouse. That's not polite, Porfiry Petrovich, and look here, I may very well not permit it, sir! I'll rise up and I'll tell you the whole truth to your face. Then you'll see how I despise you all!" He caught his breath with difficulty. "What if I'm wrong, though? What if it's only a delusion and I'm all wrong? Losing my temper from inexperience? What if I just don't have the guts to go through with my vile role? Maybe it was unintentional? Their words were all ordinary, but there was something in them. Words that might normally have been said. Yet there was something. Why did he come straight out and say 'at her place'? Why did Zamiotov add that I spoke *cleverly*? Why that particular tone? Yes . . . the tone . . . Razumikhin was sitting right here; why didn't anything seem wrong to him? Nothing ever seems wrong to that innocent dope! Fever again! Did Porfiry wink at me awhile ago or didn't he? Probably nonsense. Why should he wink? Maybe they want to play on my nerves, or provoke me? Either it's all a delusion, or *they know*! Even Zamiotov is insolent. . . . Or is he? He changed his mind overnight. I had a feeling he'd change his mind! He seems at home here, yet he's here for the first time. Porfiry's not treating him like a guest, he's sitting with his back to him. They're in cahoots! *Because of me!* They were certainly talking about me before we came in! Do they know about that business in the apartment? Get it over with! When I said I ran away to rent an apartment yesterday, he let it pass. He didn't pick it up. . . . I was pretty smart to get that in about the apartment. Come in handy later! . . . Could be said I was delirious! . . . Ha-ha-ha! He knows about all of yesterday evening! He didn't know about Mother's arrival! . . . So the old witch wrote the date down in pencil, did she! . . . You're laying it on thick. I won't give myself away! These still aren't facts, though. They are mere illusion. No, you give me the facts! The apartment's not a fact, either. It's delirium. I know what to tell them. . . . Do they know about the apartment? I won't leave till I find out! Why did I come? Losing my temper just now. . . . That's a fact, if you like! My God, how irritable I am! Maybe it's all for the best. The role of a sick man. . . . He's sounding me out. He'll take me by surprise. Why did I come?" All this flashed through his mind like lightning.

Porfiry returned in a moment. He seemed suddenly gayer. "I've got a hangover from your party, my friend. . . . I seem shot to pieces, somehow," he said laughingly to Razumikhin, in a very different tone.

"Was it interesting? I think I left just as it was really getting interesting: Who won?"

"Why, no one, of course. We arrived at the eternal questions and soared off into the clouds."

"Can you imagine what we got onto last night, Rodia: is there such a thing as crime or isn't there? All talking their heads off, like I told you!"

"What's so unusual about that? An ordinary social question," Raskolnikov replied absently.

"That's not the way the question was formulated," Porfiry noted.

"Not quite, it's true," Razumikhin agreed at once, plunging on and getting all excited as usual. "You see, Rodion. Listen and tell me what you think. I'd like to know. I practically crawled out of my hide arguing with them yesterday, and I was waiting for you. I told them about you and said you were coming. . . . It began with the socialist point of view, which is well known. Crime is a protest against the abnormality of the social order—just that, and nothing more, no other causes admitted, and that's that!"

"There he goes again, laying it on thick!" said Porfiry Petrovich. He grew visibly livelier and laughed every time he looked at Razumikhin, which egged the latter on all the more.

"N-not to be admitted!" Razumikhin heatedly broke in, "I'm not laying it on thick! I'll show you their books. It's always 'the influence of the environment' with them, that's all they know! They love that phrase! If society were constructed normally, therefore, all crimes would disappear at once because there would be nothing to protest against and we'd all become righteous in a flash. Nature doesn't count; nature gets chased away; nature's not supposed to exist! They won't have mankind developing along some *living* historical path to the end, turning finally of itself into normal society; but on the contrary, a social system emerging from some kind of mathematical brain that's going to reconstruct mankind and make it in one moment righteous and sinless, quicker than any life process, no living or historical path needed! Instinctively they don't like history, and that's why. 'Ugliness and stupidity, that's all it is,' everything can be explained by stupidity alone. That's also why they don't like the life process. A *living soul* isn't called for. A living soul demands life; a living soul doesn't obey mechanical laws; a living soul is suspect; a living soul is retrograde! And this thing here, maybe it reeks of carrion, maybe it's made out of rubber; anyway, it's not alive, it doesn't have a will of its own; anyway, it's servile and won't rebel! And in the long run it turns out everything boils down to how you lay the bricks, how you arrange the rooms and corridors in a phalanstery! The phalanstery's all set, but nature's not quite ready for the phalanstery. Nature wants life, the life process isn't over yet, too early for the graveyard! You can't vault over nature with logic alone. Logic indicates three instances—but there are a million! The easiest way to solve the problem is to cut short the million and reduce everything to the problem of comfort alone! Temptingly clear, no need to think! That's the main point, having no need to think! The life secret crammed into eight pages!"

"Now he's off again, beating the big drum! You have to hang on to him," Porfiry laughed. "Just imagine"—he turned to Raskolnikov—"yesterday evening. Six of them arguing in one room! And tanked up ahead of time on punch, at that. Can you picture it? No, my friend, you talk nonsense. 'Environment' accounts for a good deal in crime, I assure you."

"I know myself it accounts for a good deal. But, tell me: a man of forty violates a girl of ten—is it Environment drove him to it, or what?"

"Well, now, strictly speaking, yes, Environment," Porfiry remarked with surprising gravity. "The crime against the girl is very, very likely accounted for by Environment."

Razumikhin almost went into a frenzy. "Well, if you like, I'll *prove* to you, right here and now," he roared, "that the only reason you have white eyelids is because the Church of Ivan the Great is a hundred yards high, and I'll prove it clearly, precisely, in a progressive manner, and with liberal overtones even! I will! Do you want to bet?"

"I accept! By all means, let's hear him prove it!"

"He's always joking, damn it!" Razumikhin cried. He leaped up and waved his hand. "Well, you're not worth talking to! He does it on purpose—you don't know what he's like, Rodia! Yesterday he took their side, just to make fools of them all. What he said yesterday—oh, God! They were as pleased as could be! And he can keep that sort of thing up for two weeks running. Last year he assured us for some reason that he was going to enter a monastery; and he kept it up for two months! Not long ago he took it into his head to say he was getting married and everything was set for the wedding! He even had a new suit made. We started sending him congratulations. Then it turned out there was no bride, nothing! All a mirage!"

"There you go talking nonsense again! I had the suit made first. The new suit made me think of kidding you all a bit."

"Are you really such a joker?" Raskolnikov asked casually.

"Did you think I wasn't? Wait. I'll fool you, too—ha-ha-ha! No, I'll tell you the whole truth. Speaking of such problems—crimes, little girls, Environment (matters I've always been interested in anyway)—I'm reminded of a little article you wrote, 'On Crime,' or something like that, I forget the exact title. I had the pleasure of reading it a couple of months ago in the *Periodical*."

"My article? In the *Periodical Review*?" Raskolnikov asked in surprise. "I really did write an article about six months ago on a book I'd read. It was at the time I left the university. But I sent it to the *Weekly Review*, not the *Periodical*."

"Well, it got into the *Periodical*."

"The *Weekly Review* ceased to exist, and so they didn't print. . . ."

"That's right. But just as it was ceasing to exist, the *Weekly Review* joined forces with the *Periodical Review*, and that's why your little article appeared two months ago in the *Periodical Review*. You mean you didn't know about it?"

Raskolnikov really hadn't known anything about it.

"My goodness, they must owe you some money for that article! But what a strange fellow you are! You're so isolated you're not even in touch with what concerns you most directly. And that's a fact."

"Bravo, Rodia! I didn't know either!" Razumikhin shouted. "I'll run down to the library today and look that issue up! Two months back? What's the date? Doesn't matter. I'll find out. There's a deal for you! And he wouldn't say!"

"How did you know it was my article, though? It's signed with an initial."

"By chance, and just the other day. Through the editor. I know him. . . . I was extremely interested."

"If I remember correctly, I was examining the psychological state of the criminal through the whole course of a crime."

"That's right. And you maintain that the act of carrying out a crime is always accompanied by illness. Very, very original, but personally that wasn't the part of your article that really interested me. There was a certain idea slipped in at the end, unfortunately you only hint at it, and unclearly. . . . In short, it contains, if you recall, a certain reference to the notion that there may be certain kinds of people in the world who can . . . I mean not that they are able, but that they are endowed with the right to commit all sorts of crimes and excesses, and the law, as it were, was not written for them."

Raskolnikov smiled at this deliberately distorted amplification of his idea.

"How's that? What do you mean? The right to commit crime? Not because of the 'influence of the Environment,' I hope?" Razumikhin asked with a certain anxiety.

"No, no, not for that reason at all," Porfiry replied. "The heart of the matter is that in this gentleman's article all people are divisible into 'ordinary' and 'extraordinary.' The ordinary must live obediently and have no right to transgress the law—because, you see, they're ordinary. The extraordinary, on the other hand, have the right to commit all kinds of crimes and to transgress the law in all kinds of ways, for the simple reason that they are extraordinary. That would seem to have been your argument, if I am not mistaken."

"What do you mean? It can't possibly be like that?" Razumikhin muttered, bewildered.

Raskolnikov smiled again. He understood at once what was going on and the direction in which they were trying to push him. He remembered the article, and decided to accept their challenge.

"That's not quite the way I put it," he began simply and modestly. "Still, I must admit, you've got the gist of it. Even completely right, if you wish." He seemed to enjoy agreeing that it was completely right. "The only bone I have to pick is I don't really insist these extraordinary people are absolutely bound and always obliged to commit excesses, as you say. Such an article wouldn't even have been allowed in print, I don't believe. I merely suggested that the 'extraordinary' man has the right . . . I don't mean the official right; but he has the inner right to permit his conscience to transgress . . . certain obstacles, but only if the execution of his idea— which might involve the salvation of all mankind—demands it. You were so good as to say my article was unclear. I'll try to clarify it for you as best I can. Perhaps I'm not wrong in believing that's what you'd like me to do? Permit me, then. I believe that if circumstances prevented the discovery of a Kepler or a Newton from becoming known except through the sacrifice of a man's life, or of ten, or a hundred, or as many as you please, who prevented this discovery or blocked its path as an obstacle, Newton would have the right, he would even be obliged . . . to remove these ten men, or these hundred men, so he could make his discoveries known to all mankind. But it doesn't at all follow from this that Newton had the right to kill anyone he felt like, or go thieving in the marketplace every day. What's more, as I recall, my article goes on to develop the notion that all the . . . well, for example, the lawgivers and architects of our humanity, from the most ancient on through the Lycurguses, Solons, Mohammeds, Napoleons, and so forth—they were all criminals, to a man. Even if only because they violated the old law in giving a new one—law handed down by their fathers and considered sacred by society. Nor did they stop short of bloodshed if blood could be of use to them, and sometimes this blood was quite innocently and bravely shed, in defense of the old law. You might even take note that these benefactors and architects of our humanity have been for the most part especially fierce at shedding blood. I conclude, in brief, that not only great men, but even those who are just a little out of the common ruck—those, I mean, who have something the least little bit new to say—must absolutely by their very nature be criminals. More or less, of course. Or else they can't get out of the common ruck, and in the common ruck, of course, they cannot consent to remain, again because of their very nature. I believe they are even morally obliged not to consent. You see, in brief, there's nothing specially new here so far. It's been in print a thousand times. As for dividing people into ordinary and extraordinary, it's a bit arbitrary, I agree, but I don't insist on exact figures. I believe only in the basic conception. Merely that people *in general* are divided by a law of nature. The lower part, ordinary people I mean, just stuff, so to speak, good only to reproduce their own kind. The other part consists of people in the true sense. I mean those who are gifted, those who have the talent to shape a *new word* in the context of their environment. The subdivisions, of course, are endless. Yet the distinguishing features of both parts are clear enough. I mean the first part is mere stuff, generally speaking; people conservative by nature, sedate, who live obediently and who like being obedient. I believe they are morally obliged to obedience, because that's their role in life. For them there is definitely nothing degrading about it. In the second part, all transgress the law. They incline to be destroyers, according to their abilities. Of course, their crimes are relative and varied. They call for the destruction of the present in the name of something better for the most part, in their different ways. If for the sake of their idea they need to transgress, even over a corpse, over blood, I believe they may in all conscience grant themselves the inner permission to transgress, even over blood. Depending, however, on the idea and its scope. Note that. My article only speaks in this sense of their right to crime. We began with the juridical problem, remember. But there isn't much reason to fret. The mass almost never concedes them this right, and more or less insists on punishing and hanging them, and thus quite rightly fulfills its conservative role. Only in later generations the same mass places those it has hanged on a pedestal and more or less worships them. The first part is always master of the present, the second of the future. The first preserves the world and causes it to multiply numerically; the second moves the world and leads it to its goal. They have the same right to exist. I believe they have an equal right, and—*vive la guerre éternelle*—until the New Jerusalem, of course!"

"So you still believe in the New Jerusalem?"

"I believe," Raskolnikov answered firmly. He was looking at the ground as he said this. Throughout his long tirade he had been staring at a point on the rug.

"And . . . and . . . and . . . do you believe in God? Forgive my curiosity."

"I believe," Raskolnikov repeated, raising his eyes to Porfiry.

"And . . . and . . . do you believe in the resurrection of Lazarus?"

"I . . . I believe. Why do you want to know all this?"

"Do you believe literally?"

"Literally."

"Yes, I see . . . I was just curious. Excuse me. But permit me—I return now to what we were talking about—they aren't always hanged. Some, on the contrary—"

"Triumph during their lifetime? Oh, yes. Some manage even during their lifetime, and then—"

"They begin to do some hanging themselves?"

"If need be. Even the majority, you know. Your remark, in general, is quite apt."

"I thank you. Tell me this, though. How do you go about telling the extraordinary ones from the ordinary? Are they marked from birth? I believe we need to be a little more accurate here, a somewhat more external definition, so to speak. Forgive me for the natural anxiety of a practical man of goodwill, but wouldn't it be possible to introduce a special kind of clothing, for example, or have them wear something, or stamp them with something or other? Because, you'll agree, if there should be any kind of mixup and somebody from the one part should imagine he belonged to the other part, and if he started 'eliminating all obstacles' as you so felicitously put it, then there's a—"

"Oh, it happens quite frequently! That's even more apt than the remark you made a while back."

"I thank you."

"Don't mention it. You must consider, though, that a mistake is possible only for the first part, I mean the 'ordinary' people, as I perhaps not very successfully called them. In spite of their innate tendency to obedience, there must be quite a few who, because of a certain whimsicality of nature not even a cow is denied, love to imagine themselves as advanced people, 'destroyers,' and to get in on the 'new word,' and quite sincerely, mind you. At the same time they often don't notice the *really* new people, and even hold them in contempt as a backward and low-thinking lot. But I don't believe there can be any significant danger here. The truth is you have little to be anxious about because they never go far. They could, of course, be whipped from time to time for getting carried away, and to remind them of their place; but nothing more. You don't, in fact, need anyone to carry it out. They'll whip themselves. They're very good citizens. In some cases, friend would perform the service for friend; in others, it would be self-inflicted. . . . They'd take all sorts of public penance on themselves at the same time—it would all be so pretty and edifying. You don't, in short, have much to worry about. . . . It's a law."

"Well, you've calmed me down some on that angle, anyway. Here's trouble again, though. Please tell me if there are lots of people of the kind who have the right to cut down others, the 'extraordinary' ones? You understand, of course, I'm quite ready to bow down to them. But you'll

agree, it would be a bit, ah, sticky, wouldn't it, if there were
an awful lot of them, ah?"

"Oh, you shouldn't worry about that, either," Raskolnikov continued in the same tone. "Generally, people with a
new idea, even those barely capable of something *new,* are
born most rarely. It's even peculiar how rarely. All that's
clear is that the birth cycle, all these divisions and subdivisions, must quite surely and precisely be determined by
some law of nature. It hasn't been discovered yet, of course,
but I believe it exists and will be discovered some day. The
great mass of people, the raw material, the stuff, exists on
this earth solely for the purpose of eventually—through
some effort, some mysterious process, some crossing of races
and species—straining and bringing forth the man out of a
thousand who is at least to some extent independent. One
out of ten thousand might be born of still greater independence. I speak roughly, by way of example. Still greater, one
out of a hundred thousand. Men of genius, out of millions.
And the great geniuses, the summits of mankind—perhaps
one will appear on earth out of many thousands of millions.
I have not, in short, had a look into the retort in which all
this takes place. Undoubtedly there is a definite law, though.
There must be. This cannot be chance."

"Are you both joking?" Razumikhin cried out. "Are you
kidding each other, or what? Here they sit, pulling each
other's legs! You serious, Rodia?"

Silently Raskolnikov raised his pale and almost grieving
face to the level of Razumikhin's, and said nothing in reply.
Beside this quiet, mournful face, Porfiry's unconcealed, ob-
trusive, irritating, *discourteous* sarcasm seemed strange to
Razumikhin.

"Well, old pal, if you're really serious . . . Of course, as
you say, it's not new. We've read and heard it a thousand
times. What's really *original* here, what really belongs to you
alone, is, to my horror, that you permit bloodshed *according
to conscience.* And, if you'll excuse me, that you're even so
fanatical about it. . . . So that must be the main point of
your article. What bothers me is this permission *according
to conscience.* That . . . that, if you ask me, is even more
appalling than official legal permission. . . ."

"Absolutely right, even more appalling," responded
Porfiry.

"You must have got carried away! It's a mistake. I'll read

the article. . . . You got carried away! You couldn't possibly believe that . . . I'll read it."

"This isn't in the article. Only some implications," Raskolnikov said.

"Yes, yes," Porfiry could not sit still. "I almost see what your attitude to crime is. But . . . you'll excuse me for being such a nuisance (I'm bothering you a lot, and I'm really sorry!) and, don't you see, a little while ago you reassured me about any possible mixup of the parts and divisions, but here I go worrying again about various practical aspects! Well, what if some young fellow starts imagining he's a Lycurgus or a Mohammed—of the future, of course—and he decides he's going to remove all obstacles. . . . You might say he had a long campaign ahead of him and he's going to need money on the way. . . . Well, let's say he starts preparing himself for the campaign . . . you know?" From his corner Zamiotov suddenly let out a snort. Raskolnikov did not even raise his eyes.

"I must agree," he answered calmly, "that there really would be such cases. The vain and the stupid especially will go for that bait, and young people in particular."

"There, you see. Well, so what about it?"

"Why, just this." Raskolnikov smiled. "I am not to blame for it. That's the way it is and always will be. Here, he"—with a nod at Razumikhin—"was just saying I permit bloodshed. What if I do? Society, with its prisons, exiles, investigators, hard labor, is all too secure. What is there to worry about? Look for the thief!"

"Well, and if we find him?"

"That's his tough luck."

"You are so logical. What about his conscience, though?"

"What business is that of yours?"

"Well, for humanitarian reasons, let's say."

"If he has one, let him suffer. If he realizes his mistake. That's his punishment, on top of hard labor."

"And what about the real geniuses?" Razumikhin asked. "The ones who have the right to cut people down. Must they not suffer at all, even for the blood they've spilled?"

"Why *must*? It's not a question of permitting or forbidding. If he pities his victim, let him suffer. For broad understanding and deep feeling, you need pain and suffering. I believe really great men must experience great sadness in the world," he said pensively, in a tone that was not even conversational. Lifting his eyes, he looked pensively at them all, smiled, and picked up his cap. He felt he was too calm, compared with how he had come in a while ago. Everyone rose.

"Well, sir, you may swear at me or not, be angry or not, but I can't resist it," said Porfiry, "allow me one more little question (I know I've been bothering you a lot!), one tiny little idea I wanted to mention, just so I don't forget it, really. . . ."

"All right. Let's hear your little idea." Raskolnikov, serious and pale, stood waiting before him.

"It's like this, you see. . . . I'm not sure I know the best way of putting it . . . the idea is in itself a bit whimsical . . . it's a psychological idea. . . . There you are, though. When you wrote that article . . . it couldn't be, though, could it, he-he! you thought yourself—well, just a little bit, now, you know—one of those 'extraordinary' men, somebody who has a *new word* to say . . . I mean in your sense. . . . Well?"

"It might very well be," Raskolnikov contemptuously replied.

Razumikhin made a movement.

"And if that were so, you might have decided yourself . . . well, in view of the setbacks and limitations in your day-to-day life . . . maybe even to hurry mankind progressively along a bit . . . to transgress an obstacle? Let's say, for example, to murder or to rob?"

Somehow he suddenly winked again with his left eye and laughed inaudibly, exactly as he had done a little while ago.

"If I had actually transgressed," Raskolnikov answered with defiant, haughty contempt, "I certainly would not tell you about it."

"No, no, I was interested really just for a better understanding of your article, merely from the literary point of view, sir. . . ."

"Fff, how brazen and obvious it is!" Raskolnikov thought with disgust.

"Allow me to note," he replied dryly, "that I do not consider myself a Mohammed or a Napoleon . . . or anyone of that kind. So I can't give you a satisfactory explanation as to how I would act in their shoes."

"Oh, well, bosh, who among us in old Rus nowadays doesn't consider himself a Napoleon?" Porfiry, with appalling familiarity, said suddenly. Even the intonation of his voice seemed particularly clear this time.

"Wasn't it some future Napoleon who finished our Aliona

Ivanovna off with an ax last week?" Zamiotov barked suddenly from the corner.

Raskolnikov fell silent and looked hard and steadily at Porfiry. Razumikhin frowned darkly. Even before this he had begun to suspect something was going on. He looked around angrily. A moment of gloomy silence passed. Raskolnikov turned to leave.

"Going already?" Porfiry said sweetly, holding out his hand in an extremely friendly way. "I'm very, very glad to have met you. And don't worry about your report. Just write the way I told you. . . . Or best of all, come call on me there yourself . . . in a couple of days . . . or even tomorrow. I'm there around eleven. We'll fix it all up . . . we'll talk. . . . You were one of the last people *there.* You may be able to tell us something," he added with a good-natured air.

"Do you want to question me officially, with all the formalities?" Raskolnikov asked harshly.

"Why, whatever for? That's not called for at all . . . for the time being. You misunderstood. You see, I never let a chance go by. And I've already spoken with all her other customers . . . I gathered some testimony from the others . . . but you, as the last one . . . Oh, yes, by the way!" he exclaimed, lighting up suddenly about something and turning to Razumikhin, "I just remembered! What's wrong with me! Wasn't it you who kept nagging me about this Nikolashka. . . . Well, I myself know, I myself know"—he turned to Raskolnikov—"the fellow is in the clear, but what could I do, though? And then I had to go bother this Mitka. . . . Here's the point of the matter, the whole crux. . . . When you were going along the stairs that time . . . allow me . . . was it about eight o'clock?"

"About eight," Raskolnikov answered, with the unpleasant sensation simultaneously that perhaps he should not have said it.

"And while you were climbing the stairs about eight o'clock, did you perhaps see an apartment open on the second floor. . . . Remember? And two workmen, or maybe just one? They were painting, didn't you notice? It's very, very important for them!"

"Painters? No, I didn't see them," Raskolnikov answered slowly, as though he were dredging his memory. He was at the same time straining every nerve and swooning with agony to puzzle out as quickly as he could where the trap was, and whether he had overlooked anything. "No, I didn't see them. Nor an apartment open like that. I didn't notice anything. . . . On the fourth floor, though"—by now he saw the trap, and exulted—"I remember there was a government clerk moving out of his apartment . . . opposite Aliona Ivanovna's . . . I remember . . . I remember that clearly. . . . The men were carrying a couch out and pressed me to the wall . . . Painters, though . . . No, I don't recall any painters . . . and I don't think any apartment was open. No. There wasn't any—"

"What are you up to, anyway!" Razumikhin suddenly cried out, as though coming to his senses and realizing something. "The painters were painting on the day of the murder, and he was there three days before that. Wasn't he? What are you asking?"

"Fff! Got mixed up!" Porfiry clapped himself on the forehead. "Damned if I know which side is up in this case!" He turned to Raskolnikov as though he were actually going to apologize. "We need so badly to find out if anyone saw them in that apartment around eight o'clock, it made me imagine you, too, might be able to say. . . . Completely mixed up!"

"You better be more careful," Razumikhin remarked morosely.

They were already in the hall when he said this. Porfiry Petrovich conducted them all the way to the door with extraordinary graciousness. They both went into the street frowning and sullen, and for several steps they did not utter a word. Raskolnikov took a deep breath.

6

"I don't believe it! I can't believe it!" Razumikhin repeated, perplexed, trying as hard as he could to refute Raskolnikov's arguments. They were approaching Bakaleev's house, where Dunia and Pulcheria Alexandrovna had long been expecting them. Razumikhin kept stopping along the way in the heat of the conversation, embarrassed and disturbed by the fact that they were for the first time speaking clearly about *that*.

"Don't believe it, then!" Raskolnikov replied with a cold and careless smile. "As usual, you noticed nothing. But I was weighing every word."

"You don't trust anybody, that's why you keep weighing . . .

Hmm . . . Actually, I agree. Porfiry's tone was pretty strange.
And especially that bastard Zamiotov! You're right, he was
up to something. . . . But why? Why?"

"He changed his mind overnight."

"It must be the other way around, though! If they were
brainless enough to have such an idea, they would try hard
as they could to hush it up and hide their cards, so as to
swoop down later. . . . Now, though—it's brazen and
careless!"

"If they had facts, I mean real facts, or if there were any
kind of foundation to their suspicions, then they'd really try
to hide their cards in the hope of winning more—and what's
more, they would have made a search long ago! But they
don't have a single fact, not one, it's all illusion, all up in
the air, only a fleeting idea. So they're trying to get me by
being brazen. Maybe he just got mad because he doesn't
have any facts, and blew his top in indignation. Or maybe
he has something in mind. I think he's a clever man. . . .
Maybe he wanted to scare me by hinting he knows. . . .
That's his psychology, my friend. . . . Anyway, it's vile explaining all this. Let's drop it!"

"It's insulting, yes, insulting! I know what you mean!
But . . . since we've mentioned it openly now—and it's great
we finally got around to mentioning it openly, and I'm
glad!—I might as well tell you frankly I noticed they were
up to something quite a while ago. I noticed this idea of
theirs. Barely noticeable, of course. Still just hatching. But
why even just hatching? How dare they! Where, where does
it all come from? If you only knew how mad I was! What
do you mean . . . just because a poor student, ground down
by destitution and acute depression, on the eve of a cruel
illness, with delirium perhaps already beginning to affect him
(note that!), suspicious, touchy, aware of his own worth,
brooding in his corner for six months without seeing a soul,
in rags, wearing boots without soles . . . just because he
stands in front of some cops and suffers their abuse; and
then an unexpected debt gets shoved under his nose, an
expired I.O.U. from Chebarov; and the fresh paint stinks
and it's eighty degrees and the air is fetid; there's a whole
bunch of people, a story about somebody's murder (somebody just seen the day before), and all this on an empty
stomach! And who wouldn't pass out! And then to base
everything on this! To hell with them! I know it's exasperat-
ing, but if I were you, Rodia, I'd laugh in their face. Why,

I'd spit in their eye. I'd let them have it smart and neat in a proper way and let it go at that. To hell with them! Cheer up! Shame on you!"

"He put that well," Raskolnikov thought. Aloud he said: "To hell with them? But they'll ask me questions again tomorrow. Why should I enter into explanations with them? And I'm indignant that I lowered myself to Zamiotov's level in the tavern yesterday. . . ."

"To hell with it! I'll go to Porfiry myself! I'll squeeze him—a cousin's privilege, you know. Let me get to the bottom of it with him. As for Zamiotov . . ."

"So it got through to him at last," thought Raskolnikov.

"Wait!" Razumikhin yelled, grabbing him suddenly by the shoulder. "Wait! You're all wet! I've got it! You're all wet! Well, what kind of a trick is it? You say the question about the workmen was a trick? Just think, though. If you had really *done* it, would you have said you saw them painting the apartment? And the workmen? On the contrary. You wouldn't have said you saw anything even if you did! Who would testify against himself?"

"If I had done *that,* I would certainly have said I saw the workmen and the apartment," Raskolnikov said reluctantly and with evident disgust.

"But why speak against yourself?"

"Because only peasants and the most inexperienced novices deny everything at inquests as soon as it comes up. If a man's been around at all, he'll certainly try to admit all the external and incontrovertible facts as much as he can. Only he'd look for other reasons. He'd try to introduce some special and unexpected feature of his own, which would give them a completely different significance and show them in a different light. Porfiry could well have expected me to answer like that, for plausibility to say I saw them, then introduce my own explanation."

"And then he would have told you right off the workmen couldn't have been there two days beforehand, so you must have been there on the day of the murder around eight o'clock. He would have gotten you on a triviality!"

"Yes, that's what he was counting on. He thought I'd hurry to answer as plausibly as possible and I'd forget the workmen couldn't have been there two days before."

"But how could you forget that?"

"Couldn't be easier! You catch crafty men on the most trivial details. The craftier he is the less likely he'll suspect they could catch him on something simple. The craftiest man has to be caught on the very simplest thing. Porfiry isn't as dumb as you think."

"He's a bastard after this!"

Raskolnikov could not help laughing. Yet his own liveliness struck him as odd, and so did the eagerness of his explanation. He had kept up the preceding conversation with gloomy disgust, obviously because he had to and for ulterior motives. "I get myself too worked up about some points," he thought.

Almost at that very moment, however, he somehow became suddenly anxious, as though an unexpected and alarming thought had just struck him. His anxiety mounted. They had almost reached the entrance to Bakaleev's house.

"You go on in," Raskolnikov said suddenly. "I'll be back right away."

"Where you going? We're practically there!"

"I have to, have to. Business . . . I'll be back in half an hour. Tell them. . . ."

"It's up to you. But I'm going with you!"

"Damn it, you want to torment me too!" he cried out, and with such bitter irritation, such despair in his look, that Razumikhin dropped his hands. He stood on the porch a little while and watched morosely as Raskolnikov strode rapidly in the direction of the crossing. Finally, grinding his teeth and clenching his fists, swearing all the while he would squeeze Porfiry like a lemon that very day, he went upstairs to reassure Pulcheria Alexandrovna, by then alarmed at their long absence.

When Raskolnikov reached his own house, his forehead was wet with sweat and he breathed heavily. He hurried up the stairs, entered his unlocked apartment, and immediately put the door on the latch. Then, scared out of his wits, he plunged to the corner, to the very hole in the wallpaper where he had laid the things, thrust his hand in, and felt around carefully inside for several moments, going carefully over every nook and cranny in the wallpaper. Finding nothing, he rose and took a deep breath. He had suddenly imagined, while approaching Bakaleev's house, that one of the things, a chain of some sort, or a stud, or even a piece of the paper in which some of the things had been wrapped, with the old woman's handwriting on it, might somehow have eluded him and lost itself in some chink, to turn up suddenly and confront him with unexpected and irrefutable evidence.

He stood there as if in thought, and a strange, submissive, half-foolish smile played on his lips. Finally he took his cap and quietly left the room. His thoughts were confused. Pensively he went down and out to the gate.

"Why, there he is in person!" said a loud voice. He raised his head.

The janitor stood in the doorway of his little room and was pointing straight at him for the benefit of a short man who looked like some kind of artisan. He was dressed in loose coveralls and vest, and from a distance looked a lot like a woman. His head, with a greasy cap on it, was bowed, and he seemed all hunched up. From his flabby, wrinkled face, he might have been about fifty. Tiny, bloated eyes looked out, morosely, sternly, discontentedly.

"What is it?" Raskolnikov asked, approaching the janitor.

The artisan squinted at him from beneath lowered brows, looking him over carefully and closely, without hurrying. Then he turned slowly and went out through the gate into the street without saying a word.

"Why, what is it!" Raskolnikov exclaimed.

"That guy was asking if a student lived here. He mentioned your name and asked who you were living with. Then you came. I pointed you out. And he left. That's it." The janitor was a bit perplexed, too, but not much. After thinking about it a little, he turned and slithered back into his hole.

Raskolnikov hurried after the artisan and saw him cross to the other side of the street at the same steady, unhurried pace, eyes on the ground, as though thinking something over. He soon overtook him, but walked behind for a little while. Then he drew abreast of him and looked sideways into his face. The artisan noticed him immediately, threw him a quick look, but dropped his eyes again. They walked like that for a little while, one beside the other, without saying a word.

"You were . . . asking for me?" Raskolnikov said finally, yet somehow he said it very softly. The artisan gave no answer and did not even look at him. Again they were silent.

"Well, what do you mean coming and asking . . . then silence . . . what is this, anyway?" Raskolnikov's voice faltered. Somehow the words refused to come out clearly.

This time the artisan lifted his eyes and gave Raskolnikov

an ominous and somber look. Suddenly he said in a quiet but clear and distinct voice: "Murderer!"

Raskolnikov walked beside him. All of a sudden his legs felt horribly weak, a cold shiver ran up his back, and for a moment his heart seemed to stop. Then it suddenly started beating as though it had come unhinged. They walked about a hundred steps in this way, side by side, once again in complete silence.

The artisan never glanced at him.

"How dare you . . . what . . ." Raskolnikov murmured almost inaudibly. "Who do you think you're accusing of murder?"

"*You,*" he said still more precisely and emphatically, with a smile that seemed at once full of hatred and triumphant, "are a murderer," and again he looked straight at Raskolnikov's pale face and into his glazed eyes.

They were approaching the intersection. The artisan turned up the street to the left and walked on without a further glance. Raskolnikov stopped where he was and for a long time gazed after him. He saw the other man walk about fifty steps, turn and look at him as he stood there immobile. Though he could not see clearly, Raskolnikov thought that this time too the other man smiled his coldly hateful and triumphant smile.

Raskolnikov turned around and went back to his garret with a slow, faltering step, knees trembling, feeling as though a terrible chill had passed over him. He took off his cap, put it on the table, and stood there motionless beside it for ten minutes. His strength drained, he lay down on the couch; and painfully, with a weak moan, stretched out. His eyes were closed. He lay like that for half an hour.

He thought about nothing. Thoughts or the fragments of thoughts, images of one kind or another flickered in his mind without order or connection. Faces of people seen long ago in childhood, or met somewhere only once and not even remembered; the bell tower of a certain church; the billiard table in a tavern somewhere and some officer at the billiard table; the smell of cigars in some basement tobacco store; a saloon; a back staircase, completely dark, drenched with slops and strewn with eggshells; and from somewhere the sound of Sunday church bells ringing . . . Object followed object, and they went around and around like a whirlwind. Some of them he even liked, and he tried to hang on to them, but they went out like candles, and he felt that something inside him was holding him back, but not very hard. Sometimes it even felt good. His light chill did not pass, but that, too, almost felt good.

He heard Razumikhin's hurried steps and his voice, closed his eyes, and pretended to be asleep. Razumikhin opened the door and stood for a while on the threshold, as though thinking something over. Then he stepped quietly into the room and cautiously approached the couch. Nastasia could be heard whispering.

"Don't bother him. Let him sleep it off. He can eat later."

"You're right," Razumikhin said.

They went out cautiously and closed the door. Another half hour passed. Raskolnikov opened his eyes and stretched out again on his back, clasping his hands behind his head. . . .

"Who is he, this man sprung from the ground? Where has he been? What has he seen? He has seen everything, that's without doubt. But where was he standing at the time? Where did he watch *from?* Why has he emerged only now from under the floor? And how could he have seen? Is it possible? Hmm . . ." Raskolnikov grew colder and shivered. "The jewel box Nikolay found behind the door, that too, was that possible? Clues? If you overlook one infinitesimal detail the clues grow to an Egyptian pyramid! A fly flew by—and saw! Is it really possible?"

And he suddenly felt with contempt how he had weakened, physically weakened.

"I should have known," he thought with a bitter smile. "And how did I dare, when I knew myself, when I had the *feeling,* take that ax and shed blood! I should have known beforehand . . . Ah, but I did know beforehand!" he whispered in despair.

At times he would linger motionless before one thought or another.

"No, such people aren't made like that. The real *master* to whom all is permitted storms Toulon, commits a butchery in Paris, *forgets* an army in Egypt, *wastes* half a million men on his Moscow campaign, and gets off with a pun at Vilna. And when he dies they dedicate monuments to him. So it follows that *all* is permitted. No, it's clear, such people are made of bronze, not flesh and blood!"

An unexpected tangential thought suddenly almost made him laugh.

"Napoleon, the pyramids, Waterloo—and that vile, skinny clerk's widow, that wizened old bag, the pawnbroker woman

with the red trunk under her bed—well, how could even
Porfiry Petrovich make a stew of that one! Where's the pot
it would stew in! Basic esthetics would get in the way. Would
Napoleon sneak up to an old bag like that along her bed!
Oh, hell!"

For whole minutes he felt he was delirious. He was lapsing
into a feverish, ecstatic condition.

"The old bag's rubbish!" he thought heatedly and impetu-
ously. "She may even have been a mistake; anyway, she's
beside the point! The old woman was only a disease I
wanted to step over as quick as I could. . . . To step over, ah,
to transgress . . . I didn't kill a person, I killed a principle! I
killed that principle, but step over—well, I didn't step over.
I stayed on this side. . . . All I could do was kill. Couldn't
even do that, it would seem. . . . Principle? Why did that
fool Razumikhin abuse the socialists a little while ago? A
diligent, industrious lot, concerned with 'universal happiness' . . . No, life is given to me but once, and I will not
have it again. I don't want to wait for 'universal happiness.'
I want to live myself, or better not to live at all. And so? I
just didn't want to pass my hungry mother by, clutching my
ruble in my pocket while I waited for 'universal happiness.'
'I'm carrying my little brick, so to speak, for universal happiness, and that's why my heart is at peace.' Ha-ha! Then why
did you pass *me* by? I only live once, you see, and I, too,
want—Eh, I'm an esthetic louse and nothing more," he
added suddenly, and laughed like a madman. "Yes, I'm
really a louse," he went on. He fastened on the thought,
reveling in it, playing *and* picking at it for comfort, "because
in the first place I'm pondering the fact that I'm a louse.
Because in the second place I've been assuaging an all-
benevolent providence for a whole month, calling it to witness that I undertook what I did, not, you might say, for my
own lusts and desires, but that I had in view a superb and
agreeable end—ha-ha! Because in the third place, in carrying it out I proposed to stay as much as possible within
the bounds, to observe measure and balance and arithmetic.
Of all the lice I chose the one that was absolutely the most
useless, and when I killed her I intended to take from her
only as much as I needed for the first step, and neither more
nor less (and so the rest would have gone to a monastery
according to her will—ha-ha!). . . . And so, and so, I am
decisively a louse," he added, grinding his teeth, "because I
am myself nastier and fouler than the louse that was killed,

and I had the *feeling* beforehand I'd tell myself this *after* I killed! Is there a horror like it! The pettiness! The villainy! Oh, how I understand the prophet on horseback with his sword: Allah wills it; quivering flesh, submit! And the prophet is right, absolutely right, when he stations a damn good battery across a street and blasts the just and the unjust together, no explanations accepted! Quivering flesh, submit! And—*have no desire,* because . . . that's not your business! . . . Oh, not for anything, not for anything, shall I ever forgive that old hag!"

His hair was damp with sweat; his trembling lips were parched; his immobile gaze was fixed on the ceiling.

"My mother, my sister, how much I loved them! Why do I hate them now? Yes, I hate them, I physically hate them, I cannot bear to have them beside me. . . . A while ago I went up to Mother and kissed her, I remember. . . . To embrace her and to think that if she only knew . . . could I have told her then? Coming from me that would have been . . . Hmm! *She* must be the same as I am," he added, exerting an effort to think, as though struggling with the delirium that seized upon him. "Oh, how I hate that old hag now! If she came to, I think I'd kill her again! Poor Lizaveta! Why did she have to turn up at that point! . . . Strange though, wonder why I almost don't think of her, as if I hadn't killed her at all? . . . Lizaveta! Sonia! Poor creatures, meek, with meek eyes . . . Dear ones! . . . Why don't they weep? Why don't they moan? . . . They give everything away . . . they look out meekly and gently. . . . Sonia, Sonia! Gentle Sonia! . . ."

He lost consciousness. It seemed strange to him he didn't remember how he could have gotten out into the street. The evening was already late. The twilight deepened, a full moon gleamed brighter and brighter; yet somehow the air was exceptionally stuffy. Crowds of people walked along the streets. Some were going home from work. Others were strolling. It smelled of lime, dust, stagnant water. Raskolnikov walked along, mournful and preoccupied. He remembered quite well that he had left the house with some purpose in mind, that he had to do something, and in a hurry, but he had forgotten just what it was. Suddenly he stopped and saw a man standing on the other side of the street on the sidewalk, beckoning to him with his hand. He walked across the street toward him, but suddenly the man turned and walked off as though nothing had happened,

with his head down, without turning around or giving any
sign that he had called him. "Did he call or didn't he?"
Raskolnikov thought, as he started in pursuit. But before he
had gone ten steps, he suddenly remembered him and was
frightened. It was the same artisan of a while back, in the
same loose coveralls and with the same stooped figure.
Raskolnikov walked at a distance. His heart was pounding.
They turned into a side street. The other still did not turn
around. "Does he know I'm following him?" Raskolnikov
thought. The artisan entered the gate of a certain large
house. Raskolnikov approached the entry as quickly as he
could and started looking to see if the other were watching
him or if he would call him. And, in fact, when he had
passed through the entryway and was already in the yard,
the other turned and again seemed to beckon to him.
Raskolnikov passed straight through the entryway, but the
artisan was no longer in the yard. That must mean he had
gone up the first staircase. Raskolnikov hurried after him.
He could, in fact, hear measured, unhurried footsteps of
some sort two flights up. Strange, the staircase seemed somehow familiar! That window there on the first floor. Mournfully and mysteriously the moonlight filtered through the
glass. Look at the second floor. Damn! This was the very
same apartment in which the workmen had been painting. . . .
Why had he not recognized it at once? The footsteps of the
man who was walking up ahead died away. "That must
mean he stopped or he's hidden himself away somewhere."
There was the third floor. Should he go on? How quiet it
was. Appalling, even . . . But he went on. The sound of his
own footsteps frightened and disturbed him. God, how dark
it was! Very likely the artisan had hidden himself in a corner
around here somewhere. Ah! An apartment opened wide
onto the staircase. He thought for a moment, and went in.
In the entryway it was very dark and empty, not a soul, as
though everything had been moved out. Quietly, on tiptoe,
he went into the living room. The whole room was brightly
steeped in moonlight. Everything was as it had been: chairs,
the mirror, the yellow couch, and the pictures in their
frames. An immense round copper-red moon peered straight
through the windows. "The moon is what makes it so quiet,"
Raskolnikov thought. "Likely it's riddling a riddle now." He
stood there and waited. He waited a long time. The quieter
the moon was, the stronger his heart beat. It even began to
hurt. Everything was silent. Suddenly there came the sound

of an instantaneous, dry crack, like the snapping of a twig, and everything died down again. An awakened fly suddenly collided with the windowpane in flight and buzzed plaintively. At that very moment he noticed in the corner between the small cupboard and the window a woman's coat hanging on the wall. "What's that coat doing here?" he thought. "It wasn't here before." He approached very quietly. He had the feeling someone might be hiding behind the coat. Cautiously he drew the coat aside with his hand and saw that a chair stood there, and the old hag was sitting on the chair in the corner, all huddled up, with her head bent over so he could not see her face. But it was her, all right. He stood over her. "She's afraid!" he thought, and quietly he freed the ax from the loop and struck the old woman on the crown of her head, once, and then again. Strange, though. She did not stir under the blows. As if she were made of wood. He was frightened. He bent over her more closely and began to examine her. But she only sank her head down lower still. Then he crouched all the way down to the floor and looked up from below into her face. He looked and turned icy cold. The old hag was sitting there and laughing. She was shaking with quiet, inaudible laughter, bracing herself with all her might so he wouldn't hear her. Suddenly he thought the bedroom door opened slightly, and it seemed as if people were laughing there, too, and whispering among themselves. Fury seized him. With all his might he began to smash the old woman on the head, but with every blow of the ax the laughter and whispering from the bedroom became louder and louder, while the old hag laughed, spluttering like a blown flame. He tried to run away, but the front hall was already full of people; the doors facing the stairs were wide open; and on the landing, on the stairs, and all the way down, people were standing with their heads together, all looking, yet they were all hiding themselves from him, they were waiting. They fell silent! . . . His heart shrank; his feet would not move. His feet were rooted to the spot. . . . He tried to cry out. And woke up.

He was breathing heavily. Strange, though. The dream seemed still to be going on. His door was wide open, and a man he didn't know at all stood on the threshold and was examining him intensely.

Barely had Raskolnikov managed to open his eyes when he instantly closed them again. He lay on his back and did not stir. "Is the dream going on or isn't it?" he thought, and again he raised his eyelids, just imperceptibly, to have a look. The stranger stood in the same place and continued to gaze at him. All of a sudden he stepped cautiously over the threshold, closed the door carefully behind him, went up to the table, and waited a moment. All this time he did not take his eyes off Raskolnikov. Then softly, without a sound, he sat down on the chair beside the couch. He put his hat on the floor, to one side, then leaned on his cane with both hands, his chin on his hands. It was apparent that he was prepared to wait a long time. As far as Raskolnikov could make out through fluttering eyelids, the man before him was stout, no longer young, and had a thick, fair, almost white beard. . . .

About ten minutes passed. It was still light, but night was falling. It was altogether quiet in the room. Even from the stairway there was not a sound. There was only a large fly that buzzed and beat against the windowpane, with which it had collided in flight. At last, finding the silence unbearable, Raskolnikov sat up on the couch.

"Well, tell me. What is it you want?"

"Ah, but I knew you weren't asleep, only pretending," the stranger oddly answered, laughing calmly. "Allow me to introduce myself . . . Arkady Ivanovich Svidrigailov."

PART FOUR

1

"Could I still be dreaming?" Raskolnikov thought once more. He scrutinized his unexpected visitor cautiously and mistrustfully.

Perplexed, he finally said aloud: "Svidrigailov? Absurd! It can't be!" This exclamation did not seem to surprise the visitor.

"I've come to see you for two reasons. One, I wanted personally to meet you, because I've been hearing interesting and flattering things about you for some time. Secondly, I fancy you won't refuse me a little help in a certain project of mine that touches directly on the interests of your dear sister, Avdotia Romanovna. Because of certain, ah, prejudices, she wouldn't even admit me into her yard by myself, without an introduction. But with your help, I could count—"

"You count badly," Raskolnikov interrupted.

"Permit me to ask, did they arrive just yesterday?"

Raskolnikov did not reply.

"It was yesterday, I know. I just arrived two days ago myself. Well, sir, let me say this to you, Rodion Romanovich. Mind you, I don't consider it necessary to justify myself, but let me say this much. In actual fact, what was so particularly criminal about the part I played in this whole matter—I mean, if judged without prejudice and with common sense?"

Raskolnikov went on gazing at him in silence.

"I pursued a defenseless girl in my own home, and I 'offended her with my infamous proposals'—is that it? (I'm getting a little ahead of myself!) Just suppose, however, that I, too, am a man, *et nihil humanum* . . . in a word, that I can be attracted and fall in love (and of course that doesn't happen to us according to our will) . . . and everything's accounted for in the most natural manner. The whole question boils down to this: am I a monster or am I a victim? Well, you may ask, what do you mean, 'victim'? Well, when I proposed to my object that she run away with me to

America or Switzerland, I might have been nourishing the most worthy sentiments all along, and I might even have been planning our mutual happiness! Reason is passion's slave, is it not? Heavens, for all you know I might have hurt myself far more than I hurt her!"

"That's not the point at all," Raskolnikov interrupted with disgust. "To put it bluntly, you are repulsive. Nobody wants to know whether or not you were right, they just want you to leave and get the hell out!"

Svidrigailov suddenly burst out laughing. He laughed in the most blatant manner. "Well, I can't seem to take you in, can I? Here I thought I'd try to put something over, but you got the point right away."

"You're still trying to put something over."

"And what if I am? What if I am? It's what they call the *bonne guerre,* isn't it?—and I'm certain 'putting something over' is absolutely allowed! But, in any case, you interrupted me. Be that as it may, I assure you once more, there would have been no unpleasantness if it had not been for that incident in the garden. Martha Petrovna—"

"They say you sent off Martha Petrovna, too," Raskolnikov rudely broke in.

"So you heard that, did you? How could you help it. . . . Well, as for your question, I really don't know what to say to you, though my conscience is absolutely clear in the matter. I mean, you mustn't think anything of that sort frightens me. It was all gone into in complete detail and perfectly properly. The medical investigation revealed a stroke caused by bathing immediately after a heavy meal and what was almost a full bottle of wine. Furthermore, it couldn't have revealed anything else. . . . No, sir. I spent some time thinking it over. Especially while I was sitting in the train on the way here. I thought: didn't I contribute to all this . . . bad luck . . . by upsetting her morally in some way, or something of that sort? Even that, I concluded, was definitely out of the question."

Raskolnikov laughed. "What a fine concern!"

"But why do you laugh? Just think: I only hit her twice with the switch. There weren't even any traces that showed. . . . You mustn't think I'm a cynic. I can assure you I know just how beastly it was on my part and all that. I also happen to know for certain, mind you, that Martha Petrovna was actually quite pleased with what you might call this little diversion of mine. The episode with your sister had been exhausted to the dregs. And there was Martha Petrovna, forced to sit home for the third day. She had nothing to show around in town, and everybody was bored stiff with that letter of hers—you heard about her reading that letter? And all of a sudden these two strokes of the switch fell as if from heaven! First thing she did was order the carriage harnessed! I won't even go into the fact that there are times when women find it very very agreeable to be offended, all their apparent indignation to the contrary notwithstanding. They all have times like that. Man in general enjoys offense—haven't you noticed? But women especially. You might even say it's all they've got to live on."

At one point Raskolnikov thought he might get up and leave and put an end to the interview, but a certain curiosity, even a certain self-interest, kept him awhile.

"Do you enjoy fighting?" he asked absentmindedly.

Svidrigailov replied calmly: "No, not much. I almost never fought with Martha Petrovna. We lived quite harmoniously, and she was always content with me. During our seven years together I used the switch only twice in all (not counting a third time that was extremely ambiguous anyway). The first time was two months after our wedding, as soon as we arrived in the country. The last time is the one we're talking about. And you thought I was a monster, a reactionary, a serf owner? He-he . . . And by the way, Rodion Romanovich—do you remember how, some years ago (it was in the days when people still believed in the beneficent effects of publicity), a certain nobleman got taken over the coals by all the newspapers. . . . I've forgotten his name . . . you remember, he whipped some German girl in a railroad car . . . I think it was the same year *Century* magazine had that scandal (you remember, the woman who read 'Egyptian Nights' aloud in public? Those dark eyes! And wherefore art thou fled, golden time of our youth!). Well, sir, I think this: I don't have a very deep sympathy for the gentleman who whipped the German girl, because in actual fact . . . well, what is there to sympathize with! And yet I feel obliged to point out that from time to time one comes across such provocative German girls it would seem to me there isn't a single progressive who can vouch for himself with certainty. At the time there wasn't anybody who looked at the matter from this point of view. Nevertheless, this is the point of view that's the humane one, really!" When he said this, Svidrigailov suddenly burst out laughing again. It was clear to Raskolnikov he was a man who had his mind set on something, a man who was keeping something to himself.

"It must be several days now since you've talked to anybody," Raskolnikov said.

"Just about. You're probably surprised to find me so easygoing?"

"No. I'm surprised to find you *too* easygoing."

"Because the rudeness of your questions didn't offend me? Is that it? Why should I be offended? You asked, I answered," he said with a remarkable expression of good humor. "You know," he added pensively, "there's nothing that interests me much. Especially now I'm not doing anything . . . You may very well think I'm after something— I said so myself— especially since I have business that concerns your sister. But I tell you frankly—I'm very bored! These last three days especially. I was actually delighted I found you. . . . Now, don't get angry, Rodion Romanovich, but to me it seems as if you're terribly strange yourself, somehow. Whatever you say, you've got something inside you; inside you now, I mean 'now,' not just this very moment, but 'now' in general. . . . Well, well; I won't, I won't; don't frown! But I'm not such a bear as all that."

Raskolnikov looked at him darkly. "You might not be a bear at all. It strikes me you come of quite good society. At least, you know how to behave respectably sometimes."

"Well, I'm not particularly interested in anybody's opinion," Svidrigailov replied dryly and with even a touch of arrogance. "Why not be vile?—it's a suit that goes well with our climate . . . especially if you have a natural bent for it," he added, laughing again.

"I heard you know lots of people here. You are, as they say, not without connections. So why do you come to me—unless you have some purpose in mind?"

"That's true. I know people here," Svidrigailov said, avoiding the main point. "I've seen them already. I've been lounging around for three days now. I acknowledge them, and it seems they acknowledge me. Of course, I'm well dressed and considered far from poor. Even the peasant reform didn't hit us badly. Woods and water meadows—the income hasn't been lost. But . . . I won't go back. I was sick of it even before. I've been here three days and I haven't really talked to anybody. . . . Here's a city for you! How, pray tell, did it ever come to pass—a city of clerks and students of every conceivable kind! You know, there was a lot I never noticed when I used to hang around here some eight years ago. . . . Now I pin all my hope on anatomy alone, by God!"

"What do you mean, anatomy?"

"As for these clubs, Dussot's Restaurant, these promenades of yours—progress, yes . . . well, you can have it," he went on, again ignoring the question. "Who wants to be a swindler, anyway?"

"You were a swindler, too?"

"How could I not? There was a whole crowd of us about eight years ago, all highly respectable. We used to pass the time. We were people with manners, mind you. Some were poets, some capitalists. Have you noticed, by the way, that in our Russian society generally you'll find the very best manners among those who have been kicked around? Just now I've let myself go a bit, living in the country, and all that. Well, anyway, they put me in jail that time, for debt. On account of a dirty Greek from Nezhin. That's where Martha Petrovna came in. She made an arrangement and bought me out for thirty thousand, silver. (I was in debt for seventy thousand in all.) So I married her according to law and she had me shipped off at once to her place in the country, like some kind of treasure. She was five years older than I was. She was very much in love. For seven years I didn't leave our village. All her life, mind you, she kept that document against me, in somebody else's name, for those thirty thousand rubles. And if I should ever take it into my head to rebel—straight into the jug! She would have done it, too! Women don't find all this contradictory, you know."

"And if it hadn't been for the document you would have flown?"

"I don't know how to tell you. It wasn't the document that hindered me. I didn't feel like going anywhere. Twice Martha Petrovna herself suggested I go abroad, when she saw how bored I was. What was the point! I'd been abroad before; I was always miserable. It's not just that you watch the sun rise over the Bay of Naples and the sea and somehow you feel sad. What's most sickening is that you really do feel sad about something! No, it's better at home. You can at least blame other people and justify yourself. I guess I could go on an expedition to the North Pole, because *j'ai le vin mauvais* and I find drinking repulsive; but except for liquor there's nothing left. I've tried it. By the way, you know what, they say Berg's flying over Iusupov Park Sunday in a huge balloon, and he'll take passengers for a fee, not so?"

"Would you fly?"

"I? No . . ." Svidrigailov muttered as if he really were putting his mind on it, "it's just that . . ."

"What's he really up to?" Raskolnikov thought. "What is going on?"

"No, it wasn't the document that hindered me," Svidrigailov went on thoughtfully. "I didn't leave the village on my own account. Not quite a year ago Martha Petrovna gave me the document as a birthday present. She threw in quite a bit of money, too. Of course, she had quite a pile. 'See how much I trust you, Arkady Ivanovich?' She really did say something of that sort. Don't you believe she said that? You know, I got to be a pretty good landlord in the village, though. I'm well known in the neighborhood. I also had books sent. At first Martha Petrovna approved. Then she worried I might study too much."

"You seem to miss Martha Petrovna a lot?"

"I? Maybe I do. Maybe I really do. By the way, do you believe in ghosts?"

"Ghosts? What kind?"

"Ordinary ghosts, that's what kind!"

"And you—do you believe in them?"

"Well, yes and no, *pour vous plaire*. . . . What I mean to say is, it's not exactly—"

"You see them, or what?"

Svidrigailov looked at him strangely.

"Martha Petrovna deigns to visit me," he said. His mouth was twisted into a sort of strange smile.

"What do you mean, she deigns to visit?"

"Well, she's come three times now. First I saw her the day of the funeral, an hour after I got back from the cemetery. That was the day before I left. The second time was the day before yesterday, on the road, at dawn, at the Maly Visher station. Third time was two hours ago at the apartment where I'm staying, in my room. I was alone."

"Wide awake?"

"Completely. Wide awake all three times. She comes, talks for a minute, and leaves through the door. I even seem to hear her."

"Why was it I thought something like this was happening to you!" Raskolnikov said this suddenly, astonished that he said it. He was quite excited.

"You do-on't say? That's what you thought?" Svidrigailov asked in surprise. "Really? Well, didn't I tell you we had a certain something in common, ah?"

"You never said it," Raskolnikov replied sharply and fervidly.

"Didn't I say it?"

"No!"

"I thought I did. A while ago, when I came in and saw you lying there with your eyes closed, pretending—I said to myself on the spot, 'That's the very man!' "

"What do you mean—the very man? What are you talking about?" Raskolnikov cried out.

"What? I really don't know what," Svidrigailov murmured sincerely. He seemed genuinely confused. They were silent a moment, and looked each other full in the face.

"What nonsense!" Raskolnikov exclaimed indignantly. "What does she say to you when she visits?"

"Her? Well, she just talks about little things, really. Banalities. Such is man. You know, it even makes me mad. The first time she came in, I was tired, you realize—the funeral, the ceremony, the lament, the meal; finally I found myself alone in my study, I lit up a cigar, I was thinking—she came in through the door. 'Arkady Ivanovich,' she says, 'you had a lot to do today and you forgot to wind the clock in the dining room.' I really had been winding that clock every week for the last seven years, and if I ever forgot she'd remind me. Next day I started out for here. I got to the station at day-break. I'd slept badly that night, I was upset, my eyes were heavy; I had some coffee. All of a sudden Martha Petrovna sits beside me with a pack of cards in her hands. 'Shouldn't I tell your fortune, Arkady Ivanovich, for the road?' She was a master at reading the cards. Well, I can't forgive myself not letting her read them! I ran away. I was frightened, and then, it's true, the train bell rang. Today I was sitting around, dyspeptic, after the most disgusting meal brought in from some kitchen. I was sitting there smoking. Suddenly Martha Petrovna comes in again, all dressed up in a new green silk dress with a very long train. 'Hello, Arkady Ivanovich! How do you like my dress? Anis'ka doesn't make them like that.' (Anis'ka is the dressmaker in our village, used to be a serf, went to Moscow to learn her trade—a good kid.) She stands there and turns around to show it to me. I look at the dress and then I look her carefully in the face. I say to her, 'Martha Petrovna.

Why do you insist on coming here and bothering me with such banalities?' 'Oh, good heavens, my dear fellow, can't you even be bothered a little!' I say to her, to tease her: 'I'd like to get married, Martha Petrovna.' 'That's to be expected from you, Arkady Ivanovich. But it doesn't do you much honor, running off to get married, when you've hardly managed to bury your first wife. Well, if you'd only pick the right one . . . but neither you nor she would be happy; and decent people would only laugh.' Then she gathered herself up and left. I even thought I heard her train rustle. Damn nonsense, isn't it, ah?"

"Yes, and then you might even be lying about the whole thing, might you not?" said Raskolnikov.

Svidrigailov answered thoughtfully, as if he had not noticed the rudeness of the question: "I rarely lie."

"And before all this—did you ever see any ghosts?"

"Nn . . . no. Only once in my life, six years ago. I had a servant called Fil'ka. He'd just been buried, but I forgot about it, and yelled, 'Fil'ka, my pipe!' He came in and went straight to the cabinet where I keep my pipes. I sat and I thought: 'He's doing this to revenge himself on me,' because just before he died we had a big fight. 'How dare you come in to me with your elbows out,' I told him. 'Beat it, you scoundrel!' He turned, went out, and never came in again. I didn't tell Martha Petrovna at the time. I wanted to have a requiem performed for him, but then I thought better of it."

"Go see a doctor."

"I don't need you to tell me I'm sick. Although, really, I don't know with what. Still, I think I'm five times as healthy as you are. I didn't ask you if you believe people see ghosts. I asked you if you believe ghosts exist."

"No, I wouldn't believe it for anything!" Raskolnikov shouted, practically in a rage.

Svidrigailov murmured, as if to himself: "What is it they usually say?" He looked away and bowed his head a little. "They say: 'You're sick. So what you see is just delirium. Doesn't exist.' The logic's not very strict here. Ghosts appear only to the sick, I agree. But all that proves is that ghosts can appear only to the sick. Not that they don't exist in their own right."

Raskolnikov irritably insisted: "Of course they don't!"

Looking at him hard, Svidrigailov went on: "They don't? You think they don't? What if we look at it this way, though (you can help out here): You might say that ghosts are the scraps and fragments of other worlds, their beginning. Of course, a healthy man has no way of seeing them, because a healthy man is above all an earthbound man; so for order and fullness he must live his life in the here and now exclusively. The moment he's sick, though, the moment the normal earthbound order of his organism is violated, the possibility of another world begins to make itself felt, and the sicker he gets the closer in touch he is with the other world, so when a man dies completely he goes straight over into the other world. I've been debating this a long time. You can follow me, if you have faith in a future life."

"I don't have faith in a future life," Raskolnikov said.

Svidrigailov sat absorbed in thought. Suddenly he said: "What if there are only spiders there—or something of that sort?"

"That's insane," thought Raskolnikov.

"We always imagine eternity as a conception impossible to grasp, something enormous, immense! Why must it inevitably be enormous? Just think of a single little room—a bathhouse in one of our backwater villages, something like that, sooty, spiders in all the corners—and that's all there is to eternity. You know, sometimes that's the way it strikes me."

"You mean, you mean to tell me," said Raskolnikov with a queasy feeling, "you mean you can't imagine anything more comforting than that, more just?"

Svidrigailov replied, smiling vaguely: "More just? How do we know? Maybe it is just. I'll tell you something. If I had my way, that's exactly the way I would have made it!"

This horrible answer made Raskolnikov shudder. Svidrigailov raised his head, gave him a penetrating look, and suddenly burst out laughing.

"Who would have thought it!" he roared. "Half an hour ago we'd never even seen each other. We consider ourselves enemies. There's unsettled business between us. So we've tossed our business aside and taken off into literature! When I said we were berries from the same field, wasn't I right?"

"Be so kind," said Raskolnikov irritably. "Let me ask you to explain yourself. Tell me as quick as you can why you do me the honor of this visit . . . and—and—I'm in a hurry, I don't have much time. I want to go out. . . ."

"Of course, of course. Your sister, Avdotia Romanovna, is going to marry Peter Petrovich Luzhin, is she not?"

"Would you mind leaving any question about my sister out of this? If you really are Svidrigailov, I don't understand how you have the nerve even to mention her name in my presence. . . ."

"She's what I came here to talk about. How can I not mention her?"

"All right. Speak up. But hurry."

"I'm sure you already have your own opinion of Mr. Luzhin. He's a relative of mine on my wife's side. Even if you've only seen him for half an hour, even if you've only heard something about him at second hand, if it rang true, you've formed an opinion. He is no match for Avdotia Romanovna. If you ask me, she is rashly and magnanimously making a sacrifice of herself for the sake . . . for the sake of her family. After all I'd heard about you, it struck me that you might be rather pleased if this marriage could be broken up without any harm to your interests. Now that I've met you personally, I'm quite sure of it."

"You're being very naïve. Excuse me. I meant to say 'brazen,' " said Raskolnikov.

"You mean I'm out for my own gain. Don't worry, Rodion Romanovich, if I were out for my own profit I wouldn't speak out so plainly. I'm not a complete fool, you know. On that subject, I'll let you in on a certain psychological curiosity. Before, when I was justifying my love for Avdotia Romanovna, I said I was myself the victim. You might as well know I don't feel any love for her anymore, none at all, and I must admit myself, it's odd, because I really did feel something—"

"Idleness and dissipation!" Raskolnikov interrupted.

"Yes, I'm a dissipated and an idle man. Yet your sister has such qualities, even I couldn't help being impressed. But it's all nonsense, as I see now myself."

"Have you known this for long?"

"I became aware of it some time ago, and the day before yesterday, almost at the very moment I arrived in Petersburg, I was conclusively convinced. As recently as Moscow, though, I still imagined I was going to try for Avdotia Romanovna's hand and compete with Mr. Luzhin."

"Excuse me for interrupting, but couldn't you please cut this short and get to the point? I'm in a hurry. I have to go out."

"With the greatest pleasure. After I arrived here I decided to undertake a certain . . . voyage. I wanted to make the necessary preliminary arrangements. My children were left at their aunt's. They're rich, and they don't need me personally. What kind of a father am I, anyway! For myself I took only what Martha Petrovna gave me a year ago. For me, that's enough. Excuse me, I'm getting to the main point. Before this voyage, which I might take yet after all, I'd like to finish with Mr. Luzhin, too. Not that I find him particularly objectionable, but he was the one who caused my quarrel with Martha Petrovna, when I found out she'd cooked up this wedding. I'd like to arrange a meeting with Avdotia Romanovna now, with your help; in your presence, if you like. I'd like to explain to her how she not only cannot expect the least good out of marrying Mr. Luzhin, but most likely would suffer positive harm. Then I'd like to ask her pardon for all those recent unpleasantnesses, and I'd like to ask permission to present her with ten thousand rubles and facilitate the break with Mr. Luzhin. I'm sure she wouldn't mind breaking with Mr. Luzhin, if only the possibility presented itself."

"Well, you really, really are mad," exclaimed Raskolnikov, not even so much angry as astonished. "How dare you talk like this!"

"I knew you'd raise objections. Well, in the first place, even though I'm not rich, I do have these ten thousand rubles at my disposal. That is, I really don't need them. If Avdotia Romanovna didn't take them, I'd probably use them in some stupider way. That's one. Two: my conscience is quite at peace. I make this proposal without any calculation. You may believe it or not. Later, you and Avdotia Romanovna both will have to admit it is true. The point is I really did cause your worthy sister a certain amount of trouble and unpleasantness. Since I'm genuinely sorry, I'd really like—not to buy myself off, not to pay for the unpleasantness, but—simply to do her some good, on the grounds that I'm not trying to assert the exclusive privilege of doing wrong. If there were even a millionth part of cunning in this proposal I'm making, I wouldn't be putting matters so bluntly and I wouldn't have suggested only ten thousand— just five weeks ago . . . to her . . . I suggested more. Anyway, it's possible, very, very soon now, I might marry a certain girl. That alone ought to eliminate any suspicion of some design against Avdotia Romanovna. I might close by saying that if she married Mr. Luzhin, Avdotia Romanovna would be taking the same money, only from another party. . . .

Now, don't get angry, Rodion Romanovich. Consider the matter calmly and dispassionately." As he said this, Svidrigailov himself was extremely calm and dispassionate.

"I beg you to finish," said Raskolnikov. "It's unforgivably impudent, in any case."

"Not in the least. Or else man may only do harm to man in this world, without any right to do the least crumb of good—and all because of empty, conventional formalities. That's absurd. If I should die, let's say, and leave your sister this amount in my will, you mean to say she'd refuse to accept it even then?"

"It might very well be."

"Well, that's as good as no. What's more, no is no; so be it. And yet, ten thousand makes a fine pile on occasion. Anyway, I beg you to convey what I said to Avdotia Romanovna."

"No, I will not convey it."

"In that case, Rodion Romanovich, I'd be forced to seek a personal interview myself. That might upset her."

"You won't seek a personal interview if I do convey it?"

"Really, I don't know what to say. I'd very much like to see her once more."

"Not a hope."

"Too bad. But then you don't know me. Can't tell, though; we might get to know each other better."

"You think we will get to know each other better?"

"And why not?" Svidrigailov said, and smiled. He rose and took his hat. "I didn't really want to trouble you, you know; and I didn't even bank much on coming here. And yet, you know, your face struck me some time ago this morning—"

"Where did you see me some time ago this morning?" Raskolnikov asked, disturbed.

"Accidentally . . . I still think you have something in you that resembles me. Don't worry, now, I won't be a nuisance. I managed to get along with swindlers, and I didn't bore Prince Svirbey—he's a distant relative of mine and a grandee. I could write about the Rafael Madonna in Mrs. Prilukov's album, and I lived with Martha Petrovna for seven unrelieved years, and in the old days I used to spend the night at Viazemsky's flophouse, and maybe I'll fly in a balloon with Berg."

"Very well. May I ask if you're planning to leave on your journey soon?"

"What journey?"

"Why, that 'voyage' . . . you mentioned it yourself."

"On a voyage? Ah, yes! In actual fact, I did tell you about the voyage. . . . Well, it's a broad question. . . . If you only knew what you were asking, though!" he added, and all of a sudden, briefly and loudly, he burst out laughing. "Maybe I'll get married instead of going on this voyage. They're finding me a bride."

"Here?"

"Yes."

"When did you manage that?"

"And yet I'd very much like to see Avdotia Romanovna once. I'm asking seriously. Well, good-bye. . . . Oh, yes. I almost forgot. Convey to your sister, Rodion Romanovich, that Martha Petrovna left her three thousand in her will. That really is so. Martha Petrovna made the arrangements a week before her death. I was there at the time. In two or three weeks, Avdotia Romanovna can get the money."

"Are you telling the truth?"

"Yes, the truth. Convey it to her. Well, sir—your servant. The place I'm staying isn't at all far from you."

Going out, Svidrigailov bumped into Razumikhin in the doorway.

2

It was almost eight o'clock. They both hurried to Bakaleev's, to get there ahead of Luzhin.

"Who was that?" Razumikhin asked as soon as they were out in the street.

"Svidrigailov. The landowner. Where my sister was insulted when she worked in their house as a governess. She left because he was chasing her around. She was driven away by Martha Petrovna, his wife. Later this Martha Petrovna asked Dunia for her forgiveness. A little while ago she suddenly died. She's the one they were talking about a while back. This man frightens me, I don't know why. He came here right after his wife's funeral. He's very strange, and he's made up his mind about something. . . . As though he knew something . . . Dunia's got to be protected from him . . . that's what I wanted to tell you, you hear?"

"Protected! Why, what could he do to Avdotia Romanovna? Well, anyway. I'm grateful to you for talking to me like that, Rodia. . . . We'll protect her, we will! . . . Where's he living?"

"I don't know."

"Why didn't you ask? Ah, well. Too bad. But I'll find out!"

After a brief silence, Raskolnikov asked: "You saw him?"

"Well, yes. I took notice. I took good notice."

"Did you see him clearly?" Raskolnikov insisted. "In detail?"

"Why, yes, I remember him clearly. I'd know him in a thousand. I have a good memory for faces."

Again they fell silent.

";Hmm . . . better . . ." murmured Raskolnikov. "But if you hadn't . . . I thought . . . well, it seemed . . . the whole thing might have been a fantasy."

"What are you talking about? I don't quite follow."

Raskolnikov twisted his mouth into a smile. "Well, you all say I'm insane. I thought maybe I really was insane and what I saw was just a ghost."

"What are you saying?"

"Who knows! Maybe I've been insane all along. Maybe everything that's happened these last few days was just my imagination. . . ."

"Oh, come on, Rodia! They've upset you again! Well, what did he say? What did he come for?"

Raskolnikov did not reply. Razumikhin thought for a moment. "Well, then, listen to my report," he began. "I came to your place. You were asleep. Then we ate, and then I went to Porfiry's. Zamiotov's still there. I tried to start in, but nothing came of it. I couldn't get anything across properly. They simply don't understand and cannot understand, and it doesn't bother them in the least. I led Porfiry aside to the window and started talking, but again, for some reason, it didn't come off. He looks away—I look away. Finally, I put my fist under his jaw and I told him, one relative to another, I'd brain him. He just looked at me. I spat and left, and that's all. It's awfully dumb. I didn't say a word to Zamiotov. Look, though. I thought I'd made a mess of it, but an idea popped into my head as I was going down the stairs, and I saw the light. What do we care, the two of us? If you were in any kind of danger or anything like that— well, okay, certainly. But what's it to you! It has nothing to do with you, so to hell with them. We'll have the last laugh, and if I were you I'd go on kidding them along. Later they'll be ashamed of themselves! Later we'll rub it in. For now, though, let's have a good laugh!"

"Yes, of course," Raskolnikov replied. "What will you say tomorrow, though?" he thought to himself. A strange business; yet until now it had not once entered his head what Razumikhin would think when he found out. Having thought of it, Raskolnikov looked at him intently. He had very little interest in Razumikhin's report of his visit to Porfiry. So much had gone by since then, and so much had been added!

In the corridor they ran into Luzhin. He had appeared punctually at eight o'clock and was looking for the apartment. All three of them went in together, but without greeting each other or so much as a glance. The young men went on ahead while Peter Petrovich, for appearances' sake, loitered a bit in the front hall while taking off his coat. Pulcheria Alexandrovna immediately stepped forward so as to meet him at the threshold. Dunia greeted her brother.

Peter Petrovich entered, and fairly politely, though with doubled solemnity, greeted the ladies. But he looked as though he'd been a little put out and hadn't yet had time to recover. Pulcheria Alexandrovna, who also seemed embarrassed, immediately hastened to seat everyone at the round table, on which a samovar boiled away. Dunia and Luzhin sat at opposite ends of the table. Razumikhin and Raskolnikov sat across from Pulcheria Alexandrovna— Razumikhin closer to Luzhin, and Raskolnikov beside his sister.

A momentary silence arose. Slowly Peter Petrovich took out a scented cambric handkerchief and blew his nose, with the air of a man of goodwill who has just received some slight affront to his dignity and has firmly resolved to demand an explanation. While still in the front hall he had wondered whether he should not leave his coat on and go away, punishing both the ladies with this stern emphasis, letting them feel it immediately. Yet he could not bring himself to do so. He was a man who did not like uncertainty, and something here had to be cleared up. Since his order had been so flagrantly violated, something must be up, and he'd better find out what it was in ample time. Everything was in his hands, and there would always be the chance to punish.

"I trust you had a pleasant journey," he said in an official tone to Pulcheria Alexandrovna.

"Thank God, it was, Peter Petrovich."

"I'm very glad to hear it. You didn't get overtired?" he said to Dunia.

"I'm young and strong and I don't get tired," Dunia said, "but it was a hard trip for Mother."

"What can one do? The railroads in our country are very long. Our so-called Mother Russia is vast. Much as I wanted to, there was no way I could meet you yesterday. But I trust everything went without inconvenience?"

"Oh, no, Peter Petrovich, we were very downhearted," Pulcheria Alexandrovna hastened to declare, with a special emphasis, "and if God himself, as it would seem, hadn't sent Dmitry Prokofich to us, I simply don't know what we would have done. Here he is, Dmitry Prokofich Razumikhin," she added, introducing him to Luzhin.

"Why, yes, I had the pleasure . . . yesterday," Luzhin muttered, with a hostile sidelong glance at Razumikhin. Then he scowled and fell silent. All in all, Peter Petrovich was one of those people, very polite in society, who even flaunt special claims to politeness, but who lose their grip as soon as things do not go their way, and become more like flour sacks than lively and amiable cavaliers. Once more, silence descended. Raskolnikov was stubbornly silent; Avdotia Romanovna did not want to break the silence prematurely; Razumikhin had little to say. And so Pulcheria Alexandrovna started worrying again.

"You heard that Martha Petrovna died," she began, taking refuge in her major standby.

"Yes, ma'am, I heard. I was immediately informed, and one of the reasons I came was to tell you that Arkady Ivanovich Svidrigailov left hastily for Petersburg immediately after his wife's funeral. At least that's what I heard from a reliable source."

"To Petersburg?" Dunia asked anxiously, and exchanged a glance with her mother. "Here?"

"Precisely, ma'am, and, of course, not without some end in view, bearing in mind the haste of his departure and, in general, the circumstances preceding it."

"Good Lord!" Pulcheria Alexandrovna exclaimed. "Does that mean he isn't going to leave Dunia in peace even here?"

"I don't think either you or Avdotia Romanovna need to

feel specially anxious—if you yourselves have no wish to enter into any kind of relationship with him, that is. For my part, I'm tracking him down now, trying to find out where he's staying. . . ."

"Oh, Peter Petrovich, you won't believe how much you frightened me just now!" Pulcheria Alexandrovna went on. "I've seen him only twice, and to me he seemed horrible, horrible! I'm sure he was the cause of Martha Petrovna's death."

"About that, one can't say. I have reliable information. I won't argue, maybe he helped things along, so to speak, by the way he insulted her. In general, I agree with you, as far as his conduct and moral character are concerned. I don't know whether he is a wealthy man or how much Martha Petrovna actually left him. I'll find out about that quite soon. Meanwhile, he's back in St. Petersburg with at least some monetary means at his disposal, and he'll no doubt take up his old ways again. As men of his type go, he's the most depraved and vice-ridden there is! I have some reason to believe that Martha Petrovna, who was unlucky enough to fall in love with him eight years ago and buy out his debts, served him in another way, too. Through her effort and her sacrifices alone a criminal case was covered up at the very start. This had a dash of brutal and, I might say, fantastic homicide in it, for which he might well have had to go romping off to Siberia. That is the kind of man he is, if you want to know."

"Good heavens!" Pulcheria Alexandrovna exclaimed. Raskolnikov listened attentively.

"Are you telling the truth when you say you have precise information about it?" Dunia asked sternly and insistently.

"I say only what I heard from the deceased Martha Petrovna myself, in confidence. It should be pointed out that the case is quite obscure from a legal point of view. A certain woman named Resslich used to live here, and I believe she still does. She's a foreigner and a small-scale money lender who also engages in other activities. From a long time back, Mr. Svidrigailov had very close and mysterious relationships with this Resslich. A distant relative, a niece of some sort, was living with her, a deaf and dumb girl of about fifteen, maybe only fourteen, whom this Resslich hated beyond all measure, and whom she grudged every crust. She would even beat her inhumanly. One day the girl was found hanging in the garret. The verdict was suicide.

After the usual procedure, the case ended at that, but a later report came to light that the child had been . . . cruelly outraged by Svidrigailov. True, it was all obscure. The report came from another German, a notorious woman who could not be trusted. In the long run, thanks essentially to Martha Petrovna's efforts and money, the report was not made. Everything remained confined to rumor. This rumor was highly indicative, though. By the way, Avdotia Romanovna, you must have heard that story about the man Phillip, when you were at their place, the one who died of ill treatment about six years ago, before serfdom had been abolished."

"I heard, on the contrary, that this Phillip hanged himself."

"Precisely so, ma'am, yet it was Mr. Svidrigailov's constant and systematic persecution and his exactions that forced or, better to say, *inclined* him to a violent death."

"I don't know that," Dunia answered dryly. "All I heard was a very strange story that this Phillip was a kind of chronic depressive, a kind of homespun philosopher. The servants used to say, 'He read himself silly.' They said he hanged himself more from Mr. Svidrigailov's laughter than from his blows. While I was there, he treated the servants very well. They were actually very fond of him, though they did blame him for Phillip's death."

"I see, Avdotia Romanovna, that you are somehow suddenly inclined to justify him," Luzhin noted, twisting his mouth into an ambiguous smile. "Actually, he is a cunning man, and seductive where the ladies are concerned. Martha Petrovna, who died so strangely, may serve as a lamented example. I merely wished to make my advice available to you and your dear mother—since he will undoubtedly try again to see you. As for me, I am firmly convinced the man will undoubtedly disappear into debtors' prison again. Martha Petrovna had her children in mind and never intended to settle anything on him, and if she did leave him something it could only have been a bare minimum, something insignificant and ephemeral, something that would not last a man of his habits for even a year."

"Peter Petrovich, I beg you," Dunia said, "please let's stop about Mr. Svidrigailov. It depresses me."

"He has just been to see me," Raskolnikov said suddenly, breaking his silence for the first time. There were exclamations on all sides. Everyone turned to him. Even Peter Petrovich was aroused. "He came in an hour and a half ago, when I was asleep. He woke me up and introduced himself. He was quite cheerful and at ease and really hoped that we would become friends. Among other things, Dunia, he's quite anxious to see you, and he asked me to arrange a meeting. He has a proposition for you. He told me what it was. In addition, he told me definitely that a week before her death Martha Petrovna managed to leave you three thousand rubles in her will, Dunia, and you'll be able to get this money in a very short time."

"Thank the Lord!" Pulcheria Alexandrovna exclaimed, and crossed herself. "Pray for her, Dunia, pray!"

"That's a fact," burst out Luzhin.

"Well, and what else?" Dunia said quickly.

"He said he himself was not rich and the whole estate was left to his children, who were at their aunt's. He said he was staying somewhere not far from me, but I don't know where. I didn't ask. . . ."

"But what, what in the world does he want to propose to Dunia?" the terrified Pulcheria Alexandrovna asked. "Did he tell you?"

"Yes, he told me."

"What?"

"I'll tell you later." Raskolnikov fell silent and turned to his tea. Peter Petrovich drew out his watch and looked.

"I have business to attend to, so I won't be in your way," he said with a rather piqued expression, and began to get up from the table.

"Wait, Peter Petrovich," Dunia said. "You intended to spend the evening. What's more, you yourself wrote there was something you'd like to have Mother explain."

"Precisely so, Avdotia Romanovna," Peter Petrovich said emphatically as he sat down again, still holding his hat in his hands. "I really wanted to have an explanation with you and your worthy mother, about quite important details, actually. But since your brother cannot, in my presence, explain certain proposals of Mr. Svidrigailov, I do not wish to and cannot explain . . . in the presence of others . . . certain quite, quite important details. What is more, my fundamental and most earnest request was not fulfilled. . . ."

Luzhin put on an aggrieved air and lapsed into dignified silence.

"Your request that my brother not be present at our meeting was not fulfilled solely on my insistence," Dunia said. "You wrote that my brother had insulted you. I think this must be cleared up immediately and you two should be reconciled. If Rodia really did insult you, he *should* and he *will* beg your pardon."

Peter Petrovich immediately assumed a swaggering tone. "There are some insults, Avdotia Romanovna, which one cannot forget with the best will in the world. There is always a line it's dangerous to cross, for once you step across, you cannot turn back."

"Actually, that's not what I was talking about, Peter Petrovich," Dunia broke in with a trace of impatience. "You do understand, don't you, that our whole future now depends on whether all this can be cleared up and composed as quickly as possible? I tell you frankly from the very start, I can't look at it any other way, and if you have any regard for me at all this whole incident must be brought to an end today, even if it may be hard for you. I repeat: if my brother is to blame, he will apologize."

"I am amazed you put the question like that, Avdotia Romanovna." Luzhin grew increasingly irritated. "I may value you, so to speak, I may even adore you, yet it is quite quite possible for me to dislike someone in your household. Though I aspire to the bliss of your hand, I cannot at the same time take upon myself responsibilities that are incompatible—"

"Ah, don't be so quick to take offense, Peter Petrovich," interrupted Dunia with feeling, "and be the clever and generous man I have always considered and wish to consider you to be. I've given you a solemn promise; I am your fiancée. Trust me. Believe I'm capable of judging impartially. My taking on the role of judge is as much a surprise to my brother as it is to you. When I received your letter today, I asked him to be sure and come to our meeting, but I told him nothing about my intentions. You understand. If you two are not reconciled, I have to choose between you: either you or him. That's the way it is. I don't want to make a mistake choosing. For your sake I'd have to leave my brother; for my brother's sake I'd have to leave you. What I want to find out now for certain is whether he is a brother to me. And about you, whether I am dear to you, whether you value me. Whether you are a husband to me."

"Avdotia Romanovna," said Luzhin, making a wry face, "your words mean too much to me. What is more, I must say, in view of the place I have the honor to occupy in relation to you, they are actually offensive. Not even to speak of this strange and offensive comparison, on the same level, between me and . . . an impertinent young man. By your words you admit the possibility of breaking the promise you gave me. 'Either you or him,' you say—showing me how little I signify for you. . . . I cannot let this pass, considering the relations and . . . the obligations existing between us."

"What!" Dunia exploded, "I place your interest beside everything I have treasured in my life until now, everything that until now has been my *whole* life—and suddenly you're offended because I assign you too *little* worth!"

Raskolnikov smiled silently and caustically. Razumikhin could hardly sit still. But Peter Petrovich did not accept this retort. On the contrary, he became all the more captious and irritable, as though he were just hitting his stride.

"One should love one's future life companion, one's husband, more than one's brother," he said sententiously. "In any case, I cannot be put on the same level. . . . I just insisted I could not explain everything I intended to in the presence of your brother, but now I intend to turn to your worthy mother for a needed explanation on one quite fundamental point that has been a source of great offense to me. Yesterday," he said to Pulcheria Alexandrovna, "your son, in the presence of Mr. Rassudkin . . . or . . . that's it, isn't it? Excuse me, but I have forgotten your name"—he bowed politely to Razumikhin—"your son offended me by distorting an idea of mine, which I had communicated to you in personal conversation over coffee; namely, that marriage to a poor girl who had already experienced some trouble in life was in my opinion more advantageous from a matrimonial point of view than marriage to a girl who always had what she wanted, for it was more conducive to morality. Your son deliberately exaggerated the significance of my words to the point of absurdity, and accused me of malicious intentions, basing himself, as I see it, on correspondence from you personally. I'd be happy, Pulcheria Alexandrovna, to have you convince me to the contrary and thereby ease my mind. Could you tell me in what terms you actually conveyed my words to Rodion Romanovich in your letter?"

"I don't remember," Pulcheria Alexandrovna faltered. "I conveyed them as I understood them. I don't know how Rodia conveyed them to you. . . . He may have exaggerated something."

"Without encouragement from you he could not have exaggerated."

"Peter Petrovich," said Pulcheria Alexandrovna with dignity, "the proof that Dunia and I did not take your words badly is that we are *here*."

"Well put, Mother," said Dunia approvingly.

"So I'm to blame?" said Luzhin, taking offense.

"Now, look, Peter Petrovich, you're blaming everything on Rodion, but in a letter a while ago you yourself wrote something about him that wasn't true," said Pulcheria Alexandrovna, taking heart.

"I don't recall having written anything that was not true."

Without turning to look at Luzhin, Raskolnikov said harshly: "You wrote that I gave money away yesterday, not to the widow of a man who'd been run over, as was actually the case, but to his daughter, whom I'd never seen till yesterday. That was to put me at odds with my family, and you added some dirty expressions about the behavior of a girl you don't know. It's all meanness and slander."

"Excuse me, sir," Luzhin replied, trembling with anger. "In my letter I enlarged on your activities solely in response to your mother's and sister's request that I describe them: how I found you and what kind of impression you made on me. As to what you've alluded to in my letter, be so good as to find even one unjust line. I mean, prove that you did not waste your money. Prove there were no disreputable members in that family, however unfortunate."

"I think you and your whole reputation are not worth the little finger of that unfortunate girl at whom you are casting a stone."

"Does that mean you'd invite her into the company of your mother and sister?"

"If you must know, I've already done that. Today I asked her to be seated beside my mother and beside Dunia."

"Rodia!" exclaimed Pulcheria Alexandrovna. Dunia blushed. Razumikhin knitted his brows. Luzhin smiled caustically and arrogantly.

"Avdotia Romanovna, you may see for yourself," he said, "whether agreement is possible. I hope the matter is clear and at an end, once and for all. I shall withdraw, not to interfere further with the delights of a family reunion or with the communication of secrets." He rose from the table and picked up his hat. "But while I'm leaving, I make so bold as to note—I hope in the future to be exempt from such meetings and such, so to speak, compromises. In this matter I would especially appeal to you, worthy Pulcheria Alexandrovna, the more since my letter was addressed to you and to no one else."

Pulcheria Alexandrovna was a bit offended. "You seem to be taking us completely into your power, Peter Petrovich. Dunia told you why your wish wasn't carried out. She meant well. Anyway, you write as though you were issuing orders. Am I to consider your every wish an order? I tell you it's the other way around—you ought to show particular delicacy and tact to us, because we have thrown up everything and come here. Because we trusted you. Whatever happens, we are practically in your power."

"Pulcheria Alexandrovna, that isn't altogether fair. Especially at the present moment, when it's just been announced Martha Petrovna left you three thousand in her will—come at the right moment, judging by the way you've been speaking to me."

"According to that, one could guess you'd really been counting on our helplessness," Dunia noted irritably.

"In any case I cannot count on it now, and I especially don't want to interfere with communication of the secret proposals of Arkady Ivanovich Svidrigailov, which he entrusted to your brother and which, as I can see, have a fundamental significance for you, maybe even rather a pleasant one."

"Oh, my God!" exclaimed Pulcheria Alexandrovna. Razumikhin could not sit still on his chair.

"Aren't you ashamed of yourself now, Sister?" asked Raskolnikov.

"I'm ashamed, Rodia," Dunia said. She turned to Luzhin, pale with anger. "Peter Petrovich, you get out of here!"

Peter Petrovich hadn't quite expected such an ending, it would seem. He had too much confidence in himself, in his power, and in the helplessness of his victims. Even now he did not believe it. He paled, and his lips quivered.

"Avdotia Romanovna, if I go out this door now, after such a dismissal, you may count on it, I will never return. Think it over carefully! I give you my solemn word."

"What insolence!" Dunia cried, rising swiftly from her place. "I don't want you to come back anyway!"

"What? So tha-a-at's how it is, ma'am!" Luzhin exclaimed, refusing up to the very last to believe in such an outcome, and so losing the thread completely, "and so that's it, is it! But you know, Avdotia Romanovna, don't you, that I could sue for this!"

"What right do you have talking to her like that!" Pulcheria Alexandrovna interrupted hotly. "How could you sue? What rights do you have? Do you think I'd give my Dunia to a man like you? Get out, leave us altogether! We have ourselves to blame for having gotten mixed up in a bad business, and I blame myself most of all. . . ."

"Nevertheless, Pulcheria Alexandrovna"—Luzhin was in a rage—"you bound me with your promise, and now you're going back on it, and . . . besides . . . besides, throughout . . . I was involved in, so to speak, expenses. . . ."

That was so characteristic of Peter Petrovich that Raskolnikov, white with anger though he was, and with the effort of restraining it, suddenly let himself go and burst out laughing. But Pulcheria Alexandrovna was beside herself.

"Expenses? Now, what expenses would those be? Surely you don't mean our trunk? The conductor took it for you for nothing. My God, you say we bound you! You forget, Peter Petrovich—it was you who bound us, hand and foot, and not we you!"

"Enough, Mother dear, please, that's enough!" Dunia pleaded. "Peter Petrovich, please be so kind, leave!"

"I am leaving, *madame*—but one last word!" he said, by now almost out of control. "It seems your dear mother has quite forgotten I resolved to take you after the talk of the town, so to speak, had carried gossip concerning your reputation all over the district. For your sake I disregarded public opinion, and since I reinstated your reputation, it was quite natural for me to expect a fitting return, even to demand some gratitude from you. . . . And only now have my eyes been opened! I see myself that in disregarding the public voice I have acted quite, quite recklessly—"

"Does he want his head smashed, or what!" cried Razumikhin, leaping from his chair and ready for action.

"You are a mean and spiteful man!" said Dunia.

"Not a word! Not a move!" Raskolnikov exclaimed, holding Razumikhin back. Then he approached Luzhin so they were almost face to face, and he said quietly and distinctly: "Please get out of here! Not a word more, or else . . ."

For a few moments Peter Petrovich looked at him, pale face distorted with anger, then turned and walked out. Toward Raskolnikov he felt a rare and baleful hatred. He blamed him and him alone for everything. Even as he went down the stairs he still imagined his case might not yet be completely lost, and, as far as the ladies were concerned, might even be "quite, quite" recoverable.

3

The main point was that right up to the last moment he had not expected it to turn out that way. To the last moment he had blustered along without admitting even the possibility that two destitute and defenseless women could get out from under his power. Conviction was reinforced by vanity and by a degree of self-assurance that might best be called self-infatuation. Peter Petrovich had pulled himself up by his own bootstraps. He was morbidly used to admiring himself. He had a high opinion of his mind and abilities. Sometimes when he was alone he used to admire his face in the mirror. What he loved and valued most, however, was the money he had made by hard work and other ways. It was his money that made him the equal of everything higher than himself.

When he bitterly reminded Dunia that he had decided to take her in spite of her bad reputation, he had spoken quite sincerely. He even felt profoundly indignant about such "black ingratitude." Yet when he proposed to Dunia he had known very well the groundlessness of those rumors, long since publicly refuted by Martha Petrovna herself and long since abandoned by the whole town. He himself would not have denied that he had known all this all along. And yet he valued his decision to bring Dunia up to his own level and regarded it as heroic. Telling Dunia this just now, he was expressing his own most cherished secret notion, one that he had more than once admired himself for holding in the past, and he failed to understand how others could not but admire him for his heroism. Raskolnikov he had visited with the feeling of a benefactor, prepared to gather in the fruits of his virtue and to hear the sweetest compliments. As he descended the staircase he considered himself insulted in the highest degree, and his virtue unrecognized.

Dunia he simply needed. She was necessary. It was unthinkable for him to forgo her. For a long time, for years, he had dreamed voluptuously of getting married, but he went on piling up money, waiting. In his inmost self, he went on dreaming ecstatically of a poor, virtuous girl (she was inevitably poor), quite young, quite pretty, of good family, and well educated, quite timid, one who had been through a lot of bad luck and who would defer to him completely, who would consider him all her life as her savior, would admire, submit to, and venerate him—him alone. How many little dramas, how many delicious episodes, his imagination had created on this wanton and seductive theme as he rested quietly from his labors! After all these years, the dream had been all but realized: Dunia's beauty and breeding had struck him. The helplessness of her situation had excited him greatly. She was even more than he had dreamed about—here was a girl, proud, virtuous, of strong character, with education and breeding superior to his own (he felt that), and she would be slavishly grateful to him all her life because he was heroic, and she would belittle herself reverently before him, while he enjoyed complete and unlimited power over her! With this in mind he had, not long before this, after long deliberation and delays, made up his mind to a decisive change in his career. He decided to embark on a more extensive round of activity, at the same time passing over little by little into a higher sphere of society, about which for some time he had cherished voluptuous thoughts. . . . In short, he made up his mind to have a try at Petersburg. He knew one could get "quite, quite" a lot through women. The fascination of a charming, virtuous, and educated woman could smooth his path remarkably, could attract people, create an aura . . . and now, it was all ruined! This present unexpected, grotesque disruption was like a bolt from the blue. It was a horrible joke, an absurdity. All he had done was swagger a bit, he hadn't even said what he meant, he'd just been joking, carried away—and it had ended so seriously! And by this time, in his own way, he had even fallen in love with Dunia and was ruling over her in his dreams. Then suddenly—no! Tomorrow—tomorrow, all this would have to be restored, mended, patched up. The main thing was to crush this insolent young pup, this whippersnapper who was to blame for everything. Involuntarily, with a painful sensation, he remembered Razumikhin, but on that score soon calmed down. "Not on the same level!" Actually, the man he was most seriously afraid of was Svidrigailov. . . In short, there was a lot that needed to be done. . . .

* * *

"No, it was me. I am more to blame than anyone," Dunia said, throwing her arms around her mother and kissing her. "I was tempted by his money—but I swear, Rodia, I did not imagine he was such a despicable man. If I had seen through him sooner, I wouldn't have been tempted! Don't blame me, Rodia!"

"God has delivered us! God has delivered us!" Pulcheria Alexandrovna muttered, but she said it as if somehow she were still not aware of everything that had happened.

They all cheered up. In five minutes they were even laughing. From time to time, however, Dunia turned pale and frowned as she remembered. Pulcheria Alexandrovna could not even have imagined how glad she would be. That morning she had still thought of the break with Luzhin as a terrible calamity. Razumikhin, however, was in ecstacy. He still did not dare express it fully, but he trembled all over as in a fever, as if a great weight had been lifted from his heart. Now he would have the right to devote the rest of his life to them, to serve them. . . . Now, come what may! Yet he was more timid than ever in pursuing any thoughts beyond that, and his own imagination frightened him. Raskolnikov alone sat in the same spot as before, morose and distraught. He had insisted most that Luzhin leave, but now he seemed the least interested in what had happened. Dunia could not help thinking he was still quite angry with her, and Pulcheria Alexandrovna glanced at him apprehensively.

"What in the world did Svidrigailov say to you?" Dunia asked, going up to him.

"Ah, yes, yes!" Pulcheria Alexandrovna exclaimed.

Raskolnikov raised his head. "He wants to give you ten thousand rubles. He also says he wants to see you again, in my presence."

"See her! Not for anything in the world!" Pulcheria Alexandrovna exclaimed, "and how dare he propose giving her money!"

Raskolnikov related (fairly dryly) his conversation with Svidrigailov, but he left out Martha Petrovna's appearances so as not to have to go into unnecessary detail. He felt disgust at the idea of carrying on any kind of conversation at all, except the most necessary.

"What did you say to him?" Dunia asked.

"At first I told him I would convey nothing to you. Then he said he would find you out himself, by any and all means. He said his passion for you had been a whim, and he now felt nothing toward you. . . . He doesn't want you to marry Luzhin. . . . In general, he was incoherent."

"How do you account for him, Rodia? How did he strike you?"

"I must admit I don't much understand it. He said he wasn't rich, yet he offers ten thousand. He announces he wants to go away somewhere; ten minutes later he's forgotten what he said. All of a sudden he says he wants to get married and a girl's been proposed for him. . . . He certainly has some end in mind, and most likely it's bad. Yet somehow it's hard to imagine he'd go about it so stupidly if he had designs on you. . . . Of course, I refused the money on your behalf, once and for all. Everything considered, he struck me as very strange, maybe even . . . a touch insane. But I could be wrong. He might have been trying to pull something. I gather Martha Petrovna's death made an impression on him."

"May she rest in peace!" said Pulcheria Alexandrovna. "I will always, always pray to God for her! Well, what would become of us now if it weren't for those three thousand! It's as though they fell from Heaven! Ah, Rodia, you know we had only three rubles left to our name this morning, and all Dunia and I could think of was pawning her watch somewhere as quickly as possible, not to have to ask that man for anything so long as he didn't think of it himself."

Dunia seemed somehow overly struck by Svidrigailov's proposal. She stood there, pondering. "He thought up something horrible," she said to herself, almost in a whisper, shuddering slightly. Raskolnikov noted this excessive terror.

"Looks like I'm going to be seeing more of him," he said to Dunia.

"We'll watch out for him! I'll track him down!" exclaimed Razumikhin. "I won't take my eyes off you! Rodia's given me permission. He said to me himself just now: 'Watch my sister.' Will you permit me, Avdotia Romanovna?"

Dunia smiled and held out her hand to him, but her face was still anxious. Pulcheria Alexandrovna looked at her timidly. Nevertheless, the three thousand apparently were of some comfort to her.

Fifteen minutes later they were all plunged into the liveliest conversation. Even Raskolnikov, though he didn't talk much, listened attentively. Razumikhin held forth. "And why—why should you leave!" He flowed rapturously into an impassioned speech. "What would you do there, in that town? Here the main point is you're all together, and you need one another—oh, yes, you are needed, and how! Believe me! For a little while yet, anyway. . . . Take me in as a friend, a partner, I assure you we'll get quite an enterprise going. Listen. I'll explain the whole project to you in detail. This morning it all flashed into my head, even before anything happened. . . . Here's what. I have an uncle (I'll introduce you—he's a terribly adaptable, highly respectable old geezer!), and this uncle of mine has a thousand rubles saved up. He himself lives on a pension and is not in any need. Couple years ago, he wanted me to take this thousand and pay him six percent on it. I understand, all right—he just wants to help me out. But last year I didn't need it. This year I thought I'd wait till he got here, then I'd take it. So if you put up another thousand out of your three—we're in business, and it's enough to start with. We can be partners. What'll we go into?"

Razumikhin then began to unfold his project, and explained at some length how little most publishers and booksellers knew their business, whereas actually decent publications sold well and made a profit, sometimes even a considerable profit. For two years Razumikhin, who had been working for others, had been brooding about the publishing business. He knew three European languages fairly well, in spite of the fact that he had told Raskolnikov his German was *"schwach"* about a week ago, when trying to persuade him to take on half the translating work and with it the three rubles' advance—he'd been laying it on then, and Raskolnikov knew he had been laying it on.

"Why—why should we let a chance like that go by, when we've got one of the most important things we need—our own money?" Razumikhin had lathered himself up. "Of course, it takes a lot of work, but we'll work hard. You, Avdotia Romanovna; myself; Rodion. . . . Other publications make a good profit now! The mainstay of the enterprise is the fact that we'll really know what should be translated. We'll translate and publish and study all at the same time. Now, I can be of use, because I have some experience. I've been hanging around publishers for two years now, and I know their business inside out—they're not in it for love, and why should we let the chance go by! I know myself, and I've been keeping it a secret, two or three such works that would bring in a hundred rubles a book just for the idea of translating and publishing them, but I wouldn't take even five hundred rubles per book for the idea. And you know, if I told one of those publishers, he'd back and fill, that's how dumb they are! As for the business end—printing, paper, sales—you trust that to me! I know my way around! We'll start on a small scale and expand. Anyway, we'll get back what we put in and still have enough to live on."

Dunia's eyes sparkled. "I very much like what you're saying, Dmitry Prokofich," she said.

"Of course, I don't know anything about it," Pulcheria Alexandrovna said, "maybe it really is a good idea; then again, God knows. It's new, untried. Of course, we have to stay around here awhile yet. . . ." She gazed at Rodia.

"What do you think, Rodia?" Dunia said.

"I think he has a very good idea," he replied. "There's no point dreaming of a publishing firm prematurely, but there's no doubt five or six books could be published successfully. I know a work that would sell well, too. As far as his knowing how to manage the business is concerned, there's no doubt he knows the business. . . . You'll still have time to talk that over."

"Hurrah!" Razumikhin shouted. "Wait. There's an apartment here in this very house, belongs to the same owners. It's a special, separate apartment—doesn't connect with these, and it's furnished. The price is moderate; it's got three little rooms. Why not rent it for the time being? I'll pawn your watch for you tomorrow and bring you the money, then it can all be arranged. The main thing is the three of you could live together, Rodia would be able to live with you. . . . Why, Rodia, where are you going?"

"Rodia—you're not leaving?" Pulcheria Alexandrovna asked with a touch of fear.

"At a moment like this!" Razumikhin shouted. Dunia looked at her brother with incredulous astonishment. His cap was in his hands. He was getting ready to leave.

"You talk as though you were lowering me into my grave or saying good-bye to me forever," he said, somehow oddly. He seemed to be smiling yet not smiling. "Who knows? Maybe it really is the last time we'll see each other," he added unexpectedly. He had been thinking to himself; it seemed somehow to say itself aloud.

"What is the matter with you!" his mother cried.

Dunia asked rather strangely: "Where are you off to, Rodia?"

"I've really got to go," he answered vaguely, as though

he were hesitating about what he wanted to say. But in his pale face there was a look of sharp determination. "I wanted to say . . . on the way here . . . I wanted to tell you, Mother . . . and you, Dunia, it would be better if we . . . separated for a while. I don't feel well, I'm not at ease . . . I'll come later. I'll come myself, when . . . I can. I love you. I'll remember you. . . . Leave me! Leave me alone! That's the decision I made, I made it a while back. The decision I made. . . . Whatever happens to me, whether I go to wrack and ruin or not, I want to be alone. Just forget me. That would be better. . . . Don't go asking around about me. When I have to, I'll come myself, or I'll call for you. Maybe everything will come back to life! But now, if you love me, renounce. . . . Or else, I feel I'll come to hate you . . . Good-bye!"

"Good Lord!" Mother and sister were both terribly alarmed. Razumikhin, too.

"Rodia, Rodia, make it up with us," his poor mother exclaimed. "Let us be as before."

He turned slowly to the doorway and walked slowly out. Dunia approached him. "Rodia! What are you doing to Mother!" she whispered, giving him a look that burned with indignation.

He looked at her dully. "It's nothing. I'll be back, I will come!" he muttered half aloud as though he didn't really know exactly what he wanted to say, and left the room.

"Wicked, heartless egoist!" Dunia cried.

"He's ca-razy—but not heartless! He's out of his mind! Don't you see that? Then you're the one who's heartless!" Razumikhin whispered to her, at the same time squeezing her hand hard. "I'll be right back!" he said to the petrified Pulcheria Alexandrovna. He ran out of the room.

Raskolnikov was waiting for him at the end of the corridor. "I knew you'd come after me," he said. "Go back and stay with them. . . . Be with them tomorrow . . . and always. I'll . . . be back, maybe . . . if I can. Good-bye!" He left without offering his hand.

"But where are you going? What are you up to? What's the matter with you? How can you carry on like this!"

Raskolnikov stopped once more. "Once and for all—don't ever question me about anything. I can't answer. . . . Don't come to see me. Maybe I'll come here. . . . Leave me, but *don't* . . . leave them. Do you understand me?"

It was dark in the corridor. They were standing near the

lamp. For a moment they looked at each other in silence. All his life Razumikhin would remember this moment. Raskolnikov's burning and intent gaze seemed to keep growing stronger, pierced into his consciousness and into his soul. All of a sudden Razumikhin shuddered. Something strange seemed to have passed between them. . . . An idea had slipped through, a kind of hint; something terrible, hideous, suddenly understood on both sides. . . . Razumikhin turned pale as a corpse.

"Now do you understand?" Raskolnikov said suddenly, his face twisted with pain. "Turn around. Go back to them," he suddenly added, turned swiftly, and left the house.

I will not now attempt to describe how it was at Pulcheria Alexandrovna's that evening, how Razumikhin went back in, how he calmed them down, how he protested that Rodia needed to rest because of his illness, protested that Rodia would undoubtedly be back, that he would visit them every day, that he was very much upset, that he shouldn't be irritated; that he, Razumikhin, would keep track of him, that he would get him a good doctor, a better one, a whole consulting board of doctors. . . . In short, from that evening on, Razumikhin took his place with them as a son and brother.

4

Raskolnikov went straight to the house on the canal embankment where Sonia lived. It was an old green house of three stories. The janitor gave him some vague directions as to where Kapernaumov the tailor lived, and in a corner of the yard he found an entryway to the dark, narrow stairs. Mounting to the second floor, he came out on a gallery that ran around it on the side toward the yard. As he groped his way in the dark, uncertain as to where the door to Kapernaumov's might be, a door opened three steps away from him. Automatically he took hold of it.

"Who is it?" a woman's voice asked uneasily.

"It's me. . . . I've come to see you," Raskolnikov replied, and entered a tiny hallway. Here, on a broken chair, stood a candle in a crooked copper candlestick.

"God, it's you!" Sonia exclaimed weakly, and stopped as though rooted.

"Which is your room? Is it this way?" Trying not to look at her, Raskolnikov passed on into her room as quickly as he could. A moment later Sonia followed, carrying the candle. She put it down and stood there completely distraught, inexpressibly agitated, and obviously alarmed by his unexpected visit. The color rushed to her pale face, and her eyes filled with tears. She felt sick and ashamed and delighted. Raskolnikov turned away quickly and sat down on a chair near the table. He took the room in at a glance.

It was a large but very low room, the only one the Kapernaumovs rented out. A locked door on the left led to their apartment. Across from it, in the wall on the right, there was another door, which was always kept tightly locked. That led to another, separate, neighboring apartment. Sonia's room was like a tool shed. It had a highly irregular rectangular shape, which gave it a grotesque aspect. A wall with three windows facing the canal embankment cut across the room at an angle, so that there was one terribly sharp corner that plunged into depths one could not even discern in the weak light. The other corner was too disproportionately wide. In the whole large room there was almost no furniture. On the right in the corner there was a bed. Beside it, closer to the door, was a chair. Along the same wall as the bed, by the door that led to the other apartment, stood a simple deal table covered with a bluish tablecloth; near the table were two chairs with rush seats. By the opposite wall, close to the sharp corner, stood a small chest of drawers, made of plain wood, which seemed lost in the void. That was all there was in the room. The yellowish, stained, shabby wallpaper had turned dark in all the corners. That meant the room was damp, and full of soot and smoke in the winter. Its poverty was obvious. There were not even curtains around the bed.

Sonia gazed silently at her visitor, who without standing on ceremony was examining her room so attentively. At last she even began to tremble, as though she were standing before the judge who would decide her fate.

"I'm late. . . . Is it eleven?" he asked, still without turning his eyes on her.

"Yes," Sonia murmured. "Oh, yes, it is!" she added hastily, as if she could avoid everything that way. "The clock just struck in my landlord's apartment. I heard it myself. . . . It *is* late."

"I've come to you for the last time," Raskolnikov said

morosely, though this was only the first time. "I may never see you again. . . ."

"You're . . . leaving?"

"I don't know. . . . Everything . . . tomorrow . . ."

"You won't be at Katherine Ivanovna's tomorrow?" Sonia's voice trembled.

"I don't know. Everything . . . tomorrow morning. . . . That's not the point. I came to say one word. . . ."

He lifted his brooding gaze and suddenly noticed that while he was seated, she remained standing in his presence. "Why are you standing? Sit down," he said suddenly. His tone of voice had become soft and gentle.

She sat down. For a moment he looked at her kindly, almost compassionately. "How skinny you are! Look at your hand! Transparent. Fingers like a corpse's." He took her hand, and Sonia smiled weakly.

"I've always been that way," she said.

"When you were living at home?"

"Yes."

"Certainly. Of course!" he said abruptly, and his expression and the sound of his voice again changed suddenly. He looked around once more. "You rent this from the Kapernaumovs?"

"Yes, I do. . . ."

"They're there, behind that door?"

"Yes. . . . They have the same kind of room."

"They live all in one room?"

"Yes, in one."

"In your room I'd be afraid at night," he noted somberly.

"My landlords are decent, kind people," Sonia replied, as though she were still bewildered and unused to the situation. "And all the furniture and everything . . . it's all theirs. They're very considerate, too, and the children come see me often. . . ."

"They stutter, don't they?"

"Yes, they do. . . . He stammers, and he's lame. His wife, too . . . She doesn't stammer, she just doesn't say everything quite right. She's a very kind woman. He's a former house serf. There are seven children . . . only the eldest stammers; the others are just sick . . . but they don't stammer. . . . But how did you," she asked with a certain surprise, "happen to know about them?"

"Your father told me. He told me all about you. . . . About how you left at six o'clock and came back at nine, and how Katherine Ivanovna knelt by your bedside."

Sonia looked embarrassed. "I thought I saw him today," she whispered hesitantly.

"Whom?"

"My father. I was walking along the street, just outside, on the corner, at ten o'clock. He seemed to be walking ahead of me. I even wanted to go to Katherine Ivanovna's."

"You were street-walking?"

"Yes," whispered Sonia abruptly, lowering her eyes, embarrassed again.

"Katherine Ivanovna used to just about beat you, didn't she, when you were living at your father's?"

"Oh, no, what are you . . . how could you . . . no!" Sonia looked at him, almost frightened.

"You love her, then?"

"Her? Why, of cou-ourse!" Sonia drew the words out plaintively, and suddenly folded her arms in distress. "You see. . . . If you only knew her. She's completely like a child. . . . And her mind's all mixed up . . . from grief. But how clever she used to be . . . how generous . . . how kind! You know nothing, nothing about her. . . . Ah!"

Sonia said this as though in pain and despair, agitated and wringing her hands. Her pale cheeks flushed again, and there was suffering in her eyes. She was very deeply moved and she wanted terribly to express something, to speak out, to intercede. A kind of *insatiable* compassion, if one may put it that way, suddenly etched itself into all the lines of her face.

"Beat me! How could you think such a thing? Good Lord, beat me! And if she did beat me, what of it! Well, what of it? You know nothing, nothing about it. . . . She's so unhappy, ah, how unhappy she is! And sick. . . . She looks for what's right. . . . She's pure. She has such faith that there must be a 'right' in everything, and she makes demands. . . . Even if you tortured her she wouldn't do what wasn't right. She doesn't know it's not possible for people to do 'right' to each other, so she gets upset. . . . Like a child, like a child! She is righteous, righteous!"

"But what will become of you?" Sonia looked at him questioningly. "They're left on your hands, aren't they? True, it was that way before, too, your dead father used to come asking you for something to drink. Well, what will become of you now?"

"I don't know," said Sonia mournfully.

"Will they stay there?"

"I don't know. They owe rent. I heard that the landlady

said today she wanted to get rid of them, and Katherine Ivanovna says she for one won't stay another minute."

"What makes her so sure of herself? Does she rely on you?"

"Oh, no, you mustn't say that! We are as one, and we'll live as one." Sonia was agitated again, even irritated, and she seemed like some angry little bird, like a canary. "And what can she do? I ask you, what can she do?" she asked, excited and agitated. "How much she cried today, how much she cried! Her mind is slipping—didn't you notice? It's slipping; one minute she worries like a child that everything should go well tomorrow, there should be food and everything . . . next, she wrings her hands and spits up blood and suddenly starts to beat her head against the wall as if she were desperate. Then she comforts herself all over again. She relies on you a lot. She says you're her helper now, and she'll borrow a little money somewhere and go back to her hometown with me, and she'll run a boarding school for girls of good family, and she'll take me on as supervisor, and a quite new and glorious life will begin for us—so she throws her arms around me and kisses me, she comforts me, and she has such faith, such faith in those fantasies of hers! How can one contradict her? She's been washing, cleaning, mending, all day long. She drags the wash basket into the room all by herself with her own feeble hands, she gasps for breath, and she collapses gasping on the bed. This morning we went shopping together to the market to buy Polia and Lida some shoes because theirs are all worn out. But the money we'd figured on wasn't enough, not nearly enough. But she picked out such sweet little booties, because she has taste, you don't know . . . she burst out crying there in the shop, in front of all the attendants, because there wasn't enough. She was so pathetic to look at. . . ."

"Well, it's understandable after all that why you . . . live as you do," Raskolnikov said with a bitter smile.

"Then you don't feel sorry for her? You don't pity her?" Sonia leaped up again. "But I know you gave away the very last that you had, and without even seeing anything. . . . And if you had seen it all—good Lord, I don't know how many times I drove her to tears! Why, only last week! Yes, I did! Just a week before his death. I was cruel! And think how often, how often I did it! Oh, I've been miserable thinking about it all day, and now, too." From the pain of remembering, Sonia wrung her hands as she spoke.

"So it was you who were cruel?"

"Oh, yes, I was, I was! I went to see them that time," she continued, weeping, "and my dead father, he said, 'Read me, something's hurting my head . . . Sonia,' he said, 'read me . . . here's a book. . . .' He had a book he got from Andrei Semionovich, from Lebeziatnikov—he lives there, and he always used to get hold of such funny books. I don't want to read, so I said, 'It's time for me to go'; anyway, what I'd come to see them for was to show Katherine Ivanovna some collars. Lizaveta the peddler had brought me some collars and cuffs, real cheap, nice ones, practically new, with embroidery on them. Katherine Ivanovna liked them a lot. She put them on and looked at herself in the mirror. She liked them an awful lot. 'Sonia,' she says, 'give them to me, please.' She liked them so much she even asked *please*. And where could she wear them? Well, they just reminded her of her happy time long ago! She looked at herself in the mirror and admired herself. She doesn't have any clothes at all, not any—she hasn't had anything decent to wear for a long, long time, and mind you, she'd never ask anything from anybody; she's proud. She'd sooner give her own last scrap away. And these little things pleased her so much she even asked for them! But I hung on to them. 'What good will they do you, Katherine Ivanovna?' I said. That's just how I said it: *what good?* I should never have said that to her! She looked at me, she got so terribly, terribly sad, because I refused, it was pathetic to look at her. . . . She wasn't sad because of the collars, mind you, but because I refused her. I could see that. If I could only take it all back now and start all over again, all those words I used. . . . Well, I. . . . Still—you don't care do you?"

"Did you know Lizaveta the peddler?"

"Yes. . . . Did you know her, then?" Sonia asked with a certain surprise.

Without answering her question, Raskolnikov said after a pause: "Katherine Ivanovna has consumption, a bad case. She'll die soon."

"Oh, no, no, no!" Sonia grasped both his hands with an unconscious gesture, as though imploring him that she should not.

"Yet it would be better if she died."

"No, not better, not better, not better at all," she repeated helplessly, frightened.

"What about the children? Where could they go, if not to you?"

"I don't know!" cried Sonia, and she grasped her head, almost in despair. Clearly this thought had occurred to her often, and he had merely raised it again.

"And what about now, while Katherine Ivanovna is still alive? Suppose you get sick and carried off to the hospital, what then?" he persisted mercilessly.

Sonia's face was twisted by a terrible fear. "What are you saying, what are you driving at! It just can't happen!"

"What do you mean, can't happen?" said Raskolnikov with a harsh smile. "You're not insured, are you? So what will become of them? They'll go out in the street in a batch; she'll cough and beg and knock her head against a wall somewhere like today; and the children will cry. . . . She'll drop there; they'll carry her off to the hospital; she'll die; and the children—"

"Oh, no! God will not permit it!" burst at last from Sonia. She listened and looked at him imploringly, clasping her hands in mute supplication, as if everything actually depended on him.

Raskolnikov arose and started pacing the room. A minute passed. Sonia stood there, with arms and head hung down, in terrible dejection. "Can't you save? Put something away for a rainy day?" he asked. He had stopped suddenly in front of her.

"No," Sonia whispered.

"Of course not! But have you tried?" he added with a flicker of mockery.

"I tried."

"And it didn't work! That goes without saying! Why bother to ask!"

Again he paced the room. Another minute passed. "You don't get customers every day, do you?"

Sonia was even more embarrassed than before, and the color rushed to her cheeks. "No," she whispered with a painful effort.

"The same thing will happen to Polia, no doubt," he said suddenly.

"No! No! It can't be! No!" Sonia cried out loudly and desperately, as though she had suddenly been wounded with a knife. "God will not permit such a horror!"

"He permits others."

"No, no! God will protect her—God!" she repeated, beside herself.

"Maybe there's no God at all," Raskolnikov said with a certain malevolence. Then he laughed and looked at her.

All of a sudden Sonia's face became terribly transformed; spasms and tremors passed rapidly across it. She looked on him with unutterable reproach, wanting to say something, unable to get anything out. Suddenly she burst into bitter tears and covered her face with her hands.

After a pause, he said: "You say Katherine Ivanovna's mind is going. Your own mind is going."

Five minutes passed. He paced silently up and down without looking at her. Then he went up to her. His eyes flashed. He took her by the shoulders with both his hands and looked straight into her grieving face. His glance was dry, inflamed, piercing; his lips trembled violently. Suddenly and swiftly he stooped all the way down, fell to the floor, and kissed her foot. Sonia drew back from him in horror, as from a madman. Actually, he looked quite mad.

"What are you doing that for, to me of all people?!" she muttered, and turned pale. Her heart pulsed with great pain.

He rose at once. "It wasn't you I bowed down to. I bowed down to all of suffering humanity," he said wildly, and walked off to the window. "Listen"—after a minute he turned to face her—"I told a blackguard just now he wasn't worth your little finger . . . I told him I did my sister an honor today by seating her beside you."

"What did you say that for! Was she there?" Sonia exclaimed in alarm. "An honor! Sitting beside me! But I . . . I'm dishonorable, a terrible sinner. What in the world were you saying!"

"I said what I said not because of your dishonor or your sin, but because of your great suffering. It's true, though, that you're a terrible sinner," he added, practically enraptured. "Mostly because you've mortified yourself and sold yourself *in vain*. There's a horror for you, a real horror. You live in this muck that you hate, and all the time you know yourself—all you have to do is open your eyes—you won't help anybody this way, you won't save anybody from anything! Tell me, then, finally"—he was almost in a frenzy—"how can you abide such shame and degradation inside you up against their opposite—such holy feelings? Wouldn't it have been better, a thousand times more 'right'—and more clever, too—if you'd gone and jumped in the river and ended everything at once!"

"But what would become of them?" Sonia asked weakly, looking at him with suffering eyes, yet at the same time not at all surprised by his suggestion. Raskolnikov looked at her strangely.

So she had thought of it herself. She might well have thought it over many times, quite seriously and desperately, how she might end it all; so seriously, she was not now much surprised by his suggestion. She had not even noticed how harsh his words were. Nor had she grasped the meaning of his reproaches, nor his peculiar view of her shame—that much was clear to him. Still, he knew very well how awfully she had been torn at the thought of her dishonorable and shameful position. And what was it, he thought, prevented her putting an end to it once and for all? For the first time he grasped what those poor little orphan children meant to her, and that pathetic, half-crazy Katherine Ivanovna, with her consumptive cough, beating her head against the wall.

Yet it was equally clear to him that with her character and with what little education she had received, she could not possibly remain the way she was. Since she couldn't bring herself to jump into the river, how could she have endured such a lot so long and not gone out of her mind? A fortuitous social manifestation—he knew, of course, that's what Sonia's lot was—unfortunately, far from unique, and not even exceptional. Its very fortuitousness—that slight amount of education and her whole previous life—might well have served to finish her off the first step she took in the way of depravity. What kept her going? Depravity? The shamefulness touched her obviously only mechanically. There was still not a drop of real depravity in her. He could see that. She stood transparent before him.

"Three possibilities for her," he thought. "Throw herself into the canal; wind up in the madhouse; or . . . at long last, plunge into depravity headlong, stupefying the mind and petrifying the heart." The last seemed most disgusting. Because he was young and skeptical, abstract—and therefore, cruel—he could not help believing the last way out the most likely.

"Can that be right?" he said to himself. "This pure creature—in the long run will she deliberately let herself be sucked into this rotten, stinking sump? Has she started being sucked in already? Can it be she's managed to last it out till now only because vice no longer seems quite so disgusting to her? No, that can't be!" he cried, as Sonia had a short while back. "No, what's kept her from the canal up to now has been her notion of sin, and *them, those*. . . . And if she hasn't gone out of her mind. . . . But who says she hasn't gone out of her mind? Is she in her right mind? The way she talks? Does anybody in his right mind argue that way? Can she sit there above her own perdition, right over the stinking sump that's already started to suck her in, and wave it all away and stop up her ears when she's told of the danger? What's she doing, waiting for a miracle? Probably. Isn't that derangement?"

He lingered stubbornly on this thought. As an answer, it appealed to him more than any other. He started looking at her more intently. "You pray a lot to God, Sonia, don't you?" he asked her.

She looked up at him for a moment with a sudden flash in her eyes, and she pressed his hand firmly with her own. "What would I be without God?" she whispered swiftly and energetically.

"Yes," he thought, "that's the way it is."

"And what does God give you in return?"

Sonia was silent a long time, as if she could not answer. Her frail chest heaved. "Be quiet! Don't ask! You don't deserve an answer!" she suddenly cried, and she looked at him sternly and angrily.

"Yes, that's the way it is," he said again to himself, "that's the way it is."

"He does everything!" she whispered swiftly, again lowering her eyes.

"That's the answer," he told himself as he examined her with avid curiosity, "and an explanation of the answer, too!" With a new, strange, almost painful feeling, he began scrutinizing this pale, thin, odd-shaped, and angular little face, those meek blue eyes that could flash such fire, such stern, forceful passion; that small body, still trembling with anger and indignation—and all this seemed more and more strange to him, almost impossible. "She's a holy fool," he told himself, "a holy fool!"

There was a book lying on the bureau. Pacing up and down, he had noticed it every time he went by. He picked it up and looked at it. It was the New Testament in Russian translation. The book was old and worn and bound in leather. "Where did you get this?" he cried to her across the room. She stood where she was, three steps from the table.

"Somebody brought it to me," she said with seeming reluctance, and without looking at him.

"Who brought it?"

"Lizaveta. I asked her to."

"Lizaveta! Strange!" he thought. Everything about Sonia seemed stranger and more wondrous to him at every moment. He carried the book to the candle and started leafing through it. Suddenly he asked: "Where's the passage about Lazarus?" Sonia stared stubbornly at the ground and did not reply. She stood turned slightly sideways to the table.

"The part about the resurrection of Lazarus—where is it? Find it for me, Sonia."

She gave him a sidelong look. "Not where you're looking. . . . It's in the fourth Gospel," she whispered sternly, without moving toward him.

"Find it and read it to me," he said. He sat down and got ready to listen, propping his elbows on the table and leaning his head on his hand. "Look for me on the road to prison in about three weeks. I guess I'll be traveling that road, if worse doesn't happen," he muttered to himself.

Hesitantly Sonia walked up to the table. She did not quite trust Raskolnikov's strange request. Yet she picked up the book. "Haven't you read it?" she asked, throwing him a quick glance across the table. Her voice became even more severe.

"Long ago . . . when I was a child. Read!"

"You never heard it in church?"

"I . . . haven't been going. Do you go often?"

"N-no," Sonia whispered.

Raskolnikov grinned. "I understand. . . . Does that mean you won't be going to your father's funeral tomorrow?"

"I'll go. Last week I went once, too. . . . I had a memorial service done. . . ."

"For whom?"

"Lizaveta. She was killed with an ax."

His nerves became even tenser. His head started spinning. "You were a friend of Lizaveta's?"

"Yes. . . . She had a sense of what was right . . . once in a while she used to come here . . . she wasn't allowed . . . We used to read together, and . . . talk. She will see God."

The words sounded strange to him. And here was something else that was new. Mysterious meetings with Lizaveta.

Both of them, holy fools. "Watch out," he thought, "or you'll turn into a holy fool yourself—it's catching!" Suddenly, with force and some irritation, he cried out: "Read!"

Sonia hesitated. Her heart was pounding. For some reason she did not dare read to him. Almost in anguish he beheld this "unhappy madwoman." She whispered softly, as though she were out of breath: "Why? You don't really believe, do you?"

"Read! I want you to!" he insisted. "You read to Lizaveta!"

Sonia opened the book and found the place. Her hands trembled and her voice would not come out. Twice she began and could not get past the first syllable. " 'Now a certain man was sick, named Lazarus, of Bethany,' " she said at last, with effort, yet all of a sudden. After the third word, her voice tightened. Her breath went, and her chest constricted.

Raskolnikov understood in part why Sonia could not bring herself to read to him. All the more savagely and irritably he seemed to insist on her reading. He understood only too well how hard it was for her now to expose and betray everything that was *her own.* He understood that these feelings really did somehow constitute her present *secret,* and perhaps they had done so for a long time, ever since her adolescence, perhaps, ever since the time when she'd still been with her family, beside her unfortunate father and her stepmother crazed with grief, among the hungry children, the horrible shrieks and reproaches. Yet at the same time he knew too, and for certain, that although she was miserable and terribly afraid of something as she tried reading now, she was at the same time, and in spite of all her misery and all her fears, painfully eager to read, and to read *to him,* to read so he heard, and *right now,* come what may! He read this in her eyes, understood it from her enraptured excitement. . . . She controlled herself, suppressed the spasm in her throat that had strangled her voice at the beginning of the passage, and continued her reading of the eleventh chapter of the Gospel of John. She went on reading up to the nineteenth verse: " 'And many of the Jews came to Martha and Mary, to comfort them concerning their brother. Then Martha, as soon as she heard that Jesus was coming, went and met him: but Mary sat still in the house. Then said Martha unto Jesus, Lord, if thou hadst been here, my brother had not died. But I know, that even now, whatso-

ever thou wilt ask of God, God will give it thee.' " Here
she paused again, shamefacedly anticipating that her voice
would tremble and break. . . .

" 'Jesus saith unto her, Thy brother shall rise again. Martha saith unto him, I know that he shall rise again in the
resurrection at the last day. Jesus said unto her: *I am the
resurrection and the life:* he that believeth in me, though he
were dead, yet shall he live: And whosoever liveth and believeth in me shall never die. Believest thou this? She saith
unto him' "—and as though it hurt her to breathe, Sonia
read on, strongly and distinctly, as though she were herself
making a confession to all who listened—" 'Yea, Lord: I
believe that thou art the Christ, the Son of God, which
should come into the world.' "

She paused, swiftly lifted her eyes to *him,* but regained
control of herself as quickly as she could and began to read
further. Raskolnikov sat and listened without stirring. He
did not turn his head. His elbows were still on the table, and
he looked askance. They arrived at the thirty-second verse.

" 'Then when Mary was come where Jesus was, and saw
him, she fell down at his feet, saying unto him, Lord, if
thou hadst been here, my brother had not died. When Jesus
therefore saw her weeping, and the Jews also weeping which
came with her, he groaned in the spirit, and was troubled.
And said, Where have ye laid him? They said unto him,
Lord, come and see. Jesus wept. Then said the Jews, Behold
how he loved him! And some of them said, Could not this
man, which opened the eyes of the blind, have caused that
even this man should not have died?' "

Raskolnikov turned and looked at her nervously. That's
just the way it was. She trembled already, in a real fever.
He had expected it. She was coming to the tale of that
greatest, immense miracle, and a feeling of triumph possessed her. Her voice rang metal-clear; triumph and joy
sounded in it and strengthened it. Her eyes misted over and
the lines blurred, but she knew what she was reading by
heart. At the last verse—" 'Could not this man, which
opened the eyes of the blind . . .' " she lowered her voice.
Fervently, passionately, she enacted the doubt, the reproach
and censure of the blind, unbelieving Jews, who in a minute
now would fall as though struck by thunder, weep and
believe. . . . "And *he . . . he,* too, is blind and unbelieving.
Now he, too, will hear, he, too, will have faith, yes, yes! This

very moment now," she dreamed, and trembled in joyful
expectation.

" 'Jesus therefore again groaning in himself cometh to the
grave. It was a cave, and a stone lay upon it. Jesus said,
Take ye away the stone. Martha, the sister of him that was
dead, saith unto him, Lord, by this time he stinketh: for he
hath been dead *four* days.' " She vigorously stressed the
word *four*. " 'Jesus saith unto her, Said I not unto thee, that,
if thou wouldest believe, thou shouldest see the glory of
God? Then they took away the stone from the place where
the dead was laid. And Jesus lifted up his eyes, and said,
Father, I thank thee that thou hast heard me. And I knew
that thou hearest me always: but because of the people
which stand by I said it, that they may believe that thou
hast sent me. And when he thus had spoken, he cried with
a loud voice, Lazarus, come forth. *And he that was dead
came forth*,' " she read loudly and ecstatically, trembling and
shivering, as though she were seeing it before her very eyes,
" 'bound hand and foot with graveclothes: and his face was
bound about with a napkin. Jesus saith unto them, Loose
him, and let him go. *Then many of the Jews which came
to Mary, and had seen the things which Jesus did, believed
on him.*' "

Past this she did not and could not read. Closing the book,
she rose quickly from her chair. "That is all about the resurrection of Lazarus," she whispered sternly and abruptly
without moving, her eyes askance, not daring, somehow
ashamed, to meet his. She went on trembling. The candle
end had long been flickering out in its crooked holder, dimly
illuminating in this beggarly room the murderer and the harlot, who had so strangely come together here to read the
Eternal Book. Five minutes passed, or more.

Raskolnikov frowned, and suddenly said out loud: "I
came to talk about a certain business matter." He rose and
went to Sonia. Silently she raised her eyes to him. His gaze
was especially harsh, and it expressed a kind of savage
determination.

"Today I abandoned my family," he said, "my mother
and my sister. I won't go back to them now. I've broken
with them completely."

"But why?" Sonia asked, stunned. Meeting his mother
and sister a while back had made an extraordinary impression on her, though she was not exactly clear herself of what

kind. She received the news of his break with something approaching horror.

"You are all I have now," he added. "Let's go together . . . I came to you. We're both damned, so let's go together."

His eyes glittered. "Like a madman's," Sonia thought.

"Go where?" she asked, afraid. Involuntarily, she moved back a step.

"I don't know. I just know it's the same road. I know that for certain, and that is all I know. One goal!" She looked at him and understood nothing. She only knew that he was terribly, infinitely unhappy.

"If you told them, not one of them would understand," he said, "but I understand. I need you. That's why I came."

"I don't understand," whispered Sonia.

"You'll understand later. Haven't you done the same? You, too, have transgressed . . . you found within yourself you were able to transgress. You laid hands on yourself, you took a life . . . *your own*—what's the difference! You could have lived a fine life, and here you'll wind up on Haymarket Square. . . . But you won't be able to stand it. If you're *alone,* you'll go out of your mind, like me. You behave as though you're mad already, so we have to go the same way together. Let's go!"

"Why? Why are you like this?" Sonia was strangely, restlessly stirred by his words.

"Why? Because you can't stay like this, that's why! In the long run you have to think things over seriously and look the facts in the face and not weep like a child or cry out, 'God won't permit it!' Well, what would happen if in fact you were carted off to the hospital tomorrow? The mad consumptive will die soon, but the children? You mean to tell me Polia won't come to a bad end? Haven't you seen the children on the street corners? Their mothers have sent them out to beg. I've learned where and how those mothers live. Children can't stay children there. A seven-year-old is vicious and a thief. Yet children are the image of Christ. 'Theirs is the kingdom of heaven.' He bade us honor and love them. They are the future of mankind. . . ."

"But wh . . . , what can be done?" said Sonia, weeping hysterically and wringing her hands.

"What can be done? Smash what has to be smashed, once and for all—that's all there is to it; and take the suffering on oneself! What, you don't understand? You'll understand later. . . . Freedom and power, but the main thing is power!

Over all trembling flesh and over the whole ant heap! . . .
That's the goal! Remember that! Those are my parting
words to you! I may be talking to you for the last time. If
I don't come tomorrow you'll find out for yourself, then
you'll remember what I'm saying now. Sometime later, over
the years, as life goes on, maybe you'll understand what they
mean. If I come tomorrow I'll tell you who killed Lizaveta.
Good-bye!"

Sonia trembled all over from fear. "Do you really know
who killed her?" she asked, frozen with horror and looking
at him wildly.

"I know, and I'll tell you. . . . You alone! I've chosen
you. It's not for your forgiveness I'll come. I will simply tell
you. Long ago I chose you to tell; when your father was
telling me about you; when Lizaveta was still alive—I
thought of it. Good-bye. Don't give me your hand.
Tomorrow!"

He left. Sonia stared after him as if he were mad. But she
felt like a madwoman herself. Her head spun. "Good Lord!
How does he know who killed Lizaveta? What did those
words mean? It's terrible!" And yet *the thought* never entered her head! "How terribly unhappy he must be! He
has abandoned his mother and his sister. But why? What
happened? What does he have in mind?" What was it he had
been telling her? He had kissed her and said . . . he had said (yes,
he had said it clearly) he could not live without her. . . .
"Oh, heavens!"

Sonia spent the whole night in fever and delirium. Every
now and then she would jump up, weep, wring her hands,
and then sink back into a feverish sleep in which she
dreamed of Polia, Katherine Ivanovna, Lizaveta, the reading
of the Gospel, and him . . . pale face and burning eyes . . .
Kissing her feet, weeping . . . O God!

Beyond the door on the right, beyond the door that separated Sonia's apartment from the apartment of Gertrude
Karlovna Resslich, was an intervening room that had long
stood empty; it belonged to Mrs. Resslich's apartment, and
she had put it up for rent. There was a notice posted on the
entryway, and stickers on the windows opening out to the
canal embankment. Sonia was long since used to thinking
of this room as unoccupied. Yet all that time, Mr. Svidrigailov had been standing by the door in the empty room. Hidden there, he had been listening. When Raskolnikov left, he
had stood there pondering for a while, and then had tiptoed

back to his room, which was next to the empty one. Without making a sound, he had picked up a chair and had brought it right up to the doorway that led to Sonia's room. The conversation had struck him as entertaining and significant, and he had enjoyed it very, very much. He had enjoyed it so much he had brought a chair over for future occasions, such as tomorrow, so he would not have to suffer again the discomfort of standing on his feet for a whole hour and he could make himself more comfortable and enjoy himself thoroughly in every respect.

5

When Raskolnikov entered the police station the next morning at exactly eleven o'clock and went to the department of criminal investigation to ask to be announced to Porfiry Petrovich, he was rather surprised at how long they kept him waiting. At least ten minutes passed before he was called in. The way he figured, they should have pounced on him at once. Meanwhile he stood in the waiting room, and people who had no interest in him at all walked past him both ways. In the next, officelike room, several clerks were sitting and writing away. It was obvious not one of them had the slightest idea who or what Raskolnikov was.

With a restless and suspicious gaze he examined his surroundings, checking to see if somebody had been secretly assigned to keep tabs on him and make sure he didn't leave. There was nothing of the kind. About him he saw only faces occupied with petty official tasks, and various other people, and not one of them would care in the least if he were to take off in any direction at all at that very moment. He became more and more firmly convinced that if yesterday's puzzling figure, that phantom who had appeared from the bowels of the earth, had really known and seen everything, they could scarcely allow him, Raskolnikov, to stand here now, waiting so peacefully. Would they simply have waited around until eleven o'clock when he himself saw fit to put in an appearance with a request? Either the man had as yet reported nothing, or . . . or simply he knew nothing, had seen nothing with his own eyes (and how could he have seen anything?), and so everything that had happened to him yesterday was a phantasm too, magnified by his sick and inflamed imagination. He had leaned to this even the day before, when his fears had been deepest and his desperation greatest. As he thought it out all over again and prepared himself for a renewal of the struggle, he suddenly felt he was trembling, and he seethed with indignation at the thought that he was terrified before the prospect of confronting the odious Porfiry Petrovich. He felt the most terrible thing of all was having to meet this man again. He hated him without measure, infinitely, and even feared he might somehow give himself away through this very hatred. His indignation was so strong the trembling immediately ceased. He steeled himself to enter in a cold, sharp manner, and he vowed he would remain silent as much as he could, he would look and listen, and this time, come what may, he would suppress his pathological irritation. At that moment he was called in to Porfiry Petrovich.

Porfiry Petrovich was alone in his office. It was a room neither large nor small, and contained a large desk stationed in front of an oilcloth-covered couch, a bureau, a closet in the corner, and several chairs—all government furniture made of polished yellow wood. In a corner of the back partition, there was a closed door. That meant there must be still other rooms on the other side of the partition. As soon as Raskolnikov came in, Porfiry Petrovich shut the door through which he had entered, and they were alone. He received his visitor with what was apparently a cheerful and polite manner, and it was only after a while that Raskolnikov noticed he seemed embarrassed, as though he had been taken suddenly by surprise or caught at something secret and obscure.

"So, my most worthy friend, here you are! In our neck of the woods . . ." Porfiry Petrovich offered him both his hands. "Well, do sit down, old man! But then, you might not like to be called 'my most worthy friend' or 'old man' just like that, *tout court.* Please don't think I'm being too familiar. . . . Over here, please. On the couch." Raskolnikov sat down without taking his eyes off him.

The phrase "in our neck of the woods," the apologies for familiarity, the French expression, all this meant something. "He offered both hands, but he didn't give me one; he withdrew it in time," flashed suspiciously through his mind. Each watched the other, but as soon as their glances met, both quickly dropped their eyes.

"I brought you this statement . . . about the watch . . . here it is. Is it correct, or should I copy it over?"

"What? Statement? Ah, so. Don't worry, that's exactly right," he said, as if he were about to leave and was in a hurry. After he said this, he picked up the statement and glanced over it. "Yes, that's exactly right. Don't need another thing," he said in the same hurried tone. He put the statement down on the desk. A minute later, when they were already discussing something else, he picked it up again and carried it over to his bureau.

"I think you said yesterday you'd like to ask me . . . as a matter of form . . . about my acquaintance with . . . the murdered woman?" Raskolnikov began again. "Why did I insert that '*I think*'?" went through his mind in a flash. "And why does it bother me I inserted that '*I think*'?"

Suddenly he sensed that his nervousness, because he was alone with Porfiry and near him, because of a few glances, had grown rapidly to monstrous proportions . . . and it was terribly dangerous. His nerves were tense and his agitation mounted. "It's bad. Bad! I'll say too much again."

"Yes, yes, yes! Relax! There's no hurry, no hurry at all," muttered Porfiry Petrovich as he paced up and down beside the desk, aimlessly it would seem, darting now to the window, now to his bureau, now back to the desk, sometimes evading Raskolnikov's suspicious gaze, sometimes stopping suddenly dead still and looking at Raskolnikov point-blank. All the while, his short, stout, round figure seemed to roll strangely in various directions, bouncing off the corners and all the walls like a ball.

"We'll manage it, we'll manage! Do you smoke? Have any on you? Here, have a cigarette. . . . You know, I'm entertaining you here, but the apartment where I live is through there, beyond the partition. I get it free from the government. I'm out of it for a while now. Repairs, you know. But almost done. An official apartment's not a bad deal—ah? Don't you think?"

"Not a bad deal," Raskolnikov replied, almost with a sneer.

"Not bad at all, not bad," Peter Petrovich repeated, as though some quite different thought had actually dawned on him. "Yes, not bad!" he all but shouted. Suddenly he looked up at Raskolnikov, stopping two paces away from him. His idiotic reiteration to the effect that an official apartment was not a bad thing contradicted too starkly in its vulgarity the serious, thoughtful, and enigmatic gaze that he now directed at his visitor.

Raskolnikov's malice was more than ever stirred, and he could no longer resist a mocking and rather indiscreet challenge. "You know what," he said all of a sudden, looking at him almost insolently and as though his own insolence pleased him, "I believe there's a kind of juridical rule of thumb, isn't there, sort of a tradition that investigating attorneys follow—you start off obliquely, trifles, or serious matters if you will, so long as they're absolutely irrelevant, just to encourage, or, you might say, divert, the man you're interrogating, put him off guard—then all of a sudden you take him completely by surprise, the most crucial and dangerous question, bang on the head—isn't that right? I think it's referred to in all the textbooks and regulations, isn't it?"

"Well, well, so . . . you think I was telling you about my official apartment for . . . that—ah?" As he said this, Porfiry Petrovich screwed up his eyes and winked. Something merry and sly flitted across his face; the wrinkles on his forehead smoothed themselves out, his eyes narrowed, the lines on his face relaxed, and suddenly he let himself go in a prolonged nervous laugh, body heaving and shaking all over, as he looked Raskolnikov straight in the eye. The latter broke out laughing too, forcing himself a bit. When Porfiry saw him laughing, he in turn laughed so hard he almost turned purple. Suddenly Raskolnikov's disgust overcame all his caution. He stopped laughing. He frowned. He looked at Porfiry long and with hatred. While Porfiry's deliberate, prolonged laughter went on, Raskolnikov did not take his eyes off him. The lack of caution, however, seemed not to be one-sided. Porfiry Petrovich seemed to be laughing right in his visitor's face, not much troubled by the fact that the visitor hated it. This struck Raskolnikov as quite significant. He realized that Porfiry Petrovich had probably not been embarrassed at all; on the other hand, he, Raskolnikov, seemed to have fallen into a trap. Something was obviously up of which he knew nothing, a purpose of some sort; it could be that everything was already set and would at this very moment reveal itself and burst upon him. . . .

He went straight to the point immediately, rising from his place and picking up his cap. "Porfiry Petrovich," he began resolutely, but with a rather strong show of irritability. "Yesterday you said you wanted me to come for some kind of questioning." He especially stressed the word "questioning."

"I came. If you have anything you need to ask me, ask. If not, please allow me to leave. I'm in a hurry. I have business to attend to. . . . I have to be at the funeral of that clerk who was run down by horses the other day. I think you . . . know about him, too," he added, and was immediately angry with himself for adding it, which then immediately irritated him even more. "I'm fed up with all this, you hear, and I've been fed up for a long time, too! It's partly this made me sick . . . in short," he almost shouted, feeling at the same time that the phrase about his illness had been even more out of place, "in short, please interrogate me, or let me go at once . . . and if you interrogate me, do it according to regulations, no other way! Or else I won't allow it. So for the time being, good-bye. There isn't much for the two of us together now."

"Heavens! What *are* you talking about? What would I have to interrogate you about?" clucked Porfiry Petrovich, suddenly and at the same time changing the tone of his voice and the expression of his face and instantly ceasing to laugh. "Now," he fussed, "don't worry about it, please," and he rushed off again in all directions, and then all of a sudden he tried to get Raskolnikov to sit down. "There's no rush, no rush, these are all trifles! And I'm so glad you finally have come to see us. . . . I consider you my guest. As for laughing, I sincerely hope, Rodion Romanovich, old man, that you'll forgive me. That's your full name—Rodion Romanovich—isn't it, old man? I'm nervous. Your remark was witty, and you made me laugh a lot. You know, sometimes I shake like India rubber for half an hour on end. . . . Sense of humor! The way I'm built, I'm afraid I might even have a stroke. Do sit down, won't you? Please do, old man. Or I might think you're angry . . ."

Raskolnikov remained silent. He listened and watched, still frowning angrily. He sat down, yet he hung on to his cap.

"Rodion Romanovich, old man, one thing I'll tell you about myself," Porfiry went on, fussing about the room as before and seeming to avoid looking his visitor in the eye, "to explain my character, I mean. I'm a bachelor, you know, unsociable and unknown, and what's more I'm a man who's gone to the end of his road, set in his ways, gone to seed, and . . . and . . . have you noticed, Rodion Romanovich? Here, I mean here in Russia, especially here in our Petersburg circles, when two intelligent men, not well acquainted,

but with a certain respect for each other, let's say—you and
me, for example—when they get together it takes them all
of half an hour before they can find something to talk about.
They go numb in each other's presence; they're both terribly
embarrassed. Now, everybody has something they can make
conversation about. Ladies, let's say, fashionable, high-toned
people; they always have something to make conversation
about; *c'est de rigueur.* Yet people of the middle sort, like
you and me—I mean thinking people—are all embarrassed
and tongue-tied. Now, I ask you, old man, why does that
happen? Is it because sociability doesn't interest us, or because we're so honest we don't want to fool each other, or
what? Ah? What do you think? Come on, now; put your
cap down. It's as though you were going to leave, and it
makes me feel awkward. . . . While I, you see, I am so
glad . . ."

Raskolnikov put down his cap and went on listening, silent, serious, and sullen, to Porfiry's vacuous, confused babble. "What's he up to? Does he really want to distract my
attention, babbling away like that?"

"I'm afraid this isn't the right place, and I can't offer you
any coffee; but why not take five minutes and just sit down
with a friend and relax?" Porfiry chittered away without
pausing. "All these official duties, you know . . . well, you
mustn't be offended, old man, if I walk up and down. You
must excuse me, old man, I am very much afraid of of-
fending you, but I simply have got to move about like that.
I sit all the time, and I'm very glad to be able to walk
around for five minutes or so . . . hemorrhoids, you know . . .
I keep intending to do gymnastics for the cure; they say that
state councillors, senior state councillors, even privy councillors, mind you, enjoy going down to the gym for a little
skip-rope. Well, there you are; that's science for you
nowadays. . . . That's the way it is. . . . As far as my duties
here are concerned, I mean interrogations and all that kind
of formality . . . I do believe you mentioned interrogations,
now, didn't you; well, you know, really, Rodion Romanovich, old man, sometimes these interrogations are more
confusing to the interrogator than to the man he's
interrogating. . . . You just now said something about that
yourself, old man, quite rightly, too, and wittily." (Raskolnikov had said nothing of the kind.) "A man gets all mixed
up—yes, yes; he gets all mixed up! Always pounding on the
same thing, too; one and the same thing, always, like a

drum! Well, the big reform is under way, isn't it, and from now on we'll be called by a different name, anyway, won't we, he-he-he! As for our juridical rules of thumb, as you so wittily put it, I agree with you thoroughly. Well, now, anybody who's under arrest, even the dumbest peasant, knows they'll start out lulling him with irrelevant questions (to use your felicitous phrase)—who doesn't know that?—and then suddenly, smacko! right on the head with the butt end—he-he-he!—right on the head, as you put it, he-he! So you really thought when I mentioned my official apartment, I wanted you—he-he! You're an ironical man. Well, I won't! Oh, yes, but since one phrase recalls another and an idea evokes another one, since you mentioned the regulations a while back in connection with being interrogated . . . now, what's the use of regulations, anyway! You know, in many cases all that formality is rubbish. Then there are times when if you just talk a little in a friendly way—well, it pays. The regulations won't ever go away—oh, on that point, let me reassure you. Yet what, I ask you, is at the heart of the regulations? An investigator can't be cramped with the regulations every step he takes. His work's one of the liberal arts, in its own way—or something of that sort . . . he-he-he!"

For a moment Porfiry Petrovich held his breath. He'd been chattering away without pause—now senselessly pouring out empty phrases, now suddenly inserting these enigmatic expressions, then falling back on nonsense again. He was practically running around the room, moving his fat little legs more and more rapidly, looking constantly at the floor, his right arm thrust behind his back and his left arm waving in the air, constantly tracing any number of gestures, which seemed always curiously inappropriate to his words. Then Raskolnikov noticed that he seemed to pause briefly a couple of times while scurrying about the room. Near the doorway. As though he were listening . . . "Is he waiting for something, or what?"

"Still, you were absolutely right," Porfiry started up again, gazing at Raskolnikov cheerfully and with extraordinary good humor. It made Raskolnikov shudder, and instantly put him on his guard. "You really were right when you mocked our little police formalities with such wit, he-he! You know, these (some of them, certainly) profound psychological devices of ours—well, they're quite absurd. Yes, if you like, they're quite useless, really, if they're terribly cramped by the regulations. Yes . . . well, here I go talking about the regulations again. Well, let's suppose I perceive, or better, I suspect somebody. Some case I'm handling, let's say, and I take this fellow to be guilty . . . You study law, don't you, Rodion Romanovich?"

"Yes, I did."

"Well, then, I might say this is a little precedent for you, for your future interest. . . . I mean, you mustn't think that I presume to teach you—why, just look at the articles on crime you've been publishing! No, no. I'm just presenting it to you as a fact, a bit of a precedent. Now, let's say, for example, I consider some man or another or a third guilty; why, I ask you, should I bother him too soon—even if I had evidence against him, eh? I'm bound, for example, to arrest one man as quickly as possible, yes, but then another may have quite a different character, really; so why shouldn't I let him run around town a bit! He-he! No, I can see you don't quite understand, so I'll spell it out. Let's say I arrest him too soon—well, I give him a kind of moral support, don't I? He-he Are you laughing?" It had never occurred to Raskolnikov to laugh. He sat there, lips pressed together, without taking his burning gaze from the eyes of Porfiry Petrovich. "Yet that's the way it goes, especially with some people. Men are quite, quite different, you know, and only experience can tell. A while ago you were kind enough to mention evidence. Well, all right, there's evidence. Let's say there's evidence. But you know, old man, evidence can cut both ways, and usually does. Say I'm an investigator, a professional. I must confess all that means is that I'm only human. I'd like to have a case you could call mathematically clear; I'd like to have evidence of the order of twice two equals four—direct and unmistakable proof! Yet if I went and arrested him before the time was ripe, even though I'm absolutely sure it's *him*—well, you see, I'd be depriving myself of the means to incriminate him further. And why so? Because I provide him with what you might call a clear-cut position; I define him psychologically, so to speak, I give him comfort, and he withdraws from me into his shell. He understands at last that he's a prisoner. I've been told that at the Battle of Sevastopol, right after Alma, the really clever people were afraid the enemy might launch an immediate and direct attack and capture Sevastopol at once. When they saw the enemy digging trenches, meaning he preferred a normal siege, these clever people rejoiced and felt comforted. That gave them at least another two months—that's how long a normal siege would have to take! You're laughing again, you don't believe me? Of course, you're right. Oh, absolutely right! These are all particular instances, I agree. The case in point is certainly a special one. But, my dearest Rodion Romanovich, that's what you really have to watch out for. The typical case, the one for which all the legal rules and regulations were designed, for which they were figured out and written up in books, doesn't exist at all; because every case, every crime, as soon as it takes place in real life, turns immediately into a completely special case, and you know, sometimes it's not in any way like anything that happened before. Sometimes you get the funniest cases of that sort. Now, suppose I leave this gentleman completely alone . . . I don't run him in, I don't bother him; but every minute of every hour I let him know, or at least I let him suspect, that I know everything right down to the dirt under his fingernails; day in and night out I follow him, I keep constant watch on him, and since he's always in a state of doubt and terror his head will really start swimming, and he'll come of his own will; yes, and he'll do something that will be like twice two; that will have what you might call an aspect of mathematical certainty; and that's just fine and dandy. Now, the case I'm citing could even be that of an ignorant peasant, but with our good friend the clever man of today—especially if he has a touch of cultivation—it's dead certain! You have to know where this touch of cultivation lies. And, yes, nerves, too. You've forgotten about nerves, now, haven't you? Nowadays everybody's sick, aren't they? Puny, irritable. And how bilious everybody is! Well, that gives us a lot to work on. So why should I worry if he gads about a bit with his hands free? Let him. Let him run around awhile. Let him. I know I've got him where I want him and he isn't going to get away! Anyway, where would he go? He-he! Abroad? Your Polish gentleman, now, would get away abroad, but not him; and especially since I keep track of him and I have taken measures. Maybe into the depths of our hinterland? Well, now, you know, it's inhabited by peasants—regular, crude Russian peasants. Our cultivated man of today, you know, he'd sooner take the hoosegow than live with a bunch of foreigners like our peasants, he-he! Of course, this is all nonsense, and quite superficial. What does 'getting away' mean? That's conventional. The main point is elsewhere. Not just that he isn't going to get away from me—he has no place to get away to. *Psychologically* he won't get away from me. He-he! Some way of putting it, eh? Even if he had someplace to get away to, he wouldn't get away from me. It's like a law of nature. Did you ever see a moth and a candle? Well, that's just like him; he'll go on circling around me, like around a candle. Freedom will lose its charm. He'll start brooding and weaving. He'll weave a net around himself. He'll worry himself to death! That's not all, either. If I give him enough rope, he'll do me a nice mathematical job, all by himself, like twice two. . . . And he'll keep circling around and around me, smaller and smaller circles, and—plop! He'll fly straight into my mouth, and I will swallow him. Yes, and that will be very nice, he-he-he! Don't you believe me?"

Raskolnikov did not reply. He sat pale and motionless and kept staring with the same concentration into Porfiry's face. "A fine lesson!" he thought, turning cold. "Not even cat and mouse anymore, like yesterday. Still, he's not just showing off his power in front of me, or just provoking. He's much too clever for that. He's got something else in mind—but I wonder what it is? Ach, it's all bunk, pal. You're trying to scare me, and you're bluffing. You have no proof, and that man yesterday—he doesn't exist. You just want to throw me off-balance. You want to get me good and sore, and then you can spring the trap. Only you're wrong. You're going to get caught short, caught short! But why? Why is he taking such pains to provoke me? Is he counting on my sick nerves, or what? No, pal, you're mistaken. You may have something all set up, but you'll get caught short. . . . Well, now, let's have a little look-see at what you've got set up there. . . ."

And he braced himself hard as he could to prepare for a terrible and unknown catastrophe. At moments he felt like flinging himself on Porfiry and strangling him on the spot. This rage of his—it was what he had feared even when he came in. His lips were parched and his heart was pounding. And yet he resolved to keep silent and not breathe a word for the time being. He realized that this was the best tactic in his position; he would not only not be saying too much himself, but with his silence might even irritate the enemy and get him to say too much instead. At least that was what he hoped.

"No, I see you don't believe me. You think I'm just making silly jokes," Porfiry started in again, merrier and merrier, gayer and gayer, giggling constantly with pleasure, and beginning again to circle about the room. "You're quite right, of course. Even my figure was cut by the Lord himself to rouse only comic thoughts in others. A buffoon, yes. Still. I'll tell you something. And I'll tell it over again, too, Rodion Romanovich, old man, you—you'll excuse me, I'm an old man—you're still young, in the prime of youth, you might say, and so you value the human intellect above all things, the way all young people do. The play of intellect and the conclusions of abstract reasoning fascinate you. You know, that's just the way it was with the former Austrian *Hofkriegsrat,* as far as I can judge about military matters. On paper they had smashed Napoleon and taken him prisoner. At headquarters they had it all figured out and toted up in the cleverest way. But then, you see, General Mack went and surrendered with all his army, he-he-he! Oh, I can see, I can see, Rodion Romanovich, old man, you're laughing at me—me, I'm such a civilian, and here I go taking all my examples from military history. Well, what can I do? It's a weakness. I like military matters. I like them so much I read all these military accounts. . . . I distinctly missed my calling. I really should have served in the military. Well, now, perhaps I would never have made a Napoleon, but I could have become a major. . . . Yes, he-he-he! Well, my dear fellow. Now I'll tell you the whole truth in solemn detail. I'm talking about that *special case.* . . . Reality and character, my dear sir, are quite important matters, and sometimes they undermine the staunchest plans! Ah, you'd better listen to the old man. Rodion Romanovich, I speak seriously." As he said this Porfiry Petrovich, who was barely thirty-five, really seemed to age all of a sudden. Even his voice changed. He seemed to shrivel up somehow. "What's more, I'm an open man. . . . Am I open, or not? What do you think? I think I am, really. Here I am, letting you in on all these matters gratis, he-he! Well, there you are. Let me go on. I think cleverness is a splendid thing, yes. It's nature's ornament, you might say, one of our great comforts in life—and my goodness, what tricks it can play. You might well ask how a poor old court investigator was going to make it all out, since he's bound to get carried away by fantasies of his own, too—he's only human, after all! The thing is that human nature helps this poor investigator out! Youth does not pause to reflect on that, however, preoccupied as it is with cleverness, 'striding over all obstacles,' as you deigned to put it in that most clever and crafty way. Let's say he tells a lie, the man I'm talking about, the *special case,* that incognito, and he lies extremely well, in the most crafty manner. He'll win out, you might think, enjoy the fruits of his cleverness, but no—he walks into the most interesting, the most prominent possible place and falls in a faint, 'plop!' Well, there's his illness, it's true, and sometimes it does get stuffy in those rooms, but still! Still, it makes you think! He told a lie splendidly, but he couldn't take human nature into account. That's how insidious it is! Then again, he'll get carried away by the play of his cleverness and he'll start making a fool of the man who suspects him. He'll pretend to turn pale, as if he were play-acting. Yet somehow he turns pale *too naturally,* too much like the truth—and there again, it makes you think! Even if you've been fooled at first, if you know what's what, you'll sleep on it and think it over. And so it goes, at every step! And that's not all. He'll start plunging ahead of himself. He'll butt in where nobody asked him. He'll start talking all the time about what he should obviously keep quiet. He'll start weaving allegories. He-he! He'll drop by and start asking questions like, 'Why didn't they haul me in long ago?' He-he-he! Mind you, he might be the very cleverest kind of man—a psychologist or a litterateur! Ah, human nature is a mirror—yes, a mirror. The most limpid mirror, sir. Behold and admire—there you are! Rodion Romanovich, why have you turned so pale? Does it feel stuffy? Shall I open the window?"

"Oh, please don't bother," Raskolnikov said, and all of a sudden burst out laughing. "Please don't bother."

Porfiry paused, facing him, waited, then suddenly burst out laughing too. Raskolnikov rose from the couch and brought his quite hysterical laughter to an abrupt end.

"Porfiry Petrovich!" he said loudly and distinctly, though his legs were trembling so he could hardly stand. "I see clearly at last that you really do suspect me of the murder of that old woman and her sister Lizaveta. As for me, I tell you I've been fed up with this whole thing for a long time now. If you should find you have the right to prosecute me legally, then prosecute. If you can arrest me—arrest away. But I won't allow you to laugh in my face and torment me." All of a sudden his lips were quivering, his eyes burned with uncontrollable anger, and his hitherto restrained voice rang out. "I won't allow it, sir!" he shouted suddenly, bringing his fist down on the table with all his might. "Do you hear that, Porfiry Petrovich? I won't allow it!"

"Oh, good heavens, now what's the matter!" Porfiry Petrovich gasped, apparently very much alarmed. "Rodion Romanovich, old man! My friend, my good fellow! What's the matter with you?"

"I won't allow it!" Raskolnikov shouted again.

"Hush, old man! They'll hear, you know, they'll come in! Well—just think—what will we tell them!" Porfiry Petrovich whispered in horror, bringing his face close to Raskolnikov's face.

"I won't allow it, I won't allow it!" Raskolnikov repeated mechanically, but suddenly also in a complete whisper.

Porfiry turned swiftly and ran to open a window. "Let some fresh air in! And you could use a little drink of water, my friend—you're quite hysterical, you know!" And he ran to the doorway to ask for some water, but there turned out to be a pitcher of water right there in the corner. "Have a drink, old man," he whispered, and rushed up to him with the pitcher. "It should help." Porfiry Petrovich's actions seemed so natural, and his anxiety so genuine, that Raskolnikov fell silent and began to examine him with a wild curiosity. He did not, however, take any water.

"Rodion Romanovich, my dear fellow! you'll drive yourself crazy that way, I assure you. My, my. Come, have a drink! Come on, now, just a drop!" He forced him to take the glass. Mechanically Raskolnikov lifted it to his lips; then he recollected himself and put it on the table in disgust.

"Yes, you did have a slight touch of hysteria, you see! If you go on like that you'll bring your old sickness back, my dear." Porfiry Petrovich clucked sympathetically, though he still looked a bit shaken. "Heavens! How can you not take better care of yourself? Dmitry Prokofich came to see me yesterday—and, well, agreed; yes, agreed that I have a foul and poisonous nature, and yet, my oh my, what isn't being made out of that! Heavens! He came yesterday, after you left; we ate dinner, and he talked and talked and I just threw up my hands. Well, well, my goodness! Maybe you sent him? Do sit down, old man; make yourself comfortable, for Christ's sake!"

"No, I didn't! But I knew he'd gone to you, and I knew why he went," Raskolnikov answered sharply.

"You knew?"

"I knew. What of it?"

"Well, just that I know some of your other little deeds, too, Rodion Romanovich, old man. I know everything. I know, you see, how you tried *renting an apartment;* around nightfall, getting dark, and you started ringing the bell; you asked about the blood and got the workmen and the janitors all mixed up. You see, I understand the state of mind you were in—that evening, I mean. . . . By God, you'll just drive yourself crazy that way, you'll go around and around! You boil with indignation. Righteous indignation at the wrongs you've suffered—first from fate, then from the local police. So you rage up hill and down dale, sort of trying to get everybody to commit himself as soon as possible. So you can have done with it once and for all. Because you're fed up with these stupid suspicions—isn't that right? That's about the way you feel, isn't it? You're not the only one buzzing around me, though. You've set Razumikhin buzzing, too. He's too *good* a man for that—you know it yourself. You're sick, he's virtuous; he'll catch your disease. . . . When you calm down, old man, I'll tell you something. . . . For Christ's sake, do sit down! Please rest. You look awful. Do make yourself comfortable."

Raskolnikov sat down. He stopped shivering and began to feel hot all over. Tensely, and in deep astonishment, he attended Porfiry Petrovich, who hovered around him with a friendly solicitude. Yet he did not believe a single word he said, although he was aware of a strange inclination to believe. Porfiry's words about the apartment had taken him completely by surprise. "I don't get it. He knows the incident and he tells me all about it himself!" he thought.

"Yes, I once had a case like that, a sick psychological case," Porfiry went on, talking rapidly. "This fellow glued a murder charge to himself and tried hard to make it stick. He cooked up a regular hallucination, presented facts, described circumstances, got everybody all muddled and mixed up— and why? Quite unintentionally he had been partly the cause of the murder, but only partly, and when he found out he had given the murderers the opportunity, he started brooding; it began to haunt him and affect his mind; then he went completely off, and he wound up convincing himself that he really was the murderer! The High Court finally examined the case, and the poor fellow was acquitted and put under care. Thanks to the High Court! Tch-tch-tch-tch. So what are you up to, old man? If you keep abusing your nerves impulsively you could wind up in delirium—going around ringing doorbells at night and asking about blood! You see, I learned all this psychology in the course of my practice. I understand what makes a man sometimes want to jump out of a window or from a belfry—it's a very tempting impulse. It's the same with ringing doorbells. . . . Sickness, Rodion Romanovich, sickness! You've been neglecting your disease. You should consult an experienced medico—what's the good of that fat fellow! You're delirious! You go around doing all this in delirium!"

For a moment everything positively whirled around Raskolnikov. "Is it possible," flashed through his mind, "is it possible he's lying now, too? Impossible, impossible!" He pushed that idea away from him, sensing in advance to what a degree of rage and fury it might lead him, sensing that rage might drive him out of his mind.

"I wasn't delirious," he cried out, "I was fully conscious!" He strained his every faculty to penetrate Porfiry's game. "Conscious, do you hear! I was fully conscious!"

"Yes, I hear—and I understand! Yesterday also you said you weren't delirious. You were even specially emphatic about it! Yes, I understand everything you can possibly say! E-eh! Listen here, Rodion Romanovich, my friend and benefactor. Consider this one circumstance. If you were really guilty, you see, if you were somehow mixed up in this damned business—excuse me—would you go around insisting you weren't delirious and did all this fully conscious? Would you insist on it so particularly, so stubbornly? Well, now, forgive me, but would you, would you really? Likely to be quite the opposite, I think. Because if you felt involved, it stands to reason you'd insist you were delirious. Wouldn't you? Not so? It is, isn't it?"

There was something sly in the question. Raskolnikov recoiled to the very back of the couch, away from Porfiry, who was bending over him. Silently and stubbornly he stared at Porfiry, bewildered.

"For that matter, about Mr. Razumikhin—I mean, whether he came on his own yesterday or at your instigation. You really should have said he came on his own and tried to hide your sending him! Yet you don't try to hide it at all, you see! You actually insist it was at your instigation!" Raskolnikov had never insisted on this. A shiver passed along his back.

"You keep lying," he said slowly and weakly, twisting his mouth into a painful smile. "Once more you want to show me you know my whole game, know my answers before I give them." He could almost sense that he was no longer weighing his words as he should. "You want to frighten me . . . either that, or you're just laughing at me." He kept staring at him steadily as he said this. Suddenly a boundless hatred glittered again in his eyes. "You keep lying!" he cried. "You know very well that the criminal's best gambit is not to hide what doesn't have to be hidden, not to hide anything when he doesn't have to. I don't believe you!"

"What a difficult fellow you are to pin down!" Porfiry sniggered. "There's no coping with you, old man. Some kind of monomania's got you. So you don't believe me? I think you do believe me, though. Just believe me a bit and I'll persuade you all the way. Because I really like you, and I sincerely wish you well." Raskolnikov's lips quivered. "Yes, I do. And let me tell you," he went on, taking Raskolnikov lightly by the arm in a friendly fashion, a little above the elbow, "let me tell you emphatically, you better keep an eye on that disease of yours. What's more, your folks are here now, and you've got to think about them. You ought to soothe and comfort them, and you do nothing but scare them—"

"What business is that of yours? How do you know all this? Why are you so interested? Is it because you're watching me, and you want me to know that?"

"Look here, old man. You just told me all about it yourself. You're so excited you don't even notice how you let everything out of the bag, not just to me, to others, too. I also learned a lot of interesting details from Mr. Razumikhin yesterday. No, sir, you interrupted me; but I tell you, for all your cleverness, this suspiciousness makes you lose the commonsense view of things. Let's go back to the subject of doorbells, for example. I handed you this precious jewel (didn't I?) this fact (it's a whole fact, you see!) gratis—me, the investigator! And you don't see anything in that? Now, if I suspected you—even a little—would I have done a thing like that? On the contrary. I would have begun by lulling your suspicions, not letting on I already knew this fact. I'd draw you off in the opposite direction. Then, suddenly—like a blunt edge on the skull, to use your expression—I'd smash you with it. And what were you doing, sir, in the murdered woman's apartment—I'd say—ten o'clock at night, almost eleven? And why did you ring the doorbell? And why those questions about the blood? And why did you try to confuse the janitors by inviting them to the police station, to the precinct lieutenant? That's how I'd have acted if I had even a grain of suspicion of you. According to all the regulations, I should have made you testify. I should have made a search. I should even have arrested you. . . . So it must mean I don't harbor any suspicions, or I would have acted differently! I repeat, sir, you've lost hold of common sense, and you don't see a thing!"

Raskolnikov's whole body shook. Porfiry Petrovich noticed it all too clearly. "You keep lying!" Raskolnikov cried. "I don't know what you're driving at, but you keep lying. . . . You were talking differently a while ago. I couldn't be wrong. You're lying!"

"Lying? Me?" said Porfiry, evidently annoyed, yet preserving an extremely good-humored and ironical expression, as though he couldn't care less what Mr. Raskolnikov thought of him. "Me lying? . . . But how did I treat you? Me, the investigator! Prompting you myself, giving you every means for your defense, and bringing in all that psychology on your behalf. Sickness, I said, delirium; he was insulted, he was depressed, there were all those policemen, and all that sort of thing. Ah? He-he-he! By the way, I might as well tell you, while I'm at it, all those psychological defenses, those alibis and excuses, are extremely thin—and they cut both ways. Sickness, you might say, delirium, hallucination, I imagined it, I don't remember! Be that as it may. But why, old man, should these particular hallucinations come up in your sickness and delirium? Why these and not others? There might well have been others, too, not so? Not so? He-he-he-he!"

Raskolnikov looked at him proudly and contemptuously. "In short," he said loudly and emphatically, and he got up and pushed Porfiry slightly aside as he did so; "in short, I want to know: do you consider me under suspicion or *not*? Say it, Porfiry Petrovich, definitely and conclusively, as quick as you can, right now!"

"What a business this is. My, what a business I'm having with you," said Porfiry with a completely benign, sly, unperturbed expression on his face. "What do you want to know for? What do you want to know so much for? They haven't even started bothering you yet! Why, you're like a child asking to play with fire! And why are you so upset? And why do you come thrusting yourself upon us? For what reasons? Ah? He-he-he!"

"I tell you once more," cried Raskolnikov in a rage, "I can't put up with any more—"

"What? Uncertainty?" interrupted Porfiry.

"Don't provoke me! I won't have it! I tell you I won't have it! I cannot and I will not have it! You hear! You hear!" he shouted, and pounded his fist on the table.

"Why, hush, hush! They'll hear you! I warn you seriously: watch yourself. I am not joking, sir!" Porfiry said in a whisper. His face did not wear the good-natured, womanish, frightened expression of a while ago. He was now giving a direct order. He knitted his brows sternly, as though he were at once resolving all mysteries and ambiguities. This was only for a moment, however. Bewildered, Raskolnikov suddenly fell into a real frenzy. Strangely enough, he obeyed the order to speak more softly, although he was in the most powerful paroxysm of fury.

"I won't allow myself to be tortured," he suddenly whispered. At the same time he acknowledged inwardly, with pain and hatred, that he could not help obeying the order. This drove him to a still greater fury. "Arrest me, search me, but be so kind as to proceed according to the regulations—and don't play with me! Don't you dare—"

"Well, now, don't get upset about the regulations," Porfiry interrupted with his former sly grin, as though he actually enjoyed gloating over Raskolnikov. "I invited you here quite informally, old man. Just to be friendly, you might say!"

"I won't have your friendship. I spit on it! Do you hear? What's more, I'm taking my cap and I'm leaving. Well, what do you say now? Do you intend to arrest me?" He seized his cap and walked to the doorway.

"But what about my little surprise? Don't tell me you don't want to have a look at it?" Porfiry sniggered, again taking him just above the elbow and stopping him in the doorway. He was evidently getting more playful and gayer, and this drove Raskolnikov wild.

"What little surprise? What are you talking about?" he asked, suddenly standing still and looking with fear at Porfiry.

"A little surprise, sir. It's sitting right here behind my door, he-he-he!" He pointed his finger at the closed door that led to his official apartment. "I even locked it in so it wouldn't run away."

"What are you talking about? Where? What?" Raskolnikov walked to the door and wanted to open it, but it was locked.

"It's locked, sir. Here's the key."

And he actually showed him a key that he had taken out of his pocket.

"You keep lying!" screamed Raskolnikov, no longer able to restrain himself. "You're lying, you damned clown!" And he flung himself on Porfiry, who retired to the doorway, but without a trace of panic.

"I understand everything, everything!" He approached Porfiry. "You're lying and taunting me so I'll give myself away—"

"You can't give yourself away any more than you have already, Rodion Romanovich, old man. Why, you've gone into a state. Don't shout, or I'll call my men, sir!"

"You're lying! Nothing will happen! Call your men! You knew I was sick, and you wanted to work me into a fury so I'd give myself away—that was your aim! No, first you produce the facts! I've got it all down. You don't have any facts. All you have are some low, dirty guesses from Zamiotov! You knew my character and you wanted to put me in a state, then suddenly clobber me with those priests and deputies of yours. . . . So you're waiting for them, ah? What are you waiting for? Where? Let's have it!"

"What deputies do we have here, old man! You're dreaming! Why, we can't do that. According to the regulations, as you say—why, you don't know what's involved, my dear fellow. . . . All the same, the regulations won't fly away, sir. You'll see for yourself," Porfiry muttered, listening at the door. At that very moment, something that sounded like a commotion could be heard in the next room, right by the door.

"Ah, they're coming!" Raskolnikov exclaimed. "You sent for them! You were waiting for them! You were counting— Well, let's have out with them all—deputies, witnesses, whatever you want . . . come on! I'm ready! Ready!"

At this point, however, something strange happened, which was so unexpected and so out of the ordinary that neither Raskolnikov nor Porfiry Petrovich could have counted on such a denouement.

Later, when he would recall this moment, it would present itself to Raskolnikov in the following manner:

The commotion that had been heard behind the door suddenly grew loud, and the door opened a little. "What's going on?" Porfiry Petrovich exclaimed indignantly. "I warned you. . . ."

For the moment there was no answer, but clearly there were several men on the other side of the door, and they seemed to be pushing somebody around. "Well, what's going on there?" Porfiry Petrovich repeated, alarmed.

"They've brought in the prisoner Nickolay," a voice said.

"He's not wanted! Get him out of here! Wait! How did he get in? It's highly irregular!" Porfiry shouted, rushing to the doorway.

"Well, you see, he—" the voice began again, and suddenly stopped.

For a few seconds or so only, a real struggle took place. Suddenly somebody seemed to shove somebody else forcibly aside, and right after that, a very pale individual walked straight into Porfiry Petrovich's office. His appearance, at first glance, was very strange. He stared straight ahead as though he didn't see anybody. His eyes flashed with determination, yet at the same time his face was deathly pale, as though he were being led to his execution. His lips, entirely drained of color, trembled slightly. He was still quite young, dressed like a workman, of medium height and rather thin. His hair was cropped in a circle, and he had lean, delicate features. The man he had unexpectedly shoved aside pursued him into the room and managed to grab him by the shoulder. It was his escort. But Nikolay pulled his arm away and broke free again. Several onlookers crowded into the doorway. Some tried to get in. It all took place almost all at once.

"Get out, it isn't time yet! Wait till you're called! What's the idea, bringing him in ahead of time?" Porfiry Petrovich muttered, extremely annoyed, as though he had been taken by surprise. Suddenly, however, Nikolay went down on his knees.

"What are you doing?" Porfiry shouted, astounded.

"I'm guilty! I sinned! I am the murderer!" Nikolay suddenly proclaimed, as though he had some trouble catching his breath, but in a fairly loud voice.

For ten seconds or so there was silence; they were all struck dumb. Even the escort drew back and did not approach Nikolay. He withdrew to the doorway mechanically, and stood there motionless.

"What did you say?" Porfiry Petrovich exclaimed, recovering from his momentary stupefaction.

"I'm . . . the murderer. . . ." Nikolay repeated after a brief silence.

"What . . . you . . . what are you . . . Whom did you murder?" Porfiry Petrovich was apparently at a loss. Nikolay again remained silent for a bit.

"Aliona Ivanovna and her sister Lizaveta Ivanovna—I . . . killed them . . . with an ax. A darkness came over me," he added suddenly, and again fell silent. All this time he remained on his knees.

For several moments Porfiry Petrovich stood there as though he were brooding; suddenly he roused himself again and gesticulated at the unbidden witnesses. Instantly these disappeared, and the door was closed. Then he looked at Raskolnikov, who was standing in the corner staring wildly at Nikolay. He moved in Raskolnikov's direction. Then suddenly he paused, looked at him, looked at Nikolay, again at Raskolnikov, and again at Nikolay. Suddenly, as though seized, he swooped down on Nikolay again.

"What do you mean plunging on ahead with that darkness of yours?" he shouted at him almost maliciously. "I didn't ask you whether a darkness came over you or not. . . . Just tell me: did you kill them?"

"I am a murderer . . . I'll make a statement. . . ." Nikolay proclaimed.

"Hah! What did you kill them with?"

"An ax. I had it ready."

"Hah, he's in a hurry! By yourself?"

Nikolay did not understand the question.

"Did you kill them by yourself?"

"By myself. And Mitka's not to blame. He didn't have anything to do with it."

"Well, don't rush this Mitka business, eh! Well, tell me. What were you . . . what were you doing running down those stairs that time? The janitors ran into both of you, didn't they?"

"That time . . . when I ran out with Mitka . . . I did that for a cover. . . ." Nikolay replied, as though he were hurrying through something he had prepared beforehand.

"Just as I thought!" Porfiry darkly exclaimed. "He's not using his own words," he muttered, as though to himself. Suddenly he caught sight of Raskolnikov again. He had evidently been so absorbed with Nikolay that for a moment he had even forgotten Raskolnikov. Suddenly recollecting himself, he seemed even disconcerted. "Rodion Romanovich, old man! Please excuse me"—he hurried up to him—"this just won't do. Please . . . There isn't much for you here . . . and I myself . . . well, you see what surprises! If you don't mind . . ." Taking him by the arm, he showed him to the door.

"Looks as though you weren't expecting this," Raskolnikov said. He had as yet no clear understanding of anything, yet managed to take heart.

"Yes, and you didn't expect it either, old man. Look how your hand is trembling, he-he!"

"You're trembling too, Porfiry Petrovich."

"Yes, I'm trembling too. I didn't expect it!" They were standing in the doorway. Porfiry was waiting impatiently for Raskolnikov to leave.

"But why don't you show me your little surprise?" Raskolnikov said suddenly.

"His teeth haven't stopped shaking in his mouth, and listen how he talks. He-he! You *are* an ironical person! Well, then—till soon."

"If you ask me, it's *good-bye*!"

"As the Lord disposes, sir, as the Lord disposes!" said Porfiry with a rather crooked smile.

Walking through the office, Raskolnikov noticed many people were looking at him intently. In the waiting room, in the crowd, he caught a glimpse of both the janitors from *that* house—the ones he had summoned by night to the police station. They were standing there waiting for something. As soon as he walked out onto the staircase, however, he suddenly heard Porfiry Petrovich's voice behind him again. He turned around and saw the latter running after him, all puffing and steaming.

"Just one word, Rodion Romanovich. As to what we were talking about, it's as God disposes. In any case, according to the regulations I've got to ask you a few questions . . . and so we'll be seeing each other after all, sir." Porfiry paused in front of him with a smile. "After all, sir," he repeated. One might have supposed he wanted to say something else, but somehow it didn't quite come out.

"I hope you'll excuse me, Porfiry Petrovich, for what just went on . . . I lost my temper," Raskolnikov began, so relieved he could hardly resist showing off.

"It's nothing at all, nothing at all," Porfiry chimed in almost joyfully. "I, too . . . I have a nasty temper, I must admit, I must admit! Well, anyway, we'll be seeing each other. If God so disposes, we'll be seeing quite a lot of each other, quite a lot!"

"And we'll get to know each other through and through?" said Raskolnikov.

"And we'll get to know each other through and through," Porfiry assented, and he frowned and looked very solemnly at Raskolnikov. "Are you off to a birthday party now?"

"To the funeral."

"Why, of course, to the funeral! Make sure you look after your health, now. Yes, your health . . ."

"Well, for my part, I hardly know what to wish you!" Raskolnikov said. He had already begun descending the stairs. Suddenly, however, he turned around to Porfiry again. "I'd like to wish you more success, but then, you see, don't you, what a comical profession you're in!"

"Why comical?" Porfiry Petrovich, who had also turned to leave, immediately pricked up his ears.

"Well, here's this wretched Mikolka you've been grilling—the way you do—you must have been at him day and night, rehearsing him: 'You're the murderer, you did it, you're the murderer. . . .' And now he's confessed you're starting to pick him apart again. 'You're lying,' you tell him, 'you're not the murderer! You couldn't be! You're not using your own words!' So how can you stand there and say your profession isn't comical?"

"He-he-he! You noticed I told Nikolay just now he wasn't using his own words?"

"How could I not?"

"He-he. Clever. Clever, yes. You notice everything! Yes, a really playful mind! You have a gift for latching onto the comical side of things . . . he-he! It's Gogol, they say, don't they, among writers I mean, who had this quality in the highest degree?"

"Yes, Gogol."

"Yes, of course. Gogol, of course . . . A very good day to you."

"A very good day . . ."

Raskolnikov went straight home. He was so bewildered and confused he threw himself down on his couch as soon as he got home. For a quarter of an hour he sat there, just resting, trying to collect his thoughts as best he could. He did not even try to figure out Nikolay. He felt stunned. He felt there was something astonishing, something inexplicable in Nikolay's confession, something he could not hope to understand just now. Yet Nikolay's confession was a real fact. The consequences of such a fact seemed immediately apparent to him. The lie could not help but be discovered, and then they would be after him again. But at least he would be free until then, and he absolutely had to do something on his own behalf, because danger was inevitable.

To what degree, though? His position became clearer. He remembered *in outline,* in its general shape, the whole recent scene with Porfiry, and he could not help shuddering in horror. Of course, he still did not know all Porfiry's aims, nor could he intuit all his calculations of a while ago. Still, part of the game had been exposed, and no one could grasp better than he how closely that "move" in Porfiry's game had threatened him. A little bit more and he. . . . He *might* have given himself away completely. Porfiry knew the morbidity of his nature and had seen through him at a glance, and even though he had acted a little too decisively, he had hardly been mistaken. It seemed clear that Raskolnikov had already managed to compromise himself too far. And yet as far as *facts* were concerned—they hadn't any. Everything was still just relative. But was that right? In the state he was in, could he really grasp what was going on? Couldn't he be mistaken? What result had Porfiry really been aiming at today? Did he really have something up his sleeve? And what was it? Was he actually expecting something, or not? How would they have parted if it had not been for that unexpected incident with Nikolay?

Porfiry had revealed almost his whole game. He had taken a chance. He had revealed it, and Raskolnikov thought that if Porfiry had more up his sleeve, he would have revealed that, too. What could the "surprise" have been? A joke, or what? Did it mean something or didn't it? Could he have been implying something, something resembling the presence of a fact, a positive accusation? That man yesterday?

Where had he dropped from? Where was he today? If Porfiry had anything positive at all, it must have had something to do with that man yesterday. . . .

He sat on the couch with his head bowed, elbows on his knees, hands covering his face. He was still trembling all over. Finally he rose, took his cap, pondered, and started toward the doorway. He somehow felt that for today, at least, he was certainly safe. Suddenly he felt what was almost a sense of joy. He wanted to make his way to Katherine Ivanovna's as quickly as possible. He was, of course, late for the funeral, but he could make it in time for the feast, and there he would see Sonia. He thought for a moment, and a sickly smile played upon his lips. "Today! Today!" he said to himself. "Yes, this very day! So it must . . ." As he was about to open the door, it seemed suddenly to begin to open of itself. He shuddered and leaped back. Slowly and quietly the door opened, and all of a sudden a figure appeared— the man who had yesterday sprung *from underground.*

He paused on the threshold, looked silently at Raskolnikov, and took a step into the room. He looked just as he had yesterday—the same shape, dressed the same, yet in his face and in his glance something seemed to have changed considerably. He looked somewhat downcast, and he stood there a little while and heaved a deep sigh. All he had to do was place the palm of his hand on his cheek and tilt his head to one side, and he would have looked completely like a woman.

"What do you want?" asked Raskolnikov, terrified.

The man was silent. Suddenly he made a deep bow, almost to the ground. At least, he touched the ground with one finger of his right hand.

"Who are you?" Raskolnikov exclaimed.

"I am guilty," the man softly proclaimed.

"Of what?"

"Of evil thoughts."

They looked at each other.

"I was angry. That time when you came around. Maybe you were drunk. You asked the janitors to come along to the police station, and you started asking about the blood. I was angry because they thought you were drunk and left you alone. I was so angry I couldn't sleep. I remembered your address. So yesterday we came here and inquired—"

"Who came?" Raskolnikov asked, little by little beginning to recollect.

"I did. I mean, I wronged you."

"So you live in that house?"

"Yes. I was standing at the gate with some others that time, if you remember. We've had our little workshop there since way back. We're furriers, artisans, we bring our work to the house, but mostly I was angry because . . ."

Suddenly the whole scene by the gates the day before yesterday came back to Raskolnikov clearly. Besides the janitors, there had been several men and women standing there. He remembered a voice that had proposed taking him directly to the police station. He could not remember the face of the person who had spoken, and even now he didn't recognize it, but he remembered that at the time he had given an answer, had even turned to him. . . .

That must be the solution to yesterday's horror. Most horrifying of all was the thought he had actually almost come to ruin over such a *trivial* circumstance. It turned out that except for the business about renting an apartment and those conversations about the blood, the fellow had nothing to say. Which meant that Porfiry likewise had nothing except that act of *delirium*. No facts except psychology, which is *double-edged*. Nothing positive. That meant if no more facts turned up (and more facts mustn't turn up! they mustn't! they mustn't!)—well, then . . . What could they do to him? Even if they arrested him, how could they pin anything on him? That also meant Porfiry had only just learned about the apartment and hadn't known anything about it before.

"Did you tell Porfiry this today? About my coming?" he exclaimed, struck suddenly by an idea.

"What Porfiry?"

"The investigator."

"I told him. The janitors wouldn't go. So I went."

"Today?"

"A minute or so before you. I heard everything—how he tormented you."

"Where? What? When?"

"Right there. I was sitting there all the time, behind the partition."

"You don't say? *You* were the surprise? But how? Good Lord!"

"When I saw the janitors didn't want to go with me," the artisan began, "because, they said, it's late, and the police would ask why they waited so long, I got mad, and I couldn't sleep, so I started looking around. Yesterday I found out, and then today I went. The first time I came, he wasn't there. When I came back in an hour, they wouldn't let me in. The third time I came, they let me in. I started telling him what was what, and he started thumping up and down the room and beating his chest. 'What are you doing to me,' he says, 'you bandits? If I'd known about this business I'd have had him dragged here by escort!' Then he ran out, called somebody, and talked to him in the corner; then he started cursing me out again and asking me questions. And he blamed a lot on me. I told him everything, and I said when I spoke to you yesterday you didn't dare answer me, and you didn't recognize me. Then he started running around again, beating his chest, getting mad and running around, and when they announced about you—'Well,' he says, 'slip in behind the partition. Sit there awhile. No matter what you hear, don't stir.' Then he brought me a chair and locked me in. 'It may be,' he says, 'that I'll call you in.' Then, when they brought Nikolay in, he sent me away. 'I'll need you again,' he says, 'I've still got some questions to ask you. . . .'"

"Did he question Nikolay while you were there?"

"They sent me away right after they sent you; then they started questioning Nikolay." The artisan stopped, and all of a sudden he made another bow, touching the floor with his finger.

"Forgive me for my evil thoughts and for slandering you."

"God will forgive you," Raskolnikov replied, and as soon as he said this the artisan bowed to him, not all the way down this time, but only at the waist. Then he turned slowly and left the room. "It's all double-edged. Now everything is double-edged," Raskolnikov repeated, and he left the room more boldly than he had at any time before.

"We'll keep fighting," he said with a malicious grin as he went down the stairs. The malice was directed at himself. He recalled with contempt and shame his own "faintheartedness."

PART FIVE

1

The morning after his disastrous declaration to Dunia and
Pulcheria Alexandrovna had a sobering effect even on Peter
Petrovich. Little by little, and to his great annoyance, he
had to recognize as acknowledged and irrevocable fact
something that yesterday had seemed to him fantastic, and
though he knew it had happened, still seemed in a sense
impossible. All night the black serpent of wounded vanity
had gnawed at his heart. As soon as he got out of bed, Peter
Petrovich looked at himself in the mirror. He had feared he
might be bilious, but everything seemed all right for the time
being, at least as far as that was concerned. As he looked
at his pale, well-bred face, turning slightly to fat as of late,
Peter Petrovich actually felt a moment's consolation. He was
fully convinced he could find himself some other bride, and
a better one at that. But he recalled himself immediately
and spat energetically to one side, and this evoked a silent
but sarcastic smile from his young friend and roommate,
Andrey Semionovich Lebeziatnikov. Taking note of that
smile, Peter Petrovich held it against his young friend's account. Recently he had managed to reckon up a great deal
against that account. His malice doubled when he suddenly
realized that he should not have told Andrey Semionovich
about what had happened yesterday. It was the second mistake he had made yesterday on the spur of the moment,
while he was irritated, and because he was too outgoing. . . .
All morning long, as though fated, unpleasantness followed
unpleasantness. Even in the Senate he had a kind of setback
in the case he'd been pleading there. The landlord of the
apartment he had rented with his impending marriage in
mind irritated him particularly. He'd been having it remod-
eled at his own expense, and this landlord, who was some
kind of *nouveau riche* German shopkeeper, couldn't be persuaded to break the lease they had just signed, and was
demanding the full recompense provided for in the contract—in spite of the fact that Peter Petrovich had returned
the apartment to him almost completely redone. Similarly,

the furniture store wouldn't return a single ruble of the deposit he had left on the furniture he had bought, but which had not yet been delivered to the apartment. "I can't just go and get married for the sake of the furniture!" gritted Peter Petrovich to himself. At the same time a desperate hope flashed once again through his mind. "Is it really the end? Is everything over and hopelessly done with? Couldn't I really try again?" The thought of Dunia beguiled his fancy. He felt tormented. If he could have killed Raskolnikov by wish alone, Peter Petrovich would certainly have immediately pronounced this wish.

"I made another mistake not giving them any money," he thought, returning sadly to Lebeziatnikov's room. "And why the hell was I such a damned Jew? There wasn't even any point to it! I thought I'd keep them in short supply awhile and then rescue them, so they'd think I was providential—and now look at them! . . . T'foo! If I'd given them, let's say, a thousand and a half for a dowry to tide them over—for presents and all those little packages and parcels and jewelry and all that junk, for dresses from Knopf's or from the English department store—I would have had a much better case . . . considerably stronger! They wouldn't be able to turn me down so easily now! They're the kind of people who'd certainly consider it a duty to return money and presents if they turned me down; but returning them would be pretty difficult and painful. And conscience would bother them. How could they suddenly drive away a man who had been so generous up to that point, and also fairly tactful? Hmmm! I missed the chance!" And gritting his teeth again, Peter Petrovich at that moment called himself a fool—to himself, of course.

With this conclusion in mind, he returned home twice as angry and irritated as when he had left. The preparations for the funeral feast in Katherine Ivanovna's room attracted his curiosity. He'd heard this feast mentioned the day before. He even seemed to recall that he'd been invited. Given his own troubles, however, he had let it slip by. He hurried in so he might inquire of Mrs. Lippewechsel (who was looking after things around the laden table while Katherine Ivanovna was at the cemetery), and he learned that the feast was to be on a grand scale, that almost all the tenants had been invited, among them even some the deceased had never known, that in spite of his previous quarrel with Katherine Ivanovna, Andrey Semionovich Lebeziatnikov had also been invited, and, finally, that he himself, Peter Petrovich, had not only been invited but was expected with great eagerness, since he was obviously the most distinguished guest among all the tenants. Amalia Ivanovna too had been invited with great ceremony, in spite of past unpleasantnesses, and that was why she was taking charge of things now and fussing about so one might almost think she derived some pleasure out of all this; and although she was dressed in mourning, everything she wore was new and of silk; she was dressed up in her finery, and proud of it. All this suggested something to Peter Petrovich, and he walked past into his little room, that is, into Lebeziatnikov's room, lost in thought. He had discovered that Raskolnikov, too, was to be among the guests.

For some reason, Lebeziatnikov was spending the whole morning at home. With this gentleman, Peter Petrovich had a relationship that was rather strange, and yet, in part, quite natural. Peter Petrovich looked down on him and hated him immeasurably, and had done so almost from the very day he had moved into his room; yet at the same time he seemed a bit afraid of him. During his Petersburg sojourn he stayed with him not just because he was tight and wanted to save money. That may have been the most important reason, but there was another reason, too. In the provinces he had heard that this former ward of his was one of the foremost of the young progressives; he had even heard that he played a significant role in strange and legendary circles, and that astounded Peter Petrovich. For the powerful, omniscient circles that held nothing sacred and "exposed" everybody had for a long time frightened Peter Petrovich with a special kind of fear—quite undefined. Of course, back in the provinces, and by himself, he could not even remotely have conceived of goings-on *of this kind.* He had heard, like everyone else, that there were some progressivists or nihilists or muckrakers or whatever you called them in Petersburg, but like many others, he distorted and exaggerated the sense and significance of these names to the point of absurdity. For some years he had been most of all afraid of *exposure,* and this was the main reason for his constant and exaggerated unease, especially as far as his dreams of transferring operations to Petersburg were concerned. In this regard he was, as they say, *scared stiff,* the way small children sometimes are. Some years ago, back in the provinces, at the very beginning of his career, there had been two cases in which people of some importance in the province (people to whom he had up to that time attached himself and who had been his patrons) had been cruelly "exposed." One case ended in scandal; the other practically in an uproar. And so Peter Petrovich proposed, when he arrived in St. Petersburg, to find out immediately what it was all about, and if need be search out and ingratiate himself with "our younger generation." For this he relied on Andrey Semionovich. It will be recalled that while visiting Raskolnikov he had already acquired the practice of rounding out certain well-known borrowed phrases.

Of course, he soon found out that Andrey Semionovich was a very mean-spirited, simpleminded man. But this did not impel him to change his mind nor did it discourage him in any way. Even if he had been convinced that all the progressivists were equally foolish, it would not have softened his unease. Actually, he had no interest in any of the doctrines, ideas, or systems with which Andrey Semionovich had assaulted him. He had his own purpose. He needed to find out, as quickly as he could, what was going on *here,* and in what manner. Did *these people* have any power, or didn't they have any power? Was there anything to be scared about, or not? If he should happen to go into something or other, would they expose him, or would they not expose him? And if so, for what, and, in general, what were they exposing people *for* these days? And if they really were strong, could he not perhaps fall in with them and somehow or other lead them off his track? Was it necessary, or wasn't it? For example, perhaps he could advance his career by actually using these very people? In short, hundreds of questions came up.

Andrey Semionovich was a scrawny and scrofulous little man who worked in some government office, and had amazingly fair hair and mutton-chop whiskers of which he was very proud. His eyes were almost always ailing. He was rather softhearted, but his talk sounded very self-assured and sometimes even quite arrogant. In contrast with his pathetic figure, this almost always seemed funny. Nevertheless, he was considered one of the more respectable tenants at Amalia Ivanovna's. That meant he did not get drunk, and paid his rent on time. In spite of all this, Andrey Semionovich really was a bit dense. He had passionately committed himself to "progress" and "our young generation"—one of that innumerable motley legion of half-baked vulgarians and meddling know-it-alls who will immediately attach themselves to the most fashionable idea current, if only to vulgarize it and instantly caricature everything they serve, sometimes with the greatest sincerity.

In spite of the fact that he was quite good-natured, Lebeziatnikov, too, was beginning to find his roommate and former guardian insufferable. It happened both ways, as if by chance, and it was mutual. No matter how dense Andrey Semionovich was, he gradually became aware that Peter Petrovich was pulling a fast one; that secretly Peter Petrovich held him in contempt; and that he was "not what he pretended to be." He'd been trying to explain Fourier's ideas and Darwin's theory to him, but, especially lately, Peter Petrovich had begun to listen with what seemed too sarcastic an air, and had even started insulting him. Peter Petrovich was beginning to surmise that Lebeziatnikov was a rather vulgar and stupid man, and a bit of a fibber to boot, and had no important connections even among people who thought as he did, but merely repeated what he heard from somebody else. He didn't even seem to know his own business of *propaganda* properly, because he got too confused—and so how could he ever "expose" anybody! Nevertheless, we should note in passing that during the past week and a half (especially at the beginning) Peter Petrovich had been all too eager to receive compliments from Andrey Semionovich, even some rather strange ones. He would not object, for example, and would remain silent, when Andrey Semionovich ascribed to him readiness to assist in the rapid future construction of a "commune" in the red-light district. Or, not to interfere with Dunia if she decided to take a lover the very first month of their marriage. Or, not to baptize their future children. And so on and so on, all in this vein. Peter Petrovich, as usual, did not object to having such things ascribed to him. He allowed himself to be praised for them. That was how pleasant he found any praise at all.

That morning, for some reason, Peter Petrovich had cashed in some 5 percent bonds, and he sat at the table counting over the heaps of bank notes. Andrey Semionovich, who almost never had any money, paced up and down the room, trying to pretend that those heaps meant nothing at all to him. Peter Petrovich, for instance, would never believe that Andrey Semionovich could really be indifferent to so much money. For his part, Andrey Semionovich thought Luzhin was quite capable of thinking this of him and of trying to provoke him by piling up the bank notes to remind him of his insignificance and of the great difference that presumably existed between them.

Yet he was incredibly irritable and inattentive, in spite of the fact that Andrey Semionovich had launched into the theme that he liked best to expound to him: the establishment of a new, special kind of commune. The brief retorts and remarks torn from Peter Petrovich between the clicking of the buttons of his abacus were laced with the most obvious, deliberately rude mockery. The "humanist" Andrey Semionovich ascribed Peter Petrovich's mood to the effects of yesterday's break with Dunia. He was itching to get to this subject as soon as possible. There he had something to say that was progressive and instructive, which might comfort his worthy friend and would "undoubtedly" serve his further development.

"What sort of funeral feast are they preparing at . . . that widow's place?" Peter Petrovich suddenly asked, interrupting Andrey Semionovich at just the most interesting point.

"As if you didn't know. Why, I spoke to you yesterday on this very subject, and I expounded an idea about all these rituals. . . . Anyway, I heard her invite you, too. You were talking with her yesterday yourself."

"I never thought the destitute fool would squander on a funeral feast all the money she received from that other fool . . . Raskolnikov. Even just walking through there, I was amazed. Such preparations going on—wines! Quite a few people invited—devil knows what kind!" Peter Petrovich seemed to be leading the conversation to some aforeseen goal. "So you say she invited me, too?" he added suddenly, raising his head. "When was that? I don't remember. Anyway, I won't go. What would I do there? I just mentioned to her yesterday in passing that as the destitute widow of a civil servant she might be eligible for a special grant of a year's salary. You think that's why she might be inviting me? He-he!"

"I don't intend to go either," Lebeziatnikov said.

"I should think not! You thrashed her with your own hands. It's understandable you should feel touchy about it, he-he-he!"

"Who did? Thrashed whom?" Lebeziatnikov was startled, and even blushed.

"Why, you did; that Katherine Ivanovna. A month ago—

you know what I mean! I just heard about it yesterday, though. . . . Well, there you are—that's what convictions amount to! So, the woman question didn't make out so well! He-he!'' Peter Petrovich, as though he had calmed down, began clicking on the abacus again.

"That's all stupid slander!'' cried Lebeziatnikov, who was constantly touchy about any reference to this incident. "It wasn't like that at all! It was different. . . . You heard it wrong; malicious gossip! I was only defending myself. She attacked me first, with her fingernails. . . . She pulled out a whole sideburn. . . . I trust every man has a right to defend his own person. What's more, I permit no one to use force on me. . . . It's a principle. Why, that's practically despotism. What should I have done? Just stand there? All I did was push her away.''

"He-he-he!'' Luzhin went on laughing maliciously.

"You're just digging away at me because you're in such a wicked mood yourself. . . . But it's all rubbish and irrelevant—irrelevant to the woman question. Completely! You don't understand. I might even have thought that if it's accepted a woman's a man's equal in everything, even physical strength (there are some who maintain that), it would follow there should be equality here, too. Of course, later I decided essentially such a question should not come up, because there wouldn't be any fights, because in the future society fights are unthinkable . . . and because, of course, it's strange to look for equality in fighting. I'm not that stupid. There are such things as fights, though. . . . I mean, later on there won't be any . . . now, though, there still are . . . ah, blast! To hell with it! You've got me all mixed up! That's not the reason I won't go to the funeral feast. I simply won't go on principle, so as not to take part in the nasty superstition of a funeral feast; that's the reason! Still, one might go, if only just to laugh at it. . . . But it's a pity there won't be any priests. Or I would definitely go.''

"That is, you would break bread with someone, and then you'd spit on her, no matter who it was invited you. Isn't that right?''

"I wouldn't spit. I'd protest. I'd have a useful purpose. Indirectly, I'd be expounding our propaganda. Every man is obliged to expound and instruct, and perhaps the fiercer the better. I might throw out an idea, a seed. . . . From this seed a fact will grow. How am I insulting them? At first they might feel insulted, but later they'll see for themselves

I've done them good. Look how they accused the Terebiev girl—the one who's in the commune now—the time she left her family and . . . gave herself. Then she wrote her mother and father she didn't want to live among superstitions and she was going to enter into a liberal marriage . . . they said she was too blunt, one should write more gently to fathers, spare them as much as possible. I think that's all rubbish, one shouldn't be gentler at all. Quite the contrary, quite the contrary—that's just where one has to protest. There's Varents. She'd been living with her husband seven years. She left her two children. And right off she wrote her husband: 'I realized I could not be happy with you. I will never forgive you for deceiving me by concealing from me the existence of another form of organization of society by means of the commune. I learned about all this not long ago from a very high-minded man to whom I'm completely devoted, and he and I are going to found a commune together. I speak frankly because I consider it dishonest to deceive you. Do as you like. Do not think you can get me back. You are too late. I wish to be happy.' That's the way to write such a letter!"

"But isn't that the Terebiev girl you once told me was about to take on her third liberal marriage?"

"Only her second, actually—if you look at it right. But what if it were her fourth or her fifteenth? It's all bosh! If I ever regretted my mother and father were dead, it's certainly now. Several times I've dreamed how I'd scorch them with protest if they were alive! I'd really have set it up. . . . Talk about a 'lost sheep'—bah! I'd have shown them! I'd have given them a surprise. Really, it's a pity I don't have anybody!"

"So you could give them a surprise! He-he! Well, have it your own way," said Peter Petrovich. "Tell me, though. You know the dead man's daughter, don't you? I mean the puny little one! Tell me, is it all true, what they say about her, eh?"

"What about it? In my opinion—I mean, I'm personally convinced it's the most normal condition for a woman. Why ever not? I mean, *distinguons*. In our society, of course, it's not quite normal, because the condition is forced; but in the future it will be quite normal, because it will be free. Even now, though, she had the right: she had suffered. That was her reserve, her capital, you might say, which she had a right to use any way she wanted. In the future society, of course, there will be no need for capital reserves; but her role would have a different meaning. It would be conditioned rationally and harmoniously. As far as Sofia Semionovna personally is concerned, I tend to regard her actions as an energetic and personalized protest against the way society is organized, and I respect her profoundly for it. And when I look at her I even rejoice!"

"I heard it was you who had her thrown out of the apartment!"

Lebeziatnikov practically burst a blood vessel. "That's another slander!" he shrieked. "It wasn't like that at all, not at all! I tell you, it wasn't like that! Katherine Ivanovna twisted it around, because she didn't understand a thing! And I wasn't making advances to Sofia Semionovna at all! I was merely contributing to her development, quite disinterestedly, trying to arouse in her a protest. . . . All I wanted was protest; she couldn't have stayed here in the apartment anyway!"

"Did they invite her into the commune, or what?"

"You're trying to turn everything into muck—but you're not succeeding. Allow me to point that out to you. You don't understand anything! In the commune there are no such roles. The commune is organized so there should be no such roles. In the commune this role will change its entire present nature, and what is stupid here will become clever there, what is unnatural here under present circumstances will become quite natural there. Everything depends on circumstance and a man's environment. Environment is everything; the man himself nothing. But Sofia Semionovna and I are on good terms even now, which may serve you as proof that she never considered me her enemy or assailant. Yes, I'm trying to entice her now into our commune, but only on quite, quite different terms! What's so funny! We want to establish our own special commune, but only on broader terms than the old ones. We have gone further in our convictions. There's more we're against! If Dobroliubov were to rise from his grave, I would argue with him. And I'd send Belinsky packing! Meanwhile, I go on developing Sofia Semionovna. She has a beautiful, beautiful nature!"

"Well, this—eh—beautiful nature—you make use of it, eh? He-he!"

"No, no! Oh, no! On the contrary!"

"Well, so it's on the contrary! He-he-he! Do tell."

"But believe me! Why, what motives could I have for

concealing it from you, I ask you! On the contrary, I find it strange myself. With me she seems somehow intensely, timidly chaste and shy!"

"And you, of course, go on developing her . . . he-he! You show her all this shyness is bosh?"

"Not at all! Not at all! How coarse you are! How stupid, even—forgive me—you don't understand the word 'development!' You don't understand a-a-anything! Oh, God. How . . . unprepared you are yet! We seek woman's liberty, and you have only one thing on your mind. . . . Quite apart from the question of chastity and feminine modesty (surely they are useless and even superstitious things in themselves), I fully, fully countenance her chastity with me, because in this I see the expression of all her free will, all her right. Of course, if she herself said to me, 'I want you'—I'd consider myself lucky. Because I like the girl a lot. But for now, certainly, for now, at least, no one could treat her more politely and considerately than I do, or with greater respect for her dignity. . . . I wait and I hope—and that is all!"

"You'd do better to give her a little something. I bet you never even thought of that."

"You don't understand a-a-anything, as I said! Of course, her situation is what it is, but that's a different question—altogether different! You simply despise her. Observing a phenomenon you mistakenly consider worth despising, you deny a human being humane consideration. You still don't know what she's like! I'm only sorry she stopped reading and doesn't borrow books from me anymore. Before, she used to borrow them. Shame, too, that with all her energy and will to protest (which she's already demonstrated once) she still doesn't show much self-reliance or independence—she's not against much—so she could tear herself loose completely from other prejudices and . . . stupidities. In spite of that, she understands the other questions very well. She understands the hand-kissing question superbly, for example. I mean that a man insults a woman, that he implies her inequality, when he kisses her hand. We discussed the problem in the commune, and I passed the argument on to her immediately. And she also listened carefully when I told her about the French workers' associations. Right now, I'm explaining the question of free entry into rooms in the future society."

"And what's all that about?"

"The question was debated recently: does a member of

the commune have the right to enter another member's room, a man's or a woman's, at any time . . . well, it was decided, he has the right. . . ."

"Well, and what if he or she is occupied by urgent needs at the moment, he-he!"

Andrey Semionovich actually lost his temper. "You always think of that—about those damned 'needs!'" he screamed with hatred. "I'm goddamned mad, and sorry I mentioned those goddamned needs to you so prematurely when I was explaining the system. Goddamn it to hell! That's always the stumbling block for your ilk—you're always ready to tear something apart before you even know what it's about! And self-righteous about it! Just as though you had something to be proud of! Goddamn it! I said several times, you can only explain this whole question to initiates at the very end, when they're already convinced of the system, when they're developed and on the right path. You might tell me, by the way, what you find so shameful and repulsive in cesspools? I'm ready, I'd be the first to go clean out any cesspool you like! Without even any spirit of self-sacrifice! It's just a job—a worthy activity, useful to society. As good as any other. Actually superior, you might say, to the work of some Raphael or Pushkin—because it's more useful."

"And nobler, nobler—he-he-he!"

"What do you mean, nobler? I don't understand such expressions in the context of a definition of human activity. 'Nobler,' 'more generous'—that's all bosh. Absurdities, old prejudice words that I reject! Everything that's *useful* to mankind is noble! I understand one word only: *useful*! Snicker as much as you please, that's the way it is!"

Peter Petrovich laughed a long time. He had already finished counting his money and had put it away. For some reason, though, some of it was still on the table. This very "cesspool question," for all its banality, had served several times as the occasion for disagreement and heated argument between Peter Petrovich and his young friend. The funny part was that Andrey Semionovich really did lose his temper. Luzhin, on the other hand, would just let off some steam. At that moment particularly, he wanted to make Lebeziatnikov angry.

"You're just angry and argumentative because of your failure yesterday," Lebeziatnikov burst out at last. In spite of all his "independence" and all his "protests," he somehow did not dare oppose Peter Petrovich, and maintained a respectful attitude to him that he somehow retained from former years.

"But tell me," Peter Petrovich interrupted haughtily and with annoyance, "I wonder if you could . . . I mean, are you really . . . what I mean is, on sufficiently intimate terms with the young person mentioned . . . well, to ask her to come in here a moment . . . into this room? It looks like they're all back from the cemetery by now. . . . I can hear them walking around. . . . I'd like to see that—er—person."

"But what ever for?" Lebeziatnikov asked in surprise.

"Because I'd like to. I must. Today or tomorrow I'll be leaving here, so I'd like to let her know . . . But if you don't mind, you stay here too. That would be better. Otherwise, God knows what you'd be thinking."

"I wouldn't think anything . . . I was just asking. If you have business with her, nothing could be simpler than calling her in. I'll go right now. You can certainly be sure I won't stand in your way."

In five minutes or so, Lebeziatnikov actually did return with Sonia. She entered, greatly surprised, and, as usual with her, feeling shy. She always felt shy on such occasions and was very timid in the presence of new faces or new acquaintances. She had been that way ever since childhood, and all the more so now. . . . Peter Petrovich greeted her "kindly and politely," yet with overtones of a certain gay familiarity, appropriate, or so it seemed to Peter Petrovich, in such a solid citizen as himself with regard to such a young, you might say such an *interesting,* creature. He hastened to "make her feel at home," and had her sit down across the table facing him. Sonia sat down, looked around—at Lebeziatnikov, at the money lying on the table, then suddenly again at Peter Petrovich, from whom, as though she were chained to him, she did not again remove her eyes. Lebeziatnikov gravitated to the door. Peter Petrovich rose, signaled to Sonia to remain seated, and stopped Lebeziatnikov in the doorway.

"Is that fellow Raskolnikov there?" he asked Lebeziatnikov in a whisper.

"Raskolnikov? Yes. Yes, but so what? He just now came in; I saw him. . . . So what?"

"Well, so I especially request you to stay here with us, and not to leave me alone with this . . . young lady. It's a silly business, but God knows what they might think. I would not want Raskolnikov to comment on it *there*. . . . Do you understand what I mean?"

"I understand. Yes, I understand!" It came to Lebeziatnikov in a flash. "Well, you have the right. . . . Of course, personally I think your fears are a little farfetched . . . but, anyway, you have the right. I'll remain if you like. I'll stay here by the window and won't get in your way. I think you have the right. . . ."

Peter Petrovich returned to the couch, sat down facing Sonia, looked at her carefully, and assumed an extremely dignified, even rather stern expression. As much as to say: "Don't you try to make anything of this, madam." Sonia was overcome with embarrassment.

"First of all, Sofia Semionovna, my apologies to your esteemed mother . . . That's right, isn't it? Katherine Ivanovna does act as a mother to you, doesn't she?" Peter Petrovich began, very dignified, but still fairly gently. It was apparent he had the friendliest intentions.

"Yes, sir. That's right. Just so. As a mother, sir," Sonia replied hastily and timidly.

"Well, I hope you will please excuse me to her and tell her, due to circumstances beyond my control, I'm afraid I can't be at your place for the cakes . . . I mean, for the funeral feast, in spite of your mother's kind invitation."

"Yes, sir. I'll tell her. Right away!" And Sonia got up hastily.

"That isn't *quite* all—" Peter Petrovich stopped her, smiling at her simplicity and social awkwardness. "You obviously don't know me very well, my dear Sofia Semionovna, if you think I would disturb a person like yourself and call you in to see me for such a trivial reason, which concerns only me, personally. I had something else in mind."

Sonia hastily sat down. The gray and rainbow-colored bills, still on the table, flashed again in her eyes, but she quickly turned her face away from them and raised it toward Peter Petrovich. It suddenly struck her as terribly improper that *she* should be looking at someone else's money. She fixed her gaze on the golden lorgnette Peter Petrovich was holding in his left hand and on the massive, extremely handsome ring, set with a yellow stone, he wore on the middle finger of that hand. Suddenly she averted her eyes from that, too, and, at a loss, wound up once more looking straight into Peter Petrovich's eyes. After an even more dignified pause than the previous one, he continued.

"Yesterday, I had an opportunity in passing to exchange a few words with the unfortunate Katherine Ivanovna. A few words were all I needed to learn that she is in an—er—abnormal condition, if I may put it that way."

"Yes, sir . . . in an abnormal condition," Sonia hastily confirmed.

"To put it more simply and clearly—she is sick."

"Yes, sir. More simple and clearer . . . yes, sir. She is sick."

"So. You see, then, from feelings of humanity and—and, you might say, compassion, I for my part would like to be useful in some way, since I see her inevitably unhappy lot. It would seem this whole destitute family now depends on you alone."

"May I ask, sir"—Sonia suddenly rose—"what it was you said to her yesterday, sir, about the possibility of a pension? Because yesterday she told me you were going to see to it she got a pension. Is that true, sir?"

"Not at all. In a way that's even silly. I merely hinted at the temporary aid given the widow of a civil servant who has died in the service—if she knows somebody influential to look out for her interests—but it would seem your departed father not only did not serve out his time, but, recently, he wasn't working at all. In short, there might have been some hope—extremely ephemeral, though, because essentially there is no real right to aid in this particular case, quite the contrary, even. . . . So she'd thought of a pension already—ha-ha-ha! A clever lady!"

"Yes, sir, about a pension . . . Because she is trusting and good-hearted, and because she's good-hearted, she believes everything, and—and—and that's the way her mind works. . . . Yes, sir . . . excuse me, sir," Sonia said, and again she got up to leave.

"But, allow me. You still haven't heard what I have to say."

"It's true, sir. I haven't heard," Sonia murmured.

"Well, then, please sit." Sonia got all mixed up, and sat down again for the third time.

"Since I see the position she's in, with those unfortunate children, as I said before, I'd like to be useful in some way—as much as I can, of course, as much as I can, and no more. We might, for instance, take up a subscription in her benefit, or a lottery . . . or something of that sort. In the way these things are done—by those who are close to the person involved, or even by strangers, for that matter—in general, by people who want to help. That was what I intended to inform you about. It could be done."

"Yes, sir. That would be a good thing, sir. . . . For that, sir, God will . . ." Sonia murmured, looking at Peter Petrovich intently.

"It could be done. Later, we'll . . . I mean, we could get it started even today. This evening we'll get together and talk it over, and we'll lay the foundation, so to speak. Come see me here around seven o'clock. I hope Andrey Semionovich will join us, too. . . . But . . . One thing I'd like to warn you about in advance. That's why I made so bold as to disturb you, Sofia Semionovna, and call you in here. I don't believe one can, I think it may even be dangerous, to give Katherine Ivanovna money personally. Today's funeral feast is the best proof of that. She hasn't a crust for tomorrow, you might say . . . no shoes, nothing; and she goes out and buys Jamaica rum, and even Madeira, it would seem, and—and—and coffee. I saw it as I passed through. Tomorrow you'll be hard up again, down to your last crust. That's ridiculous. Therefore, I personally think the subscription ought to take place in such a way that the unfortunate widow, so to speak, knows nothing about the money, that the only one who'd know, let's say, would be you. Am I right?"

"I don't know, sir. What she did today was only . . . once in a lifetime . . . she wanted very much to do him honor, in memory . . . she's a clever woman, sir. . . . But just as you like, sir; and I will be very, very, very . . . they will all consider you . . . and God will . . . and the orphans, sir . . ." Sonia could not get it out, and began to weep.

"There, there. Well, you will keep it in mind, won't you? Now, as a kind of start, please be so good as to accept a small sum from me personally, in the interests of your relative. I'd very much like my name not to be mentioned in this connection. There you are. Since I have, so to speak, some concerns of my own, I am in no position to offer more. . . ." Peter Petrovich handed Sonia a ten-ruble note, which he had carefully unfolded. Sonia took it, blushed, jumped up, murmured something, and quickly began to take her leave. Peter Petrovich solemnly accompanied her to the door. She left the room at last, excited and distressed, and returned to Katherine Ivanovna in a state of extraordinary confusion.

During all this time, Andrey Semionovich had either stood

by the window or paced about the room, not wanting to interrupt the conversation. After Sonia left, he suddenly went up to Peter Petrovich and solemnly offered him his hand.

"I heard everything and I *saw* everything," he said, lingering especially on the word "saw." "That was noble. I mean, it was humane! You wanted to avoid her gratitude—I saw! I must admit to you that in principle I cannot sympathize with private charity, because not only does it not radically root out the evil, but nourishes it even more; nevertheless, I cannot help but admit I looked on what you did with pleasure. Yes, yes, I do like it."

"Ah, that's all bosh!" muttered Peter Petrovich, a bit nervous, looking a little askance at Lebeziatnikov.

"No, it is not bosh! A man who's been humiliated and upset, as you were by what happened yesterday, who is yet capable of thinking of the misfortune of others—such a man, sir . . . though, mind you, he's making a social mistake— nevertheless, he is worthy of respect! I must admit I didn't expect it of you, Peter Petrovich, especially because of your ideas. . . . Oh, how your ideas hold you back! How much yesterday's bad luck upset you for instance!" the kindly Andrey Semionovich exclaimed, feeling once more quite favorably disposed to Peter Petrovich. "And why, why must you really have this marriage, this *legal* marriage, my dear, noble Peter Petrovich? What good is this *legality* in marriage? Well, hit me if you like, but I'm glad—glad, I tell you—that it didn't come off, that you are free, that you haven't been completely ruined for service to mankind. I'm glad. Now, you see—I've said my piece!"

"Because I don't want to wear horns and bring up somebody else's children in one of your liberal marriages—that's why I need a legal marriage," Luzhin said, in order to say something. He seemed especially preoccupied with something.

"Children? You mentioned children?" Andrey Semionovich trembled like a war horse that has just heard the trumpet call to battle. "Children are a social question, and one of the first importance, I agree. There's a different way of solving it, though. There are some who actually deny children completely, as they do any hint at the family. We'll talk about children later, but right now we'll take up the subject of horns! I must admit I have a weakness for it. In the future lexicon that nasty Pushkinian hussar expression is unthinkable. Anyway, what does it mean—'horns'? Oh, what an error! What horns? Why horns? What bosh! It is precisely in a liberal marriage, on the contrary, that there will cease to be such a thing! Horns are no more than the natural consequence of any legal marriage, so to speak—its repair, a protest—in this sense you might say horns are not even degrading. . . . Assuming the ridiculous, if I should ever find myself in legal wedlock, so to speak, I'd even be glad to wear your bloody horns. I'd say to my wife: 'Dear friend, up to now I merely loved you; but now I respect you, because you have known how to protest!' You laugh? That's because you cannot tear yourself loose from your prejudices! Damn it, I know very well how unpleasant it is to be deceived in a legal marriage; but it is only the vile consequence of a vile fact, a situation in which both partners are degraded. When horns are worn openly, as in a liberal marriage, they no longer exist—they are unthinkable, and they even cease to be called horns. On the contrary, your wife will merely be showing you how much she respects you; she'd consider you incapable of opposing her happiness, sufficiently developed not to torment her because she's taken a new husband. Damn it, I think sometimes that if I ever married (legally or liberally, it doesn't matter)—I myself would bring my wife a lover if she took too long finding one. 'Dear friend,' I'd say to her, 'I love you; but even more than that, I would like you to respect me—here!' Isn't that the way? Is that the way, or isn't it?"

Peter Petrovich snickered as he listened, but was not particularly amused. He did not even listen closely. He was really thinking of something else, and at last even Lebeziatnikov noticed this. Actually, Peter Petrovich was excited, and as he went on thinking, he rubbed his hands together. Later, all this came back to Andrey Semionovich, and he remembered. . . .

2

It would be hard to say just what reason prompted Katherine Ivanovna's disordered mind to this incomprehensible funeral feast. Practically ten of the almost twenty rubles she had received from Raskolnikov for Marmeladov's funeral had been squandered on it. Perhaps Katherine Ivanovna thought she was obliged to the departed to honor his memory "properly," so all the tenants would know (Amalia Ivanovna particularly) that not only was he "no worse than they, but maybe even quite a bit better," so none of them had the right to "turn up their noses" at him. Most influential, perhaps, was that special *pride of the poor,* due to which, when certain social ceremonies that custom imposes on everyone have to be carried out, many destitute people drain their last savings and spend the last pennies they have saved merely to be "no worse than others," so others would not somehow "reproach" them. It was probably now, precisely at the moment when she seemed abandoned by everyone on earth, that Katherine Ivanovna wanted to show all those "low and nasty tenants" that she "knew how to live and knew how to entertain," and that it was not to fill her present miserable lot she had been brought up. On the contrary, she had been brought up in a "noble, one might say an aristocratic home, a colonel's home," and what she had been groomed for was not to scrub floors with her own hands or to launder her children's rags at night. Such paroxysms of pride and vanity sometimes take hold of the poorest, meekest people, and turn into a provocative and irresistible craving. And Katherine Ivanovna was by no means of the meek; she could be destroyed by circumstances, but it was not possible to *crush* her morally—that is, to intimidate or subordinate her will. Moreover, what Sonia had said about her was quite true; her mind was getting mixed up. Of course, there was nothing positive or conclusive, but during that whole past year she had suffered too much for her mind not to have undergone some harm. The powerful onslaught of consumption, as the medical authorities inform us, also contributed to the derangement of her mental faculties.

A great quantity or variety of wines, there really was not; nor any Madeira. That was an exaggeration. But there was liquor. There were vodka, rum, and Lisbon brandy, all of the poorest quality, but in fairly large quantity. In addition to the traditional rice and raisin cakes, there were three or four other kinds of dishes (pancakes, among other things), all from Amalia Ivanovna's kitchen, and two samovars were set up simultaneously, for tea and punch, to be served after the meal. Katherine Ivanovna had directed the purchases herself, with the help of one of the tenants, a miserable little Pole who, for God knew what reason, lived at Mme. Lippewechsel's, and who had been commandeered for Katherine Ivanovna's errands and had been running around all

the previous day and that morning, shaking his head and
hanging out his tongue, as though he were doing his best to
attract attention in this way. He kept running to Katherine
Ivanovna over every little detail, and he even ran to the
market to look for her, and he kept calling her *pani chorun-
zina,* and drove her finally to distraction, though she had
said at first that without this "obliging and generous" man
she would have been entirely lost. It was like Katherine
Ivanovna to depict the first person that came her way in the
best and brightest colors, praise him so much she would
make him uneasy, invent in his favor all kinds of imaginary
attributes, believe in them herself quite sincerely, and then
suddenly become disenchanted all at once, snub him, hold
him in contempt, and violently send packing the man she
had only a few hours before literally bowed down to. By
nature she was easily amused, gay, and peaceable, but constant failure and bad luck had made her so *fiercely* hope and
crave that all should live in peace and joy, and *not dare* to
live otherwise, that the slightest dissonance in life, the least
little failure, would drive her immediately practically into a
frenzy, and she could turn in a single flash from the brightest
hopes and fantasies to cursing fate, smashing and scattering
everything that came to hand, and beating her head against
the wall. Amalia Ivanovna had suddenly acquired exceptional status and respect in Katherine Ivanovna's eyes, perhaps for no other reason than that Amalia Ivanovna had
decided to throw herself wholeheartedly into all the details
of the funeral feast. She had undertaken to set the table,
provide the tablecloth and crockery and so on, and to prepare the food in her own kitchen. As she was about to go
to the cemetery, Katherine Ivanovna had entrusted her with
plenary powers and left her in charge at home. And, indeed,
everything had been excellently prepared. The tablecloth
was even fairly clean, and although the crockery, the forks,
the knives, the glasses, and the cups were all of different
kinds, and even of different shapes and sizes, having been
collected from among the various tenants, still, everything
was in its place at the appointed time, and Amalia Ivanovna,
feeling she had carried out her job extremely well, met those
who returned from the cemetery with a certain pride, all
dressed up in a bonnet with new mourning ribbons and in
a black dress. This pride, though earned, did not for some
reason please Katherine Ivanovna: "You might even think
that without Amalia Ivanovna the table could not have been

set at all!" Nor did she like the bonnet with the new ribbons:
was that stupid German woman proud by any chance of
being the landlady or consenting out of the goodness of her
heart to help her poor tenants? Out of the goodness of
her heart! Katherine Ivanovna's father had been a colonel,
practically governor, and sometimes his table had been set
for forty persons, so that the ilk of Amalia Ivanovna—or,
better to say, Ludwigovna—wouldn't even have been allowed in the kitchen. . . . However, Katherine Ivanovna
decided not to express how she felt until the time was ripe,
though she had made up her mind it would be necessary to
put Amalia Ivanovna in her place that very day—otherwise,
God only knew what she might not fancy about herself. In
the meantime, she merely treated her coldly.

Still another unpleasantness irritated Katherine Ivanovna.
Except for the little Pole (who hopped around the cemetery
in his own peculiar way), almost none of the tenants had
shown up at the funeral; and only the most poverty-stricken
and insignificant of them had shown up for the feast, many
of them not quite sober—what one might expect from trash
like that! The older, the more respectable, tenants all stayed
away as though on purpose, as though they had conspired
together. For instance, Peter Petrovich Luzhin (one might
call him the most highly respectable of all the tenants) had
not shown up; and yesterday evening Katherine Ivanovna
had let the whole world know (Amalia Ivanovna, Polia,
Sonia, and the little Pole, that is) that this was a fine and
generous man with the most imposing connections and with
a position of eminence, who was the former friend of her
first husband, who had been a guest in her father's house,
and who had promised to do everything he could to petition
a sizable pension for her. Let us note here that whenever
Katherine Ivanovna praised anybody's connections or position in life it was quite disinterestedly, without any element
of personal calculation, with no vested interest at all, for the
sheer pleasure of elevating by praise and of attaching a
greater value to the person praised.

In addition to Luzhin, and probably "copying him," that
"nasty scoundrel Lebeziatnikov" had not shown up either.
"Did he think he *was* somebody, or what? We only invited
him to be polite, because he knows Peter Petrovich and
shares a room with him, so it would have been awkward not
to invite him." Also missing were a certain high-toned lady
and her daughter ("an old maid"), who had only been living

a short time in Amalia Ivanovna's rooms but had already
lodged several complaints about the noise and hubbub that
issued from the Marmeladovs' room, especially when the
late departed had come home drunk. Katherine Ivanovna
had learned all this from Amalia Ivanovna during one of
those quarrels when the latter was threatening to throw the
whole family out and when she had shouted at the top of
her voice that the Marmeladovs were disturbing "fine tenants from whom the little finger" they were not worth. Katherine Ivanovna deliberately decided to invite this lady and
her daughter, though she supposedly was not worth their
"little finger," all the more since whenever they had met the
woman had turned haughtily away, so she obviously needed
to grasp the fact that there were some people "more delicate
than that in their thoughts and feelings, who sent out invita-
tions unbegrudgingly"—and thus it might dawn on them that
Katherine Ivanovna herself was not used to living like this.
She had made up her mind to explain this to them at the
table, and she'd also tell them about her departed father's
governorship, and indirectly, in passing, she would point out
there was nothing to turn away from so haughtily when they
met and it was extremely stupid to do so. The stout lieutenant colonel had not come either (actually, he was a retired
lieutenant), but it seemed he had been "out cold" since
yesterday morning.

In short, these were the only ones who came: the little
Pole; a shabby little clerk in a greasy jacket, with blackheads
and a repulsive odor, who said nothing; a deaf and almost
totally blind old man who had once worked in some post
office and whom someone, for some unknown reason, had
been supporting at Amalia Ivanovna's since time immemo-
rial; some drunken former lieutenant (actually he was a former quartermaster) also showed up, with the loudest, most
unpleasant laugh, and ("Imagine!") without a vest; and
somebody who had gone straight to the table without so
much as a nod to Katherine Ivanovna; and finally somebody
came in a dressing gown because he didn't have any clothes,
but this seemed so improper that somehow, through the
combined efforts of Katherine Ivanovna, Amalia Ivanovna,
and the little Pole, he was eased out; on the other hand, the
little Pole had managed to bring two other little Poles with
him, who had never lived at Amalia Ivanovna's and who
had never even been seen around before. All this irritated
Katherine Ivanovna extremely. For whom had all this been

prepared? In order to make room, the children had not been seated at the table, which, even as it was, practically filled the room; they sat by a suitcase laid for them in the rear corner, with the little ones seated on a bench, and Polenka (as the "big sister") looking after them, feeding them, and wiping their noses—they were "decent children," after all! And so Katherine Ivanovna simply felt obliged to face them all with redoubled dignity, and even with hauteur. At some she looked especially sternly, and condescendingly asked them please to be seated at the table. For some reason she seemed to hold Amalia Ivanovna responsible for everyone who had not shown up, and suddenly began to treat her with great negligence, which the landlady noted immediately and which she resented in the extreme. Such a beginning hardly foreshadowed a happy end. Finally they were all seated.

Raskolnikov came in just when they had returned from the cemetery. Katherine Ivanovna was terribly pleased to see him—first, because he was the only "educated man" among all the guests, and "as was well known," he was being prepared "to fill an endowed chair at the local university in the next two years," and second, because he immediately and respectfully requested her pardon for the fact that, in spite of his desire to, he had not been able to attend the funeral. She practically threw herself on him, seated him on her left at table (Amalia Ivanovna sat at her right), and in spite of her constant concern that the food be served properly and with enough for everybody, in spite of the racking cough that interrupted her constantly and stifled her sentences (these past two days the cough seemed to have become worse), she kept constantly turning to Raskolnikov, and in a half whisper hastened to pour out to him all her pent-up feelings and all her righteous indignation at the failure of the funeral feast. And yet her indignation frequently gave way to the most unrestrained and abandoned laughter at the expense of the assembled guests—for the most part, however, at the expense of the landlady.

"That nut is to blame for everything. You know who I'm talking about. Her. About her." And Katherine Ivanovna indicated the landlady. "Look at her. Her eyes just popped. She knows we're talking about her and can't understand what we're saying, so she pops her eyes. Ugh, an owl! Ha-ha-ha! . . . Cough-cough-cough! What do you think she wants to prove with that bonnet of hers! Cough-cough-

cough! Have you noticed she wants everybody to think she's looking after me, doing me an honor by being here? I asked her, as a respectable woman, to invite the better kind of people, those who really knew the late departed. And just look who she invited—sluts, clowns! Look at the one with the dirty face: kind of a walking snot! And the little Polacks—ha-ha-ha! K-khee-k-khee! Nobody ever saw them here before, nobody. I never saw them, either. Well, I ask you, what did they come for? There they sit, all in a row. Hey, there, *pan*!" she suddenly shouted at one of them, "have you had any pancakes? Have some more! Come on, have some beer! Don't you want any vodka? Look: he's up and bowing—look, look. Must be terribly hungry, poor people! It's nothing, let them eat! At least they don't make a hubbub, but, eh . . . it's true, I'm worried about the landlady's silver spoons! Amalia Ivanovna," she said, almost aloud, turning to the landlady, "I warn you ahead of time—if they should by chance steal your spoons, I'm not responsible! Ha-ha-ha!" she burst out, turning again to Raskolnikov and pointed at the landlady and rejoicing in her own sally. "She doesn't get it, she still doesn't get it! Sits there with her mouth wide open. Just look: an owl, a regular owl, a barn owl in brand-new ribbons, ha-ha-ha!"

This turned into an unbearable coughing fit that lasted five minutes. There was some blood on her dress, and drops of sweat stood out on her forehead. She silently showed Raskolnikov the blood. Scarcely having caught her breath, she immediately started whispering to him again with extraordinary animation, red stains standing out on her cheeks.

"You see, I trusted her with what you might call a most delicate mission (inviting that lady and her daughter), do you know what I mean? It required the utmost poise and tact, but she managed it so that stupid hayseed, that insolent creature, that provincial nobody, just because she's some major's widow or something and came here to curtsy her way through all the right places, appealing for a pension, and just because she pencils her eyes and powders and rouges herself when she's pushing fifty-five (everybody knows it) . . . and a creature like that not only did not think it fitting to show up but did not even bother to send an excuse, as the most ordinary politeness would require! I cannot understand why Peter Petrovich did not come. And where is Sonia? Where has she gone? Ah, there she is—at last! Sonia, where in the world have you been? Strange that you should be so unpunctual, even at your father's funeral. Rodion Romanych, let her sit beside you. Here is your place, Sonechka . . . take whatever you want. Have some of the jellied meat, that's the best. They'll bring the pancakes in a minute. Have the children had some? Polenka, do you have everything to eat over there? Cough-cough-cough! Very well. Be a good girl, Lenia. And you, Kolia, stop swinging your legs. Sit up like a nice boy should. What did you say, Sonia?"

Sonia immediately hastened to pass on to her Peter Petrovich's apology, trying to speak loudly so all could hear, and careful to use the most respectful turns of phrase, which she made up and embroidered on and attributed to Peter Petrovich. She added that Peter Petrovich had insisted she tell Katherine Ivanovna that he would come as soon as he possibly could to consult in private *on business,* and they would arrange whatever could be done, and discuss plans for the future, and so forth and so forth. Sonia knew this would soothe Katherine Ivanovna and calm her down. It would flatter her, and (most important) her pride would be appeased. She sat down beside Raskolnikov, greeted him hastily, and gave him a fleeting and curious look. Afterward, however, she seemed to avoid glancing at him or talking to him. She seemed a little distracted, although she looked Katherine Ivanovna full in the face so as to please her. For lack of clothes, neither she nor Katherine Ivanovna was in mourning. Sonia was wearing something darkish, some shade of brown, and Katherine Ivanovna the only dress she had, a dark cotton with stripes. The report on Peter Petrovich went over well. Katherine Ivanovna listened to Sonia with an air of dignity, then inquired a little portentously about Peter Petrovich's health. After that she whispered in a scarcely audible voice to Raskolnikov that it really would have been odd for an important, dignified man like Peter Petrovich to drop in on such "unusual company," for all his devotion to her family and his former friendship with her father.

"And that is why I am especially grateful to you, Rodion Romanych, that you did not refuse my invitation even under the circumstances," she added almost aloud. "I am convinced, however, that it was only your special friendship for my poor departed husband that impelled you to keep your word."

Once more, proudly and with dignity, she surveyed her

guests, and with a sudden note of special concern she inquired loudly of the deaf old man across the table whether he might not want some more roast and whether he'd had some port. The old man did not answer and for a long time could not understand what was being asked him, though his neighbors were prodding him for the fun of it. He only stared open-mouthed around him, and this made the general hilarity flare up still higher.

"What an idiot! Look at him, look at him! What did they bring him for? As for Peter Petrovich, I always had confidence in him," Katherine Ivanovna said to Raskolnikov. "And, of course, he's not like these—" harshly and loudly and with an extremely stern expression she addressed Amalia Ivanovna, who quailed as she spoke, "not like these poof-powdered, draggle-tail creatures my father wouldn't have had even as cooks in his kitchen; if my dear departed husband ever did them the honor of inviting them, it was only out of the infinite kindness of his nature."

"Yes, sir, he sure loved to drink. Oh, boy, did he love to drink all right!" the retired quartermaster suddenly shouted, draining his twelfth glass of vodka.

"My late departed husband really did suffer from that weakness," Katherine Ivanovna suddenly swooped down on him. "But he was a kind man and a gentleman, and he loved and respected his family. The only trouble was because he was so kind he would believe all kinds of low-down people, and God knows who he drank with, people not worth the soles of his shoes! And Rodion Romanovich, just think. They found a gingerbread rooster in his pocket: he was dead-drunk, but he remembered his children."

"Roo-ooster? Did you say roo-ooster?" yelled the quartermaster. Katherine Ivanovna did not stoop to reply. She thought about something and sighed.

"You probably think, as they all do, that I was too hard on him," she went on, addressing Raskolnikov. "But it isn't so! He respected me. He respected me very, very much! He was a kindhearted man! Sometimes I'd feel so sorry for him! He'd sit there in the corner and he'd look out at me, and I'd feel so sorry for him I'd want to go over and stroke him, and then I'd think to myself: If you stroke him, he'll just go and get drunk all over again. The only way you could hold him back a little was to be stern."

"Yes, he sure used to get the kinks taken out of his hair!

Happened more than once!" roared the quartermaster, and poured down another glass of vodka.

"Some fools not only need their hair pulled, they could use a whack with a good broomstick—and I'm not talking about my late departed husband, either!" Katherine Ivanovna snapped back. The red spots on her cheeks shone more and more brightly, and her chest heaved. Another moment and she would be ready to start an incident. Many sniggered. They would have liked that. They started whispering to the quartermaster and urging him on. They obviously wanted to set the pair off.

"A-a-allow me to a-a-ask, on what account, *madame,*" the quartermaster began, "I mean, on whose . . . decent account . . . you just now dei-eigned . . . Oh, well, who needs it, anyway! Bosh! A widow! A poor widow! I beg your pardon. . . ." And he downed another vodka.

With disgust, Raskolnikov sat and listened silently. He ate merely out of politeness, nibbling a little at the food Katherine Ivanovna kept putting on his plate so he would not offend her. He was gazing intently at Sonia. But Sonia was becoming more and more concerned and alarmed. She had a premonition the feast would not end well, and she observed Katherine Ivanovna's mounting irritation with terror. Among other things, she knew quite well the main reason the provincial ladies had received Katherine Ivanovna's invitation so haughtily was Sonia herself. Amalia Ivanovna had told her the mother had actually been offended by the invitation and had asked how she could possibly seat her daughter alongside *that whore.* Sonia had the feeling that Katherine Ivanovna somehow knew about this, and an insult to Sonia meant more to her than an insult to her personally or to the children or to her husband; in brief, it was a mortal insult and Sonia knew Katherine Ivanovna would never calm down as long as she had not "shown those draggle-tails they both . . ." et cetera, et cetera. At that moment, as though fated, somebody from the other end of the table sent Sonia a plate with a carving in black bread of two hearts pierced by an arrow. Katherine Ivanovna flared up and immediately proclaimed loudly across the table that whoever had sent it was, "of course, a drunken jackass." Amalia Ivanovna also had a foreboding something would go wrong. She had been profoundly offended by Katherine Ivanovna's haughtiness. In order to divert the company's bad mood and fix its attention on some other subject, and perhaps to raise herself in the general esteem, she suddenly began, for no apparent reason, to talk about some acquaintance of hers, "Karl from drugstore," who had been driving in a cab one night and the "driver wanted killing him, and Karl, he begged and he begged he should not and he cried and the driver's hands he folded and he vas frightened and from his fear his heart vas pierced." Katherine Ivanovna smiled, but immediately remarked that Amalia Ivanovna should not tell anecdotes in Russian. The latter was even more offended, and retorted that her "vater aus Berlin vas fery, fery important man and crept always mit hands into pocket." The mocking Katherine Ivanovna would not let it pass and laughed horribly, so that Amalia Ivanovna began to lose even the last traces of her patience and could scarcely control herself.

"Just look at that barn owl!" Katherine Ivanovna immediately whispered once more to Raskolnikov. She seemed almost cheerful. "She wanted to say: 'He kept his hands in his pockets,' but it came out, 'He crept into pocket,' k-khee-k-khee! Have you noticed, Rodion Romanovich, how all the Petersburg foreigners, I mean mostly Germans, God knows where they come from, are all more stupid than we are! Now, I ask you, how can you say, 'Karl from drugstore from fear his heart vas pierced,' and instead of tying up the cab-driver, 'his hands he folded'—like a snot-nosed kid's—'and vept and becked and becked fery much.' The idiot! And she thinks it's very touching and doesn't suspect how stupid she is! I think that drunken quartermaster is smarter than she is! At least it's clear he's a sot and he's drowned his last wits in drink, but here you have all these orderly, solemn . . . Eesh, there she sits, all goggle-eyed. She's angry! Angry! Ha-ha-ha! K-khee-ke-khee-ke-khee!"

Taking cheer, Katherine Ivanovna immediately began to wander off into various particulars, and all of a sudden she told him of how (with the aid of the pension she would get) she would open a boarding school for well-born young ladies in her hometown. Raskolnikov had not yet heard this from Katherine Ivanovna herself, and she immediately launched into the most enticing particulars. Suddenly she had in her hands that same "testimonial" of which the departed Marmeladov had informed Raskolnikov when he told him in the saloon that his wife had done the shawl dance when she graduated from the institute "in the presence of the governor and suchlike people." This testimonial, obviously, was now supposed to serve as evidence of Katherine Ivanovna's qualifications to run a boarding school; but the main point was that it had been kept in reserve expressly with the aim of demolishing "both those poof-powdered draggle-tails," in the event they might show up at the funeral feast, and clearly to point out to them that Katherine Ivanovna came from the most decent, the most . . . "one might even say, aristocratic" home, a colonel's daughter, and no doubt a good deal better than certain adventuress-types who seem to have proliferated so abundantly in recent times. The testimonial was immediately passed around among the drunken guests. Katherine Ivanovna did not object. It really did indicate *en toutes lettres* that she was the daughter of a middle-grade civil servant who had been awarded a decoration, and that she was therefore in fact *almost* a colonel's daughter. Getting excited, Katherine Ivanovna soon launched a detailed description of her future beautiful and peaceful life back in her hometown. She spoke of the teachers she would hire to give lessons in her boarding school; of one worthy old gentleman, the Frenchman M. Mangot, who had taught Katherine Ivanovna French at the institute and who was now retired and living in the town, and who would undoubtedly be glad to work for her at a very reasonable salary. Finally, she touched on the subject of Sonia, who would accompany her back to the town and who would "help with everything." Here somebody at the end of the table suddenly snorted. Katherine Ivanovna tried to pretend not to pay any attention, to regard the laughter with contempt. At the same time she raised her voice and started speaking animatedly about Sofia Semionovna's undoubted abilities to serve as her assistant, of her "modesty, patience, self-effacement, decency, and cultivation," and she stroked Sonia on the cheek and then stood up and kissed her twice, with great feeling.

Sonia blushed, and Katherine Ivanovna suddenly burst into tears. She said she was a "weak-nerved, overstrung fool," and it was time to put a stop to this nonsense, and since the food was gone it was time to serve tea. At this very moment Amalia Ivanovna, by now thoroughly offended since she had not taken the least part in the entire conversation and because nobody so much as listened to her, suddenly ventured on a final attempt, and though she had some inner misgivings, made so bold as to confer on Katherine Ivanovna the extremely pithy and profound observation that in her future boarding school she would need to see to it that "ze girruls" had clean linen ("*die Waesche*") and that she "opsolutely het to hev eine gute Dame to look out gut fuer ze linen," and also to make sure "ze girruls did not no novels on ze qviet read at night." Genuinely overstrung and very tired, Katherine Ivanovna, who was by now thoroughly sick of the funeral feast, immediately "put down" Amalia Ivanovna by saying she was "talking rubbish" and that she understood nothing; that worrying about *die Waesche* was the matron's job, not that of the directress of a respectable boarding school; and as far as reading novels was concerned, it was simply not a decent subject and she begged her to be quiet about it. Amalia Ivanovna flared up. Getting really angry, she remarked that she only "vished her vell," and she "vished her fery vell," and it was a long time since she "geld fuer ze apartment had paid." Katherine Ivanovna immediately "put her down" by saying that she was lying when she claimed to "vish her vell," because only the evening before, while the late departed still lay stretched out on the table, she'd been tormenting her about the apartment. To this Amalia Ivanovna answered, with her own logic, that, "Zees lady I hef invited, but zees lady don't come pecause zis lady are deshent lady and cannot come to lady who not deshent iss." Katherine Ivanovna immediately retorted that since she herself was a slut, she could have no notion of what true decency was. Amalia Ivanovna found this insufferable, and immediately declared that her "fater aus Berlin vas fery, fery important man and crawled mit hands into pocket, and eferyfing he did so: poof-poof-poof!" and in order to give a more vivid picture of her "fater," Amalia Ivanovna leaped up from her chair, thrust both her hands into her pockets, puffed out her cheeks, and began to make some rather strange sounds, something like "poof-poof," to the loud laughter of all the tenants, who deliberately egged Amalia Ivanovna on in the hope of starting a fight. This Katherine Ivanovna could not abide; and immediately, and so all could hear, she "rapped out" that maybe Amalia Ivanovna never had a "fater" at all but was just some drink-sotted Petersburg Finn, and probably had formerly lived around in people's kitchens, or maybe even worse. Amalia Ivanovna turned red as a lobster and screeched that maybe Katherine Ivanovna "het no fater at all," but *she* "het fater aus Berlin und he vore long coat and alvays he vent poof-poof-poof!" Katherine Ivanovna replied contemptuously that her background was known to all, and

in the testimonial that was going the rounds it said in black
and white that her father was a colonel; and that Amalia
Ivanovna's father (if indeed she had a father at all) was a
Petersburg Finn of some sort who sold milk; but most likely
she had no father at all, because to this day nobody knew
what her patronymic was, Ivanovna or Ludwigovna. At this
point Amalia Ivanovna, totally enraged, pounded her fist on
the table and started screaming that she was Amal-Ivan and
not Ludwigovna, that her father was called Johann "und he
vass burgomeister," and that Katherine Ivanovna's fater
"vass never no burgomeister." Katherine Ivanovna rose
from her chair, and in an outwardly calm voice (though she
turned pale and her chest was heaving) told her that if she
once more made so bold as to put her "dirty little fa-
therling" in the same class with her own dear papa, she
would tear off that bonnet of hers and trample it underfoot.
When she heard this, Amalia Ivanovna started rushing
around the room, screaming at the top of her lungs that she
was the landlady and that Katherine Ivanovna had to get
out that very minute. For some reason, she started rushing
around the table, picking up the silver spoons. Pandemo-
nium broke loose. The children burst out crying. Sonia was
about to try to restrain Katherine Ivanovna; but when Amalia Ivanovna all of a sudden shouted out something about
the yellow ticket, Katherine Ivanovna pushed Sonia aside
and flung herself on Amalia Ivanovna to carry out immediately her threat about the bonnet. At this moment the door
opened, and on the threshold of the room stood Peter Petrovich Luzhin. He stood, and scrutinized the company with
a stern, attentive gaze. Katherine Ivanovna rushed to him.

3

"Peter Petrovich!" she exclaimed. "You at least will protect
me! Teach this stupid creature that she doesn't dare behave
like that to a decent, respectable woman in misfortune, that
there is a court for such cases. . . . I'll take it to the governor-
general himself. . . . She'll answer for it. . . . Since you
remember my father's hospitality, defend my orphans."

"Allow me, *madame* . . . Please, allow me, *madame*."
Peter Petrovich waved her aside. "As you must know, I
never had the honor of knowing your dear father . . . allow

me, *madame*"—someone burst out laughing—"and as for your indecent squabbles with Amalia Ivanovna, *madame,* I have no intention of getting involved . . . I'm here on my own account . . . and I'd like to have an explanation immediately with your stepdaughter Sofia . . . what is her patronymic? Ivanovna, I believe. Isn't that so? Please let me through."

Edging around Katherine Ivanovna, Peter Petrovich made his way to the opposite corner, where Sonia was. Katherine Ivanovna stood there as though hit by lightning. She failed to understand how Peter Petrovich could deny her father's hospitality. Once she had made up this story she fervently believed in it. The dry, matter-of-fact, implicitly threatening tone Peter Petrovich used also struck her.

His appearance calmed everyone else down, too, little by little. Not only was this serious and businesslike gentleman out of place in this company, it seemed quite clear he had come for some important reason, because only something unusual could have brought him here, and something was clearly about to take place, something would happen. Raskolnikov, who had been standing beside Sonia, drew aside to let him pass. It was as though Peter Petrovich took no notice of him. A minute later Lebeziatnikov also appeared in the doorway. He did not come into the room, but stood there as though especially curious, almost amazed. He listened, but for some time he did not seem to be able to understand.

"Perhaps I'm interrupting you, I'm sorry, but I've come on fairly important business," Peter Petrovich said, as though addressing no one in particular. "I'm even glad there's an audience. Amalia Ivanovna, I humbly beg of you, in your capacity as landlady of the apartment, please pay special attention to what I am about to discuss with Sofia Ivanovna. Sofia Ivanovna," he continued, turning directly to the astonished Sonia, who was terribly frightened even before he began.

"Sofia Ivanovna, there has disappeared from my table (I refer to the table in my friend's room—my friend Andrey Semionovich Lebeziatnikov), immediately following your visit, a government-accredited bank note of the value of one hundred rubles. If you should happen to know and would show us where this bank note is now, I give you my word of honor, and I call upon all here to witness, that the matter will end there. If not, I shall be forced to take quite serious measures, and in that case . . . you will have only yourself to blame!"

The room was completely silent. Even the children stopped crying. Sonia turned deathly pale, looked at Luzhin, and could not reply. It was as though she still did not understand. A few moments passed.

"Well, *madame,* which is it?" Luzhin asked, looking at her intently.

"I don't know . . . I don't know anything," Sonia said at last in a weak voice.

"Oh? You don't know?" Luzhin asked. Again he was silent for a few seconds. "Think a moment, *mademoiselle,*" he·began sternly, but as though he were still exhorting. "Think it over. I'm willing to give you a little more time for reflection. Please take note that it goes without saying that a man of my experience would not have taken the risk of accusing you so directly if I were not quite convinced; because if a direct public accusation in such an instance turns out to be false, or even merely mistaken, in some way I would have to answer for it myself. This I am aware of. I cashed in several five percent bonds this morning, for my own needs, at a face value of three thousand rubles. I jotted down the account in my little notebook. When I got home— Andrey Semionovich is my witness—I started counting the money. When I counted out two thousand, three hundred rubles, I put them away in my notebook and put the notebook away in the side pocket of my overcoat. There were about five hundred rubles left on the table, including three hundred-ruble bills. That was the moment you arrived—at my invitation. All the time you·were in my presence you seemed extremely perturbed. At least three times during the conversation you got up and for some reason hastened as if to leave, although our conversation was by no means over. Andrey Semionovich can serve as witness to all that. You yourself, *mademoiselle,* would probably not refuse to confirm I invited you through Andrey Semionovich for the sole purpose of discussing with you the bereaved and helpless position of Katherine Ivanovna, your relative (whose funeral feast I was unable to attend)—as well as how useful it would be to arrange a subscription, a lottery, or some such thing, in her benefit. You thanked me, and even shed tears. I tell you all this just as it happened; in the first place, to remind you; in the second place, to show you that not the least impression has been erased from my memory. I then took

a ten-ruble note from the table and gave it to you in my
own name, in your relative's interests, and as a kind of first
contribution. All this Andrey Semionovich saw. I then accompanied you to the door. For your part, you were quite
perturbed. After that, I was alone with Andrey Semionovich,
and conversed with him for about ten minutes. Andrey Semionovich then left, and I turned my attention to the table
and the money lying on it. I meant to count it and put it
away. That is what I had been doing before. To my surprise,
one of the hundred-ruble notes did not seem to be there.
Be so kind as to think it over. I could in no way suspect
Andrey Semionovich; I'm even ashamed to suggest it. Nor
could I be mistaken in my accounting, because the moment
before you came I had just finished all my accounting and
found the sum correct. You yourself will agree: considering
how perturbed you were, how anxious to leave, and the fact
you held your hands on the table for some time; and finally,
considering your social position and the habits associated
with it—I felt myself horribly *forced* (even against my will,
mind you!) to become suspicious. It is cruel, of course, but
it is justified! I would like to say once more, and to add,
that in spite of my *certain* conviction, I know there is nevertheless in my present accusation a certain risk involved for
me. As you see, however, I could not let it pass. I rebelled,
and I will tell you why. Entirely, *madame,* entirely on account of your most black ingratitude! What do you mean?
In the interests of your terribly destitute relative, I invite
you, I offer you a contribution of ten rubles (which is all I
can afford), and you—tell me, now, tell me in front of these
people here—tell me how I am repaid for such a deed! No,
ma'am, that is not good! A lesson is called for. Think it
over. What is more, I beg you as your true friend—at this
moment you could not have a better friend—think hard! Or
I will be merciless! Well, ma'am, what have you to say?"

"I didn't take anything," Sonia whispered in horror. "You
gave me ten rubles. Here, you can have them." Sonia took
her handkerchief from her pocket, found the knot, untied
it, removed the ten-ruble note, and held it out in her hand
to Luzhin.

"So you refuse to acknowledge the other hundred rubles?" he
said urgently and reproachfully, without taking the bill.
Sonia looked about her. They were all gazing at her—such
terrible, stern, mocking, hate-filled faces! She looked at

Raskolnikov. He was standing by the wall, arms folded, and he looked at her with burning eyes.

"Oh, God!" burst from Sonia.

"Amalia Ivanovna, it will be necessary to inform the police, so I most humbly beg you for the time being to send for the janitor," said Luzhin quietly and even tenderly.

"*Gott der barmherzige! Und* I knowed she vas geshtealing!" Amalia Ivanovna threw up her hands.

"You knew it, did you?" Luzhin interposed. "Then there must have been at least *some* foundation for such a conclusion. I beg you, most worthy Amalia Ivanovna, to remember these words—and remember, too, that they were spoken in front of witnesses."

A loud hubbub suddenly arose on all sides. Everybody started shuffling around.

"Wha-a-at!" Katherine Ivanovna suddenly exclaimed, recovering herself. As though she were tearing loose from something, she rushed at Luzhin. "What! You accuse her of theft? Sonia? Oh, you scoundrels, scoundrels!" Rushing over to Sonia, she gripped her in a viselike embrace. "Sonia! How dared you take ten rubles from him? You stupid girl! Here, give it to me! Give me those ten rubles right now. Here!" Snatching the note from Sonia, Katherine Ivanovna crumpled it in her hand, and with a backhanded stroke flung it straight at Luzhin's face. The pellet hit him in the eye and fell to the ground. Amalia Ivanovna rushed forward to pick up the money. Peter Petrovich lost his temper.

"Restrain this madwoman!" he shouted. Several more faces appeared in the doorway beside Lebeziatnikov's; among them, the two provincial ladies', peeping in.

"What! Madwoman? I'm the one supposed to be mad, eh? You f-fool!" Katherine Ivanovna shrieked. "You're the one who's a fool, you shyster lawyer, you low-down, no good, vile, nasty man! Sonia—Sonia take money from him! Sonia a thief! Why, she'd sooner give you money, you fool!" And Katherine Ivanovna burst into hysterical laughter. "Did you see the fool?" She rushed around the room, nudging everybody and pointing to Luzhin. "What! You, too?" She had caught sight of the landlady. "You were right there on the spot, weren't you, you sausage-maker! Backing him up that Sonia 'vas geshtealing,' you vile Prussian chicken leg in a crinoline! Ah, you . . . you . . . Well, she hasn't been out of the room. As soon as she came here from seeing you, you scoundrel, she sat down right here beside Rodion Romanovich. Well, search her! Since she hasn't gone out anywhere, the money must still be on her! So, search her and see! But if you don't find it, you'd better watch out, my little pigeon, you'll answer for it! To the Sovereign, I'll go to the Sovereign, to the merciful Tsar himself, and I'll throw myself right down at his feet, this very day! I—an orphan! They will allow me! You think they won't allow me? You lie—I'll get through! I'll—get—through! So you were counting on her meekness, were you? That's what you were counting on? Well, brother, that is why I am so bold! You are heading for a fall! Search her! Well, go on, search her!" And Katherine Ivanovna pulled furiously at Luzhin, and dragged him over toward Sonia.

"I'm ready. I will answer for it . . . but take yourself in hand, *madame*, take yourself in hand! I can see all too well that you are bold! But . . . how . . . how can I?" muttered Luzhin. "The police should be here. Still, there are more than enough witnesses even now . . . I am ready. Still, for a man, it is awkward. . . . Perhaps with the help of Amalia Ivanovna . . . although, I must say, that is not the way it is done . . . But how can I?"

"Whoever you want! Let whoever wants to search her!" Katherine Ivanovna shouted. "Sonia, empty your pockets! There, see, I told you, you monster, this one's empty! Here's where her handkerchief was—the pocket's empty—see! Here's the other pocket. There—see! You see!"

Katherine Ivanovna did not so much turn the pockets inside out as wring them dry, one after the other. From the remaining right pocket, however, there dropped a piece of paper, which described a parabola in the air and fell at Luzhin's feet. Everyone saw it. Many cried out. Peter Petrovich bent down, with two fingers picked the paper up from the floor, held it up for everyone to see, and unfolded it. It was a hundred-ruble bank note folded in eight. Peter Petrovich showed the bill around to everyone.

"Thief! Out of my apartment. Help, polizei!" howled Amalia Ivanovna. "Siberia for them! Out!"

Exclamations flew from all sides. Raskolnikov silently fixed his eyes on Sonia, occasionally switching them swiftly to Luzhin. Sonia stood rooted to the spot, as though struck dumb; it was almost as though she were not even surprised. Suddenly the color rushed to her face; she cried out and covered her face with her hands.

"No, it wasn't me! I didn't take it! I don't know!" she

cried with a heart-rending wail, and threw herself into Katherine Ivanovna's arms. The latter put her arms around her and pressed her close, as though trying to protect her from everything.

"Sonia, Sonia! I don't believe it! You see I don't believe it in spite of all appearances!" Katherine Ivanovna cried, rocking her in her arms like a child, kissing her again and again, catching at her hands and kissing them as though she would devour them. "What stupid people, to think you would steal! Oh, God! How stupid you are, stupid!" she cried, addressing them all. "You don't know her heart, you don't know what kind of a girl she is, you just don't know how good she is! She, steal! Why, she'd take off her last dress, sell it, and go naked, in order to give you what you needed—that's the kind of girl she is! She took a yellow ticket because the children were wasting away from hunger—she sold herself for us! Ah, my dear dead husband, look what a funeral feast you have! Oh, God! Well, why don't you defend her? Why are you all just standing there? Rodion Romanovich! Why don't *you* stick up for her? Do you believe it, too? None of you are worth her little finger—not one! None, none! God! *You* defend her, then!"

Poor, consumptive, abandoned Katherine Ivanovna's lament seemed to have a powerful effect on her audience. There was so much suffering and misery in that pain-racked, disease-wasted face and parched, blood-flecked lips, the hoarsely crying voice, the violent lament so like a child's wail, the trusting, childlike, yet at the same time desperate plea for protection, that everyone felt sorry for the unfortunate woman. At least Peter Petrovich seemed to feel immediately sorry.

"Madame!" he exclaimed in an imposing voice. "This does not reflect on you! No one accuses you of complicity or assent, especially since it was you who emptied her pockets and brought the whole thing out. It follows that you must have been quite unaware. Oh, I am quite ready, quite ready to feel sympathy—if, so to speak, it was poverty drove Sofia Semionovna to this. But, *mademoiselle,* why wouldn't you own up? Were you afraid of the disgrace? Taking the first step? You lost your head, perhaps? Understandable, quite understandable . . . But how did you ever let yourself get started on such bad habits? Gentlemen!" he addressed everyone present. "Ladies and gentlemen! Feeling pity, and feeling what you might call compassion, I am, if you like,

even now prepared to forgive—in spite of the personal insults I have received. May your present disgrace serve as a future lesson to you, *mademoiselle*," he said to Sonia, "and as for me, I will take the matter no further, and so be it; I will cease. Enough!"

Peter Petrovich looked askance at Raskolnikov. Their eyes met. Raskolnikov's blazing look seemed ready to reduce him to ashes. Katherine Ivanovna, however, seemed to hear nothing more. She kept embracing and kissing Sonia as though she had gone out of her mind. The children also had gathered around Sonia, and flung their little arms around her and embraced her from all sides. Polenka, who did not quite understand what was going on, seemed submerged in tears, sobbing hysterically as she buried her pretty little face, swollen from weeping, on Sonia's shoulder.

"How low-down that is!" a loud voice suddenly sounded in the doorway.

Peter Petrovich quickly looked up.

"What a low-down thing!" Lebeziatnikov repeated, looking him steadily in the eye. Peter Petrovich actually seemed to give a start. Everybody noticed it. They remembered it later. Lebeziatnikov strode into the room. "And you were so bold as to refer to me as a witness?" he said as he approached Peter Petrovich.

"What do you mean, Andrey Semionovich? What are you talking about?" muttered Luzhin.

"I mean you're a . . . slanderer—that's what I mean," Lebeziatnikov said angrily, looking at him severely with his blind little eyes. He was terribly angry. Raskolnikov devoured him with his eyes, as though he were seizing and weighing every move and every word. Once again, silence. Peter Petrovich almost lost his head, especially at first.

"If you mean me . . ." he began haltingly, "why, you must be out of your mind!"

"Oh, I'm in my right mind, all right. It just so happens that *you* are a scoundrel! Oh, how low-down that was! I heard everything, I waited on purpose so I could understand everything—but I must admit, even now, it doesn't seem quite logical. What for? Why did you do it? I don't understand."

"Why, what did I do! Stop speaking in these trashy riddles! Perhaps you've had one too many?"

"Perhaps *you've* had one too many, you low-down man—but not me! I never drink vodka, because it is against my principles! Just imagine. He—he himself—he gave Sofia Semionovna that hundred-ruble note with his very own hands. I saw it, I am witness, and I'll swear to it! He—he—" Lebeziatnikov repeated, addressing them all.

"Have you gone out of your mind, you milksop?" Luzhin screeched. "You all heard her confirm that all she got from me was ten rubles. How could I have given her anything after that?"

"I saw it, I saw it," Lebeziatnikov kept shouting, "and I'm ready to take an oath, even though it's against my principles, an oath in court, any kind you want, because I saw how you slipped it to her when she didn't notice! Fool that I was, I thought you were slipping it to her out of charity! When you were saying good-bye to her in the doorway, when she turned away and you were shaking her hand—with your other hand, your left hand, you slipped the bank note into her pocket on the sly. I saw you do it!"

Luzhin turned pale.

"You're spinning dreams!" he said brazenly. "How could you see a bank note when you were standing by the window? You dreamed it up . . . with your nearsighted eyes. You're raving!"

"No, I didn't dream it up! And even though I was standing a good ways away, I saw everything—I saw it all! True, it was fairly hard to see the bank note from the window (you're right about that), but one thing made me sure it was a hundred-ruble bill. Because before you gave Sofia Semionovna the ten-ruble bill, I saw you pick up a hundred-ruble bill from the table. I saw it since I was standing quite close at the time. It gave me an idea immediately, so I didn't forget you had a bill in your hands. You folded it and held it squeezed tight in your hand all this time. Then I forgot about it again, but when you started getting up, you shifted it from your right hand to your left and almost dropped it. I remembered it, because here again I got a notion into my head you wanted to do something charitable for her without my knowing it. So you can imagine how I started taking note. Well, I saw how you managed to slip it into her pocket. I saw it. I'll swear to it on oath!" Lebeziatnikov almost choked. There were exclamations on all sides, mostly of amazement, but also some of a more threatening tone. Everybody pushed in the direction of Peter Petrovich. Katherine Ivanovna rushed over to Lebeziatnikov.

"Andrey Semionovich, I was wrong about you! Protect

her! You're the only one who's for her! She's an orphan—
it was God sent you! Oh, thank you, Andrey Semionovich,
my dear friend, thank you!" Almost out of control, Katherine Ivanovna went down on her knees before him.

"Poppycock!" cried Luzhin, infuriated to the point of
rage. "You're spouting poppycock, sir! 'I forgot, I remembered, I remembered, I forgot!' What does that mean! Does
it follow I deliberately planted it? Why? For what purpose?
What do I have in common with this—"

"Why? That's what I don't understand—but I know that
what I'm saying is true. I am so completely unmistaken—
you loathsome, criminal man—I even remember how the
question actually arose in my mind at the very moment I
thanked you and shook your hand. Why did you slip it into
her pocket on the sly? I mean, really, why on the sly? Just
because you wanted to hide it from me, because you knew
it was against my principles, because I'm against private
charity, because it doesn't change anything radically? Well,
I decided you really must be touchy about giving away such
sums while I was around, and I also thought, well, maybe
he wants to surprise her, so she'll be astonished when she
finds a hundred rubles in her pocket. There are benefactors
who like to postpone the effect of their good works—that
much I know. I also thought maybe you wanted to test her—
I mean, when she found it, would she come and thank you,
that sort of thing. Then I thought you wanted to avoid hearing her express her gratitude, and, well, how do you say it,
so the right hand or something wouldn't know . . . in short,
something like that. . . . Well, what I didn't think of after
that! So I decided I'd think it all over later. Anyway, I
thought it would be indelicate to let you know I knew your
secret. And yet a problem immediately popped into my
head: that Sofia Semionovna might lose the money before
she had a chance to take note of the good deed. That's why
I decided to come here, call her over, and let her know she
had a hundred rubles in her pocket. While I was at it,
though, I dropped in at the Kobyliatnikovs' first, to bring
them a copy of *A General Exposition of the Positive Method*
and tell them to read Piderit's article, and the one by
Wagner, too. After that I came here, and just look what was
going on! Well, now, could I have had all those thoughts
and reflections if I really hadn't seen you put a hundred
rubles in her pocket?"

By the time Andrey Semionovich had finished his long,

drawn-out reflections and brought his speech to such a logical conclusion, he was terribly tired, and the perspiration actually dripped from his face. Although he knew no other language, he could not express himself properly in Russian, and he seemed to have completely exhausted himself, all at once as it were; and after his forensic feat he even seemed to have grown thinner. Nevertheless, his speech produced an extraordinary effect. He had spoken with such ardor and such conviction, that everyone had apparently believed him. Peter Petrovich felt his case was going badly.

"What do I care if all kinds of stupid questions happen to pop into your head!" he shouted. "That's no proof, sir! You could have dreamed all this up in your sleep, and that's that! And what's more, I tell you, you lie, sir! You are lying, and you are slandering me—because you've got something against me—because you're mad I don't go along with your freethinking and atheistic social proposals, that's what it is!" This turn did Peter Petrovich no good, however. On the contrary, there was grumbling on all sides.

"So that's what you're up to, is it!" shouted Lebeziatnikov. "You're talking nonsense! Call the police, and I'll take an oath! There's only one thing I cannot understand: why did he take a chance on such a low-down act! Oh, you miserable, vile man!"

"I can explain why he took a chance on such an act, and if necessary I'll take an oath myself!" Raskolnikov said at last in a firm voice, and stepped forward. He seemed firm and calm. One look at him, and it seemed clear to everyone he really did know what was going on, and everything was solved.

"It's all clear in my own mind now," continued Raskolnikov, addressing Lebeziatnikov directly. "From the very beginning I suspected there was a vile, dirty trick afoot. I suspected this because I know some special circumstances, which I will now explain to everyone. They are at the bottom of the whole business. Your invaluable testimony, Andrey Semionovich, has finally made it all clear to me. I beg you to listen, all of you. This gentleman"—he pointed to Luzhin—"was engaged not long ago to a certain young lady; my sister, actually, Avdotia Romanovna Raskolnikov. But when he arrived in Petersburg day before yesterday and we met for the very first time, we quarreled, and I threw him out of my room. There are two witnesses to that. This man is very spiteful. . . . Day before yesterday I still didn't know he was living here with you, Andrey Semionovich, but on the very same day that we quarreled (the day before yesterday, that is), he was witness to the fact that as a friend of the late Mr. Marmeladov, I gave his wife Katherine Ivanovna some money for the funeral. He immediately wrote my mother a note and informed her that I'd given all my money away, not to Katherine Ivanovna but to Sofia Semionovna, and used the most vile expressions to refer to . . . to Sofia Semionovna's character, I mean, he commented on the character of my relations to Sofia Semionovna. All this, you understand, to set me at odds with my mother and sister, trying to convince them I was taking the last money they had, with which they were trying to help me, and squandering it for indecent purposes. Yesterday evening, with my mother and sister there, and in his presence, I restored the true picture, pointing out I hadn't given the money to Sofia Semionovna, but to Katherine Ivanovna for the funeral, and that the day before yesterday I still hadn't met Sofia Semionovna and had never even seen her face to face. To all this I added that he, Peter Petrovich Luzhin, with all his fine qualities, was not worth as much as Sofia Semionovna's little finger, though he had such a low opinion of her. He asked me whether I would ask Sofia Semionovna to sit down beside my sister and I replied that I had already done so that very day. Because my mother and sister refused to quarrel with me on the grounds of the slanders he provided, he got carried away and started saying unforgivably rude things to them. There was a decisive break, and he was thrown out of the house. It all happened yesterday evening. Now, your attention, please. Suppose he had managed to show Sofia Semionovna was a thief. . . . First, he would have demonstrated to my sister and mother he'd been almost right in his suspicions; that he'd been right to lose his temper at my putting Sofia Semionovna in the same class as my sister; so in attacking me, he was only guarding my sister's honor—his fiancée's. In short, he might after all this even set me at odds with my family again while he entered their good graces. I won't even mention that he would have revenged himself personally on me, for he had reason to presume that Sofia Semionovna's honor and happiness were very dear to me. There you have all his double-entry bookkeeping. That's how I figure this business! That's the whole reason—can't be anything else!"

In this way, or approximately so, Raskolnikov finished his

speech. It had been frequently interrupted by exclamations from the audience, which nevertheless listened carefully. Inspite of the interruptions he had spoken harshly, calmly, precisely, clearly, firmly. His harsh voice, his convinced tone, and his stern face produced an extraordinary effect on everyone.

"Yes, yes,—so it is!" Lebeziatnikov confirmed ecstatically. "It must be so; when Sofia Semionovna came into our room he was actually asking me if you would be here. Hadn't I seen you among Katherine Ivanovna's guests? That was why he called me over to the window on the sly. So it must follow he absolutely had to have you here! That's the way it is—exactly the way it is!"

Luzhin was silent and smiled contemptuously, yet he was quite pale. He seemed to be thinking of a way to get out. He might well have been glad to throw the whole thing up and leave, but that was almost impossible at the moment. It would have meant a direct admission of what he had been accused of, particularly that he really had slandered Sofia Semionovna. Moreover, his audience, which had been drinking, was too excited. Even though he had not understood everything, the quartermaster was shouting louder than anyone, proposing certain measures that would have been most unpleasant for Luzhin. But there were some who were not drunk; they had been gathering from all the rooms. All three of the little Poles were terribly worked up. "*Pan* swindler!" they kept shouting at him, and muttering threats of some sort in Polish. Sonia was listening intently, but looked as though she did not understand anything either, as if she were just recovering from a faint. Feeling he was her only defense, she simply did not take her eyes off Raskolnikov. Katherine Ivanovna was breathing hoarsely and with difficulty and seemed terribly exhausted. Amalia Ivanovna stood there more stupidly than anyone, her mouth hanging wide open, as if she were unable to figure anything out at all. All she saw was that Peter Petrovich had somehow fallen. Once more Raskolnikov was asking to speak. This time, however, he wasn't given a chance to finish; everybody was shouting, and they all crowded around Luzhin with threats and abuse. Peter Petrovich, however, did not turn coward. Seeing that his plan for accusing Sonia had completely fallen through, he resorted to brazening it out.

"Allow me, gentlemen, allow me. Don't shove. Let me pass!" he said, pushing his way through the crowd. "And do me a favor. Don't threaten. I assure you, nothing will come of it, you'll get nothing, I'm not afraid of you. On the contrary—you gentlemen will have to answer for concealing a criminal case by use of force. The thief was more than exposed, and I shall prosecute. In court they are not so blind, and they're not . . . drunk, and they won't believe two declared atheists, revolutionaries, and freethinkers who happen to be accusing me for personal revenge, as they stupidly acknowledge themselves. . . . Well, sir, allow me!"

"Just you get your smell out of my room immediately! Be so kind as to get out. Everything is finished between us! And when I think of how I racked my hide to explain to him . . . two whole weeks!"

"I told you some time ago that I was leaving, Andrey Semionovich, and when I told you, you kept urging me to stay. Let me add only that you are a fool, sir. I do hope you find some cure for your mind, and for your nearsightedness. Allow me, gentlemen!"

He pushed his way through, but the quartermaster would not let him get away with merely a few shouts of abuse. Grabbing a glass from the table, he flourished it in the air and let fly at Peter Petrovich. The glass, however, flew straight at Amalia Ivanovna. She screamed. The quartermaster lost his balance brandishing the glass, and collapsed under the table. Peter Petrovich made his way to his own room, and within half an hour he was gone.

Sonia, shy by nature, had been quite aware of her own social vulnerability; she knew that anyone could insult her and get away with it. And yet until that very moment she had thought she might somehow avoid trouble by being careful and meek and humble to everybody. Her disillusionment was more than she could bear. In the long run, of course, she could endure anything with patience and almost without a murmur—even this. For this first moment afterward, however, it was too much. In spite of the triumph of her justification, she had felt, after her first fear and the first stupor, when she could grasp and picture clearly what was going on, a helplessness and an outrage that painfully constricted her heart. She became hysterical. Finally, she fled from the room and ran home. She left at about the same time as Luzhin. When Amalia Ivanovna was hit by the glass (to the loud merriment of those present), she too found it unbearable to have to suffer for what was not her fault.

With a shriek, she hurled herself upon Katherine Ivanovna, whom she considered to be to blame for everything.

"Get out of the apartment! At once! March!" With this, she began to grab anything that came her way that happened to belong to Katherine Ivanovna and hurled it to the floor. Half dead anyway, almost unconscious, pale and breathing hard, Katherine Ivanovna leaped up from the bed (on which she had sunk, exhausted) and flung herself on Amalia Ivanovna. But the struggle was too uneven; the latter brushed her aside like a feather.

"What! Isn't it enough I've been godlessly slandered—does this creature have to turn on me too! What! Throwing me out of my home the day of my husband's funeral? They enjoy my hospitality first—and then, out into the street with my poor orphans! But where will I go?" the miserable woman howled, sobbing and catching her breath. "God!" she suddenly shouted, her eyes flashing, "is there no justice! Whom shouldst thou protect if not us, thy orphans? Ah, we shall see! There is right and justice on earth—there is, and I shall seek it out! Now then, wait, you godless creature! Polenka, you stay with the children. I'll be right back. Wait for me—out in the street if you have to! We shall see if there is justice in the world!"

Flinging over her head that very same green woolen shawl to which the departed Marmeladov had referred in his story, Katherine Ivanovna pushed her way through the disorderly and drunken crowd of tenants still thronging the room, and weeping and wailing ran out into the street—with the direct aim of immediately finding justice, come what may. Terror-stricken, Polenka crouched on the trunk in the corner where, with her arms around the two little ones, who were trembling all over, she awaited her mother's return. Amalia Ivanovna swept about the room, screaming, wailing, hurling anything that got in her way to the floor, and making a great row. The tenants bawled away in hopeless confusion. Some were recounting what had happened; others quarreled and cursed; still others struck up some songs. . . .

"High time I left," Raskolnikov thought. "Well, then, Sofia Semionovna, let's see what you say now!" And he made his way to Sonia's apartment.

In spite of the fact that he carried so much of his own horror and suffering in his heart, Raskolnikov had been a bold and energetic advocate of Sonia's cause against Luzhin. Having suffered so much that morning, he rejoiced in the chance to cast off his own inner sensations, which were becoming unbearable, not to mention the degree to which his urge to come to Sonia's aid had been purely personal and heartfelt. Moreover, there were moments when the thought of his meeting with Sonia excited him terribly: he would *have to tell her* who killed Lizaveta, but he could foresee his own terrible anguish, and he seemed to be trying to brush it aside. And therefore, when he exclaimed on leaving Katherine Ivanovna's—"Well, then, Sofia Semionovna, let's see what you say now!"—he was obviously in a rather excited state, elated by his recent victory over Luzhin. And yet by the time he got to Kapernaumov's apartment he suddenly felt helpless and afraid. Before the door, he paused thoughtfully and with a strange question: "Do I need to tell who killed Lizaveta?" It was a strange question, because he felt simultaneously that not only was it impossible not to tell, but that even to postpone the moment of telling for a short time was beyond him. He did not yet know why it was beyond him; he merely *felt* it was so, and this anguished awareness of his impotence before necessity almost crushed him. In order not to think about it anymore and not to go on suffering, he quickly opened the door, and looked at Sonia from the threshold. She was sitting with her elbows on the table, hiding her face in her hands; but when she saw Raskolnikov she got up quickly, and went toward him as though she had been expecting him.

"What would have happened to me if you hadn't been there!" she said quickly, meeting him in the middle of the room. This was evidently all she had been in a hurry to tell him. It was what she had been waiting for.

Raskolnikov walked to the table and sat down on the chair from which she had just risen. She stood in front of him, a couple of steps away, exactly like yesterday. "Well, Sonia?" he said, and suddenly became aware that his voice was trembling. "You know the whole business was based on

your 'social position' and the habits associated with it! Did
you understand?"

Distress showed on her face. "Don't talk to me like you
did yesterday!" she said. "Please, don't even begin. There's
been enough suffering. . . ." She smiled hastily, afraid that
perhaps he would resent the reproach. "I was foolish to
leave. What's going on there now? I wanted to go back, but
then I thought, well . . . you'd be coming."

He told her Amalia Ivanovna was throwing them out of
the apartment and that Katherine Ivanovna had run off
somewhere, "looking for justice."

"Oh, God!" Sonia leaped up. "Let's go quickly. . . ." She
grabbed her cloak.

"It's always the same!" Raskolnikov shouted in irritation.
"They are all you think about! Stay here with me."

"But . . . Katherine Ivanovna—"

"She certainly won't go far. Now that she's run out of the
house, she'll come to you herself," he added peevishly. "If
she doesn't find you home it will be your fault." Agonizingly
undecided, Sonia sat down on a chair. Raskolnikov fell silent, staring at the floor and mulling something.

"Let's assume that Luzhin didn't want to this time," he
began, without looking at Sonia. "But if he had wanted to,
if it had entered into his calculations, he could have had you
tossed into jail—if I hadn't been there, and Lebeziatnikov!
Ah?"

"Yes," she said weakly. "Yes!" she repeated, distraught
and alarmed.

"I might very well not have been there! Lebeziatnikov
turned up entirely by chance." Sonia was silent. "Well, what
if you had landed in jail—what then? Remember what I
said yesterday?"

Again she did not answer. He waited.

"And I thought you'd cry out again, 'Oh, don't say that,
stop!' " Raskolnikov laughed, but it seemed forced. "What?
Silence?" he asked after a minute. "Still? But we have to
talk about something, don't we? I'd really like to know how
you'd solve a certain 'question'—as Lebeziatnikov might put
it." He was apparently beginning to get mixed up. "No, I
mean it. I'm serious. Sonia, pretend you knew ahead of time
what Luzhin had in mind—I mean, you knew for certain
Katherine Ivanovna and the children would have been ruined and you, too. I know you take no account of yourself,
so that's why I say 'you, too.' But also Polenka . . . because

she's going to follow the same path. Well, there we are. If all this were suddenly left up to you to decide . . . if one or the other should live in the world . . . I mean, should Luzhin live and commit abominations and Katherine Ivanovna die? . . . How would you decide? Which of them should die? I ask you."

Sonia looked at him uneasily. She could sense some special meaning in this halting, roundabout speech. "I had a feeling you'd ask me something like that," she said, and she looked at him searchingly.

"All right, you did. But how would you decide?"

"Why do you ask the impossible?" Sonia said with distaste.

"You mean it's better for Luzhin to live and commit abominations! You don't even dare decide?"

"But how can I know God's will . . . and why do you ask what shouldn't be asked? Why these empty questions? How could it ever depend on my decision? And who ever made me judge of who was to live and who not live?"

"Once God's will gets mixed up in it, nothing will be done," growled Raskolnikov morosely.

"Better say what you want to say straight out!" Sonia exclaimed painfully. "You're leading up to something. You surely didn't come here just to torment me!" She could not restrain herself, and suddenly burst into bitter tears. He looked at her somberly. About five minutes passed.

At last he said quietly: "Of course you're right, Sonia." Suddenly he had changed. His deliberately insolent and helplessly defiant tone disappeared. Even his voice had suddenly grown weak. "I said yesterday I wouldn't come to ask forgiveness, yet I almost started out by asking forgiveness. . . . When I said what I did about Luzhin and God's will, I was thinking of myself. . . . Sonia, I was asking forgiveness. . . ." He wanted to smile, but there was something helpless and incomplete in it. He bowed his head and covered his face with his hands.

Suddenly he felt a strange, unexpected sensation, a kind of bitter hatred for Sonia. As if he were himself surprised and frightened by this, he suddenly lifted his head and looked at her intently; but he found her disturbed and painfully troubled gaze upon him. She loved him. His hatred disappeared like a phantom. No. He had mistaken one feeling for another. All it meant was the time had come. He covered his face with his hands again and bowed down his head. Suddenly, he turned pale, got up from the chair, looked at Sonia, and without saying a word sat down again mechanically on her bed. In his awareness this moment seemed horribly like the moment he had stood behind the old woman, the ax already free of the loop, when he had felt there was "not a moment to lose."

"What's the matter with you?" asked Sonia, feeling terribly apprehensive.

He was unable to utter a word. This was not at all the way he had intended to *declare himself* to her, and he did not understand himself what was happening to him now. She quietly went up to him, sat on the bed next to him, and waited, without taking her eyes off him. Her heart pounded and she had a sinking feeling. The situation became intolerable. He turned his deathly pale face to look at her; his lips twisted helplessly, straining to say something. A horror passed through Sonia's heart.

"What's the matter with you?" she repeated, drawing back a little.

"Nothing, Sonia. Don't be frightened. Rubbish. Really, when you think of it—rubbish," he muttered, with the look of a man raving. "But why did I come to torment you?" he suddenly asked, and looked at her. "Why, really? Sonia, I keep asking myself that question. . . ."

A quarter of an hour back he might actually have asked himself that question. Now he uttered it quite helplessly, hardly aware of what he was saying, while he felt his whole body shudder incessantly.

"How you torment yourself!" she said, distressed, looking at him closely.

"It's all rubbish! Sonia . . ." For some reason he suddenly smiled wanly and helplessly for a couple of seconds. "Do you remember what I wanted to tell you yesterday?"

Sonia waited uneasily.

"As I was leaving I said maybe I was saying good-bye to you forever, but if I came today I would tell you . . . who killed Lizaveta."

Her whole body suddenly shuddered.

"Well, that's what I came to tell you."

"Then yesterday, you really . . ." she whispered with difficulty. "But how do you know?" she asked quickly, as though suddenly coming to her senses. She began to breathe heavily. Her face grew paler.

"I know."

For a minute she was silent. "Does that mean they found *him*?" she asked timidly.

"No, they haven't found him."

Scarcely audibly, and again after almost a minute of silence, she asked: "Then how do you know?" He turned to her, and looked at her very intently.

"Guess," he said, and he smiled his former contorted and helpless smile. A shudder seemed to pass along her entire body.

"You're . . . why are you . . . frightening me so?" she said, smiling like a child.

"I must be a great friend of *his* . . . since I know," Raskolnikov said, looking steadily at her face, as though he no longer had the power to take his eyes away. "He didn't want to kill . . . this Lizaveta. He killed her . . . accidentally. He wanted to kill the old woman . . . when she was alone . . . and he came . . . and then Lizaveta came in . . . and he was there . . . and he killed her."

Another horrible minute passed. They looked at each other.

"Can't you guess?" he suddenly asked. He had that familiar sensation of hurling himself down from a steeple.

"N-no," Sonia whispered, almost inaudibly.

"Take a good look."

As soon as he said it another old, familiar sensation suddenly turned his soul to ice: he looked at her, and suddenly he seemed to see in her face the face of Lizaveta. He remembered clearly Lizaveta's expression as he approached her with the ax and she backed away from him toward the wall with her arm raised in front of her and a completely childlike fear in her face, like little children who, when they suddenly begin to be frightened of something, look at it steadily and uneasily and then start to back away, stretching out a tiny arm and ready to burst out weeping. Sonia was like that now: helpless, with the same fright, she looked at him for a while—and suddenly raising her left arm before her, her fingers barely touching her chest, she got up slowly from the bed and backed further and further away from him, but with her gaze all the more steadily fixed on him. Suddenly her horror seemed to communicate itself to him, too. The same expression of fright appeared on his face, and he looked at her in exactly the same way, and almost with the same *childlike* smile.

"Did you guess?" he whispered at last.

"Oh, my God!" she wailed. She collapsed helplessly on the bed, with her face in the pillow. But after a moment she quickly got up again and quickly moved closer to him. She seized both his hands, holding them with her thin fingers in a viselike grip. Again she looked steadily into his face, as though fastening herself to him. With this last desperate look, she wanted to search out and capture some last frail hope for herself. But there was no hope. There was no doubt. So it *was*! Even later, when she remembered this moment, she thought of it as strange and eerie. Why, actually, had she seen *at once* that no doubt remained? Could she say, for instance, that she really had foreseen something like this? And yet, as soon as he told her, it suddenly seemed to her that she actually had foreseen precisely *this*.

"Enough, Sonia! Don't torture me!" he begged. That was not the way he had planned his revelation, but *that* was the way it had turned out.

She leaped up as though possessed, and wringing her hands, walked to the center of the room; but she turned quickly and sat down again beside him, almost shoulder to shoulder. Suddenly she shuddered as if pierced. She cried out and flung herself down at his knees, not knowing why herself.

"Why, why did you take this upon yourself!" she said in despair. Rising from her knees, she threw her arms around his neck and hugged him very tight.

Raskolnikov recoiled, and looked at her with a melancholy smile. "How strange you are, Sonia. Embracing me and kissing me after I've told you *about that*. You don't know what you're doing."

"No, no, there is nobody, there is nobody anywhere in the world now unhappier than you!" she said as though in a frenzy, without having heard his remarks. Suddenly she burst into hysterical weeping.

A feeling he had not known for a long time surged into his soul and softened it at once. He did not resist. Two tears started from his eyes and hung from his lashes. He said almost with hope as he looked at her: "Then you won't leave me, Sonia?"

"No, no, never, nowhere!" Sonia cried out. "I'll follow you, I'll go anywhere! Oh, my God! . . . How miserable I am! But why, why didn't I know you before? Why didn't you come to me before? Oh, my God!"

"I've come now."

"Yes, now! Oh, but what's to be done now! . . . Together! Together!" she repeated as though oblivious, and again she embraced him. "I'll go with you to Siberia! We'll go together!" Something seemed to sting him to the quick, and his former caustic, almost arrogant smile played upon his lips.

"Maybe I still don't feel like going to Siberia, Sonia," he said.

Sonia looked at him quickly. After her first passionate and agonized feeling of sympathy for the unfortunate man, the terrifying idea of the murder once again stunned her. In the altered tone of his words she suddenly heard the murderer. She looked at him with astonishment. She still did not know why or how or for what it had been done. Now these questions all flared up at once into her conscious mind. And again she could not believe it: "Him—a murderer! Is that possible?"

"What is it all about, and where am I?" she asked, profoundly bewildered, as if she were not fully conscious. "But how could you—a man like you? How could you bring yourself to do such a thing? What is all this?"

"Stop, Sonia!" he said with a certain weariness, almost with indignation. "I did it to steal."

She stood as though thunderstruck, but suddenly she exclaimed: "You were hungry! You . . . wanted to help your mother? Yes?"

"No, Sonia, no," he muttered, and he turned away and hung his head. "I wasn't that hungry . . . I actually did want to help my mother, but . . . even that isn't altogether true . . . don't torture me, Sonia!"

Sonia wrung her hands. "But is it really all true! Oh, my God, what kind of truth can it be! Who could believe it? And how could you—how could you give away the last you had, when you had murdered to steal! Aaaah!" she suddenly cried out—"the money you gave Katherine Ivanovna . . . that money . . . Oh, my God, was it—"

"No, Sonia," he interrupted her hastily. "Don't worry— not that money. It was money my mother sent me by way of a merchant, and I received it when I was sick, the same day I gave it away. . . . Razumikhin saw . . . he even got it for me . . . it was my money, my own, really mine." Sonia listened to him in bewilderment, trying as hard as she could to make something out of it. "As for *that* money . . . well, I'm not even sure there was really any money there," he added softly, and as though lost in thought. "I took a purse from around her neck, a suede purse . . . it was full, packed tight. . . . But I didn't look inside; because there wasn't time, must have been . . . Well, as for the things, there were some studs and chains and whatnot—I buried the purse and all the things in somebody's backyard on Voznesensky Prospect under a stone . . . the next morning. . . . It's all still there. . . ."

Sonia was listening as hard as she could. "Why, then? You said you did it to steal . . . but you didn't take anything?" she asked quickly, clutching at straws.

"I don't know . . . I still hadn't decided—whether I'd take the money or wouldn't take it," he murmured, once again as though he were deep in thought. Suddenly recollecting himself, he grinned swiftly and briefly. "What rubbish I do babble, do I not?"

The thought flashed through Sonia's mind: "Is he mad?" But she abandoned it. No, this was different. And yet she understood nothing!

"Do you know, Sonia," he said suddenly, and with a kind of inspiration, "you know what? If only I had killed because I was hungry"—he emphasized every word and looked at her mysteriously but sincerely—"I'd be . . . *happy* now! You know that?" After a moment, he exclaimed with a kind of despair: "What's it to you? Why should you care I just confessed I did wrong? Why should you care about winning this stupid triumph over me? Ah, Sonia, was this the reason I came to you!" Again Sonia wanted to say something, but she remained silent. "That's why I asked you yesterday to go with me. You're the only one I have left."

"Go where?" Sonia asked uncertainly.

"Not stealing, not killing. Don't worry. Nothing like that." He grinned bitterly. "We're not the same sort. . . . Sonia, you know, I only just realized where I was asking you to go yesterday. . . . But yesterday, when I asked you, I still didn't know myself where I meant. I asked you for one thing only, I came for one thing only: don't leave me. You won't leave me, will you, Sonia?" She squeezed his hand. "Why did I tell her? Why did I reveal myself to her!" a minute later he exclaimed in desperation, looking at her out of a bottomless misery. "You're waiting for me to explain, Sonia, aren't you? You're sitting and waiting, I can see it. What shall I tell you? You won't understand, you'll just wear yourself out suffering . . . because of me! Well, now, you're crying and embracing me again—and what are you embracing me for? Because on my own I couldn't bear it, and came to dump my burden on somebody else: 'If you suffer, too, I'll find it easier!' Can you love that kind of scoundrel?"

"Yet you're in pain, aren't you?" cried Sonia.

That same feeling surged up again in his soul, and again softened it for an instant. "Sonia, I have a wicked heart. Note that well. It can explain a lot. I came here because I'm wicked. There are some who wouldn't have come. But I'm a coward and a . . . scoundrel! But let it go! It's not what I mean . . . I've got to talk now, but I don't know how to begin. . . ." He stopped and pondered. "A-a-ah, we're not the same sort!" he cried again. "We're not a pair. And why, why did I come! I'll never forgive myself for it!"

"No, no, it's good you came," Sonia exclaimed. "It's better I should know—much better!"

He looked at her in pain.

"Maybe you're right!" he said, as though making up his mind. "All right. So be it! It was like this: I wanted to make myself a Napoleon; that's why I murdered. . . . Well, now do you understand?"

"N-no," whispered Sonia timidly and naïvely. "Talk, go on, talk! I'll understand, I'll understand it all *inside*!" she entreated.

"You'll understand? All right, we'll see!" He fell silent and thought it over a long time.

"It's like this. Once I asked myself a question sort of like this: suppose Napoleon had been in my place, without Toulon or Egypt or the passage across Mont Blanc to launch his career, but instead of those beautiful monumental, epoch-making events there had been simply some absurd old hag, a stinking clerk's widow, and she had to be killed so he could steal some money from her trunk (for his career, mind you)—well, suppose there had been no other way—would he have brought himself to do a thing like that? Would he have shrunk back because it wasn't monumental enough, because it was . . . sinful? Well, as I say, this 'question' tormented me for a terribly long time, so I felt horribly ashamed when it finally occurred to me—all of a sudden, somehow—not only would he not have shrunk back, it would never have occurred to him that what he was doing wasn't monumental . . . and he wouldn't have understood what there was to shrink back from. If he had no other way he would snuff her out—just like that, without hesitating,

without even thinking about it. . . . Well, and as for me . . .
I overcame my reluctance . . . I snuffed her out . . . on the
example of my authority. . . . That's exactly how it was, you
know! You think it's funny? Yes, Sonia, the funniest thing
is I think maybe that's exactly how it was. . . ."

It was not funny to Sonia at all. "You had better tell
me directly . . . without examples," she begged, even more
uncertainly, and scarcely audibly. He turned to her, looked
at her sadly, and took her by the hands.

"You're right again, Sonia. But it's all rubbish, practically
pure blather! Look. I guess you know my mother has almost
nothing. My sister had her education by accident and was
condemned to drag out her life as a governess. All their
hopes rested on me. I studied, but I couldn't support myself
at the university, and after a while I had to quit. Even if I'd
made it, I might (with luck) in ten or twelve years hope to
become some kind of teacher or petty official at a thousand
rubles a year. . . ." He spoke as if by rote. "Meanwhile, my
mother would have withered sadly and anxiously away, and
I wouldn't be able to console her in any case. As for my
sister . . . well, even worse for her! . . . Yes, and how can
you spend your whole life avoiding every issue, turning aside
from everything, forgetting your mother, and putting up politely with insults to your sister? For what? So that when
you've buried them, you can take on a new batch—a wife
and children—then leave them, too, without a crust or a
scrap? Well . . . I decided I'd use the old woman's money
to get a start, and I wouldn't torment my mother. I'd use it
for my keep at the university, for my first steps after the
university—and I'd do everything in a big way, thoroughly,
so I'd make a completely new career and start off on a new
and independent path. . . . Well . . . that's all there is to
it. . . . Well, of course, killing the old woman—that was bad.
But enough!" he stumbled weakly to the end of the story
and hung his head.

"Oh, no, no," Sonia mournfully exclaimed, "how could it
be like that. . . . No, that isn't it, not like that!"

"No, you can see it isn't right! Yet I was telling the
truth, sincerely!"

"But what kind of truth is that! Oh, my God!"

"Sonia, I only killed a louse—useless, vile, pernicious."

"A human being a louse!"

"Of course I know she's not a louse," he replied, looking
at her strangely. "Anyway, I'm talking nonsense, Sonia," he

added, "I've been talking nonsense for a long time. . . . You're right. It isn't at all like that. The reasons are quite, quite, quite different! I haven't talked to anyone for a long time, Sonia . . . I have a bad headache."

His eyes blazed with a feverish light. He was almost delirious. An uneasy smile strayed about his lips. Beneath his excited emotional state, his terrible helplessness could be glimpsed. Sonia knew how he suffered. Her head, too, began to spin. He spoke so strangely. Some of it seemed clear, yet—"How, but how? Oh, my God!" And she wrung her hands in despair.

"No, Sonia, it isn't right!" he began again, suddenly lifting up his head as though a sudden turn of thought had struck him and excited him all over again. "It isn't right! Better . . . you should suppose (yes! really better), you should suppose I'm vain, envious, malicious, slimy, vengeful, well . . . if you like, slightly insane. (Let's say it and get it over with! They were talking about my being insane—I heard them!) A while ago I told you I couldn't support myself at the university. Well, you know—maybe I could have. My mother would have sent me enough to pay what I needed for fees, and I could have earned what I needed for food and clothing; I really could have! I could have given lessons at half a ruble a lesson, just the way Razumikhin does! But I got angry and didn't want to. I really got *angry* (that's the right word!), and I hid myself in the corner of my room like a spider. You've been in my kennel, you've seen . . . Ah, Sonia, you know, low ceilings and tight rooms cramp the mind and the soul! How I hated that kennel! And yet I didn't want to leave it. I deliberately didn't want to! For days on end I didn't leave, and I didn't want to work and I didn't even want to eat. I just lay there. If Nastasia brought me something, I'd eat. If not, the day would pass. I made a point of not asking, because I was angry. Nights I had no light. I'd lie in the dark, I just wouldn't earn enough money for candles. I was supposed to study, so I sold my books. On my table, notes, notebooks, there's dust finger-thick. Best of all I liked to lie there and think. I thought all the time. . . . And all the time I had such different, strange dreams. I couldn't begin to tell you the dreams I had! But it was only then I started imagining that— No, that's not so! Again I'm not telling it right. . . . I kept asking myself why I was so stupid; and if others were stupid and I knew they were, didn't I want to be cleverer? Then, Sonia, I learned it takes too long to wait for everybody to get clever. . . . What's more, I learned it would never happen; people won't change, nobody can reform them, and it's not worth the effort! Yes, that's right! It's the law of their being. . . . Their law, Sonia! That's right! I know now, Sonia, that whoever is strong and self-confident in mind and spirit has power over them! Whoever is bold and dares has right on his side. Whoever can spit on the most people becomes their legislator, and whoever dares most has the most right! So it has been in the past, and so it will always be! Only a blind man can't see it!"

Raskolnikov looked at Sonia as he spoke, but no longer cared whether she understood or not. The fever took possession of him. He was in a kind of dark ecstasy. (It had really been too long since he had spoken with anyone!) Sonia realized that this dark catechism had become his creed and his law.

"Then I figured out, Sonia," he continued triumphantly, "that power is given only to him who dares to stoop and seize it. There's only one thing that matters, just one thing: you have to dare! Then a certain idea popped into my head for the first time in my life, an idea nobody had ever thought of before me! Nobody! I suddenly realized, clear as day, that not a single soul had so far dared, and would not dare, to bypass all this nonsense, simply take it all by the tail and shake the hell out of it! I . . . I wanted to *dare,* and I killed. . . . I only wanted to dare, Sonia—that's the whole reason!"

"Ah, quiet, be quiet!" Sonia exclaimed, throwing up her hands. "You abandoned God, and God has stricken you and turned you over to the Devil!"

"So as I lay in the dark, Sonia, figuring it all out, that was the Devil confusing me—eh?"

"Quiet! You mustn't laugh, blasphemer! Nothing. You don't understand anything! Oh, my God! He understands nothing, nothing!"

"Hush, Sonia, I'm not laughing. I know it was the Devil who led me on. Hush, Sonia, hush!" he repeated, gloomy and insistent. "I know it all. I thought it all over, and that's what I whispered to myself as I lay there in the dark. . . . I carried on a debate with myself, down to the last little detail, and I know it all, all of it! How I hated all that chatter— God, how I hated it! I wanted to forget everything and start over again, Sonia, and stop the chatter! Do you think I plunged headlong like a fool? No, I was clever about it—

that's how I came to grief. For instance, don't you think I knew that if I started cross-examining myself as to whether I had the right to this power or not, the conclusion would follow that I didn't have the right? Or if I put the question: is a human being a louse?—it would follow a human being was not a louse *for me,* but a louse only for him who doesn't give it a thought, who goes straight ahead without any questions . . . Just because I spent so many days tormenting myself about whether Napoleon would have done it or not, I must have pretty well sensed I was not Napoleon. I put up with all this torment of chatter, Sonia, and I wanted to shrug it all off. I wanted to kill without casuistry, to kill for myself, for myself alone! I didn't want to lie about it even to myself! I didn't kill to help my mother—that's rubbish! And I didn't kill to provide myself with means and power for becoming a benefactor to mankind. Rubbish! I simply killed; I killed for myself, for myself alone. Whether I'd become anybody's benefactor or spend my whole life like a spider catching everybody in my web and sucking the living juices out of them—at that moment it *should* have been all the same to me! . . . And, Sonia, when I killed—money wasn't the main thing I needed. It wasn't money I needed, it was something else. . . . Now I know all this. . . . Understand me. Maybe following the same path I would not have committed another murder. There was something I had to know—something else—something else that pushed me on. I had to know, and I had to know right away: was I a louse like all the rest, or was I a man? Could I transgress, or could I not? Did I dare to stoop and take, or didn't I? Was I mere trembling flesh, or did I have the *right*—"

"To kill? The right to kill?" Sonia threw up her hands.

"A-a-ah, Sonia!" he exclaimed irritably, and wanted to make some objection, but instead kept a contemptuous silence. "Don't interrupt me, Sonia! There was just one thing I wanted to prove to you: that the Devil led me on, and then he made it clear to me I didn't have the right, because I'm exactly the same species of louse as all the rest! He laughed at me. That's why I'm here now! If I weren't a louse, would I have come to you? Listen. The time I went to the old woman's, I was just going to *give it a try.* . . . You must know that!"

"And you killed her! You killed!"

"What do you mean, *killed*? Is killing done like that? The way I did it? Sometime I'll tell you what it was like. . . .

Did I kill the old hag? No, not the old hag—I killed myself! I went there, and all at once I did away with myself forever! But it was the Devil killed the old hag—not me! Enough, Sonia, enough, enough! Let me be," he cried out suddenly in shuddering misery, "let me be!" He put his elbows on his knees and pressed his head in his hands, as in a pair of tongs.

"How you're suffering!" Sonia cried out in anguish.

"Well, tell me what I should do now!" he said, suddenly raising his head and looking at her, his face monstrously distorted with despair.

"What should you do!" she exclaimed, and leaped suddenly from her seat. And all of a sudden her eyes, which had been full of tears, were flashing. "Rise!" She seized him by the shoulder. He raised himself, looking at her almost in amazement. "Go now. Go this very moment, and stand at the crossroads; bow down, and first kiss the earth which you have defiled; then bow down to the whole world, to the four points of the compass, and say aloud, for all men to hear: 'I have killed!' Then God will send you life again. Will you go? Will you go?" she asked him, trembling as in a fit, seizing both his hands, pressing them firmly in her own, and looking at him with a burning gaze.

He was amazed and even dumbfounded by her sudden ecstasy. "Are you talking about Siberia, Sonia? Does that mean I have to give myself up?" he asked morosely.

"You must accept suffering and redeem yourself by it; that's what you must do."

"No! I won't go to them, Sonia."

"But what about living? How will you live your life? And with what!" Sonia exclaimed. "Can you do it? How will you talk to your mother? What will become of them now? What will become of them! But what am I talking about! You've already abandoned your mother and sister . . . haven't you! You've already abandoned them, abandoned them! My God!" she cried out, "he surely knows all this already! How, then, how can you live all alone, without a human being! What will become of you now!"

"Don't be childish, Sonia," he said softly. "What am I guilty of, as far as they're concerned? Why should I go? What would I tell them? It's all a mere phantom. . . . People are used up by the millions, and it's considered a virtue. They're swindlers and villains, Sonia! . . . I won't go. What would I say? I killed, but didn't dare take the money and stashed it away under a stone?" he added with a bitter grin. "Why, they'd have to laugh at me themselves. They'd say: he was a fool not to take it. A coward and a fool! They wouldn't understand a thing, Sonia, not a thing! And they aren't worthy of understanding. Why should I go? I won't go. Don't be childish, Sonia. . . ."

"You'll wear yourself out," she said, stretching out her hands to him in desperate supplication.

"*Still*—maybe I wasn't being fair to myself," he noted gloomily, as though thinking it over. "Maybe I'm *still* a man and not a louse, and maybe I condemned myself too hastily. . . . Maybe I'll *still* put up a fight." A haughty smile played upon his lips.

"To bear such torment! And for all your life! All your life!"

"I'll get used to it," he said pensively and morosely. "Listen," he began a minute later. "Enough crying. It is time for action. I came to tell you, they're looking for me now. They'll catch me. . . ."

"Oh, no!" cried Sonia, frightened.

"You see, you cried out! You'd like me to go to Siberia, and yet you're frightened? But, look. I won't give myself up. Not to them. I'll struggle with them, and they won't be able to do anything. They don't have any real evidence. Yesterday I was in great danger. I thought I was finished. But things are better today. All their evidence is double-edged. I mean, I can turn their accusations to my advantage—understand? And I will. Because I've learned my lesson now . . . They'll certainly put me in jail, though. If not for one accident, they might even have arrested me today; they might *still* arrest me today. . . . But it's nothing, Sonia. I'll go to jail . . . then they'll have to let me out. Because they don't have a shred of real evidence, and won't have, I give my word. They can't convict anybody with what they have. Well, enough . . . I just wanted you to know. . . . I'll try to work it so my mother and sister can find out, yet not get frightened. . . . Anyway, it looks like my sister is secure now . . . and so, my mother, too. . . . Well, that's all there is to it. But be careful. Will you come visit me in jail when I'm there?"

"Oh, I will! I will!"

The two sat side by side, mournful and dejected, as though they had been washed up alone on a deserted shore after a storm. He looked at Sonia and sensed how much her love

was on him; strangely, it suddenly felt weary and painful to
be loved like that—a strange and terrible sensation! On his
way to Sonia's he had felt she was his only hope and his
only way out. He had thought he would be able to unload
at least part of his torment, and now, all of a sudden, when
she turned to him with all her heart, he suddenly felt and
realized that he was infinitely more miserable than he had
been before.

"Sonia," he said. "Maybe you had better not come see
me when I'm in jail."

Sonia did not reply. She wept. A few minutes passed.
Unexpectedly and all of a sudden she asked: "Do you wear
a cross?"

He did not at first understand her question.

"You mean you don't? Here, take this one. It's made of
Cypress. I have another one that's made out of brass. Lizaveta gave it to me. I once exchanged crosses with Lizaveta.
I mean, she gave me her cross and I gave her my icon. I'll
wear Lizaveta's now, and you take this one. Take it . . . it's
mine! I tell you it's mine!" she reassured him. "We will
suffer together. Together we will bear the cross!"

"Give it to me!" said Raskolnikov. And yet, although he
did not want to upset her, he immediately withdrew the
hand he had held out for the cross.

"Not now, Sonia. Better later," he added, to comfort her.

"Yes, yes, that's better, better." She seized the remark
eagerly. "When you go to suffer, you will put it on. Come
to me, and I will put it on you. We will pray together, and
then we'll go."

At this moment someone knocked at the door three times.

"Sofia Semionovna, may I come in?" said a polite and
familiar voice.

Sonia ran to the door in fright. The albino face of Mr.
Lebeziatnikov looked into the room.

5

Lebeziatnikov looked worried. "I have come to you, Sofia
Semionovna. Excuse me . . . I thought I'd find you here,"
he suddenly addressed Raskolnikov. "I mean I didn't think
anything of *that* sort . . . but I really did think . . ." Then
he turned away from Raskolnikov and suddenly blurted out

to Sonia: "Look, over at our place, Katherine Ivanovna has gone out of her mind." Sonia cried out. "I mean, at least it looks that way. But we don't know what to do about it, that's the trouble! She came back; it looked like she'd been thrown out of someplace; maybe beaten, too. . . . She'd run off to see Semion Zakharych's former boss, but he wasn't home. He was dining out at some general's place. . . . So imagine, off she went to where they were dining . . . to this other general's place. And imagine, she just stood there and said she wanted to see this former boss of Semion Zakharych, and while he was still at the table. You can picture what happened. Of course, they threw her out; she says she personally shouted at him and threw something at him. You can just picture it. Why they didn't arrest her, I don't understand! Now she's telling everybody, including Amalia Ivanovna—only it's hard to understand, she shouts and carries on so. . . . Oh, yes: she cries out that since everybody has abandoned her, she'll take the children and go out on the street with a barrel organ, and the children will sing and dance, and she will, too, and collect money, and every day she'll stand under the general's window. . . . 'Let them see,' she says, 'how the decent children of a state official have to go out on the streets and beg!' She beats the children and they cry. She's teaching Lenia to sing 'The Hamlet' and the little boy to dance. Polenka, too. She's ripped all their clothes, and she's made them caps, like actors. She says she'll carry a frying pan and beat it for music. . . . She won't listen to anything . . . Just imagine. How can she do it? It's simply impossible!"

Lebeziatnikov would have gone on, but Sonia, who had been listening to him with bated breath, suddenly grabbed her cloak and hat and ran out of the room, putting them on as she ran. Raskolnikov followed close on her heels, and Lebeziatnikov behind him.

"She's undoubtedly gone out of her mind!" he said to Raskolnikov, as they came out on the street. "I said 'it looks that way' because I didn't want to frighten Sofia Semionovna, but there isn't any doubt. They say when somebody has consumption, the little tubercles go to the brain. Pity I don't know any medicine. I tried to persuade her, but she wouldn't listen."

"You told her about the little tubercles?"

"Well, not exactly about the little tubercles. She wouldn't have understood, anyway. What I mean is, if you can show a person logical proof that essentially he's got nothing to cry about, he'll stop crying. That seems clear. Don't you think he'd stop crying?"

"That would make life too easy," Raskolnikov replied.

"Oh, come now, please. It's pretty difficult for Katherine Ivanovna to understand, of course. Did you know that in Paris they've already performed some serious experiments, trying to cure the insane on the basis of logical proof alone? There was a professor there—he died recently—a real scientist—he thought you could cure people that way. His basic notion was that insanity isn't an organic defect, but, you might say, a logical mistake, a mistake in judgment, an incorrect way of looking at things. He would refute his patients step by step, and—you know—they say he got results! It's true he used sprays, too, so the results may be subject to some doubt. . . . At least, so it would seem. . . ." Raskolnikov had not been listening for some time. When they reached his own house, he nodded to Lebeziatnikov and turned in at the entry. Lebeziatnikov recovered himself, looked about, and ran on ahead.

Raskolnikov entered his garret and stood in the middle of it. Why had he turned in here? He looked at the yellowish strips of disintegrating wallpaper, the dust, the couch. . . . From the yard came a sharp, incessant knocking, as of someone somewhere hammering nails. . . . He went to the window, rose up on tiptoe, and gazed out into the yard for a long time with a look of extraordinary attention. The yard was empty. Whoever was hammering was invisible. Some windows were open on the wing to the left. There were some sick-looking potted geraniums on the windowsills. Beyond the windows, the laundry was hung out to dry.. . . He knew it all by heart. He turned away and sat down on his couch.

Never, never till now had he felt so horribly alone.

Again he felt he could really get to hate Sonia; especially now that he'd just added to her misery. Why had he gone to her to beg for her tears? Why did he have to poison her life that way? Oh, it was nasty!

"I'll stay alone!" He suddenly made up his mind. "She won't come to the prison!" About five minutes later he raised his head and smiled strangely. It was a strange thought that had suddenly occurred to him: "Maybe it would really be better to go to Siberia."

He did not remember how long he sat there, vague

thoughts swarming in his head. Suddenly the door opened, and Avdotia Romanovna came in. She first stopped and looked at him from the threshold, just as he had looked at Sonia a while ago. Then she came in and sat down facing him, in the same chair she had sat in yesterday. He looked at her silently, as though his mind were blank.

"Don't be angry," said Dunia, "I just came for a minute." She looked thoughtful, but not stern. Her eyes were clear and soft. He saw she had come in a loving mood.

"Well, now I know everything, *everything.* Dmitry Prokofich explained everything to me. They're persecuting you, aren't they? Tormenting you, because of a stupid, vile suspicion . . . Dmitry Prokofich said there wasn't any danger and it was foolish for you to be so horrified. I don't look at it that way. I *realize,* I really do, how disturbing all this must have been to you. And you're so indignant, it could have permanent effects. That's what worries me. I don't judge you for leaving us. I don't presume to judge. I'm sorry I reproached you earlier. I can't help feeling, if I'd been bearing such a burden, I would have taken off too. I won't say anything to Mother *about this.* I'll keep telling her you say you'll come soon. Don't worry about her. *I'll* calm her down. But don't worry her, either. Come at least once. Remember, she's your mother! Well, I just came to say"—Dunia started getting up from her chair—"well, if you ever need me, anything I can give . . . my life . . . call me, and I'll come. Good-bye!" She turned sharply and walked to the door.

"Dunia!" Raskolnikov stopped her, got up and went over to her. "This Razumikhin, Dmitry Prokofich—he's a very good man."

Dunia blushed slightly. She waited a moment and said: "Well?"

"He's a practical, hard-working, honest man, and he's capable of loving deeply. . . . Good-bye, Dunia." Dunia flushed and seemed suddenly worried.

"When you give me . . . advice like that—does that mean . . . good-bye forever?"

"Never mind . . . good-bye. . . ." He turned away and went to the window. She stood there, looked at him uneasily, and left in alarm.

No, he had not behaved coldly to her. There had been a moment (the very last) when he had longed terribly to hold her tightly in his arms and *say good-bye* to her, even *tell* her; but he could not even bring himself to offer her his hand. "She'd probably shudder afterwards if she remembered I embraced her. She'd say I stole her kiss," he added to himself several minutes later. "Will she survive *this*, or not? . . . No, she won't. *Such* women don't survive. Such women never survive. . . ." He thought of Sonia.

A fresh breeze blew in from the window. Outside, the light no longer shone so brightly. All of a sudden he picked up his cap and left.

Of course he could not, nor would he, concern himself about his illness; but all this incessant excitement and all the inner horror could not pass without consequences. If he was no longer on his back in a fever, maybe it was because the constant inner excitement kept him alert and on his feet; but only artificially, and for the time being.

He wandered without aim. The sun was setting. Recently a special kind of misery had begun to make its mark on him. There was nothing especially sharp or searing about it; yet it breathed something permanent, eternal, foretelling hopeless years of this cold and deathly misery, foretelling a kind of eternity on a "square yard of space." At dusk this sensation began to torment him even more than usual.

"Well, you get these damn stupid little infirmities, and they're purely physical and depend on the way the sun sets or some such thing, and then you have to watch out or you'll do something really stupid! Wind up going to Dunia, let alone Sonia!" he muttered bitterly.

Somebody called him. He looked up, and Lebeziatnikov rushed up to him.

"Just imagine. I've been at your place. I was looking for you. Just imagine. She did what she said she'd do—took the children off! Sofia Semionovna and I had an awful time finding them. She was beating a frying pan, making the children dance. The children were crying. They'd stop at crossings and in front of shops. With a stupid crowd following them. Come on!"

"And Sonia?" Raskolnikov asked in alarm, hurrying after Lebeziatnikov.

"Simply out of her mind. I mean, it's not Sofia Semionovna who's out of her mind, but Katherine Ivanovna. Anyway, Sofia Semionovna's out of her mind, too. But Katherine Ivanovna's completely out of her mind. She's definitely insane. They're being taken to the police station. You can imagine what that will do. . . . They're by the canal now, near Voznesensky Bridge, not far from Sofia Semionovna's. Quite close."

By the canal, not very far from the bridge and not more than two houses from where Sonia lived, a crowd was gathering. A large number of street urchins, boys and girls, came running. They could already hear Katherine Ivanovna's hoarse, broken voice at the bridge. It really was a strange scene, the kind that could draw a crowd. Katherine Ivanovna, in her old dress, her green, light wool shawl, and a battered straw hat (tilted and hideously crushed on one side), really was in a state of absolute frenzy. She was tired and short of breath. Her agonized, consumptive face seemed more stricken than ever (moreover, a consumptive always looks sicker and more disfigured outdoors in the sunlight than at home), and her overly excited mood had not worn off; every moment she seemed to become more and more aroused. She would rush over to the children, shout at them, coax them, instruct them before the crowd how to dance and what to sing, start explaining why it was necessary, fall into despair at their incomprehension, beat them. . . . Then she would rush to the crowd; if she noticed a halfway reasonably well-dressed man who had stopped to look, she would immediately launch into her explanations. Just look what children from "a decent, you might even say from an aristocratic home" had come to. If she heard laughter or anything derogatory, she would fling herself on the presumptuous ones and start quarreling with them. Some laughed. Others shook their heads. Everyone found the madwoman and her thoroughly frightened children strange. There was no frying pan; at least, Raskolnikov didn't see it. Instead of beating on a frying pan, Katherine Ivanovna kept time by clapping her withered hands when she made Polenka sing and Lenia and Kolia dance. She would start singing herself, but always break off at the second note and start coughing painfully, at which she would fall into despair, curse her coughing, and even weep. What made her wildest of all were Kolia's and Lenia's tears, and their fear. She'd actually tried to dress the children up in street-singer costume. The boy wore a red and white turban and was supposed to look like a Turk. There hadn't been enough material for Lenia's costume. She simply wore a red knitted worsted nightcap that had belonged to the late Semion Zakharych. Stuck in the cap was a white ostrich feather, a kind of family heirloom that had belonged to Katherine Ivanovna's grandmother and that she had rescued from the trunk. Polenka wore her usual dress. She was watching her mother timidly and with perplexity and would not leave her side, hiding her tears, guessing her mother's madness and looking around uneasily. The street and the crowd frightened her terribly. Sonia kept following Katherine Ivanovna, weeping, begging her to come back home; but Katherine Ivanovna was implacable.

"Stop, Sonia, stop!" she gabbled, breathing hard and coughing. "You don't know what you're asking, just like a child! I told you I won't go back to that drunken German woman. Let them all see, let all Petersburg see, how the children of a decent father beg for alms—a father who worked hard and faithfully all his life and who even, you might say, died in the service." This was a fantasy Katherine Ivanovna had created for herself, and by now she believed in it blindly. "Let that nasty little general see them, let him. And you're stupid, Sonia: what else can we do? We've worried you enough. I don't want to anymore! Ah, Rodion Romanych, it's you!" she exclaimed when she saw Raskolnikov, and rushed over to him. "Please explain to this little idiot there's nothing better to be done! Even organ-grinders make do, and anybody can tell we're a poor, decent family of orphans reduced to poverty, and that general will lose his position, you'll see! We'll stand under his window every day, and if the Sovereign should pass, I'll go down on my knees and I'll thrust these children forward and I'll point to them: 'Protect them, Father!' He is father to orphans, he is merciful, he will protect—you'll see, and as for that little general . . . Lenia! *Tenez vous droite!* You, Kolia, now you'll dance again. What are you sniveling for? Always sniveling! Well, what is it, what are you afraid of, you idiot! My God! What shall I do with them, Rodion Romanych! If you only knew how stupid they are! Well, what can you do with children like that!"

Almost weeping herself (it did not hinder her incessant babbling), she showed him the whimpering children. Raskolnikov tried to persuade her to return, and even said, thinking he might act on her vanity, that it was not seemly for her to go about the streets as organ-grinders did, since she was preparing herself to become the headmistress of a respectable girls' boarding school.

"A boarding school, ha-ha-ha! Great bells beyond the mountains!" cried Katherine Ivanovna, her laughter immediately giving way to a fit of coughing. "No, Rodion Ro-

manych, the dream has passed! They've all abandoned
us. . . . As for that wretched little general . . . You know,
Rodion Romanych, I threw an inkwell at him. There was an
inkwell on the table in the anteroom by the visitors' book
which everybody had to sign; and I signed, and I threw it
and ran away. Oh, the villains, the villains! But damn them
all; I'll provide for these children myself now. I won't kow-
tow to anybody! And we've tormented her enough. . . ."
She indicated Sonia. "Polenka, how much did we take in?
Show me. What? Only two kopecks? Oh, the mean creatures! They won't give us anything; they just run after us
and waggle their tongues! Well, what is that monkey laughing at?" She pointed to somebody in the crowd. "It's all
because that Kolia's so stupid; he's causing all the trouble!
Polenka, what's the matter with you? Speak French to me;
parlezmoi français. But I taught you, you know; surely you
know a few phrases! Or else how can they tell you're well-
brought-up children from a decent family, and not like all
the other organ-grinders. We're not putting on a Punch-and-
Judy show in the streets, we're singing a respectable drawing-
room song. Ah, yes! What shall we sing? You keep interrupting
me, and we . . . Don't you see, Rodion Romanych, we
stopped here to choose something we could sing. Something
Kolia can dance to, also . . . because, as you might imagine,
we have to do it all without preparation; we have to get
together and rehearse it carefully; then we'll make our way
to Nevsky, where there are lots more people of a better
sort, and they'll notice us right away. Lenia knows 'The
Hamlet'. . . . Only, it's 'Hamlet,' 'Hamlet,' all the time—
everybody sings it! We've got to sing something much more
respectable. . . . Well, what comes to your mind, Polia? You
might at least help your mother out a little! I have no memory, no memory, or else I'd remember! We can't really sing
'A Hussar On His Saber Leaning.' . . . Ah, let's sing *'Cinq
sous,'* in French! But I *taught* it to you, I taught it to you!
The main point is it's in French. They'll see at once you're
gentry children, and that will be much more touching. . . .
We might even try *'Malborough s'en va-t-en guerre,'* since
that's a children's song and it's used in all aristocratic houses
when they rock children to sleep:

> *Malborough s'en va-t-en guerre,*
> *Ne sait, quand reviendra . . ."*

she began to sing. "But no. '*Cinq sous*' is better! Now then,
Kolia—hands on your hips, quickly. And you, Lenia, you
keep turning, too, in the opposite direction. Polia and I will
sing and clap hands!

> *Cinq sous, cinq sous,*
> *Pour monter notre ménage . . .*

K-khee-k-khee-k-khee!" And she went off into a fit of
coughing. "Straighten your dress, Polia, the shoulders have
slipped down," she said through her coughing, gasping for
breath. "It's especially important you behave nicely and
mind your manners now, so everybody can see you are gentry children. I did say at the time the bodice ought to be
cut longer and made of two widths. But you have to have
it your way, Sonia. 'Shorter and still shorter,' so now it's
turned out the child looks perfectly dreadful. . . . Why are
you all crying again! What for, stupids! Well, Kolia, start,
quickly, hurry, hurry—oh, what an insufferable child! . . .
Cinq sous, cinq sous. . . . Another policeman! Well, what
do you want?"

A policeman was indeed pushing his way through the
crowd. At the same time, however, a gentleman in civil service uniform and a cloak, a solid civil servant of about fifty,
with a medal around his neck (this last point pleased Katherine
Ivanovna and impressed the policeman), made his way up to
them and silently handed Katherine Ivanovna a three-ruble
note. On his face was an expression of genuine compassion.
Katherine Ivanovna took it, and politely, even ceremoniously,
bowed to him.

"I thank you, my dear sir," she began loftily, "the reasons
that have compelled us . . . take the money, Polenka. There
are, as you see, decent and magnanimous people, immediately ready to help a poor gentlewoman in distress. You
see before you, my dear sir, decent orphans, with the most
aristocratic connections, you might even say. . . . And that
wretched little general sat there eating grouse . . . and
stamped his feet at me for disturbing him. 'Your Excellency,'
I said, 'protect these orphans, since,' I said, 'you knew the
late Semion Zakharych, and since the nastiest villain slandered his daughter on the very day of his death—' That
policeman again! Protect us!" she appealed to the civil servant. "Why is that policeman pushing this way? We already

ran away from one the likes of him on Meshchansky . . .
well, idiot, what is it you want?"

"Well, it's not allowed on the streets. Be so good as not
to disturb the peace."

"You're the one who disturbs the peace! It isn't as though
I had a barrel organ. What business is it of yours?"

"You need a permit for a barrel organ. As for you, you're
gathering a crowd, carrying on like that. Where are you
staying, please?"

"What do you mean, a permit!" yelled Katherine Ivanovna. "I buried my husband today—that's my permit!"

"*Madame, madame,* calm yourself," the official began.
"Come along. I'll take you. . . . It's unseemly here in the
crowd . . . you're unwell . . ."

"My dear sir, my dear sir, you know nothing!" Katherine
Ivanovna shouted. "We're going to Nevsky. Sonia, Sonia!
Where did she get to? Now she's also crying! Why, what *is*
the matter with all of you? Kolia, Lenia, where are you
going?" she exclaimed suddenly, in alarm. "Oh, the stupid
children! Kolia, Lenia—where *did* they get to?"

What had happened was that Kolia and Lenia, scared out
of their wits by the crowd and by the outbursts of their mad
mother, and to top it all seeing what they thought was a
policeman about to arrest them and drag them off somewhere, took each other suddenly by the hand, as though
by plan, and ran off. Weeping and wailing, poor Katherine
Ivanovna tried to catch up with them. She was a terrifying
and pathetic sight—running, weeping, panting. Sonia and
Polenka chased after her.

"Bring them back, Sonia, bring them back! Oh, you stupid, ungrateful children! Polia, catch them! It's for your sake
I—" She stumbled and fell headlong.

"She's hurt, she's bleeding! Oh, my God!" Sonia exclaimed, bending over her.

Everybody ran up and crowded around. Raskolnikov and
Lebeziatnikov were among the first; the official also hurried
up, and behind him the policeman, who was muttering, "Eh-
h-hm," and waving his hand, anticipating trouble. "Go on,
go on!" He drove off the people who were crowding around.

"She's dying!" someone yelled.

"She's gone out of her mind!" said somebody else.

"Lord preserve us!" said one woman, crossing herself.
"Did they catch the two little ones? Ah, here they come.
The older one caught them. . . . E-eh, they're off their nut!"

When they examined Katherine Ivanovna more closely, however, they saw she hadn't hurt herself on the stone as Sonia had imagined, but that the blood staining the roadway came spurting from her lungs and out of her mouth.

"I knew it, I could see," the official muttered to Raskolnikov and Lebeziatnikov. "That's consumption. The blood spurts up and chokes them. Not long ago I saw it happen to a relative of mine. A glass and a half of blood and all of a sudden . . . But what can we do now? She's going to die."

"This way—to my place," Sonia pleaded. "I live right here! That house there—the second one . . . To my place, quickly, quickly!" She swept from one to the other. "Send for a doctor. . . . Oh, my God!"

Thanks to the official's efforts it was organized, and even the policeman helped carry Katherine Ivanovna. They carried her to Sonia's place, almost gone, and put her on the bed. Blood continued to flow, but she seemed to come to her senses. Not only Sonia, Raskolnikov, and Lebeziatnikov, but also the official and the policeman had squeezed into the room. Some of the crowd had followed them right up to the doorway, but the policeman had dispersed them. Polenka brought in Kolia and Lenia by the hand. They were trembling and weeping. Some of the Kapernaumovs had also gathered: Kapernaumov himself, lame and one-eyed, a queer-looking man with bristly side-whiskers and bristly hair standing up in a mass on one side; his wife, who had a perpetually frightened look, and some of their children, faces stiffened into a look of permanent surprise, and with wide open mouths. Suddenly, in the midst of all this crowd, Svidrigailov turned up. Raskolnikov looked at him in astonishment, not having seen him in the crowd before and not knowing where he had come from.

They spoke of a doctor and a priest. The official, though he whispered to Raskolnikov that a doctor would be superfluous now, nevertheless had one sent for. Kapernaumov himself ran to fetch one. Meanwhile, Katherine Ivanovna was getting her breath back. The blood subsided for a while. She gazed with a painful but steady and penetrating look at the pale and trembling Sonia, who was wiping the drops of perspiration from her forehead with a handkerchief. Finally she asked to sit up. They raised her up on the bed, supporting her on both sides.

"Where are the children?" she asked in a weak voice. "Did you bring them, Polia? Oh, you stupids! Why did you run away . . . Ach!" The blood still flecked her parched lips. She swept the room with her eyes, taking it in.

"So that's how you live, Sonia! I haven't been to your place, not even once . . . and now I was brought here. . . ." She looked at her in anguish. "We sucked you dry, Sonia. . . . Polia, Lenia, Kolia, come here. . . . Well, here they are, Sonia—all of them. Take them . . . I'm handing them to you . . . all they can get from me! The ball is over! Kha! . . . Put me down. Let me die in peace!" They laid her down again on the pillow. "What? A priest? Don't need him . . . where did the money come from? I don't have any sins! God has to forgive me anyway. . . . He knows how I've suffered. . . . And if he won't forgive me, what difference will a priest make!"

She became increasingly restless and delirious. At times she would give a start, sweep the room with her eyes, for a moment recognize everyone; but delirium would take over again immediately. She breathed hoarsely and heavily. Something seemed to rattle in her throat.

"I said to him, 'Your Excellency!' " she cried out, resting after each word, "that Amalia Ludwigovna . . . ah! Lenia, Kolia, hands on hips, hurry, hurry, *glissez–glissez, pas-de-basque!* Tap your feet. . . . Be graceful.

Du hast Diamanten und Perlen . . .

How does it go on? we might sing that. . . .

Du hast die schoensten Augen,
Maedchen, was willst du mehr?

Well, of course that's the way it goes! '*Was willst du mehr*'— he's making it up, the dunce! Ah, yes; then there is:

In the noonday heat, in a vale of Daghestan . . .

Oh, how I loved . . . I loved that song to distraction, Polenka! . . . You know, your father . . . used to sing it when he was courting me. . . . Oh, those days! Yes, we could sing that one; we might sing that! But how does it go, how does it go . . . well, now, I've forgotten . . . come on, now, remind me, how does it go!" She was extremely excited, and tried to raise herself up. Finally, in a terrible, hoarse, broken voice, she began, shrieking and panting for breath at every word, with a look of mounting terror:

"In the noonday heat! . . . in a vale . . . of Daghestan! . . . With a bullet in his breast! . . .

Your Excellency!" she suddenly wailed with a broken howl and a flow of tears, "protect these orphans! Knowing the hospitality of the late Semion Zakharych . . . aristocratic, you might say! . . . Kha!" She gave a shudder, and suddenly came to her senses. She glanced at everyone with a kind of horror, but immediately recognized Sonia. "Sonia," she said meekly and gently, as though surprised to see her there before her. "Sonia, darling—you here, too?" They raised her up again. "Enough! . . . It's time! . . . Good-bye, you poor thing! . . . They've finished off the old nag! She's ovestrai—overstrained!" she cried in bitter despair, and her head dropped on the pillow.

Again she dropped into a coma, but this time not for long. Her yellow, pale, parched face tilted up and back, her mouth fell open, her legs stiffened out and quivered. She gave a deep, deep sigh, and died.

Sonia fell on the corpse, put her arms about it, and lay still in that position, with her head pressed against the dead woman's withered breast. Polenka fell at her mother's feet and kissed them, weeping without restraint. Kolia and Lenia, who still did not understand what was going on but sensed that it was quite terrible, put both arms on one another's shoulders, stared straight into each other's eyes, and suddenly opened their mouths at the same time and began to howl. They were both still in costume: one in the turban, the other in nightcap with ostrich feather. And how did that "testimonial" suddenly appear on the bed beside Katherine Ivanovna? It was lying there near the pillow; Raskolnikov saw it.

He went to the window. Lebeziatnikov joined him there.

"She's dead," said Lebeziatnikov.

"Rodion Romanovich, I must have a few words with you," said Svidrigailov, coming up to them. Lebeziatnikov immediately yielded his place and retired tactfully. Svidrigailov led the astonished Raskolnikov back a little further into the corner. "I'll take care of all this—I mean the funeral, I'll pay for it. You know it will take money, and as I told you, I have plenty to spare. I'll take these two little birds and this Polenka and I'll put them in the best orphanage I can find, and I'll settle a thousand and a half rubles on each of them till they come of age, so Sofia Semionovna doesn't have to worry about them. Yes, and I'll pull her out of the mud, too; because she's a good girl, isn't she? Well, sir, you can tell your sister, that's how I used her ten thousand."

"What is the object of all this philanthropy?" Raskolnikov asked.

"E-e-eh! What a mistrustful man!" Svidrigailov laughed. "But I told you, I have this money to spare. Well, suppose it's simply out of a feeling of humanity—won't you allow that? She wasn't a 'louse,' you know"—he indicated the corner where the dead woman lay—"not like some old pawnbroker woman. Well, I mean, you'll agree: 'Should Luzhin really live and commit abominations, or should she die?' And if I don't help out—well, 'Polenka will go the same way. . . .' Won't she?"

He said this with a sort of gay, *winking* connivance, yet without taking his eyes off Raskolnikov. Hearing his own phrases as he had expressed them to Sonia, Raskolnikov turned pale and icy cold. He quickly stepped back and looked wildly at Svidrigailov.

"How do . . . you know?" he whispered, scarcely drawing his breath.

"Well, you see, I live here behind the partition, at Madame Resslich's. Here's Kapernaumov, and there's Madame Resslich, an old and very devoted acquaintance. I'm a neighbor."

"You?"

"Me," Svidrigailov went on, rocking with laughter. "I can honestly assure you, my dearest Rodion Romanovich, that you have been of astonishing interest to me. You know, I told you we would get to know each other better—I predicted it to you. Well, then, here we are. You'll see what an easygoing man I am. You'll see it's possible to get along with me. . . ."

PART SIX

1

A strange time began for Raskolnikov: as though a fog had suddenly rolled in before him and imprisoned him in a desperate and heavy solitude. Recalling this time later, after a long time had passed, he thought his consciousness must have kept flashing on and off, with several dim, dark intervals, right up to the final catastrophe. He was absolutely convinced he had been mistaken about many things at the time; the duration of time of certain events, for example. At least, when he recalled them later and tried to clarify to himself what he recalled, he learned a lot about himself, especially since he also had information from others at his disposal. He would confuse one event with another, for example; still another, he would take as the consequence of an event that had taken place only in his imagination. At times he was gripped by a painful anxiety that would turn into panic. He also remembered, however, that there were minutes, hours, and perhaps even days full of apathy, which gripped him as though to spite his former terror—an apathy so overwhelming that it resembled mortal illness. In general, in these last days, he seemed to be trying to escape from a full and clear understanding of his position. Certain vital facts that demanded an immediate explanation weighed on him especially. Yet how happy he would have been to free himself and escape from these concerns, although forgetting them threatened him with complete and inevitable ruin.

Svidrigailov worried him especially: you might say he seemed to concentrate on Svidrigailov. Since the time Svidrigailov had all too clearly expressed those dreadful words in Sonia's room, the time of Katherine Ivanovna's death, the ordinary flow of his thoughts seemed disrupted. Although this new fact disturbed him terribly, Raskolnikov made no haste to get to the bottom of it. Sometimes he would suddenly find himself somewhere in a distant and solitary part of the city, in some sad tavern. Alone at his table and lost in thought and scarcely recalling how he had got there, he would suddenly remember Svidrigailov. Suddenly it would become disturbingly clear to him he would have to have a talk with this man as soon as possible, and come to a final decision if he could. Once, out somewhere beyond the city limits, he even imagined he'd arranged a meeting there with Svidrigailov and was waiting for him to show up. Again, he woke up before dawn on the ground, somewhere in some bushes, and he could scarcely remember how he had got there. Two or three days after Katherine Ivanovna's death, however, he did meet Svidrigailov a couple of times, always near Sonia's, where he now and again made his way, but always for barely a moment. They always exchanged a few words, but never talked about the main issue, as though they had agreed between them to keep it silent for the time being. Katherine Ivanovna's body lay in its coffin. Svidrigailov made all the arrangements for the funeral and kept himself busy. Sonia, too, had her hands full. When they last saw each other Svidrigailov told Raskolnikov he had settled the problem of Katherine Ivanovna's children and settled it successfully; thanks to certain connections of his he had been able to locate people who helped him place all three orphans immediately in establishments that were quite suitable for them; the money set aside for them had also helped a lot, because it was easier to place orphans who had some savings than orphans of the destitute. He also said something about Sonia, and said he would come see Raskolnikov in a day or so, mentioning that he "would like his advice," really had to talk to him, there were certain things . . . This conversation took place on the landing by the stairs. Svidrigailov had been looking intently into Raskolnikov's eyes. Suddenly he broke off, lowered his voice, and asked: "What's the matter with you, Rodion Romanych? You don't seem to be yourself. Really! You listen and look as though you weren't taking anything in. Cheer up. Just wait till we have our little chat. It's a pity I'm so busy, though; I mean, with my own affairs and other people's— Ah, Rodion Romanych," he added all of a sudden. "What all men need is air, air—yes, air. . . . First of all!"

He suddenly stepped aside to make way for the priest and deacon, who were on their way upstairs. They were going to perform the mass for the dead. According to Svidrigailov's arrangements, masses for the dead were to be performed twice a day, meticulously. Svidrigailov went on his way. Raskolnikov stood there, thought for a moment, and then followed the priest into Sonia's room.

He stood in the doorway. Quietly, ceremoniously, and sadly the service began. Since childhood he had always felt in the awareness of death and in the experience of death's presence something oppressive and mystically horrifying; and it was a long time since he had heard the mass for the dead. And there was something else about it now that was too horrifying and disturbing. He looked at the children: they were all on their knees beside the coffin, and Polenka was crying. Behind them, sobbing timidly, Sonia prayed softly. Suddenly it occurred to Raskolnikov: "She hasn't looked at me once the past few days or said a word to me." The sun lit up the room; the smoke of incense rose in clouds; and the priest was reading the prayer for the dead. Raskolnikov stood up during the entire service. The priest, as he gave his blessing and was saying good-bye, looked about him, a little perplexed. After the service, Raskolnikov went up to Sonia. Suddenly she took both his hands and leaned her head on his shoulder. This brief gesture amazed Raskolnikov. It certainly was strange. What, not the slightest disgust, not the slightest aversion to him? Not the slightest trembling in her hand? Here was a kind of infinity of self-abnegation. So, at least, he interpreted it. Sonia said nothing. Raskolnikov pressed her hand and left. He felt terribly depressed. If he could have gone off somewhere and remained completely by himself, even for the rest of his life, he would at that moment have considered himself blessed. The fact of the matter was that although he had been almost always alone of late, he had in no way been able to feel that he was alone. Sometimes he would hike outside the city or along the highway, and once he even entered a kind of small wood; but the more solitary the place was the more he would be aware of some close and disturbing presence, which was not so much frightening as somehow extremely aggravating, and he would go back to the city as quickly as he could, mingle with the crowd, go into a tavern or saloon, or to a bazaar or the Haymarket. He seemed to feel easier there, and more alone. In one hash joint, early one evening, they were singing songs. He sat there a whole hour listening, and later he remembered that he had actually enjoyed it. But toward the end he got up suddenly, uneasy again, as though a twinge of conscience had suddenly started to fret him. As though he thought: "What am I doing sitting here listening to songs, as though I had nothing else to do!" And yet he had an inkling at the same time that this wasn't the only thing bothering him. Something demanded an immediate solution; but what it was he could not put into words or even conceive. Everything bunched itself into a kind of cloud. "No, a struggle would be better! Better Porfiry again . . . or Svidrigailov . . . The sooner there's a challenge, some kind of attack, the better . . . Yes! Yes!" he thought. He left the hash joint and almost broke into a run. Then the thought of Dunia and his mother for some reason threw him into a panic. This was the night he had awakened just before dawn in the bushes on Krestovsky Island, trembling all over feverishly. He got home in the wee hours of the morning. After a few hours of sleep the fever passed, but he woke up late. It was two o'clock in the afternoon.

This was the day of Katherine Ivanovna's funeral, he remembered, and he was glad he had not attended. Nastasia brought him something to eat. He ate and drank with a hearty appetite, almost greedily. His head was clearer, and he felt calmer than he had these last three days. He even wondered fitfully about his former bursts of panic. The door opened and in came Razumikhin.

"Ah! He's eating. That means he's not sick!" Razumikhin said. He took a chair and sat down at the table facing Raskolnikov. He was worried and did not try to hide it. He spoke with obvious annoyance, but without hurrying and without especially raising his voice. He seemed to have something special, something even rather exceptional on his mind. "Listen," he began determinedly. "The way I feel, to hell with you, and everybody else, too. Because I can see now—I see clearly—I don't understand a thing. Please don't think I came to butt in. Hell, I don't give a damn! If you told me all your secrets, maybe I wouldn't even listen—I'd just say to hell with you, and I'd walk out. I just came to find out personally, once and for all—well, number one, is it true you're insane? You see, there's a theory current (well, *there*, somewhere) you're insane, or you lean strongly in that direction. I can assure you, I'm rather strongly inclined to that theory myself; in the first place because of your stupid and rather nasty actions (which can't be explained), and in the second place because of the way you treated your mother and sister not long ago. If a man weren't mad he'd have to be a monster and a villain to act as you have to them. Consequently, you must be insane."

"Is it long since you've seen them?"

"Just now. Since that time, haven't you seen them at all?

Where, if you don't mind telling me, have you been slouching off to? I've been here three times. Your mother has been seriously ill since yesterday. She wanted to come here. Avdotia Romanovna tried to hold her back, but she wouldn't listen. 'If he's sick,' she says, 'if he's really going out of his mind, who's to help him if not his mother?' We all came here, because we didn't want her to go alone. Right up to your door we kept trying to calm her down. We went in; you weren't there. So she sat down right here. She sat here for ten minutes, and we stood by in silence. She got up, and she says: 'If he leaves he must be well, and if he's forgotten his mother, it's unseemly and shameful for her to wait at the door and beg for affection as for alms.' She went home and lay down. Now she has a fever. 'I see,' she says, 'he has time for his *girl*.' She assumes this Sofia Semionovna is your *girl*, your fiancée or your sweetheart, I don't know. I went to Sofia Semionovna's right away, because, brother, I wanted to find out what was going on. Well, I looked in, and there's the coffin, and the kids are crying. Sofia Semionovna is trying their mourning clothes on them. You're not there. I excused myself and left, and I reported to Avdotia Romanovna. That meant rubbish, there was nothing to this business about your *girl*; most likely, then, insanity. But here you sit, wolfing down boiled beef as if you hadn't eaten for three days. All right, let's assume that madmen eat, too; but even though you haven't said a single word to me, you're . . . no madman! I'll swear to that. Above all, you're no madman. So to hell with you all, because there's a mystery here, a secret of some kind; and I don't intend to break my head over your secrets. So I came to let off some steam," he concluded, rising, "get it off my chest. I know what I have to do now!"

"What do you want to do now?"

"And what business is it of yours what I want to do now?"

"Watch out, you'll wind up getting drunk!"

"What . . . what makes you so sure?"

"Hah! What a question!"

Razumikhin was quiet a minute. "You always were a very rational man, and you've never been insane, never!" he suddenly remarked with heat. "So be it. I'll go get drunk! Good-bye!" And he made a motion to leave.

"I was talking about you, Razumikhin, I think it was the day before yesterday—to my sister."

"About me! But where could you have seen her the day

before yesterday?" Razumikhin stopped suddenly and even turned slightly pale.

"She came here alone, she sat here, and she talked with me."

"Her!"

"Yes, her."

"What did you say . . . I mean, about me?"

"I told her you were a very good, honorable, and hard-working man. I didn't tell her you loved her. She knows that herself."

"Knows it herself?"

"Well, what a question! No matter where I go or what happens to me, you'd be their salvation. I, so to speak, entrust them to you, Razumikhin. I say this because I really know how you love her and I'm convinced your heart is pure. I also know she's capable of loving you, and she may even love you already. Now, you decide—after all, you know best—if you need to get drunk or not."

"Rodia, look . . . Well . . . Oh, hell! But where is it you want to go? Look, if it's all a secret, okay, let it be! But I'll . . . find out . . . I'm convinced it's bound to be some kind of rubbish, some awful trifle, and you just cooked it all up yourself. Still, you're a marvelous guy! A marvelous guy!"

"I was actually about to tell you when you interrupted me just now that you were being rational a while ago when you decided not to pry into these mysteries and secrets. For the time being, let it go; don't get upset. You'll find out everything in good time, when you need to know. Somebody told me yesterday that what a man needs is air, yes, air, air! I want to go to him now and find out what he meant."

Razumikhin stood there, thoughtful and agitated, and tried to put something together. "A political plotter, that's what he is!" he thought suddenly to himself. "Of course! And he's about to take a decisive step of some sort—of course, that's it! It couldn't be anything else, and . . . and . . . Dunia knows. . . ."

"So Avdotia Romanovna comes to see you?" he said aloud, weighing his words. "And you want to go see a man who says we need more air, more air, and . . . and then there's the letter . . . that must be part of the same business, too," he concluded as if to himself.

"What letter?"

"She received a letter today, and it upset her very much.

Very much. Too much. I mentioned you and she asked me to keep quiet. Then . . . then she said maybe we'd be parting soon, then she started thanking me warmly for something. Then she went to her room and locked herself in."

Thoughtfully, Raskolnikov asked again: "She received a letter?"

"Yes, a letter. You didn't know? Hmm." They both fell silent. "Good-bye, Rodion. Brother, I . . . there was a time . . . anyway, good-bye. You see, there was a time . . . Well, good-bye! I have to go, too. I won't drink. Don't need to, now . . . so you were wrong!"

He was in a hurry. After he had already gone out and practically closed the door behind him, however, he suddenly opened it again and said, looking off to the side: "By the way! Do you remember that murder? Well, you know— Porfiry and the old woman and all that? Well, they found the murderer. He confessed and provided evidence. It was one of the workmen—the painters—remember? Just think, I even defended them. And would you believe it—that whole business of the fight with his friend and the laughing on the stairs while the janitor and the two witnesses were on their way up—he set it all up deliberately, as a blind. What cunning, what presence of mind for a lout like that! Hard to believe, but he explained it himself. He confessed everything. Was I ever wrong! Still, I think he is a genius at deception and the quick answer and putting one over on the law, so there's nothing to be so surprised about! As if such people didn't exist. The fact that he didn't hold out, and confessed, makes me believe him all the more. Makes more sense . . . But was I ever wrong! I just about climbed up the wall for those guys!"

"Would you mind telling me where you learned this and why it interests you so much?" Raskolnikov asked with obvious agitation.

"What a question! He asks why it interests me! Well, I found out from Porfiry, among others. Actually I found out almost everything from him."

"From Porfiry?"

"From Porfiry."

"And what . . . what does he think?" asked Raskolnikov apprehensively.

"He explained it to me quite well. Psychologically—the way he does."

"He explained it to you? Himself?"

"Yes, himself. Well, good-bye. I've still got something to tell you, but later. Right now there's work to be done. There was a time . . . when I thought . . . Well, anyway. Later! Why should I drink now—you got me drunk without any liquor. I tell you I'm drunk, Rodia! I'm drunk without any liquor. Well, so. Good-bye! I'll be back quite soon."

He went out. As he walked slowly down the stairs Razumikhin made up his mind conclusively: "He's a political plotter, that's what he is, of course! And he's gotten his sister into it. That would be quite, quite in character for Avdotia Romanovna. They had some meetings. . . . She dropped a hint, too. Judging by a lot of what she said . . . and between the lines . . . and her hints . . . that's really the way it is! How else explain the whole mess? Hmm! And I almost thought . . . Oh, my God, what was it I almost thought! That was an eclipse, all right, and it was my fault! He was the one brought on the eclipse, that time in the corridor, near the lamp. Hell! What a nasty, coarse, vulgar notion of mine! Good old Nikolka confessed. . . . Now those things he did will all be explained, like everything else! The sickness, the strange things he did; even before, when he was still at the university, what a gloomy and morose character he was. . . . But what did that letter mean? I guess there's something in that, too. Who was it from? I suspect . . . Hmm. No, I'll find out all about it." He remembered and thought over everything he knew about Dunia, and his heart sank. He tore himself from the spot and ran on.

As soon as Razumikhin had left, Raskolnikov got up and turned to the window; he ambled over to one corner, then another, as though he had forgotten how cramped his kennel was, and . . . sat down again on his couch. He felt like a new man. Once more, struggle! That meant there was a way out! "Yes, it means there's a way out!"

It had all grown too airless, too confined; the pressure had begun to crush him; a kind of stupefaction had come over him. Ever since the scene with Mikolka, at Porfiry's, he had been gasping for air, feeling cramped and hemmed in. That same day there had been the scene at Sonia's; he had conducted and concluded it very, very differently from the way he had somehow conceived it before . . . and that meant he had weakened—on the spot and considerably! All at once! And he had agreed with Sonia, he had actually agreed with her, hadn't he, in his heart he had agreed, that he could not go on living alone with such a matter weighing on him!

But Svidrigailov? Svidrigailov was a riddle. . . . Svidrigailov worried him, true, but that was different. He might have to lock horns with Svidrigailov, too. But Svidrigailov might also be a total way out. Porfiry was another matter.

Porfiry had explained everything to Razumikhin; Porfiry himself had explained it to him *psychologically*! Started dragging in that damned psychology again! But Porfiry? How could he believe for even a moment that Mikolka was guilty after their encounter, before Mikolka's appearance, when they had stood face to face—an encounter which could only be interpreted *one* way? (The whole scene had flashed through Raskolnikov's mind several times these past few days in bits and pieces; yet he could not endure remembering it as a whole.) They had spoken such words then, they had made such moves and gestures, exchanged such glances, some things had been said in such a tone of voice, and they had reached such a pass that afterward no Mikolka—whom Porfiry could read backward and forward from his first word and gesture—no Mikolka could shake the foundation of his convictions after that.

And, think! Even Razumikhin was beginning to suspect! Their encounter in the corridor near the lamp had not been lost. And so he dashed off to Porfiry. . . . And what did *he* have in mind, leading Razumikhin on like that? What could he have been aiming at? Diverting his attention to Mikolka? Still, he must have had something in mind; there was a purpose here—but what? A lot of time had gone by since that morning, it was true—much too much. But neither sight nor sound of Porfiry. Well, of course, it made things worse. . . . Deep in thought, Raskolnikov took his cap and was about to leave the room. It was the first day all this while that he at least felt himself to be in sound mind. "I have to settle with Svidrigailov," he thought, "as quickly as possible and come what may. Porfiry seems to be waiting for me, too." At that moment such a hatred swelled up in his weary heart, he could have killed either of these two, Svidrigailov or Porfiry. And if he were not capable of it now, he would be later. "We'll see, we'll see," he kept repeating to himself.

As he opened the door onto the landing, however, he suddenly bumped into Porfiry himself. Porfiry had come to him. For a moment Raskolnikov went numb. Yet, strangely, he was not much surprised, and almost not even afraid of Porfiry. He shuddered, but quickly, instantly, composed himself. "The denouement, perhaps! But how did he manage to creep up so softly, like a cat, without me hearing a thing? Could he have been eavesdropping?"

"You weren't expecting a visitor, Rodion Romanych," cried Porfiry Petrovich, laughing. "I've been meaning to drop by for some time. I thought I might just stop by for five minutes or so and see how things were. Going out somewhere? I won't keep you. I'll smoke just one little cigarette, if you don't mind."

"Do sit down, Porfiry Petrovich, do sit down," Raskolnikov seated his visitor with such an obviously pleased and friendly expression, he would have been surprised himself if he could have seen it. They were getting to the bottom of the barrel! There are times when a man, after having survived half an hour of mortal terror with a cutthroat, suddenly finds, with the knife finally touching his skin, that his terror has vanished. He sat down right in front of Porfiry and looked at him without blinking. Porfiry frowned, and started lighting a cigarette.

"Well, go on and speak! Speak!" seemed to want to spring from Raskolnikov's heart. "Well, why—why, why don't you speak?"

2

"Ah, these cigarettes!" Porfiry Petrovich said at last, having finished lighting up, and blowing out the smoke. "They're bad for you, really bad, but I can't give them up! I cough, my throat tickles, and I'm short of breath. I'm a coward, you know. I went to see a specialist the other day; he gives each patient at *least* half an hour's examination. When he looked at me he actually burst out laughing. He poked around and listened. 'By the way,' he says, 'tobacco's not good for you. Your lungs are distended.' Well, but how can I give it up? What would I replace it with? I don't drink, that's the trouble. He-he-he, the trouble is I don't drink! Everything's relative, Rodion Romanych, everything's relative!"

"What's he up to? Is this his old routine, or what?" Raskolnikov thought with disgust. Suddenly he recalled the whole recent scene of their last encounter, and the feeling he had had then came surging back.

"I came to see you the day before yesterday, though, in

the evening—didn't you know?" Porfiry went on, examining the room. "I came into this room, into this very room. I happened to be walking by, just like today, and I thought— come on, I'll pay him a little visit. I came up and the room was wide open; I looked around, waited—I didn't bother telling the maid—then I left. Don't you lock up?"

Raskolnikov's face clouded over more and more. Porfiry seemed to guess his thoughts.

"I came to have an explanation with you, my dear Rodion Romanych—yes, an explanation! I owe you an explanation," he went on with the flicker of a smile, and he even tapped Raskolnikov lightly on the knee, yet almost at the same instant his face assumed a serious and preoccupied expression; to Raskolnikov's amazement, there even seemed to be a certain sadness in it. He had never yet seen or even surmised the possibility of an expression like that on Porfiry's face. "A strange scene passed between us last time we met, Rodion Romanych. And I guess the scene of our first meeting was pretty strange, too; but then— Well, by now it's all one! Here's what: I may be very much to blame as far as you're concerned, and I do feel that. Do you remember how we parted company? Your nerves were screaming and your knees were knocking, and so were mine. And you know, it ended up kind of indecently between us, not like *gentlemen*. Still, we are *gentlemen*; that is, we are first and foremost *gentlemen*; need to remember that, yes. And you recall, don't you, it reached a point . . . that was positively indecent, wasn't it."

"What's he up to? Who does he take me for?" Raskolnikov asked himself with astonishment, lifting up his head and looking Porfiry straight in the eyes.

"I figured it would be better for us to deal openly with each other now," Porfiry went on, tilting his head back a little and lowering his eyes, as though he no longer wished to trouble his former victim with his look, and as though he were holding in contempt his former tricks and ruses. "No, scenes and suspicions of that sort can't go on for long. Mikolka settled matters for us then, or I don't know what might have happened between us. That damned artisan fellow was sitting there behind my partition—can you imagine it? Of course, you know all this; and I know he called on you afterward. But what you were supposing at the time was not true: I hadn't sent for anybody, nor had I made any arrangements as yet at the time. You may ask why I hadn't.

What can I say? I was a bit stunned myself at the time. I'd hardly arranged to send for the janitors. (I'm sure you noticed the janitors as you went by.) Then, quick as a flash, I had an idea. You see, even then, Rodion Romanych, I was firmly convinced. I thought, all right, I'll let one go for a while, but I'll grab the other by the tail. I won't let the one I want get far, not the one I want. I suppose that you are by nature quite irritable, Rodion Romanych—too much so, really, given the other basic qualities of your character and your heart, and I flatter myself in believing that I have managed to understand them to some degree. Well, of course, even a man like me could calculate that someone doesn't just get up and blurt out everything he's been hiding under his fingernails. If it happens, it's generally because you've brought him to the end of his endurance; but in any case it's rare. Even I could calculate that far. No, I thought, what I need is some little detail, just one merest crumb of a little detail—just one, but one I can really grab hold of. A solid fact, though; not just psychology in a vacuum. Because, I thought, if a man's guilty, you can certainly expect to get something substantial out of him, anyway; you can even count on the most unexpected results. That time I counted on your character, Rodion Romanych; most of all on your character! I relied on you a great deal at the time."

"But you . . . why do you talk this way?" Raskolnikov muttered at last, without even having thought the question through properly. He wondered: "What's he talking about? Can he really believe I'm innocent?"

"Why do I talk this way? You might say I came to have an explanation with you. I consider it my sacred duty. I want to go over everything with you—how it was, a full account of that whole dark episode, you might say. Rodion Romanych, I made you suffer a great deal. I am not a monster. I, too, understand, you know, what it's like for a man to drag all that around with him—a man who's depressed, but proud, imperious, and impatient. Especially impatient! Anyway, I believe you are the most decent kind of person; one who even has traces of magnanimity—though I don't agree with all your views, and I consider it my duty to tell you so in advance, frankly and quite sincerely, because, above all, I have no wish to deceive. Since I met you I have felt drawn to you. Perhaps you laugh? You have a right to. I know that from the first glance you didn't take to me, and essentially, why should you? But, take it anyway you like, I'd still like to correct that impression as best I can and show you that I'm human, too, and I have a heart and a conscience. I speak sincerely."

Porfiry Petrovich paused with dignity. Raskolnikov felt immersed in a new kind of fear. The idea that Porfiry might consider him innocent suddenly began to frighten him.

"I hardly need to tell you everything as it happened, in precise order," said Porfiry. "I think that would be superfluous. Anyway, I couldn't do it. How could it ever be explained in detail? First there were rumors. What kind, who started them, and when . . . and how you actually got involved in the case—I think that's all superfluous, too. As far as I am concerned personally, it began with an accident, a complete coincidence, which could just as easily not have happened. Which one? Hmm. That, too, I think, is hardly worth mentioning. Rumors and coincidences: everything combined into a single idea. I admit openly (once you start admitting things, you'd better admit everything), I was the first one to pounce on you at the time. Well, let's say it was the old woman's marks on all the pledged items, et cetera, et cetera—it's all rubbish, certainly. One could check off a hundred little tidbits of that sort. I also happened to learn about your little scene in the police station, quite by chance, but not just any old way—from a particularly fine storyteller, who, without realizing it, heightened the scene amazingly. It all added up to the same thing, yes, one and the same thing, Rodion Romanych, my boy! Well, how could I avoid taking that tack? A hundred rabbits don't make a horse, a hundred suspicions don't make a proof, as the English proverb says; and after all, that's only common sense—and yet, and yet, what about the passions, you still have to reckon with the passions, for your investigator's a man, too, after all, isn't he? Then I remembered that little essay of yours, in the journal—you recall, we talked about it in detail during your first visit. I jeered at you, but only to provoke you to go on. I repeat, you are very impatient, Rodion Romanych, and sick. You are bold and proud and serious, and you have been through a great deal, you've been through a great deal—I knew all that long ago. I am familiar with all these moods, and as I read it your little essay seemed quite familiar. It was thought out on sleepless nights and in a state of wild excitement, heart heaving and pounding, and with suppressed enthusiasm. It's dangerous, though—this proud, suppressed enthusiasm in a young man! I jeered at you at the time, but I'll tell you now that I'm terribly fond—I mean as an admirer—of this first, youthful, passionate experimenting with the pen. Smoke—mist—a chord sounds in the mist. Your essay's absurd and fantastic, but there's such a sincerity keeps flashing through it, such a youthful, incorruptible pride, such desperate boldness; and it's rather somber, your essay; well, but that's to the good, yes. I read that essay of yours and I put it aside, and . . . as I put it aside I thought: 'That man's heading for trouble!' So with a preliminary like that, tell me, how could I avoid getting carried away by what followed! But, of course, how could I say anything, how could I make any assertion? I merely took note of it at the time. Anything in it, I thought? Nothing, practically nothing, maybe nothing at all. And it isn't seemly for me, an investigator, to get carried away; yes, quite unseemly; and there's Mikolka to deal with, and he's got facts. Oh, yes, as many facts as you like! And he's even brought in his own psychology. I have to deal with it; it's a matter of life and death, after all. Why am I explaining all this to you now? Because I want you to know, so you won't blame me for my spiteful behavior that time. I tell you sincerely I was not being spiteful. Yes, he-he! You think I did not have your place searched at the time? I did. Yes, he-he, I did, while you were lying here sick in bed. Not personally, not officially; but I did, yes. Your apartment was examined down to the last little hair while the trail was still fresh, but—*umsonst*. Well, I thought: this man will come of his own accord, and he'll come quite soon. If he's guilty, he will certainly come. Somebody else might not, but this one will certainly come. Do you remember how Mr. Razumikhin started spilling the beans? That was planned, to get you worked up; we started a rumor on purpose so he would tell you, because Mr. Razumikhin isn't the man to restrain his indignation. Mr. Zamiotov was the first to be struck by your anger and your open daring. Well, I mean, suddenly blurting it out in a tavern—'I killed her!'—just like that! Too daring, yes, too bold; and if it should be he's guilty, I thought, then he's a hard fighter! That's what occurred to me at the time, yes. So I waited. I waited as hard as I could. After all, you simply squashed Zamiotov, and . . . the point is, you know, this damned psychology is double-edged and cuts both ways! Well, I waited. And lo and behold, God presents you—you come! My heart started pounding. Ah! Well, why did you come? And the way you laughed—your laughter on the way in—

remember? And I saw through you then as if I were looking through glass. Yet if I hadn't been waiting for you in such a special mood, I would not have noticed anything special about your laughter. That's what it means to be in a receptive mood. And Mr. Razumikhin at the time—and, ah, yes! the stone—the stone, you remember; the stone, yes; you know, the one you hid the things under? Well, I could picture it clearly in a back garden somewhere. You told Zamiotov it was in a back garden, didn't you? And you said so again in my presence? Then you started expounding your article to us that time; you began to interpret, and it seemed as if you were using every word in a double sense, as if each word had another word sitting underneath it! Well, you see, Rodion Romanych, that's how I came to the end of my road; I rammed my head into the barrier and came to my senses. I asked myself what I was doing. If you so desire, I told myself, you can explain it all down to the last detail from the opposite point of view, and it will make even more sense. It was sheer agony! No, I thought, I better get hold of some little detail! When they told me about all that bell-ringing I gasped, and a shudder ran through me. Now, there's a little detail for you, I thought! There it is! I didn't ponder it much at the time; I simply didn't want to. I would have given a thousand rubles of my very own money just to have been able to have seen you at that moment *with my own eyes*: how you walked a hundred paces beside that artisan fellow, how he called you 'murderer!' to your face, and how you walked a hundred steps without daring to ask him a question! Well, and what about that chill down the spine? And all the bell-ringing when you were sick and half delirious? Then how could it come as a surprise to you, Rodion Romanych, that I played with you the way I did at the time? Why did you come at that very moment? It does seem, doesn't it, as though somebody were pushing you from behind? It did, by God, and if Mikolka hadn't separated us . . . Remember Mikolka? Have you kept that little encounter in mind? It was a thunderbolt, wasn't it! Thunder crackling from a cloud—a bolt from the blue! And how did I react? I didn't believe in that bolt, not in the slightest—you could see for yourself! Not by a long shot! After you left, he answered some points very sensibly, and I really was surprised, but even then I didn't believe him two kopecks' worth! That's what they mean when they say hard as concrete. No, I thought, *morgen frueh*! Mikolka has nothing to do with it!"

"Razumikhin just told me you're in the process of accusing Nikolay now, and you've convinced Razumikhin . . ." His breath failed him, and he did not finish. He had listened in inexpressible alarm as the man who had seen right through him doubled back on himself. He was afraid to, and did not, believe it. In the continued ambiguity, he looked for and snatched at anything that might be more precise or conclusive.

"That Mr. Razumikhin!" Porfiry Petrovich exclaimed; he seemed to rejoice in the question the otherwise silent Raskolnikov had asked. "He-he-he! Yes, Mr. Razumikhin had to be decoyed off. Two's company, three's a crowd. Mr. Razumikhin is wrong; anyway, he is an outsider. He came running up to me white as a sheet. . . . Well, God bless him, let's let him go, he's got no business here! As for Mikolka, would you like to know what kind of person he is, at least as I understand him? First, he's immature, still a child; and not that he's a coward, but sensitive, a kind of artist type. Yes, really. You mustn't laugh at me for explaining him like that. He is innocent and completely impressionable. He has feelings; he is a fantast. He can sing and dance, and they say he can tell stories so people gather from all around to listen. And he'll go to school and he'll laugh himself silly because somebody somehow crooked a finger at him; and he'll drink himself senseless, not because he's a drunkard, but just every now and then, when people buy him drinks; he's like a child still. He went and stole that time, and didn't know it himself: if he picked it off the ground, where does stealing come in? Did you know he was a Raskolnik? Well, not a Raskolnik exactly, but a member of one of those religious sects. There were members of his family who were Runners; they'd "run" away from worldly involvement. He himself actually spent two years, not long ago, under the spiritual tutelage of some holy elder in some village. I learned all this from Mikolka and his Zaraisk friends. What's more, he himself was moved to run off into the wilderness! He had the spirit, would pray to God at night, read the old 'true' books and reread them, for hours on end. Petersburg had a powerful effect on him, especially liquor and women. He was impressionable, yes; and he forgot about the elder and all that. I know a certain artist here who took a great liking to him, and he used to go over to his place, but then this case came along! Well, he panicked—tried to hang himself, run away! What can be done about the notion the common people have of the law? Some find the mere word 'trial' terrifying. Who's to blame! Maybe the new courts will have some effect here—I hope to God they do! Well, now, in jail it seems he remembered the honorable elder, and the Bible turned up again, too. Do you know what they mean, Rodion Romanych, when they talk of taking suffering upon themselves? They don't mean suffering for anybody in particular, just 'got to go do some suffering'! That means, *accept* suffering; and if it's from the authorities, so much the better. Once I remember one of the meekest prisoners doing time, a whole year in jail, and he read the Bible all the way through, lying on the stove nights; he read it and he reread it, and, you know, one day, for no reason at all, he picked up a brick and heaved it at the warden. The warden hadn't done him any wrong, mind you. And the way he heaved it, too! He deliberately missed by a yard, so nobody would get hurt! Well, you know what happens to a prisoner who assaults an official; so he 'took suffering upon himself'! And so that's what I suspect now, you see, that Mikolka wants to 'take suffering upon himself,' or something like that. Actually, I know it even from the facts, yes. He just doesn't know that I know. You mean you won't admit that our people produce fantastic characters of this sort? Yes, many. Now the elder is beginning to have some effect again, especially after that business with the noose. Anyway, he'll come around and tell me everything himself. You think he'll hold out? Wait! He'll deny it yet! From hour to hour I expect him to come and retract his testimony. I've grown quite fond of this Mikolka, and I'm studying him carefully. You know, he-he! he replied quite cleverly to some points. He'd obviously latched onto the information he needed and prepared himself with some skill. But on other points he was completely at sea—didn't know a blessed thing, never heard of it; and he himself doesn't even have an inkling that he never heard of it! No, Rodion Romanych, old man, it wasn't Mikolka! This is a fantastic, a somber case—contemporary, an incident of our time, yes, when the heart of man has grown dark; when you hear people cite the phrase, 'blood refreshes'; when the whole meaning of life is expounded in terms of comfort. Here we have bookish dreams, yes, and a heart troubled by theories; here we discern a determination to make a first step, determination of a special sort, though. This fellow made up his mind, all right, but then it was as though he'd fallen from a mountain or dropped from a steeple, as though he had not walked to the crime on his own two feet. He forgot to close the door behind him, yet he killed—killed two people—to prove a theory. He killed, but as for stealing money, he wasn't up to it; and whatever he did manage to grab, he stashed away under a stone. The torment he suffered crouching behind the door, with the doorbell ringing, and the pounding at the door, wasn't enough for him. No, he had to come back later to the empty apartment, half delirious, to hear once again the sound of that bell, and experience that chill running down his spine. . . . Well, all right, let's suppose he was sick, but what about this: he committed murder, yet continues to consider himself an honorable man; he looks down on people and walks around like a pallid angel. . . . No, Rodion Romanych, old boy, this has nothing to do with Mikolka—no Mikolka here!" These last words, after all that had been said, and so much like a disavowal, were entirely too unexpected. Raskolnikov quivered all over, as though he had been transfixed.

"So, then . . . who . . . killed . . .?" he asked in a gasping voice, unable to hold out longer. Porfiry Petrovich rolled back in his chair, almost as though he were taken by surprise and astonished at the question.

"What do you mean, who killed?" he asked as though he could not believe his own ears. "Why, Rodion Romanych, *you* killed! You committed the murders, yes," he added almost in a whisper, in a completely convinced tone of voice.

Raskolnikov leaped up from the couch, stood there for a few seconds, and sat down again without saying a word. Suddenly his whole face began to twitch in faint spasms.

"Your lip's quivering again, just like last time," Porfiry Petrovich murmured, almost as though in sympathy. After some silence, he added: "It would seem, Rodion Romanych, that you haven't understood me quite correctly, and that is why you are so amazed. I really did come to tell you everything and bring the case out into the open."

"I didn't do it," Raskolnikov whispered, as frightened little children do when they are caught at the scene of the crime.

"No, it was you, Rodion Romanych; it was you, all right; you and nobody else," Porfiry whispered sternly and confidently.

They both fell silent, and their silence lasted for a weirdly long time, for about ten minutes. Raskolnikov leaned his elbows on the table and kept running his fingers through his hair. Porfiry Petrovich sat quietly and waited. Suddenly Raskolnikov looked at Porfiry with contempt.

"You're up to your old tricks again, Porfiry Petrovich! Still the same old ways. How come you don't get sick of them?"

"Oh, stop that! What are tricks to me now? It might be different if there were witnesses here; but we are alone, whispering only to each other. You can see for yourself I didn't come to hunt you down and catch you like a rabbit. Whether you confess or not—it's all the same to me at this moment. I'm convinced in my own mind, no matter what you say."

"Why did you come here, then?" Raskolnikov asked irritably. "I will ask you my former question: if you consider me guilty, why don't you haul me off to jail?"

"Well, there's a question for you! I'll answer point by point. First, it's not to my advantage to arrest you straight off like that."

"What do you mean, not to your advantage! If you're convinced, it's your duty—"

"Come, now, what if I am convinced? For the time being these are just my dreams. Why should I arrest you? So you can have a *respite*? You know yourself, since you ask. Should I, for instance, bring that artisan fellow in to confront you? Well, you'd say to him: 'Were you drunk, or weren't you? Who saw me with you? I simply took you for drunk, and you really were drunk.' What would I say to you then, especially since your line's more plausible than his; the only thing in his evidence is psychology—and given his looks that's even unseemly—and you would have hit the nail on the head, because he does drink, the bastard, he's a terrible drunkard and only too well known for it. I've already told you myself quite frankly, several times now, that this psychology business is double-edged, and that second edge will cut sharper and seem much more plausible, and so far that's all I have on you. I am going to arrest you, anyway, and I even came here myself (quite against the rules) to let you know in advance (also against the rules) it won't be to my advantage. But in the second place, I came to you because . . ."

"In the second place, yes?" Raskolnikov was still out of breath.

"Because, as I told you just now, I believe I owe you an explanation. I don't want you to take me for a monster, especially since I am sincerely well disposed to you, whether you believe it or not. So, in the third place, I came to make a frank and open proposal: give yourself up and confess. This would have more advantages for you than you can count; and for me, too, because it will be off my back. Well, have I spoken frankly with you, or haven't I?"

Raskolnikov thought for a minute. "Listen, Porfiry Petrovich, you said yourself, didn't you, that all you have to go on is psychology, and yet you've passed over into mathematics. What if you're making a mistake yourself now?"

"No, Rodion Romanych, I'm not making a mistake. I have one little clue. Yes, I discovered this little clue a while ago; the Lord sent it."

"What little clue?"

"I am not going to tell you, Rodion Romanych. Anyway, I don't have the right to put it off any longer. I'm going to arrest you. So you figure it out: by *now* it's all the same to me. So it must be for your sake alone. I swear to God it would be better, Rodion Romanych!"

Raskolnikov smiled maliciously. "That's not only funny, you know, it's even shameless. Suppose I were guilty (mind you, I'm not saying I am!), what would be the point of my giving myself up and confessing, when you say yourself I'd just be going to jail *for a respite*?"

"Ah, Rodion Romanych, you fasten on words too literally; maybe it wouldn't be quite altogether *for a respite*! It's only a theory, after all, and mine at that, and how much of an authority do you take me for? Maybe I'm hiding something from you even now. I'm not supposed to lay all my cards on the table, am I? He-he. The second matter, as to what advantage it would be? Surely you know the kind of reduction you'd get in your sentence? Think of the time you'd be giving yourself up! Figure it out for yourself. Just as another man has confessed and confused the whole case. And I swear to you before God himself I'll fix it up for you and arrange things *there* so your confession will come as a complete surprise. We'll junk the psychology business, and I'll bring all the suspicions against you to nothing, so your crime will appear as a kind of lapse; because, in all conscience, a lapse is what it was. I am an honest man, Rodion Romanych; I will keep my word."

Raskolnikov maintained a sad silence and hung his head. He thought for a long time, and at last he smiled again, but this time his smile was meek and sad. "Eh, I don't want it!"

he said, as though he were coming out entirely into the open with Porfiry. "It's not worth it! I don't want your reduction of sentence!"

"That's just what I was afraid of!" Porfiry exclaimed hotly and as though involuntarily. "Just what I was afraid of—that you wouldn't want our reduction of sentence."

Raskolnikov gazed at him sadly and solemnly.

"Ah, don't despise life!" Porfiry went on. "You have a lot of it still ahead of you. How can you say you don't want a reduction of sentence? How can you not want it! You're an impatient man!"

"What did you say, that I had a lot of ahead of me?"

"Life! Are you a prophet, or what? How much do you know? 'Seek and ye shall find.' Perhaps there is God's hand in this. And it's not forever, you know—the chains. . . ."

"Reduction of sentence . . ." Raskolnikov laughed.

"Well, is it the bourgeois disgrace that scares you, or what? Maybe you don't know yourself what you're scared of; you're young, after all! Whatever it is, you should not be scared or ashamed of giving yourself up and confessing."

"Oh, to he-ell!" Raskolnikov whispered with contempt and disgust, as though he did not even wish to speak. He started getting up again, as if he wanted to go out somewhere, but then he sat down in evident despair.

"To hell, is it, eh! You've lost confidence in yourself, so you think I'm flattering you grossly. Have you really lived so long, though? Do you really know so much? You invented a theory; now you're ashamed because it went wrong, because it turned out to be not so original after all! True, it turned out to be pretty low-down, but it still doesn't mean you're such a hopeless villain. You're no villain! At least you didn't deceive yourself for long; you traveled straight to the end of the road. You want to know the kind of man I think you are? I think you're the kind of man who would stand there and smile at his torturers while they were tearing out his guts—if only he could find faith or a god. Well, find one and you'll live. First of all, you've been needing a change of air for some time. Why not? Suffering is also a good thing. Go and suffer. Mikolka might have been right, you know, to want suffering. I know it's hard to believe, but give yourself up to life directly, without sophistry; don't puzzle over it. Don't worry. It will carry you straight to shore and set you on your feet. What shore? How should I know! I only believe you still have a lot for which to live. I know you take my words as a prepared sermon of some sort; but maybe you'll remember them later, and the memory might come in handy. That's why I'm talking. After all, it's lucky you only killed an old woman. If you had thought up some other theory, you might have done something a hundred million times more awful! You still have something for which to thank God. And you know, maybe God is saving you for something. So buck up, and be a little less afraid. Are you frightened at the great task that stands before you? No, it would be shameful to be afraid of that. Since you've taken the step you've taken, brace yourself. That's justice. Do what justice demands. I know you don't believe it—but, by God, life will sustain you. Later you'll accept yourself again. Air is what you need now—air, air!"

Raskolnikov gave a start.

"And who are you?" he exclaimed. "What kind of prophet are you? From the height of what majestic tranquility do you utter these oracular prophecies?"

"Who am I? I am a man who has been used up, that's all. If you like, I am a man who's been around and has some feeling and knows a thing or two, but who's been all used up. But you—that's another story. God has prepared a life for you. Yet who knows? Maybe yours, too, will only pass like smoke, will come to nothing. Well, what is it? That you'll be passing over to a different class of people? Not the comfort you'll be missing, is it? A man with a heart like yours? Would it be that nobody will see you for a long, long time? But it's not a matter of time, it's a matter of you yourself. Rise like the sun, and everyone will see you. First and foremost, the sun has got to be the sun. Smiling again? Because I'm such a Schiller? I bet you even think I'm trying to put one over on you! Well, maybe I really am, he-he-he! Maybe you shouldn't take my word, Rodion Romanych, maybe you shouldn't ever quite believe me. I agree, that's really the way I am. I'd just like to add this. The extent to which I'm a low-down character, and the extent to which I'm honest—I should think you could judge for yourself!"

"When do you think you'll arrest me?"

"Well, I guess I can let you wander around for a day or two yet. Think it over, my friend, and pray to God. I swear to God you'd be better off."

"What if I run away?" Raskolnikov asked, smiling rather strangely.

"You won't run away. A peasant would. A fashionable

progressive would—the lackey of someone else's idea—all you have to do is show him the tip of your finger, and like that character in Gogol's play, he'll believe anything you wish for the rest of his life. You don't believe in your theory anymore, though, do you? What would sustain you if you ran away? What would you do on the run? It's rough and nasty on the run; what you need above all else is life and a definite position, and air to go with it—and, I ask you, would that do for air? If you run away, you'll come back on your own. *You can't get along without us.* Even if I locked you in a cell—well, you'd sit there a month or two or three; then you'd suddenly remember my words, and you'd come forward yourself; maybe it would even come as a surprise to you. An hour before you wouldn't even know you were going to confess. I tell you I'm even convinced you would 'bring yourself to accept suffering.' You don't have to take my word for it now, but dwell on it. Suffering is a great thing, Rodion Romanych; don't be blinded by the fact that I've grown fat, because I know—don't laugh—there is an idea in suffering. Mikolka's right, you know. No, Rodion Romanych, you won't run away."

Raskolnikov rose from his seat and picked up his cap. Porfiry Petrovich rose also. "Going for a walk? Looks like a fine evening if we don't have a thunderstorm. That would be better, though, if it cleared the air. . . ."

He picked up his cap, too.

"Porfiry Petrovich, you mustn't, please, take it into your head I confessed to you today," said Raskolnikov, grimly obstinate. "You're a strange man, and I listened to you only because I was curious. But I haven't confessed anything to you. . . . Remember that."

"Well, I reckon I'll remember. Why, just look at him—he's trembling. Don't worry, my boy, have it your way. Go for a little walk, but don't stroll too far. I still have one small request to make of you," he added, lowering his voice. "It's a bit ticklish, but important. If—I mean, just in case—I don't believe you would, mind you; I think you're quite incapable of it—but in case, well, I mean—in case it should occur to you within the next forty or fifty hours to end things differently, in some fantastic kind of way—sort of lay hands on yourself—an absurd proposition, I am sure you will forgive me—well, what I mean is—leave a brief but circumstantial note. A couple of lines, that's all—just a couple of lines—and refer to that stone. It would be nicer. Well, sir, good-bye . . . I wish you pleasant thoughts and good beginnings!"

Porfiry left. He looked weary, somehow, and seemed to avoid looking at Raskolnikov, who went to the window and waited with irritated impatience for Porfiry to emerge onto the street and walk on out of sight. Then he himself hastily left the room.

3

He hurried to Svidrigailov's. He himself did not know what it was he could hope for from this man. Yet the man had a kind of mysterious power over him. Once aware of this, he could not rest. And anyway, the time had come.

On the way he was worried by one question in particular. Had Svidrigailov been to see Porfiry? As far as he could tell (and he would have sworn to it), he had not. He went over everything, recalled Porfiry's entire visit, and decided: no, he had not. Of course he hadn't. But even if he hadn't yet been—would he go?

He believed he would not go for the time being. Why? He could not explain that, either. Even if it had been possible, he would not have racked his brains over it now. It all tormented him, and yet it was not primarily what was on his mind. A strange business—perhaps nobody would believe it—but he was worried only a little, and sporadically, by his immediate fate. It was something different that bothered him, something far more important, far more extraordinary; it concerned nobody but him, but it was the most important thing. In addition, he felt an immeasurable moral weariness, although his reasoning faculty was working better that morning than it had all these past days.

After everything that had happened, was it worthwhile trying to win out against all these new miserable obstacles? Was it worthwhile plotting to prevent Svidrigailov from going to Porfiry? To study, to pry into, to lose time over the likes of Svidrigailov? Oh, how sick he was of it all!

Nevertheless, he hurried to Svidrigailov's. Wasn't he expecting something *new* from him—a sign, a way out? People clutch even at straws! Was it not fate, was it not some kind of instinct that was bringing them together? Maybe it was only weariness, desperation. Maybe he didn't want Svidrigailov, but somebody else; only it was Svidrigailov who happened to have turned up. Sonia? Well, what would he go to Sonia for now? To implore her tears again? Sonia appalled him, anyway. Sonia represented an implacable verdict, an irreversible decision. It was either her way or Svidrigailov's. At the moment especially, he was in no shape to see her. No, it was better to try Svidrigailov, wasn't it? What was he up to? Within himself he could not help realizing that he really had needed Svidrigailov for some reason for a long time.

But what could they have in common? The evil they had done could not have been the same. What's more, the man was quite unpleasant; obviously, he was unusually depraved, undoubtedly sly and treacherous, perhaps quite evil. There were strange stories about him. True, he had done something for Katherine Ivanovna's children; but who knew for what purpose or what it meant? He had all kinds of strange projects and intentions.

There was another idea that glimmered steadily in Raskolnikov's mind of late, and it disturbed him terribly. It disturbed him so much, he tried to drive it away. Svidrigailov, he thought, had been hovering around him, and still hovered; Svidrigailov had learned his secret; Svidrigailov had once had designs on Dunia. Suppose he still had them? And he almost certainly still did. Since he had learned the secret, suppose he decided to use it as a weapon against Dunia? The thought tormented him sometimes, even in his sleep. Now that he was on his way to Svidrigailov's, however, it struck him consciously, for the first time, with a stark clarity. The very idea provoked in him a somber rage. First it changed everything, even his own position. It meant he would have to reveal his secret to Dunia at once. It meant that to divert Dunia from some possible rash step, he might have to give himself up. The letter? That very morning Dunia had received a letter! Whom did she know in Petersburg who would write her? Luzhin? True, Razumikhin was keeping an eye out, but Razumikhin didn't know anything. Should he tell Razumikhin? Raskolnikov was repelled at the thought.

He made up his mind that in any case he had to see Svidrigailov as soon as he could and get it over with. Here, thank God, he didn't have to worry about particulars so much as the heart of the matter. If Svidrigailov turned out

to be plotting something against Dunia, then if only he could
be strong enough to . . .

During this entire past month, Raskolnikov had grown so
weary he could resolve such problems only in one way. "To
kill him," he thought in chill despair. Inside he felt heavy
and oppressed. He stopped in the middle of the street to
see where he was and which way he was going. He was on
Obukhovsky Prospect, about thirty or forty steps from the
Haymarket, which he had just passed. The whole second
floor of the house on his left was a tavern. Its windows were
all wide open, and judging by the figures moving about in
the windows, it was packed. There was singing in the main
hall, a clarinet, a violin, and somebody beating a Turkish
drum. And the shrill voices of women. He wanted to go
back. He could not think why he had turned onto Obukhovsky Prospect. Then, suddenly, he saw Svidrigailov, who was
sitting by a wide-open window, behind a tea table, with a
pipe clenched in his teeth. Raskolnikov was surprised to the
point of shock. Svidrigailov was looking him over silently,
observing him; and it struck Raskolnikov immediately that
Svidrigailov seemed to want to get up and sneak away before Raskolnikov noticed him. Raskolnikov pretended he
had not noticed him, and looked off in another direction
while actually continuing to observe him out of the corner
of his eye. His heart beat anxiously. Svidrigailov obviously
did not want to be seen. He removed the pipe from his
mouth and evidently wanted to leave; but as he moved his
chair back and rose he probably realized suddenly that
Raskolnikov had seen him and was watching. There was an
encounter that resembled the scene of their first meeting,
when Raskolnikov had been asleep. Svidrigailov's face broke
into a roguish smile, which spread and spread. Each was
aware the other was observing him. Finally Svidrigailov
burst into a loud laugh.

"Well, here I am!" he yelled from the window. "Come
on in if you want!"

Raskolnikov went up to the tavern. He found Svidrigailov
in a very small back room, which had a single window. It
was just off the main hall, where merchants, officials, and a
motley crowd sat drinking tea at twenty small tables, accompanied by the bellowing of a desperate male choir. From
somewhere came the click of billiard balls. On the table
before Svidrigailov stood an opened bottle of champagne
and a half-full glass. Also in the room were a young boy

with an accordion and a robust, red-cheeked girl of eighteen in a tucked-up striped skirt and a ribboned Tyrolean hat, a singer, who in spite of the chorus going full blast next door was singing some vulgar song in a rather hoarse contralto accompanied by the accordion. As Raskolnikov came in Svidrigailov interrupted her: "Well, that's enough!"

The girl cut short her singing at once and stood there with a kind of dignified attentiveness. Her cheap little song, too, she had sung with a solemn and dignified expression on her face.

"Hey, Phillip, a glass!" Svidrigailov shouted.

"I won't drink any wine," Raskolnikov said.

"As you like. It wasn't for you. Katia, have a drink! That's all for today—run along!" He poured her a full glass of wine and pulled out a yellowish bill. Katia drank it up at once the way women drink wine, in twenty short swallows but without stopping. She took the bill, kissed Svidrigailov's hand, which, quite solemnly, he allowed her to kiss, and left the room. The boy with the accordion followed her. Svidrigailov had called them both in from the street. He had scarcely been living in Petersburg a week, yet everything around him seemed to be on some sort of patriarchal footing. By now the tavern waiter Phillip was also "an old pal" and made up to him. They shut the door to the main hall. Svidrigailov seemed at home in this room, and possibly he spent days on end there. The tavern was dirty, filthy, not even second-rate.

"I was on my way to your place. I was looking for you," Raskolnikov began, "but for some reason I turned off the Haymarket Square onto Obukhovsky! I never turn off there or come this way. From the Haymarket I usually turn to the right. This isn't even the way to your place. It so happened I turned, and there you were! Strange!"

"Why don't you say it right out: it is a miracle!"

"It might just have been a coincidence!"

"What a mentality these people have!" Svidrigailov laughed. "Even if they believed in a miracle they would not admit it! As you said, it 'might' just have been a coincidence! Ah, when it comes to voicing what their own opinions really are, what sniveling little cowards they all turn out to be, Rodion Romanych, you simply can't imagine! Of course, I don't speak about you. You have your own opinion and you're not afraid of it. That is how you captivated my curiosity."

"No more than that?"

"Why, I should think that enough." Svidrigailov was apparently in a state of exhilaration, but only a little. He had drunk no more than half a glass of wine.

"I think you came to see me before you discovered I was capable of having what you call 'my own opinion,'" Raskolnikov noted.

"Well, that was different then. We each have our own ways. But as far as the miracle is concerned, you would seem to have been dozing off lately. I told you about this tavern myself. Your coming here was no miracle. I told you where it was. I showed you how to get here, and I even told you when you might expect to find me here. Don't you remember?"

"I forgot," Raskolnikov answered in surprise.

"I believe so. I told you twice. The location would seem to have registered automatically in your memory. You turned this way automatically and came here without knowing what you were doing. When I told you, you know, I didn't think you'd understood. You betray yourself easily, Rodion Romanych. And what is more, I'm convinced lots of people in Petersburg go around talking to themselves. It's a city of the half insane. If we had such a thing as scholarship, our doctors, jurists, and philosophers might contribute the most valuable studies dealing with Petersburg, each in his own profession. Not many places bring to bear such gloomy, harsh, and strange influences on the spirit of man as Petersburg. Just think of the climate alone! And it's the administrative center of all Russia, so its character is imprinted on everything! Still, that's not the business at hand. But you know, I've caught sight of you several times when you didn't know I was watching. As you leave your house, you hold your head straight. Twenty paces, and you lower it. You put your hands behind your back. You look, but it's obvious you don't see anything, either straight ahead or to the sides. Then your lips start to move and you're talking to yourself. Once in a while one of your hands goes out in a speechifying gesture. Then, for a long time, you just stand still in the middle of the road. That really won't do at all. Somebody besides myself might notice you, and that would not be to your advantage. To me it's essentially all one; I won't try to cure you; but you know what I mean."

"Yet you're sure they're following me?" Raskolnikov asked, giving him a searching glance.

"No, I'm not sure of anything," replied Svidrigailov, as though surprised.

"Well, then, suppose we leave me out of it," Raskolnikov muttered, frowning.

"All right, suppose we leave you out of it."

"I'd rather you told me why—since you come here to drink and since you told me twice I could find you here—why, when I stood in the street and looked through the window just now, you jumped up and wanted to leave? I noticed that quite distinctly."

"He-he! And why, when I was standing in your doorway that time, why did you lie on your couch with your eyes closed pretending to be asleep, when you weren't asleep at all? I noticed that quite distinctly."

"I might have had . . . my reasons . . . you know that yourself."

"I might have had my reasons, too; though you will never know them."

With his right elbow on the table, Raskolnikov leaned his chin on the fingers of his right hand and stared intently at Svidrigailov. For a minute he examined the face that had struck him even before as remarkable. It was a strange face, rather like a mask, white and ruddy, with ruddy scarlet lips and a light blond beard and still fairly thick blond hair. The eyes were somehow too blue, and their gaze too ponderous and immobile. There was something terribly unpleasant about this handsome and unusually well-preserved face. Svidrigailov's clothes were summery, colorful, and light; his shirt was especially colorful. On his finger he wore a huge ring, set with an expensive stone.

Suddenly, coming straight out into the open with trembling impatience, Raskolnikov said: "Now I suppose I have to deal with you, too! If you want to hurt somebody you may well be the most dangerous man in the world, but for my part I don't want it tormenting me any longer. I want to show you directly that I don't set as high a store on my skin as you probably think. You know, I came to tell you to your face that if you're still nursing any of your former intentions concerning my sister and you plan to make use of something you've discovered recently, I will kill you before you can have me locked up. I give you my word of honor. You know I'm capable of keeping it. Secondly, if there's anything you want to tell me—because all this time I've had the feeling there was something you wanted to say to me—out with it quickly! Because time is valuable. Maybe, even quite soon, it will be too late."

"Where is it you're off to in such a hurry?" Svidrigailov asked, looking at him curiously.

"Each of us has his ways," said Raskolnikov sullenly and impatiently.

"You're the one who challenged me to be frank just now, but the first question I ask, you refuse to answer," Svidrigailov noted with a smile. "It looks as if you think I've had ulterior motives all along, so you're suspicious. Well, that's quite understandable, given your position. As much as I would like to get along with you, I wouldn't presume to try to convince you of the contrary. By God, the game is not worth the candle! Besides, there wasn't anything special I wanted to talk to you about."

"Then what did you want? Why were you always hanging around?"

"Why, you were simply an interesting subject for observation. The fantastic nature of your position rather appealed to me—that's all there was to it! Besides, you're the brother of somebody who was of some interest to me, and there was a time when I frequently heard a lot about you from this very person. So I came to the conclusion you have a great deal of influence on her. Isn't that enough? He-he-he! Still, I must admit, your question is complicated, and I find it difficult to answer. Well, for instance, it wasn't exactly on business you came to see me now, was it, but to find out something new? Isn't it so? Isn't it?" Svidrigailov insisted with his roguish smile. "Well, now, just imagine, on my way to Petersburg, on the train, I was counting on *you* to tell me something a bit new, so I might be able to borrow a little something from you. You see how rich we are!"

"Borrow what?"

"How shall I explain? Do I even know? You see the kind of place I spend my time in. I enjoy it. I mean not so much that I enjoy it, but one has to sit somewhere. Well, take poor Katia, now—you saw her? Of course, if I were a glutton or a club gourmet or something . . . but, you know, this is all I can eat!" He pointed a finger at the small corner table on which there were the remains of a horrible beefsteak and a potato on a metal plate. "Have you eaten, by the way? I've had a bite and don't want anymore. I don't drink liquor at all, for instance. Nothing but champagne. Even champagne—just one glass an evening, and it gives me a headache at that. I ordered this one to help me pull myself together, because I'm getting ready to go somewhere and you see me in a very special mood. That's why I jumped up like a school-boy a little while ago, because I thought you'd hinder me. But I think"—he drew out his watch—"I could spend an hour with you. It's half past four now. If there were only something I could be, you know: well, a landowner, say, or a father, or a cavalry officer, or a photographer, or a journalist . . . but there's nothing, no profession! Sometimes it even gets tedious. Really, I thought you might tell me something a little new."

"But what kind of man are you, and why did you come here?"

"What kind of man am I? But you know. I'm of the gentry class. I served two years in the cavalry, then I knocked around here in Petersburg, then I married Martha Petrovna and lived in the country. That's my biography!"

"It seems you're a gambler?"

"No. What kind of gambler would I be? A swindler is not a gambler."

"So you were a swindler?"

"Yes, I was a swindler."

"What happened? Did you get beaten up?"

"Sometimes. So?"

"Well, you might have challenged them to a duel . . . that often livens things up."

"I won't contradict you, and I don't mind telling you I'm not good at rationalization. I must admit I came here as quick as I could, mostly on account of the women."

"So soon after you buried Martha Petrovna?"

"Well, yes." Svidrigailov smiled with winning frankness. "And so? It seems you find something bad in the way I talk about women?"

"You mean, do I find something bad in depravity?"

"In depravity! Oh, so that's our tack, is it? Still, one thing at a time. First I'll answer you about women in general. I'm in the mood to talk. Tell me, why should I hold myself back? Why should I give up women, if that's the way I'm inclined? At least it's an occupation."

"Depravity's all you hope for here, then?"

"Well, and what if it is depravity! You have depravity on the brain. But I like a straight question, anyway. At least in this depravity there's something you can count on, even something basic and natural—not subject to fantasy—something that's there, like a constant red-hot needle in the blood, always setting it on fire, something that will go on for a long time, not so easily quenched, perhaps not even with the years. . . . Surely it's an occupation of sorts. Don't you agree?"

"Why so gay? It's a disease, and a dangerous one."

"What do you mean? That it's a disease, I agree—like everything that exceeds measure; and here you inevitably transgress all measure. Still, it's different for different people. That's number one. Number two: of course, you have to keep to measure in everything; calculation, even if it's vile; what can we do about it? If you're not like that, it's quite likely you might very well have to go and shoot yourself. A decent, respectable man is obliged to be bored, I agree; and yet, you know—"

"But you—could you shoot yourself?"

"Oh, come, come!" Svidrigailov parried the question in disgust. He added hastily: "Do me a favor—don't talk about that." He said this without any of the brassy fanfare of his previous words; even his face seemed to change. "I confess it is an unforgivable weakness—but what can I do? I am afraid of death, and I don't like hearing it talked about. Did you know I was a mystic of sorts?"

"Ah! Martha Petrovna's ghost! Does that mean it still appears?"

"Don't talk about it. It hasn't appeared in Petersburg. To hell with it!" he exclaimed, rather irritated. "No, we had better talk about . . . yes, well . . . Hmm! There isn't much time. I can't stay with you long. It's a pity! There might have been something to communicate."

"What's on your mind—a woman?"

"Yes, a woman; something that came up by mere coincidence . . . but it's not what I wanted to talk about."

"Well, but the loathsomeness of this whole business— hasn't it had any effect on you yet? Have you lost the strength to stop?"

"So you pretend to have strength, do you? He-he-he! Just now you really surprised me, Rodion Romanych. Of course, I knew you would beforehand. And you presume to lecture me, do you, on depravity and esthetics! What a Schiller you are! What an idealist! Of course, it's all as it should be— surprising if it were different—yet even so, it does seem strange. . . . Ah, it's a pity there isn't time, because you're such an absolutely fascinating subject! Do you like Schiller, by the way? I'm terribly fond of him."

"What a cheap braggart you are!" said Raskolnikov with a certain disgust.

"No, I swear to God I'm not!" Svidrigailov replied, laughing, "but I won't argue. Let me be a cheap braggart. Why not brag a little—there's no harm in it. For seven years I lived in the country at Martha Petrovna's; so when I run into an intelligent man like you—intelligent, and in the highest degree interesting—I'm only too glad to natter away. What's more, I drank this half glass of champagne and it's already gone to my head a little bit. The main point is, there is one thing I am all worked up about, but about that I'm going to . . . keep quiet. But where you going?" Svidrigailov asked, suddenly alarmed.

Raskolnikov had started to get up. He was beginning to feel oppressed and stifled and a bit awkward about having come here. He was convinced Svidrigailov was the emptiest and most worthless scoundrel in the world.

"E-eh! Sit down, stay awhile," Svidrigailov pleaded. "Ask them to bring you some tea. Do sit down. I won't jabber any more nonsense—about myself, I mean. Well, now, if you like—I'll tell you something. How a woman 'saved' me, if I may use your idiom. It will even be an answer to your first question, because this person is your sister. May I tell you? We'll kill some time that way."

"Go ahead, but I hope you—"

"Oh, don't worry! Even in a nasty, empty man like me, Avdotia Romanovna can inspire only the very deepest respect."

4

"You might know—I think I actually told you myself," Svidrigailov began, "I once served a term in the debtors' prison here for a huge sum, and without the slightest means or prospect of paying it. There is no point in going into the details of how Martha Petrovna bailed me out. I'm sure you know to what degree of stupefaction a woman can sometimes fall in love? She was an honest woman, not stupid by any means, but completely uneducated. Now, would you believe it: this extremely jealous and honest woman, after a number of terrible outbursts and reproaches, decided to lower herself and make a kind of bargain with me, which she kept all the time we were married. The point is, she was considerably older than me and always went around with a clove in her mouth. I was brutal enough and honest enough in my own way to tell her frankly I could not be completely faithful to her. This acknowledgment drove her frantic, and yet my coarse frankness seemed in some way to please her, too. 'If he tells me in advance,' she must have thought, 'he must not really want to fool me.' Well, you know, that's the first thing for a jealous woman. So after floods of tears we arrived at a kind of oral compact: first, that I would never leave Martha Petrovna and always remain her husband; second, that I would never go anywhere without her permission; third, that I would never take a permanent mistress; fourth, that in return for all this Martha Petrovna would allow me to have my pick of the maids from time to time, but only if she were privately informed; fifth, that God forbid I should ever fall in love with a woman of our own class; sixth, if it should happen, which God forbid, that I should be visited by any kind of grand and solemn passion, then I was obliged to reveal same to Martha Petrovna. On this last point, though, Martha Petrovna seemed fairly relaxed. She was an intelligent woman and could not regard me as anything but a skirt-chaser and debauchee, not so constructed as to fall in love. But you know, an intelligent woman and a jealous woman are two different matters—that was precisely the rub. And yet there are some people, you know—in order to judge them impartially, you must first renounce a number of the a priori views and the habitual attitudes we normally hold concerning the people and things that commonly surround us. I've a right to expect something from your judgment, more than from anyone else's. You may already have heard a great deal about Martha Petrovna that was ridiculous and absurd. She really did have some very foolish habits. But I tell you frankly—I sincerely regret those innumerable sorrows of hers of which I was the cause. I suppose that's enough—a very seemly *oraison funèbre* to the tenderest of wives from the tenderest of husbands. When we happened to quarrel I would keep silent for the most part and would not get irritated, and this gentlemanliness on my part almost always achieved its aim. It had an effect on her and even pleased her. There were times she was even proud of me. But she couldn't bear that sister of yours. How

she ever brought herself to risk taking such a beauty into
the house as governess is beyond me! I explain it by the
fact that Martha Petrovna was an impulsive and susceptible
woman and that she fell in love with your sister herself—
literally fell in love with her. Ah, that Avdotia Romanovna—
well, you know! At first glance I understood perfectly well
this was a bad business, and (what do you think?) I decided
I wouldn't even look at her. Believe it or not—she took the
first step herself. And would you believe that Martha Petrovna even went so far as to get angry with me at first for
my perpetual silence on the subject of your sister and for
my seeming indifference to her perpetual infatuated outbursts on that subject? I don't understand myself what she
wanted. Well, of course, Martha Petrovna went and told
Avdotia Romanovna all about the dirt under my fingernails.
She had the unfortunate habit of telling absolutely everybody all our family secrets and of complaining about me
incessantly to everybody. And so how could she overlook
such a fine new friend? I suppose I was their sole subject
of conversation, and no doubt Avdotia Romanovna learned
of all those dark, mysterious tales people associate with
me. . . . I'd be willing to bet you've heard them, too?"

"Yes, I have. Luzhin even accused you of causing the
death of a child. Is it true?"

"Please do me a favor; let these vulgarities rest in peace,"
Svidrigailov said morosely and with disgust. "If you insist
on hearing all that nonsense, I'll tell you about it specially
sometime; but now—"

"He mentioned some valet of yours in the country, that
you had a hand in that, too."

"Please do me the favor—enough!" Svidrigailov interrupted, again with obvious impatience.

"Wasn't that the same valet who came to you after he
died to fill your pipe? You told me about him yourself."
Raskolnikov grew more and more irritable.

Svidrigailov looked hard at Raskolnikov, who thought for
a moment he saw a malicious sneer flash in that look, yet
Svidrigailov restrained himself and answered very politely:
"Yes, that was the one. I can see you're quite interested in
all this. I shall consider it my duty, at the first convenient
opportunity, to satisfy your curiosity on all points. Damn it!
I see I really strike some people as a romantic character.
You may judge for yourself what a debt I owe Martha Petrovna for telling your sister so many strange and mysterious

things about me. I don't dare judge the impression it made; but in any case it was to my advantage. In spite of her natural revulsion, in spite of my perpetually gloomy and repellent expression, she began to pity me, to pity a fallen man. When a girl starts *pitying*—watch out, she's in danger. She starts wanting to 'save' you and bring you to reason; revive you and recall you to more decent goals; restore you to a new life and new work—I guess you know the sort of thing they can dream up. I saw immediately that the little bird was flying straight into the net; so, for my part, I got ready. Are you frowning, Rodion Romanych? Relax. As you know, sir, it all came to nothing. (Damn it, I'm drinking a lot!) You know, from the very beginning, I thought it was a pity fate hadn't arranged for your sister to be born in the second or third century of our era, the daughter of some local ruler or a proconsul in Asia Minor. No doubt she would have been among the martyrs; and when they seared her breast with red-hot irons, she would no doubt have smiled. She'd have deliberately chosen that path; and in the fourth or fifth centuries, she would have gone out into the Egyptian desert and lived there thirty years, on roots, ecstasies, and visions. That's all she thirsts for; she asks to take someone else's suffering upon herself, and right away! And if she can't she'll throw herself out the window. I heard something about a certain Mr. Razumikhin. They say he's a sensible young man (and so his name would indicate—*razum*, 'good sense'—he must be a seminarist); well, let's hope he takes good care of your sister. In brief, I understood her, and that does me honor, I think. At the time, though—I mean when we first met—well, you know how it is; you're somehow more frivolous then, more stupid, you don't have any perspective and don't see what you should. Damn it, why does she have to be so beautiful? It's not my fault! In brief, it began for me with an outburst of the most irresistible passion. Avdotia Romanovna is terribly chaste—to an unheard-of degree. (I say this about your sister as a fact, please note. In spite of the breadth of her mind, she is chaste, perhaps to the point of morbidity; and it will do her harm.) At that time we had a girl at our place called Parasha—black-eyed Parasha—who'd just been brought from another village, a chambermaid I hadn't seen before. Quite pretty, but unbelievably stupid. She burst into tears and raised a cry all over the household, and there was a scandal. Once, after dinner, Avdotia Romanovna deliberately sought me out alone on a path in the garden, and with her eyes flashing she *demanded* I leave poor Parasha in peace. That was practically our first conversation together. Of course, I considered it an honor to grant her wish, and I tried to assume an air of confused embarrassment; in brief, I didn't play the role badly. Then our negotiations began, our secret conversations, sermons, lessons, appeals, entreaties, even tears—would you believe it, even tears! You can see the power a passion for propaganda holds over some girls. Naturally, I blamed everything on fate; I pretended I was craving and thirsting for the light; and finally, I brought into play the greatest and most reliable instrument for the subjugation of the feminine heart—an instrument that has never yet let anybody down, that has a decisive effect on each and every woman without exception. That instrument is well known: flattery. There is nothing in the world more difficult than candor, and nothing easier than flattery. If there is a hundredth of a fraction of a false note to candor, it immediately produces dissonance, and as a result, exposure. But in flattery, even if everything is false down to the last note, it is still pleasant, and people will listen not without pleasure; with coarse pleasure, perhaps, but pleasure nevertheless. And no matter how coarse flattery may be, it seems always at least half true. This holds for all stages of development and all social classes. With flattery even a vestal virgin can be seduced, not to mention ordinary people. I can hardly remember without laughing how I once seduced a certain lady who was quite devoted to her husband, her children, and her virtues. How gay it was, and how little work! In her own way, at least, the lady really was virtuous, though. My whole tactic consisted of being perpetually overwhelmed, and I prostrated myself before her chastity. I flattered shamelessly. As soon as I managed a hand squeeze, or even a glance, I would reproach myself for having taken it by force; I would reproach myself (aloud, of course) and say that she resisted, and so much, that I could not have possibly gotten anywhere with her if I hadn't been so wicked; that in her innocence she had not anticipated my duplicity and had yielded without intending to, without knowing, without being aware; and so on and so on. In brief, I got what I wanted, but my lady remained quite convinced she was innocent and chaste, performed all her duties and obligations, and had fallen quite by chance. How furious she was with me when I told her I thought that all in all she'd been as much after pleasure as I myself. Poor Martha Petrovna was also terribly susceptible to flattery. If I had wanted to, I could certainly have had her whole estate turned over to me, even while she was still alive. (Still, I'm drinking an awful lot of wine, and I'm nattering.) I hope you won't be angry if I tell you I began to produce the same effect on Avdotia Romanovna. But I was stupid and impatient and spoiled the whole business. Several times, once especially, Avdotia Romanovna took an awful dislike to the look in my eyes—would you believe it? In brief, I had a kind of fire in them which would flare up stronger and stronger and more unguardedly, and which frightened her and finally she came to hate it. There's no point in going over the details, but we had a falling-out. Then I pulled another boner. In the crudest way, I allowed myself to mock her propaganda, all those moral appeals. Parasha came on the scene again, and not only her—in brief, Sodom flared up. Ah, Rodion Romanych, if you could only have seen, just once in your life, the flash of your sister's eyes at times. I'm drunk now. I've emptied a whole water glass of champagne. But it doesn't matter—I'm telling the truth. I assure you, I have dreamed of that look. Finally, I couldn't stand hearing the rustle of her dress. I had never imagined I could reach such a state; I really thought I was suffering from epilepsy. In brief, I simply had to arrange a reconciliation, but it was no longer possible. What do you think I did then? Oh, the stupidity to which rage will drive a man! Don't ever do anything in a rage, Rodion Romanych. Calculating that basically Avdotia Romanovna was a beggar—oh, excuse me, I didn't mean to—still, isn't it all one, as long as it expresses the idea? I mean, in brief, she lives by the work of her hands, she has her mother to support, and you—ah, damn it, you're frowning again—and so I decided to offer her all my money (at that time I could have realized about thirty thousand), on condition she run off with me to Petersburg. It goes without saying I was ready to swear eternal love, promise happiness and so forth and so on. I was so far gone, believe it or not, if she'd said to me, 'Slit Martha Petrovna's throat, or poison her, and marry me'—I would have done it immediately! But it all ended with the catastrophe you already know about. You can judge yourself how mad I was when I learned Martha Petrovna had dug up that vile scribbler Luzhin and practically masterminded a match—which essentially would have come to the same thing as what I had proposed. Isn't that so? Isn't it? Well, isn't it? I notice you're listening to what I'm saying pretty carefully. . . . You're an interesting young man. . . ."

Impatiently Svidrigailov banged his fist on the table. He was flushed. Raskolnikov saw clearly that the glass and a half or so of champagne that he had drunk (sipping slowly in short swallows) had had a bad effect on him; he decided to take advantage of the opportunity. Raskolnikov was quite suspicious of Svidrigailov. "After all this, I'm fully convinced you came here with my sister in mind," he said openly, without restraint, hoping to provoke Svidrigailov further in this way.

"Oh, come, now; come, come." Svidrigailov suddenly seemed to pull himself together. "I told you, didn't I . . . Anyway, your sister can't stand me."

"I'm quite convinced she can't. That isn't the point."

"Ah, you're convinced she can't?" Svidrigailov screwed up his eyes and smiled mockingly. "You are right. She doesn't like me. Still. In what passes between husband and wife, lover and lover, you should never be too sure. Always, there's one little corner the world doesn't know about, which only the two of them know about. Are you sure Avdotia Romanovna regarded me with disgust?"

"I've noticed from some of your words and expressions as you talked you still have your own views and the most pressing designs on Dunia. It goes without saying, they are vile."

"What! Did I really use words and expressions of that sort?" said Svidrigailov suddenly, in the most naïve alarm, not paying the slightest attention to the adjective describing his designs.

"Yes, you did. What are you afraid of, for instance? Why, all of a sudden, did you just get scared?"

"Scared? Me? Afraid? Me afraid of you? You've got more reason to be afraid of me, *cher ami*. But what nonsense . . . And yet I can see I'm a little high. Again I almost went too far. To hell with the wine! Hey, there, some water!" He grabbed the bottle and heaved it unceremoniously out the window. Phillip brought some water.

"It's all bosh," Svidrigailov said, wetting a napkin and applying it to his head. "I can settle your wagon and reduce your suspicions to dust. Do you happen to know, for instance, that I'm getting married?"

"You told me that before."

"I did? I forgot. But I couldn't have told you for certain, because I hadn't even seen my bride. I only had my designs. Now, though, I've got a bride, and it's all arranged. If I didn't have this pressing business, I'd certainly take you to her family's place right now, because I'd like your advice. Oh, damn! Only ten minutes left. Just look what time it's getting to be. But I'll tell you about this marriage of mine because it's an interesting little item—in its own way, of course. Where are you off to? Are you leaving again?"

"No, this time I'm not leaving."

"Not leaving at all? We'll see! I'll take you there, I really mean it, and I'll show you my bride. Only not now. It will soon be time for you to go. You go to the right, me to the left. You know this Resslich woman? I mean, you know, the Resslich at whose place I live—ah? Listening? No, well, you know, she's the one they say, you know, one of her girls jumped in the drink, in the winter, you know. . . . Listening? Are you listening? Well, she fixed it all up for me. You lead a dull life, she said. Why not live it up a little. Of course, as you know, I'm a gloomy man, dull. You think I'm light-hearted? No, gloomy. I do no harm, but I brood in the corner. Sometimes nobody talks to me for three days. But this Resslich's a fox; I'll tell you what she had in mind. She figured I'd get bored, throw my wife over, and leave; then she'd get the wife and put her in circulation—within our own class, of course, or even higher. There's this invalid father, she tells me, a retired official. For three years now he's been sitting in a chair—legs won't carry him, and there's the mother; a sensible lady, she says, this mama. There's a son who has a job in the provinces, but he won't help. And a married daughter, but she won't even come see them; and (as if their own weren't enough) they have two small nephews on their hands. And so they took their youngest daughter out of school before she finished. She's not quite sixteen yet. That means in a month (when she'll be sixteen) she can be married off. She's for me. We went there, and how silly it was at their place. I presented myself: landowner, widower, of good family, with such and such connections and with savings. And if I'm fifty and she is only sixteen—what difference does that make? Who'd pay any attention to that? Pretty alluring, isn't it? Yes, alluring. Ha-ha! You should have seen me talking things over with papa and mama—worth paying admission, just to see me then! She comes out and curtsies. Imagine, she's still wearing a short skirt—an

unopened bud, and she colors up and blushes like the dawn.
(They'd told her all about it, of course.) I don't know how
you feel about feminine faces; I think these sixteen-year-
olds, with their eyes still childlike, their modesty, their sweet
little tears of shyness—I think what they have is better than
beauty. She was a little picture in her own right, what's
more. Fairish hair in tight little curls like a lamb's coat,
puffed-out bright red little lips, and her feet—how charming!
Well, we made our acquaintance; I said I was in a hurry
because of domestic circumstances; and on the very next
day—the day before yesterday, that is—we were engaged.
Since then, whenever I go there I take her on my knee at
once and I don't let her down. . . . Well, she colors up like
the dawn, but I keep kissing her. Of course, mama's impressed
upon her sternly: this is your husband and all that, and that's
the way it has to be. In brief, just dandy! You know, being
engaged might even be better than being a husband. It's
what they call *la nature et la verité*! Ha-ha! Once or twice I
talked things over with her. The girl's far from stupid. Once
in a while she looks at me kind of sideways, and it burns
right through me. But you know, she has a face like a Raphael Madonna. The Sistine Madonna's face is fantastic, isn't
it—the mournful face of a holy fool. Doesn't it strike you
so? Well, she looks like that. The day after we were engaged
I brought fifteen hundred rubles: one set of diamond jewelry, another of pearl, and a silver case—a great big one,
with all kinds of things inside—and even her little Madonna's face flushed with pleasure. Yesterday I sat her on my
knee, but I must have been rather too unceremonious about
it—she blushed, and the little tears came to her eyes; and
she didn't want to show it, but she was all on fire herself.
Everybody went out for a minute, and I was alone with her.
Suddenly she flings herself around my neck (on her own,
for the first time)—she embraces me with both her sweet
little arms, she kisses me and swears she'll be a good, faithful, and obedient wife to me, she'll make me happy, she'll
devote her whole life to me, every minute of her life, and
all she'd ask of me would be *my respect alone,* and beyond
that, she says, 'I want nothing, nothing, no presents of any
kind!' I'm sure you'll agree: hearing such a declaration of
confidence from such a little sixteen-year-old angel, with the
tint of maidenly modesty on her cheeks and the tears of
enthusiasm in her eyes—it's fairly alluring, isn't it? Don't
you agree that it's alluring? It *is* worth something, isn't it?

Ah? It's worth . . . So, listen . . . you will come and see my bride . . . only not right now!"

"In brief, this monstrous age difference rouses your lust! Is that really the way you're going to get married?"

"What do you mean? Of course. Every man thinks of himself; he is happiest who knows best how to pull the wool over his own eyes. Ha-ha! But tell me how it is that you've gone over so completely to the side of virtue? You'll have to pardon me, old man—I'm just a poor sinner. He-he-he!"

"And yet you made arrangements to provide for Katherine Ivanovna's children. But you had your own reasons for that . . . now I understand."

"But I love children, in general. I am very fond of children." Svidrigailov laughed. "Along that line I could tell you about a very curious little episode that's still going on. The very first day I got here I visited some sewers of various kinds. Well, after seven years away, I simply hurled myself into them. Probably you've noticed I haven't been in any hurry to get together with my own crowd, my former friends and acquaintances. Well, I'll get along without them as long as I can. When I lived in the country at Martha Petrovna's, you know, the memory of all those secret places and little dives which offer so much to a man who knows his way around used to torture me out of my skin. Damn it all! The masses drink too much; our educated youth burns itself idly out building fantasies, castles in the air, crippling itself with theories; from somewhere or other the Jews have swooped down on us, stashing all money away; and everything else heads for debauchery. When I first arrived in this town, that's the familiar smell I smelled. I happened to drift into a so-called dance hall one evening. A terrible sewer—but then, I really like my sewers a little dirty—well, they were dancing a cancan the like of which in my time simply didn't exist. There's progress for you. Suddenly I see a girl of about thirteen, dressed most charmingly, dancing with a real virtuoso; another one watches her. Her mother sits on a chair by the wall. Well, you can just imagine what a cancan that was! The girl is embarrassed. She blushes. Finally she takes offense and starts crying. The virtuoso grabs her, twirls her around, and starts showing off in front of her. Everybody laughs and laughs—at times like that, I just love our crowds, even the cancan crowd—they laugh, they shout: ' 'At's the way to do it! No place to bring children!' Well, hell, I don't give a damn if they're being reasonable or unreasonable, or how they salve their conscience! I spotted my place right away! I sat down near the girl's mother, mentioned that I'd just arrived in town, too. I remarked how ignorant everybody was here, how they didn't seem to know real quality, or show the proper respect. I let her know I had a lot of money, offered them a lift in my carriage. Then I drove them home and got acquainted. They only just got here, and live in some garret they rent. She said she and her daughter could take my acquaintanceship only as an honor. I find out they haven't a penny to their name; they've come to petition for some kind of official favor. I offer my services and money. I discover they went to the dance hall by mistake—they thought it was a place that gave dancing lessons! Well, I propose for my part to help further the girl's education in dancing and French. They accept gladly. They consider it an honor. . . . We're still friends. . . . If you like, we'll go there sometime. Only not right now!"

"Stop, I've had enough of your filthy anecdotes, you depraved, low-down voluptuary!"

"A Schiller! Our own Schiller! A very Schiller! *Où va-t-elle la vertu se nicher?* I'm going to go on telling you these little tales on purpose, you know, just to hear you protest. Delightful!"

"Ah, no doubt! And don't you think I find myself absurd at this moment?" Raskolnikov muttered angrily.

Svidrigailov gave a full-throated laugh. Finally he called Phillip, paid, and started to get up. "Well, I guess I'm drunk, *assez causé!*" he said. "Delightful!"

"No doubt you find it delightful," said Raskolnikov, getting up too. "I guess it's delightful for a dried-up husk of a debauchee to tell his adventures, especially in these circumstances and to a man like me, even as he plots a monstrous design of the same sort. . . . It sets him on fire."

"Well, if that is so," said Svidrigailov, looking surprised and scrutinizing Raskolnikov, "if that is so, you're a fair cynic yourself. At least you've collected some material along that line. There's a lot you can understand, yes, a lot . . . and you can do a lot, too. . . . But that's enough. I'm genuinely sorry I've had so little time for a talk with you, but don't go away. . . . Wait. . . ."

Svidrigailov left the tavern. Raskolnikov followed him. Svidrigailov was not very drunk. The wine had gone to his head for a moment, but the stupor was dissipating itself rapidly. Something preoccupied him quite a bit, something quite important; he frowned. Evidently something he expected agitated and disturbed him. Over the last few minutes he had somehow suddenly changed, grown coarser and more facetious. Raskolnikov noticed it, and also became alarmed. Quite suspicious of Svidrigailov, he decided to follow him.

They came out on the sidewalk.

"You go to the right, I'll take the left; or, if you like, the other way around. Only—*adieu, mon plaisir,* till our next happy meeting!"

And he turned right, in the direction of the Haymarket.

5

Raskolnikov followed him.

"What's this!" said Svidrigailov, turning around. "Didn't I tell you—"

"I'm not going to let you out of my sight."

"Wha-a-at?"

Both stopped, and each scrutinized the other carefully, as though measuring.

"From all your half-drunken stories," said Raskolnikov sharply, "I reach the *positive* conclusion you not only have not abandoned your filthy plots against my sister, you're more than ever obsessed with them. This morning, I know, my sister received a letter. You've hardly been able to sit still. . . . Suppose you did manage to pick up some kind of wife along the way—that doesn't mean a thing. I want to make sure personally." Yet Raskolnikov hardly knew himself what he wanted at that moment, or what it really was he wanted to make sure of personally.

"So that's how it is! Shall I call the police immediately?"

"Call away!"

For a minute they stood there facing each other once again. At last the expression of Svidrigailov's face changed. Noting that Raskolnikov was not frightened by his threats, he suddenly assumed the gayest and friendliest air.

"What a character you are! I purposely avoided mentioning your little affair, though it goes without saying my curiosity is killing me. A fantastic business. I was going to put it off to some other time—but, really, you're enough to provoke the dead. . . . Well, come along. But I tell you in advance: I'm only going home for a minute to pick up some money; then I'm going to lock up the apartment and get a cab. I'm off to the islands for the whole evening. How far are you planning to come along?"

"For the time being, to the apartment. Not to yours, to Sofia Semionovna's; to excuse myself for not being at the funeral."

"As you like, but Sofia Semionovna's not home. She's taken the children to see a certain lady, an old lady of rank I used to know quite well, who now supervises a number of orphanages. I charmed this lady by bringing some money for all three of Katherine Ivanovna's fledglings, and I offered some money to the institution as well. Finally, I told her Sofia Semionovna's story, grisly details and all, keeping nothing back. It produced quite an effect. And so Sofia Semionovna was granted an appointment at such and such hotel, where for the time being, while she's in from her *dacha,* this lady friend of mine stays."

"It doesn't matter. I'll go anyway."

"As you like, but don't expect my companionship—what do I care! Well, here we are at the house. You know, I bet you're suspicious because I've been extremely delicate and haven't pestered or cross-examined you so far . . . know what I mean? You think that's unusual. I bet that's it! Well, that shows where delicacy gets you."

"And listening at doors!"

"Ah, so that's it!" Svidrigailov laughed. "Yes, I suppose I would have been surprised if you had let that go without comment. Ha-ha! I suppose I did get some inkling of what you'd been up to . . . what you were telling Sofia Semionovna . . . but so what? Maybe I'm completely at sea and don't understand a thing. Explain it to me, old boy, for God's sake! Fill me in on these newfangled principles of yours."

"You couldn't hear a thing; you're talking nonsense!"

"Oh, that's not what I meant, not that (though I did hear a thing or two, by the way)—no, that's not what I meant. It's just that you ooh and ah all over the place! The Schiller in you keeps stirring. Now you tell me: don't listen behind doors. If that's the way you feel, why don't you inform the authorities? You know, tell them: I did such and such, for such and such reasons; it so happens there was a tiny mistake in my theory. If you believe it's wrong to listen behind doors but perfectly all right to crack open old women's skulls with whatever comes to hand whenever you feel like it, you'd best take off to America, the quicker the better! Away, young man—there may still be time! I speak sincerely. You mean you don't have any money? I will pay for the trip."

Raskolnikov interrupted with disgust: "I'm not thinking about that at all."

"I understand—you mustn't put yourself out, though; you don't have to talk a lot if you don't want to—I understand the kind of problem must be bothering you. Moral problems, eh? The man and the citizen: that kind of problem? You should forget it. What good does it do you now? He-he. You mean, for all that, you're still a man and a citizen? If that's the way it goes, you shouldn't have started something that wasn't really your style. I suppose you could shoot yourself. Or don't you feel like it?"

"You're trying to get me mad so I'll leave."

"What a queer bird you are! Well, we've arrived. After you up the stairs. Look, there's the door to Sofia Semionovna's. Look. Nobody home. You don't believe me? Ask at Kapernaumov's—she leaves her key with them. Ah, here's Madame de Kapernaumov herself, ah? What's that? (She's a little deaf. . . .) She's gone out? Where? Well, there you are—now you've heard. She's not home, and maybe won't be till late in the evening. Well, come into my place, then. You wanted to come see me too, didn't you? Well, here we are at my place. Madame Resslich isn't home. That woman's always busy at something; but she's a good woman, I assure you. She might have been of service to you, too, if you'd been a little more sensible. Well, then, please watch; I'm taking this five percent bond out of the bureau drawer (look, I still have quite a few left!), but this one's going to be cashed today. Were you watching? I don't have much more time to lose. Lock the bureau, lock up the apartment, and there we are on the stairs again. If you like, we'll take a cab! But I'm heading for the islands. Wouldn't you like to come along for the ride? I'm taking this cab to Elagin Island, so what do you say? You won't? You've given up? Come on, let's go for a ride. It doesn't matter. Looks like it's going to rain, but it doesn't matter. We'll put the hood up. . . ."

Svidrigailov was already sitting in the cab. Raskolnikov decided his suspicions were unfounded, at least for the moment. Without a word, he turned and walked back in the direction of the Haymarket. If he had turned even once along his way, he would have seen that Svidrigailov hadn't driven more than a hundred paces before paying off his cab and dismounting back onto the sidewalk. By then he had turned the corner and could not see. A profound sense of disgust drove him away from Svidrigailov. "How could I have expected anything from that depraved, filthy sensualist, even for a moment!" he exclaimed involuntarily. Raskolnikov judged too hastily, too impulsively; there was something about Svidrigailov that at least endowed him with a certain originality if not mysteriousness. As for his sister, Raskolnikov remained convinced Svidrigailov would by no means leave her in peace. Yet it became too difficult, too unbearable, to have to go on thinking about all this, over and over again.

After twenty steps he became deeply pensive, as was usual for him when he was alone. Crossing the bridge, he stopped by the rail and stared into the water. At that moment, Avdotia Romanovna was standing a little further along the same bridge. He had passed her as he started across the bridge, but had walked past without noticing her. Dunia had never before seen him this way on the street, and she felt almost frightened. She stopped, and didn't know whether to call out to him or not. Suddenly she noticed Svidrigailov approaching hurriedly from the direction of the Haymarket.

His approach seemed cautious and secretive. He stopped before the bridge, on the sidewalk, trying hard as he could to prevent Raskolnikov from seeing him. He had noticed Dunia some time ago and signaled to her. By these signs he seemed to be pleading with her not to arouse her brother's attention, calling her to come over to him. Dunia did so. Quietly, she passed her brother and approached Svidrigailov.

"Let's go," Svidrigailov whispered to her. "Quickly. I don't want Rodion Romanych to know about our meeting. I must tell you I sat with him in a tavern not far from here. He sought me out there himself. I had a hard time shaking loose. He knows something about my letter to you and has some suspicion. I know you didn't tell him, of course—but if you didn't, who could it have been?"

"We've turned the corner," Dunia said. "My brother won't see us now. I tell you I won't go with you any further. Tell me everything here. You can say all that needs to be said right here on the street."

"In the first place, I can't possibly tell you this on the street; second, you must hear what Sofia Semionovna has to say. Third, I will show you certain documents. . . . Well, then, finally: if you don't agree to come to my place, I refuse to discuss the matter any further and will go away immediately. But I'd like you to remember that an extremely curious secret of your beloved brother is entirely in my hands."

Dunia paused indecisively and threw a penetrating glance at Svidrigailov. "What are you afraid of?" he remarked calmly. "The city's not the country. Even in the country you did me more harm than I did you, but here—"

"Has Sofia Semionovna been told?"

"No, I didn't say a word to her, and I'm not entirely sure she's home. Still, she's probably home. She buried her stepmother today; it's no day to go visiting. I don't want to say anything about this before the time is ripe. I even have some misgivings about letting you know. The slightest indiscretion would amount to a betrayal. I live right here—right here in this house, the one we're approaching. That's our janitor. He knows me quite well. You see, he's bowing. He sees I'm walking with a lady and he will certainly have noticed your face, and that should reassure you if you're suspicious and afraid. Forgive me for speaking so bluntly. This apartment of mine, I sublet. Sofia Semionovna lives next door, and she sublets her room, too. The whole floor is crawling with tenants. Why be scared, like a child? Or am I really so very terrible?" Svidrigailov's face twisted into an indulgent smile, though he was not quite up to smiling. His heart was pounding and his breath turned thick in his lungs. To hide his mounting excitement, he deliberately spoke louder. Dunia, however, had not noticed his peculiar excitement. She was too irritated by his remark about her being scared as a child of him and his terrifying her.

"I know you're a man . . . without honor. But I'm not afraid of you in the least. Go on," she said, apparently calm, although her face was very pale.

Svidrigailov stopped at Sonia's apartment.

"I'll see if she's home, if you don't mind. No, she's not. Too bad! But she's likely to come home very soon, I know. If she went out it must have been to see a certain lady about the orphans. Their mother died. I got myself involved in that, too, and made the arrangements. If Sofia Semionovna isn't back here in the next ten minutes, I'll make a point of sending her to see you—this very day if you like. Here is my door. Here are my two rooms. Behind that door lives my landlady, Mrs. Resslich. Now, look here, and I'll show you my major documentation: this door leads from my bedroom into two quite empty rooms that are normally rented out. Here they are . . . you have to look a little more carefully at this. . . ."

Svidrigailov occupied two fairly spacious furnished rooms. Dunia looked around mistrustfully, but noticed nothing special either in their furnishing or in their disposition; although she did notice that, for instance, Svidrigailov's apartment was sandwiched in between two almost uninhabited apartments. One did not enter his rooms directly from the corridor, but through the landlady's two rooms, which were almost empty. Svidrigailov unlocked a door that led out from his bedroom and showed Dunia the vacant apartment. Dunia paused in the doorway. She did not understand why she was being asked to look, but Svidrigailov hastened to explain.

"Look here—the second large room. Note the door; it's locked. Beside the door there's a chair, just one chair in the two rooms. I brought it from my own apartment so I could listen more comfortably. On the other side of the door stands Sofia Semionovna's table. She was sitting there, talking with Rodion Romanych. Sitting on this chair, I overheard them, two evenings in a row, about two hours each time. So, naturally, I could learn something that way—don't you think?"

"You listened in?"

"Yes, I listened in. Come to my place now. There's nowhere to sit here."

He led Avdotia Romanovna back to his own living room and asked her to sit down. He sat at the other end of the table, at least a couple of yards away, and yet his eyes must have flared in the way that had once so frightened Dunia. She shuddered, and looked about her mistrustfully once more. Her gesture was involuntary. Apparently she did not wish to manifest her mistrust. But the isolated location of Svidrigailov's apartment struck her at last. She felt like asking if the landlady, at least, were home, but out of pride she did not ask. Anyway, there was a far greater pain gnawing at her heart than fear for herself. She suffered unendurably.

"Here is your letter," she began, and put it on the table. "But is it really possible, what you write? You seem to refer to a crime that my brother committed. The hint was obvious, so you don't dare try to talk yourself out of it now. I might as well tell you that I've heard this foolish story before you even mentioned it, and I don't believe a single word. It's a nasty and absurd suspicion. I know the incident and why it was thought up. You couldn't possibly have any proof. But you promised to prove it—so, speak up! You might as well know in advance, though, I don't believe you! I don't believe you!" Dunia said this very rapidly, hurrying through it; for a moment the color rushed to her face.

"If you didn't believe me, why did you risk coming alone to see me? Why did you come? Curiosity?"

"Don't torment me. Speak up!"

"You've a brave girl, that goes without saying. I thought, by God, you would ask Mr. Razumikhin to bring you here! But he wasn't with you or hanging around anywhere near you—I noticed that. It was brave. I suppose it means you wanted to spare Rodion Romanych. But everything about you is divine. . . . As for your brother—what shall I say? You saw for yourself the shape he's in, didn't you?"

"That isn't all you have to go on, is it?"

"No, it isn't. I have his own words. Two evenings in a row he came here to see Sofia Semionovna. I showed you where they sat. He made a full confession to her. He's a murderer. He killed the old woman, the official's widow, the pawnbroker, with whom he himself used to pawn things. He killed her sister, too—the clothes dealer called Lizaveta—who chanced to walk in as her sister was being murdered. He killed them both with an ax he brought with him. He killed so he could rob them, and he did rob them. He took some money and various things. . . . All this he passed on to Sofia Semionovna, word for word. She is the only one who knows his secret. But she had no part in the murder—either by word or deed. On the contrary, she was horrified, just as you are now. But don't worry. She won't betray him."

"Impossible!" Dunia muttered with deathly pale lips; her breath came hard. "Impossible! He didn't have any reason at all, no motive. . . . It's a lie! A lie!"

"He robbed; that was his motive. He took the money and the things. True, by his own confession he didn't make use of either the money or the things. He hid them away somewhere under a stone, and that's where they still are. But only because he didn't dare make use of them."

"Could he really steal? Rob? Is it likely he could think only of that?" Dunia cried out, and leaped from her chair. "But you know him; you've seen him. Could he really be a thief?" She seemed to be pleading with Svidrigailov. She had forgotten all her fears.

"Avdotia Romanovna, there are thousands and millions of nuances and complexities in such matters. Suppose the man who steals is a thief; he knows, at least within himself, that he's a villain. But you know, I once heard about a certain respectable gentleman who broke into the post office. In his case—who knows—maybe he actually thought he was doing the right thing! If some third party had told me, it goes without saying, I wouldn't have believed it, just as you didn't. I had to believe my own ears, though. And he explained all the reasons to Sofia Semionovna. At first she didn't believe her own ears, either. But finally she believed her eyes. She believed her own eyes. You see—he told her himself, personally."

"What were . . . the reasons!"

"It's a long story, Avdotia Romanovna. We have here— how shall I express it to you—a kind of theory, you know the kind of thing; where I might find, for instance, that one single evil act is permissible so long as its main purpose is good. A hundred good deeds and only one evil one! And of course, to a talented young man with an outsize sense of self-esteem, it's offensive to realize that if he only had, for instance, three thousand rubles or so, his whole career, his whole future, might well be different—and yet he doesn't have those three thousand. Add to that a sense of irritation from going hungry, from his cramped quarters, from his rags, from a hyperacute awareness of the beauty of his social position, along with that of the position of his sister and mother. And most of all, vanity—pride and vanity—although, God knows, all this might well have been mixed in with his good impulses, too. . . . You mustn't think I'm accusing him of anything. Anyway, it's not my business. We have here also some sort of personal theory of his own—not such a bad theory—by which people are divided, you see, into those who are raw material and those who are special people. I mean, those who are so lofty the law was not written for them, but on the contrary, they themselves make the law for the other people, the raw material, the garbage. It's not such a bad theory, nothing special; *une théorie comme une autre.* He was terribly taken with Napoleon. I mean, he was really taken personally by the fact that there have been people of genius who never stopped to look at any one solitary evil act, but strode on their way without giving it a thought. Seems he imagined he too was a man of genius—I mean, he was convinced for a while. He has suffered much and still suffers from the notion he was able to construct such a theory, and yet unable to stride on his way without reflecting. So it must follow he is not a man of genius. Well, for a young man of such self-esteem, it is humiliating, especially in our time. . . ."

"But his conscience? Do you deny he has any moral feeling? Do you think he's really like that?"

"Ah, Avdotia Romanovna, nowadays everything's all mixed up. But there never was any intrinsic moral order in such matters anyway. Russians, in general, are people of a certain breadth. They are broad like their land, and they are exceptionally strongly drawn to the fantastic and the disorderly. But the trouble consists of being broad without any special genius. Surely you remember how we used to talk about such things when we were alone together, sitting on the terrace in the garden after supper. You even reproached me for being broad in that manner. Who knows, we may have been having our discussion just as he was lying here thinking his own thoughts. As you know, Avdotia Romanovna, we don't have any especially sacred traditions in our educated society; it's as if somebody patched something together the best he could out of books, one way or another, or extracted it out of the ancient chronicles. But those would be the scholars, and they're all blockheads in their own way, you know, so it's even indecent for a man of the world to be like that. Anyway, you know, in general, how I think; I certainly don't go around accusing anybody. I belong to the idle classes myself, and I mean to go on belonging to them. We've discussed all this more than once. Once I was even lucky enough to arouse some interest on your part in my conclusions. . . . Avdotia Romanovna, you are quite pale!"

"I know his theory. I read an article he wrote in a journal about people to whom everything is permitted. . . . Razumikhin brought it to me."

"Mr. Razumikhin? Your brother's article? In a journal? There is such an article? I didn't know. Curious! But where are you off to, Avdotia Romanovna?"

"I want to see Sofia Semionovna," Dunia said in a weak voice. "How do I get through to her place? She may have come back. I really must see her now. Let her . . ." Her breath literally failed her, and she could not speak.

"Sofia Semionovna won't be back till tonight. At least, so

I suppose. She should have come back soon, but since she didn't, she'll probably be quite late. . . ."

"Ah, so you're lying! I see . . . you lied . . . you were lying all along! I don't believe you, don't believe you, don't believe you!" Dunia cried out in a real frenzy, completely losing her head. Almost in a faint, she dropped back in the chair Svidrigailov hastened to pull up for her.

"Avdotia Romanovna, what is the matter with you! Pull yourself together! Here's some water. Drink a little. . . ." He sprinkled a little water on her. Dunia shuddered and came to her senses. "Well, quite an effect!" Svidrigailov muttered to himself, frowning. "Avdotia Romanovna, do calm down! You should know that he has friends. We'll save him; we'll give him a hand. Would you like me to take him abroad? I have money. In three days I'll get a ticket. As for his committing a murder, he can still do a great many good deeds, so it will all balance out. Do calm down. He may yet become a great man. Well, how are you now? How do you feel?"

"You wicked mocker! Let me go. . . ."

"But where? Where would you go?"

"To him. Where is he? Do you know? Why is this door locked? This was the door we came through, but now it's locked. When did you manage to lock it?"

"What we were talking about just now—we couldn't blare it forth to all the rooms, could we? I'm not mocking at all. I was just sick of this kind of talk. Where are you going in a state like that? Or do you want to give him away? You'll drive him to a frenzy and he'll give *himself* away. You should know that they're following him; they're on his trail already. You'd only betray him. Wait. I saw him and spoke to him just now. He can still be saved. Sit down. Wait. Let's think it through together. That's why I called you, so we could talk about it alone and think it over carefully. Do sit down!"

"How can you save him? Can he really be saved?" Dunia sat down. Svidrigailov sat beside her.

"It all depends on you, on you, on you alone," he began, eyes flashing. He spoke almost in a whisper, stumbling over some of the words and, in his excitement, unable even to get some of them out. He was trembling. Dunia recoiled and moved further away from him in alarm. "You . . . only your word, and he's saved! I . . . I'll save him. I have money; I have friends. I'll send him off right away, and I'll take a passport out myself. Two passports. One for him, the other mine. I have friends, practical people . . . You want me to? I'll get a passport for you, too . . . and for your mother . . . what do you need Razumikhin for? I love you, too . . . I love you incredibly. Let me kiss the hem of your dress—let me, please! I can't bear hearing it rustle. Say to me: do this!—and I'll do it! I'll do anything. I'll do the impossible. Whatever you believe in, I'll believe, too. I'll do anything, anything! Don't look, don't look at me like that! Don't you know you are killing me. . . ."

He was beginning to rave. All of a sudden something happened to him, as though he had suddenly been hit on the head. Dunia leaped up and ran to the door. "Open up! open up!" she cried, calling to anyone through the door, shaking it with her hands. "Open up! Isn't anybody there?"

Svidrigailov got up and pulled himself together. A malicious and mocking smile began slowly to play about his still trembling lips.

"Nobody's home," he said quietly. "The landlady is out. There is no use your crying out like that. You will just get yourself upset over nothing."

"Where's the key? Open the door at once, you vile man! At once!"

"I lost the key. I can't find it."

"Ah? So you're going to use force!" said Dunia, turning very pale. She rushed into a corner, where she quickly shielded herself behind a small table. She did not scream. She fixed her eyes on her tormentor and warily watched every move he made. But Svidrigailov did not move. He stood facing her from the opposite end of the room. Outwardly, at least, he had even brought himself under control. But his face was as pale as before, and the mocking smile did not leave it.

"You mentioned 'force,' Avdotia Romanovna. If it's force, then you may judge that I have taken measures. Sofia Semionovna's not at home. It's a long way to the Kapernaumovs'—five locked rooms. Finally, I'm at least twice as strong as you are. I don't, what's more, have much to be afraid of, because you cannot appeal—after all, you don't want to betray your brother in the process, do you? Nobody would believe you anyway: why would a single girl go alone to a man's apartment? So that even if you sacrifice your brother, you would have little to show for it. Rape is quite difficult to prove, Avdotia Romanovna."

"Scoundrel!" Dunia whispered indignantly.

"As you like. But please note, I said that only as a suggestion of sorts. It's my personal conviction you are absolutely right: rape is an abomination. I was merely trying to say there needn't be anything on your conscience, even if . . . you wanted to save your brother voluntarily in the way I'm suggesting. It would simply mean you were submitting to circumstances; to force, if you will; if you insist on putting it that way. Think it over. Your brother's fate and your mother's are in your hands. And I would be your slave all my life. . . . I will wait here. . . ." Svidrigailov sat down on the couch about eight steps away from Dunia. She no longer had the slightest doubt about his determination. She knew him. . . .

Suddenly she drew a revolver from her pocket, cocked it, and supported the hand in which she held it on the small table. Svidrigailov leaped up from his seat.

"Aha! So that's how it is!" he exclaimed, surprised, yet smiling maliciously. "Well, that changes the matter entirely. You're making it a great deal easier for me, Avdotia Romanovna! Where did you get that revolver? Not from Mr. Razumikhin, surely? Bah! It's mine! An old friend! Just think, I was looking everywhere for it! So the shooting lessons I had the honor of giving you in the country have not been wasted."

"It's not your revolver. It's Martha Petrovna's—whom you murdered, you evil man! You had nothing of your own in her house. I took it when I began to suspect what you were capable of. If you dare move one step, I swear I'll kill you!" Dunia was in a frenzy. She held the revolver at the ready.

"And what about your brother?" Svidrigailov said, without moving from the spot. "I ask out of curiosity."

"Denounce him if you like! Don't move! Stand still or I'll shoot! I know that you poisoned your wife; you're a murderer yourself!"

"Are you firmly convinced I poisoned Martha Petrovna?"

"You did! You implied as much to me. You told me about poison . . . I know you went to get some . . . you had it all ready. . . . Undoubtedly it was you . . . you villain!"

"Even if true, it was your fault . . . you would have been the cause."

"You lie! I always hated you! Always!"

"Come, Avdotia Romanovna! Apparently you have forgotten how in the zeal of your propaganda you began to yield and to melt. . . . I saw it in your eyes. Do you remember that evening in the moonlight, when the nightingale sang?"

"You lie!" Fury blazed in Dunia's eyes. "You lie, you slanderer!"

"Lie? I lie? Very well, if that's the way you want to put it, I told a lie. It doesn't do for women to remember things like that." He smiled. "I know you will fire, you lovely little beast. All right. Fire away!"

Dunia raised the revolver, deathly pale, her lower lip turning white and trembling, her large, dark eyes flashing fire. Steeling herself, she looked at him, judging the distance, waiting for him to make the first move. He had never seen her so beautiful. It seemed as if the fire blazing from her eyes as she lifted the revolver seared through him, and his heart shriveled with the pain. He moved a step, and a shot rang out. The bullet grazed his hair and buried itself behind him in the wall. He paused and laughed softly.

"A wasp stung me! Flew straight for my head . . . What? Blood!" He drew out a handkerchief to wipe away the blood that ran in a thin stream down his right temple; the bullet must have just broken the skin at the top of his skull. Dunia lowered the revolver and looked at Svidrigailov, not so much with fear as with a kind of wild incomprehension. She seemed not to understand what she had done or what was going on.

"You missed! Fire again; I'll wait," Svidrigailov said softly, still smiling, yet somehow gloomily. "Or else I might grab you before you cock it again."

Dunia shuddered, quickly cocked the revolver, and raised it. "Leave me alone!" she said desperately. "I swear I'll fire again . . . I'll kill you. . . ."

"But, of course . . . at three paces, you can't miss. And if you don't kill me . . . then . . . ." His eyes flashed, and he moved two paces forward.

Dunia pulled the trigger, and the gun misfired.

"You didn't load it properly. No matter! You still have one bullet left. Fix it. I'll wait."

He stood not two paces away from her. He waited, looking at her with a wild determination, a feverishly passionate and serious look. Dunia grasped that he would die sooner than let her go. And now, of course, at less than two paces, she would kill him!

All of a sudden she threw away the revolver.

Svidrigailov said in surprise, "She threw it away!" and drew a deep breath. Something seemed to lift from his heart, and it may not only have been the weight of his fear of death; he seemed at the moment scarcely even aware of that. It was release from a more melancholy and more somber feeling, which even he himself could not have fully defined. He went up to Dunia and gently put his arm around her waist. She did not resist but, trembling like a leaf, looked at him with imploring eyes. He wanted to say something; his lips made a grimace, but nothing came out.

"Let me go," Dunia said imploringly. Svidrigailov shuddered. She spoke in a tone different from the one she had used before.

"You don't love me?" he asked softly.

Dunia shook her head in the negative.

"And . . . you could . . . never . . .?" he whispered in despair.

"Never!" Dunia whispered.

For a moment a terrible, mute struggle took place in the soul of Svidrigailov. He looked at her somehow in a way that was beyond words. Suddenly he removed his arm, turned around, strode quickly to the window, and stood there in front of it.

Another moment passed.

"Here's the key." He took it from his left coat pocket and put it behind him on the table, without looking, and without turning around to face Dunia. "Take it, and go now! Quickly!"

He stared steadily at the window. Dunia went to the table to take the key.

"Quickly! Quickly!!" he repeated, still without moving or turning around. A terrible note sounded in that "quickly."

Dunia understood; grasped the key and rushed to the door. She opened it quickly and tore from the room. A moment later, beside herself, she was running like a madwoman to the canal embankment and toward the Voznesensky Bridge.

Svidrigailov stood at the window for about three minutes longer. Then he turned slowly, looked around, and softly drew the palm of his hand across his forehead. A strange smile twisted his face, a weak, sad, pitiful smile, a smile of despair. The blood, which had already clotted, stuck to his hand. He looked angrily at the blood. Then he wet a towel

and cleaned off his temple. The revolver Dunia had thrown
away had landed near the doorway, and it caught his eye.
He picked it up and examined it. It was a small three-shot
pocket revolver of an old-fashioned make. It had two
charges and one cap left, and could still fire once. He medi-
tated; pocketed the revolver, picked up his hat, and went
out.

6

All that evening, until ten o'clock, he spent in taverns and
dives, going the rounds from one to the other. Somewhere
he even came across Katia, who sang him another cheap
song, this time about somebody, "a scoundrel and a tyrant,"
who ". . . started kissing Katia. . . ."

Svidrigailov treated Katia and the accordion-player and
the male choir and the waiters and two odd little clerks to
drinks. He had actually taken to these clerks because their
noses were bent; one's to the right, the other's to the left—
and this had struck Svidrigailov's fancy. They dragged him
finally into some pleasure garden where he paid even their
entrance fee. In this garden there was a rather skimpy three-
year-old fir tree, and three bushes. Also, a "Vauxhall" had
been set up—actually a bar, though they also served tea—
and beyond that were several green tables and some chairs.
A chorus of pretty awful singers and some drunken Munich
German, painted as a clown with a red nose, but with an
extremely melancholy expression on his face for some reason, entertained the audience. The clerks quarreled with
some other clerks, and a fight broke out. They asked Svidrigailov to arbitrate. For a quarter of an hour he tried, but
there was so much yelling, nobody could make anything out.
One of them, it seemed likely, had stolen something, and
had even managed to dispose of it to some Jew who had
turned up, and once he had sold it he tried to get out of
sharing the proceeds with his companion. The object that
had been sold would seem to have been a teaspoon belonging to the vauxhall. Once they discovered the loss in the
vauxhall, the matter began to take on troublesome proportions. Svidrigailov paid for the spoon, rose, and left the garden. All this time he himself had not drunk a single drop
of liquor. In the vauxhall, he had merely ordered some tea,

more for the sake of form than anything else. The night, meanwhile, was stifling and gloomy. By ten o'clock, terrible storm clouds gathered from all directions. Thunder burst, and the rain poured down like a waterfall. The water did not fall in drops, but lashed the earth in torrents. Lightning flashed constantly, and one could count to five during every flash. Drenched to the skin, he went home, locked himself in, opened up his bureau, took out all the money, and tore up a couple of sheets of paper. The money he put in his pocket. He had wanted to change his clothes, but having glanced at the window and heard the storm and the rain, he waved his hand, took his hat, and went out without locking his apartment. He went straight to Sonia's; she was at home.

She was not alone—four of the Kapernaumov children surrounded her. Sofia Semionovna was treating them to tea. She greeted Svidrigailov silently and respectfully and looked with surprise at his drenched clothing, but did not say a word. The children immediately ran off in indescribable terror. Svidrigailov sat down near the table, and asked Sonia to sit down beside him. Shyly she prepared herself to listen.

"Sofia Semionovna, I may be going off to America," Svidrigailov said, "and since this is probably the last time I'll be seeing you, I came to make certain arrangements. Well, did you get to see that lady today? I know what she told you—you don't have to say." Sonia made a gesture and blushed. "Those people have their own way of looking at things. Your sisters and your brother are taken care of; I've deposited money in each of their names, and it's all signed and attested in the proper form. Anyway, you better take these receipts, just in case. Here, take them! Well, then, that's done. Here are three five percent bonds; they come to three thousand in all. Take them; they're for you. You don't have to tell anybody; let it remain between the two of us, no matter what you might happen to hear. They'll come in handy, Sofia Semionovna, because it's no go living the way you've been living, and anyway, you don't have to anymore."

"You've been so kind to me, sir, and to the orphans, and to my dead stepmother," Sonia said hastily. "If I've thanked you so little up to now, you mustn't think—"

"Ah, that's enough, enough."

"But about this money, Arkady Ivanovich—I'm very grateful to you, but I won't be needing it now. Please don't think I'm being ungrateful; but I will always be able to earn enough for myself. If you are pleased to feel so generous, this money—"

"It's for you, Sofia Semionovna, it's for you; and if you don't mind, without all these discussions, because I don't have much time. You can use it. Rodion Romanovich has two paths: a bullet in the head, or the road to Siberia." Sonia looked at him wildly and shuddered. "Don't worry. I learned about it from him, and I'm no gossip. I won't tell anybody. You had the right idea when you told him to go give himself up. That would be much better for him. If he sets out on the road to Siberia, you will follow him, won't you? Won't you? Well, won't you? If you do that, you'll need money. For his sake—you understand? If I give it to you, it's the same as giving it to him. What's more, you did promise Amalia Ivanovna you'd pay her what was owed her. I heard you. Why, Sofia Semionovna, do you insist on assuming such contractual obligations? Katherine Ivanovna was in debt to the German woman, not you; so to hell with the German woman. You can't live in the world that way. Well, if somebody should ask you sometime—tomorrow or the day after, say—about me or my affairs (and they *will* ask you!), don't mention my visiting you now; don't show the money to anybody; and don't tell anybody I gave it to you. Well, good-bye now." He rose from the chair. "Say hello to Rodion Romanych. By the way, you might let Mr. Razumikhin keep the money for the time being. You do know Mr. Razumikhin, don't you? Of course. Not a bad guy. So, take it to him tomorrow or . . . when the time is right. Till then, you better hide it."

Sonia got up from her chair, too, and looked at him in fear. She wanted very much to say something, to ask something, but at first she did not dare, and anyway she did not know how to begin.

"Why should you . . . how can you . . . go out while it's raining so?"

"Since I'm getting ready to go to America, why should I be afraid of a little rain, he-he? Good-bye, Sofia Semionovna, my dear! A long life to you—you're of use to others. By the way . . . tell Mr. Razumikhin, would you, that I asked to be remembered to him. Just like that. Tell him, Arkady Ivanovich Svidrigailov asks to be remembered to you. Without fail." He went out, leaving Sonia amazed, frightened, and vaguely but somehow insistently suspicious.

It later turned out that he made another very eccentric

and quite unexpected visit that evening between eleven and twelve. The rain had not yet stopped. At twenty minutes of twelve, soaking wet, he entered the cramped little apartment of the parents of his promised bride on the third block of Vasilievsky Island on Maly Prospect. He had some difficulty getting himself let in, and at first he produced great consternation. When he so wished, however, Arkady Ivanovich could be a man of the greatest charm, so that the original conjecture (fairly acute) of the fiancée's parents, to the effect that Arkady Ivanovich was drunk and out of control, quickly dropped of its own weight. The softhearted but sensible mother wheeled out the invalided parent in his chair to see Arkady Ivanovich, and in her usual manner proceeded to launch into some rather farfetched questions. (She was a woman who never posed questions directly, but always began by smiling and rubbing her hands, and then, if there was something she really needed to know—for example, when it might be convenient for Arkady Ivanovich to have the wedding—she would begin with intense and almost avid questions about Paris and about the court life there; and only by a kind of orderly progression would she proceed from Paris to approach the third block on Vasilievsky Island.) At some other time all this would certainly have inspired some considerable respect; on this occasion, however, Arkady Ivanovich somehow seemed impatient, and wanted to see his fiancée right away, although he'd been told to begin with his fiancée had already gone off to bed. Needless to say, the bride made her appearance. Arkady Ivanovich informed her directly that because of a very important circumstance he was obliged to leave Petersburg for a while; and so he had brought her fifteen thousand rubles in silver and bank notes, and he was asking her to accept them as a kind of gift from him, since he had made up his mind some time ago he would give her this little trifle before the wedding. There was no very logical connection established between the gift and his immediate departure, or why he had to come in the rain at midnight to present it; nevertheless, it came off quite well. Even the required aah's and oh's, the queries and exclamations, were muted and restrained; still, this most sensible of mothers expressed the most ardent gratitude, properly emphasized with tears. Arkady Ivanovich rose, laughed, kissed his fiancée, patted her on the cheek, reassured her he'd be back soon; and he noticed that along with the childish curiosity in her eyes there was something of a mute and solemn question. He thought for a moment and kissed her again. As he did so, he felt genuinely annoyed that his present would be put immediately under lock and key by the most sensible of mothers. When he went out, he left everybody in an unusually excited state. But the tenderhearted mama, speaking rapidly in a half whisper, resolved some of their main perplexities by reminding them that Arkady Ivanovich was a big man, a man of affairs, rich, with important connections, and God only knew what went on in his head. If he felt like it, he went on a trip; if he felt like it, he gave money away. There just wasn't anything to be surprised at. Of course, it was strange to come visiting all soaked from the rain. But take Englishmen, for instance—they were even more eccentric. Anyway, these high-society people didn't care what was said about them and didn't stand on ceremony. He might even go around like that on purpose, just to show he wasn't scared of anybody. It was important not to breathe a word of this to anybody, because God alone knew what might not yet come of it, so the money had to go immediately under lock and key, and wasn't it lucky that Fedosia had been sitting in the kitchen through it all, but the main thing was never, never, never to breathe a word of this to that old witch Resslich, and so on and so on. They sat there whispering until two in the morning. The fiancée, however, went back to bed much earlier, astonished and a little sad.

Meanwhile, at the stroke of midnight, Svidrigailov crossed the Tuchkov Bridge on his way to the Petersburg side. The rain had stopped, but it was windy. He started shivering. For a moment, with a kind of special, questioning curiosity, he looked at the dark waters of the Little Neva. Soon, though, it seemed cold standing there above the water; he turned and walked to the Bolshoy Prospect. He strode on and on, for almost half an hour, along the endless Bolshoy Prospect, stumbling more than once in the darkness on the wooden paving blocks, but searching constantly and intently for something on the right side of the street. Somewhere around here, at the very end of the prospect, he had noticed a wooden hotel—but a big one—not long ago while riding by. As far as he could recall, it was called something like the Adrianople. He had not been wrong. A hotel of that sort in such an out-of-the-way place was a landmark he couldn't miss even in the darkness. It was a long wooden, blackened building, in which, in spite of the late hour, some lights still burned and some signs of activity were still apparent. He went in and asked the ragged attendant who met him in the corridor for a room. The attendant looked Svidrigailov up and down, pulled himself together, and led Svidrigailov directly to a remote room, stifling and cramped, somewhere at the very end of the corridor in a corner under the staircase. There was no other; they were all taken. The attendant looked at him inquiringly.

"You have tea?" Svidrigailov asked.

"Yes, sir."

"Something to eat?"

"Veal, sir; and vodka and sandwiches, sir."

"Bring me some veal and some tea."

"Nothing else?" the attendant asked, somewhat surprised.

"Nothing, nothing!"

"You sure?"

"Yes."

The attendant withdrew, quite disenchanted.

"Must be a good place," Svidrigailov thought. "Wonder why I didn't know it? I must look like somebody back from a night out who's already loaded up on his way. I wonder, though, who stops here and spends the night."

Svidrigailov lit a candle and looked more closely at his room. It was a cell so tiny he could hardly stand up in it, and there was one window. A very dirty bed; a plain, painted table and a chair occupied almost the whole room. The walls seemed simply a few boards knocked together, with worn-out wallpaper, the yellowish color of which could still be distinguished, but so dusty and shredded the pattern had disappeared. Part of the wall and ceiling were at an angle, as if for an attic, but due actually to the staircase. Svidrigailov deposited the candle, sat down on the bed, and started to think. But a strange incessant whispering in the next cubicle, mounting at times to a shout, finally engaged his attention. He had heard the whispering since he came in. He listened. Somebody was abusing somebody else with reproaches that might have been almost a matter for tears, but only one voice could be heard. Svidrigailov rose, shielding the candle with his hand. At once a crack of light became visible on the wall. He went up to it and looked through. In a room a little bigger than his own were two guests. One, coatless, quite curly-headed, and with a red, puffy face, struck an orator's pose, feet set apart to keep his balance, beating himself on the chest and reproaching the other man, in a tone resonant with pathos, for being a vagrant, of no standing, whom he had pulled out of the mire, and whom, anytime he wanted, he could drive back into the muck, with only the raised finger of the Almighty to witness. The subject of this reproach sat on his chair with the look of a man who wants very badly to sneeze but somehow can't quite. Every so often he threw a sheepish, fuddled look at the orator, but obviously had no idea what he was talking about and hardly even heard anything. On the table there was a lit candle, an almost empty pitcher of vodka, some glasses, bread, cucumbers, and a pot of stale tea. Having taken in the scene, Svidrigailov turned away from the crack disinterestedly and sat down again on the bed.

The attendant returned with the veal and the tea, and could not keep himself from asking once more if there were anything he wanted. Receiving a negative response once more, he withdrew conclusively. Svidrigailov fell on the tea to warm himself up, and drank a whole glass; but he could not bring himself to eat a bite of food—his appetite had left him completely. He was obviously beginning to run a fever. He took off his coat and jacket, wrapped himself in a blanket, and lay down on the bed. He felt annoyed. "Better for the occasion if I were in good shape," he thought, and grinned. The room was stifling; the candle burned feebly; outside, the wind sounded; somewhere in a corner a mouse scratched; the whole room smelled of mice and something leathery. He lay there and seemed to daydream; thought followed thought. Maybe, if he tried, his imagination could get a grip on something. "Beneath this window there must be some kind of garden," he thought, "the trees are sighing. I must admit I don't care for the sighing of trees on a dark, stormy night—it gives me the creeps!" He remembered walking past Petrovsky Park a little while ago, and even thinking about it disgusted him. And he fleetingly recalled the Tuchkov Bridge and the Little Neva, and a chill seemed to run through him again, as it had while he stood, not long ago, over the water. "I never in my life liked water, not even as part of the landscape," he thought, and he suddenly smiled again at a certain strange thought. "You'd think now, of all times, I'd be indifferent to these fine points of esthetics and comfort, whereas actually I'm fussier, like some animal that insists on finding the right place. . . . I should really have turned in at the Petrovsky! No doubt it seemed dark—cold—he-he! As if I needed pleasant sensations! Why not snuff out the candle, in any case?" He put it out. "My neighbors have turned in," he thought; there was no light showing through the crack. "Well, this would be a good time for you to come complaining, Martha Petrovna. It's dark; an appropriate place; a unique moment. Of course, that's exactly why you won't come. . . ."

For some reason he suddenly remembered how an hour before he had enacted his plot against Dunia he had urged Raskolnikov to commit her to Razumikhin's care. "Actually, I probably said it to whip up my own enthusiasm, just as Raskolnikov guessed. What a scoundrel that Raskolnikov is, though! He's taken on a big load. In time he'll be a big scoundrel—when he gets all the nonsense out of him. But right now he's *too* eager to live! His kind are all cowards on that point. Well, to hell with him. Let him do as he likes. What do I care?"

And still he could not sleep. Little by little, the image of Dunia he had seen not long ago began to take shape, and suddenly he shivered. "No. That's got to be dropped now," he thought, recovering himself. "Got to think about something else. Strange and funny: I never hated anybody much; revenge never especially appealed to me. That must be a bad sign—a bad sign! I didn't like arguing, either, and I never got excited—also a bad sign! How much, how much I promised her . . . pah, to hell with it! But somehow she might have made a new man of me. . . ." Clenching his teeth, he ceased. Again he saw Dunia's image as she had appeared after she fired the first time, when she had lowered the revolver, terribly frightened, and she had seemed petrified, so that he could have seized her twice over without her being able to lift a hand in her own defense, had he not reminded her. He remembered how he seemed to have taken pity on her at that moment, how his heart seemed to be stifling him. . . . "Eh, to hell with it! Thoughts again. Got to drop all that. Drop it!"

He was beginning to doze off. His fevered shivering abated. Suddenly he thought he felt something running over his arm and over his leg under the blanket. He shuddered. "Pah, damn it! Must be a mouse!" he thought. "Because I left the veal on the table. . . ." He was terribly reluctant to uncover himself and get up in the cold air, but suddenly something unpleasant once again slithered over his leg. He tore off the blanket and lit the candle. Shivering from his feverish chill, he stooped to examine the bed. Nothing. He shook the blanket, and a mouse suddenly darted out onto the sheet. He tried to catch it, but the mouse flashed from one side to the other in zigzags without running off the bed, slipped away from under his fingers, ran over his hand, and darted under the pillow. He threw off the pillow, but instantly felt something leap on his chest, slither along his body and down his back, under his shirt. He shivered and woke. In the room it was dark. He lay on the bed wrapped up in his blanket, as before. The wind fretted at the windowpane. "Eh," he thought indignantly, "disgusting!"

He got up and sat on the edge of the bed with his back to the window. "Better not to sleep at all," he resolved. And yet the cold and the damp leaked from the window. Without rising, he drew the blanket to him and wrapped it around himself. He did not light the candle. He did not think about anything, nor did he want to think; but fantasies formed one after the other; fragments of thoughts flashed out, without beginning or end and without connection. He seemed to be dozing off again. Was it the cold, the dark, the damp, was it the wind fretting at the windowpane and shaking the trees outside, which evoked in him some stubborn and fantastic inclination or desire? Yet he had begun by seeing nothing but flowers. He imagined a charming landscape, a bright, warm, almost a hot day, a holiday, Trinity Sunday. A rich, sumptuous country cottage in the English style, all overgrown with clumps of sweet-smelling flowers, the whole house surrounded by flower beds; a porch twined by climbing plants and surrounded by roses; a bright, cool staircase covered with sumptuous carpeting and lined with rare flowers in Chinese vases. He took special note of the bouquets of tender white narcissus in water-filled vases on the windowsills, inclining outward on their bright green, long, thick stems, with a powerful aromatic smell. He did not want to leave them behind, but he mounted the stairs and entered a large, high room, and here too, once again, there were flowers everywhere, by the windows, near the doors opening out on the terrace, on the terrace itself—everywhere. The floor was strewn with fragrant, freshly cut grass; the windows were open; the fresh, light, cool breeze stirred in the room; birds chirped beneath the windows. In the middle of the room, resting on tables covered by white satin shrouds, was a coffin. The coffin was lined with white Neapolitan silk and edged with a thick white ruche. Garlands of flowers were twined about it on all sides. Inside lay a young girl, all in flowers, in a white tulle dress, arms tightly folded over her breast as though carved out of marble. Yet her loose, bright yellow hair was damp; there was a garland of roses on her brow. Her profile, already stiffened, seemed stern, and also as if carved of marble, but on her pallid lips the smile seemed to bespeak some vast and unchildlike offense and an enormous protest. Svidrigailov knew this girl. She had neither icon nor lighted candles by her coffin, and no prayers were heard. She had committed suicide, drowned herself. She was only fourteen, but her life had been broken and she had destroyed herself, outraged by an offense that had horrified and appalled her childlike sensibility and infused that soul of angelic purity with a sense of undeserved shame, wrenching from her a last despairing cry that went unheard and was brazenly cursed on a dark night in the gloom, in the cold, in the damp thaw, while the wind howled. . . .

Svidrigailov woke up. He rose from the bed and strode to the window. Haltingly, he found the catch and opened it. The wind roared furiously into the tight little cubicle and seemed to cling like hoarfrost to his face and to his chest, protected only by his shirt. There must have been something like a garden beneath the window, and it seemed like a pleasure garden at that. A chorus probably sang there in the daytime, and they served tea at small tables. But now drops of water flew through his window from the trees and bushes, and it was dark as the grave, so that one could just barely make out some dark stains that denoted material objects. For about five minutes Svidrigailov leaned his elbows on the windowsill and stared out into the darkness unable to tear himself away. Out of the gloom and the night came the sound of a cannon shot, and after it another.

"Ah," he thought, "the signal! The water is rising. By morning it will be seeping into the low places, into the streets, flooding basements and vaults. The cellar rats will be swimming out, and people will start hauling their junk to the upper floors in the wind and the rain, wet and cursing. . . . What time is it now, though?" No sooner had he thought this when somewhere close by, ticking away as if in a great hurry, a wall clock powerfully struck three. "Aha! It will be light in an hour! What am I waiting for? I'll go out now, straight to the Petrovsky; I'll choose a big bush there somewhere, all dripping with rain, so when you just barely brush it with your shoulder, a million drops

shower down on your head. . . ." He moved away from the
window, shut it, lit the candle, put on his jacket and overcoat
and hat, and took the candle out into the corridor to look
for the attendant (asleep somewhere in his cubicle, with rubbish and candle ends piled around him), so he could settle
with him for the room and leave the hotel. "It is the very
best moment. I couldn't choose a better one!"

For some time he walked up and down the long, narrow
corridor without finding anybody, and he was about to yell
out when suddenly, in a dark corner, between an old cupboard and the door, he saw something strange, and it
seemed to be alive. He leaned over, holding the candle, and
saw a child—a girl of about five, no more, in a sopping
wet dishrag of a dress, weeping and shivering. Apparently
unafraid of Svidrigailov, she fixed her large, dark eyes on
him in blank surprise, sniffling now and then, as children do
who have been crying for a long time and only just stopped
and begun to calm down, yet who still cannot help suddenly
sniffling again. The little girl's face seemed pale and exhausted; she was stiff with cold. "But how did she get here?
She must have sneaked in for cover and not slept all night."
He started questioning her. The little girl suddenly livened up
and began to babble at him in her childish way—something
about her "mommy," and her "mommy would beat" her for
some kind of cup she had "bwoken." The little girl talked
on and on. Somehow he managed to make out that she
was her mother's unloved child; and her mother was some
perpetually drunken scullion, probably from this very hotel,
who had beaten and terrified her. The girl had broken one
of her "mommy's" cups, and was so frightened she had run
away that same evening. She had probably been hiding
somewhere out in the rain for a long time, finally making
her way in, hiding behind the cupboard, and crouching there
in the corner all night long, weeping and shivering from the
damp and the dark and from the fear she would be beaten
within an inch of her life. Gathering her in his arms, he
returned to his room and deposited her on the bed. He
began to undress her. The dilapidated shoes on her bare
feet were so wet, it looked as if they had been in a puddle
all night. After he undressed her, he stretched her out on
the bed and wrapped her in the blanket from head to foot.
She fell asleep immediately. After he had done all this he
began once more to brood.

"Look how I've gotten myself involved again!" he thought,

with a heavy, angry feeling. "Absurd!" Indignantly he picked up the candle, meaning to search out the attendant, come what may, and leave as soon as possible. "The little bitch!" he thought as he opened the door, yet he turned once more to have a look at the girl, to see whether or not she was asleep. Cautiously, he lifted the blanket. The girl was soundly, blissfully asleep. She had warmed up under the blanket, and the color returned to her pale cheeks. Strangely, however, the color seemed brighter and deeper than seemed possible for a normal childish flush. "Fever," Svidrigailov thought. Or wine; it was as if somebody had given her a whole big full water glass to drink. Her scarlet lips seemed hot and burning—and what was that? Suddenly it seemed to him that her long, dark eyelashes stirred and fluttered as if they were about to lift, and a sly, sharp little eye peered out from under them; an eye that winked at him in an unchildish way, as though she were not asleep, but pretending. And so it was. Her lips were parting in a smile; the little corners of her mouth quivered as though she were still restraining herself; and then she let go completely. She was laughing, laughing openly. Something brazen and provocative radiated from that completely unchildlike face. It was corruption. It was a harlot's face, the brazen face of a venal French whore. Abandoning concealment, she opened her eyes wide. They wandered over him with a shameless, burning look; they were inviting him; they were laughing. . . . There was something infinitely horrible and outrageous in that laughter, in those eyes, in all the lewdness in the child's face. "What? A five-year-old!" Svidrigailov whispered in genuine horror. "It's . . . it's what?" But now she was turning the whole of her burning little face toward him, stretching out her arms. "Oh, you damned . . .!" Svidrigailov cried out in horror, raising his hand over her. . . . But at that very moment he woke up.

He was on the same bed, still wrapped in the blanket. The candle had gone out, and full daylight was brightening in the windows.

He sat up angrily, hurting all over. "Nightmare all night!" His bones ached. Outside, the fog was very thick, and nothing could be seen. It was almost five. He had overslept! He got up and put on his jacket and overcoat, which were still damp. Feeling the revolver in his pocket, he took it out and adjusted the percussion cap. Then he sat down, took a notebook from his pocket, and on the most conspicuous, the opening page, he wrote a few lines in a large hand. He reread them, pondering, his elbows on the table. The revolver and the notebook lay there at his elbow. The flies, wakened now, clustered around the untouched portion of veal on the table. For a long time he stared at them, and finally, with his free right hand, he tried to catch one. Although he tired himself out trying, he couldn't seem to catch a fly. Finally, noting himself at this interesting occupation, he pulled himself together, shuddered, got up, and resolutely left the room. A minute later he was out in the street.

A thick, milky fog had settled over the city. Svidrigailov walked along the dirty, slippery wooden pavement toward the Little Neva. He fancied he saw the waters of the Little Neva risen high overnight, Petrovsky Island, the wet footpaths, the wet grass, the wet trees and bushes, and, at last, *that very bush.* . . . Irritated, he started looking at the houses so he could think of something else. He met neither pedestrian nor cab along the prospect. The bright yellow little wooden houses looked dreary and dirty with their shutters closed. The cold and the damp gripped his whole body, and he started shivering. Now and then he would notice advertisements in the stores, and he read each one diligently. The wooden pavement came to an end. He was beside a large stone house. A dirty little dog, a bitch shivering with cold, ran across the street in front of him, tail between its legs. A drunk in a greatcoat lay face down across the sidewalk. Svidrigailov looked at him and walked on. A high watchtower loomed on his left. "Bah!" he thought, "why go to Petrovsky? This place is as good as any. At least I'll have an official witness. . . ." At this new thought he almost grinned, and turned onto Siezhinsky Street. There was the big building with the watchtower. A small man was leaning his shoulder up against the big locked gates. Wrapped in a gray army coat, he was wearing a brass "Achilles' helmet" on his head. His sleepy glance touched coldly on the approaching Svidrigailov, and he had that expression of long-suffering querulousness that has been stamped without exception on all Jewish faces. For some time Svidrigailov and Achilles looked at each other in silence. Finally it struck Achilles as improper that a man who wasn't drunk should be standing there, three steps away, without saying a word.

Still without stirring or changing his position, he asked: "Nu, vat you vont—ah?"

"Nothing, friend. How are you?" said Svidrigailov.

"Diss is no place."

"My friend, I am leaving for abroad."

"Abroad?"

"America . . ."

"America?"

Svidrigailov drew the revolver and cocked it. Achilles raised his eyebrows.

"Nu, vot! Diss for jokes is no place!"

"Why not?"

"Because . . . Vy, because diss is no place."

"It's all one, my friend. It's a fine place. If anybody asks you, tell them I went—well, tell them I went to America."

He placed the revolver at his right temple.

"Nu, here you can't! Diss is no place!" Achilles shook himself awake, and the pupils of his eyes distended and grew wider and wider.

Svidrigailov pulled the trigger.

7

That same day, but between six and seven in the evening, Raskolnikov was approaching the apartment in Bakaleev's house where Razumikhin had arranged for his mother and sister to stay. Entry to the stairs was from the street. Raskolnikov seemed to hesitate as to whether he should go in or not; yet he would not have turned away for anything. His mind was made up. "Anyway, they don't know anything yet, so it's all one," he thought. "And by now they're used to thinking that I'm odd. . . ." His clothes were in terrible shape, dirty and shredded and torn from a whole night spent out in the rain. He seemed almost disfigured from exhaustion, exposure, physical weariness, and a struggle with himself that had gone on for twenty-four hours. He had spent the whole night alone, God knew where. But at least he had made up his mind.

He knocked at the door, and his mother opened. Dunia was not at home. Even the maid happened to be out at the moment. At first Pulcheria Alexandrovna was speechless from happy astonishment; then she seized him by the arm and pulled him into the room.

"Well, you're here after all!" she began, joyfully catching her breath. "Rodia, don't be angry with me for greeting you in this stupid way, with tears. Actually I'm laughing, not crying. You think I'm crying? No, I am delighted. The tears come—it's just a stupid habit of mine. Since your father died, everything makes me cry. My dear, sit down. You're tired—you must be; I can see. Oh, you've gotten yourself all muddy."

"I was out in the rain yesterday, Mother," Raskolnikov began.

"No—oh, no!" Pulcheria Alexandrovna interrupted, leaping up. "You thought I would start questioning you, as I used to, like an old woman. Don't worry. I understand, you see; I understand everything. I've learned how you do things here now, and I can see myself it's better. So I've made up my mind once and for all: how can I expect to understand your motives or ask you to account for them to me? Lord only knows the plans and activities you have in that head of yours, or the ideas that crop up there; so I guess I shouldn't go around asking you what you're thinking. You see, I . . . Oh, Lord! Why am I dashing around like a madwoman? . . . You see, Rodia, I am reading the article you wrote in that magazine for the third time now. Dmitry Prokofich brought it to me. When I saw it—well, I sighed. I thought to myself: you're a fool—see what he's busy with— this is the whole secret! Scholars are always like that. Perhaps at this very moment he has some new ideas in his head and he's thinking them over. And what do I do but bother him and get him mixed up. Well, so, I read it, my dear. Of course, there was a lot I didn't understand. Anyway, that's the way it has to be. How could I?"

"Show it to me, Mother."

Taking the journal, Raskolnikov glanced swiftly at his article. In spite of its contradicting his present situation and condition, he experienced the strange, bittersweet sensation every author experiences (let alone one who is only twenty-three) who sees himself in print for the first time. This lasted only a moment. After a few lines he frowned, and a terrible melancholy seized him. At once his whole spiritual struggle of these last months came back to him. In disgust and irritation, he flung the article down on the table.

"I may be stupid, Rodia, but I can tell that you will soon be one of the top people in our learned world, maybe the very top. And they dared think you were mad! Ha-ha-ha! You may not know it, but that's what they really did think. Ah, the miserable worms, how could they understand what

it means to have brains! Even Dunia almost believed it—as
if it were possible! Twice in his life, your late father sent
things in to the journals; poems the first time (I still have a
notebook stashed away I'll show you sometime), then a
whole novel (I copied it out for him myself; I asked to), and
how we both prayed for it to be accepted, but it wasn't! Six,
seven days ago, Rodia, when I looked at your clothes I
worried myself silly—how you lived, what you ate, what you
went around in—but now I see I was being stupid again.
Because if you felt like it, with your mind and talent, you
could immediately have anything you wanted. I suppose you
don't want to for the time being and you're busy with more
important matters."

"Isn't Dunia home, Mama?"

"No, Rodia, she's not. Quite often I don't see her at
home. She leaves me alone. Dmitry Prokofich comes to visit
with me, bless him, and he talks about you all the time. He
loves and respects you, my dear. I'm not saying your sister
has been terribly disrespectful to me; I'm not complaining,
mind you. She has her nature and I have mine. She seems
to be clutching some secrets of her own. Well, I have no
secrets of any sort that I keep from either of you. Of course,
I'm convinced Dunia is much too clever a girl, and besides,
she loves us both . . . still, I don't know where it will lead.
You see how happy you've made me now that you've
dropped by, but she has gone for a walk. When she comes
back I'll say to her: your brother came while you were out,
and where have you been spending your time? Rodia, you
mustn't spoil me. If you can come, do; if you can't, it doesn't
matter; I'll wait. In any case I'd know you loved me, and
that's all I need. I'll be reading your works, and I'll be hearing about you from everybody, and once in a while you
might come see me yourself—what could be better? Here
you are now, to comfort your mother, and you know, I can
see—" At this point Pulcheria Alexandrovna burst into
tears. "There I go again! Don't look at me, I'm silly! Oh,
Lord, why am I sitting here!" she exclaimed, jumping from
her place. "There's coffee, and I haven't even offered you
any! That's an old woman's selfishness for you! I'll be right
back—right back!"

"Mama, forget it, I'm going now. That's not why I came.
Please listen." Pulcheria Alexandrovna moved timidly in his
direction. "No matter what had happened, Mama dear, no
matter what you had heard about me, what people said to

you about me—would you still love me as you do now?"
He asked this all of a sudden, as if it flowed out of him, as
if not thinking about his words or weighing them.

"Rodia, what's wrong with you, Rodia? How can you
even ask such questions! Who is going to say anything to
me about you? Anyway, whoever came to me, I wouldn't
believe anybody—I'd simply chase them away."

"I came to assure you I've always loved you, and I'm
glad we're alone, even that Dunia's not here," he continued,
carried away by the same impulse. "I came to tell you
frankly: you won't be happy, but you should know your son
loves you right now more than he does himself; and everything you've thought about me—that I'm cruel and don't
love you—it was unjust. I'll never stop loving you. . . . Well,
I guess that's enough. I thought I should do this; make a
beginning. . . ."

Pulcheria Alexandrovna embraced him silently, pressed
him to her breast and wept softly.

"I do not know what is the matter with you, Rodia," she
said at last. "I thought all along we were simply getting on
your nerves; but now I see you have some great calamity
taking shape, and that's why you are sad. I had a feeling
about this for a long time, Rodia. Forgive my mentioning
it. I think about it all the time and don't sleep nights. Last
night all night long your sister had a fever, and she talked
about you in her sleep the whole time. I caught a thing or
two, but didn't understand. All morning long I've been pacing up and down like a convict, waiting for something awful
to happen—and now it has come! Rodia, where are you
going, Rodia? Are you off on a journey?"

"I'm off on a journey."

"I thought so! If you want, I could go with you, you know;
Dunia, too. She loves you. She loves you very much. And
Sofia Semionovna, she could come with us, if you want. I'd
even accept her gladly as a daughter, you see. Dmitry Prokofich would help us to go together . . . but . . . where is
it . . . you're off to?"

"Good-bye, Mama dear."

"What? This very day!" she cried, as if losing him forever.

"I can't . . . It's time . . . I really have to—"

"And I can't go with you?"

"No, but you can pray to God for me on your knees.
Your prayer might reach."

"Come here and let me make the sign of the cross over

you and bless you! Like this . . . There, there. Oh, God, what are we doing!"

Yes, he was glad nobody was there and he was alone with his mother. It seemed as if after all that terrible time his heart had softened at once. He fell down before her and kissed her feet. The two of them embraced and wept. This time she was not astonished and asked no questions. She had understood for some time that something terrible was happening to her son, that a terrible time had come for him.

"Rodia, my darling, my firstborn!" she said, weeping. "You are just like you were as a little boy. You used to come up and hug and kiss me just like that. When your father was still alive, and times were hard, you comforted us simply by being there with us; and after I buried your father, how often we would hug each other like now, and weep over his grave. If I cry so long now, it's because I have a mother's heart, and it senses trouble. As soon as I saw you the first time—remember, that evening when we first arrived—I guessed it all, just from the way you looked at me, and my heart skipped a beat; and as soon as I opened the door today, as soon as I saw you, I thought, well, the hour has come. But you're not leaving right away, Rodia, are you?"

"No."

"You'll come see me again?"

"Yes . . . I'll come."

"Rodia, don't be angry; I know I shouldn't ask any questions. I know I shouldn't; but tell me, just in a few short words—will you be going far?"

"Very far."

"What will you do there? Do you have a job? Will there be a career for you?"

"Whatever God sends . . . but pray for me. . . ."

Raskolnikov went to the door, but she clung to him and looked at him in despair. Her face was twisted with horror.

"Enough, Mama dear," Raskolnikov said, regretting deeply that he had decided to come.

"It's not for good? You're still not leaving for good? You'll come, won't you? You'll come tomorrow?"

"I'll come. Yes. Good-bye."

At last he tore himself away.

It was a fresh, warm evening. Since morning the weather had cleared. Raskolnikov went to his apartment, hurrying. He wanted to get everything over with before sunset, but until now he had not wanted to see anybody. As he climbed up to his apartment he noticed that Nastasia tore herself away from her samovar and followed him steadily with her eyes. "Is there anybody in my place?" he thought. In disgust, he thought it might be Porfiry; but when he got to his room and opened the door, he saw Dunia. She sat there alone, profoundly lost in thought. She seemed to have been waiting a long time. He paused at the threshold, and she rose from the couch in alarm, standing straight in front of him. The gaze she fixed intently upon him expressed horror and inextinguishable grief. From her look alone, he grasped immediately that she knew everything.

"You want me to come in or go away?" he asked mistrustfully.

"I've been at Sofia Semionovna's all day. We were both waiting for you. We thought you would certainly go there."

Raskolnikov entered and sat down, exhausted. "I'm a bit weak, Dunia. Very tired. At this moment I should have liked complete control of myself." He darted a glance at her mistrustfully.

"Where were you all night long?"

"I don't remember too well. I wanted to make up my mind once and for all, Sister, you see, and many times I walked close to the Neva. That much I remember. I wanted to put an end to it there . . . but I couldn't. . . ." he whispered, glancing mistrustfully again at Dunia.

"Thank God! How terrified we were of just that, Sofia Semionovna and I! That means you still believe in life—thank God, thank God!"

Raskolnikov smiled bitterly. "I didn't believe. Yet I was hugging Mother just now, and we were crying. I don't believe. Yet I asked her to pray for me. God knows how it works, Dunia dear—I don't understand any of it."

"You were at Mother's? Did you tell her?" Dunia exclaimed, frightened. "You didn't tell her, did you?"

"No, I didn't tell her . . . in words. But she understood a lot. She heard you talking in your sleep last night. I'm convinced she half understands. Maybe I did a foolish thing, dropping by like that. I don't even know why I did it. I'm a vile man, Dunia."

"A vile man, yet ready to go suffer. You are going, aren't you?"

"I'm going. Right now. Yes, it was to avoid the shame of it I wanted to drown myself, Dunia; but I thought as I stood over the water—if I thought I was strong till now, why should I fear shame at this point? Dunia—is that pride?"

"It is pride, Rodia."

A light seemed to flash in his dulled eyes; it was as though he liked the idea that he was still proud. "You don't think—do you, Sister—I was simply afraid of the water?" he then asked with a hideous grin, looking her in the face.

"Oh, Rodia, stop!" Dunia exclaimed bitterly.

The silence lasted a couple of minutes. He sat there, head bowed, looking at the ground; Dunia stood at the other end of the table and looked at him with anguish. All of a sudden he got up. "It's late. Time to go. To give myself up now. But I don't know why I am going to give myself up." Large tears flowed down her cheeks. "You are crying, Sister. But can you give me your hand?"

"Did you doubt it?" She embraced him tightly. "By going to suffer, surely you wash away half your crime?" she cried, pressing and hugging and kissing him.

"Crime? What crime?" he suddenly shouted, in a kind of sudden rage. "Killing a foul, noxious louse! An old pawnbroker woman no good to anybody, who sucked the life juices of the poor—why, for killing her I'll be forgiven forty sins! I don't think about it, and I don't think about washing it away. Why does everybody push 'crime, crime!' at me? Only now do I see clearly the full depth of my mean-spiritedness, now that I've already decided to accept this unnecessary shame! Just because I'm worthless and have no talent, maybe also for my own advantage, as . . . Porfiry . . . suggested!"

"Brother, what are you saying!" Dunia cried out in despair. "You have shed human blood!"

"Which they all shed," he interrupted, almost frantic. "Which cascades, and always has, down upon the earth like a waterfall, which they pour like champagne, and for which they are crowned on the Capitoline and called the benefactors of mankind. Look a little harder and you'll see! My own intentions were good, as far as people were concerned. I would have done hundreds, thousands of good deeds, instead of this one stupidity—not even stupidity, just clumsiness. Because the whole idea wasn't quite as stupid as it seems now that it's failed . . . (Everything seems stupid when it fails!) Performing this stupidity, I wanted to make myself independent, to take the first step, to acquire the means; then everything would have been canceled by the relatively immense good. . . . I couldn't even take the first step. . . . Because I'm—vile! That's what it all comes to! Anyway, I refuse to look at it your way. If I had made it I would have been crowned, but now—off to jail!"

"Brother, what are you saying! That isn't so at all!"

"Ah, not the right form! Esthetically, not such very good form! Well, I really don't understand why blasting people with bombs or a barrage is better form. Finicking over esthetics is the first sign of impotence! . . . I never, never realized this more clearly than now, and I understand my crime less than ever! I have never, never felt stronger or more convinced than now!"

The color even returned to his pale, exhausted face. In the middle of his last outburst, however, his eyes desperately met Dunia's; and he found in that look so much anguish for him that involuntarily he came to his senses. Any way you looked at it, he felt, he had made these two poor women miserable. Any way you looked at it, he had been the cause. . . .

"Dunia, darling! If I'm guilty, forgive me. Though if I'm guilty, I cannot be forgiven. Good-bye! Let's not quarrel. It's time—it's high time. Don't follow me, I beg you; I still have a call to make. . . . You go now, and stay with Mother. I beg you to! It's the last and the greatest request I have to make of you. Don't ever leave her. When I said good-bye to her, she was in such anxiety I don't think she can bear it—she'll die or go out of her mind. Be with her! Razumikhin will be with you both. I spoke to him. . . . Don't weep for me. I'll try to be brave and honest as long as I live, even though I'm a murderer. Maybe you'll hear my name sometime. I won't disgrace you; you'll see. I may yet prove . . . Well, good-bye for now," he hastened to conclude, noticing that strange expression again in Dunia's eyes as he spoke these last words and made these last promises. "Why are you crying so? Don't cry, don't cry. We won't part forever! . . . Oh, yes! One moment! I forgot. . . ."

He went to the table, picked up a thick, dusty book, opened it, and took out a small portrait he had placed between two pages, a watercolor on ivory. It was a portrait of the landlady's daughter, his former fiancée, who had died: the same strange girl who had wanted to enter a nunnery. For a moment he looked at that expressive, sickly little face; then he kissed the portrait and handed it to Dunia.

"I used to talk to her a lot. *About that,* too," he said

pensively. "To her alone. I confided a lot that later came terribly true. Don't fret"—he looked at Dunia—"she didn't agree, just as you didn't, and I'm glad she's not here. The main point is everything's going to start over; there will be a clean break!" he cried, but soon returned to his melancholy state. "Oh, yes, everything. But am I ready for it? Do · I want it! I'm supposed to face an ordeal, they say. But why these ordeals that don't make sense? What for? What will I be able to realize better than I do now after twenty years of hard labor, crushed by suffering and idiocy, when I'm senile and impotent? What will there be left to live for? Why should I consent to live like that? Oh, when I stood over the Neva at dawn today, I knew I was vile!"

Finally they both left. It was hard for Dunia, but she loved him. She went, but after she'd gone about fifty steps she turned once more to look at him. He was still visible. When he came to the corner, he also turned. Their looks met for the last time. As she looked at him he waved his hand impatiently, with some annoyance, signaling for her to go; and he himself turned sharply around the corner.

"I'm wicked, I see that," he thought, ashamed a moment later of that gesture to Dunia. "I'm not worth it—why do they have to love me so? If only I were alone and nobody loved me and I never loved anybody! *All this wouldn't have happened!* I wonder whether my spirit will humble itself sufficiently in the next fifteen or twenty years so I'll snivel meekly when confronted, and call myself a criminal? I will, yes, I really will! That's why I'm being sent off to hard labor; that's what they're after. . . . Look at them scurrying up and down the street! Every last one of them by his very nature is a criminal and a scoundrel, and worse—an idiot! If anybody tried to get me off exile and hard labor, they'd all go mad with righteous indignation! Oh, how I hate them all!"

He pondered. By what process was he humbling himself before them all, by what process had it come about that he would humble himself without even thinking about it, and without conviction? But why not? That was, of course, the way it had to be. Wouldn't twenty years of constant oppression finally wear him down? Water wears down stone. "Afterwards, what would there be left to live for? Why do I go now, when I know as if it were written in a book that it really will be like that and cannot be different!"

For perhaps the hundredth time since yesterday evening he asked himself that question; but he went anyway.

8

When he entered Sonia's room dusk was already falling. Sonia had been waiting for him all day in terrible agitation. She and Dunia had waited together. Having remembered Svidrigailov's words of the day before, that Sonia "knew," Dunia had come that morning. We will not relate the details of their conversation, or the tears the women shed, or how close they came to feel to one another. From this meeting Dunia at least carried away the consolation that her brother would not be alone. He had come to Sonia first with his confession. When he needed a human presence he had sought one in her. Wherever fate might send him, she would follow. Dunia did not need to ask; somehow, she knew it would be that way. She regarded Sonia with a kind of awe; so much so, it was almost embarrassing at first. Sonia, on the other hand, was close to tears, because she considered herself unworthy even so much as to look at Dunia. The beautiful look on Dunia's face when she had bowed to her with such consideration and respect the time they had first met at Raskolnikov's, had remained in her mind ever since as one of the most beautiful and most unattainable visions of her life.

Dunia had finally lost patience and left Sonia, to wait for her brother in his apartment. She thought he might go there first. Left alone, Sonia really was terrified at the thought he might really put an end to himself by suicide. The same thought frightened Dunia. All day each had kept trying to convince the other with all possible arguments that it couldn't be, and they had been calmer when together. Now that they had gone separate ways, neither could think of anything else. Sonia remembered how Svidrigailov had said to her the day before that Raskolnikov had two paths—Siberian exile, or . . . And she knew his vanity, his arrogance, conceit, and disbelief. "Can weakness of spirit and fear of death alone force him to live?" she finally thought in despair. Meanwhile, the sun was already setting. She stood sadly in front of the window and stared at it hard, but all she could see was the main wall, unwhitewashed, of the next house. When she was completely persuaded of the unhappy man's death, he finally walked into her room.

A joyous cry burst from her, but when she looked hard at his face she paled.

"All right," he said, grinning. "I've come for your crosses, Sonia. You were the one who sent me to the crossroads. What's wrong? Now the time's come, are you afraid?"

The tone struck Sonia as strange, and she looked at him, astonished. A cold shiver ran along her body. But a minute later she realized both the tone and the words were a pretense. He kept looking into the corner, as though he were trying to avoid looking her straight in the face.

"You see, Sonia, I calculated it would be more to my advantage this way. One circumstance . . . Well, it's a long story, and not much point. You know the only thing makes me mad, though? To think all the stupid animal snouts will gather together now and gape and stare at me and ask me stupid questions I'm going to have to answer, and they'll wag their fingers—that's what's annoying. . . . Pah! You know, I'm not going to go to Porfiry. I'm sick of him. I'd rather go to my old friend Gunpowder. I'd certainly surprise him. I'd certainly have an effect on him! I've got to be calmer, though. I'm too bilious lately. Believe it or not, I almost shook my fist at my sister just now, because she turned around to look at me for the last time. What a nasty state of mind I'm in—look what I've come to! Well, now, come on—where are the crosses?"

Silently Sonia took two crosses from a drawer, one of Cypress and one of brass, crossed herself, made the sign of the cross over him, and put the Cypress cross around his neck and over his chest.

"That's a symbol, I suppose. Means I'm taking the cross upon myself, ha-ha! As if till now I hadn't suffered! Cypress—that's for the common people; brass—that was Lizaveta's. You take that one. Show me, would you? Is that the way she wore it . . . then? I know of two other brass crosses like that, and a silver one and a small icon. I threw them down on the old woman's breast that time. They're really what I should be wearing now, by the way. . . . I'm getting everything mixed up; I forget what I'm doing. I'm kind of distraught! You see, Sonia, what I really came for was to let you know in advance, so you'd be informed. . . . I guess that's all there is to it . . . all I came for. (Hmm. Still, you know, I thought I'd have more to say.) You're the one who wanted me to go, weren't you? So I'm going to go to jail, and thy will be done. Why are you crying? You, too? Stop! Enough. How difficult all this is for me!"

His feelings were roused, however; his heart shrank as he looked at her. "And this one—what about her?" he thought to himself. "What am I to her? Why is she crying? Why is she seeing me off like my mother did, or Dunia? She's going to be my nursemaid!"

"Cross yourself; pray at least once," begged Sonia in a timid, quivering voice.

"Oh, as you like! As often as you wish! And with a pure heart, Sonia, with a pure heart . . ."

Yet what he wanted to say was something else.

He crossed himself several times. Seizing her shawl, Sonia flung it over her head. It was probably the green "family" shawl Marmeladov had once referred to. It occurred to Raskolnikov, but he did not ask. He already had some sense of how distraught he was, and how terribly edgy. That was what he was afraid of. Suddenly it struck him that Sonia intended to accompany him.

"What are you doing! Where are you going? Stay here! Stay here! I'm going alone!" he cried out in petty irritation, and almost furious; he strode to the door. "What's the need for a whole procession!" he muttered as he went out.

Sonia remained in the middle of the room. He had not even said good-bye to her; he had already forgotten her; he was possessed by mocking and rebellious doubt.

"Is this the way—is this the way to do it?" he thought once more as he descended the stairs. "Is it really impossible to stop where I am and put everything right again . . . and not go?"

But he kept on walking. Suddenly he realized with a kind of finality that there was little point in putting questions to himself. As he emerged onto the street he remembered he had not said good-bye to Sonia and she had remained in the middle of the room in her green shawl, frozen in her tracks by his outburst. For an instant he stopped. In that same instant another thought suddenly burst upon him, as though it had been lying coiled, waiting to confound him once and for all. "Why did I go see her now? I told her, on business; but what business? I didn't have any business! Just to tell her I was *going*? So what? How important! Do I love her? Surely I don't? I drove her away like a dog just now. Did I really want the crosses? Oh, how low I've fallen! No, what I wanted was her tears; I wanted to watch her fear; I

wanted to see her aching, suffering heart! I had to have
something to hang on to, a chance to linger and watch a
human being suffer! And I once dared to aspire, to hope
and to dream! What a beggar I am, what a nobody! How
vile, vile!"

Walking along the canal embankment, he no longer had
far to go. Yet when he reached the bridge he paused,
crossed in the wrong direction, and headed for the Haymarket.

Avidly he looked to the right and to the left, staring intently at every object, yet finding nothing on which he could
fasten his attention. Everything was slipping away. "In a
week or a month they'll be carting me off somewhere in
one of those prison vans and along this bridge, and maybe
I will look at the canal, and will I remember it as it is now?"
flashed through his mind. "That signboard—how will it feel
to be reading those letters then? They've spelled it 'Cam-
pany'—must remember that *a,* the letter *a*—I must look at
it a month from now, the same *a.* How will it strike me
then? What will I feel and think? My God, how con-
temptible . . . all these . . . things I'm worrying about! Of
course . . . in its own way . . . it's interesting . . . (Ha-ha-
ha! What am I thinking of!) I must be going dotty, bragging
to myself. Why do I have to mock myself? Pah! How they
shove! Must have been that fat German shoved into me.
Wonder if he knows who he shoved? An old woman and a
child, begging. Funny. She thinks I'm better off than she is.
Well, I'll give her something just to see what happens. Hmm,
wonder where this five-kopeck piece in my pocket came
from? Here you are, old girl. . . . Take it!"

"God keep you!" sounded the plaintive voice of the beggar woman.

He came to the Haymarket. He did not like being shoved
around by the crowd, he did not like it at all, and yet he
made his way to where the crowd was thickest. To be left
alone he would have given everything in the world; yet he
sensed that he would not be alone, not for a single minute.
In the crowd, a drunk was acting up. He kept trying to
dance, staggering sideways as he tried. The crowd proceeded
around him. Raskolnikov pushed his way through the crowd,
watched the drunk for a few minutes, and suddenly burst
into a short, spasmodic laugh. A minute later he had forgotten the drunk and no longer even saw him, though he was
looking straight at him. Finally he walked away without even

remembering where he was. When he came to the middle of the square, however, he felt a sudden impulse; a sensation possessed him at once and seized all of him, body and mind.

Suddenly he remembered Sonia's words: "Go to the crossroads, bow down to the people, kiss the earth because you have sinned against it, too, and say aloud to the whole world: 'I am a murderer!'" As he remembered, he shook all over. The blind melancholy and anxiety of the recent past, but especially of the last few hours, oppressed him to such a degree that he simply plunged into the possibility of this new, whole, and complete sensation. It came upon him suddenly like a kind of nervous fit; took fire first as a single spark in his soul, and suddenly, like flame, seized everything. Everything seemed to melt inside him, and tears flowed. He dropped to the earth where he stood. . . .

He was on his knees in the middle of the square. He bowed down to the earth. With joy and pleasure he kissed the dirty earth. He rose and bowed down once more.

A youth nearby remarked: "Eesh, he's plastered!" And laughter sounded.

One of the artisans added: "It's to Jerusalem he's going, my friends; and he says good-bye to his children and his motherland. He bows to the whole world, and he's kissing our capital city of St. Petersburg and the ground it's built on." He was a bit drunk.

"The guy's still young," a third one put in.

"And from a decent class of people, it would seem," said someone in a more matter-of-fact tone of voice.

"Nowadays you can't tell who's decent and who ain't."

These comments restrained Raskolnikov. The words, "I killed," which had perhaps been ready on his tongue, died inside him. Nevertheless, he bore the shouting calmly, and without looking around walked straight down a side street in the direction of the police station. He saw something flash ahead of him, but was not surprised. Already he had felt that somehow that was how it had to be. At the Haymarket, as he had bowed to the earth for the second time, about fifty paces away and slightly to the left, he had caught a glimpse of Sonia. She hid from him behind one of the wooden booths on the square, and that meant she must have followed him his whole sorrowful walk. At this moment Raskolnikov sensed and understood, once and for all, that Sonia would be with him always from now on, and would follow him to the ends of the earth, wherever fate might send him. His heart heaved. . . . But now he had come to the fated place.

He entered the yard boldly. He had to go up to the third floor. "I still have to climb up," he thought. It seemed as if the fated moment were still a long way off. There was still a lot of time left. He could still change his mind.

And there was the same litter again: the same eggshells on the spiral staircase, again the doors of apartments wide open, the same kitchens reeking of the same steam and stench. Raskolnikov had not been here since that time. His legs turned numb and buckled, but he kept going. He stopped for a moment to catch his breath, to straighten up and go in *like a man*. But he thought suddenly, reflecting on this impulse of his: "What for? Why? If I must drink this cup, does it make any difference? The fouler the better!" At this moment there flashed in his imagination the figure of Ilia Petrovich Gunpowder. Did he actually have to go to *him*? Couldn't he go to somebody else? Why not Nikodim Fomich? Should he turn around right now, and go perhaps to the home of the superintendent? At least it would all be handled in a homey manner. . . . No, no! To Gunpowder, to Gunpowder! If he had to drink, he might as well drink it down all at once. . . .

Turning cold, and scarcely conscious, he opened the door to the station. There were very few people inside this time; a janitor of some sort and some other simple soul. The policeman on duty did not even look up from behind his partition. Raskolnikov passed on to the next room. "Maybe I still don't have to speak," flashed within him. In this room was a person, undoubtedly one of the clerks, but dressed in mufti, settling himself at a desk and about to write something. Another clerk sat in the corner. Zamiotov wasn't there. Nikodim Fomich, naturally, wasn't there either.

"Nobody here?" Raskolnikov asked, addressing the person at the desk.

"Who is it you want?"

"A-a-ah! 'Not a sound to be heard, not a sight to be seen, but the Russian spirit . . .' How does that fairy tale go? I forget! M-my c-compliments!" a familiar voice suddenly exclaimed.

Raskolnikov shuddered. It was Gunpowder. He suddenly emerged from the third room. "Fate itself," Raskolnikov thought. "Why is he here?"

"Come to see us? What's the occasion?" Ilia Petrovich

exclaimed. (He was evidently in excellent spirits, and even a bit exalted.) "If it's on business, you've come early. I'm here myself by chance. . . . But if there's anything I can do . . . I confess . . . what's your name, by the way? Excuse me. . . ."

"Raskolnikov."

"Of course, Raskolnikov! You don't think I really forgot, do you! I surely hope you don't think I'm a . . . Rodion Ro . . . Ro . . . Rodionych, isn't that right?"

"Rodion Romanych."

"Yes, yes, of course! Rodion Romanych, Rodion Romanych! I had it on the tip of my tongue. I even checked it a number of times. I confess I've sincerely regretted I had that . . . you know, with you . . . they told me later, I learned you were a young writer, a scholar, even . . . and you were just starting out, so to speak. . . . Oh, Lord! What writer or scholar hasn't started out by trying something original! My wife and I, we both respect literature—my wife with a real passion! Literature and being artistic! Granted you're a gentleman—then all you need is talent, knowledge, judgment, genius, and you can get anything else you want. A hat—well, I ask you now, what does a hat signify? A hat's nothing, I can buy one at Zimmerman's; but what's under the hat, what the hat keeps and covers—that I can't buy, sir! . . . I confess I even wanted to come see you and explain myself; you see, I thought maybe you . . . Well, anyway, let me ask, is there anything I can do for you? I hear some of your family has arrived?"

"Yes, my mother and sister."

"I've had the honor and pleasure of meeting your sister—a charming and cultivated person. I confess I regretted losing my temper with you that time. It was too bad! And if I leaped to conclusions about your fainting fit— it was all brilliantly explained to me later! Ferocity and fanaticism! I can understand your indignation. Are you by any chance changing apartments because of your family's arrival?"

"N-no, I just . . . I came to ask . . . I thought I'd find Zamiotov here."

"Oh, yes! You two got to be friends, didn't you? I heard about it. Well, Zamiotov's not with us anymore. You missed him. Yes, sir, we've lost Alexander Grigorevich! As of yesterday his presence is not to be encountered; he's transferred . . . and when he transferred he even tangled

with everybody . . . that's how rude he is. . . . He's a feath-
erbrained little pipsqueak, nothing more; once he even
showed some promise; but what can you do with them, these
brilliant young men of ours! He wants to take some kind of
examination, but our boys just talk and brag a little, and
that's all the examination ever comes to. Not like you, for
example, or that Mr. Razumikhin there, your friend. You
picked a scholarly career, and you're not going to let a couple failures beat you down! As far as the little ornaments
and appurtenances of life are concerned, for you—*nihil est*;
you're an ascetic, a monk, a hermit! . . . For you it's a pen
behind the ear, a book, scholarly researches—that's what
makes your spirit soar! I myself partly— Have you read
Livingstone's memoirs?"

"No."

"I've read them. Awful lot of nihilists around nowadays,
though; well, I know, it's understandable, of course; the
times we live in, I ask you. By the way, if I may . . . you're
not a nihilist, now, are you? Answer frankly, now, quite
frankly!"

"N-no . . ."

"Now, you know you can be quite frank with me; don't
hold back; just imagine you're all alone by yourself! Business is one thing, and—You thought I was going to say
'*pleasure*'—no, sir, you didn't guess right! I wasn't going to
say 'pleasure,' I was going to say one's feelings as man and
citizen, one's feelings of humanity and love for the Almighty. I may be an official person and in the service, but
I always feel obliged to give an account of myself as man
and citizen. . . . You were about to say something about
Zamiotov, though. Now, Zamiotov's a man who would
raise a rumpus in the French manner, with a glass of champagne or Don wine in front of him in a house of ill repute—
that's the kind of guy your Zamiotov is! While I, perhaps,
have been burning, so to speak, with devotion and lofty
feelings, and what's more, I have significance, I'm a man
of rank, I have a position! I'm married and I have children.
I do my duty as a man and citizen, and who is he, may I
ask? I talk to you as a person ennobled by education. And
just look at those new midwives spreading all over the
place. . . ."

Raskolnikov raised a questioning brow. Ilia Petrovich had
obviously risen from table not very long ago, and his words
nattered and fell around Raskolnikov like empty husks. Yet

in part Raskolnikov understood them somehow, and he looked inquiringly at the lieutenant without knowing how it would all end.

"I'm talking about those crop-haired dolls," the garrulous Ilia Petrovich continued. "I call them midwives. I think it's appropriate. Ha-ha! They all flock to the academy to learn anatomy; well, tell me now, suppose I get sick, you don't think I'd call a doll in to cure me, do you? He-he!" Ilia Petrovich laughed and laughed, thoroughly pleased at his own witticisms.

"Let's admit there's an incredible thirst for knowledge; why not get an education and let it go at that? Why abuse it? Why insult decent people the way that scoundrel Zamiotov does? Why did he insult me, I ask you? Look how these suicides have been spreading all over the place—you simply can't imagine. They all spend the last money they've got and go and kill themselves. The dolls do it, young boys, kids, old people. . . . Only this morning we had a report about some gentleman who'd arrived in town not long ago. Nil Pavlych—hey, Nil Pavlych! What was that gentleman's name—the one we had a report on just now—the one who shot himself over on the Petersburg side?"

Someone from the other room answered hoarsely and indifferently: "Svidrigailov."

Raskolnikov gave a start. "Svidrigailov!" he exclaimed, "Svidrigailov shot himself!"

"You mean you know Svidrigailov?"

"Yes . . . I know him. . . . He hasn't been here long. . . ."

"That's right, he hasn't been here long; lost his wife; a man of dissolute behavior; and all of a sudden he shot himself, and so scandalously, you can't imagine. . . . He left a few words in his notebook, that he's dying in sound mind and that nobody be blamed for his death. They say he had money. How did you happen to know him?"

"I'm . . . an acquaintance . . . my sister lived with them, as a governess. . . ."

"Aha, aha, aha . . . Maybe you could tell us something about him, then? Didn't you suspect anything?"

"I saw him yesterday . . . he . . . was drinking wine. . . . I knew nothing."

Raskolnikov felt as if something had fallen on him and was crushing him.

"You've turned kind of pale again. Air's so damn stuffy in here. . . ."

"Yes, I think I had better go now," Raskolnikov muttered. "Excuse me for disturbing—"

"Oh, please! Whenever you like! It was a pleasure, and I'm happy to say . . ."

Ilia Petrovich even held out his hand.

"I just wanted . . . to see Zamiotov. . . ."

"I understand, I understand; it was a pleasure."

"I'm . . . very glad . . . good-bye, sir." Raskolnikov smiled.

He went out; he swayed. His head spun. He had no feeling of whether he was standing on his legs or not. He began to descend the stairs, leaning his right hand on the wall. He thought some janitor holding a register bumped into him, making his way upstairs to the station; some mutt started barking rapidly somewhere downstairs; and a woman shouted and threw a rolling pin at it. He came out into the yard. There, not far from the gate, stood Sonia, numb and deathly pale; and she looked at him with a wild look. He stopped before her. There was something painful and tortured in her face, something desperate. She threw up her hands. A ghastly, lost smile forced its way to his lips. He stood there and grinned. Then he turned back upstairs to the station.

Ilia Petrovich had sat down and was rummaging through some papers. Before him stood the peasant who had bumped into Raskolnikov on the stairs.

"A-ah? You again! Leave something behind? Why, what's the matter?"

With color draining from his lips and with a fixed stare, Raskolnikov went quietly up to him, right up to the table. He leaned on it with one hand and tried to say something, but he could not. All that came out were some incoherent sounds.

"You're not well—a chair! Here, sit on the chair, sit down! Water!"

Raskolnikov sank down on the chair, but did not take his eyes off the quite unpleasantly startled face of Ilia Petrovich. For a moment each stared at the other and waited. Somebody brought some water.

"It was I—" Raskolnikov began.

"Drink some water."

He pushed the water away with his hand and said quietly but distinctly, pausing between words: "It was I who killed the old pawnbroker widow and her sister Lizaveta; I killed them with an ax and robbed them."

Ilia Petrovich opened his mouth. People came running from all sides.

Raskolnikov repeated his testimony.

EPILOGUE

1

Siberia. On the banks of a broad, deserted river stands a town, one of Russia's administrative centers; in the town is a fortress; in the fortress, a prison. In the prison Rodion Raskolnikov, transported convict second-class, has been confined for the last nine months. Almost a year and a half have passed since the day of his crime.

The legal proceedings had passed without great difficulty. The criminal supported his own testimony firmly, clearly, and precisely, without confusing the circumstances or attempting to soften the account of them in his favor, without distorting the facts or forgetting even the most insignificant detail. He related the whole story of the murder down to the smallest item; he explained the mystery of the *pledge* (the piece of wood with the metal strip), which had been found in the murdered woman's hand. He told in detail how he had taken the keys from her, and he described the keys and the chest and what was in it. He even enumerated some of the objects it contained. He explained the riddle of Lizaveta's murder. He told how Koch had knocked on the door, and the student behind him. He recounted everything they had said to each other; and how he, the criminal, had run down the stairs and heard the cries of Mitka and Mikolka; how he had hidden in the vacant apartment; and how he had gone home. He pointed out in conclusion the stone in the yard on Voznesensky Prospect, under which the purse and the other items were found. In brief, the case was clear. The investigators and judges were quite surprised that he had not made use of the purse and other items but had hidden them under a stone, and even more so that he could not remember in detail all the items he had stolen, and was even wrong about how many there were. In particular, the statement that he had not once opened the purse and did not even know how much money there was in it seemed improbable. There turned out to be three hundred and seventeen silver rubles and three twenty-kopeck pieces; some of the larger bills, which had been on top, had gotten quite moldy from lying under the stone. A long time was spent trying to find out why the accused had lied about this one circumstance when he had correctly and of his own free will confirmed everything else. There were, finally, some (the "psychologists" especially) who even admitted he really might not have looked into the purse, and so didn't know what was in it; and since he hadn't known, had hidden it away under the stone. For this very reason, however, they concluded that the crime itself could not have been committed except in a fit of temporary insanity, so to speak, while the criminal was pathologically obsessed with murder and robbery, without any further aims or calculations of personal gain. Incidentally, this was supported by the recently fashionable theory of temporary insanity, which is applied so often in our time. Moreover, Raskolnikov's former depressive condition was attested to in detail by many witnesses; by Dr. Zosimov, by his former friends, by his landlady, by the maid. It greatly facilitated the conclusion that Raskolnikov was not quite an ordinary murderer, criminal, and thief, and that his was a somewhat different case. To the great annoyance of those who advanced this opinion, the criminal scarcely tried to defend himself. In response to the final questions—what exactly could have inclined him to murder and what prompted him to commit robbery—he replied quite clearly and with the crudest precision that his motive had been his bad situation, his poverty and helplessness, his desire to firm the foundations of his career with the help of the at least three thousand rubles that he had expected to find at the murdered woman's. He had decided on murder because of his weak and irresponsible character, exasperated, moreover, by privations and failures. When asked what had impelled him to declare his guilt, he replied he was sincerely repentant. All this was almost too crude. . . .

And yet the sentence proved more merciful than could have been expected, given the nature of the crime, and this may have been because the criminal not only made no attempt to justify himself, but even seemed to want to inculpate himself still further. All the strange and special circumstances of the case were taken into account. There was not the slightest doubt of the criminal's pathological and destitute condition in the period before the crime was committed. The circumstances surrounding the accidental murder of Lizaveta actually served to support the latter hypothesis. A man in the process of committing two murders forgets that the door is wide open! Finally, he confessed at a time when the case had become unusually tangled as a result of the false confession made in a fit of depression by the religious fanatic (Nikolay), when there was no clear evidence and almost no suspicion as to the real criminal (Porfiry Petrovich had fully kept his word)—all this definitely helped to soften the lot of the accused.

There were some other circumstances that came up quite unexpectedly, and these, too, favored the man on trial. The former student Razumikhin dug up the information somewhere, and testified to the effect that the prisoner Raskolnikov, when he had been at the university, had used his last resources to help a poor, consumptive fellow student, and had practically supported him over a period of six months. When this student died, Raskolnikov had looked after his old invalid father, who was still alive, and whom the dead student had supported and kept by his own efforts almost since the age of thirteen, and Raskolnikov had finally placed this old man in a hospital, and when he, too, had died, Raskolnikov had paid for his funeral. All this information had a certain favorable effect on the determination of Raskolnikov's fate. And his former landlady, the mother of his dead fiancée, the widow Zarnitsyn, attested that when they had been living in their other house (the one at Five Corners), a fire had once broken out at night, and he had rescued two small children from an apartment that was already in flames, and he had gotten himself scorched in the process. It was investigated assiduously and turned out to be well attested by many witnesses. In brief, the trial ended with a sentence to hard labor of the second-degree, for a period of only eight years in all, the court having considered his confession and the circumstances mitigating his guilt.

At the very beginning of the trial Raskolnikov's mother took sick. Dunia and Razumikhin found it necessary to remove her from Petersburg for the duration of the trial. Razumikhin chose a town along the railroad not far from Petersburg, so he could keep up regularly with the course of the trial and at the same time see Avdotia Romanovna as often as possible. Pulcheria Alexandrovna turned out to have some rather peculiar nervous ailment that was accompanied by mental derangement, if not constantly, at least from time to time. When Dunia had returned from her last meeting with her brother, she found her mother quite sick—feverish and delirious. That same evening she consulted Ra-

zumikhin on how to reply to her mother's inquiries about
Raskolnikov, and for her mother's sake the two of them
invented a whole story about Raskolnikov's departure for
one of Russia's distant borders on a private commission,
which in the long run would bring him both fame and
money. They were nevertheless struck by the fact that Pulcheria Alexandrovna never questioned them about it, either
then or later. On the contrary, she, too, seemed to have a
whole story at hand about her son's sudden departure. In
tears, she would tell how he had come to bid her good-bye;
at the same time, she let it be known by insinuations that
many important and mysterious circumstances were known
to her alone; Rodia had many very powerful enemies, and
he even had to go into hiding for a while. As for his future
career, she, too, thought it would undoubtedly be brilliant,
as soon as certain hostile circumstances improved. She assured Razumikhin her son would in time be a person of
some importance to the state, as his brilliant essay and his
literary flair already indicated. This essay she read constantly, sometimes even aloud; she went to bed with it practically beside her. And yet she almost never asked where
Rodia really was, in spite of the fact that it was obvious
they avoided the subject in her presence, which in itself
might well have aroused her suspicion. At last they began
to worry about Pulcheria Alexandrovna's strange silence on
several points. She did not, for example, complain that he
didn't write letters, whereas formerly, with Raskolnikov in
Petersburg, she had lived in the sole expectation of receiving
a letter soon from her beloved Rodia. This latter circumstance seemed completely inexplicable and greatly disturbed
Dunia. The thought occurred to her that her mother had a
sense of something awful in her son's fate and feared to
inquire because she might discover something even more
awful. Anyway, Dunia saw clearly that Pulcheria Alexandrovna was not in sound mind.

Several times, however, she herself would lead the conversation to a point where, if one answered her, it would be
impossible not to refer at least to Rodia's whereabouts.
When the answers, willy-nilly, turned out to be unsatisfactory or suspicious, she would turn suddenly very sad,
gloomy, and taciturn, a mood that would last a very long
time. Dunia saw at last how difficult it was to go on lying
and improvising, and concluded it was better, on certain
points, to keep silent altogether. Still, it became clearer and

clearer, until it was obvious, that her poor mother suspected something awful. Dunia recalled her brother's mentioning that Pulcheria Alexandrovna had heard her talk in her sleep the night before that last fateful day, after her encounter with Svidrigailov. What had she heard? Sometimes after several days or even weeks of morose, gloomy silence and mute weeping, the patient would become rather hysterically animated and would all of a sudden start talking, and almost never stop, about her son, about her hopes for his future. . . . Sometimes her fantasies were quite strange. They humored her, they agreed with her (she herself may have seen clearly they were only humoring her), and yet she went on talking. . . .

Five months after the prisoner's confession, he was sentenced. Razumikhin, whenever possible, went to see him in prison; and Sonia, too. At last it came time to part. Dunia promised her brother it would not be permanent, and so did Razumikhin. In the latter's youthful, active brain a project had already taken shape, of spending the next three or four years acquiring the basis of a fortune, and after a certain amount of money had been accumulated, moving to Siberia, where the soil was fertile but people and capital were scarce, settling in the town where Rodia would be, and . . . they could all begin a new life together. When they said good-bye, they all wept. Raskolnikov had brooded a great deal these last days; he inquired about his mother and worried about her constantly. He even seemed to suffer a good deal on her account, to Dunia's alarm. Learning in detail of his mother's illness, he became very gloomy. With Sonia he was for some reason particularly uncommunicative the whole time. She had been making plans for some time, with the help of the money Svidrigailov had given her, to follow the convict gang in which he was being dispatched. It never came up between Raskolnikov and her, but they both knew that's the way it would be. During their farewell meeting he smiled strangely in response to his sister's and Razumikhin's fervid assurances about their happy future together when he got out of prison, and he predicted his mother's illness would soon end in disaster. At last he and Sonia set off.

Two months later Dunia and Razumikhin got married. The wedding was quiet and sad. Porfiry Petrovich and Zosimov were among the guests. All this time Razumikhin had worn the look of a determined man. Dunia believed blindly in all his projects. Indeed, she could not help but believe in

them; his iron will was there to be seen. He began attending
lectures at the university again, to finish his course of studies. They both made plans for the future, firmly reckoning
on moving to Siberia within five years. Until then they were
relying on Sonia. . . .

Pulcheria Alexandrovna gladly gave her blessing to her
daughter's marriage, but after it took place she seemed to
grow even sadder and more preoccupied. In order to afford
her a moment's pleasure, Razumikhin told her about the
sick student and his father and how Rodia had been burned
and even laid up for a while after saving two children from
their death the year before. Both these items of information
sent the already disturbed Pulcheria Alexandrovna practically into raptures. She talked about them all the time, entering into conversation on the subject on the street or
anywhere, even though Dunia always accompanied her. No
sooner did she secure a listener of any kind—in a public
conveyance, in a shop, anywhere—than she brought the conversation around to her son, his article, how he had helped
the student, how he had been burned in a fire, and so on.
Dunia did not know how to restrain her. In addition to the
dangers of overexcitement, there was the possibility someone might recall the name Raskolnikov from the recent trial
and mention it. Pulcheria Alexandrovna even discovered the
address of the mother of the two children who had been
saved from the fire, and she determined to go see her. At
last her disturbance reached an extreme. She would break
suddenly into tears at times; she fell ill frequently and would
become feverishly delirious. One morning she declared
forthrightly that Rodia would be back soon according to her
calculations; when they had said good-bye, he had told her
to expect him back in nine months. She started cleaning up
the apartment, getting it ready for their reunion; she got a
room ready for him (her own), and dusted the furniture and
washed and hung out a new set of curtains, and so on.
Though alarmed, Dunia said nothing, and even helped get
the room ready to welcome her brother. After an alarming
day given to fantasies, happy delusions, and tears, she took
sick; by morning she was running a temperature and was
delirious. A fever set in; within two weeks she died. In her
delirium she uttered words indicating she surmised more
about her son's awful fate than they had suspected.

Raskolnikov did not learn of his mother's death for a long
time, even though he had been in touch with Petersburg

from the very beginning of his settlement in Siberia. It was arranged through Sonia, who wrote to Razumikhin's address in Petersburg punctually every month, and every month received a punctual reply. To Dunia and Razumikhin, Sonia's letters seemed at first a bit dry and unsatisfactory; later, however, they found the letters could not have been better, for they provided the fullest possible and most precise account of their unfortunate brother's lot. Sonia's letters contained the most ordinary, everyday events, a very simple and clear description of Raskolnikov's surroundings in convict exile. Nor did she include an account of her own hopes or doubts about the future, nor of her own feelings. Instead of attempting to interpret his spiritual condition and inner life, she related facts only—his own words, for example; detailed information about his health; what exactly he seemed to want at the time she had last seen him; what he had asked her to do, and so on. All this was communicated in great detail. In the end, the image of their unfortunate brother seemed to emerge of itself, clearly and precisely drawn; since it was based on solid fact, there could be no mistake.

Yet Dunia and her husband could draw but cold comfort from this information, especially at first. Sonia wrote that he was perpetually gloomy, taciturn, and scarcely even interested in the news she told him every time she saw him, as culled from the letters she received; that he asked about his mother from time to time; and that when she saw he seemed to surmise the truth, she told him, finally, of his mother's death, and to her surprise even this news had no very strong effect on him, or, at least, so it seemed, as far as she could judge by external appearances. But she did write that in spite of the fact he seemed so self-absorbed and somehow shut off from everybody, his attitude to his new life was straightforward and direct; he clearly understood his position, expected nothing better in the near future, had none of the frivolous hopes so common to men in his shoes, and was surprised by hardly any of the circumstances of his new environment, so different, after all, from anything he was used to. She wrote that his health was satisfactory. He went to work, which he tried neither to avoid nor to seek out. He was practically indifferent to food, but since the food was so bad (except on Sundays and holidays), he was finally glad to accept some money from her, Sonia, to buy some daily tea for himself; he begged her not to worry about anything else and made it plain that her fussing over him only annoyed him. Sonia went on to write that he lived in the prison with the other convicts; she had not seen the inside of the prison but assumed it was crowded, ugly, and unhealthy; he slept over a felt pad on a wooden bunk; and he had no desire to arrange things differently—not because of any preconceived plan or intention, but because he paid no heed and seemed not to care about his lot. Sonia wrote frankly that he not only took no interest in her visits (particularly at first) but seemed almost annoyed with her, was taciturn and even rude in her presence. In the end, however, these meetings became habitual for him and practically a necessity, so he would even feel quite miserable if she took sick for a few days and was unable to visit him. She would see him on holidays by the prison gates or in the guardhouse, where he would be brought to visit with her for a few minutes. On weekdays she would see him at work, visiting him either in the workshops, or at the brickkilns, or in the warehouses on the bank of the Irtysh. About herself, Sonia wrote that she had actually managed to acquire a few acquaintances in town and some patronage; she was doing some sewing, and since there were practically no dressmakers in town, a number of households had already come to rely on her as a necessity. What she did not mention was that through her Raskolnikov, too, received some of the privileges of patronage from the authorities, that his work assignments had been eased, and so on. In Sonia's last letters Dunia had noticed an unusual anxiety and alarm, and finally Sonia wrote that Raskolnikov had estranged himself from everybody; the convicts in his prison did not like him; he was silent for whole days on end; and he was growing very pale. All of a sudden, in her last letter, Sonia wrote that he had fallen quite seriously ill and he was confined in the prisoners' ward of the hospital. . . .

2

He was sick a long time; yet it was not the horrors of convict life, the hard work or the food or the shaved head or the ragged clothes, which broke him. What did he care about these! On the contrary, the hard work actually pleased him; even though he suffered physically, the work at least earned him several hours of calm sleep. As for the food—the bowls of watery cabbage soup with cockroaches floating in it—what did he care? As a student in the old days he often had not had even that. His clothing was warm and suited to this kind of life. As for the chains, he actually was not aware of them. Should his shaved head and prison clothes have shamed him? Before whom? Sonia? Since Sonia was afraid of him, why should he be ashamed before her?

And yet, why not? He was ashamed even before Sonia, and he made her suffer for it by treating her coarsely and contemptuously. But it wasn't the shaved head and the chains that made him ashamed. His pride was deeply wounded, and it was from wounded pride that he took sick. How happy he would have been if only he could have considered himself guilty! He could have borne all, even the shame and disgrace. And yet, while judging himself severely, even his embittered conscience could find no specially terrible guilt in his past, except for what was simply a *blunder*, the sort of thing that might happen to anyone. What he was really ashamed of was that he, Raskolnikov, had come to grief so blindly, hopelessly, deafly and stupidly, by some decree of blind fate, and had to resign himself to such "meaninglessness" and make the best of such a decree if he wanted any peace at all for himself.

In the present, anxiety without aim or object; in the future, a perpetual sacrifice, productive of nothing—that was what faced him on earth. And if in eight years he would be only thirty-two and could still begin a new life, what difference did it make? What did he have to live for? What could he look forward to? What was he after? Mere existence? He had been ready a thousand times in the past to stake his existence on an idea, a hope, even a fantasy. Mere existence had always been too small for him; he had always wanted something bigger. It may have been only because of the strength of his desires that he had once considered himself a man to whom more was permitted than to others.

If only he could feel remorse—searing remorse, shattering the heart, banishing sleep—the kind of remorse that conjure up the noose and the whirlpool! He would have rejoiced! Agony and tears—that, too, is life! But he felt no remorse for his crime.

He might at least rage at his stupidity, as before he had raged at those hideous and stupid acts leading him to prison. Now that he was in prison, however, *free,* on his own, he reexamined all his former actions only to find them by no means so hideous and stupid as they had seemed at that fateful time.

He thought: "In what way was my idea any stupider than the other ideas and theories that have swarmed and clashed in the world, one after the other, since the world began? All you have to do is look at it from a disinterested and completely independent point of view, free of the common preconceptions, and surely, if you do that, my idea turns out to be not quite so . . . grotesque. Ah, critics and five-kopeck philosophers, why stop always halfway!

"Why does what I committed seem so hideous to them?" he said to himself. "Because it was a crime? What does that word mean—'crime'? My conscience is at rest. Of course, I overstepped, illegally; of course, the letter of the law was violated; blood was spilled. Very well, satisfy the letter of the law—take my head, why not?—and let it go at that! Given that, of course, we have quite a few human benefactors who did not inherit power but seized it for themselves; they should have been executed at their very first steps. But they followed their steps through, and so *they were right;* and I didn't follow through, so it turns out I did not have the right to permit myself that first step."

It was the only sense in which he acknowledged his transgression: simply that he hadn't followed it through, and had gone and confessed.

He also regretted not having killed himself. Why had he stood overlooking the river, and preferred, after all, to confess his guilt? Was his desire to live so strong? And was it so hard to overcome? Hadn't Svidrigailov, who feared death, overcome that desire?

He posed the question in anguish, and failed to understand that even as he had looked down into the river he had perhaps sensed a profound lie within himself and in his convictions. He did not understand that this feeling might have been a token of the future break in his life, of his future resurrection, his future new view of life.

He was more inclined to regard it as the mere dead weight of instinct, from which he had been unable to break loose and which he had lacked the vigor to step beyond, because he was weak and worthless. He looked at his fellow prisoners and was amazed at how much even they loved life, how much they treasured it! It even struck him that they valued life more in prison than they had when they were at large. How much agony some of them must have been through—

the tramps, for instance. Could an odd ray of sunlight really mean so much, or the dense forest, or some cold spring in the wilderness, seen once, perhaps, three years ago, and now dreamed of as though of a rendezvous with some beautiful mistress, the green grass around it, and a small bird singing in the bush? Observing further, he noticed still more inexplicable examples.

He certainly did not notice much of the life around him in prison, and he did not really want to notice. He lived looking out of the corners of his eyes, so to speak, and he found it loathsome and unbearable to look more directly. Yet he began to feel some surprise finally, and he started noticing, willy-nilly as it were, what before he had not even suspected. What surprised him the most was the terrible, impassable gulf between himself and the others, as if he and they were of different nations. He and they looked at one another distrustfully and with hostility. The main reasons for this cleavage he knew and understood; yet formerly he would not have admitted these reasons were so profound and powerful. There were also some exiled Poles in the prison, political offenders. They simply considered everybody an ignoramus and a slave and sneered down at everybody from on high. But Raskolnikov could not look at it that way. He saw clearly that these ignoramuses were much cleverer about a lot of things than the Poles. There were also some Russians who held this folk too much in contempt—a certain former officer and two seminarists. Raskolnikov clearly noted their mistake.

Everybody disliked and avoided him. Finally they even came to hate him. Why? He did not know. There were some far more criminal than he, and even these held him in contempt, laughed at him, laughed at his crime.

"You're a gentleman!" they told him. "You shouldn't have been walking around with an ax—not a gentleman's business!"

During the second week in Lent it was his turn to fast, along with the rest of his barracks. With the others, he went to church to pray. For some reason he did not understand there was a quarrel one day; they all fell on him at once in a fury. "You're an atheist! You don't believe in God!" they shouted at him. "You should be killed!"

He had never talked to them about God or faith, yet they wanted to kill him as an atheist; he remained silent and did not contradict them. One convict flung himself on him in a real frenzy. Calmly and quietly Raskolnikov stood his ground; not an eyebrow twitched and not a face muscle quivered. A guard managed to get between him and the murderer in time, or blood would have been spilled.

There was one other question to which he had no answer. Why were they all so fond of Sonia? She did not try to ingratiate herself with them. They saw her rarely, sometimes only at work when she would come for a mere moment to catch a glimpse of him. Nevertheless, everybody knew her, knew she had followed *him* here, knew how she lived and where she lived. She gave them no money, did nothing special for them. Once only, at Christmas, she brought a gift for the whole prison—some pies and some white rolls. Nevertheless, little by little, closer and closer ties were formed between them and Sonia. She wrote their letters for them, mailing them to their kin. Relatives who came to town to visit with them left things and even money for them in Sonia's hands, on the instruction of the convicts. Wives and sweethearts knew her and went to see her. When she came to see Raskolnikov at work, or when she met a party of prisoners on their way to work, they would all take their caps off, and they would all greet her: "Sofia Semionovna, ma'am, you're our tender, aching mother!" So spoke these coarse, branded convicts to this tiny, skinny creature. She smiled as she greeted them, and when she smiled at them they loved it. They loved even the way she walked, and would turn around and watch her go past, and they would praise her. They even praised her for being so small; they didn't know what to praise her for next. When they were sick, they went to her for treatment.

He was in the hospital through Lent and Easter. When he was recovering, he recalled the dreams he had had while still delirious and feverish. While sick, he had dreamed the whole world was condemned to suffer a terrible, unprecedented, and unparalleled plague, which had spread to Europe from the depths of Asia. Except for a small handful of the chosen, all were doomed to perish. A new kind of trichinae had appeared, microscopic substances that lodged in men's bodies. Yet these were spiritual substances as well, endowed with mind and will. Those infected were seized immediately and went mad. Yet people never considered themselves so clever and so unhesitatingly right as these infected ones considered themselves. Never had they considered their decrees, their scientific deductions, their moral convictions and their beliefs more firmly based. Whole settlements, whole cities and nations, were infected and went mad. Everybody was in a state of alarm, and nobody understood anybody; each thought the truth was in him alone; suffered agonies when he looked at the others; beat his breast; wept and wrung his hands. They did not know whom to bring to trial or how to try him; they could not agree on what to consider evil, what good. They did not know whom to condemn or whom to acquit. People killed each other in a senseless rage. Whole armies were mustered against each other, but as soon as the armies were on the march they began suddenly to tear themselves apart. The ranks dispersed; the soldiers flung themselves upon each other, slashed and stabbed, ate and devoured each other. In the cities the alarm bells rang for a whole day. Everybody was called, but nobody knew by whom or for what, and everybody was on edge. The most ordinary trades were abandoned, because everyone proposed his own ideas, his own criticisms, and they could not agree. Agriculture came to a halt. In some places, knots of people would gather together, reach some agreement, and swear not to separate; no sooner was this accomplished, however, than something quite different from what they had proposed took place. They started accusing each other, fighting each other, and stabbing away. Fires blazed up; hunger set in. Everything and everybody went to wrack and ruin. The plague spread and moved on. In the whole world only a few people were able to save themselves: the pure and the chosen, predestined to begin a new race of men and a new life, to renew and purify the earth; but these people were not seen anywhere by anybody, and nobody heard their voices or their words.

It bothered Raskolnikov that this senseless piece of delirium echoed so mournfully and painfully in his memory, so that for a long time the impression made by these feverish dreams did not pass. By the second week after Easter, warm, clear spring days had come. The windows were open in the prisoners' ward. They were barred, and a sentry paced underneath. While he had been sick in the ward, Sonia had only been able to visit him twice. She had to request permission each time, and it was hard to get. But she would come often to the hospital yard and stand beneath the windows, especially in the evening, sometimes merely to stand in the yard for a moment and look at the windows, even if only from a distance. Once, early one evening, Raskolnikov, almost completely recovered, had fallen asleep; when he woke he accidentally went over to the window; and suddenly, at the hospital gates in the distance, he saw Sonia. She stood there as if she were waiting for something. At that moment something seemed to pierce his heart. He shuddered and left the window as quickly as he could. Sonia did not come the next day or the next, and he noted that he waited for her with anxiety. At last he was discharged. When he got back to the prison he learned from the convicts that Sofia Semionovna was ill, home in bed and not going out anywhere.

He was very worried and sent for word of her. He soon learned her illness was not dangerous, and when she found out he was worried about her, Sonia sent him a penciled note informing him she was much better, that all she had was an ordinary cold, and that soon, quite soon, she would come see him at work. When he read this note, his heart beat strongly and painfully.

The day was again clear and warm. Early in the morning, about six, he made his way to the riverbank to work in a shed where a workshop and kiln for baking and hammering alabaster had been set up. Only three workers were sent there. One of the convicts went back to the fortress with a guard for some tool. The other began gathering wood and stuffing it into the kiln. Raskolnikov walked out of the shed to the riverbank, sat down on some logs piled beside the shed, and looked out over the broad, deserted river. From the high bank a broad vista opened out. A scarcely audible song wafted from the far bank. There, on the boundless steppe, flooded with sunshine, the black dots of nomad tents could barely be seen. There freedom was; and people lived who were quite different from the people on his side of the river. There time seemed to have stood still, as though the age of Abraham and his flocks had not yet passed. Without moving, Raskolnikov sat and looked, his eyes fixed upon the scene. Thought gave way to daydreams, to contemplation; he was not thinking of anything, but a kind of melancholy nagged and disturbed him.

Suddenly Sonia appeared beside him. She had approached almost without being heard, and sat down at his side. It was quite early, and the morning chill had not yet lifted. She wore a shabby old burnoose and her green shawl. There were still some signs of illness on her face, which had sunken and grown thinner and paler. She gave him a happy, welcoming smile, but, as usual, held her hand out to him timidly.

She always held her hand out to him timidly; sometimes she didn't even hold it out at all, as if she were afraid he might reject it. He always seemed disgusted when he took her hand, always met her as though he were annoyed, and sometimes he remained stubbornly silent the whole time of her visit. Sometimes he terrified her, and she went away deeply grieved. But now their hands did not separate; he looked at her swiftly, said nothing, and let his gaze drop to the ground. They were alone. Nobody could see them. The guard had turned away.

He did not know himself how it happened, but suddenly something seemed to seize him and hurl him to her feet. He wept, and embraced her knees. At first she was terribly frightened, and her face turned completely pale. She jumped up and looked at him and shivered. But at the same time, at that very moment, she understood everything. A boundless joy illuminated her eyes. She understood. For her there was no longer any doubt he loved her. He loved her infinitely. At long last the moment had come. . . .

They wanted to say something, but could not. Tears came. They were both pale and thin; yet in those pale, sickly faces there already glowed the light of the renewed future, resurrection to a new life. Love resurrected them; the heart of one contained infinite sources of life for the heart of the other.

They resolved to wait and be patient. There were seven years to go; and until then how much unbearable pain, what infinite happiness! He knew that he was born again. He felt himself completely renewed in his very being. And she—she lived only his life!

The evening of that very day, with the barracks locked, Raskolnikov lay on his bunk and thought of her. It even seemed to him as if all the convicts who had been his enemies looked at him differently now. He even chatted with them, and they replied politely. Surely that was the way it had to be. Everything had to change now, did it not?

He thought of her. He recalled how he had constantly caused her pain; he recalled her pale, skinny little face. These memories did not grieve him now; he knew the infinite love with which he would redeem her suffering.

What did they amount to, *all* those torments! Everything—even his crime, even sentence and exile—seemed to him now, in his first outburst of feeling, strange and superficial, as though it had not actually happened to him. He could not think very long or steadily about anything that evening or focus his mind on anything; nor did he come to any conscious decision; he had merely become aware. Life replaced logic, and in his consciousness something quite different now had to elaborate and articulate itself.

Under his pillow lay the New Testament. He picked it up mechanically; it belonged to her, the one from which she had read him the resurrection of Lazarus. At the beginning of his exile he had suspected she would bother him with religion, keep talking to him about the Gospels, and shove books at him. To his great surprise she did not mention such a thing once and never even offered him the Gospels. He had asked her for the New Testament himself, not long before his illness, and silently she had brought it to him. Since then he had not even opened it.

Nor did he open it now, but he thought: "Can her beliefs not be mine, too? Her feelings and aspirations, at least . . ."

She, too, felt agitated all that day, and that night she even took sick again. She was so happy, she was almost frightened of her joy. Seven years, *only* seven years! At the beginning of their happiness they were both prepared at moments to look on these seven years as on seven days. At the time he did not know that a new life had not been given him for nothing, that it would have to be bought dearly, that he would have to pay for it with a great deed in the future. . . .

That is the beginning of a new story, though; the story of a man's gradual renewal and rebirth, of his gradual transition from one world to another, of his acquaintance with a new reality of which he had previously been completely ignorant. That would make the subject of a new story; our present story is ended.

The End! You made it baby!
(what a good. last page, no?)

now read it again

AFTERWORD
The Dream of the Suffering Horse

Dostoyevsky wrote *Crime and Punishment* between 1864 and 1866, as Russia began a troubled transition to modernity with a series of far-ranging but ultimately unsuccessful reforms. The rights of "man and citizen," as Ilia Petrovich ironically puts it in the novel, were much on his mind.

Around "man and citizen" there clustered other polarities: freedom and repression, criminality and the law, the individual and society, reason and faith. And still another, which for almost any other novelist might have seemed awkward close to the same company, but which Dostoyevsky stationed at its heart: death and rebirth.

If the title has an abstract, didactic ring, calling to mind Beccaria's treatise *On Crimes and Punishments* of the previous century, there is nothing abstract or didactic about the novel itself. Close acquaintance, however, reveals it to be, nevertheless, an amazingly "literary" work, suffused with an awareness of the literature and public issues of the time, and concerned to an unusual degree with ideas, beliefs, and attitudes. For Dostoyevsky, an idea always has skin around it, and a human personality. As Berdiaev said of him, Dostoyevsky explored pathological states and the psychology of high tension, the realm of "obsession" and "possession," because it was there one could most clearly and dramatically see the human consequences of an idea carried ruthlessly through its logical conclusion.

The receding of the sea of faith that caught Matthew Arnold's ear at Dover Beach was Dostoyevsky's anxiety, too, though he tried to convince himself and others that the primitive Christianity of the Russian peasant offered other alternatives. In Europe, Dostoyevsky saw the triumph of M. Hommais and Mr. Gradgrind (the literary prototypes of Peter Petrovich Luzhin), and with them of the petty "rational self-interest" idea of the bourgeoisie. To Dostoyevsky, urban bourgeois industrial Europe, with its legalisms, abstractions, love of formalities, its arid doctrines of, on the one hand, political economy, economic man, utilitarianism,

Malthusianism, social Darwinism; and on the other, socialist materialism and social utopianism, seemed indeed, as he put it, "a graveyard."

But a graveyard dear to the Russian, where he went, like Raskolnikov in his dream, with votive offerings for the dead, to bow before the Dutch paintings and the English churches. Dostoyevsky was in London in 1862, and saw the Crystal Palace, built of glass like a greenhouse, displaying the latest in Victorian technology, the object of utopian hopes that connected increase in technical knowledge with moral progress. Dostoyevsky's close enemy, that saint of the revolution, Nikolai Chernyshevsky, saw the Crystal Palace as a dazzling beacon of "enlightened self-interest," though in his calculations (see his utopian novel, published in 1863, *What Is to Be Done?*) self-interest led to socialism, not to the triumph of M. Hommais. At this time, Dostoyevsky does not seem to have been particularly interested in socialism as such (the only real socialist in *Crime and Punishment* is the good-natured simpleton, Lebeziatnikov), but the idea of self-interest was another matter.

Responding to Chernyshevsky with his *Notes from Underground,* Dostoyevsky, in that supremely brilliant book, created a perverse hero who, by the ruthless application of reason and absolute insistence on the primacy of the self, equates the Crystal Palace with an ant heap and obedience to rational laws as an abject and imprisoning conformity that precisely denies the self. For the self that feels itself infinite all laws are confining, including the law that two and two makes four. "Two and two makes five, if I want it to!" cries the underground man. At a number of points the underground man sounds like Svidrigailov, at some like Raskolnikov. His logic calls all norms and formulas and conventions into question. Humanitarian reform, he points out, may be the response of fine feelings to the presence of suffering in the world, but it may also be an excuse for indifference, an alleviation that permits people not to respond. "One thing you can say in favor of corporal punishment," writes the underground man, "it's better than nothing!"

Near the Crystal Palace moiled the poor, the numberless and abysmally wretched London poor to whom the Malthusians and social Darwinists urged indifference on principle. What appalled Dostoyevsky most was the prostitutes, among whom he noticed young girls, children. In *Crime and Punishment,* the Crystal Palace turns into a pleasure house, a cafe on the European model, where one drinks tea or champagne and reads the newspapers, and where the prostitutes walk outside. For Dostoyevsky, the corruption and suffering of children is the world's ultimate evil, and its presence in the world really does call the existence of God into question. There are times when Dostoyevsky's moral passion is not so remote from Chernyshevsky's.

In *Crime and Punishment*, at least, his quarrel is not with socialism, and even less with the attempt to alleviate suffering. It is rather, and on a very high level, with *rebellion*, with the refusal to accept God's world and its fundamental condition, mortality. For Dostoyevsky, rebellion is crime and crime is rebellion. In Russian, he plays on the noun "crime" (*prestuplenie*) and the verb "to transgress" (*perestupit'*), which means both transgressing and overstepping.

After beginning *Crime and Punishment*, Dostoyevsky must have read Napoleon III's *History of Julius Caesar* (1865), in which the revival of Bonapartism from 1848 on found its official expression, and which must have provided him with grist for his mill. There are many juicy passages about the "man of destiny" to whom the ordinary rules of morality do not apply. In literature, of course, the Napoleonic theme is older than Napoleon and dates back at least to the Renaissance and the first untwining of the purely secular from the traditional-religious. There are almost all the plays of Christopher Marlowe; and above all (a work to which Dostoyevsky obviously owed very much indeed), Shakespeare's *Macbeth*. The first Napoleon, however, had (directly or indirectly) inspired a whole literature featuring somewhere the brilliant and ambitious young man of no particular hereditary station in society who aspires not only to create his own destiny but to move the destiny of the world, and the price his ambition forces him to pay; the theme of the self-made man who aspires to change the world, for whom crime-rebellion seems a kind of virtue rather than a transgression. During the two decades or so after the failure of the revolutions of 1848, with the triumph of *Machtpolitik*, the emergence of Germany (that parvenu among nations), and the Second Empire of Napoleon III in France, with its deliberate propagandistic evocation of the Napoleonic legend, the theme in literature sprouted a new and vigorous crop. I need only mention that Tolstoy's *War and Peace* was written at about the same time as *Crime and*

Punishment and that installments of the two novels actually appeared together in three issues of the same journal.

The drawing of Raskolnikov owes much to both the early and the late literary manifestations of the Napoleonic theme. Among the late, there are Bazarov, the "nihilist" hero of Turgenev's *Fathers and Sons* (1862), and Rakhmetov, the iron-willed hero (he trains himself in asceticism by sleeping on a bed of nails) of Chernyshevsky's *What Is to Be Done?* Among the early, Rastignac, Balzac's student hero who defiantly shakes his walking stick at Paris from Montmartre and who ponders the problem of the unknown mandarin (a fellow student asks him if he would consent to the death of a Chinese mandarin completely unknown to him, if his fortune depended on it; Raskolnikov poses the same problem to Sonia); and Julien Sorel, the hero of Stendhal's *The Red and the Black,* who secretly nourishes himself on Napoleon's memoirs. Most significant, however, since he helped inspire Dostoyevsky's method as well as reinforcing his confidence in the modern significance of the theme, was Hermann, the hero of Pushkin's remarkable short story "The Queen of Spades" (1834).

Like Raskolnikov, Hermann resembles Napoleon without the inner consistency to carry the resemblance into effective action. His assault on the "secret" of the old countess is like Raskolnikov's murder of the old pawnbroker woman. In "The Queen of Spades," Pushkin uses (with most extraordinary insight) the possibilities of the dream as an area of human experience where, for literary purposes, the allegory and symbolic generality of the medieval morality play or the old-fashioned dream book could be combined with psychological verisimilitude and convincingness. Pushkin's story is also explicitly about the unconscious, about a will beneath the individual's conscious will, manifest in action, contradicting, negating, making a mock of what the individual thinks his real will is. In Pushkin's story, it is the death wish; in Dostoyevsky's, the will to live struggling desperately against the death wish. Both manifest themselves in dreams. Dostoyevsky combined the psychological insight and method of Pushkin's story with the charged atmosphere trembling on the edge of hallucination of the knocking-at-the-gate scene in *Macbeth* into what he called his own "fantastic realism."

All the major characters of *Crime and Punishment* bear the allegoric names of a medieval morality play. Raskolnikov is a schismatic (*raskolnik*) who has willfully cut himself off from his fellow men. Dostoyevsky emphasizes his fastidiousness and his "disgust" with people. Yet it is a disgust born of love, magnanimity, and great expectations. In the modern world of receding faith and calculating self-interest, Raskolnikov is the Russian Everyman. Cutting himself off from people, he refuses to acknowledge that he is like everybody else. Everyman turns out to be a murderer. But Dostoyevsky's genius makes him a murderer who is also just like us, forces us to identify with him very closely.

He is a murderer capable of redemption. Indeed, Dostoyevsky asks us to believe that in a future that lies outside the novel he will become a "great man" in a sense different from the one he originally imagined—possibly a great saint. Again and again Dostoyevsky asks the reader to look back on present events from some vague future vantage point, where the assumption is that Raskolnikov has "come through," and which, more than the flashbacks or occasional recapitulations, breaks up the linear sequence of the novel and helps to imbue it with a sense of time imbedded in timelessness, like one of those paintings in which a saint in Heaven looks down on the scene of his own past martyrdom.

Early in the novel Raskolnikov, physically and spiritually exhausted, wanders into the suburbs of Petersburg and drops wearily to sleep under a bush. He dreams of his childhood. That day he has received a letter from his mother in which she refers to that idyllic time when his father was alive and the family lived together. In the dream his father takes him to visit the graves of his brother and grandmother. The occasion (including the old priest in the cemetery church) has an air of domestic ritual, a taming and sweetening of the presence of death, which the tavern along the road and the roistering crowd of peasants interrupt with a grim, cruel, ineluctable reminder of that presence.

The weary nag and her outsize load is one of those casual images from everyday life our unconscious seizes upon and turns to its own symbolic purposes. In dreams, we invest the concrete and the commonplace with our own deepest meanings. Dostoyevsky precedes his description of the dream with a rather stiff little introduction on the vividness and artistry dreams occasionally display; Raskolnikov's first dream, however, is remarkable for its symbolic rather than its merely descriptive eloquence. It anticipates and foreshadows and at the same time compresses into a single scene almost the entire action of the novel. At the same time, it is completely convincing as a dream—not Dostoyevsky's, but Raskolnikov's.

The drunken peasant Mikolka in lashing at the mare punishes his own sense of helplessness and inadequacy. Precisely because the old nag cannot pull such a load Mikolka insists on piling it higher and higher, heavier and heavier. He is not a Christian, somebody in the crowd shouts. He is a rebel against his own weakness, poverty, and limitation. The nag is *his,* his property, at his disposal, the external part of himself of which he *can* dispose, and a symbol of the inner part, the trembling of the flesh. Since he is not strong enough to tolerate her weakness and inadequacy for the pull of his ambition, he destroys her. Part of the crowd makes a joke of his rage and joins in. "Go get an ax!" somebody shouts. Finally, Mikolka does in the nag with a crowbar.

Later Raskolnikov associates the old nag with Sonia, with Katherine Ivanovna, with Lizaveta, with his own mother—the eternal victims. In the dream he clearly identifies himself with the sufferings of the horse; the boy Raskolnikov breaks from his father's protecting, restraining arms, and throws his own arms around the horse's neck. Desperately his father calls to him: ". . . it's not our business!"* The boy sobs. He kisses the horse and flings himself in a fury on Mikolka.

But Raskolnikov also identifies himself with Mikolka. When he wakes he thinks: thank God, this is only a dream! But immediately afterward: "Will I really? . . . Will I really take the ax, will I really hit her on the head, split open her skull. . . . Good Lord, will I really?" And he shakes like a leaf. He feels a sense of release and liberation. "I renounce that damned . . . dream of mine!" he says. Yet this statement in itself identifies the dream of the horse with his fantasy of killing the pawnbroker woman, and in a deeper sense than he knows the dream has been a decision. *What* decision is made clear by the "superstitious" significance he attributes to a chance conversation overheard at the Haymarket, about Lizaveta. In this way, the opportunity to murder "presents itself," and chance becomes the language of necessity.

After the crime, Raskolnikov is torn between getting rid of the traces and grasping them more closely to him. He

---

*This is the only appearance of Roman Raskolnikov, although the letter refers to him; and later, Rodion's article on crime reminds Pulcheria Alexandrovna of the fact that his father used to write poems. Thus he assumes his father's image (the image of a loved and kindly failure, but still a failure) in her eyes.

thinks not only of washing away the blood, but also of throwing away the few pledges and trinkets and bits of petty cash he has managed to plunder (presumably the object of the crime) into the river or the canal. Throughout the novel, water is used as the symbol of regeneration and rebirth; the water of life. But also the water of death and oblivion, as at the end of the novel, when Raskolnikov, before he becomes aware of Sonia's presence, contemplates flinging himself into the Neva. It is perhaps also one of the effects of the city that the wellspring of life turns at moments into the river of death. The water will wash away Raskolnikov's crime, but, since he has identified himself with his crime, it will wash him away, too. With one part of his mind Raskolnikov will not let go of the crime or its traces, and he grasps the frayed edges of bloodstained cloth to him as a baby clings to a fetish; as part of himself, as part of his fundamental identity in the world.

Nor will the crime let go of him. He has a second dream, as vivid and terrifying as the first. In it the "man from nowhere," who as a conscience figure or superego is a sterner, more consistent, more competent version of the father in the first dream as well as the actual artisan who accused Raskolnikov, beckons him eerily back to the scene of the crime. He finds himself eternally in the same room, wielding the same ax against the obscenely mocking old witch who will not die. Like the fly buzzing against the windowpane, he cannot get out. "It was not the old pawnbroker woman I killed," he realizes, "it was myself." Yet Lizaveta, the innocent and chance victim, whose fate was nevertheless inexorably tied to the old pawnbroker woman's, and who is the equivalent of the innocent victim in Raskolnikov, does not appear in the dream, and it would seem her memory is repressed by Raskolnikov until, quite startlingly, Sonia prompts him, and it leaps out. Raskolnikov planned his crime (the plans had always a certain unreality; nevertheless, they obsessed him) as he lay on his couch in the hot and stifling tightness of his garret, dazzled by the career the theft would make possible, the hundred good deeds which would transform the crime into virtue. The darling of his mother and sister, who are sacrificing themselves for him, he must make himself a hero to justify their love. (If not for their love, he thinks much later, *"All this wouldn't have happened!"*) The dream of the horse provides him with the first indication (still not entirely conscious) that the general wel-

fare is not his real motive; that he must kill in order to try
to overcome the victim in himself, to prove that he is a
Napoleon, not "a louse," an over-, not an under-man, Mikolka, not the horse.* The second dream tells him that he
has not succeeded; actually, he interprets it as indicating that
he was indeed the victim. Not that there are no over-men,
but simply that he was not one; that he failed.

In addition to the three dreams (the third I will discuss
below), Raskolnikov has three visions or daydreams or hallucinations, which play a slightly different and only slightly
less important role in the structure of the novel. If Raskolnikov's sleeping dreams are a concretely imaged representa-
tion of the drama, the *action,* the *plot* of his soul's
development, in which the techniques of allegory and realism are combined, his waking dreams indicate the psychological setting, the background against which this development
takes place, and are symbolist in a Baudelairian sense.**
They establish "correspondences" between Raskolnikov's
inner life and the concrete physical world in which he lives.
They link the world of everyday reality with the *associations*
and *connotations* of Raskolnikov's conscience.

In the first daydream, after the dream of the horse and
before the murder, Raskolnikov sees an oasis in the desert,
a caravan, the parching-hot desert sands, the aridity of gold,
and the cool trickle of water that makes life and an oasis
possible. The whole scene has a painful, slow, arrested quality, with a shiver of coolness running through it, like a cold
compress applied during a fever. The desert and the urban
metropolis of St. Petersburg are subtly associated. (Afterward, on his way to the crime, Raskolnikov wonders why
there are no fountains in the city.) More than the "Waste
Land" of the modern metropolis, however, the desert suggests an allegory for the world as such, through which man
passes as a caravan through the desert. It suggests gold and
the scramble for gold (not only the color of the sand; cara-

---

*Not only art, but also life, imitates art. Friedrich Nietzsche, who ad-
mired Dostoyevsky immensely, and especially *Crime and Punishment,*
in his last conscious act before he collapsed in a coma in the streets of
Turin and into the insanity that lasted the rest of his life, threw his
arms around the neck of a horse a cabby was belaboring with the whip.
See W. J. Kaufmann, *Nietzsche,* Cleveland and New York, Meridian
Books, 1962, p. 57.
**After a decade of relative neglect, it was the Russian symbolists who
rediscovered Dostoyevsky at the turn of the century.

vans, after all, engage in trade) and thus the theme of self-interest, rational calculation, and "double-entry bookkeeping" later embodied in Luzhin. It is also Egypt and the Holy Land, suggesting Egyptian slavery and the flight into Egypt, but introducing also the Napoleonic theme; for we are reminded later of Napoleon's Egyptian adventure and the cavalier way in which he abandoned "an army in Egypt." The oasis in the desert also suggests the theme of Lazarus. It is the wished-for water of life, the possibility of renewed life, which at the end of the novel, after the hot, dry summer, comes pouring down in torrents, sending Svidrigailov out to suicide and Raskolnikov to confession.

In the second, Raskolnikov associates his crime with the aggressive manner of Gunpowder (the explosive lieutenant) and its victims with his landlady (the mother of his former fiancée). I refer, of course, to his hallucination of the beating on the stairs. Before he loses consciousness, slipping into a long delirium, Raskolnikov takes a cold swallow of water.

In the third, which takes place in the Epilogue, the feverish, pathological, supercharged atmosphere recedes, and the vision seems to emerge naturally out of the calm observation and contemplation of an objective scene. Raskolnikov looks out over the Siberian river and sees the nomad tents, which remind him of Abraham and biblical times, and, in their timelessness, of all new beginnings, an eternal order and a fresh start. The act of looking out over a river suggests an analogue with the many times in Petersburg he has paused along the Neva to admire the celebrated prospect. "The marvelous view always left him with an unexplained chill . . ." In the stench-filled city, the panorama is impressive but not a vision. And yet it is the experience of the city that makes the experience of Siberia possible.

Setting the novel in St. Petersburg, Dostoyevsky chose a locale that conspired with his imagination at every point to produce symbols at once striking and apt for his theme and yet casually and realistically commonplace. When Dostoyevsky wrote, it was a city of almost a million people in a country that was overwhelmingly rural. Unlike London and Paris, St. Petersburg was founded as an act of will; in this sense, a *planned* city; and it was founded in modern times (1703), a purely secular city that assumed its characteristic shape, form, and architecture during the eighteenth century, the age of reason and enlightenment.

A modern poet (Mandelstam) has called it "the typographical city," in a striking metaphor that compares its streets with the lines of a galley proof, and many writers have dwelt on its "bookishness"—the city not only of sharp-angled streets, architectural ensembles, uniform rows, planned linear perspectives, but also quite literally the center of the book trade, the city of clerks, officials, students and artisans, police and professors, the overdeveloped intellectual and administrative center of a vast and impoverished rural land. It was also a city of the tricks of light, with "white nights" in summer, almost perpetual darkness in winter; a city of fantasy and hallucination. Socially, it was not only a place where extremes met, but one in which *all* social classes were uprooted and often lived side by side—the wealthy parvenu, the nobleman gone to seed, the beggar, the prostitute, the student; renting rooms and corners and apartments in the teeming, huge low-slung buildings that had been partitioned and repartitioned—a city of startling social proximities. It is the urban wasteland, the "unreal city" of T. S. Eliot; but a genuine historic Russian city as well.

When he moved as a student to the "typographical" city, Raskolnikov left not only his mother and sister but also the protective, ritualized, ceremonial way of life of the countryside. Yet he clings to fragments of the traditional faith of his childhood. When Porfiry asks him if he still believes in the New Jerusalem, he answers grimly that he does—and in the resurrection of Lazarus, too. At the crossroads, he still senses the primitive symbolism of the cross, and after the janitors (when he has returned to the building in which he committed murder) refuse to take him to the police station as he requests, he pauses at the crossroads in the middle of the road and looks "as though he expected to hear the last word from somebody outside himself." Later, inspired by Sonia, he falls down at the same crossroads and kisses the ground. Once, looking for Svidrigailov, he pauses to talk with a rude peasant who fascinates him because he is "a Zaraisky man"—he comes from the same place as Raskolnikov. And so does the house painter Mikolka, who takes Raskolnikov's guilt so astonishingly upon himself, and who has the same name (surely not by chance) as the peasant in the dream of the horse. "There are no more families!" Dostoyevsky wrote elsewhere; and he might well have added, in the same sense: there are no more churches either. The shreds and patches of his early life that Raskolnikov brings with him to the city are useless until he discovers them anew in terms of his own experience. After that he must reconstitute a family—not out of marriage to Sonia, or through the old tie with his mother and Dunia—but out of humanity as a whole, all mankind.

While each of the important characters in *Crime and Punishment* is a "double" of Raskolnikov—or better, a special mirror in which he can see, if he looks with seeing eyes, some aspect of himself—Sonia and Svidrigailov play a special role as his "*semblables,*" and come to represent the forces within himself that are struggling for the possession of his soul.

"Sonia" is the diminutive for "Sofia," Greek for "wisdom." She is characterized by an "*insatiable* compassion," and the adjective "insatiable" sits oddly on her, since we are told that she has remained inwardly "chaste" in her corrupting profession. If the Marmeladovs as a family are out of Dickens (which is not to deny them a life of their own)—Sonia is out of George Sand. Interesting as she is, there is something incomplete about her, something still "literary." In my memory, her physical presence recedes to a pair of widely staring, injured eyes. Two small details linger beside: that she once refused Katherine Ivanovna a bauble, out of some stubborn residual possessiveness; and that she once read, with interest and aptitude, Lewes' *Physiology,* borrowed from Lebeziatnikov.* It would seem that she resembles Dunia in more than her capacity to suffer, and one can see her, pale but determined, in the lines of a number of high-minded causes, given only a slightly different turn of circumstance. She is not so much a force as a *presence.*

Svidrigailov, as soon as he steps into the novel, threatens to walk away with it. Dostoyevsky is far less explicit about him than about Raskolnikov; perhaps for this very reason he is more memorable and haunting, a more vivid, yet also a more mysterious, and somehow a more *modern*, character.

His name does not yield to allegorical interpretation, although it suggests Polish-Lithuanian ancestry, like "Dostoyevsky," and might hint at some hidden identification. For this, actually, there is better; clearer evidence. He is the only character besides Raskolnikov whose dreams and inner life we are *shown*; the only one besides Raskolnikov we inhabit.

*George Henry Lewes (1817–1878) lived with George Eliot from 1854 until his death, and was, in addition to being a famous popularizer of science and philosophy, and a Comtean positivist, a sturdy champion of women's rights.

More suggestive is his first name: Arkady. Svidrigailov has lived in Arcadia, for seven years, on Martha Petrovna's estate. And it would seem he, too, has a literary source after all, if a shadowy one: he is a fantastic Russian version of Rousseau's "natural man"—the natural man of the *Social Contract,* but also the *carefully educated* natural man of *Emile,* whose instructress (Martha Petrovna), in teaching him to know his feelings and be true to them and providing him with an external point of reference, never leaves him alone for a moment and makes him extremely dependent on her.

A number of commentators have noted a certain anti-intellectual tendency in *Crime and Punishment.* Raskolnikov, they have pointed out, moves in the direction of human community when he attends to his feelings, his spontaneous reactions; and he moves away, in the direction of aggression, isolation, and self-will, as soon as he thinks. Razumikhin, however, is as much an intellectual (if not so bold and original) as Raskolnikov, and his very name implies "intellect." What Dostoyevsky means to expose, then, is not reason or intellect as such, but the danger of intellectual pride, of intellect detaching itself from emotion and instinct and tradition and proclaiming itself autocrat. But if intellect is dangerous and destructive when invested with autocratic powers, so are feelings and emotions. Svidrigailov is Rousseau's natural man; pure impulse and spontaneous feeling, but outside morality, beyond good and evil. He is felt instantly as far more threatening and sinister than the merely-calculating Luzhin. Yet he is also strangely appealing and attractive, and it is far from certain that when Dunia, resisting his violence, tells him she could never love him, she is being entirely truthful.

Svidrigailov does not calculate, and he has managed somehow to detach himself entirely from the moral will, if not absolutely from conscience. He acts only on impulse. His talk is generally perceptive free association; it lacks coherence. In the interests of passion, however, he is capable of planning shrewdly, and he is an accomplished seducer. But his passion is hollow at the core, and he is weary and bored with it; at the same time he hopes a "different" passion (Dunia) will redeem him.

His impulses are as often generous as they are destructive and aggressive, but one kind turns into the other with bewildering and uncontrolled rapidity. He has no confidence in moral standards and asks Raskolnikov to "suspend preju-

dice." Nor has he any confidence in reason: "Reason is passion's slave, is it not?" And he assumes, like Hobbes and
unlike Rousseau, the "*bonne guerre*" of the state of nature,
the war of all against all.

The domineering Martha Petrovna has given his life whatever shape it has had. Incidental sexual indulgences with the
maids are part of that shape. These he reports dutifully to
Martha Petrovna. Sex, he tells Raskolnikov, is at least
"something you can count on, something basic and natural,"
and above all "not subject to fantasy"—though he is certainly wrong there, he clings to the basic instincts as his last
hold on the earth.

Like the narrator of *Notes from Underground,* he has a
disconcerting way of calling all moral judgments into question ("Am I a monster or am I a victim?") and shifting
attention from the victim to the man who is *tempted.* He
shrugs off the account of a peculiarly lurid crime by re-
marking: ". . . one comes across such provocative German
girls . . ." A rapist, possibly a murderer, certainly responsible
for at least three deaths, he saves lives with as little "prejudice" as he destroys them. And, as he says, he is genuinely
fond of children.

Children attract him fatally, for they are, without trying,
everything that Svidrigailov's careful training has failed to
make him—sensual and innocent at the same time. Svidrigailov cannot be a child again; the gates of Eden are closed to
him. Aggression inevitably corrupts his affection, and the
hurt, shivering child of his dream turns before his eyes into
a grinning harlot.

For Svidrigailov, especially since the death of Martha Petrovna, all boundaries and distinctions, all definitions, have
broken down; he can no longer tell the difference between
sleep and waking, dream and reality, life and death. Casually
the dead visit him. Reality and hallucination change places.
He speaks of getting married again or going to America, and
associates these two possibilities with the unspoken third, of
killing himself. He tries to seduce, then to rape, Dunia. He
fails. Then the three possibilities merge into each other.
Going to America and getting married seem the same as
suicide. In his last moments he goes through the motions of
a vaudeville farce. The doorman protests the *inappropri-
ateness,* and the very expression on his face *tempts* Svidrigailov to raise the pistol and pull the trigger.

When he hears of Svidrigailov's suicide, Raskolnikov is in

the police station trying to confess. The lesson of the master prompts him to hold back from his new life a little and give death one more try. Again Sonia's felt presence saves him, and he finds his way back to the road to Siberia. In Siberia he has his third and final dream, in which the meaning of his crime is made clear to him. Unlike the other two, this dream is told indirectly, as an allegory—already interpreted for us and somehow less convincing. The dream of the proud microbes might well have made a masterpiece for any less-inspired writer, but it lacks the imaginative symbolic power of the dream of the horse. In any case, Raskolnikov's redemption and resurrection lie outside the novel. It is true, of course, that not long after *Crime and Punishment,* Dostoyevsky began work on *The Idiot,* which was to be a psychologically convincing novel about the kind of completely good man Raskolnikov might have turned out to be. Prince Myshkin, however, no longer resembles the pale Napoleonic criminal. Somehow, for all the magnificence of Dostoyevsky's effort, his Great Sinner never did quite manage to turn into the longed-for Great Saint. Dostoyevsky was a Christian, but he also lived almost entirely in the modern world.

—SIDNEY MONAS

SELECTED BIBLIOGRAPHY

Works by Fyodor Dostoyevsky

Poor Folk, 1846
The Double, 1846
An Honest Thief, 1846
White Nights, 1848 (Signet Classic 0451-523768)
Uncle's Dream, 1859
The Friend of the Family, 1859
The Insulted and the Injured, 1861
The House of the Dead, 1862
Notes from Underground, 1864 (Signet Classic 0451-523768)
Crime and Punishment, 1866 (Signet Classic 0451-527232)
The Gambler, 1866
The Idiot, 1868–69 (Signet Classic 0451-524926)
The Eternal Husband, 1870
The Possessed, 1871–72 (Signet Classic 0451-524861)
A Raw Youth, 1875
The Dream of a Ridiculous Man, 1877
   (Signet Classic 0451-523768)
A Diary of a Writer, 1873–81
The Brothers Karamazov, 1879–80
   (Signet Classic 0451-523881)
Letters of Fyodor Dostoyevsky

Selected Biography and Criticism

Bakhtin, Mikhail. *Problems of Dostoevsky's Poetics*. Ed. and trans. Caryl Emerson. Intro. Wayne Booth. Theory and History of Literature, vol. 8. Minneapolis: University of Minnesota Press, 1984.

Copleston, Frederick C. *Philosophy in Russia*. Notre Dame, IN: Notre Dame University Press, 1986.

Debreczeny, Paul, and Jesse Zeldin. *Literature and National Identity. Nineteenth-Century Russian Critical Essays*. Lincoln: University of Nebraska Press, 1970.

Dowler, Wayne. *Dostoevsky, Grigor'ev, and Native Soil Conservatism.* Toronto: University of Toronto Press, 1982.

Fanger, Donald. *Dostoevsky and Romantic Realism. A Study of Dostoevsky in Relation to Dickens, Balzac, and Gogol.* Cambridge: Harvard University Press, 1967.

Frank, Joseph. *Dostoevsky, the Miraculous Years, 1865–1871.* Princeton: Princeton University Press, 1995.

Holquist, Michael. *Dostoevsky and the Novel.* Princeton: Princeton University Press, 1977.

Ivanov, Vyacheslav. *Freedom and the Tragic Life: A Study in Dostoevsky.* Trans. Norman Cameron. Ed. S. Konovalov. New York: Noonday Press, 1971.

Jackson, Robert L. *Dostoevsky's Quest for Form: A Study of His Philosophy of Art.* New Haven: Yale University Press, 1966.

———, ed. *Twentieth Century Interpretations of Crime and Punishment. A Collection of Critical Essays.* Englewood Cliffs, NJ: Prentice-Hall, 1973.

Levitskii, Sergei A. *Ocherki po istorii russkoi filosofii.* Moscow: Kanon, 1996. [In Russian]

Mackenzie, David, and Michael W. Curran. *A History of Russia and the Soviet Union.* Third ed. Belmont, CA: Wadsworth Publishing Co., 1987.

Mirsky, Dmitri. *History of Russian Literature.* Ed. Francis J. Whitfield. New York: Knopf, 1949.

Mochulsky, Konstantin. *Dostoyevsky: His Life and Work.* Trans. Michael A. Minihan. Princeton: Princeton University Press, 1967.

Peace, Richard. *Dostoevsky: An Examination of the Major Novels.* Cambridge: Cambridge University Press, 1971.

Riasanovsky, Nicholas V. *A History of Russia.* Fourth ed. New York: Oxford University Press, 1984.

Rosenshield, Gary. *Crime and Punishment: the Technique of the Omniscient Author.* Lisse: Peter de Ridder Press, 1978.

Ryan, John K., ed. *The Confessions of St. Augustine.* Garden City, NY: Image Books, 1960.

Steiner, George. *Tolstoy or Dostoyevsky.* New York: Knopf, 1959.

Terras, Victor, ed. *Handbook of Russian Literature.* New Haven: Yale University Press, 1985.

Ware, Timothy. *The Orthodox Church.* London: Penguin Books, 1993.

Wasiolek, Edward, ed. *Crime and Punishment and the Critics.* San Francisco: Wadsworth Publishing Co., 1961.

————. *Dostoyevsky: The Major Fiction*. Cambridge: M.I.T. Press, 1964.

————, ed. and trans. *The Notebooks for Crime and Punishment*. Chicago: Chicago University Press, 1967.

Wellek, René, ed. *Dostoyevsky: A Collection of Critical Essays*. Englewood Cliffs, N.J.: Prentice-Hall, 1962.